Mastering Fear

Mastering Fear

Women, Emotions, and Contemporary Horror

Rikke Schubart

BLOOMSBURY ACADEMIC
NEW YORK • LONDON • OXFORD • NEW DELHI • SYDNEY

BLOOMSBURY ACADEMIC
Bloomsbury Publishing Inc
1385 Broadway, New York, NY 10018, USA

BLOOMSBURY, BLOOMSBURY ACADEMIC and the Diana logo are trademarks
of Bloomsbury Publishing Plc

First published in the United States of America 2018

Copyright © Rikke Schubart, 2018

For legal purposes the Acknowledgments on p. xix–xx constitute an extension of this copyright page.

Cover design: Louise Dugdale
Cover image: *The Babadook*, 2014, Causeway films/Smoking Gun Productions/ DR/Collection Christophel/ArenaPAL

All rights reserved. No part of this publication may be reproduced or transmitted in any form or by any means, electronic or mechanical, including photocopying, recording, or any information storage or retrieval system, without prior permission in writing from the publishers.

Bloomsbury Publishing Inc does not have any control over, or responsibility for, any third-party websites referred to or in this book. All internet addresses given in this book were correct at the time of going to press. The author and publisher regret any inconvenience caused if addresses have changed or sites have ceased to exist, but can accept no responsibility for any such changes.

A catalog record for this book is available from the Library of Congress.

ISBN: HB: 978-1-5013-3671-3
ePDF: 978-1-5013-3673-7
eBook: 978-1-5013-3672-0

Typeset by RefineCatch Limited, Bungay, Suffolk
Printed and bound in the United States of America

To find out more about our authors and books visit www.bloomsbury.com and sign up for our newsletters.

With all my love

*To
Ditte and Rasmus*

*To
My mother
Susanne Schubart*

Fear is like fire. It can cook for you. It can heat your house. Or it can burn it down.

CUS D'AMATO, MIKE TYSON'S TRAINER[1]

Breaking habits is a little like breaking your own bones. What should keep you trying is the knowledge that by experiencing the world from a very different perspective, you will enrich your life considerably.

MIHALY CSIKSZENTMIHALYI, *CREATIVITY*[2]

---

[1] Michael J. Apter, *Danger: Our Quest for Excitement* (Oxford: Oneworld Publications, 2007), eBook, 56.
[2] Mihaly Csikszentmihalyi, *Creativity: Flow and the Psychology of Discovery and Invention*, HarperCollins eBooks, 2007, Kindle edition, 360.

CONTENTS

List of Illustrations xiii
List of Tables xviii
Acknowledgments xix

Introduction: Approaching the Problem 1
Playing with Horror 1
Unpleasant and Fun 3
Only Humans have Gender 6
Defining Horror 7
The Structure of *Mastering Fear* 10

1 The Dark Stage 15
EMOTIONS 16
What are Emotions? 18
System 1 and System 2 21
Positive and Negative Emotions 25
The Horror Experience 26
GENDER 29
Throwing Like a Girl 30
Thinking Like a Woman 33
Gender and Change 35
Evofeminism 37
PLAY 40
What is Play? 41
Play Fighting 42
From Animal Play to Human Play 44
Playing on the Edge 46
Aggression 50
Three Basic Horror Narratives 52
Horror as Play 54

Child 57

2 Mud, Blood, and Magic: Genre and Gender in *Pan's Labyrinth* 59

Pan's Labyrinth (2006)

Anchor Points and Default Rules 60
Into the Labyrinth 62
Fairy-Tale Expectations 64
With a Child's Eyes 65
The Meaning of Mud 66
A Task and a Monster 69
Beauty Meets the Beast 70
A Trial and Disobedience 72
The Meaning of Magic 73
The Fantastic and the Melodrama 74
Hero or Victim? 76
A Final Anchor Point 77

3 The Bio-Logic of Vengeance in *Let the Right One In* 79

Let the Right One In (2008)

The Vampire Triptych 80
The "Piggy Game" 81
Play Fighting and Cruel Play 83
Sex and Gender: "I am not a girl" 85
From Friends to Lovers: The *Romeo and Juliet* Theme 87
The Bio-Logic of Justice 89
The Ethics of Vengeance 91
Scar as Passage and Border 93
Conclusion 95

Teen & Emerging Adult 97

4 "She Made a Choice": Werewolf Affordances and Female Character Development 99

Wilderness (1996), *Ginger Snaps* (2000), *Hemlock Grove* (2013–2015), *Bitten* (2014–2016)
Lycanthrophy 100
Werewolf Affordances 101
Wilderness: Wolf as Zen Master 103
Ginger Snaps: Menarche as Mayhem 107
Menarche: Disease and Shame 109
Hemlock Grove: A Crazy Vargulf 110
Fantastic Transformations 112
Explosive Plasticity as Character Development 116
Deep Ecology 117
Bitten: The Neofeminist Wolf 119
Sex and the Single Werewolf 120
Mastering Change and Desire 122
The Evofeminist Werewolf 125

5 Lust, Trust, and Educational Torture: *The Vampire Diaries* 129

The Vampire Diaries (2009–2017)
Sexual Selection Theory Revisited 130
Caroline: Stupid and Shallow 134
The Sexual Emotions 135
Abuse and Self-Confidence 137
Managing Lust and Love 139
Trust, Pain, and Play 141
Friends and a Climate of Trust 143
Restoring Trust 144
Who Do You Trust? 145
Trust, Educational Torture, and Change 146
The Doubling of Choices 148

Adult 151

6 Disgust and Self-Injury: *In My Skin, Martyrs, Black Swan* 153

In My Skin (2002), *Martyrs* (2008), *Black Swan* (2010)

Disgust 154
New French Extremity 157
Self-Injury 158
In My Skin: Fascinating Flesh 159
Cut N Slash Transgression 161
A New Ethics of Viewing 163
Martyrs: Third Wave French Extremity 164
When Self-Injury is Comforting 166
The White Mouse 167
The Feel-Bad Experience 169
Black Swan: A "Delicate Cutter" 170
Ordinary Disgust 171
"To Beauty" 172
The Magic Circle and the Moral Circle 173
Conclusion 175

7 The Maternal Myth: Birth, Breastfeeding, Mothering 177

Inside (2007), *Grace* (2009), *The Babadook* (2014)

Mother: The Good, the Bad, and the Real 178
Inside: "Completely Unwatchable" 180
Terror and a Real Maternal Body 182
Who is the Good Mother? 185
Grace: "It's All About Maintaining Your Diet" 187
Milk: "A Whole New Level of Freaky" 189
Mother Discourses 190
The Babadook: "This Monster Thing" 192
Meta-Play 193
Princess Play and Monster Play 195
Wild, Deep, and Dark Play 197
Conclusion 201

Middle Age 203

8 Home and Road: Carol's Change in *The Walking Dead* 205

The Walking Dead (2010–)

Graphic-Novel Carol and Television Carol 206
Change 208
House and Home 210
Home Is Where You Die 211
Alexandria 213
The Chronotope of the Road 214
The End of the Road 216
Stepping Up 218
"You Have to Change" 220
Two Kinds of Freedom 222
Eudaimonia 224
Surviving Middle Age 227

9 Age Anxiety and Chills: Jessica Lange and *American Horror Story* 229

American Horror Story (2011–)

The Emotion of Interest 231
Fiona, Supreme Witch 233
Ageism 234
Millennials and WAGs 235
The Bad Mother 238
Sex, Love, and Hell 239
Freaks and Chills 241
Piecing Together Elsa Mars 243
Lange Doing Lange 245
The Void of Identity 247

Old 251

10 Abyss and Peak: The New Old Woman 253

Penny Dreadful (2014–2016)
Penny Dreadful and Patti LuPone 254
The Old Woman 256
Joan: Witch and Wise Woman 257
The Witch in History 260
Dr. Seward: Scientist and Survivor 262
The Wise Woman in the White Room 264
Cool and Edgy 267
The New Old Woman 269

Exit: Playing the Ball Back to the Universe 273

Appendix 1. A Note on Age 275
Appendix 2. Table 3. Horror, Age, and Learning 279
Notes 281
Bibliography 325
Filmography 341
Index 345

LIST OF ILLUSTRATIONS

1.1 To be a werewolf affords a woman to kill with a single nail transformed into a claw. Elena (Laura Vandervoort) is about to get even with a molester from her childhood in *Bitten*: Season 1, Episode 10 ("Caged"). © Space, 2014.   30
2.1 Ofelia (Ivana Baquero) in her new, pretty dress and an intertextual nod to Alice's dress in *Alice's Adventures in Wonderland* from 1865. *Pan's Labyrinth* (*El laberinto del fauno*, 2006, Guillermo del Toro). © Estudios Picasso, Tequila Gang and Sententia Entertainment, 2006.   68
2.2 Jamie (Christian Bale) is covered in mud and saluted by American POWs in a Japanese prisoner-of-war camp during the Second World War. *Empire of the Sun* (1987, Steven Spielberg). © Amblin Entertainment and Warner Bros, 1987.   68
3.1 Eli (Lina Leandersson) looks like a girl. *Let the Right One In* (2008, Tomas Alfredson). © EFTI, Sandrew Metronome Distribution Sverige AB, Filmpool Nord, 2008.   86
3.2 Eli's (Lina Leandersson) scar in *Let the Right One In* (2008, Tomas Alfredson). © EFTI, Sandrew Metronome Distribution Sverige AB, Filmpool Nord, 2008.   94
4.1 Werewolf Alice (Amanda Ooms) dreams that she is caged and about to be operated on in Ben Bolt's British three-part mini-series *Wilderness* (1996). © Red Rooster Film & Television Entertainment and Carlton Television, 1996.   104
4.2 Alice (Amanda Ooms) retreats into a wildlife reservation where she with smooth CGI transforms from woman.... *Wilderness* (1996). © Red Rooster Film & Television Entertainment and Carlton Television, 1996.   105
4.3 ... and into wolf. *Wilderness* (1996). © Red Rooster Film & Television Entertainment and Carlton Television, 1996.   106
4.4 Sixteen-year-old Ginger (Katharine Isabelle) gets her first period after being bitten by a werewolf in *Ginger Snaps* (2000, John Fawcett). © Copperheart Entertainment, Water Pictures, Motion International, 2000.   108
4.5 The social outcast Ginger (Katharine Isabelle) becomes assertive, sexy, and self-assured after being bitten. *Ginger Snaps*

4.6	(2000, John Fawcett). © Copperheart Entertainment, Water Pictures, Motion International, 2000.	108
4.6	Young and insecure Christina (Freya Tingley) with her friends, the sexually experienced twins. *Hemlock Grove*: Season 1, Episode 2 ("The Angel"). © Netflix, 2014.	111
4.7	Christina's (Freya Tingley) face graphic and visceral transformation into a werewolf in *Hemlock Grove*: Season 1, Episode 12 ("Children of the Night"). © Netflix, 2014.	113
4.8	Petite teenager Christina (Freya Tingley) becomes a huge white werewolf. *Hemlock Grove*: Season 1, Episode 12 ("Children of the Night"). © Netflix, 2014.	114
4.9	The beautiful young werewolf Elena (Laura Vandervoort) is a supernatural SYF (single young female) in Canadian show *Bitten*: Season 1, Episode 1 ("Summons"). © Entertainment One, Hoodwink Entertainment, No Equal Entertainment, 2014.	120
4.10	Elena's (Laura Vandervoort) change from human into werewolf is rendered in smooth CGI. *Bitten*: Season 1, Episode 5 ("Bitten"). © Entertainment One, Hoodwink Entertainment, No Equal Entertainment, 2014.	123
4.11	Elena's (Laura Vandervoort) limbs slowly elongate into wolf limbs. *Bitten*: Season 1, Episode 5 ("Bitten"). © Entertainment One, Hoodwink Entertainment, No Equal Entertainment, 2014.	124
4.12	The transition from human to wolf in *Bitten* has no blood or gore as in *Hemlock Grove*. *Bitten*: Season 1, Episode 5 ("Bitten"). © Entertainment One, Hoodwink Entertainment, No Equal Entertainment, 2014.	124
5.1	Caroline (Candice Accola) can fling rapist Damon to the ground, now that she is no longer a weak human but a strong and an assertive vampire. *The Vampire Diaries*: Season 2, Episode 2 ("Brave New World"). © Alloy Entertainment, Bonanza Productions, Warner Bros. Television, 2010.	138
5.2	Vampire Caroline (Candice Accola) cries, when she sees her new fangs in the mirror. *The Vampire Diaries*: Season 2, Episode 1 ("The Return"). © Alloy Entertainment, Bonanza Productions, Warner Bros. Television, 2010.	140
5.3	Caroline (Candice Accola) is tortured by her father who wants to "fix" her vampirism through conditioning with pain. *The Vampire Diaries*: Season 3, Episode 3 ("The End of the Affair"). © Alloy Entertainment, Bonanza Productions, Warner Bros. Television, 2011.	142
6.1	Nina (Natalie Portman) pulls the skin off her finger in *Black Swan*, a self-injury that takes place in her imagination. *Black Swan* (2010, Darren Aronofsky). © Fox Searchlight Pictures, Cross Creek Pictures, Protozoa Pictures, 2010.	155

LIST OF ILLUSTRATIONS

6.2 Nina (Natalie Portman) cringes and makes a universal "disgust face" when she self-injures. *Black Swan* (2010, Darren Aronofsky). © Fox Searchlight Pictures, Cross Creek Pictures, Protozoa Pictures, 2010.   155

6.3 Esther (Marina de Van) self-injures in the basement, a scene which is beautifully composed and lit in chiaroscuro. *In My Skin* (*Dans ma peau*, 2002, Marina de Van). © Lazennec & Associés, Canal+, Centre National de la Cinématographie (CNC), 2002.   160

6.4 Esther (Marina de Van) is fascinated by her wounds, which she examines and reopens. *In My Skin* (*Dans ma peau*, 2002, Marina de Van). © Lazennec & Associés, Canal+, Centre National de la Cinématographie (CNC), 2002.   161

6.5 The mother in the nuclear family finds a little white mouse stuck in the drain in the garden. A meta-reflexive comment on nasty experiments. *Martyrs* (2008, Pascal Laugier). © Canal Horizons, Canal+, CinéCinéma, 2008.   165

7.1 Sarah (Alysson Paradis) holding her stomach after a car accident in French extremity film *Inside* (*À L'intérieur*, 2007, Alexandre Bustillo and Julien Maury). © La Fabrique de Films, BR Films, Canal+, 2007.   181

7.2 The Woman (Béatrice Dalle) attacks Sarah's (Alysson Para dis) stomach with scissors. *Inside* (*À L'intérieur*, 2007, Alexandre Bustillo and Julien Maury). © La Fabrique de Films, BR Films, Canal+, 2007.   182

7.3 The Woman (Béatrice Dalle) cuts Sarah's (Alysson Paradis) baby from her stomach on the stairs in Sarah's house. *Inside* (*À L'intérieur*, 2007, Alexandre Bustillo and Julien Maury). © La Fabrique de Films, BR Films, Canal+, 2007.   186

7.4 Madeline (Jordan Ladd) prepares a bottle with cow blood for her baby Grace. *Grace* (2009, Paul Solet). © Ariescope Pictures, Dark Eye Entertainment, Leoma Entertainment, 2009.   188

7.5 Wild, deep, and dark play between mother Amelia (Essie Davis) and her son Sam (Noah Wiseman) in *The Babadook* (2014, Jennifer Kent). © Screen Australia, Causeway Film, South Australian Film Corporation, 2014.   192

7.6 Amelia's sister Claire (Hayley McElhinney) and her friends performing motherhood as Perfect Mothers at the princess play birthday. *The Babadook* (2014, Jennifer Kent). © Screen Australia, Causeway Film, South Australian Film Corporation, 2014.   196

7.7 Sam (Noah Wiseman) teaches his mother to play The-Babadook-Game and hugs Amelia (Essie Davis) who is trying to kill him. *The Babadook* (2014, Jennifer Kent). © Screen Australia, Causeway Film, South Australian Film Corporation, 2014.   199

7.8 Amelia (Essie Davis) intimately hugs seven-year-old Sam (Noah Wiseman) at his first birthday party held on the day of his birthday. *The Babadook* (2014, Jennifer Kent). © Screen Australia, Causeway Film, South Australian Film Corporation, 2014.   201

8.1 In the first season of *The Walking Dead*, Carol (Melissa McBride) is a battered housewife. Her abusive husband dies in season one, she loses her daughter in season two, and in season three she becomes an able survivor. © AMC Film Holdings LLC. Courtesy Gene Page/AMC.   209

8.2 At the end of season five the group is invited into the gated community Alexandria. In season six Carol (Melissa McBride) masquerades as a lost housewife who in Alexandria has found a new "home" where she bakes cookies. *The Walking Dead*. © AMC Film Holdings LLC. Courtesy Frank Ockenfels 3/AMC.   213

8.3 Carol (Melissa McBride) travels the post-apocalyptic road with her friend and fellow survivor Daryl (Norman Reedus). *The Walking Dead*. © AMC Film Holdings LLC. Courtesy Frank Ockenfels 3/AMC.   216

8.4 In seasons four and five Carol (Melissa McBride) becomes a road warrior, an experienced killer, and the group's savior. *The Walking Dead*. © AMC Film Holdings LLC. Courtesy Gene Page/AMC.   219

8.5 Carol from *The Walking Dead* as a McFarlane action figure. © McFarlane Toys, The Walking Dead TV Series 6, 5in Action Figure, Carol Peletier.   225

8.6 Carol from *The Walking Dead* as a POP! vinyl figure. © POP! vinyl by Funko.   226

8.7 Carol (Melissa McBride) leading fellow female survivors in season eight of *The Walking Dead*. © AMC Film Holdings LLC. Courtesy Alan Clarke/AMC.   228

9.1 The Supreme Witch Fiona Goode (Jessica Lange) takes the young witches for a walk in New Orleans. *American Horror Story*: Season 3, Episode 1 ("Bitchcraft"). © Brad Falchuk Teley-Vision, Ryan Murphy Productions, 20th Century Fox Television, 2013.   237

9.2 The middle-age woman as the ultimate freak: Jessica Lange plays Elsa Mars, who in 1952 performs David Bowie's song "Life on Mars" from 1971. *American Horror Story*: Season 4, Episode 1 ("Monsters Among Us"). © Brad Falchuk Teley-Vision, Ryan Murphy Productions, 20th Century Fox Television, 2014.   241

10.1 Patti LuPone as the unruly witch Joan Clayton, who becomes mentor to Vanessa, the young witch and protagonist in *Penny Dreadful*. *Penny Dreadful*: Season 2, Episode 3 ("The Nightcomers"). © Sky/Showtime, 2015. 258

10.2 Dr. Seward (Patti LuPone) comforts hypnotized Vanessa (Eva Green) inside Vanessa's memory of her stay at the Banning clinic. *Penny Dreadful*: Season 3, Episode 4 ("A Blade of Grass"). © Sky/Showtime, 2016. 263

10.3 Dr. Seward (Patti LuPone) is a Victorian alienist and a New Old Woman who smokes, drinks, and can shoot guns. *Penny Dreadful*: Season 3, Episode 2 ("Predators Far and Near"). © Photo: Jonathan Hession/Sky/Showtime, 2016. 267

LIST OF TABLES

1   Scale of a Response to the Gender Stereotype   37
2   Horror as Play: Benefits, Narratives, and Themes   54
3   Horror, Age, and Learning   280

ACKNOWLEDGMENTS

This book has benefited from the help of so many people, I hardly know where to begin. Let me start with my editor, Katie Gallof, without whom it would never have been finished. She has been immensely positive and supportive over the years and kept faith in my project when I almost gave up. I am forever grateful. Her enthusiasm was a torch shining a light on the road, when I was lost. Thank you, Katie! Also thanks to Erin Duffy, who it has also been a pleasure to work with. And many thanks to the peer reviewers, who provided invaluable feedback that made me rethink the structure of the book and add a chapter on the old woman.

Over the years, I have had the fortune to meet wonderful colleagues around the world. When I feared my research was too strange to be worthy of the obscene amount of time I put into it, they assured me there was nothing strange about werewolves, torture, or negative emotions. They invited me to present my research and teach courses, and they read drafts of my chapters. I have benefited immensely from their feedback and in some instances also collaborations. Thank you to Angela Ndalianis for inviting me to the University of Melbourne and for reading all of my chapters and sharing her thoughts. You are one of my role models. Thank you also to Amanda Howell and Stephanie Green at Griffith University in Brisbane. They both read my chapters and shared their love of the dark fantastic, especially a love for *Penny Dreadful*. I have listened to your suggestions for making my argument clearer and my text shorter. To kill one's darlings is difficult.

I also thank the scholars from SCSMI, the Society for Cognitive Studies of the Moving Image, where I over the last seven years have presented my work. Here, I found friends, expertise, and "nerdy" research in the area of cognitive studies and bioculturalism. Especially thanks to Dirk Eitzen, who provided illuminating and meticulous editorial feedback on my article for *Projections* about positive emotions in horror; to Carl Plantinga who read the theoretical parts of this book and among other things suggested I summarize with bullet points; to Margrethe Bruun Vaage, who gave clever and diplomatic feedback on how to strengthen theory; and to Murray Smith for suggesting that I should read *The Philosopher and the Wolf*, a book that led me to ecological media theory.

At my workplace, The University of Southern Denmark, I have benefited from years of discussions with fellow scholars from media studies in my department and also with scholars outside the department. Especially thanks to Heidi Philipsen, who is marvelous at recognizing what works and doesn't work in a text and pointed me to creativity studies; to Sara Mosberg Iversen for feedback on play theory; and to many other colleagues for discussions over the years. A huge thank you also to Anne Jensen, my head of department, who gave me a year's research leave which made much of the present work here possible. Thanks also to Malin Isaksson from Umeå University who invited me to give a talk on women and horror and who was the first reader of Chapter 1 and Chapter 3. Her insightful comments made me think of gender differently.

Also thanks to my many graduate and postgraduate students, who over the years have endured courses that included horror texts, even in course topics where one would not expect such texts. Many have since told me, that my selection of films had altered their view of horror. I hope I haven't traumatized too many. Also thanks to my students in Nuuk, Greenland, who loved the horror films and with whom I had some unforgettable women's horror nights.

I am also fortunate to have friends, who are passionate about horror. Thanks to Nicolas Barbano for sharing your vast knowledge about the genre and for taking me to the cinema where we could scream together (I did most of the screaming). And thanks to Patrick Leis for being a friend with whom I can discuss all matters dark and painful.

But most of all, thanks to my two children. I started work on this book after a divorce, probably as a way to self-scare and self-heal. I truly believe horror makes us stronger and wiser. Life is a road filled with rocks, and we can't avoid those rocks. But it is up to us how we deal with them. We can step over them, walk around them, even develop the strength to carry them to the side of the road. Life is about learning. As I look back at my time of writing *Mastering Fear*, one of my fondest memories is a marvelous summer where the children, our dog Stella, and I were in a secluded cabin in the middle of the Finnish woods. Here, huddled together in a couch, we enjoyed the nightly company of vampires and werewolves from *Vampire Diaries* and *True Blood*. One might think *The Vampire Diaries* was my daughter's suggestion, but it was mine. *True Blood* was hers. And my son suggested *Stranger Things*.

Introduction

Approaching the Problem

This book analyses contemporary horror as a playground which offers negative and positive emotions to the player who is willing to engage with the genre's painful and potentially traumatizing scenarios. It asks why this play is attractive and why horror might be especially attractive to women. To put the argument in a nutshell, it is my working hypothesis that horror is play, and like play is adaptive and beneficial, so, too, is horror.

I still recall how Beth swept me off my feet when she negotiated her way out of the torture room in Eli Roth's torture porn film *Hostel: Part II* (2007).[1] Beth (Lauren German) is in a closed-down factory where costumers pay to torture and kill people. She has talked her way out of the torture chair by promising the torturer, Stuart, sex. She now has Stuart (Roger Bart) strapped in the chair and, holding a pair of scissors on his genitals, summons boss Micha so she can pay to get out. "You going to call your parents for money?" Micha asks. "No, motherfucker," Beth replies, "it's *my* money. Just get me a PDA, a SWIFT number and a recipient name. I have accounts in Switzerland, Luxembourg and the Isle of Man!" Then Micha says one must kill to leave the factory alive. "They're still gonna kill you, you stupid cunt," Stuart hisses. "What did you call me?" Beth says. Stuart: "You're a STUPID, FUCKING CUNT!" And this is when she cuts off his penis and throws it to the dogs. "Let him bleed to death," Beth says and swaggers out of the room.

I must have a mean streak because I *enjoyed* the sweet taste of payback. And then I started thinking about horror as a playground where we engage with challenging emotions, and why this is an excellent playground for women.

Playing with Horror

Austrian-British science philosopher Karl Popper points out that problems are better understood in hindsight once you have found an answer.[2] At that point your problem might turn out to be different from the one you set out to answer, which is what happened to me. *Mastering Fear* analyses fiction horror as mental play fighting and explains why horror is good for audiences, and why it can be especially good for women. However, play fighting was not part of my first work question, which was why horror, a male domain dominated by the negative emotions of pain, fear, and disgust, was attractive to women.

"The first version of my problem sprang from a two-and-a-half-decade long fascination with horror. I had always assumed horror was a male domain, and that it was natural for men to enjoy horror but unnatural for women."[3] This assumption had been confirmed countless times by people's reactions to my research. Let me illustrate. On hearing I was writing a book about the appeal of horror to women, a renowned male colleague told me, "it is natural for men to watch horror but not for women. You are the one anomaly to this biological rule." This was at a conference where I presented a draft of Chapter 2, which asks what happens when the protagonist in Guillermo del Toro's *Pan's Labyrinth* (*El laberinto del fauno*, 2006) is a girl instead of a boy. The following year, at the same annual conference, I presented a paper on Marina de Van's *In My Skin* (*Dans ma peau*, 2002), whose protagonist is obsessed with cutting and eating her skin. The next year, a German colleague said she still vividly remembered a scene I had shown—with the audio, not visual, of the protagonist self-injuring—and asked how I could enjoy such disgusting material? I used to feel guilty about my ventures into horror, not only because the territory was supposedly male, but also because I enjoyed them, which made me doubly guilty since I sided with "the enemy." However, when my German colleague approached me, my work hypothesis had by then evolved into a second version, where I analysed horror as play and asked how it was adaptive and beneficial for men as well as for women.

Before I explain further, let me illustrate the nature of this playground with another example. One of my most intense engagements with horror was with Alexandre Bustillo and Julien Maury's New French Extremity film *Inside* (*À L'intérieur*, 2008). *Inside* follows a pregnant woman, Sarah (Alysson Paradis), on the night before her planned cesarean birth, when a stranger, a woman, enters her house. I watched *Inside* on DVD with my husband, who left the room when scissors were applied to Sarah's stomach. He returned twice to ask how I could *possibly* enjoy such a *repulsive* film. "I think it is fascinating ... from a woman's point of view," I stuttered, mesmerized by the women's fight over a fetus. It was an ordeal to watch *Inside*, yet I found Sarah's delivery in a stream of blood on the stairs in her home a unique experience. Unique does *not* mean pleasant. Sarah at one point wraps duct tape around her throat to stop a bleeding wound and continues to fight even when her water breaks. She *really* deserved to live. But didn't.

So, let me return to the second version of my problem and why we enjoy horror. How can it be good for anyone, women or men, to watch such gruesomeness? It is my hypothesis that we engage with horror *as play*. Play can be painful, but is also adaptive and beneficial. And the kind of horror we choose to watch may be less determined by our sex (as the anecdote of me and my husband shows) than by our age and personality.

Unpleasant and Fun

There are many types of play, and in this book I compare horror to *play fighting*, which is when you fight for fun. Play fighting involves rules of equality and fairness, of pain and ambivalence, and it is based on the agreement that players exchange the rules of the real world with the rules of play. Play fighting is a safe place to learn things like survival skills, social rules, and creativity.

We shall see in Chapter 1, "The Dark Stage," that there is little accord among researchers about the nature of play; however, I view play as functional, beneficial, and adaptive. To fight for fun is called play fighting in non-human animals and *rough-and-tumble play* (R&T play) in humans. For brevity's sake I call non-human animals "animals" and human animals "humans," however, *we are animals too*. Also, I will use "play fighting" and "R&T play" interchangeably. Play fighting has positive and negative elements (fun and pain) and is rooted in aggression and characterized by make-believe (pretending) and mixed emotions (playing hurts but also brings other emotions). Returning to *Hostel: Part II* and *Inside*, this means watching horror can be unpleasant *and* fun, traumatizing *and* play. Horror as mental play fighting is rooted in aggression and facilitates a range of emotions, both negative emotions of pain, fear, and disgust, and positive emotions of lust, hope, trust, interest, and freedom. Furthermore, to return to women and horror, my research has led me to the conclusion that play fighting is equally natural and adaptive for women and men.

The aim of this book is to understand the function of horror, and rather than place negative emotions at the genre's core, I suggest its core is play fighting. Also, I pursue the argument that horror is adaptive for women, which is why I focus on female protagonists in contemporary film and television. Since my method is textual analysis, and I do not generate empirical data or carry out audience interviews, I can analyse representations of characters and emotions in texts but only speculate what real audiences feel and think. Thus, my analysis of responses to horror are based on what the natural sciences call "anecdotal evidence." Anecdotal evidence is not scientifically representative or valid, because anecdotes come from a researcher's personal experience and typically from situations that cannot be repeated as science requires for data to be valid (anecdotal evidence can be when a biologist observes an animal in the wild behave in a specific way in a specific situation).[4] My anecdotal evidences are from my viewings, from my knowledge of close to a thousand students' experiences after teaching horror for two decades, and from my experience with my family's and friends' viewings. My anecdotal evidence is also from what horror fans share on the Internet. Taking a hermeneutic (textual analysis) route to the experience of horror means I cannot "prove" my analyses reflect audiences' actual experiences. However, it is hard to empirically test the unpleasantness of horror, since it is not permitted in social experiments to submit test subjects to those truly traumatizing scenes I can submit myself to. To test challenging emotions on test subjects raises questions of methods and legality, and I leave these to scholars working with qualitative data and social experiments.[5]

Following the tradition of textual analysis, I have chosen texts that illustrate my problem: What is the nature and function of horror, and what is its appeal to women? My texts include American and European contemporary film and television horror with female protagonists, and are from between 2000 and 2016 with the exception of one text from 1996. My examples do not follow a historical or thematic development, but were chosen because they provide interesting material with which to discuss my hypothesis. Although they are anecdotal evidence, I believe they serve their purpose, which is to explore the complexity of horror as play and illuminate its potential use and appeal to women.

The book has two theoretical frameworks; one is *bioculturalism* and another I call *evofeminism*. They support two arguments; the first is that horror is a mental form of play fighting and a dark stage, the second is that this dark stage is especially appealing to women because it can challenge society's gender stereotype and re-author negative gender scripts. The two frameworks serve different purposes; bioculturalism is truth-based and the foundation of my argument about play, and evofeminism is a compass, pointing my biocultural approach in a specific direction, namely towards gender equality. Where bioculturalism is based on science and facts (as far as it is possible to speak of facts in science), evofeminism is thus political and based on humanism and equality, values and ethics, choice and change.[6]

Let us now return to the first version of my problem where I assumed horror was a male territory with negative emotions. This assumption changed when I ventured into bioculturalism. I had been intrigued by works on horror, among them *The Philosophy of Horror* (1990) by cognitive philosopher Noël Carroll, *Embodied Visions* by Danish biocultural film theorist Torben Grodal (2009), and *The Horror Sensorium* (2012) by Australian new media scholar Angela Ndalianis. Bioculturalism is shorthand for the merging of *natural sciences* with the *humanities*.[7] Together they make an interdisciplinary approach that embraces all areas of science. This requires longer arms than most of us are blessed with, which is why there is disagreement about most things in the field. The overall agreement is that human nature, like animal nature and all life on the planet, has evolved over successive generations, and that nature is a result of genetics, natural selection, and adaptation to the environment. The brain is understood as an organ in our body, and such things as mind, consciousness, and self are seen as generated from the brain's processing of stimuli from the environment. Research in neuroanatomy shows such processing is done mostly by automatic subsystems over which we have little influence. Yet there are such things as self and choice and free will, which I return to in Chapter 1.

While a biocultural approach, on the one hand, raises the issue if it is possible to harness the many horses of science without this becoming a wild ride, a promising aspect, on the other hand, is that bioculturalism is holistic. It embraces environment, body, and mind, and it rejects dichotomies of culture versus nature, of brain versus body, of self versus world, and "soft" ethics versus "hard" science. Popper argues research starts not with a subject matter but with a problem, and that research requires multiple theories: "[Y]ou can neither collect observations nor documentary evidence if you do not first have a problem . . . [and] . . . *there are no subject matters but only problems* which, admittedly, may lead to the rise of theories but *which almost always need for their solution the help of widely different theories*" (emphasis in original).[8] The complexity of a biocultural approach can be compared to chaos systems which are impossible to predict, yet this complexity is a necessary evil that makes possible the deeper understanding of a problem. Bioculturalism thinks the above dichotomies are interwoven and wants to explain what appears to be inexplicable: Why do we enjoy horror's unpleasant stories? Why is it good to feel fear in fiction form? And why am I not an anomaly when I watch Sarah die?

I return to play later in this Introduction and in Chapter 1, so for now we will let play and bioculturalism rest. Suffice it to say that both are ambiguous, painful, and useful. Now, what also turned out to be a challenge was the concept of gender. In my earlier writing I used psychosemiotics and concepts like a male gaze, castration anxiety, excess, and masquerade.[9] When I began work on this book, however, I shifted from feminism to postfeminism (2007, 2016) and my process of questioning horror made me question emotions, self, body, and gender.[10] Drawing from multiple strains of psychology, I ventured into cognitive psychology, ecological psychology, social and developmental psychology, and feminist phenomenology. To cut a long story short, I discarded assembled ideas from the cognitive sciences, social sciences, and phenomenology to build the framework of evofeminism, which is both biocultural and social constructivist.

Only Humans have Gender

I elaborate on evofeminism in Chapter 1, so here I shall merely outline the main points. From cognitive psychology I take the view that our ideas about gender are constructed by society and formulated as schemas, stereotypes, and scripts, which the brain uses to give meaning to the world, to construct our self, and to choose appropriate behavior. Only humans have gender. Animals have sex (male and female), but don't wear pink dresses and blue suits. Gender is a cultural construction which requires high cognitive abilities. To be female or male is a biological given, but how we *think* about ourselves as women and men is a result of society's gender stereotype. It is said that sex is innate and gender is cultural, however, neuropsychologist Melissa Hines in *Brain Gender* (2004) says this simple division is impossible to uphold since all stimuli, external and internal, pass through our brain, and behavior results from a mix of innate traits and acquired learning, and can be altered by environmental as well as situational circumstances.[11]

What kind of feminism is evofeminism? I understand feminism as a struggle for equality between women and men, and history shows a long trajectory of discrimination against women that continues today. Cognitive psychologist Cordelia Fine in *The Delusions of Gender* (2010) traces discrimination into the age of neuroscience and says, "[o]ur minds, society, and neurosexism create difference. Together, they wire gender. But the wiring is soft, not hard. It is flexible, malleable, and changeable."[12] Gender is brain software that can be rewritten. Bioculturalism is dedicated to truth, yet here, too, we find gender bias. Professor of language and communication Deborah Cameron (2015) calls society's ideas about women and men a *meta-narrative*, a story which integrates and connects ideas of gender from all areas in science and everyday life, and this story is then used to explain gender as innate and natural.[13] To change the meta-narrative, British clinical psychologist Jane M. Ussher in *Managing the Monstrous Feminine* (2006) calls for a "re-authoring process," by which she means we must rewrite our gender scripts into new scripts with more agency and freedom.[14] Negative stereotypes restrict people and make them underperform, however, as the work of social psychologist Claude M. Steele (2010) shows, we can combat negative stereotypes.[15] As you might guess, gender is a negative stereotype, and with *Mastering Fear* I want to participate in a re-authoring of the meta-narrative.

My aim with evofeminism is to alloy feminism with bioculturalism and thus use a scientific and ethical framework for discussing gender equality. I use a wide view of feminism and draw on second and third wave feminism, postfeminism, ecofeminism, neofeminism, and the recently coined fourth wave feminism.[16] The point is to further what I believe is the goal of feminism: Equality. Evofeminism is rooted in humanism and ecosophy. The latter, ecosophy, is ecological philosophy, which I return to in Chapter 4.[17] To look requires a frame of looking and, as feminist science philosopher Donna Haraway puts it, "accounts of a 'real' world do not, then, depend on a logic of 'discovery', but on a power-charged social relation of 'conversation.'"[18] Evofeminism is my power-charged conversation with science.

Defining Horror

Previous studies of horror emphasize different elements and functions. Thus, James Twitchell in his classic *Dreadful Pleasures* (1985) three decades ago said horror instructs the young in sexual behavior: "[M]odern horror myths prepare the teenager for the anxieties of reproduction ... they are fables of sexual identity."[19] A few years later, two canonical feminist works, Carol Clover's *Men, Women and Chain Saws* (1992) and Barbara Creed's *The Monstrous-Feminine* (1993), made a different argument, namely that horror reflects men's sadomasochistic fears and fantasies about women. In their view, horror was an expression of a patriarchal and misogynist society. Clover stressed the final girl—the female protagonist in the slasher film— was a stand-in for "the male viewer's ... sadomasochistic fantasies" and to see her "as a feminist development" was "a particular grotesque expression of wishful thinking."[20] Isabel Cristina Pinedo argued differently in *Recreational Terror* (1997), namely that the final girl was, indeed, a feminist development.[21] Recently, Erin Harrington in *Women, Monstrosity and Horror Film: Gynaehorror* (2017) offers a refreshingly new feminist reading of women in horror, building on Clover and Creed, and combining psychoanalyst readings with the work of Deleuze and Guattari.[22]

Taking a cognitive approach, Noël Carroll in *The Philosophy of Horror, or Paradoxes of the Heart* (1990) argued that we pay for our curiosity about the monster with the negative emotions of fear and disgust: "[T]he pleasures derived from art-horror are a function of fascination, which fascination compensates for the negative emotions engendered by the fiction." Thus, "[t]o ask what is compelling about horror ... [the] answer is the detailed account of fascination and curiosity found above."[23] In a similar cognitive reasoning, British film scholar Murray Smith (1999) links audiences' pleasures in the perverse to a revolt, not so much against morality as against moralism, and he connects horror to moral learning and moral "slumming."[24] Cynthia Freeland in *The Naked and the Undead* (2000) says we learn about evil and society's ethics. Horror films "stimulate *thoughts* about evil in its many varieties and degrees: internal or external, limited or profound, physical or mental, natural or supernatural, conquerable or triumphant."[25] Cognitive work on horror explores the idea that the genre questions society's ethics rather than it expresses our desires. In *Embodied Visions* (2009),

Grodal says horror expresses "a more basic, tribal moral system in which the world is divided into 'us' and 'them.' If some of them offend some of us, we are entitled to use any means to humiliate and eventually kill them."[26] Thus, Grodal thinks horror takes us back to an innate (primitive) morality, whereas society's morality has evolved into ethics. In recent phenomenological takes on horror, German film scholar Julian Hanich in *Cinematic Emotion in Horror Films and Thrillers* (2010) and Finnish film scholar Tarja Laine (2006, 2011) explore the physical sensations of horror. Hanich analyses the sensuous dimensions of five kinds of fear he calls "direct horror, suggested horror, cinematic shock, cinematic dread and cinematic terror,"[27] and argues our fear in cinematic horror is sensuous and links us to a collective body of co-watchers. Laine in *Feeling Cinema* (2011) says we have an emotional dialogue with a film. Rather than share a point of view with a film or a character, she says we experience "the encounter between the body of the film and the body of the spectator."[28] That is, we affectively feel we are *in* the situation the film represents. Phenomenologists focus on the affects, sensations, and feelings of horror.

In her new media approach, Angela Ndalianis in *The Horror Sensorium: Media and the Senses* (2012) explores how we connect, or *interface* as she calls it, with horror in multiple ways, and how the genre interacts simultaneously with the cognitive, emotional, and affective parts of our sensorium. According to her, horror (especially modern horror) cannot be reduced to sensations or emotions, but "is more like a ping-pong match with multiple balls in play at once—each ball representing a different way of 'being touched' by what's onscreen,"[29] which makes the analysis of a horror experience a matter of a complex interface and interaction with the fiction. Finally, cultural studies in horror, for example Kevin J. Wetmore's *Post–9/11 Horror in American Cinema* (2012), has viewed the genre as an expression of *cultural malaise*, akin to a Freudian discontent of civilization. As Wetmore writes, "[i]t is my hope that by looking into the abyss, we understand ourselves, our culture and what we may have become in the ten years since."[30]

My theory of horror as mental play fighting cuts across the above approaches. By taking play fighting and aggression as a starting point, *Mastering Fear* does not exclude the above explanations, but interacts with them. For example, horror can indeed serve as initiation ritual for young audiences, because how we play changes with age, and the emotions of horror also change according to whether protagonists are young, middle age, or old. Stories with young often have emotions of lust and trust, while stories with adults often have emotions of pain and fear, and stories with middle-age women focus on survival and have emotions like self-esteem and interest. Horror has different stories and emotions for different ages.

Most definitions use the emotion of horror as key, like Andrew Tudor in *Theories of Film,* who says horror films are "films that have in common the *intention* to horrify," and Carroll who thinks "[horror] films are designed to provoke fear."[31] The Merriam-Webster Dictionary defines "horror" as "painful and intense fear, dread, or dismay" and "intense aversion or repugnance." However, such definitions pull negative emotions to the center, which I am reluctant to do.[32] Albeit the horror genre is rooted in aggression, it is misleading to focus on negative emotions. Like play fighting, the horror genre embraces multiple emotions, and like emotions in real life, they are not experienced in isolation but are mixed. Thus, while we *hope* for Sarah's survival, we *fear* she will die and are *disgusted* by the attacks on her body. The horror genre, like play fighting, is not "about" negative emotions. It is about learning skills and acquiring abilities, among them emotional robustness, coping, social skills, flexibility, and creativity.

If we see horror as play, it becomes clear that negative emotions are accompanied by positive emotions. Horror offers more complex emotional engagement than has until now been acknowledged and it allows us to experiment, be creative, and prepare for the unexpected. Play fighting offers safe engagement with trauma and where animals play in the here and now, fiction offers what has been called a "Darwinian machine"; fiction allows humans to play with future situations and imagine possible as well as impossible scenarios (involving, for instance, supernatural forces).[33] As we shall see, humans can make more complex uses of horror as play fighting than animals can when they play for fun. Basically, our play allows us to rewrite our software.

I define horror as a dark stage where we play with *challenging emotions* and *difficult situations* that involve both negative and positive emotions. Challenging emotions range from fear and disgust to despair, anger, shame, and more, and they are challenging in the sense that they *feel* unpleasant. Mixed in with challenging emotions are other emotions like lust, trust, love, freedom, and vengeance. As for a genre definition, I agree with Carroll, Freeland, and Hanich that horror has fuzzy borders which overlap with neighbor genres, especially science fiction, the thriller, and the psychological drama, which is why some of my examples are from these genres.[34] The difference between horror and other genres is the intensity of negative emotions, however, strict border patrol is not necessary for our journey in this book.

Play fighting facilitates agency, freedom, and flexibility, and it is *not* a male terrain. If women watch less horror and play fight less than men, it is not because women are less active, more emphatic, or less aggressive. It is due to the gender stereotype. Society has long assumed aggression to be male; however, while violent crime is decreasing in the West, the percentage of violent crimes committed by women is rising.[35] Some explain this by increased equality which today allows women to express instead of suppress aggression.[36]

Aggression is innate. In horror, we play with aggression and pain and fear. Horror is a playground where players become stronger, and although not all stories end well, horror can challenge the meta-narrative, combat gender stereotype, and re-author scripts. Sarah loses her life but we, the audience, live and learn. The point of horror is not happy ends, but to face challenges and practice to master fear.

The Structure of *Mastering Fear*

The book has a theoretical chapter and nine analytical chapters. Chapter 1, "The Dark Stage," lays out the theory of horror as play with three sections on emotions, gender, and play. The analytical chapters, then, explore female protagonists in contemporary European and American horror film and television. They examine what emotions horror offers, how women are represented, and to what extent the gender stereotype is re-authored. Chapters progress chronologically from children to adolescents, from emerging adults to adults, and from middle age to old age. The idea with this design is to see if play changes as we move through what developmental psychologist Erik Erikson calls *life stages*. He described eight stages and believed each had distinct conflicts one must solve to move successfully to the next stage. His wife, Joan Erikson, added a ninth stage for old-old age, which is the eighties and nineties.[37] The idea is that as we age, we move through the life stages and solve life's changing conflicts, which are emotional, developmental, and existential. I use Erikson's life stages because I think horror is not only for an adolescent audience, but for adult audiences too. Texts range from art cinema to mainstream television, and among my heroines are innocent girls and supernatural teens, self-injurers and troubled mothers, tough-as-nails zombie survivors, age-anxious witches, and world-savvy alienists.

Chapter 1 is divided into three parts discussing emotions, gender, and play. The first part of Chapter 1 draws from cognitive psychology, emotions studies, and cognitive philosophy. Here, I discuss what emotions are, what it means to feel them, and how we construct a self. Emotions involve body, environment, and a situation. Seen from an ecological perspective, emotions arise in response to stimuli. To understand emotions, I draw on Dutch psychologist Nico Frijda (1986, 2007), and to understand how we feel emotions, I draw on neuroscientist Antonio Damasio's (2000) ideas of consciousness and self.[38] Emotions lead to actions, and in my discussion of what it means to have a self and respond to events, I combine research by neuroscientist Michael Gazzaniga (2011), Israeli neuroeconomist Daniel Kahneman (2011), and German cognitive philosopher Thomas Metzinger (2009).[39] I ask how the mind works, what role emotions play, and if there is such a thing as free will—which, apparently, there is. Yet, as Kahneman points out, the mind is ruled by heuristics and it takes cognitive effort to go against our stereotypes and scripts.

The second part of Chapter 1 relates a cognitive view of self and consciousness to gender. Are women and men's brains really different, as neuropsychologist Simon Baron-Cohen (2003, 2011) claims?[40] Or does the brain construct consciousness and self the same way, whether we are women or men? Scientists disagree, and drawing on schemas and stereotypes as cognitive software, I see gender as created by culture. Thus, if sex is biological hardware, gender belongs to software. Drawing on feminist psychology, feminist phenomenology, and feminist biology, I discuss gender in relation to mind, body, and change. The gender stereotype and Cameron's meta-narrative are real, but can be challenged. Challenging raises questions about essentialism and social construction. Are men aggressive and women emphatic? And if so, is this innate, learned, or somewhere in between, and can the human mind transcend what is "hard-wired"? I believe in flexibility of the mind, and if we cannot remove schemas and stereotypes, we can re-author them and make our own choices.

The last part of Chapter 1 takes us to the realm of play. All mammals play, and humans play in complex ways from infancy and until old age.[41] Play takes place in what French sociologist Roger Caillois (2001) calls *a pure space*, where we exchange the rules of the real world with rules of play.[42] Game studies calls this *the magic circle*.[43] Ethologist Gordon M. Burghardt (2005) has divided animal play into nine types, one of which is *play fighting*, fighting for fun.[44] When animals play fight, they learn sensorimotor skills, sexual and social skills, emotional robustness, flexibility, and creativity. When rats play, they become more resilient, courageous, and better able to deal with unexpected events, and so, too, do humans. The chapter discusses play fighting as what in sociology is called *edgework*, which is when we do dangerous activities like mountain climbing or BASE jumping. When players "work" the edge, they calculate and manage risks so they can enjoy danger without dying. Sociologist Stephen Lyng (1990) says, "[i]n edgework, the ego is called forth in a dramatic way."[45] I see horror as mental edgework and as self-work.

Research in play and edgework disagrees on the role respectively of sex and gender, both when it comes to sex differences and gender differences. Some researchers find innate differences in how boys and girls play. Others, like psychologist Michael J. Apter (2007), think there is no innate difference in regard to the sexes' innate excitement-seeking and risk-seeking instinct.[46] Also, while a lot of play research focuses on children and play as developmental, I build on the idea that we continue to play as we age, and that play is, as sociologist Thomas S. Henricks (2015) argues, essential to self-development throughout life.[47] The chapter, finally, links horror to aggression and takes inspiration from South African neuropsychologist Victor Nell (2006). Nell outlines three types of aggression which serve predation, competition, and self-defense.[48] I use Nell's work to outline three basic horror narratives: Survival horror, social horror, and identity horror.

At the end of the chapter, I summarize horror as mental play fighting and link this to the three types of aggression.

The analytical chapters, then, explore female protagonists in contemporary horror. Chapters 2 and 3 examine child horror heroines. These films, however, are not children's films. The children we find in horror represent society's ideas (scripts) about children, and they are aimed at adult audiences. Chapter 2 looks at Guillermo del Toro's *Pan's Labyrinth*. Del Toro's combination of the fantastic with war, horror, and the fairy tale illustrates how genre expectations are affected by the gender stereotype. I look at how affects are cleverly used to play with the viewer's genre and gender expectations. Chapter 3 explores the love-and-vengeance story between the twelve-year-old boy Oscar and the vampire girl Eli in Swedish film *Let the Right One In* (*Låt den rätte komma in*, 2008, Tomas Alfredson). When classmates bully Oscar, Eli tells him to strike back. "But if they . . ." he protests. "Then I will help you. I can do that," she says. It is an odd promise from a girl, but Eli turns out to be a castrated boy-vampire. The chapter discusses how the emotion of vengeance is gendered and how gender change from John Ajvide Lindqvist's novel (2004) to its Swedish film adaptation and its American remake, *Let Me In* (2010, Matt Reeves).

Chapters 4 and 5 have werewolves and vampires and the protagonists are adolescents and young adults. Chapter 4 discusses ecological psychology and werewolf affordances, and shows how female werewolves savor aggression, agency, and freedom. I examine lupine protagonists in the British television mini-series *Wilderness* (1996), John Fawcett's Canadian cult film *Ginger Snaps* (2000), and television series *Hemlock Grove* (2013–2015, Netflix) and *Bitten* (2014–2016, Space). Chapter 5 ventures into sexual selection theory with the television series *The Vampire Diaries* (2010–, CW) and supporting character Caroline. She is turned into a vampire in season two and she becomes the show's female protagonist in season seven. I focus on the emotions of lust and trust, and show how horror offers an alternative version of the sexual selection theory in a world with serial dating.

Chapters 6 and 7 examine adult women. Chapter 6 analyses three films with self-injurers: Marina de Van's French psychological drama *In My Skin*, Pascal Laugier's New French Extremity film *Martyrs* (2008), and Darren Aronofsky's psychological thriller *Black Swan* (2010). These films belong to my "identity horror" and I read the self-injury as Nell's angry aggression. Angry aggression serves self-defense, and I discuss angry aggression when it is, paradoxically, directed against one's own body. Chapter 7 focuses on the maternal myth and the mother stereotype, and I here analyse *Inside*, Paul Solet's *Grace* (2009), and Jennifer Kent's Australian ghost film *The Babadook* (2014). These deal with, respectively, wombraiding, a troubled mother with a bloodthirsty baby, and a widow mother with a six-year-old son and a monster, the Babadook. I discuss how the films use, question, and in one case re-authors the mother script.

Chapters 8 and 9 examine middle-age horror heroines. Chapter 8 looks at Carol in *The Walking Dead* (2010–, AMC). Carol was originally a minor character written to die in season one, but she became so popular that in season four she became the show's female protagonist. I examine the tropes of "home" and "road," the emotion of freedom, and I discuss Carol as subverting the gender stereotype for middle-age women. Chapter 9 is dedicated to actress Jessica Lange and her characters Fiona and Elsa in seasons three and four of *American Horror Story* (2011–, FX). Lange plays respectively an age-anxious witch and a star-obsessed owner of a freak circus. The chapter focuses on the emotion of interest and on how meta-play can subvert a negative middle-age script for women.

Finally, Chapter 10 examines the old woman in horror. I discuss two supporting characters in television series *Penny Dreadful* (2014–2016, Showtime/Sky), the witch Joan Clayton and the alienist Dr. Seward, both played by Patti LuPone.[49] In a youth-obsessed Western culture, women face ageism and sexism. To age is conventionally seen as an abyss and as death. However, in Erikson's theory of the life stages, the theme in old age is wisdom and Joan M. Erikson suggests the metaphor of a peak instead of an abyss. In old age, knowledge becomes wisdom and we here share our wisdom with our community. We become "good ancestors." LuPone's two characters show that although the old woman in horror is still today a negative stereotype, the genre also offers new and positive scripts for women.

1

The Dark Stage

One of my favorite horror scenes is in the British monster movie *The Descent* (2005, Neil Marshall), where six women go on a trip into a mountain cave system. It happens after tunnels collapse behind them and there is no turning back. They now enter an enormous cave. The bouncing rays of lights from lamps mounted on their helmets capture something white at their feet: Bones. The protagonist Sarah (Shauna Macdonald) turns on the infrared sight on her camera to see better in the dark. "Hundreds of dead animals," she concludes. One of the women has a twisted ankle and they are all terrified. What carnivorous creatures live miles down in the mountains? "What *is* this place," one asks and another yells: "Hello? Is there ANYBODY THERE?" As Sarah turns her head, the infrared light suddenly reveals a humanoid, slimy, and hungry-looking creature right behind them. At this point, I jumped in the couch and screamed out loud, which made my children come running. I assured them there was nothing to be afraid of. Mom was just enjoying herself with a movie. Really, this was just fun.

Later in the film, when several of the women are dead, Sarah has learnt that the monsters have an excellent sense of hearing but are blind. When a creature approaches, she lies still and lets it walk over her. Holding her breath, she controls instincts telling her to flee. Sarah has learnt to master her fear. We, too, learn from fiction horror. And where Sarah ultimately dies despite having learnt to control her emotions, we, the audience, live. Unlike Sarah, our lives are not at stake, because we are *playing* with fear.

In this chapter, I outline horror as a dark stage where characters may die horrible deaths, but where audiences play with fear. It is divided into three sections on emotions, gender, and play. In conclusion, I discuss how horror taps into aggression and has three basic narratives, which I call *survival horror*, *social horror* and *identity horror*. There is also a fourth narrative, which I call *creative horror*. It is when the fiction demonstrates self-awareness about its status as fiction and play, like *The Cabin in the Woods* (2012, Drew Goddard). Horror teaches us to manage challenging emotions and make difficult choices. It functions like play fighting does for animals.

However, the human mind is more complex than the animal mind, and our play with fear more complex than animal play fighting. To understand how horror teaches us to manage emotions and make choices, we will therefore first ask what emotions are, how we construct a "self," how this self becomes gendered, and what it means to play on the edge, where characters fall into the abyss and our experience can feel unpleasant, sometimes even traumatizing.

EMOTIONS

> ... stepping into the light is also a powerful metaphor for consciousness, for the birth of the knowing mind, for the simple and yet momentous coming of the sense of self into the world of the mental.
>
> ANTONIO DAMASIO (2000)

When I read neuroscientist Antonio Damasio's *The Feeling of What Happens* (2000) I realized two things: Emotions are fundamental for our construction of mind and, second, our culture associates a "knowing" mind—consciousness—with the metaphor of "light."

Before we engage with emotions and why they are relevant to an analysis of horror, I want to start with Damasio. *The Feeling of What Happens* explains how feelings are embedded in consciousness and are instrumental in the creation of mind and our sense of self. Damasio visualizes consciousness as a stage where the individual, the "I," is an actor:

> [W]e can imagine ourselves walking across the stage under the light ... Then the intensity of the light increases and as it gets brighter, more of the universe is illuminated. More objects of our past than ever before can be clearly seen, first separately, then at once; more objects of our future, and more objects in our surrounding are brightly lit. Under the growing light of consciousness, more gets to be known each day, more finely, and at the same time.[1]

Consciousness begins with an *awareness* of feelings and the ability to store this awareness—which Damasio calls the feeling-of-a-feeling—to memory. Memory is a cognitive process which requires so-called second-order neural accounts. The ability to create these second-order accounts, to store them in the brain, and to remember them at will, separates us from animals. We can remember things from our past and we can make plans for a future. Animals cannot do mental time travel or create imaginary worlds.[2] Animals share many emotions with us—they can love, hate, form friendship, be jealous, and hold grudges—but dolphins do not keep libraries in the sea, and chimpanzees do not trade stocks in the jungle. They have no abstract language, keep no archives, and do not imagine the non-existent (like vampire dolphins or zombie chimpanzees) or plan for a pension. Damasio explains that awareness of feeling—the second-order neural maps—enables memory and learning. Awareness enables meta-thinking, which is the ability to use abstract language, and meta-thinking enables choice in how we act in our world. In short, awareness of our feelings takes us to learning, choice, and free will. Because, like Sarah, you and I can learn about our emotions and we can choose to overrule our instincts. When we interact with our world, we can choose how to react. And this is where horror can teach us to face challenging situations and choose our response.

Damasio uses the metaphors "stage" and "light." The latter is from the Bible's "Let there be light," which you might recall is followed by "the earth was a formless void and darkness covered the face of the deep . . ."[3] In the West, we associate "light" with God, with what is good, and what is rational. In this mythic and binary thinking, we also, in contrast, associate "darkness" with Satan, with evil, and with chaos and irrationality.

In *Mastering Fear*, I twist Damasio's "light" and "stage" into "dark" and "dark stage." My stage is metaphor for mind, but the dark stage is also metaphor for the challenging emotions and things we fear. My darkness is frightening, but not evil or irrational. Where Damasio pictures mind bathed in light, I picture it in darkness too. Like blacklight, black holes, and black matter, darkness does not imply absence of matter. It designates things that are uncomfortable and dangerous. Like blacklight, darkness may be in a different spectrum than ordinary light. We might have to feel, before we can see. But what we feel on the dark stage is as significant to mind and consciousness as what we see in the light. In fact, the dark stage is crucial to create a resilient and strong mind, because the horror experience pushes us over the edge and forces us to fight and adapt.

Although I get ahead of myself, I want to mention Nobel prize winner and neuroeconomist Daniel Kahneman's *System 1* and *System 2*, concepts he uses to describe how the mind works. System 1 is intuitive and quick, and System 2 is deliberate and slow. We can say System 1 is hard-wired and System 2 evolves with learning and memory. System 2 is "associated with the subjective experience of agency, choice, and concentration."[4] If we remember Sarah, then System 1 makes you scream at the sight of monsters and System 2 can make you choose to pretend you are dead and let monsters walk over you.

It takes practice to use System 2 to overrule System 1 and "it is much easier to identify a minefield when you observe others wandering into it than when you are about to do so."[5] This is what horror offers: We observe characters wander into bad places, torture cellars, and deep woods, we share their emotions, and when they die, we remember their actions and we expand our skills and choices for the future.

What are Emotions?

My theoretical exchange of psychosemiotics with bioculturalism is recent, and when researching this book, I discovered my ignorance in the study of emotions. For example, cognitive scholars prefer emotions with clear cognitive aims, like fear, whereas phenomenologists and affects scholars talk of affects, feelings, and sensations rather than emotions. Emotions, it turned out, are not clearly defined. In science, and in everyday language, the word "emotions" interact and overlap with affects, feelings, sensations, mood, senses, feeling states, and drives. Most academic studies about horror leap straight from fear to why we want to feel bad. However, because I see horror as play, and because I believe horror as play involves many emotions, I want to begin by asking what emotions are.

"Emotions" is adapted from French *émouvoir*, "to stir up," which illustrates that emotions are passionate. Psychologist Richard S. Lazarus in *Emotion and Adaptation* (1991) defines emotions as "an integrative, organismic concept that subsumes psychological stress and coping within itself and unites motivation, cognition, and adaptation in a complex configuration." Lazarus says emotion theory is "centered on the relationship between a person and the environment rather than either environmental or intrapersonal events alone."[6] Taking our cue from Lazarus, emotions involve *mind*, *body*, *behavior*, and the external *world*. Emotions have evolved to give us more options than just instincts, and emotions make us flexible in how we respond to our world. Emotions give us *choices*.

Dutch psychologist Nico H. Frijda says that "emotions, moods, feelings, sentiments, and passions are not sharply separate classes of experiences."[7] Yet, he calls them "classes," and I want to look at these classes. First the *emotions*, which cognitivists say have a three-part structure: They have a physical state (facial expression, body composure, inner physical states), a cognitive content (thoughts), and action-readiness (they urge us to act). To cognitivists, thoughts are central. Cognitive philosopher and film scholar Noël Carroll separates "emotions proper" from affects, which are "responses barely mediated by thought."[8] Carroll's examples of emotions include "fear, anger, patriotism, horror, admiration, sorrow, indignation, pity, envy, jealousy,"[9] and he thinks emotions serve as "searchlights ... guiding both what we look at and what we look for."[10]

In a cognitivist frame, emotions are clearly defined. Yet, if we take a closer look at, for example, fear, things turn complex. Fear is one of the basic emotions (the others are anger, disgust, sadness, happiness, and surprise).

Fear has a universal facial expression which is recognized in all cultures, and it has cognitive content, namely danger. Legal scholar Cass R. Sunstein in *Laws of Fears* (2005) provides this definition: "I understand fear to depend on some kind of judgment that we are in danger."[11] Where Carroll and Sunstein keep fear simple, Lazarus divides fear into two types, fright and anxiety. In fright a threat is "the concrete and sudden danger of imminent physical harm," whereas in anxiety the threat is "symbolic, existential and ephemeral."[12] Anxiety is "the threat of nothingness or nonbeing, a kind of psychological death."[13] It is fear of a threat to the self, and it is argued anxiety led to religious beliefs, because religion promises immortality and alleviates anxiety. "Regardless of how it has been portrayed, there has been a great penchant for viewing anxiety as a main engine of mind."[14] Where fright concerns a literal threat, anxiety involves meta-thinking. For example, in *The Babadook* (2014, Jennifer Kent) a single mother is haunted by a ghost. But the ghost isn't real; it is her repressed sorrow, her anxiety. Her son Sam, on the other hand, is frightened his mother will kill him. And that danger is real.

Thus, at close inspection, fear can be more than one emotion. In his study of fear, film scholar Julian Hanich divides fear into five types: direct horror, suggested horror, cinematic shock, cinematic dread, and cinematic terror.[15] And Lazarus speaks of a "fright-anxiety emotion family," which includes horror, terror, fear, unease, concern, apprehension, worry, dread, awe, alarm, and panic.[16] In its simple version, the goal of fear is to avoid danger. But fear isn't always simple.

Another class of emotions are *feelings* which are diffuse mental states with no external goal. Feelings are "evanescent when attention is directed upon them" and are "awareness experienced as subjective states rather than as states of the world ... They monitor the state of satisfaction of the organism ... in a way that is accessible to reflection."[17] The mother in *The Babadook* feels anxious after the death of her husband, and she doesn't even know that she feels anxious. The monster is in her subjective state, her mind, yet she thinks it is real.

Mood, then, is a feeling state "of relatively long duration, not elicited by an external event or outlasting such an event."[18] The reason for a mood can be unknown to us. Cognitive film scholar Carl Plantinga says, "[m]oods pervade perception rather than focus it. Moods bias the subject toward making certain kinds of judgments over others, but are linked indirectly rather than directly. Moods are like frames of mind, setting a broad agenda."[19] A bad mood affects feelings, thoughts, and choices, and we can be unaware of this. In film studies, a film's mood is its atmosphere, which is an emotional state of a long duration.

Where emotions, feelings, and mood feature thoughts (cognition), the class of *sensations* are felt in the body. Sensations are for example our yuck at the sight of slimy stuff or a nerve-racking toothache. Neuroanatomist

A. D. Craig in "How Do You Feel?" (2002) says sense of self originates from body sensations, and researchers say we have not five, but close to thirty senses.[20] There is, for example, nociception, sense of pain, and chronoception, sense of time. Senses are first and foremost physical.

Psychologists also speak of *feeling states*, by which they mean the universal drives. Drives are hunger, thirst, libido, aggression, self-preservation, care of progeny, attachment to mates, exploration, and play.[21] These are, like basic emotions, innate.

Finally, the class of *affects* are our responses to stimuli. Affects are felt more or less intensely, but they remain affects until they are evaluated as being pleasant or unpleasant and become emotions. The burning sensation of my finger in a flame is an affect, and this turns into the emotion of pain when I appraise the sensation as being unpleasant and label it as "pain." A common way to differentiate emotions and affects is to say the first concerns *feeling and thinking* and the latter concerns *feeling and sensing*.[22]

Depending on the field of research, there are different definitions of what constitutes emotions. Cognitivists favor "grand" human emotions, while phenomenologists favor feeling-based emotions. However, psychologists say all the above classes are emotions. Thus, emotions, feelings, sensations, drives, mood, and affects are all emotions, albeit of different types. They must all be processed by the brain for us to register them (consciously or not), which means they involve both brain, body, and mind, whether it is our hunger, toothache, disgust, or fear. A further definition of emotions is beyond my scope, but we recognize that it is a debated issue. For example, how many emotions are there? Psychologist Paul Ekman is famous for identifying the six basic emotions, Frijda in *The Emotions* (1986) lists over thirty, and Wikipedia lists more than seventy. As an answer to the number, some say only the basic six are universal and the rest are cultural. And Belgian ethnopsychologist and philosopher of science Vinciane Despret argues in *Our Emotional Makeup* (2004) that every culture creates its own emotions.[23]

Like an ecosystem, emotions are complex. They arise from internal and external stimuli and they serve both homeostasis and social etiquette. They can be simple like a toothache or complex like jealousy, which Frijda says has a cluster of emotions (love, trust, anger, fear of loss).[24] Also, we share some emotions with animals, and cognitive ethologist Marc Bekoff and philosopher Jessica Pierce in *Wild Justice* (2009) explain how emotions like justice and gratitude are found across mammal species.[25] But meta-emotions require a meta-thinking that animals are incapable of. For example, shame, which requires self-reflection about "thoughts or actions that violate a social proscription that has been internalized."[26] Only humans can feel shame.

There are different views on emotions, and it is only recently that we are starting to understand where and why animal and human emotions differ. *Mastering Fear* uses a wide definition of emotions which includes all the above classes. My definition requires, though, that emotions, whether low-level pain or existential anxiety, are available to consciousness. That is, we can be aware of them. In Damasio's words, it means we have a second-order neural map of the emotion in our mind. If we do, we can look at the emotion and choose how to act on it. Emotions, whether basic or culturally acquired, belong to System 1. Once we learn an emotion, say, shame, it operates automatically.

Emotions point us toward actions and work automatically. Also, they are passionate and stronger than knowledge. As Frijda says, "knowing means less than seeing ... words mean less than tone of voice ... feeling means more than knowing."[27] If we want to master our emotions, we must be able to switch from System 1 to System 2. This takes us to self and consciousness.

> **SPEAKING OF EMOTIONS**
>
> - Emotions involve a subject, a world, and our engagement with the world.
> - Emotions, feelings, sensations, mood, feeling states, and affects are all emotions.
> - The brain uses two systems to process information: System 1 is intuitive and fast, and System 2 is deliberate, slow, and effortful.

System 1 and System 2

Self is linked to mind, which according to Wikipedia is "that which enables a being to have subjective awareness and intentionality towards their environment, to perceive and respond to stimuli with some kind of agency, and to have consciousness, including thinking and feeling."[28] Self and mind are connected to choice and agency and intentionality. To have a mind and a self means, among other things, to be someone who has a choice. My argument is that we play when we enter the dark stage. My argument is also that we benefit from this play, even if we feel fear. Animals don't play with things they are afraid of, so to understand more precisely how this play works, I want to examine how we construct a self.

We can separate the idea of self into *body-self* and *mind-self*, the first being our feeling of self and the second our thoughts of self. As cognitive science explains, the two interact and mind is based on a body-self. In this book, I draw on research in neuroanatomy and heuristics. Let us start with body-self. Craig (2002) explains that to feel a self, we must first perceive our body as a feeling entity. When we feel our body, we use senses like sight, hearing, smell, and touch, and interior senses like stomach ache, inner pains, and sense of balance. Our senses generate a mental image of a body.[29] Humans can imagine being sick and going to a doctor. My golden retriever Stella, however, cannot form a representational image of her body and she cannot imagine seeing a doctor. When she is sick, she seeks cover and waits to be well again. Thus, while our feeling states are similar to that of most mammals, our mental representation of our body is different. We may feel fear the same way a chimpanzee does, but we think about it differently.

Moving from body-self to mind-self is a cognitive process. Damasio says we have three selves, which he calls *protoself*, *core self*, and *autobiographical self*. A protoself registers affects. A core self can create second-order neural maps—the feeling-of-a-feeling—and eat when hungry. But only an autobiographical self can store second-order maps to memory. The autobiographical self can remember an emotion as *my* feeling of an emotion. The autobiographical self is *my* self. The feeling-of-a-feeling is accompanied by *my* perception of emotions, and the brain makes what Damasio calls a movie-in-the-brain: "The images in the consciousness narrative flow like shadows along with the images of the object for which they are providing an unwitting, unsolicited comment. To come back to the metaphor of movie-in-the-brain, they are *within* the movie."[30] When I recall events from the past, my memory is filtered by my emotions. I have no "objective" or "factual" past, only a perceived and subjective past.

Damasio explains that, "virtually all of the machinery behind core consciousness and the generation of core self is under strong gene control."[31] In Kahneman's words, the difference between core self and autobiographical self is like the difference between System 1 and System 2. My core self, System 1, registers danger in *The Descent*. The core self has feelings, but only the autobiographical self can know its feelings. "I am suggesting that 'having a feeling' is not the same as 'knowing a feeling,' that reflection on feeling is yet another step up . . ."[32] To know one's feeling—the "step up"— means to be able to examine it and respond to it. Feeling is basis for body-self, and the body-self is basis for mind-self. The mind-self, System 2, is where we find a conscious choice. Sarah's initial reaction to monsters is to scream. But like Sarah, we can learn to overrule System 1. We can learn to switch to System 2 and choose our response to a monster. But how, precisely, do we make this choice? How does consciousness work? How does it calculate the pros and cons of fleeing, hiding, or fighting?

Philosophers long imagined "self" as a homunculus who pulls the levers of the brain's machinery inside our head. But this is not how consciousness works, says neuropsychologist Michael S. Gazzaniga in *Who's In Charge* (2011).

> . . . we humans think we are making all our decisions to act consciously and willfully. We all feel we are wonderfully unified, coherent mental

machines and that our underlying brain structure must somehow reflect this overpowering sense we all possess. It doesn't. Again, no central command center keeps all other brain systems hopping to the instructions of a five-star general. The brain has *millions* of local processors making important decisions.[33]

Our self is not located in one place in the brain, but in many sections: "From moment to moment, different modules or systems compete for attention and the winner emerges as the neural system underlying that moment's conscious experience. Our conscious experience is assembled on the fly, as our brains respond to constantly changing inputs, calculate potential courses of action, and execute responses . . ."[34] What Gazzaniga calls "the interpreter module" suggests actions, constructs explanations, and when none are available, it invents one. It translates stimuli into emotions and it invents a story with us as protagonist, as "self." Yet, the question remains how the interpreter module decides which stimuli are relevant to respond to?

In another discussion of self, German cognitive philosopher Thomas Metzinger in *The Ego Tunnel* (2010) uses the metaphor of the tunnel to envision our self. His ego tunnel is a virtual construct that provides passage through the world, and we see what is at the end of the ego tunnel: "[I]n moving through this world, we constantly apply unconscious filter mechanisms, and in doing so, we unknowingly construct our own individual world, which is our 'reality tunnel.' "[35] The ego tunnel generates a phenomenal self-model, which is the body-self. Metzinger thinks our ego tunnel creates the experience of a world, *our* world. The ego tunnel tricks us into believing we have a unified self.

If you are a Freudian, you may envision self as three-layered with ego in the middle, super-ego at the top, and our subconscious at the bottom. Or, with Gazzaniga, we might envision the self as a box of Legos. Now, Metzinger suggests yet another metaphor, a neuronal cloud. He hypothesizes self comes into existence when a functional cluster of neurons communicate and form a "cloud" in our brain.[36] "At this point," says Metzinger, "it becomes something more abstract, which we might envision as an information cloud hovering above a neurobiological substrate. The 'border' of this information cloud is functional, not physical; the cloud is physically realized by widely distributed firing neurons in your head."[37] This cloud generates a first-person perspective (*my* world), agency (*my* limbs), and location (*my* sense of Here and Now). When I move my limbs, my neuronal cloud changes. When I think or feel, my cloud changes again. In this depiction of self, body and mind interact, and low-level and high-level processes join in the creation of self.

I want, with Metzinger, to envision self as a neuronal cloud that changes with any stimuli. Stimuli can be a thought, a physical action, or our emotional engagement in horror fiction where we are threatened by a monster. Like

Gazzaniga's constructed-on-the-fly self, the cloud is flexible and mobile. Our brain constantly generates options from which we choose our reactions. But again, *how* do we choose? And why would we choose something that feels unpleasant?

There have been many explanations to why we choose unpleasant emotions. For example, Danish film scholar Torben Grodal argues fiction horror regresses characters and the audience to a pre-modern state where we follow instincts and resort to "natural" violence instead of obeying the rules of our judicial system.[38] But I disagree. My argument is that the dark stage takes characters into situations where the audience can play with danger. The point of play is not to regress, but to learn. The point is to practice situations where we must overrule System 1 and engage System 2 in whatever way the situation calls for. Instead of explaining this choice as regression, perversion, or some other type of response, I argue the dark stage invites us to practice managing Systems 1 and 2, which involves overruling instincts and heuristics. The latter, heuristics, are mental short cuts the brain uses. Now, some instincts are clearly functional, such as the urge to run from danger. However, in our modern and complex environment, it may today be more adaptive to be able to choose between innate responses and a response that fits a situation. Today, flexibility is more adaptive than instincts. Instincts and heuristics may not always serve well-being, as in prehistoric time. In fact, they may run counter to our well-being.

Let me give an example which is from Kahneman and about the heuristics of choice. In an experiment, people were asked to hold a hand in painfully cold water in three trials. In the first trial, they had their hand in cold water for sixty seconds, in the second trial the water was made a degree warmer for an additional thirty seconds, and people were then asked which trial they wanted to repeat as the third trial, the first trial (sixty seconds) or the second (ninety seconds)? Eighty percent wanted to repeat the ninety seconds trial instead of the sixty seconds trial. This paradox, says Kahneman, is explained by two heuristics: first, our brain memorizes the end of events stronger than the entire experience and, second, our memorizing self overrules our experiencing self.[39]

It is striking that people do not make rational choices, which would be to choose the shortest period of pain, and people cannot see the heuristics at work. It takes practice to observe emotions and switch to System 2. We cannot change the heuristics of emotions, but we can learn to use System 2. Our knowledge about emotions does not change our nature, but it enables us to come up with a different response than what comes to mind. Knowledge, as Damasio says, leads to choice and freedom.

In his research in risk and fear, legal scholar Sunstein agrees with Kahneman that people are not rational: "[P]eople attempt to control their fear by refusing to think about the risk at all."[40] Sunstein, too, observes that we do not choose what serves us best: "People suffer from a problem of 'miswanting'; they want things that do not promote their welfare, and they do not want things that would promote their welfare."[41] We focus on short-term instead of long-term consequences, we over-estimate risks, we are governed by fears, or we ignore risks and are reckless. Also, we cannot just choose what we prefer, because there is no such thing as individual values and preferences. Values and preferences—in cognitive science called *anchor points* and *default rules*—are a product of framing, which means they are created by society. "In many domains, people's preferences are labile and illformed, and hence starting points and default rules are likely to be quite sticky ... it is unhelpful to say that regulators [institutions] should simply 'respect preferences.' What people prefer, or at least choose, is a product of starting points and default rules."[42]

Damasio says knowing emotions leads to choice in how we respond to them. Kahneman thinks we can learn to use System 2 to master System 1. And Sunstein wants us to face more risks and dangers so we become more resilient and less governed by our fears. All of this, however, requires emotional practice. To see beyond instinct, we must do cognitive work. While it is fast and easy to use System 1, because it works with "intuition, creativity, gullibility," this system is also "less vigilant and more prone to logical errors." System 2, in contrast, is linked to "sadness, vigilance, suspicion, an analytic approach, and increased effort ..."[43] System 2 takes us down a strenuous road of challenging emotions and situations. This is why we enter the dark stage. Because, ultimately, this road leads to a stronger self.

SPEAKING OF SENSE OF SELF

- Our sense of "self" arises from exterior and interior feelings.
- Our *protoself* registers feeling states, our *core self* is conscious, and our *autobiographical self* has memory. Together, they create self-awareness.
- Self is a post hoc story behind which a constant perception and processing of information is carried out by multiple brain modules.

Positive and Negative Emotions

Before moving on, I want to comment on the use of "positive" and "negative" about emotions. All emotions serve a function, which means none are "negative" in the sense that they are not necessary. They are. Fear keeps us alive when danger is near, and disgust keeps us from eating things that would make us sick. What is meant by "negative" is that these emotions feel unpleasant and our reaction is to avoid them. But to avoid unpleasant emotions does not lead to strength or wisdom. As psychologist Robert Maurer (2016) says, "fear can be a guide and a friend and it remains an essential for our survival and success in today's world as it was in the wild."[44]

Also, I must comment on the binary use of negative/positive, which suggests emotions are paired. They are not. It is tempting to use binary thinking, but philosophers Robert C. Solomon and Lori D. Stone (2002) warn it is misleading.[45] Emotions are multidimensional and cannot be paired with opposites: "Opposites depend on polarity, and polarity is just what is not available in even the simplest emotions. (What is the opposite of fear? Is it courage? Is it recklessness? Is it indifference? Is it panic? Or rage?)."[46] The positive-negative binary comes from ethics: "The positive-negative polarity as well as the conception of emotional opposites have their origins in ethics ... [it] comes out of the medieval church which in turn traces its psychology back to Aristotle."[47] The church famously paired seven sins with seven virtues.

Solomon and Stone explain the positive-negative polarity blend with three levels of meanings: Feeling (is the emotion pleasant or unpleasant?); morals (valued as good or bad); and ethics (relating to virtue and vice). When we confuse feeling, morality, and ethics, we obscure the difference between our physical experience of emotions, our cognitive appraisal of emotions, and our behavioral reaction to emotions. An emotion isn't bad; only causes and consequences can be bad.[48] Our everyday language uses "positive" and "negative" about emotions, and I do too. However, my use does not imply a moral judgment.

The Horror Experience

After Carol Clover's *Men, Women and Chain Saws* (1992) and Barbara Creed's *The Monstrous-Feminine* (1993), two ground-breaking feminist works in the study of horror, it is common to speak of sadistic men, masochistic viewer positions, and final girls as stand-ins for male audiences. However, I approach horror from an evolutionary and biocultural perspective, and since cross-gender identification and perversion are not central to play instincts, I shall examine the viewer's engagement with emotions in other terms: As emotional dialogue, as invitations to feel, with the body as a sensorium, and as a challenge to become emotional ninjas.

In the Introduction I mentioned Finnish phenomenologist Tarja Laine, who in *Feeling Cinema* (2011) talks of an *emotional dialogue* with film, where we are "making sense *with* instead of making sense *of* cinema" (emphasis in original).[49] We create meaning in a dialogue, and emotions exist in the text, in us as spectators, and as new emotions from our dialogue with the film. Films function as partners in a dialogue, they have an "emotional core," even an "emotional heart," and they are "intentional agents with emotional states that are analogous, but not identical, to human emotional states ..."[50] This dialogue is "an event that is 'a continuing interchange, neither beginning nor ending at any specific point.'"[51] Once a film is remembered and is a second-order neural map in our brain, we can continue "talking" with the film. This happened with my horror texts. For example, *Martyrs* would not leave my mind before I wrote about why Anna had to be tortured in that basement.

Greg M. Smith (2007) suggests another way to describe engagement, namely as an *invitation* to a party. Smith analyses film aesthetics—image, sound, music, framing, editing, and so on—as an emotion system which invites the viewer to feel: "Films do not 'make' people feel. A better way to think of filmic emotions is that films extend an invitation to feel in particular ways. Individuals can accept or reject the invitation ... You can properly recognize how a film is cuing you to feel and still reject the invitation by not feeling those emotions ... film does not extend a single invitation but a succession of invitations to feel, and we can accept or reject any one of them."[52] Producers can cue emotions in a film's aesthetics to solicit emotional response in audiences. A film orchestrates multiple emotion levels, both low level, such as shock, and high level where it combines, for instance, suspense, curiosity, and fear. There are many ways to create fear. You can take the "low road" or the "high road." The low road heads to the amygdala which activates the sympathetic nervous system (System 1) and triggers the fight-or-flight response. The high road "is slower because it is collecting information from other parts of our brain – particular neocortical regions that are responsible for critically evaluating information and that involve slow, conscious processes like deliberation."[53] This is System 2.

In her book *The Horror Sensorium* (2012), Australian new media scholar Angela Ndalianis analyses our body as a sensorium that interfaces with the text. When we watch a film, play a computer game, or visit a theme park, we interface with all our senses with the text. Our eyes watch the screen, our hands hold the controller, our body is moved and touched in the theme park, and so on. This interface is "where the medium and the human body collide; where they meet and affect each other in very real ways ..."[54] To Ndalianis, this meeting of the viewer's body and the medium is not identification but, like Laine and Smith also discuss, an emotional engagement. Our body, the horror sensorium, "refers both to the sensory mechanics of the human body, but also to the intellectual and cognitive functions connected to it: it's integral to the process of perceiving, and to processing the gamut of sensory stimuli the individual may experience in order to make sense of their understanding and impression of the world around them."[55]

Ndalianis compares this interfacing with "a ping-pong match with multiple balls in play at once – each ball representing a different way of 'being touched' by what's onscreen."[56] Mirror neurons make us mimic characters' body movements, we read and mimic facial expressions, we track eye movements, we scan dark caves for danger, we wonder about ominous bones, we notice genre scripts and black humor, and we, too, are terrified when monsters appear in the dark. This interfacing—or, in Laine's terms, this emotional dialogue—is strongly automatic because it is handled by System 1. Thus, a few years back I was on a train on the way to give a talk about horror. I was watching *The Descent* on my laptop to locate time codes for my presentation, and I was surrounded by fellow travelers immersed in their businesses. I told myself to look for time codes, but when the monster appeared, I screamed loudly in shock, which made passengers come and ask if I were alright? Albeit I had seen the scene many times and knew the monster was waiting, the film nonetheless pulled me so deep into the magic circle of play that my System 2 did not stop me from screaming.[57]

It is sometimes argued our fear isn't real, because the text is fiction and our emotions are aesthetic and "make-believe emotions."[58] From a cognitive position, there is no such thing as make-believe emotions. We feel emotions in our body and since we have only one sensorium, there is only the same flesh with which to feel. As Grodal explains, it is mistaken to talk about suspension of disbelief, because the "default mode of processing information is to believe it as soon as one has comprehended it, and that to disbelieve incoming information demands additional mental work."[59] That is, *first* we receive the information and *next* we process and interpret it. Thus, first I see a monster and then, if I think it is real, I run, and if I think it is not real, I block the instinct to flee (System 1) and stay in my couch (System 2).

Damasio says that to know emotions brings pain and freedom. Pain because we feel not only pleasant, but also unpleasant emotions. Freedom because we have agency. When we know our emotions, we have more choices than instincts. On the dark stage, we are invited to play with a multitude of emotions, many of them unpleasant and creating fear. I want us to enter the dark stage and play with challenging emotions so we can learn. I believe there are benefits to this play. Sociologist Margee Kerr, who researches haunted houses and rollercoasters, says we self-scare to become "emotional ninjas" (2015).[60] An emotional ninja seeks scares in the conviction she will master the challenge.

I want us to become emotional ninjas. The emotional ninja brings attention to her fear and reappraises it as a challenge which will help her become stronger. "The common thread, the defining characteristics of emotional ninjas, is mindfulness, or the ability to recognize and understand their bodies' reactions and choose the meaning they want to give it, to take the experience into their own hands and make it work for them, physically and psychologically."[61] Kerr compares this reappraisal to the "no pain no gain" athletes say about pain. The guests she interviewed in the haunted houses were frightened, yet "knowing you can leave and choosing to stay is empowering."[62] Kerr could read in the questionnaires that "people loved it, and they left the Basement feeling *wonderful*."[63]

When we play on the dark stage, we interface with a text with our full sensorium, the body, and we have an emotional dialogue where we learn to master unpleasant emotions. The horror experience turns us into emotional ninjas.

THE HORROR EXPERIENCE

- *Emotional dialogue* has emotions in a text, emotions in audiences, and new emotions arising from this dialogue (Laine).
- A film sends *invitations* to feel, which we can accept or reject (Smith).
- Our body is a *sensorium* that functions as an interface with the text, perceiving and decoding multiple sensory and cognitive stimuli (Ndalianis).
- System 1 believes the fiction world is real; to turn belief into disbelief requires additional work by System 2 (Grodal).

GENDER

Not long ago, I presented a paper on the female werewolf and lamented how rare she is. Afterwards, my audience, who were biocultural and cognitive scholars, told me this had a natural explanation: Actions like hunting, killing, and moving vigorously, appeal to men because they were hunters in prehistoric time, and a werewolf does not appeal to women because women were gatherers and nurturers. And although we no longer live in prehistoric time, nature hasn't changed. That hand of yours that holds the latest iPhone, it is assumed, still belongs to Man the Hunter and Woman the Gatherer. Well, I disagree.

Before researching this book, I shared many of the above assumptions about "natural" sex differences. I, too, believed men were innately more violent than women and women innately more emphatic, more fragile, and more sensitive than men. Today, I think different. Today, I know the topic of sex differences and gender differences is as complex as that of emotions. Obviously, men and women have different bodies. Women give birth and men have more muscle mass. Flesh *is* different. However, my interest is not flesh, but behavior. I am after mind and self and the freedom to write our own scripts. I am interested in how we can enter the dark stage to play and learn. I am after agency, choice, and freedom.

FIGURE 1.1 *To be a werewolf affords a woman to kill with a single nail transformed into a claw. Elena (Laura Vandervoort) is about to get even with a molester from her childhood in* Bitten: *Season 1, Episode 10 ("Caged"). © Space, 2014.*

The difference between sex and gender is that sex is biological, and gender is culturally constructed and socially acquired. We are born with blue or brown eyes, but we learn gender from society.[64] Animals have sex differences, *but only humans have gender*. Animals play and fight and learn. But they do not drive cars or apply makeup, or pay for gang tattoos or breasts implants. Only humans do. As Simone de Beauvoir said, "one is not born, but rather becomes, woman."

The aim of this section, then, is to present the analytical tools I use to discuss gender. My tools include a philosophy of the situated body and the lived body; the theory of schemas and stereotypes; the meta-narrative from linguistics; and the use of the incremental story to change negative stereotypes.

Throwing Like a Girl

Let us return to the female werewolf and to the objections about what is natural behavior for men and for women.

I was recommended the work by cognitive psychologist Doreen Kimura, who in *Sex and Cognition* (1999) argues men are better at targeting than women.[65] She links targeting to prehistorical time when men were hunters and women gatherers, thus men evolved skills at targeting and women didn't. Kimura makes laboratory experiments with men, women, and homosexual men throwing darts, and her results show that, "[h]omosexual men were on average significantly less accurate than heterosexual men on this targeting task, and in fact were not significantly better than heterosexual women."[66] Such laboratory experiments do not convince me. Frankly, I think they measure acquired learning and not innate abilities, and that this type of research confirms rather than questions ideas about gender and sex.

The problem with discussing sex and gender differences is that the boundaries between what is culturally learned and biological inherited are fuzzy. As I mentioned in the Introduction, neuropsychologist Melissa Hines in *Brain Gender* (2004) says it is impossible to make a clear-cut distinction between biology and culture because even simple differences like height result from interaction between genes, environment, and behavior. The difference in height between men and women have diminished today because diets change (men would grow taller because they were fed better than women).[67] Rather than draw a line between what is innate and what is learned, Hines says environment and bodies interact.

Some cognitive psychologists like to explain difference in behavior with sex differences that are located in the brain, however, Hines says, "a relationship between a brain structure and a behavior does not imply, on its own, either a causal relationship or, even if causal, that the behavior is innately determined or cannot be changed."[68] For example we may assume women are more emphatic than men, but when this is put to the test, our actions prove otherwise. In social experiments, women self-report they are more emphatic than men, but when they pass a crying baby, they do not pick the baby up more often than the men.[69] Similarly, it is assumed men have a stronger sex drive than women, but research shows women's sex drive is as strong as men's, and they are as unfaithful.[70]

So, let us return to the body, and instead of a werewolf let us look at the simple act of throwing a ball. Shortly after beginning this book, I decided to get a dog. Me and the children took Stella for walks, and one day my son scolded me for throwing a ball like a girl. "You do it like *this*," he said and sent Stella far into the fields. I shouldn't just use my arm, he explained, but my entire body to generate a *swing*. Shortly after this, I came across "Throwing Like a Girl" (1980) by philosopher Iris Young. Young quotes the psychologist Erwin Straus on girls and the ability to throw a ball. This is what Straus says:

> The girl of five does not make any use of lateral space. She does not stretch her arm sideward; she does not twist her trunk; she does not move her legs, which remain side by side. All she does in preparation for throwing is to lift her right arm forward to the horizontal and to bend the forearm backward in a pronate position ... The ball is released without force, speed, or accurate aim ...[71]

Writing in 1962, Straus found the ability to throw "the manifestation of a biological, not an acquired, difference."[72] Writing in 1980, Young disagreed.

Instead, Young argued, the girl learns to situate her body different than a boy. Women learn an ambiguous transcendence where we treat our body as an object (a thing-to-be-looked-at) and a subject. We inhibit intentionality and take up less space than men, we take shorter strides, hold our arms closer to the trunk, and we approach "physical engagement with things with timidity, uncertainty, and hesitancy."[73] We restrict our motility, take away self-confidence, tell ourselves to be self-aware—and *then* we throw like girls.

We cannot use the body as "hard" evidence about sex differences because a body is situated in history and is what Young calls "a lived body."[74] A lived body is not a clean slate. Our muscles learn movements, we learn to process affects into sensations and feelings, and our mind communicates with body parts. Our body is not simply there to throw the ball. It *learns* to throw. What we believe is a sex difference might in time turn out to be a gender difference. Thus, Kimura thinks men are better at targeting than women, but in 2016 female pitchers made history when they joined the male professional baseball league in the US.[75]

My point with anecdotes about werewolves and balls is that our assumptions about body, sex, and performances are *ideas*. The conviction that differences between men and women are innate and located in the flesh (or in the brain) is also called *essentialism*. The conviction that gender is learned is called *social constructivism*. Since I became a bioculturalist, I have also become a social constructivist. I agree with Young, who is a phenomenologist, that the body learns to sense and feel. Gender is learned, not inherited. Sport sociologist Jason Laurendeau (2008) says about women doing risk sports, that, "the ways skydivers, freeclimbers, mountaineers, or BASE jumpers, for example, 'do' risk are also – and simultaneously, and always already – ways that they negotiate gender."[76]

To use Metzinger's vocabulary, gender is a filter we use to interpret our world, and it is thus part of our ego tunnel. In a later essay, Young distinguishes between gender and what she calls the "lived body." The lived body is created by micro structures of personal experience (*my* body) and macro structures of society's gender scripts. The first is subject to *my* will while the latter, the gender script, is a situation I must negotiate: "The lived body is a unified idea of a physical body acting and experiencing in a specific sociocultural context; it is body-in-situation ... The person, however, is an actor; she has an ontological freedom to construct herself in relation to this facticity."[77]

Young believes in agency and change. It takes time to change gender scripts because they are part of the macro structures of culture, class, ethnicity, and politics. But we can change a lived body. I might not in a flash become Michael Jordan. However, I can lift and supinate my forearm, twist my trunk, and create a *swing*. Nothing, except my ideas, stops me from throwing a longer ball. Go, Stella!

> **SPEAKING OF THROWING LIKE A GIRL**
> - What we believe is a sex difference may turn out to be a gender difference.
> - When circumstances and situations change, women's performances change.
> - Women self-report they are more emphatic than men, but social experiments show men and women are equally emphatic. We may think there is difference where there is none.

Thinking Like a Woman

To "throw like a girl" requires that you *think* of yourself as a girl. In Damasio's words, it takes a second-order neural map labeled "girl" to instruct an individual she is a "girl" and, therefore, must throw in a certain way.

Cognitive psychology calls neural maps schemas and, in their elaborate forms, stereotypes and scripts. A schema, says cognitive psychologist Sandra Lipsitz Bem (1981), is "a cognitive structure, a network of associations that organizes and guides an individual's perception."[78] The schema works as a filter that sorts stimuli from the world. Bem says it, "functions as an anticipatory structure, a readiness to search for and to assimilate incoming information in schema-relevant terms.' Schematic processing is thus highly selective and enables the individual to impose structure and meaning onto the vast array of incoming stimuli . . ."[79] Once you know you are a girl, you will anticipate to behave as a girl in the future.

The gender schema extends the concept of two sexes into all other domains: Girls play with dolls and boys with balls, and man conquers the world while woman stays home to nurture the family. We understand the concept of gender at the age of five[80] and from then on we integrate the gender schema into our self-account.[81] The self-account is where we store information we think is relevant for our "self." Once the gender schema is part of our self, it is intuitively used by System 1 and now functions without our awareness. The gender schema regulates behavior "so that it conforms to the culture's definitions of maleness and femaleness" and this is how schemas become self-fulfilling prophecies.[82]

The gender schema is extended into stereotype and scripts, which are stories instructing us how to behave. Our narratives about ourself follow established scripts, and to go off-script takes deliberate effort by System 2. Social psychologist Claude M. Steele (2010) explains that positive stereotypes enhance performance and negative stereotypes suppress performance. The gender stereotype, in case you are in doubt, is a negative stereotype and suppresses performance. When women are reminded of their sex, they perform worse. Negative stereotypes suppress performances because they are social identity threats. Stereotypes function both as intrapsychic mental processes and as explicitly formulated beliefs in society. In other words, they are ubiquitous.

Steele gives an example of how stereotype functions: The gender stereotype says women are bad at math, and the Asian stereotype says Asians are more intelligent than Americans. In a social experiment, Asian-American women were divided into three groups, one primed with being Asian, a test group not primed with any information relevant to self, and a third group primed with gender.[83] The Asian-primed group performed best, the non-primed test group performed in the middle, and the gender-primed group performed worst. Two things are significant: First, the gender stereotype suppresses performance and, second, it does so without our awareness. The gender-primed women believed they had performed their best. The gender stereotype works *even when we don't see it at work*. It causes anxiety and ruminating thoughts and "a mind trying to defeat a stereotype leaves little mental capacity free for anything else we're doing."[84] The negative stereotype is "an ongoing threat to your perceived self-integrity," says Steele. "It constantly unsettles one's sense of competence and belonging."[85]

I earlier mentioned linguist Deborah Cameron and what she calls the meta-narrative. The meta-narrative are stories about men and women, stories including evolutionary stories that trace human development back over millennia, based on bones and fossils. However, explanations are often speculative because the evidence is ancient and events took place a long time ago. The evolutionary story known as Man the Hunter and Woman the Gatherer explains that men were hunters and therefore became active, vigorous, violent, and better at throwing and targeting than women. Women, on the other hand, were gatherers and stayed home with children, thus they became empathic and developed fine motor skills. The underlying gender dichotomy is "MEN – HUNT – ANIMALS – ACTIVE" and "WOMEN – GATHER – PLANTS – PASSIVE."[86] The meta-narrative, says Cameron, functions as "a larger framework into which research findings on male-female differences can be slotted, whether their immediate subject is the differing behavior of men and women in shopping malls or their differing rates of involvement in violent crime..."[87]

Feminist researchers reject the Man the Hunter story. For example, eighty percent of food was gathered and there is no evidence only men hunted.[88] Yet the meta-narrative persists and incorporates even data that contradicts it. For example, it was argued that men were better at communicating than women, because in prehistoric time men coordinated the hunt. When research showed that women talk more than men, this was called relational talk (gossip), not "real" talk. And when data then shows that female and male leaders are equally adept at communicating, the theory is that men use "transactional" language and women use "transformational" language.[89]

Again, the meta-narrative constructs difference whether there exists one or not. Feminists call evolutionary explanations "just so" stories[90] because they cannot be proven.

We find the meta-narrative in science as well as popular discourses, sometimes explicit and most of the time hardly noticeable. It is part of the situatedness of which Beauvoir wrote that, "what singularly defines the situation of woman is that being, like all humans, an autonomous freedom, she discovers and chooses herself in a world where men force her to assume herself as Other."[91] If we return to the werewolf and the girl, they are both in a meta-narrative with "the assumption that violent aggression is a normal component of male psychology."[92] However, like Straus was wrong about girls' ability to throw a ball, I think the critics of my paper are wrong too. A werewolf can be as appealing to women as it is to men. It depends on what we *want* to do with our bodies, not on what our body can do.

> **SPEAKING OF THINKING LIKE A WOMAN**
>
> - Stereotypes operate in society and are internalized in our minds. Positive stereotypes enhance performance, negative stereotypes suppress performance.
> - Gender is a negative stereotype.
> - The gender schema extends differences into other realms: Pink for girls and blue for boys.

Gender and Change

Essentialists are quick to locate differences between men and women in the body. Thus, neuropsychologist Simon Baron-Cohen in *The Essential Difference* (2004) claims, "[t]he female brain is predominantly hard-wired for empathy. The male brain is predominantly hard-wired for understanding and building systems,"[93] and suggests, "[p]eople with the female brain make the most wonderful counsellors, primary-school teachers, nurses, carers, therapists, social workers, mediators, group facilitators or personnel staff."[94] Social constructivists, in contrast, are reluctant to speak of innate differences, because they think behavior is created by schemas, and schemas change when societies change.

In the seventeenth century, it was believed women's brain fibers were more delicate than men's. In the nineteenth century, it was believed women were weaker-minded than men.[95] And today, Australian cognitive psychologist Cordelia Fine in *The Delusions of Gender* (2010) warns neuroscience is producing a 2.0 neurosexism. She disagrees with Baron-Cohen and thinks what he calls sex differences are gender differences.[96] Women are not born to be primary-school teachers, and neither are men born to build things. If we recall our discussion of mind, neither Damasio, Gazzaniga, Sunstein, Frijda, or Metzinger mention sex differences. They don't see a difference in how self and mind works in men and women.

Instead, how we *think* determines how we *act*. Despite essentialist claims about men and women's brains, experiments show that men are not more intelligent than women.[97] When it comes to bodies, performances change when circumstances change. Until 1980 women were not allowed to run marathons in the Olympic Games, because it was thought too strenuous for them. But as women gain entry to sports, they prove to be as able to run marathons and climb mountains as men.[98] Whether we "throw like a girl" or not is determined by our thoughts. And because the gender stereotype is a negative stereotype, it limits performance.

How do we change a negative stereotype? Steele says there are two things we can do: We can tell ourselves an incremental story and we can reframe a dangerous encounter to be a learning situation.[99] Steele says we can tell two stories, the incremental and the fixed story: "[T]he 'incremental' theory, which frames the ability required to meet a challenge as learnable and incrementally expandable, and the 'fixed' theory, which frames the ability as a fixed capacity that can't be meaningfully expanded but that can nonetheless limit one's functioning – the 'either you have it or you don't' theory that many people hold about intelligence."[100] The fixed story says you can't change, and the incremental story says you can improve and expand your abilities. Let me illustrate with a personal anecdote. Just before I turned forty, I told a friend I wanted to run a marathon, but this was harder for women than for men, and I was too old. He said this was nonsense. Women are as able to run as men, and if our ability to sprint deteriorates with age, our ability to run long doesn't. The only thing stopping me were my beliefs. After this conversation, I ran marathons in Venice, Warsaw, on the Chinese Wall, and on the freezing beaches in Jutland in February.

The incremental story works in two ways: It starts a "self-affirmation idea" which is "freeing up mental resources and improving performance" and it "interrupts an otherwise negative recursive process,"[101] which means it stops negative thinking. Fine says women constantly reproduce the negative stereotype: "Take a look around. The gender inequality that you see is *in* your mind. So are the cultural beliefs about gender that are so familiar to us all. They are in that messy tangle of mental associations that interact with the social context. Out of this interaction emerges your self-perception, your interests, your values, your behavior, even your abilities."[102] The negative stereotype is not part of our biological hardware, it is software, and it can be rewritten.

In the analytical chapters, I return to the question of how stereotypes are treated. Do texts merely repeat conventional stereotypes or do they critique, or perhaps even subvert them? Because it is easy to have a simple view of a

TABLE 1 *Scale of a Response to the Gender Stereotype*

THE GENDER STEREOTYPE				
reinforce	repeat	resist	reverse	re-author, subvert

text as either repeating or subverting a stereotype, I want to suggest with Table 1 the idea of a nuanced scale, where the confirmation of a stereotype is at one end, and the re-authoring at the other end, by which I mean a subversive take on the stereotype. In between there are less negative, neutral, and more positive uses of the gender stereotype.

But it is difficult to re-author a stereotype. If people are told to disregard a negative stereotype, when they meet people they hold a negative stereotype about, it has the opposite effect. Instead, says Steele, we may view such a meeting as a learning opportunity. When told to view the meeting as a learning opportunity, the negative stereotype ceases to affect behavior. This is because in a learning situation we are expected to make mistakes and not be judged. As we will see shortly, play is a learning experience where players can try and fail and try again.[103] When we play, we lift behavior out of real life and into the magic circle of play, where we judge the performance and not the player. In play, we take it for granted that we can learn new skills and expand our abilities.

> **SPEAKING OF GENDER AND CHANGE**
>
> - Stereotypes are software in the brain and software can be rewritten.
> - We can combat negative stereotypes by telling ourselves the incremental story that we can learn new skills and expand our knowledge and abilities.
> - When we reframe a situation from a threatening encounter to a learning opportunity, the negative stereotype no longer suppresses performance.

Evofeminism

Never mind which number we are on, we need to be making waves.
JANE SPENCER, "AFTERWORD: FEMINIST WAVES" (2007)[104]

Why do I call my framework evofeminism? I use the prefix *evo* for several reasons. First, I want *Mastering Fear* to be truth-based. I am not claiming to make more "objective" analyses than when I used psychosemiotics, but I want to approach horror in a new way. For me, bioculturalism, which is evolutionary, is a new approach, which I hope provides me with a clean vision to "see" my horror texts. Feminist science philosopher Donna Haraway says about feminist science that, "the goal is better accounts of the world, that is, 'science,'"[105] and that science requires a place from where we look. "Vision is *always* a question of the power to see."[106] The prefix *evo* calls attention to evolutionary theory and bioculturalism as the place from where I am looking. As said, I will abandon theories that are not truth-based in favor of theories that are, such as neural maps, the mind's use of schemas, stereotypes, and scripts, the multiple sensations of emotions, and the adaptive function of play.

Also, in using *evo*, I challenge the idea that it is not natural for women to engage with horror. In contrast, I claim women can use horror the same way as men, namely as play. A cornerstone in bioculturalism is the idea that we adapt as we evolve, and that flexibility is adaptive. When the world changes, the species with the most choices is best equipped to survive. This view is called Darwinian (after the expression "the survival of the fittest"). Darwinian theory has been used in the humanities for more than two decades, and literary scholar Brian Boyd (2009) calls fiction a "Darwinian machine" because "[b]y developing our ability to think beyond the here and now, storytelling helps us not to override the given, but to be less restricted by it, to cope with it more flexibly and on something like our own terms."[107] Creative learning reminds me of science philosopher Karl Popper. He calls scientific theories "creative evolution" and thinks the human species developed science as error-eliminating controls, "that is, controls which can eliminate errors without killing the organism; and it makes it possible, ultimately, for our hypotheses to die in our stead."[108] I see a line from fiction horror to Popper's metaphor of hypotheses as dying in our stead. In horror, characters die in our stead, and by pushing ourselves into unpleasant situations, we kill characters so we can learn. Science and fiction both evolve on the brink of death.

Evo also signals evolution. We must not see the body as destiny or the brain as a straitjacket. Despite the meta-narrative and the just-so stories about Man the Hunter, we can write new scripts. Our cognitive abilities buckles us up for a ride into the unknown future. To the question of free will, Gazzaniga says, "determinism has no meaning in this context. Human nature remains constant, but out in the social world behavior can change."[109] Our theories provide us with "plastic control" instead of "cast-iron control."[110] We are not shackled to an innate nature. Instead, we can use horror as a playground where we practice challenging emotions and dangerous situations so that we can approach our future with less fear and more choices and agency.

The second part of evofeminism is feminism, and I have taken inspiration from philosopher Cynthia Freeland, who in *The Naked and the Undead* comments on her use of cognitive theories and feminism. Freeland says, "feminist critique aims to uncover ideologies in horror films (and elsewhere) of traditional patriarchal dominance relations,"[111] but explains she finds theories about the male gaze and the abject un-illuminative. Instead she uses a "cognitivist framework [which] offers a flexible, nonreductive, and potentially illuminating framework for constructing creative feminist readings of horror films."[112] I, too, have a feminist agenda and want truth-based theories. But where Freeland refers to her work as simply "feminist" I move in a field with numerous feminisms: Here are first, second, third, and fourth wave feminism, postfeminism, neofeminism, and ecofeminism. Many of the scholars I use call themselves feminists (Beauvoir, Young, Freeland, Fausto-Sterling, Zuk, Fine), while others work with specific feminisms, like Hilary Radner (2011) writing about neofeminism, and Stéphanie Genz (2006, 2009, 2010, 2016) contributing to postfeminist theory.[113]

Where does *Mastering Fear* stand in this field? In my earlier work, I called myself feminist (1993) and postfeminist (2007, 2016). However, I have now chosen an inclusive view which draws from all types and waves of feminism. I define feminism as the struggle for equality between the sexes, and my aim is "a feminism that is not owned by anyone and can be used by all."[114] By drawing from different feminisms, I do not thereby agree with a political agenda. Postfeminism, for example, was embraced by many feminists in the 1990s, but after the 2008 recession critiqued for being neoliberal and serving privileged middle-class women.

I consider us free agents and draw from approaches that favor agency and flexibility. Such views include existentialists Beauvoir and Young, but also neofeminism and postfeminism that originate from capitalism. Thus, feminisms are contested territory. Especially postfeminism, which has been called "a frontier discourse" without center but in search of "conflict, contradiction and ambiguity."[115] Postfeminists use "femininities" in the plural because they believe there are many ways to be a person and, therefore, many ways one is a woman. Like postmodernism, postfeminism has a playful engagement with styles and performances, and do not believe there is an "essence" of femininity. British film scholar Diane Negra in *What a Girl Wants* (2009) points to a double-standard in postfeminism and says, "[p]ostfeminism continually hypes empowerment but a closer examination of its affective registers reveals a sense of stern disapproval and judgment for any manifestations of 'off-script' femininity."[116]

I agree with such critique of a neoliberal feminism. Yet, I also find it helpful to examine texts from different perspectives. We recall from Gazzaniga that the modular brain constantly uses multiple modules and systems. An answer to this multiplicity is to use multiple theories to analyse how we juggle stereotypes and scripts. These are often conflicting and contradictory, some with which we agree and others with which we disagree.[117] My aim with evofeminism is not to describe an ideal world. My aim is to understand the present world and find strategies for adaptive behavior and evolution. We may dream of a world beyond gender, however, political scientist Wendy Brown in *Edgework* (2005) asks where such a beyond is located? "This beyond is a strange place," Brown rhetorically writes.[118] Like Utopia, the beyond is imaginary. We live in a world after the Fall, by which Brown means it is postrevolutionary, and that feminists mourn the lost visions of a Utopia. We must let go of dreams of radical transformation because, "gender ... can be bent ... but not emancipated ... [it is] beyond the reach of revolution."[119]

Brown advises us to let go of mourning, because mourning creates nostalgia and resignation. "[O]nly by stumbling, only by feeling what one depended on before and with what one can now replace that dependency, does a mourning being begin to discern possibility in loss, in being free of an object [revolution] that seemed like life itself."[120] Once we let go of our dreams of Utopia we can see possibilities for change in the present. Young says the world is a situation, and it is up to the individual to take responsibility for her actions and the possibility of change.

SPEAKING OF EVOFEMINISM

- Evofeminism combines truth-based science (bioculturalism) with a politics of equality (feminism).
- Evofeminism draws from all feminisms, including first, second, third, and fourth wave feminism, postfeminism, neofeminism, and ecofeminism.
- The aim of evofeminism is to conquer the entire terrain of horror, combat the negative gender stereotype, and re-author the meta-narrative.

PLAY

Play is beyond all rationality and ethics.

FRIEDRICH WILHELM NIETZSCHE

It is commonly recognized that horror is about fear. Andrew Tudor (1974) says horror films "have in common the *intention* to horrify,"[121] Carroll

(1999) says horror films "are designed to provoke fear,"[122] and Bantinaki (2012) states, "it is enough for the purposes of this article to focus on [the horror genre's] mark, that is, the aim of generating fear and disgust in the audience."[123] Yet, we volunteer to experience horror. Why? How do we want to experience fear?

I suggest it is because in fiction horror we turn fear into play and play is separate from real life. In play, a bite is a play-bite, not a real bite, and it may hurt, but it doesn't kill. When animals play, they use play-rules to replace real-world rules. A title by Danish computer game scholar Jesper Juul, *Half-Real* (2005),[124] captures the paradox that play is real, yet not-real. Knowing we are safe, we can play with our fear. We may feel traumatized when characters die, but *we* don't die. On the dark stage, we experience death without dying and we gain emotional stamina, feel challenging emotions, and face lethal situations.

What is Play?

All mammals play. Animals spend between five and ten percent of their time on play, and an adolescent chimpanzee spends up to thirty percent. While human play can have a more complex form than animal play—say, for example, be a battle on a chess board—it is an innate drive we share with other animals. And humans are, in fact, one of the most playful species surpassed only by bonobo apes and chimpanzees.[125]

French sociologist Roger Caillois in *Man, Play, and Games* (2001) says play is free, separate from the real world, uncertain, and unproductive.[126] Play, in contrast to work, is not meant to produce something specific but is appealing for its own sake. We play in *a pure space*, a so-called *magic circle*. Dogs, for example, signal play with a bow, by wagging their tail, and by making a play face. The magic circle is a parallel world, yet boundaries between play and reality are fuzzy. Dutch play theorist Johan Huizinga says, "[g]enuine play possesses ... the consciousness, however latent, of 'only pretending' [yet in play] the distinction between belief and make-believe breaks down."[127]

Play has been categorized many ways. Caillois divides play into *agon* (competition), *alea* (chance), *mimicry* (simulation), and *ilinx* (vertigo). Caillois is critiqued for focusing on adult play, and we shall instead use ethologist Gordon M. Burghardt's categorization in *The Genesis of Animal Play* (2005):

- language play (play with sounds)
- construction play (building things)
- sensorimotor play (moving oneself)

- parallel play (playing alongside one another)
- pretend play (pretending a yarn is a mouse)
- sociodramatic play (pretend extended into role playing)
- play fighting
- rule-based play (games)
- rituals[128]

These types are all found in both animals and humans. Animals have rules and rituals too, but not cinemas or popcorn. Horror as play involves several types of play. It is *pretend* and *sociodramatic play* because it has storyworlds; it is *rule-based play* because it uses genre rules; we have *rituals* like horror film festivals and city zombie walks, even zombie runs. And, central to my definition of the genre, it is *play fighting*, because horror stages attacks on self and body.

Play Fighting

Play fighting is when animals fight for fun. It is pushing, kicking, biting, chasing one another, or fighting over the same object. Rats, socially advanced animals that are often used in experiments, play fight and have complex social play. Rats learn many things from play fighting: Motor skills, social skills, and abilities that are useful later when they fight, hunt, mate, and interact socially.[129]

Neuropsychologists Sergio Pellis and Vivien Pellis (2009) explain that play fighting involves *challenge*, *pain*, and *ambiguity*. If play fighting is to be fun, it must be neither too hard nor too easy. Consider a good horror movie. If it isn't scary, we get bored, and if it is too scary we might leave the cinema. Play fighting also involves pain. Pellis and Pellis say "that to keep playing means to accept some pain. In addition to refining their fighting skills, the subjects learn that pleasurable social interactions sometimes involve physical pain, as well as psychological pain arising from loss of control."[130] Rats learn to tolerate pain and they become robust and resilient. By determining the nature of play pain—is this too much?—they learn about the social world. "This lesson necessarily provides the basis for making finer discriminations about social events – and so training for social competency! Whatever the origin of play fighting, it contains ambiguity – 'did you mean to hurt me or not?'"[131] Another interesting feature is that animals use rules of reciprocity, fairness and equality. This means a stronger player self-handicaps so the weaker player can win. These rules ensure no one gets hurt and that players take turns in winning.

Pellis and Pellis speculate play fighting serves to prepare for the unexpected. Rats who play are "less likely to be overwhelmed by unexpected events" because they can "calibrate and match their emotional reactions to an unpredictable world."[132] Pellis and Pellis extrapolate their results from rats to humans and suggest play fighting prepares not so much for future fighting, as for the unpredictable world. "Another way to think of the play experience is as a means by which to prepare for the unexpected ... play experience in the juvenile period makes rats more resilient and better able to deal with situations."[133]

Rats and gorillas have a "play with play" or "complex play" capacity.[134] This means they can invent moves and alter the rules of play. The bigger the brain and the higher the cognitive abilities of a species, the more complex play becomes. Great apes, for example, play peek-a-boo and use theme-breaking maneuvers. We can link this "play with play" capacity to creativity, which Hungarian psychologist Mihaly Csikszentmihalyi says involves flexibility and originality: "Divergent thinking leads to no agreed-upon solution. It involves fluency, or the ability to generate a great quantity of ideas; flexibility, or the ability to switch from one perspective to another; and originality in picking unusual associations of ideas."[135]

Play fighting trains multiple skills, involves pain and ambiguity, and has rules about fairness and equality. Thus, players feel safe, even if they endure pain. Play fighting has later benefits, among which are emotional robustness and creative thinking.

Is there a sex difference in how animals play fight? Do males play fight more or differently than females? Pellis and Pellis say that since "most studies report that males engage in more play fighting than do females, play fighting may be considered a male typical behavior."[136] They speculate males play fight more than females because they are born with different levels of hormones in the brain and use play to manage aggression.[137] We here recognize the essentialist argument that men are aggressive and women empathic. Perhaps Pellis and Pellis are correct when it comes to rats. Or perhaps they use the meta-narrative to explain differences in observed behavior as caused by sex differences.

We will be cautious about transferring conclusions from animal behavior to human behavior. The relation between play fighting and real fighting may not be clear at all. Thus, New Zealand play theorist Brian Sutton-Smith points out that "in some species males do the playfighting but females do the real fighting."[138] With lions, for example, males are strongest but females do most of the hunting. And in the Copenhagen Zoo a few years back, the lionesses killed the male lion because they didn't like him. "[P]layfighting," says Sutton-Smith, "seems more like displaying the meaning of fighting than rehearsing for real combat. It is more about meaning than about making."[139]

> **SPEAKING OF PLAY FIGHTING**
>
> - Play fighting trains sensorimotor skills, sexual skills, social skills, mental robustness, and flexibility.
> - Play fighting involves challenge, pain, and ambiguity, and has rules of fairness and equality.
> - Rats, great apes, and humans have a "play with play" capacity which means they can alter play.

From Animal Play to Human Play

Play fighting in humans is called rough-and-tumble play (R&T) and involves the same behavior and skills: Sensorimotor skills, sexual skills, social skills, and to meet the unexpected.

Researchers believe play fighting facilitates a range of general skills in animals. Thus, animals who play fight become well-functioning adults and, if deprived of play, become socially dysfunctional. With human play, things are more complex. We have higher cognitive abilities than animals and we can use play in more advanced ways. Also, gender, as we recall, functions as a schema that filters stimuli and anticipates certain actions. It is difficult to explain differences in play as innate or acquired, because children learn what types of play fit their gender scripts.

Because the gender stereotype prescribes different behavior for boys and girls, it is not surprising research finds differences in how boys and girls play. In their observation of children, psychologists Anthony D. Pellegrini and John Archer find that "males are competitive and aggressive, and females are sedentary and nurturant" and "the sorts of fantasy play that girls enacted [was labeled] as 'social dramatic' and boys' play as 'thematic fantasy.' In social dramatic play, domestic and familial themes are enacted with girls 'mothering' younger children. Boys' thematic fantasy, on the other hand, has themes associated with dominance, fighting, and competition."[140] In short, girls play House and boys play Cowboy and Indians. Pellegrini and Archer observe that boys play fight twice as much in playgrounds as girls (respectively fourteen and seven percent).[141] But is this difference, then, a result of their culture or their nature?

Pellegrini and Archer don't think this difference is created by social scripts. Instead, they use the *sexual selection theory* as explanation.[142] Now, since this story is widely used in evolutionary theory and recurs in the meta-narrative, let me present it. It goes like this: In the animal world, the male is larger than the female because he hunts and he must fight other males in competition over females. Also, males are promiscuous because they must spread their genes, and the females care for offspring over a long period.[143] The idea is that humans, too, have dominant males who spread their genes to as many females. The sexual selection theory links play fighting to courtship: "[D]ominance is not an end onto itself, boys' dominance status is related to dating popularity with females."[144] The underlying idea is that dominance and aggression are male traits, and that play fighting is about sexual and social dominance.

It is striking that when the research shifts from observing animals play to observe humans play, the explanation for play fighting changes. Play fighting no longer serves general skills valuable to both males and females, instead it becomes a sexual behavior that has a narrower focus, namely courtship. However, if we turn to our close relatives, chimpanzees, Dutch ethologist Frans de Waal says male and female behavior is flexible:

> With the exception of nursing, males are capable of every behavior typical of females, and vice versa. In chimpanzees, for example, males have been known to adopt and care for orphaned juveniles, and females have been known to intimidate others by means of charging displays as impressive as those of males. It all depends on the circumstances. Most of the time, sex differences follow a specific recognizable pattern; yet in an environment that requires different responses, both sexes can and will adjust.[145]

Research in human play explains play fighting as male, and links play fighting to mating. But if we look to animals, play fighting is not limited to male sexual competition. It serves many functions for both males and females alike. And it does so in humans too, only our research may be gender biased. Feminists warn that our science does not only observe, but also construct data. Ethnopsychologist Despret says about the study of emotions: "From female rats in the lab to female monkeys and to women, with experiments and interviews, this kind of research seemed to end up with the same conclusion: emotionality differs according to one's gender . . . the research done to 'discover' the difference between male and female on the topic of sexuality is generally connected to the theme of the contrast between activity and passivity."[146]

It is, basically, impossible to "prove" that certain types of play are more natural for boys than girls, because the gender stereotype affects how parents raise children and is internalized by children from the age of five. Experiments with cooking pots, police cars, and plush toys in the hands of monkeys have demonstrated the problems in making a leap from animal play to human play.[147] With animals, both sexes play fight and benefit from this activity, and even if observations show females play fight less than males, there is no indication females become less able to fight or hunt, qualities necessary to protect and provide for their offspring.

It is my argument that both men and women benefit from play fighting. Whether men and women play fight differently is an open question. As circumstances change, behavior changes too. In areas related to physical activities and play, such as sports, youth gangs, and violent crimes, the percentage of female participants and perpetrators has been rising as gender equality has increased.[148]

Pellis and Pellis say play fighting makes an animal flexible and inventive. In other words, creative. When it comes to creativity, humans are unique. Csikszentmihalyi says, "every species of living organism, except for us humans, understands the world in terms of more or less built-in responses to certain types of sensations ... But in addition to the narrow windows on the world our genes have provided, we have managed to open up new perspectives on reality based on information mediated by symbols."[149] In addition to natural play, we can create new play spaces. We can invent chess boards, imagine storyworlds with vampires and werewolves, and pack parachutes for BASE jumping. We can use play to lift us into the unknown and unpredictable and only the meta-narrative sets limits. Humans have the cognitive abilities to reach beyond animal play.

According to Csikszentmihalyi, our cognitive play abilities are independent of sex. Creativity is an androgynous trait, and "creative and talented girls are more dominant and tough than other girls, and creative boys are more sensitive and less aggressive than their male peers." Creative people are psychologically androgynous and "a psychologically androgynous person in effect doubles his or her repertoire of responses and can interact with the world in terms of a much richer and varied spectrum of opportunities."[150] Creative play, thus, is highly adaptive. When we play fight, we become physically stronger, more robust and flexible, prepared for the unexpected, and more creative.

SPEAKING OF FROM ANIMAL TO HUMAN PLAY

- Play research can reproduce gender bias, because science not only observes and collects data, but also constructs data.
- It is problematic to transfer results from experiments with animals to humans.
- When situations change, behavior changes too. What is believed a sex difference may turn out to be a gender difference.

Playing on the Edge

Humans can play more complexly than animals. We can play fight in the imaginary worlds of chess boards, online computer games, at Live action Role Play (LARP) conventions, in the cinema.

To understand horror as play with danger I shall use the concept *edgework* from sports sociology. "Edgework" is when we do exciting and dangerous activities for fun. The edge can be a literal edge, as the edge of a cliff, however, it is used metaphorically. Sociologist Stephen Lyng (1990) uses it about risk sports like sky diving and mountain climbing, and says edgework is, "most fundamentally, the problem of negotiating the boundary between chaos and order."[151] This mental boundary is the edge. "The 'edge,' or boundary line, confronted by the edgeworker can be defined in many different ways: life versus death, consciousness versus unconsciousness, sanity versus insanity, an ordered sense of self and environment versus a disordered self and environment."[152] Lyng's examples are risk sports, where players embrace real danger and face real death. As a mountain climber puts it: "Death is so close. You could let go and make the decision to die. It feels so good."[153]

In *Danger* (2007) psychologist Michael J. Apter expands edgework to also include activities such as sexual activities, committing crimes for fun, and activities that are not physically dangerous but involve a psychological experience of danger. Apter includes fantasizing about danger and watching fiction. He mentions horror films, however, he does not discuss the viewers' use of films, he only discusses people doing physical edgework activities. Apter defines edgework through *zones*, *excitement/anxiety*, and *protective frames*. When people do edgework, they move between three zones: A safety zone, a danger zone, and a trauma zone. We feel safe in our safety zone, the trauma zone is where we face trauma and can get hurt, and the intermediary danger zone is where we move to get as close as possible to trauma without dying. The "edge" is within our danger zone, directly next to the trauma zone. It is when the mountain climber is hanging on the cliff side. It is when a player touches danger without dying.

Apter links edgework to the emotions of excitement and anxiety which both prepare for fight or flight. The two emotions are identical in terms of neurochemistry: They *feel* the same. The difference is in our assessment of our ability to cope with the situation. If we think we can manage the danger, we feel excited, and if we don't think we can manage the danger, we feel anxious. Thus, the sensory part in the two emotions is identical, but the cognitive part, and thus our action response, is different. Anxiety and excitement are intimately linked. The more anxiety, the more excitement. Thus, the closer you get to trauma, the harder stress hormones like adrenaline, cortisol, and norepinephrine kick in, and the more excited the player feels when working the edge. "In other words, one buys excitement with fear, and the greater the cost, the better the product."[154]

Apter also introduces the concepts of protective frames. They are the frames through which players look at their edgework. There are three kinds: *Confidence* frames, *safety-zone* frames, and *detachment* frames. In the first frame, the player is confident she is sufficiently skilled to survive. For example, the documentary *Into the Mind* (2013, Eric Crosland, Dave

Mossop) follows freestyle skiers who leap off mountain peaks, clearly believing they have the skills to survive. In the safety-zone frame, then, the player believes she is in a safe zone. Finally, the detachment frame is when a player thinks events are not really happening, as with fantasizing and fiction.

I argue we use horror fiction to do what I call *mental edgework*, where we wear Apter's detachment frames: This threat is not to me, but to fictional characters. In fact, the danger doesn't exist, because this is fiction and characters are played by actors. As with the assessment of anxiety/excitement, the detachment frames are created by our cognitive assessment of the situation. It happens when we use System 2 to tell ourselves this is fiction, that our emotional engagement is play, and it is safe to engage because events are not real. When characters die, no one dies in the real world. Let us recall from the discussion of emotions, that we first experience the fictional situation as real with our System 1, and next, as a secondary step, use System 2 to tell ourselves it is not real, but fiction. Apter explains, "not only is one aroused when the heroine dies in a film, but there is a sense in which one is genuinely upset . . . In fact, everything about the emotion is the same as in its 'real-life' counterpart – except that there is an awareness that it is *not* 'real-life.'"[155]

Mental edgework can be upsetting because although we tell ourselves it is play, our emotions tell us differently, namely that it feels real. This is what makes mental play human play: We can experience an ambiguously real/not-real situation, which animals cannot. We have the cognitive abilities to process conflicting information—the danger feels real, yet I know it is imagined—and use this experience in play. We can practice danger without putting our body at risk. Thus, where edgework and mental edgework share emotions of excitement and anxiety, *consequences* are different. In risk sports, players literally risk their lives, but mental edgework does not risk a player's life. We may feel traumatized from mental edgework, however, we do not die. This is how horror is mental edgework. *If* we accept the invitation to feel and *if* we enter an emotional dialogue with the fiction, *then* horror can become imaginary play fighting and mental edgework. Fiction events are not real, but our experience is; we feel real excitement and real anxiety. And while we will not lose our life, we do risk psychological trauma to a certain extent because we share character's emotions, feel their pain, and experience their death. This is why we sometimes must leave a fiction when it is "too much," so we avoid falling into our trauma zone.

The appeal and benefits of ordinary play fighting is the same for animals and humans. When we play, we learn and practice skills valuable later in life. But animals do not risk their lives in play, like people do in edgework. Why do we ski from mountain peaks, climb mountains, and skydive? What, we may ask, is the gain? People report that they learn self-control and to manage their emotions. As they grow more skilled in a risk sport, they also grow more able to push themselves further and control their emotions on the edge. They report a strong feeling of "self." Lyng reports a sky diver's description: "I wasn't thinking at all – I just did what I had to do. It was the right thing to do too. And after it was over, I felt really alive and pure." Thus, says Lyng, "[i]n edgework, the ego is called forth in a dramatic way."[156] On the edge, there is little time for doubts. We use skills without second-guessing ourselves and enter the state Csikszentmihalyi calls *flow*, where we are highly focused, lose sense of time and place, and perform our best.[157] Edgeworkers say they feel "self-realization," "self-determination," and "a purified and magnified sense of self." They feel more alive on the edge than in everyday life.

Edgework is about building and strengthening our self. In mental edgework, we put our "self" at risk too. The good horror film takes us to the edge of our abilities to endure challenging emotions and threatening situations. Our awareness of choosing danger is matched by our hope we will come out of the experience with a stronger self. Thus, tied to horror fiction is our hope of future benefits. In play research, we find this embrace of danger as, on the one hand, a threat to the self, yet, on the other hand, there is also excitement in overcoming the danger and our fear. Thus, Caillois says that *ilinx*, games of vertigo, are about falling and losing control and are "linked to the desire for disorder and destruction, a drive which is normally repressed."[158] We play with vertigo in Ferris wheels, carrousels, and haunted houses. "Vertigo is an integral part of nature, and one controls it only in obeying it."[159]

From her research in the extreme thrills of roller coasters, falls from heights, and visits to haunted places, Kerr concludes: "Thrilling experiences and self-scaring all come with a moment of confrontation and resolution, leaving us feeling good, in control, confident, and secure in our abilities and ourselves."[160] We don't like being scared, but we like *choosing* to be scared, hoping we grow stronger from the experience. Play fighting, edgework, and horror enact risk and danger, excitement and anxiety, to face and feel challenges, to push things to the limit and go over the edge, and to extend, that is, *master*, the edge. Speaking of computer games, Juul thinks games push players to win more points, use shorter play time, make more interesting choices, and become better players.[161] We don't improve by avoiding failure, only by *embracing* failure, and try again.

Is it more natural for men to do edgework than it is for women? To this question, Apter responds there is no sex difference in the excitement-seeking instinct in the sexes: "Here the data obtained so far do not support the idea that the sexes differ with respect to arousal-seeking or arousal-avoidance dominance. This implies that if men and women are different, that difference is not in terms of how much time they spend in each state, but in terms of the specific things that they do to raise or lower arousal levels when they are in one state or the other."[162] While there are, indeed, people who are low arousal-seekers and others who are high arousal-seekers, this difference depends on individual personality, not sex.[163] Apter's observation is supported by research that show men and women are, in fact, equally aggressive, but that men learn to express aggression and women learn to suppress aggression.[164]

There is also research in gender and edgework. Sociologist Jennifer Lois followed a team of voluntary mountain rescue workers for five-and-a-half years. She observed that women and men shared a narrative with a "norm of masculine emotional stoicism" which said men are strong and women weak.[165] Male rescue workers used this narrative to feel self-confident while women, reversely, would be anxious. If things went well, they did not take credit, and if things went wrong they ascribed this to being women and therefore inferior to their male colleagues. "Furthermore, even when women performed well on missions, it did not seem to boost their confidence for future situations, while conversely, men's poor performance did not erode theirs."[166] Lois did not observe any difference in men and women's ability to manage their emotions while working the edge. The difference was in the meta-narrative, their ideas about gender.

The benefits from edgework parallel those from play fighting. The player builds a stronger self when she "works" the edge and masters her emotions.

SPEAKING OF EDGEWORK

- Edgework is voluntary play with danger. Edgeworkers feel excitement and anxiety.
- Edgeworkers move between a safe zone, a danger zone, and a trauma zone. In the danger zone, they work the edge to get as close to trauma as possible.
- Edgework teaches self-management, self-control, and to manage one's emotions. Edgework is self-work.

Aggression

Play fighting is about danger and pain. Burghardt draws a direct line from animal play to humans' cruel treatment of fellow humans for fun,[167] and Caillois links vertigo to "crude and brutal forms of personality expression."[168] But although pain and violence are hallmarks of horror, the core of horror— that is, its driving engine—is not violence but aggression. We shall separate aggression from violence by seeing the first as innate behavior that serves survival, and the latter as intentional actions meant to cause harm.

In this section I discuss aggression and I take my cue from South African neuropsychologist Victor Nell's work on aggression in "Cruelty's Rewards:

The Gratifications of Perpetrators and Spectators" (2006). He defines cruelty as when we intentionally inflict pain on others, knowing that the subject feels pain and enjoying this pain. Nell thinks only humans can be cruel, because cruelty requires meta-thinking. He argues cruelty evolved from the predator's pleasure in hunting. To hunt is dangerous and strenuous and most hunts fail, which is why hunting must be affectively pleasant to be attractive to the predator. To hunt feels good before, during, and after a hunt.

Nell discusses three types of aggression: Predatory aggression; intermale territorial and sex-related aggression; and angry aggression.[169] The first is for hunting prey. The second type, territorial and sex-related aggression, serves competing for territory, for one's rank in a social hierarchy, and for a mate. The third type, angry aggression, is self-defense against a threat. The three types are neuroanatomically distinct and activate different circuits in the brain, namely *FEAR*, the *RAGE circuit*, or the *SEEKING circuit*. They function differently. RAGE is chaotic and loud and serves to scare off opponents. SEEKING is controlled and quiet, and used to stalk prey. FEAR, finally, leads to a choice between a fight-or-flight response. FEAR can draw from RAGE if the choice is to fight. RAGE and SEEKING "have separate circuits in the brain [and] the RAGE and SEEKING circuits are mutually inhibitory interactions and cannot therefore co-occur ..."[170] If you are attacked, you use RAGE to try to scare off the attacker; you use FEAR to flee; or you can activate the SEEKING circuit and, like Sarah in *Inside*, try to hunt and kill the attacker.

We can distinguish between three types of animals: *prey*, *predator*, and animals that are *both prey and predator*. A gazelle is a typical prey; it has sideways-facing eyes with horizontal pupils and can rotate eyes and head to watch out for predators. Lions and tigers, in contrast, are pure predators; they have forward-facing eyes with circular pupils designed to measure distance so they can chase prey. Humans are, like primates, both prey and predator. We can live on a vegetarian diet and we have a FEAR system to look out for predators, but we also eat meat and have forward-facing eyes with circular pupils like the tiger, and a SEEKING circuit so we can stalk prey. This dual nature might explain why horror so vividly features both roles in the hunt, namely that of predator and prey.[171]

Nell thinks man is a predator, and speaks of cruelty in men, not women. To explain the evolution from aggression to cruelty Nell uses the Man the Hunter story and sexual selection theory. Like hunting, cruelty feels affectively good and is therefore pleasant. It also signals power, which scares off other males and is attractive to women and thus serves mating. Now, Nell's argument about the benefits of cruelty is controversial and I leave further discussion of his ideas to others.[172] Our interest is in the three types of aggression, which I now turn to.

> **SPEAKING OF AGGRESSION**
>
> - Innate aggression serves hunting; fight over territory and mate; and self-defense.
> - An animal can be prey, predator, or both. Humans are both prey and predators.
> - Aggression has three neural circuits: RAGE is loud; SEEKING is quiet and for stalking prey; and FEAR leads to fight or flight.

Three Basic Horror Narratives

We will use Nell's the three types of aggression—*predation, competition,* and *self-defense*—to outline three narratives that are basic in horror: *Survival horror, social horror,* and *identity horror*. Like aggression is innate, so, too, can these be considered the genre's basic building blocks.

Survival horror shares its name with the subgenre in computer games where a player must complete a mission in a hostile environment with an under-equipped avatar. An example is *Resident Evil* (1996, Capcom) where the avatar dies innumerable times before the player develops the quick reflexes to fight off attackers and overcome obstacles.[173] Survival horror, whether it is in computer games, films, or television, has a bleak atmosphere of decay and death, and plots are about survival under primitive conditions. Typical storylines are hunting scenarios with humans reduced to prey, as in the zombie apocalypse *World War Z* (2013, Marc Forster), the post-apocalyptic *The Road* (2009, John Hillcoat), or *Predator* (1983, John McTiernan) with alien big game hunters. Whatever the monster is, undead, human, or alien, it wants to hunt and kill the protagonist. To survive one must learn to control instincts telling us to run. The lesson of survival horror is to use System 2 to explore all options and keep fighting no matter what. Characters must explore the affordances of the environment, find out who to trust (usually no one), and learn to master emotions. Basically, you're alone and the answer is not to fight harder but be smarter. Typical emotions are fear, disgust, despair, and grief, but also hope and compassion.[174]

Social horror is about relations between humans and monsters and the aim is not feeding but to carve out a niche where one can live. It is set in civilized spaces where species fight over territory, compete for social rank, and meet sexual mates, make friends, and establish families. Here, aggression is used to further "self-preservation, protection of the young, and resource competition."[175] Think of the supernatural species who hide their existence from humans in *Vampire Diaries* (2009–, CW). Nell links competitive aggression to mating, and social horror typically stages sexual encounters. If survival horror is about falling prey to predators, social horror is about learning social skills and self-management. These include fighting, flirting, making friends, and managing family ties, and social horror features sexual emotions like love, excitement, and lust, and complex emotions like trust and vengeance.

The last narrative, *identity horror*, is about holding up perimeters when you are under attack. This attack is intimate and personal, it is someone targeting *you* and *you* must defend yourself. The attack can be physical or mental, and we will understand "self" in what play psychologist Thomas S. Henricks calls *the wide sense of self*. Henrick's self has five dimensions: it is physical (body); material (possessions); social (multiple social selves); it is psychological (mind); and, finally, cultural (family or community).[176] The attack in identity horror can be on any of these dimensions. The difference between identity and survival horror is that the attack is not predation. Your life is not essential to your attacker's survival, instead you are the object of cruel play. Examples of identity horror are the leisure torture in *Hostel* and *Hostel 2* (attacks on the body), and the home-invasion subgenre, where the home is an extended part of the self, as in French-Romanian *Them* (*Ils,* 2006, David Moreau and Xavier Palud). Identity horror is about attack and self-defense, captivity and escape, and the setting is homely and claustrophobic. The attacker can be a monster, a psychopath, or a dark force inside you, as in *Black Swan* where the protagonist is delusional. Identity horror stages pain, despair, and helplessness, and often involves cognitive dissonance: Am I going crazy or is this shit really happening?

Finally, there is a fourth narrative in horror I will call *creative horror*. This narrative is not based on innate aggression as are the former three. It is instead when a text is self-aware of its status as play and as fiction. It can then become meta-play or meta-emotional, for example by asking the audience to step back and examine something from a distance. This can be the text's use of emotions, its use of genre elements or something else. This kind of narrative is linked to the play-with-play function Pellis and Pellis mention. It is when we change how we play.

SPEAKING OF THREE BASIC HORROR NARRATIVES

- *Survival horror* is about predation, the environment is hostile and primitive, and emotions are fear and disgust, but also hope and trust.
- *Social horror* is about competition and communication, it is interpersonal, and it is set in cityscapes. Emotions are sexual, social, and complex: Lust, sex, love, trust, anger, and vengeance.
- *Identity horror* is about self-defense and threats to the self in a wide sense of self which includes mind, body, possessions, friends, and world.

- *Creative horror* is a fourth narrative which has self-awareness of being play and fiction. It is not linked to basic aggression, but linked to creative use of play.

Horror as Play

Now that all our tools are in the toolbox, let us return to the function of horror. What happens when we enter the dark stage?

If we look at the research in horror, we find different suggestions. James Twitchell in *Dreadful Pleasures* (1985) said horror teaches the young about the rules of sexual behavior. Clover (1992) and Creed (1993) argued that horror showcases men's sadomasochistic fantasies and fears about women and that horror is the result of a misogynist society. Carroll (1990) thinks we satisfy cognitive curiosity about a monster, and Smith (1999) links our pleasure in the perverse to a cognitive revolt against moralism. Freeland (2000) says we learn about evil and question society's ethics. In his biocultural approach, Grodal (2009) argued horror teaches male audiences survival skills. From a phenomenological perspective, Hanich (2010) thinks we enjoy the physical sensations of fear, and Laine (2006, 2011) thinks horror lets us enter an emotional dialogue with fear and disgust. In her aesthetic approach, Ndalianis (2012) explores how we interface with horror in cognitive, emotional, and affective ways with our body, the sensorium. Finally, studies like Wetmore (2012), see the genre as an expression of cultural themes, in this case anxieties. And a study like Harrington's *Women, Monstrosity and Horror Film: Gynaehorror* (2017) sees horror as a genre to explore desires as well as anxieties around the female and fecund body, in this case.

The theory of horror as play cuts across all these approaches. Seeing horror as play, we can summarize the discussion of functions and benefits in Table 2.

TABLE 2 *Horror as Play: Benefits, Narratives, and Themes*

AGGRESSION	BENEFITS	NARRATIVES	THEMES
Predator	Sensorimotor skills	Survival horror	Hunger & hunting
Territory & mating	Sexual & social skills	Social horror	Communication
Angry	Mental robustness	Identity horror	Self-defense
Edgework	"Play with play"	Creative horror	Self-management

The first column has Nell's three types of aggression and I have added edgework as a fourth type, because it is a planned for and self-aware use of aggression as play. In the second column are the benefits, ethologists say individuals (animals and humans) gain from play fighting. The third column, then, list my basic horror narratives, to which I have added creative horror as a fourth narrative. As said, this narrative differs from the basic narratives by being self-conscious about its status as play and fiction. It involves meta-thinking and self-reflection. When humans do edgework, we know what awaits us: The BASE jumper packs a parachute, and the audience is warned by advertisement for the horror movie. The fourth column, finally, connects themes to each of the types of aggression. For example, to use horror as self-conscious mental edgework can break with stereotypes and re-author the meta-narrative. Examples are texts that play with genre rules, like the *Scream* series (1996–2011).

Corresponding to the multiple functions of horror, there are also multiple ways the audience can use the genre, a use that can change with age, sex, or individual personality. As we shall see in the analytical chapters, when protagonists are in different life phases, narratives change, and so, too, do emotions. Because I have not done audience research, I cannot say if different age groups use horror in different ways, or if male audiences use horror differently than female audiences. This research must be done by future studies. What I examine in the analytical chapters is how horror offers different protagonists, different stories with different themes, and different kinds of emotional engagements.

Most research in play examines either adult play (Caillois, Huizinga, Lyng, Lois) or child play (Erikson, Pellegrini, Pellegrini and Archer, Smith). However, I have taken my cue from animal play (Pellis and Pellis, Burghardt, Fagen), and mammals play from when they are young until old age. Play cuts across age and gender, and continues as we move through the life stages. Horror offers multiple benefits, but especially two are adaptive no matter what age or gender the viewer is: Emotional robustness (resilience) and the "play with play" capacity, which leads to flexibility and creativity. The two are connected; the more we can endure challenging emotions and situations, the better we will become at mastering System 1 and System 2. It is through mastery of emotions that we obtain choices, and choices lead to flexibility and creativity.

When we enter the dark stage, our play experience will change us. Here is how a football player describes his play: "As it gets down to game time, the personality changes, the darker side, this different person comes out. But the game itself, the physically doing it and the physically being involved and being challenged and being put to the test, that fear of failure, I enjoy it, or though I don't enjoy it, at least it provides something for me."[177] Play brings out a "darker side" and a "different person" who is willing to be "challenged." Burghardt says play "may help explain aggression, war, morality, sex (including gender differences, courtship, sex roles), drug use and risky thrill-seeking behavior, educational endeavors, cultural achievements, creativity in virtually all realms ... even the rise and fall of civilizations."[178] Burghardt, like Huizinga, thinks play is the fabric from which civilization is made.

Researchers continue to disagree about the functions of play. Some think play teaches skills and cognitive learning, others think it doesn't teach anything but just makes us happy.[179] And some play scholars think play can be a liminal space where a door is opened to self-growth and radical, even existential, change. Play can be about "disequilibrium, novelty, loss of control, and surprise" and "a field of open potentiality, an ambiguous place ... *transitional space*" (emphasis in original).[180]

On the dark stage of horror, we work the edge between excitement and anxiety, order and chaos, life and death. And even if characters lose control and fall into the trauma zone, we, the audience, will learn to master our emotions. In neuroscientific terms, we shift perspective, expand our ego tunnel, increase activity in our neuronal cloud, and tell ourselves the incremental story: Yes, horror is painful, and yes, characters die in our stead. But if characters die, we live. This is so we learn to master fear.

SPEAKING OF HORROR AS PLAY

- Horror is mental play fighting and has multiple benefits: Sensorimotor skills, sexual and social skills, emotional robustness, creativity.
- Horror is mental edgework. Edgework is when we engage in dangerous activities for fun and work the edge between danger and trauma.
- Horror teaches us to feel, control, manage, and, ultimately, master our emotions.

Child

2

Mud, Blood, and Magic:

Genre and Gender in *Pan's Labyrinth*

Guillermo del Toro's acclaimed *Pan's Labyrinth* (*El laberinto del fauno*, 2006) has been widely discussed as part of a Spanish cinema remembering its trauma from the Civil War (1936–1939), and as an example of a transnational cinema captivating a global audience with its universal themes and beautiful film aesthetics. With a Mexican auteur and its use of the Spanish Civil War (a war known as "the labyrinth"[1]), the film belongs to both contexts. However, I will discuss it from a different position. The film ingeniously plays with expectations about genre and gender, expectations that are socially constructed and which I examine in the light of what Sunstein and Kahneman call *default values* and *anchor points*. Also, albeit the film has a child protagonist, it is not a children's film. It is not aimed at the young and innocent, but at adult audiences in need of a new and "innocent" perspective.

When I rented *Pan's Labyrinth*, I mistook it for a fantasy film suitable for family viewing. I was deceived by a DVD cover promising a "magical" and "fantastic" film, a "masterpiece,"[2] and eleven-year-old protagonist Ofelia looked seven rather than eleven years old. She stood in front of an old and twisted tree with a stone arch behind her, signaling the magic land of the fairy tale. But shortly into the story, the villain, the fascist Captain Vidal, hacked a man's face to pieces with a bottle. My children, eleven and eight at the time, would later blame me for childhood trauma, and rightly so, because this explosion of violence into what we expected to be a marvelous film felt like an assault.

Pan's Labyrinth is marvelous and horrible. The story is about Ofelia (Ivana Baquero) who travels with her mother Carmen to a military post in the mountains. Carmen has married Vidal and is pregnant with his child. The fascists have won, but the resistance still campaigns against the new regime. In an old labyrinth behind the military post Ofelia meets a faun, who says she is the princess Moana and promises to return her to a magic kingdom if she can complete three tests. After the tests and a battle between the resistance and the soldiers, Vidal kills Ofelia in the labyrinth. In one ending she awakes in the magic kingdom, and in a second ending she dies in the labyrinth.

The film won more than seventy prizes, among them three Oscars, three BAFTA awards, and a Danish Bodil for best foreign film. Reviewers agreed the play with genre was a brutal and brilliant way to engage audiences. "Dark, twisted and beautiful, this entwines fairy-tale fantasy with war-movie horror to startling effect," wrote *Empire*, whose reviewer (like me) found the film's torture scenes "more uncomfortable than the full-on slicing and battering in, say, *Hostel*."[3] Reviewers noted the film's emotional impact: "[A]ll but the most cynical of adults are likely to find themselves troubled to the point of heartbreak by its dark, rich and emphatic emotions."[4]

I have chosen Ofelia as our first horror heroine because my viewing experience made me use my System 2 to think about genre and gender. I was devastated when Ofelia died: Why was the protagonist a child, and a female child? Why should she die? And why were there two endings? The chapter starts with a discussion of default rules and anchor points. I next examine the fairy tale and compare fairy-tale rules to rules of, respectively, horror, the fantastic, and the melodrama. The aim is to see how the film destabilizes genre and manipulates and challenges gender stereotype and the meta-narrative. In terms of Erikson's life stages, the film does not reflect the basic conflict of a pre-adolescent child. Instead, Ofelia's young age is used as a strategy to make the adult audience "feel" like a child and look at the world with a child's eyes. Such ideas about children's feelings and views are, of course, the ideas of adults. *Pan's Labyrinth* is a meta-film that consciously plays with genre and demands meta-thinking: What is real, and why does magic and war mix? It uses elements from the basic horror narratives, combining social horror (how to adapt in society) with identity horror (is the faun real?) and survival horror (Ofelia is almost eaten by a monster). But most of all, in its play with genre, the film uses the fourth narrative, creativity, and invites us into an emotional dialogue where we alternate between feeling with System 1 and thinking with System 2.

Anchor Points and Default Rules

Before we look at Ofelia, I want to return to heuristics and default rules, which I mentioned in the section on emotions in the previous chapter. Heuristics, we recall, govern our emotions without our knowing so. Legal scholar Cass R. Sunstein in *Laws of Fear* explains people don't have their own individual values and preferences; values and preferences are produced by default rules.

Default rules are those precepts that already exist around you; they are created by society and institutions for social control. Sunstein uses insurance as example. In one American state, an insurance company offered a low premium and no right to sue, but the customer could buy the right to sue at an additional cost. And in another state, an insurance company offered the right to sue and a high premium, and the customer could waive the right and lower the premium. In both cases, customers stuck with default rules. "Default rules of some kind are inevitable, and much of the time those rules will affect preference and choices."[5] We take default rules for granted and they "stick" in our mind and affect our future choices. We tend not to question them, because we don't notice them, and because human nature is conservative and we are afraid of new things.

An *anchor point* is an information, a value, introduced by default rules. Kahneman uses shopping in the bazaar as an example. If the seller starts out with what you think is a ridiculously high price, asking $200 for a bag, you should not begin to negotiate, but leave the shop and insist negotiations begin from a different price. The seller can then offer a new selling price, perhaps going down to $100 or $50. The new price is then the anchor point from which negotiations begin. The anchor point is *any information* that affects your calculation, and it can be a random information with no causal relation whatsoever to the situation. Kahneman gives another example, here with judges who were asked to roll a dice before they passed a sentence on a shoplifter. The dice were loaded and showed either 3 or 9. "As soon as the dice came to a stop, the judges were asked whether they would sentence the woman to a term in prison greater or lesser, in months, than the number showing on the dice ... On average, those who had rolled a 9 said they would sentence her to 8 months; those who rolled a 3 said they would sentence her to 5 months; the anchoring effect was 50%."[6] To spell this out: the random dice affected the passing of judgment.

Anchors function like real anchors: We stay close to them and "a message, unless it is immediately rejected as a lie, will have the same effect on the associative system regardless of its reliability."[7] Anchors affect us, even when random and irrelevant, like the number on a dice to the number of months in prison. And why am I talking about default rules and anchor points? Because, in the context of genre and expectations, a genre functions as default rules do. If you think you are about to watch a fantasy film, you expect the rules of fantasy to apply. New anchor points, here, are the moments with new events and emotions, which the viewer will try to fit into her viewing experience and expectations. In the case of *Pan's Labyrinth*, the beginning of the film offers both a faun and a murderous fascist, different anchor points that solicit different emotions and expectations.

Into the Labyrinth

So, let us turn to del Toro's film. *Pan's Labyrinth* opens with the sound of Ofelia's last breath as she is dying in an underground cave. A text tells us this is "Espana, 1944" and "the civil war is over. In the mountains armed groups continue the battle against the new fascist regime." The camera zooms into Ofelia's eye and a voice-over intones: "They say that long ago in the subterraneous kingdom, where there was neither lies nor pain, once lived a princess ..." The camera zooms out and time runs backward as blood flows back into Ofelia's nose and a girl runs from the dark cave back up the stairs into the sun.

The story jumps back to a week earlier when Ofelia (Baquero) and Carmen (Ariadna Gil) travel to a military post. The post is in an old mill and behind it is an old labyrinth. Carmen is due to give birth and Vidal (Sergi López) wants his son to be born where he, the father, is. On the road Ofelia sees a fairy, and on the first night the fairy takes her to the faun in a cave under the labyrinth. The faun says if she passes three tests, she can return to her kingdom. She discovers the housekeeper Mercedes (Maribel Verdú) is helping the resistance. While Vidal chases the resistance and Carmen dies giving birth, Ofelia solves her tests. The first is to obtain a key from the stomach of a big toad, the second test is to use the key to steal a dagger from a child-eating monster, the Pale Man, and the third test is to kill her infant brother, or rather *refuse* to kill him. Ofelia will rather sacrifice herself. At this moment, the faun disappears and Vidal, who has pursued her into the labyrinth, shoots her. The resistance fighters next shoot Vidal. In the first ending, Ofelia becomes princess, and in the second ending, she dies and Mercedes hums the lullaby from the film's beginning.

As indicated, the film has been discussed as an expression of Spanish memory and in terms of transnational cinema. Here I shall briefly outline the two contexts. *Pan's Labyrinth* is part of a contemporary revival of Spanish horror/Gothic cinema, which in the 1990s lifted a low-budget genre film into a high-budgeted genre film which after the millennium was called New Gothic and "sober Gothic," because it cut back on explicit violence and used suspense and mystery, to gain a wider audience. Examples are *The Others* (Alejandro Amenábar, 2001) and *Mama* (Andrés Muschietti, 2013). The creators of contemporary Spanish horror had not experienced the Civil War or Franco's 36-year dictatorship which ended with his death in 1975. Thus, these films paid as much tribute to the horror genre's past, and played with both intertextual and historical references.

In 2006, del Toro was known as an auteur working in both horror and fantasy, genres kept apart. *Cronos* (1993), *Mimic* (1997), *The Devil's Backbone* (*El espinazo del diablo*, 2001), and *Blade II* (2002) were marketed as horror films, while *Hellboy* (2004) was marketed as a comic-book-style fantasy film. Also, where *Cronos* and *The Devil's Backbone* were Spanish productions, his other films were American Hollywood productions. Del Toro had written and directed his two Spanish films, as he also did with *Pan's Labyrinth*. *The Devil's Backbone* was set during the Spanish Civil War and *Pan's Labyrinth* in 1944 after the Civil War ended. In Spain, his two films became linked to remembering the country's past, which after Franco's death was collectively shut down. In *The Spanish Gothic* (2017), Xavier Aldana Reyes discusses how "both films have come to stand for the most significant of Spanish engagements with war through the Gothic mode and they therefore need to be considered under this lens . . ."[8] After Franco's death, both right and left parties agreed to suppress the memory of the Civil War through "the pact of forgetting" with the Spanish 1977 Amnesty Law. "The direct effect of these policies was the promotion of historical ignorance and the forgetting of those civilians and opponents (especially the *maquis* who appear in *Pan's Labyrinth*) unlawfully killed and deleted from official records."[9] In the 1990s, Spain began to remember. The year after *Pan's Labyrinth* an Association for the Recuperation of Historical Memory was established, and Spain also established "the Historical Memory Law in 2007, which recognized the victims of the war and officially condemned the Francoist Regime."[10] Thus, *Pan's Labyrinth* ties into the recuperation of a national trauma.

The second context is *Pan's Labyrinth* as transnational cinema. Like *The Others*, the film uses genre to tap into "a shared iconographic language that, like the fairy tale, has transnational potential and allows for an engagement with notions of good and evil, oppression and liberation, power and insurrection."[11] Thus, where the film taps into a specific war, it also taps into universally shared storylines, themes, and characters, and uses genres widely known, such as the fairy tale, the fantastic, horror, and the melodrama. Adding to this is the unique vision of an auteur director who, for example, designed the Pale Man, a monster that today has entered a global horror mythology. Depending on one's perspective, the audience can enter the labyrinth and read *Pan's Labyrinth* as either national or transnational cinema.

As said, I want to focus on the film's ability to unsettle viewer expectations and default rules, which was my experience. I felt I navigated the tempestuous and unpredictable waters of a surprising story. My knowledge of the Spanish Civil War is limited, a historical horizon I probably share with other viewers who, like me, are not Spanish. In my Danish video rental shop, the film was marketed as a marvelous masterpiece, and when the voice-over set the story "long ago" with kings and queens and fauns and fairies, I soon forgot Ofelia's death. After all, everyone knows fairy tales have happy endings and use magic to bring people back to life. Thus, despite the events were set in fascist Spain, I thought the fairy-tale anchor points made Ofelia's world "safe." Vidal may be a villain in the "real" fascist world, but my faith in fairy-tale rules was so firm, I expected them to overrule fascism.

Fairy-Tale Expectations

But what, precisely, are the default rules in fairy tales? In *Once Upon a Time* (1970) Swiss fairy-tale scholar Max Lüthi explains that, "the fairy tale is the poetic expression of the confidence that we are secure in a world not destitute of sense, that we can adapt ourselves to it and act and live even if we cannot view or comprehend the world as a whole."[12] The fairy tale extends a safety net under our feet no matter how dark things appear.

Fairy tales did not always have happy endings, but in their bourgeois form they do.[13] Today fairy-tale scholars understand the fairy tale as "an interpretative device" that provides psychological guidance to overcome obstacles in life and are "stories to think with, stories that do not necessarily determine lives but can give children (and adults) a way to read and to understand them."[14] Fairy-tale scholar Donald Haase describes how children in the Second World War used fairy tales for comfort. A war survivor recalls: "They helped me to overcome fear, to remain undisturbed, even when the external danger and the panic of the people around me persisted. It was as if they showed me a meaningful structure of events and relationships that were superior to and more powerful than chaos – a structure in which evil did have its place and time, but not the last word."[15] In "On Fairy-Stories" (1939), J. R. R. Tolkien described the core of fairy stories as a joy which gives the reader "a sudden and miraculous grace," parallel to a Christian revelation.[16] And Marxist philosopher Ernest Bloch (1930) thought the fairy tale revolutionary was because a "little fellow" could be king.[17] These are the fairy-tale default rules.

Ofelia has brought fairy-tale books with her, and when the car stops for her mother to be sick in the side of the road, she ventures into the forest. "I have seen a fairy," she tells her mother. Likewise, the three tests are the fairy-tale element *par excellence* that heroes and heroines always solve. Fairy-tale scholar Maria Tatar divides the tests into *test*, *task*, and a *trial*. The test shows a protagonist's good character, when she is compassionate and helps supernatural beings. Next is an impossible task, which she solves with help from her new friends. And last is the trial, that proves her "strength, courage, and wit needed to defeat [her] rivals."[18]

In the first test, the faun gives Ofelia a book and three amber stones. The pages are blank, but words and drawings magically appear when needed. The book tells Ofelia to go into the forest and find a tree. "Under the tree lives a giant toad who won't let the tree grow. You must place the three magical amber stones in its mouth and take the golden key from its belly. Only that way will the tree return to life." Ofelia walks into the forest wearing a new dress and new shoes her mother has given her the same morning. She takes off her clothes before climbing into the belly of the tree where the toad covers her in spit and vomits up yellow goo. Ofelia picks the key from the vomit and returns home covered in mud and late for the Captain's dinner for the local influential people. Her mother sends her for a bath and straight to bed. Ofelia has been disobedient.[19]

Ofelia is an unconventional fairy-tale heroine. The rules for a fairy-tale hero and a fairy-tale heroine are different; the hero has "compassion and humility, coupled with simplicity or even stupidity,"[20] but a fairy-tale heroine must also be humble, beautiful, and good. If she is vain or proud, she is punished: "[F]emale protagonists are by nature just as humble as their male counterparts, but they display that virtue in a strikingly different fashion ... they are actually humbled in the course of their stories. In fact, humbled is perhaps too mild a term to use for the many humiliations to which female protagonists must submit."[21] A hero can be happy-go-lucky and do silly things like put mud in his pocket like Blockhead Hans, but heroines are "victimized" and "abased and forced to learn humility."[22]

Ofelia's beauty and costume are typical for a fairy-tale heroine, but like a fairy-tale hero, she ventures out in the world to find adventure, and although she has supernatural help (the faun and the fairies) they do not solve her tasks, unlike Cinderella who has doves to help sort out her lentils. Ofelia crawls through mud, but refuses to feel humiliated. "Hey, I am princess Moana, I am not afraid of you," she tells the toad. The mud is important, but before we feel mud, we must ask what it means to see with a child's eyes.

With a Child's Eyes

To take a child's perspective is a strategy to intensify our emotional dialogue. It reflects how the West associates children with heightened sensitivity, pre-verbal emotions, and fantastic imagination.

In *The Child in Film* (2010), British film theorist Karen Lury examines films that use a child's perspective. Her films are, like my texts, for adult audiences. Lury says children offer, "a confusing, often stuttering temporality," and "reveal the strangeness of the world in which they live."[23] The combination of the fairy tale's "long ago" with 1944 is an example of this stuttering temporality. With a child's perspective, "history is told differently, presented as magical and irrational."[24] This is because we associate children with what is irrational, magical, and with pre-verbal sensations, the affects. Thus, a "child cannot speak because as a child they are (or were) yet to become articulate (sensible)."[25] Lury argues, that we believe children are in a life phase before words (however, the children Lury discusses can speak, and are thus *not* before words) we also think they are closer to the sensory world:

> [T]he presence of the child allows for a sensual impression and response that takes the viewer beyond meaningful/meaningless silence to a more

visceral or haptic confrontation with the violence of the war-time environment ... [the fairy tale] allows for a temporal dislocation, a validation of sensory experience and a promotion of the irrational to which the child has privileged access.[26]

The strategy of seeing events through a child's eyes brings us closer to *feeling* and *sensing* the world. When Ofelia picks up a stone in the forest, the stone becomes an eye in a statue, and this is when she sees a fairy.[27] The child's perspective lets us "go deeper" than language and experience a tactile being-in-the-world-ness.

While I mostly agree with Lury's readings, I disagree that children have a more sensory relation to the world, at least not at Ofelia's age. These ideas come from the child stereotype and our scripts of what it means to be a child. British film scholar Emma Wilson in "Children, Emotion and Viewing in Contemporary European Film" (2005) similarly says the sensory is an entry point of engagement with child protagonists and notes how directors "make use of cinema's potential to evoke touch, the tactile, the haptic, drawing attention thus to space, its navigation and inhabitation, kinesthesis and containment, cocooning."[28] However, Wilson also explains the child stereotype at work in films. "[D]ominant conception of childhood innocence presumes that children exist in a space beyond, above, outside the political," and she points out that, "innocence emerges as the dominant fantasy in whose terms children have been variously represented, protected and desired."[29]

We can sum up that to use a child's eyes sets new default rules: A child is closer to the sensory world, is pre-verbal and irrational, beyond the political, exists outside of time, and is innocent. Those, at least, are the default rules in the child stereotype that steer our expectations.

The Meaning of Mud

Kahneman gave us the example of the prize in the bazaar as an anchor point for negotiations. Here I suggest del Toro uses gender as anchor points in such a clever way that we do not even notice. He used child protagonists in *Cronos* (a girl) and *The Devil's Backbone* (a boy), and in interviews called *Pan's Labyrinth* the "sister" companion to the "brother," *The Devil's Backbone*.[30] Captain Vidal is obsessed with having a son, but before the resistance kills him, they say, "your son will not even know your name." Ofelia's brother has no name, but she does, and we know her name.

In Ofelia's first test, mud is used to both conjure up and challenge our meta-narrative about gender. Lury dedicates a chapter called "Mud and Fairytales" to an analysis of mud. She argues that to the adult, mud signifies only dirt, but to the child, mud can be both a playful engagement with nature as well as part of an unpleasant world. Lury discusses *Pan's Labyrinth*, *Ivan's Childhood* (*Ivanovo detstvo*, 1962, Andrey Tarkovsky), and *Empire of the Sun* (1987, Steven Spielberg). Here, she says, mud "evoke[s] this prior meaninglessness. Mud as both a terrifying and absorbing just-is-ness; demonstrating what is exposed, what is left, when the world is turned upside down, when the fragile civilization that the child has barely understood has broken down. The contact with inanimate matter enhances the visceral, bodily sense in which the child has been 'thrown' into an encounter with the world."[31] Lury does not mention gender when she compares Ofelia, Ivan, and Jamie, but treats the three texts as having similar encounters with mud, both for characters and for the audience. However, I think the films situate children and mud differently, and we recall from Chapter 1 that we experience and appraise emotions in a situation. Therefore, let us look at the situations.

In *Ivan's Childhood* Ivan is a spy for Russian soldiers during the Second World War. He looks the same age as Ofelia and wears ill-fitting adult military clothes. In the film's start, he walks through a swamp to get to a camp for debriefing. To Ivan, mud means becoming wet and cold, but also being a brave soldier. The officer comforts Ivan and the soldiers admire him. Mud has a more dramatic function in *Empire of the Sun*, where the British boy Jamie spends three years in a Japanese prisoner-of-war camp in China during the Second World War. Jamie admires the paraphernalia of war: The airplanes, weapons, uniforms, and the courage of the soldiers. He proves his courage by sneaking out to test the area around the camp for mines. He is almost discovered by the camp commandant but hides head down in the swamp and returns covered head to toe in mud and is saluted by American POWs.

And what of Ofelia?[32] She does not wear military clothes, but a dress hand-made by her mother and new shoes. "Look! Patent leather shoes. I dreamt of such shoes when I was a child. Do you like them?" The servants notice, "she is in her pretty dress," and the housekeeper Mercedes says, "be careful that I don't stain you." The women thus lavish attention on the crackling dress and sparkling shoes. If we recall Young's description of the girl's inhibited personal space, this is an example of how a character is restricted: In her new clothes Ofelia must be careful. The dress is an intertextual nod to *Alice's Adventures in Wonderland* whose illustrator in 1865 clad Alice in a blue dress with a Peter Pan collar and puffed sleeves, a pinafore (an apron), white stockings, and flat black patent leather strap overshoes. Ofelia's dress is green and her apron without ruffles, but otherwise it looks like Alice's. The costume marks Ofelia as fairy-tale heroine and as *girl*.

Ofelia, however, will not be restricted, and if you have read *Alice's Adventures in Wonderland* you know Alice, too, is disobedient. When we compare Ofelia to Jamie and Ivan, we see that mud is presented in different

FIGURE 2.1 *Ofelia (Ivana Baquero) in her new, pretty dress and an intertextual nod to Alice's dress in* Alice's Adventures in Wonderland *from 1865.* Pan's Labyrinth (El laberinto del fauno, 2006, Guillermo del Toro). © *Estudios Picasso, Tequila Gang and Sententia Entertainment, 2006.*

FIGURE 2.2 *Jamie (Christian Bale) is covered in mud and saluted by American POWs in a Japanese prisoner-of-war camp during the Second World War.* Empire of the Sun *(1987, Steven Spielberg).* © *Amblin Entertainment and Warner Bros, 1987.*

ways: Costumes are gendered male (soldiers' clothes) and female and the boys are lauded for getting muddy while Ofelia is scolded. To Ivan and Jamie, mud means soldiering, and for Ofelia mud is part of her magical world, her play.

However, as the story progresses we understand play is also soldiering, a revolt against authority parallel to the resistance in the mountains. Ofelia is a guerilla soldier.

A Task and a Monster

The second fairy-tale test is an impossible task which the hero solves with the aid of supernatural helpers. "As soon as the hero finds himself faced with an impossible task – emptying a lake with a perforated spoon, building and furnishing a castle overnight, devouring a mountain of bread in twenty-four hours – help is at hand."[33]

The faun gives Ofelia a piece of chalk, an hourglass, and three fairies. She must go to a dangerous place where something inhuman sleeps. There will be a lavishly laid table but she must not eat or drink, or else! The book tells her: "Use the chalk to draw a door somewhere in the room. When the door opens, start the hourglass. Let the fairies lead you." Ofelia draws a door and descends along a corridor lit by torches leading the way to a cave with a table laid with delicious foods. At the end of the table sits the Pale Man, a sleeping monster with long, black fingernails. His eyeballs lie on a plate in front of him. The walls and the ceiling have paintings where he tortures and eats children, and there is a pile of children's shoes in the cave. The fairies lead Ofelia to three doors and indicate the second. Ofelia chooses the first and finds a dagger. As she leaves she eats two grapes from the table. The Pale Man wakes up, places the eyeballs in the eye sockets in the palms of his hands, and staggers towards her, hands held high above his head, a horrible spectacle. When the fairies try to stop him, he eats two of them. As Ofelia runs down the corridor, the hourglass runs out and the door closes. She draws a new door on the ceiling and barely makes it out with the Pale Man pulling at her feet. And Ofelia broke the rules: She didn't take the door indicated by the fairies, she ate from the table, and the hourglass ran out.

The task deals with time. Fairy-tale time is supposed to be unspecific and the fairy tale characterized by a "timelessness [which] derives largely from its structural disinterest in time."[34] The fairy tale can promise a "happy ever after" because it never *is*. In the first test, Ofelia entered the toad's tree, a timeless place. However, the Pale Man's cave has paintings with children being tortured on the rack, and the pile of children's shoes echoes the mountain of shoes visitors see in the Auschwitz-Birkenau death camp in Poland. The cave reeks with cannibalism, and we see fairies eaten in close-up of heads bitten off and entrails pulled from bodies.

The cave echoes two paintings: Peter Paul Rubens' 1636 painting of the Greek Titan Cronus devouring his children and Francisco Goya's 1821–1823 painting of Roman god Saturn eating his sons. It is the most famous of Goya's Black Paintings of the Spanish Civil War in 1820–1823.[35] In the myths of Cronus and Saturn it is foretold a son will kill the father, and in the Greek myth, Cronus devours his children after birth. Cronus is linked to Chronos, god of eternal time, and the cannibalism can be read as an allegory of the passing of generations and cruel patriarchy.

The task takes Ofelia to a place reeking of torture and horror, myth and war. If we are familiar with myth, we notice the shift from boy to girl: There are more girls than boys among the victims in the paintings, more girls' than boys' shoes in the pile, and the monster's next dinner is not a son, but Ofelia. Tolkien thinks fantasy opens a door to a land of magic with a better future, and that the fantastic is a fight against evil in the real world. Remember, these are our generic default rules, the rock-solid fairy-tale conventions, that del Toro destabilizes when Ofelia is pursued by a monster. What happened to the safety of fairy tales? When Ofelia returns without two of the fairies, the faun is furious. "You broke the rules," he hisses, "You will *never* see us again." But we think del Toro broke the rules by sending an innocent fairy-tale heroine into a monster's cave.

Beauty Meets the Beast

Until the Pale Man, the dual line of events with fascists and the faun have been conveyed in separate visual frames invoking different emotions. One has blood and terror, the other has tests but also help and self-confidence. But with two dead fairies we are no longer safe. The default rules of horror invade the fairy tale and this is the true horror.

This invasion feels more terrifying than my writing can express. Fairy-tale violence is *not* supposed to be bloody and terminal. "In the fairy tale, we do not see any blood flow or any wounds open up when a helping animal or someone who fails to solve a riddle is decapitated," says Lüthi.[36] Children may be killed as in *The Juniper Tree* but this is without pain and blood. Our faith in fairy-tale default rules is so strong that children use them in war as a mental shelter when the war had destroyed "the physical boundaries between outside and inside, between public and private ..."[37] Fairy tales could ease trauma, and in the Birkenau concentration camp Jewish children were allowed to perform Snow White, inspired by the Disney movie from 1937. The children used the tales to "recapture home as a place free from repressive constraints and governed by the utopian imagination."[38]

If even Nazi camp commandants respected the utopian quality of fairy tales and allowed Jewish children to perform them, it is no wonder we are shocked when a cannibal monster is about to eat Ofelia. A new anchor point is set. The Pale Man is a *real* monster who kills, like Vidal kills. The Pale Man does not belong in a fairy tale. We are familiar with the trope of the beast from the beauty and the beast tales, however, this beast is different and so, too, is our beauty. The red shoes Ofelia wears in the film's end are a nod to Dorothy's in *The Wizard of Oz* (1939), and Ofelia has dark hair, red lips, and white skin like Snow White. However, where the typical fairy-tale heroine is suitable in age to marry a prince, Ofelia is eleven years old and actor Baquero even looks younger.

Ofelia/Baquero looks like a child, not an adolescent, and I want to draw attention to two heuristics. First, a child in distress activates what cognitive theory calls innate instincts of *parent-child bonding* and of *separation anxiety*. When an adult is pursued by a monster, we share the character's fears, but the pursued is a child, and we also instinctively feel we are responsible and must save the child.[39] Thus, we fear for an adult character but are willing to sacrifice ourselves to save a child. Our character empathy, our emotional engagement, is not only deeper, but also different; it is more *involving* and requires a different *action*.

The second heuristic has to do with what cognitive theory calls *the cuteness factor*. Cognitive psychologists Gary Sherman and Jonathan Haidt (2011) describe the cuteness factor as the affective and emotional traits that trigger social interaction and hyper-mentalizing (this is, for example, compassion).[40] We experience cuteness in contrast to disgust, an emotion that makes us close off mentalizing (to mentalize is to make a mental image of something). Thus, if we find something cute, we want to cuddle and hold it, and if we find something disgusting, we shut off mentalizing. Ofelia and the Pale Man are, respectively, cute and disgusting. A cute object triggers broader social and affiliative responses—it makes us want to include it in our group. We *instinctively* want to touch and hold cute objects. Disgusting objects trigger the reverse reaction, to expel the object. Traits from our baby schemas—huge eyes, sweetness, smiles, childish features—automatically trigger cuteness.[41] Ofelia is cute with her large eyes and soft features, which stands in contrast to the Pale Man, who is a perfect example of what Hank Davis and Andrea Javor (2004) say solicits innate fear: Our fear of becoming prey and being eaten; our disgust of impure things; and our fear of beings that violate the "person file." This latter violation is when boundaries are crossed, like monsters who combine the categories of human-animal or living-dead.[42] The Pale Man is a perfect monster: He eats people, he is disgusting (his flabby white skin looks like a plucked chicken), and the eyeballs in the palm of his hands violate our person file.

In hindsight, there are signs that the marvelous will be invaded by horror. Thus, the faun looks uncanny ("a creaky, ancient creature" who is "very masculine"[43]) and just before Ofelia draws the door on the wall in her chamber, a doctor cuts into human flesh to amputate a leg on a resistance fighter. We were warned the marvelous may not be what we think, and that war costs lives in both worlds. But until the task, we thought the fairy tale was a sanctuary. Next comes the third test, the trial, where blood is spilled and a new anchor point set: Ofelia's death.

A Trial and Disobedience

In fairy tales, protagonists always get second chances, so we are not surprised the faun forgives Ofelia and gives her the third test, the trial. Tatar explains the trial "intensifies the reward (a princess and a kingdom) and the punishment (death)" and that it will morally reverse things by "enthroning the humble and enriching the impoverished" and provide narrative closure.[44]

Events in the real world are at this point depressing. Vidal has tortured a resistance fighter and shot the doctor. Carmen has died giving birth to Ofelia's brother. And the Captain has discovered Mercedes' alliance with the resistance and is about to torture her. Casualties pile up as the faun returns to Ofelia, who is locked in her room. "I have decided to give You a second chance, but You must obey *without asking any questions*." The test is for Ofelia to bring her brother to the faun. "But the door is locked," says Ofelia and the faun gives her another piece of chalk. Ofelia draws the door and sneaks into the Captain's study where she takes her brother from the crib and runs into the labyrinth, chased by Vidal. The walls magically guide her to the center, where the faun demands the "small blood sacrifice" of an innocent. When she refuses, he says, "You *promised* to obey" and asks if she is willing to give her life for her brother. Vidal reaches the center and for the first time the fascist and the fairy-tale stories meet: In a behind-the-shoulder shot from the faun's perspective we see the faun, Ofelia, and Vidal in a single frame. But cutting to Vidal's perspective, we see Ofelia talking to thin air. The first POV shot has magic, the second none, and we are confused: Is the faun real or not? Vidal takes his son and shoots Ofelia.

In the first ending, Ofelia is in the subterraneous kingdom. "This was the last test," her father the king tells her, "and the most important. You have sacrificed your own blood instead of that of an innocent." The trial was not about obedience but *disobedience*. Let us return to the stuttering resistance fighter. Vidal promises to release the man if he can count to three without stuttering, a cruel echo of the three tests. What Lury calls a "stuttering temporality" is now literal. "What a pity," says Vidal, when the captive stutters on "three." He orders the doctor to relieve the prisoner's pain so Vidal can continue the torture. The doctor instead grants the victim's wish, to be killed. When Vidal asks why the doctor disobeyed, the doctor responds: "That kind of blind obedience, without any thought, is only for people like yourself, Captain." To disobey is existential freedom, it is taking an ethical stand so a new story can begin.

In "Narrative Desire and Disobedience in *Pan's Labyrinth*" (2010), Jennifer Orme examines the film's "disobedient storytelling."[45] Vidal is obsessed with a patriarchal master narrative with himself as father and his son as the fascist future. Ofelia's fairy tale contradicts his narrative, and we can read her story as opposing the (political) real world. And by refusing to "behave" as a girl, Ofelia also opposes the gender stereotype and the metanarrative. Thus, "*Pan's Labyrinth* actively pits the monologic monovocality of Captain Vidal and fascism against the dialogic multivocality of Ofelia, Mercedes, and the fairy tale."[46] Orme concludes that if, "like Ofelia, and the film itself, you refuse to obey the narrative rules of the monologic master narrative and its storytellers, reject the primacy of mimetic realism in favor of multiple narratives and the transformative magic of the fairy tale . . . well, you may still end up dead – but only in one story."[47]

The stutterer, the doctor, and Ofelia disobey. Vidal may have the power to torture, but he has no power over stories. Like del Toro is a disobedient storyteller, so, too, is Ofelia a disobedient fairy-tale heroine. And, as Orme points out, interdiction and violation of interdiction are functions 2 and 3 in Vladimir Propp's *Morphology of the Folktale* (1928).[48] But if disobedience is a fairy-tale quality, why does Ofelia not return to life? What happened to magic?

The Meaning of Magic

The status of magic in *Pan's Labyrinth* is complex. First, we think the magic is play, but as events unfold, magic appears in ways we can only interpret as causal.

The mandrake root the faun gives Ofelia is an example. If she places it under her mother's bed and feeds it blood, it will cure Carmen. And Carmen *is* better. The Captain is furious when he finds the mandrake. "It is all that nonsense she is allowed to read! See where it leads!" Carmen throws the root in the fireplace. "There *is* no magic! Not for you or me or anyone else." But *exactly* when the mandrake screams in the flames, Carmen screams too and labor starts. The simultaneity of screams silences any objection, because simultaneity spells causality. Also, how does Ofelia escape her room if not by magic? Several scenes have shown Vidal's obsession with keys. Surely the chalk, the faun, and the magic are as real as the torture in the barn.

To Christian fantasy writers like Tolkien and C. S. Lewis, author of the *Narnia* books, magic is part of a religious world view. But magic work different than religion. French sociologist Marcel Mauss explains that where religion is an institution, magic belongs to the individual. It is "*any rite which does not play a part in organized cult* – it is private, secret, mysterious and approaches the limit of a prohibited rite" (emphasis in original).[49] An individual has no special powers in religion, but with magic, "isolated individuals can affect social phenomena."⁵⁰ Magic belongs to the disempowered and weak. As a child terrorized by war, Ofelia needs magic. And in contrast to her mother, Ofelia questions her world. Why can't they leave camp? "It is not that simple," says Carmen, "you are becoming a big girl. You will see that life is no fairy tale. The world is cruel."

Polish anthropologist Bronislaw Malinowski links magic to desire and hope. When we passionately desire something we cannot have, the primitive mind uses magic. Magic is the "extended expressions of emotion in act and in word,"⁵¹ it is the enforcement of our emotions and it supports our subjective feeling of being-in-the-world-ness. In primitive societies, "the function of myth is not to explain but to vouch for, not to satisfy curiosity but to give confidence in power, not to spin out yarns but to establish the flowing freely from present-day occurrences, frequently similar validity of belief."⁵² Through magic the disempowered can reject society's master narrative. "[T]he belief in magic, corresponding to its plain practical nature, is extremely simple. It is always the affirmation of man's power to cause certain definite effects by a definite spell and rite."⁵³ Ofelia smiles when she sees a fairy, because she has agency in a world with magic.

As I mentioned in the beginning of the chapter, fairy-tale scholars think utopian belief is fundamental to the fairy tale. Bloch saw fairy tales as "that earliest kind of enlightenment . . . consider yourself as born free and entitled to be totally happy, dare to make use of your power of reasoning, look upon the outcome of things as friendly."⁵⁴ Fairy tales are subversive because they show social action. Tolkien saw fairy stories as rebellion against a repressive political reality. Fantasy, Tolkien writes, provides *recovery*, *escape*, and *consolation*.⁵⁵ It recovers rejected desires, it provides escape from a world that has become a prison (Tolkien wrote in 1939 and was aware of Nazism), and it consoles by expressing these desires.

If the fairy tale can overcome anything, why is del Toro disobedient to default rules? Why set new anchor points with a fascist captain, a monster, and a child's death? I must insist fairy-tale rules are deeply entrenched in our mind. In fairy tales, *anything* is possible. "The fairy tale frees things and people from their natural context and places them in new relationships, which can also be easily dissolved," writes Lüthi.⁵⁶ The fairy tale knows no boundaries, not even death. Thus, "no matter how thoroughly children are killed," British literary scholar Kimberley Reynolds points out, "still *good* children come back and triumph."⁵⁷

The Fantastic and the Melodrama

But Ofelia doesn't come back. The first test cast the anchor of hope, like the fairy tale does. The second test took Ofelia to the trauma zone and cast an anchor of horror. Ofelia escaped the Pale Man, but her mother died and so, too, did the resistance fighter and the doctor. The third test takes us to the center of the labyrinth, and it casts two anchors, one of hesitation (is the faun real?) and one of sadness (as reviewers wrote, we are "troubled to the point of heartbreak"[58]). When we come to the trial, the film harnesses not two but four genres: the fairy tale, horror, the fantastic, and the melodrama.

Let me first comment on the fantastic genre, which Bulgarian structuralist Tzvetan Todorov said comes into existence when the fiction's characters and the reader hesitate between a natural and a supernatural explanation of events. The fantastic "in its pure state is represented by the median line separating the fantastic-uncanny from the fantastic-marvelous."[59] The hesitation—is the faun real?—shifts genre from fairy tale/horror to the fantastic.

When Vidal takes his son, Ofelia turns to look at the faun. He was there one moment, and is gone the next. When she says "no" to her stepfather, Vidal shoots her and several cues signal a new set of default values from the melodrama: Sad and overwrought emotions; pathos; sentimentality; a moral polarization between Good and Evil; a tragic dialect between family and individual; and a suffering female. Michael Stewart in *Melodrama in Contemporary Film and Television* (2015) says the melodrama "is a modern trans-cultural mode which by definition seeks to give a voice and form to the suffering, silenced and exiled."[60] In today's transnational cinema, the melodrama is used as political allegory. Here, "melodrama is able now to more fully complicate time, place and identity; and push morality further toward a local and global ethics of living."[61]

The use of four genres—fairy tale, horror, the fantastic, and the melodrama—generates a multivocality which has created disagreement about the film's end, or rather, endings. Orme thinks they are equally valid. Grodal, on the other hand, thinks there is only a sad end. He compares *Pan's Labyrinth* to *Gladiator* (2000, Ridley Scott), *Saving Private Ryan* (1998, Steven Spielberg), and *Hero* (2002, Yimou Zhang), which have male heroes. In the heroic melodrama, says Grodal, we find bonding, self-sacrifice, and emotions of loss, melancholy, grief, and sad tears. Heroic melodramas show a strong social bonding between people who are sad, because a hero sacrifices his life. Heroic melodrama "reaffirm bonding, albeit in the negative form."[62] To give one's life invokes "laws of moral-metaphysical exchange," because, in the logic of gift exchange, these powers now owe you.[63] Melodramas, Grodal argues, are rituals of bonding and serve the community.

I find the interpretation of heroic melodrama as bonding illuminating, however, I disagree that Ofelia is not a hero because she submits to higher powers and to her parents. "[T]he effect is . . . one of fatalism and acceptance of the negation of agency, and the primary model is infantile acceptance of omniscient parental guidance . . ."[64] But Ofelia does not submit to her mother, to her stepfather, to the faun, or to God (the film's priest is a fascist like Vidal). It is not at all clear that the melodramatic end is more valid than the fairy-tale end. Orme points out Vidal is not a trustworthy witness because Ofelia has drugged him and his vision is impaired.[65] Perhaps there is a faun? In fantastic fashion, the two endings coexist and the film stutters, producing a third fantastic end. Thus, my experience of the end was hesitation: Did Ofelia die, and was the faun real or not?

Hero or Victim?

Heroism is traditionally a male trope. Ivan and Jamie are hugged and saluted by male officers, and the heroes in *Gladiator, Saving Private Ryan*, and *Hero* are men. Elsewhere, I discuss the mythic relationship between male heroism, war, and torture.[66] To be a war hero is a male affair which until now excluded girls. So, let us ask if Ofelia is a hero or a victim.

I earlier said we instinctively react with care to a child. This reaction is innate. However, we recall from Chapter 1 that gender is soft-wired. If we react differently to a suffering boy and girl, this depends on what Frijda calls *situational meaning*, which means emotions are not in us or in events, but arise from our appraisal of events as social situations: "Emotions change when meanings change. Emotions are changed when events are appraised differently."[67] Events can be simple (a child playing in mud) or complex (a girl playing in mud in a time of war). Philosopher Robert C. Solomon proposes to use the term "paradigm scenarios"[68] to describe how emotions become meaningful in a "shift from emotional content to emotion context."[69] Solomon thinks "an emotion is not just an individual creation but is in essence 'political' – that is, it has to do with our relations with other people."[70]

Allison Mackey in "Make It Public! Border Pedagogy and the Transcultural Politics of Hope in Contemporary Cinematic Representations of Children" (2010) discusses how *Children of Men* (2006), *Babel* (2006), and *Pan's Labyrinth* (2006) mobilize the child as political symbol of the future and hope. The boys in *Children of Men* and *Pan's Labyrinth* (in this case not Ofelia, but her infant brother) represent a rejection of "a retrograde notion of the social that is organized around a culture of shared fears rather than shared responsibilities."[71] *Children of Men* is a science fiction film set in 2027 and *Pan's Labyrinth* is a fantasy film set in 1944, but both are about our contemporary war on terror. Mackey reads the children in *Pan's Labyrinth* as means to mobilize the public: "The fascist injunction to 'obey without questioning' reinforces the urgent need for disobedience in the face of authoritarianism. In the figures of the doctor, Mercedes, the rebels and Ofelia herself, there is an emphasis on compassion for others and on choosing to align oneself with them, suggesting that in a fundamental sense this film is about the power of the public."[72]

I agree with Mackey's reading of the film as political, however, I think she, like Lury, overlooks gender. If we view Ofelia as paradigm scenario, the stuttering returns. Thus, her death activates the public (the resistance), but her actions are presented as play and as different from the behavior of the children in the other films. She disobeys by playing make-believe. Like Tolkien, del Toro links political revolt to the freedom to fantasize. Remember, to believe in magic *is* rebellion. With an amalgam of politics, fairy tale, and horror, Ofelia differs from the male war heroes: Where men praise the nation with their public actions, Ofelia exposes the failure of patriarchy. Vidal is in the mountains "by free will" because he believes in a fascist Spain. And the battle is not only on public ground, as in war melodrama, but also in the bedroom, as in the family melodrama. When Ofelia is in the double bed with her mother, she asks, "Why did you have to marry?" "I have been alone so long." "You were never alone, I was with you." "One day you will understand that things have not been easy for me." The bed is where fairies come alive and Carmen dies. The forest and the bed are battlegrounds.

We cannot reduce Ofelia to one paradigm scenario with stable dichotomies of female versus male, child versus adult, play versus war, private versus public, bedroom versus forest, and marvelous versus real. Like in a 3D image, different elements come into focus depending on the contraction of our eye. Play is a coping strategy and a revolt. But in neither view is Ofelia a victim. The film destabilizes the myth of the male war hero and creates a female war hero who plays and has the courage to disobey gender, patriarchy, and the meta-narrative.

A Final Anchor Point

Films with male heroes provide narrative closure but *Pan's Labyrinth* keeps us guessing. Is Ofelia's death a happy end or a tragedy? Let me end the chapter by returning to default values and Ofelia's death as one last anchor point. How should we negotiate it?

The dead-child trope is a cliché in the melodrama. Ofelia's death is sad, but also rich with pathos. She is "dying for the narrative" as film scholar John O. Thompson puts it. Her "good death"[73] was a trope in the nineteenth century's morality tales, evangelic novels, and fairy tales where, "the dying child often experiences some kind of revelation which confirms religious teaching, thus making the death triumphant for all concerned."[74] Her death is emotional material for new beginnings. Ofelia belongs to the old world of terror and her brother to a new world of transglobal political action, yet unwritten.

As said at the beginning of the chapter, *Pan's Labyrinth* is not a horror film, yet its horror elements makes it more gruesome than many horror films. It is, as a reviewer writes, "a film that looked horror straight in the eye."[75] Its multivocality keeps us uncertain how to interpret events. In cognitive terms, uncertainty can be *cognitive dissonance*, which is when you hold conflicting beliefs, one making the other untenable. To stop cognitive dissonance we want to choose one of our beliefs. But which, magic or fascism? If we see Ofelia's actions as edgework, which in the real world is when a player "works" the "edge" of danger as leisure entertainment, then the fairy tale keeps us on the brink of danger. But in horror, characters fall into the trauma zone and may die. *Pan's Labyrinth* creates a dialectic where we, the audience, have an emotional dialogue where we continue to question events. In Kahneman's terminology, we oscillate between using our System 1 and our System 2, feeling and cognitive evaluation. And because default rules keep changing, we keep negotiating the generic rules.

Ofelia doesn't subvert the meta-narrative. From an evofeminist perspective, her death remains troubling because it echoes the female sacrifice in the melodrama. But *Pan's Labyrinth* wipes our cognitive slate clean. When Ofelia pushes herself over the edge in her play, she creates a gap between fairy tale and horror, a fantastic space open to the audience. This is an invitation to imagine a future without Vidal's patriarchy. An invitation to tell a new story.

3

The Bio-Logic of Vengeance in *Let the Right One In*

OSKAR: I don't kill people.
ELI: But you'd like to, if you could. To get revenge, right?
OSKAR: Yes.
ELI: I do it because I have to. Be me, for a little while.

LET THE RIGHT ONE IN (2008)

What would *you* do if someone made you squeal like a pig, hit you, and peed on your clothes? Hit back? And what if they were three and you were afraid to stand up for your rights? What then?

Tomas Alfredson's Swedish film *Let the Right One In* (*Låt den rätte komma in,* 2008) features two twelve-year-old children, Oskar and Eli. Oskar is bullied at school. His parents are divorced, his father is an alcoholic, and his mother is more concerned with her television shows than with her son's well-being. Then Eli moves in next door and tells him to hit back. "But they are three," Oskar protests. "Then you must hit *harder*," she says, "I'll help you. I can do that." Later, Eli hugs him and whispers: "Be me for a little while." At this point, Oskar and we know Eli is a vampire, but not that Eli is a *boy* vampire. In the novel, from which the film is adapted, Eli is called "she" until the secret is revealed. In the novel, Eli becomes Elias, a boy. In the Swedish film, however, there is just a brief shot of a scar on Eli's pubic area, a momentary hint at a lost penis, and Eli's sex remains that of a girl. In the American remake *Let Me In* (2010) there is no indication that the vampire is a boy. The vampire is, without any hints to the contrary, now a girl.

In this chapter I explore what it means to "be" Eli in Alfredson's *Let the Right One In*. Like *Pan's Labyrinth*, the film belongs to transnational art cinema and won more than seventy prizes. And like del Toro, Alfredson, too, uses a child's perspective. In *Pan's Labyrinth*, the aim of this narrative strategy was to tell a story of innocence and make a call for political action.

In *Let the Right One In*, the aim of the child's perspective is to tell a story of love and vengeance, not a story about innocence and politics, but about gender, self-esteem, and the individual's right to be a moral agent.

The chapter starts with an introduction to Alfredson's film and two related texts, the original novel and the American film adaptation. Next, I divide my discussion of *Let the Right One In* into three themes. First, I explore the theme of bullying using the concepts of moral agency and moral patiency from psychology.[1] Second, I examine the theme of love and ask what happens when the lovers are children and, furthermore, of the same sex. Last, I turn to the bio-logic of vengeance and show how *Let the Right One In* radically plays with and overturns the gender stereotype and meta-narrative.

The Vampire Triptych

Alfredson's 2008 film is adapted from John Ajvide Lindqvist's Swedish novel from 2004, *Låt den rätte komma in*, and Lindqvist wrote the screenplay for the Swedish film. The American adaptation, *Let Me In* (2010), more loosely based on Lindqvist's novel and screenplay, was written and directed by Matt Reeves. My focus is on the Swedish adaptation, and while many elements are altered, I address the changes that relate to the themes of bullying, love, and vengeance. Because the novel and the Swedish film share original and translated titles, I use *Låt den rätte komma in* about the novel and *Let the Right One In* about the Swedish film.

The novel was praised for combining horror with a coming-of-age story and the form of the social realist drama.[2] The book review in *Svenska Dagbladet* said, "'Let the Right One In' refashions the vampire myth in dirty-grey social realism and fills it with everyday boredom, supermarkets, and schoolyard bullying."[3] Oskar lives in a suburb called Blackeberg in 1981. His parents are divorced and he lives with his mother, who is psychologically fragile and distant. His alcoholic father lives on a farm in the country. At school, three classmates bully him, and when the two-hundred-year-old vampire Eli moves in next door, she tells him to hit back.

Eli lives with 45-year-old Håkan, a pedophile, who poses as her father and procures her blood in exchange for affection. And then there is a group of alcoholics in the neighborhood, three of whom fall victim to Eli. The novel interweaves four storylines, dedicating equal space to each: The bullying; the friendship and love between Oskar and Eli; Håkan's pedophilia; and a tragic love story between Lacke and Virginia, two alcoholics. When Håkan is captured by the police, Eli has to leave Blackeberg to avoid capture. However, she returns to save Oskar from being killed by the bullies. She murders two of them, and she and Oskar leave on a train with Eli in a trunk. In the tradition of social realism, the novel fuses its universal themes of love

(Eli and Oskar's relationship) and vengeance (the classmates' bullying) with socio-political themes of pedophilia and alcoholism.[4] Thus, the book has four themes and is written in the style of social realism.

Both adaptations reduce the four themes to two, love and vengeance. In the Swedish film, Håkan is still a pedophile, but in the American remake he is the vampire's companion and a genuine friend, who has aged while his friend-vampire Abby has remained a child. Eli is called Abby and Oskar is now Owen. Both adaptations have a bleak suburbia atmosphere, but only in the Swedish adaptation does Oskar's father drink, and we see the local alcoholics. In contrast to social-realist form of the novel, *Let the Right One In* uses modernist art cinema aesthetics with long slow takes in long and medium shots in the 2:35 widescreen format. The film has beautiful cinematography with crisp colors of white and blue, low-key acting, a slow tempo, and it avoids the graphic splatter effects used in the novel. While there thus are differences in themes and style, all three texts end with Eli/Abby saving Oskar/Owen from the bullies, and the two children leaving on a train.

The strategy of using a child's perspective to explore love and vengeance proved effective. *Let the Right One In* was received as not just a horror film, but a film that "falls into that category of truly great movies"[5] and, as Kim Newman noted in *Empire*, "a devastating, curiously uplifting inhuman drama."[6]

Let us now turn to *Let the Right One In* and the themes of bullying, love, and vengeance.

The "Piggy Game"

The piggy game is an example of how we humans can turn play fighting into cruel play. As said, animals can only either play or not play, but humans can turn play into cruel play, where one part enjoys the pain of the other person, who becomes a victim, who must pretend and suffer in the hope that cruel play finishes soon. What in animals is play, is turned into a power game with tormentor and victim.

In the opening scene of *Let the Right One In*, Oskar (Kåre Hedebrant) is talking to his reflection in the window at night in his room: "Squeal like a pig. Squeal!" He is repeating the words of Conny, the ringleader of the school bullies who make Oskar squeal and grunt like a pig. This is the first thing we learn about Oskar. In the novel, the bullies are called Johnny, Tomas, and Micke:

> He wrinkled up his nose like a pig's and squealed, grunted and squealed. Johnny and Micke laughed.
> "Fucking pig, go on, squeal some more."

Oskar carried on. Shut his eyes tight and kept going. Balled his hands up into fists so hard that his nails went into his palms, and kept going. Grunted and squealed until he felt a funny taste in his mouth. Then he stopped and opened his eyes.

They were gone.[7]

In the film, we see the bullies torment Oskar in recess, urinate on his clothes in the sport's room, and wait for him after school so they can whip him. Conny (Patrik Rydmark) instructs Martin (Mikael Erhardsson) to hold Oskar so Andreas can whip him. Andreas (Johan Sömnes) is uncomfortable and cries, and he will be the only survivor at the public pool where Eli saves Oskar when the bullies are drowning him. The boys exchange places, with Andreas holding and Martin whipping, and Martin hits Oskar in the face so Oskar bleeds.

The whipping scene establishes Conny as leader, Martin as second, Andreas as last, and Oskar as victim. "What happened?" Eli (Lina Leandersson) later asks when she sees the band aid on Oskar's cheek. "Some classmates." "Oskar, listen, you must hit back. You never hit back before, right? Start now. Hit back! Hard!" The novel gives no reason why Oskar is victim. "They could give a number of reasons why they had to torment him: he was too fat, too ugly, too disgusting. But the real problem was simply that he existed, and every reminder of his existence was a crime."[8] Oskar accepts the piggy game. He is passive when the bullies whip him and only thinks of vengeance when he attacks trees with his knife in the courtyard where he lives. His parents don't see what is going on, and if the teachers know, they ignore the bullying. It is just the way things are, and, we gather, how boys behave.

Oskar accepts the piggy game because he thinks of himself as a victim, or as what in psychology is called a *moral patient* which is the opposite of a *moral agent*. A moral agent is someone, who is responsible for herself and who can take care of others, and a moral patient, reversely, cannot take responsibility for herself and not be trusted to take care of others. Psychologists Kurt Gray and Daniel M. Wegner say of moral agents that, "moral agents are variously described as entities that are causally responsible for actions, as entities that can earn blame or praise for their actions, as entities that know their actions as right or wrong, or as entities that can intend."[9]

To see yourself as a moral agent means you see yourself as having agency to do right and wrong and care for yourself and others. And to see yourself as a moral patient means you think you are unable to protect yourself. The dual concept is about how we see ourselves and others. Do I have agency? The concept must be understood in a social context. Thus, a child is a moral patient to an adult, but the same child may be a moral agent to other children, who are stronger or bigger.

Experimental studies show that in our perception of being a moral agent or patient, the one excludes the other. "What is interesting though, is that the distinct categories of moral agent and moral patient *are* actually mutually exclusive" (emphasis in original).[10] If you think of someone as a moral patient, you do not at the same time perceive that person to be a moral agent. The doctor treating a patient tends to view the patient as *only* patient, and Oskar sees himself as *only* victim until Eli tells him otherwise. From Oskar's point of view, Eli is a moral agent. Her father doesn't yell at her and she is not bullied by classmates. In fact, she doesn't even go to school.

Eli was once a moral patient like Oskar. "Who are you?" Oskar asks when he discovers Eli is a vampire. "I am like you," Eli responds. Oskar doesn't understand. Eli repeats his words in the courtyard on the night she saw him: "'What are you staring at? What? Are you staring at me? Squeal, squeal like a pig.' That was the first thing I heard you say." The novel has a flashback to two hundred years ago, when Eli was castrated and impaled. But in the film, victimization is only hinted at in her words to Oskar. However, the film makes it clear that Eli knows what it means to be a child and, thus, a moral patient. She can manipulate the role as moral patient, as helpless child, to her benefit. She pretends to be a lost child when she squats in a tunnel whispering "please, help me" to a passer-by. And when Eli asks for her "father" at the hospital, she also pretends to be a child.

Play Fighting and Cruel Play

The piggy game is in both the novel and the two adaptations presented as a normal behavior for boys. We don't see girls bullying—in fact, we don't see girls playing at all in the three texts. Play fighting and cruelty is, all together, a boys' world. This world may not be nice, but it is presented as based in our nature.

Play fighting *is* natural, as we know from Chapter 1. Ethologist Frans de Waal says, "[t]he context of an industrialized multilayered society is new but the emotional undercurrent of these encounters is a primate universal."[11] We recall that human play fighting, R&T play, serves the same functions as play fighting in social mammals like rats and chimpanzees. Five to ten percent of spontaneous play in school playgrounds is play fighting and it is "remarkably similar across cultures and historical times and . . . is the one form of human play that most closely resembles the play of non-human animals."[12] You may recall, I questioned if play fighting was more natural for boys than girls, despite research reporting that male animals play fight more than females. While Pellis and Pellis report sex differences, de Waal doesn't, and biases may influence reports on animals' behavior. Leaving this question aside, *Let the Right One In* sets up the piggy game as a boy's game by only having boys play it.

One of the benefits of play fighting is that it teaches animals to interact in social situations *without resorting to violence*. Play fighting involves pain and power, and while it taps into aggression, it also arises from our innate play drive. Play fighting, we remember, has rules of fairness and self-handicapping to make play open to players despite their rank, age, or strength. "Whether it is employed by rats, hyenas, monkeys, or humans," say neuropsychologists Pellis and Pellis, "play fighting offers a level of nuance in social interactions that permits differences to be sorted out without the use of extreme violence. It would seem that adult animals that are better skilled at using the ambiguity inherent in play fighting will also be better at negotiating intricate, social worlds."[13] Play fighting teaches animals to calibrate their response to the world and it serves to avoid real fighting, which is costly for animals, who have no hospitals. In nature, less than ten percent of confrontations end as physical fights.[14]

But in humans, play fighting links to cruelty and power games. Nell (2006) argues cruelty is adaptive because it can be used to dominate others and obtain power and, ultimately, win the mating game I discussed in Chapter 1. Thus, even in children, cruelty would be natural behavior. And because we have higher cognitive-emotional abilities than animals, we can behave differently. Shame and humiliation are meta-emotions, which animals don't have. Humans may pretend to play, even if they don't like to, because to stop playing might mean to lose face and suffer a humiliation more painful than physical pain. Pellis and Pellis in *The Playful Brain* about rats' play fighting, share one of the authors' childhood memories of playing "rats" in school, a game similar to the piggy game:

> Under the guise of a smiling face and a playful demeanor, one of the bigger boys would throw you to the ground – usually in a grassed area – and then pin you on your back so that you could not move. He would then proceed with the "rats" treatment, which involved repeatedly tapping you, with his forefinger, and with an uncomfortable degree of force, on your chest, while, at the same time, shouting in your face, "rats, rats, rats . . .".[15]

Burghardt also links play fighting to cruelty: "Clearly, the most playful species is also the most deadly! We need to recognize this ubiquitous relationship if we are ever to control cruel behavior and truly understand play."[16] Play scholars, both in animal and human play studies, draw a direct line between innate play and cruel play. In the infamous Abu Ghraib prison, American soldiers' abuse of prisoners was circulated in photographs among soldiers for entertainment, and when this became publicly known, it was excused as a "college fraternity prank" on the Rush Limbaugh radio show.[17]

As said, animals cannot pretend to play and are not cruel. But in human society, play fighting can be perverted into cruel treatment of others when social institutions fail to interact on behalf of an individual, like Oskar's parents and the school fail to do.

When society fails to protect him, Oskar takes Eli's advice to hit back, which would be effective if this was fair play. It is not. When Conny tries to push Oskar into a lake during ice skating, Oskar strikes Conny with a metal rod. But when Eli leaves Blackeberg, Oskar is again on his own. One of the bullies invite him to join a swimming class, and Oskar, naively, thinks he has earned the right to be included in the boys' group. But Conny brings his older brother Jimmy, and Jimmy gives Oskar the choice between staying under water for three minutes or loose an eye. Oskar regresses to moral patiency. "And his head was pushed down further. And strangely enough he thought, *Better this. Than an eye*."[18]

We return later to Oskar and the bullies. But first, we shall look at the second theme, the love story of Eli and Oskar. This theme involves our ideas about sex and gender.

Sex and Gender: "I am not a girl"

A line between two sexes is drawn clearly by two of the three texts, the novel and the American remake, *Let Me In*. In the novel, the vampire is a boy, and in the American adaptation, the vampire is a girl. When Eli tells Oskar to hit back in the novel, the third-person narrator voice calls Eli "she," and only after Eli's secret is revealed, does Eli become Elias, and "she" becomes "he." In *Let Me In*, the bullies call Owen (Kodi Smit-McPhee) "girl" and taunt him in a girl game instead of a piggy game, and Owen calls Abby "girl."

Eli's sex is presented differently in *Let the Right One In*. Here, sex is visually represented by the vampire's exterior, its face and clothes. Sex is inferred and assumed by Oskar and by the audience. In both adaptations, the vampire is played by girl actors, Lina Leandersson (Eli) and Chloë Grace Moretz (Abby), who are beautiful and feminine with big eyes, long hair, and soft features. They look like girls. Here is the vampire's offer in the three texts to help Oskar against the bullies:

The novel:
"Yes, but what if they . . ."
"Then I'll help you."
"You? But you are . . ."
"I can do it, Oskar. *That* . . . is something I can do."
Eli squeezed his hand. He squeezed it back, nodded. But Eli's grip hardened, so hard it hurt a little.[19]

Here is *Let the Right One In*:
Oskar: But if they . . .
Eli: Then I'll help you. [Eli takes Oskar's hand]. I can do that.

And *Let Me In*:
   Abby: Then I'll help you.
   Oskar: But . . . you're a girl.
   Abby: [Abby takes Owen's hand] I'm a lot stronger than you think I am.

All three texts draw on the gender stereotype and our assumptions that boys bully, fight back, and take revenge, and girls can't fight. But only the American text uses "girl." The surprise in store for Owen is that Abby is a vampire, not that Abby is a boy.

Let me return to the difference between the novel and its Swedish adaptation. As said, the novel plays with assumptions that Eli is a girl, and it deceives the reader by calling the vampire "she." Things are different in the Swedish adaptation, more vague and ambiguous. Three scenes in *Let the Right One In* play with Eli's sex and assumptions that she is a girl. The first scene is when the vampire asks Oskar, "if I wasn't a girl would you still like me?" "I guess so. Why do you ask?" Eli leaves the matter be. The second scene is when Oskar asks Eli to go steady. The children are naked in Oskar's bed, and Oskar has his back to Eli. "Oskar, I am not a girl," she says. Oskar doesn't yet know she is a vampire, but we do, and we assume Eli means she is not *human*. In the novel, Oskar says: "What do you mean? You're a guy?" and Eli replies, "I am nothing. Not a child. Not old. Not a boy. Not a girl. Nothing."[20] In the film, Eli doesn't elaborate and Oskar says "oh, but do you want to go steady?" In the novel, we sense existential despair, but in the film, we sense loneliness and the vampire's need for emotional contact. "Do you do anything special when you go steady?" Eli asks. "No." "Is everything as

FIGURE 3.1 *Eli (Lina Leandersson) looks like a girl.* Let the Right One In *(2008, Tomas Alfredson). © EFTI, Sandrew Metronome Distribution Sverige AB, Filmpool Nord, 2008.*

before?" "Yes." "Then we can go steady." Thus, the scene changes friendship to "going steady." It does not raise the issue of two boys sleeping together, but depicts prepubescent love between a boy and a girl, the latter who happens also to be a vampire. The third scene is when Oskar watches Eli change clothes. In a brief instance, we get a close-up of Eli's pubic area, which is hairless and has a scar. Oskar doesn't ask and the camera doesn't dwell. I return to this scar at the end of the chapter.

Like all stereotypes, gender works without our conscious awareness of our assumptions. In an early draft of this chapter, I wrote Eli "posed" as a girl, and a Swedish colleague protested. She did not think Eli posed, but just dressed in whatever clothes were at hand. Oskar *assumes* Eli is a girl, which is why he gives the vampire one of his mother's dresses, and viewers *infer* Eli is a girl from appearances. This comment made me realize how cleverly the Swedish film manipulates gender.[21]

British film critic Anne Billson in her analysis of *Let the Right One In* says Eli "dumbs down" and uses "her little girl persona"[22] to fool adults. In the first kill, Eli squats in a tunnel and whispers, "help me, please help me." And at the hospital, Eli acts like a lost child looking for her "father" who was "taken by the police." Billson compares Eli to the vampire children in *Near Dark* (1987, Kathryn Bigelow) and *Interview With the Vampire* (1994, Neil Jordan) where the vampires grow mentally adult but remain trapped in a child's body. Intriguingly, Eli's denial that she is a girl can also be taken to mean that the two-hundred-year old vampire isn't a child, and that age, too, is deceptive. Thus, across all three texts, it is unclear if Eli is mentally a child or an adult. She welcomes Oskar's company, when he lends her his Rubik's cube she solves it, she eats the candy he buys for her although it makes her sick, and she chats with him in the climbing frame in the courtyard. Billson points out, "precise gender definitions are irrelevant . . . both characters are defined by their prepubescence, with their interplay remaining innocent and asexual . . ."[23] In *Let Me In*, the relation between Abby and Owen is innocent and asexual, but, like with sex, the move from the novel to its Swedish adaptation invites ambiguity and fuzzy borders between male and female and it questions what can be an appropriate love story.

From Friends to Lovers: The *Romeo and Juliet* Theme

"Just so you know, I cannot be your friend," Eli tells Oskar when they first meet, yet the two end up leaving Blackeberg together. Not only do the children become friends, theirs is also a love story. Now, the move from friendship to love is depicted differently in the three texts. As with gender, the novel and its American remake are clear that this is a love story by explicitly referring to Shakespeare's play *Romeo and Juliet*. In the novel, Eli says she quotes this play, and in *Let Me In* the play is used in class in school. But the use of *Romeo and Juliet* is more ambiguous in *Let the Right One In*. Let us look at the way these two texts invoke love.

In the novel, love is interwoven with homosexuality, pedophilia, and friendship. This is most explicitly done with Håkan, the 45-year-old pedophile who buys child prostitutes and has a criminal record of assaulting boys. Håkan sleeps with twelve-year-old Eli, but Håkan also loves Eli, who doesn't love him back. "You only love me to the extent I help you stay alive," says Håkan. "Yes. Isn't that what love is?"[24] When Håkan becomes a vampire, he brutally rapes Eli. The novel also hints at a homosexual relation between Oskar's father and a drinking buddy, and when Oscar learns Eli's nature, he wonders if he becomes a homosexual if he accepts his friend Eli as Elias. "He knew the word. Fag. Fucking fag."[25] In the novel, Eli tells Oskar she is quoting *Romeo and Juliet*, and at school Oskar asks a teacher what love is:

> "It depends on who you are, but . . . I would say that it's when you know . . . or at least when you really believe that this is the person you always want to be with."
> "You mean, when you feel you can't live without that person."
> "Yes, exactly. Two who can't live without the other . . . isn't that what love is?"
> "Like *Romeo and Juliet*."
> "Yes." [. . .]
> "What if it's two guys?"
> "Then that's friendship. That's also a form of love. Or if you mean . . . well, two guys can also love each other in that way."
> "How do they do it?"[26]

In the novel, love is referred to as friendship, as the heterosexual love in *Romeo and Juliet*, as pedophile love (Håkan's feeling for Eli), and homosexuality is hinted at in the relation between Oskar's father and the friend. Being a "fag" is a dread and a criminal act—yet the novel ends with Oskar accepting his love for boy-vampire Elias. In the novel, Oskar and Eli sleep together twice. The first time, Oskar believes Eli is a girl: "Oskar rolled over so his back was against her. She put her arms around him and he took her hands."[27] When Oskar learns Eli is a boy, he is uncertain what to make of this sex change. "Elias. *Elias*. A boy's name. Was Eli a boy? They had . . . kissed and slept in the same bed and . . . He tried to think. Hard. And he didn't get it. That he could somehow accept that she was a *vampire*, but the idea that she was somehow a *boy*, that could be . . . harder."[28] In the novel, Oskar accepts Eli as his love *and* a boy and they share a bed a second time, now as two boys.

In the American remake, as said, pedophilia and homosexuality are removed. The bullies tease Owen that he is a girl, and the assistant's feelings for Abby appear to be a deep friendship going back to when he was a twelve-year-old child. But in the Swedish adaptation, friendship, love, and homosexuality are interwoven in a complex and rather vague pattern, and show both explicitly and as a queer subtext.

The homosexuality is explicit in Håkan, who is a homosexual and pedophile in both the novel and the Swedish adaptation. The homosexuality also remains as a queer subtext in the relation between Oskar's father and the drinking buddy, who interrupts a cozy evening where Oskar is visiting his father. When the disappointed Oskar looks at the two men drinking, he finds one of Eli's notes. It says: "I must be gone and live, or stay and die." Oskar, too, must be gone if he is to live, and he hitchhikes home to Blackeberg.

However, the quote "I must be gone and live, or stay and die" is written on a piece of paper in Swedish, and the film doesn't mention *Romeo and Juliet*. Unless the audience recognizes the Swedish words as a line from Shakespeare's play, we don't know it is a quote. It is not in quotation marks, and I must admit I had forgotten the quote from when I read the novel, thus, I did not read the words in the film as an intertextual reference to *Romeo and Juliet*. In other words, a transnational audience, who is not familiar with the Swedish novel, and who also cannot read the Swedish words, cannot know they are a quote from *Romeo and Juliet*.

In the transition from friends to lovers, *Let the Right One In* offers an interpretation of Eli's missing penis in the glimpse of a scar on the vampire's body. I asked people, who had seen the film and not read the novel, if they thought Eli was a boy or a girl. They all believed Eli was a girl. Also, most did not remember the scar and those who did, didn't know what to make of it (only people who had seen the film several times remembered the scar). Thus, the scar is not a clear sign that Eli is a boy. The scar looks more like a wound than a scar, and I think it is mystifying rather than clarifying. Like Oskar, the audience doesn't know what to make of Eli's scar. And like Oskar, we still take Eli to be a girl (the audiences I asked did, and people in the diegetic story do too), and because Oskar offers her one of his mother's dresses after Eli has showered, we continue to think Eli is a girl.

I return to the scar later. Now it is time to turn to the theme of vengeance.

The Bio-Logic of Justice

Philosopher Robert C. Solomon in *A Passion for Justice* says vengeance is the flipside of justice. The two are connected, with justice being innate in mammals and vengeance being human. When Eli tells Oskar to hit back—"hit harder than you dare, *then* they'll stop"—we instinctively know Eli is right. But Oskar lacks self-esteem. When he strikes Conny with the metal rod, he wins back lost self-esteem. Self-esteem has been lost when Oskar has suffered the humiliation of being bullied, and it is time he answers the attacks on his body and his self with angry aggression. The strike with the metal rod is self-defense, and this is a natural response to an attack, and belongs to the innate aggression we in Chapter 1 located as basis of identity horror. The bullying is an attack on Oskar's self.

Through his friendship with Eli, Oskar found courage to defend himself, but after Eli has left Blackeberg, the bullying resumes. Conny brings his brother Jimmy, who is sixteen and has a knife. "You stay under water for three minutes. If you can do it, I'll just nick you. But if you can't, I'll poke one of your eyes out. An eye for an ear, right?" The scene is filmed in slow takes and is brightly lit with the light inside the public pool building, so the audience has ample time to see and feel how *unfair* this assault is. The camera cuts from Jimmy, who holds Oskar's head under water, to a clock on the wall, to Conny who starts to be afraid his brother might *kill* Oskar, to Martin starting to cry, and to Oskar who loses consciousness and starts drowning. The scene creates a strong sense of *urgency*. We must act. *Now*.

Let the Right One In has an extraordinary setup of vengeance. Usually the desire for revenge plays out in vigilante movies with men, like *Death Wish* (1974), but in our vampire triptych the vigilante is a vampire, a child, and—which feels the most contra-intuitive—a *girl*. The emotional peak in *Let the Right One In* is when a girl exacts vengeance on four boys. Vengeance is the sister of justice, and justice is an emotion we share with other mammals. So, let me recall that for animals, the emotion of justice and the fairness of play fighting is not tied to an animal's sex. Justice, plain and simple, means there are rules to social behavior, and when rules are violated, the scales of justice must be restored. This goes for humans as well as for animals.

> Morality is rather like a game: there are agreed-upon rules that everyone must follow, and there are sanctions for breaking the rules ... Social play has unique rules of engagement about how hard one can bite, about mating being off limits, and about assertions of dominance being absent or kept to a minimum ... If players don't cooperate, play can easily escalate into fighting. When animals play, they must *agree* to play. They must cooperate and behave fairly. Further, when fairness breaks down, play not only stops, it becomes impossible. *Unfair play* is an oxymoron, and this is why play is such a clear window into the moral lives of animals. (emphasis in original)[29]

The meta-narrative explains men are aggressive and women empathic, that boys bully and girls are weak. And violence is for men, certainly not for girls. But the meta-narrative is far from the bio-logic of justice.

Bekoff and Pierce, who write about animal morality, explain moral behavior is innate in mammals. Moral behavior is other-regarding behavior with norms of right and wrong and it "exists as a tangle of threads that holds together a complicated and shifting tapestry of social relationships."[30] There are three clusters of behaviors: *cooperation* with "altruism, reciprocity, trust, punishment and revenge"; *empathy* with "sympathy, compassion, caring, helping, grieving, and consoling"; and *justice* with "fair play, sharing, a desire for equity, expectations about what one deserves and how one ought to be treated, indignation, retribution, and spite."[31] Together, cooperation, empathy, and justice are the social glue that holds a group together. Without empathy there is no caring, without caring there is no cooperation, and without caring and cooperation there can be no justice. Justice is foundational to social life, be it that of animals or humans. And vengeance is part of justice.

Let the Right One In shows play fighting perverted into cruel play. In nature, the social life of animals is not filled with violence, they do not live in a sad vegetative state like Oskar's parents, or in terror like Oskar. Animals have fairness, empathy, and cooperation. A rat will not pull a lever to get food if this causes pain to another rat (one of many cruel laboratory experiments about empathy in animals).[32] A bat will help another bat give birth, although they probably never meet again.[33] And monkeys will include handicapped monkeys in the group and care for them.[34] Animal life is not terror. "It's not a dog-eat-dog world because really dogs don't eat other dogs," Bekoff and Pierce note.[35] In animal nature, the group punishes the bully. But in human civilization, the group has grown into a large-scale society, moral rules have evolved into ethics and legal justice, and play fighting has perverted into cruel play. So, if society turns a blind eye, who defends the victim of cruel play?

The Ethics of Vengeance

This is not a just world, and there is no pretending that it is. But in the end, we really are the world, there are no excuses, and justice, if it is to be found anywhere, must be found in us.

ROBERT C. SOLOMON, *A Passion for Justice*[36]

Let us now move from the biology of justice to the ethics of vengeance. Some say revenge dramas are primitive entertainment for dumb people. However, research in ethology, philosophy, and psychology agree that justice, and its sister emotion vengeance, is natural and has evolved because it has benefits.

In a chapter titled "Revenge" Frijda explains that revenge is not an emotion as such, but "there is an emotion of appraised offense that instigates desire for vengeance."[37] In animals we call it retribution, in humans revenge or vengeance, and on a mythic scale it is wrath. This emotion—"desire for vengeance"—is universal in species with higher cognitive abilities. Next to love, it is one of our most passionate emotions. The saying "time heals all wounds" is wrong because desire for revenge never ceases to burn, but, on the contrary, in time can become a raging fire returning manifold pain once suffered.

Vengeance is natural, universal, and foundational in both animal and human society. Vengeance is what Carroll calls a "proper" emotion because it has a cognitive content (remembering offense and fantasizing about vengeance), physical sensations (burning shame), and action goal (to inflict pain on the tormentor). Solomon explains vengeance is in human nature: "[o]ur sense of justice . . . is thus not a single emotion but rather a systematic totality of emotions, appropriate to our culture and our character. What I have in mind here is a holistic conception of the personality in which the whole field of one's (or one's culture's) experience is defined and framed by his or her engagements and attachments . . ."[38] Emotions bring engagement and meaning. If we feel without engaging, we become like Oskar's parents, people with no direction because they don't engage. When Oskar fantasizes about attacking Connie, he is not losing his humanity, he is holding on to it. By making Oskar believe he can be a moral agent, Eli reconnects Oskar to his lost humanity. And by making Eli care, Oskar reconnects the vampire to her lost humanity. Oskar is not "nothing" or a pig; he is a *person*.

Vengeance is natural and passionate, and because it is passionate, society surrounds it with laws. The *lex talionis*, "eye for an eye," dates back to ancient Babylonian law two millennia BC. *Lex talionis* restricts vengeance to *only* an eye for an eye, no more. In *Wild Justice* (1983) journalist Susan Jacoby describes vengeance as "a mixed substance" which appears "as a sickness of the soul and as emotional liberation; as disgrace and as honor; as an enemy of social order and a restorer of cosmic order; as mortal sin and saving grace; as destructive self-indulgence and as justice."[39] Contemporary society feels about vengeance the way the Victorians felt about sex, making it taboo and therefore more attractive, creating a tension between "moral condemnation and psychological fascination."[40] Modern society has taken vengeance from the individual and placed it with a legal system. You are not allowed to avenge your own offense. Yet our sense of justice, our desire for vengeance, is innate and passionate. Frijda writes:

> Offense to self-esteem can go deeper than shame. It can extend deeper than mere power inequality or what the term 'loss of self-esteem' usually suggests. It can extend to loss of basic pride, the sense of self-worth and of identity. It occurs when being the object of protracted maltreatment, debasement, or insult . . . All these can damage an individual's very sense of personal value. One has been treated as an object, as subhuman, as placed outside the human domain.[41]

Vengeance restores your self-worth in five ways: First, it shows your willingness to retaliate and therefore deters future insults. Second, it restores a sense of equity by rebalancing the scales of justice. Third, it restores your sense of power by reclaiming the right not to tolerate injustice. That is, you transform from moral patient to moral agent. Fourth, it restores pride. An insult suffered passively hurts your pride and creates shame. The piggy game is humiliating, and vengeance wipes away shame and damage to self-esteem and restores integrity. Finally, vengeance provides escape from pain. By inflicting pain on the perpetrator, I am relieved of my pain and this is why we want a perpetrator to feel as miserable as us; your pain takes away mine.[42] In short, vengeance has benefits. "Desire for revenge belongs to the full human response to offense and injustice. Who is not out for revenge has not been hit by the offense. The desire is not puny, or infantile, or primitive, or pathological, or immature. It is healthy, and the germ for coming to oneself again. Moreover, it is a sign of taking moral justice seriously."[43]

In the novel, two policemen discuss the meaning of the name Eli: "They're the final words that Christ uttered on the cross. 'My God, my God, why hast Thou forsaken me? *Eli, Eli, lama sabachthani?*'"[44] Witnesses describe Eli as an angel flying away with Oskar in his arms. Angels have no gender, which fits Eli as a being without genitals. The novel evokes God's wrath: "Dearly beloved, avenge not yourselves, but rather give place unto wrath; for it is written, Vengeance is mine; I will repay, saith the Lord."[45] In the novel, Eli is queer and divine, avenger and savior, a castrated, impaled and sodomized child who is also a friend, a lover, and a vampire.

Viewers of *Let the Right One In* might, however, draw on ideas about justice and vengeance from Antiquity. Here, we find vengeance in the characters of Medea and Clytemnestra in the plays of Euripides and Aeschylus, and in Antiquity divine vengeance had female form. The Greek Titaness Themis stands for divine justice, Themis' daughter Dike, a goddess, represents human justice, and the goddess Nemesis, whose name means "giving what is due" is depicted with wings. The Romans fused Dike and Themis into goddess Justitia, blindfolded, and holding a scales and a double-edged sword. In *Let the Right One In*, Eli is not an angel sent by God. Eli has become a vampire girl exacting vengeance, the essence of the goddesses of Antiquity combined.

Scar as Passage and Border

I earlier mentioned the scar on Eli's body. So, to ask what it may mean to "be" Eli, both to Oskar and to the viewer, we will return to this scar.

We see the scar when Eli visits Oskar. He now knows, Eli is a vampire and refuses to invite her into the flat. "You have to invite me in." "What happens

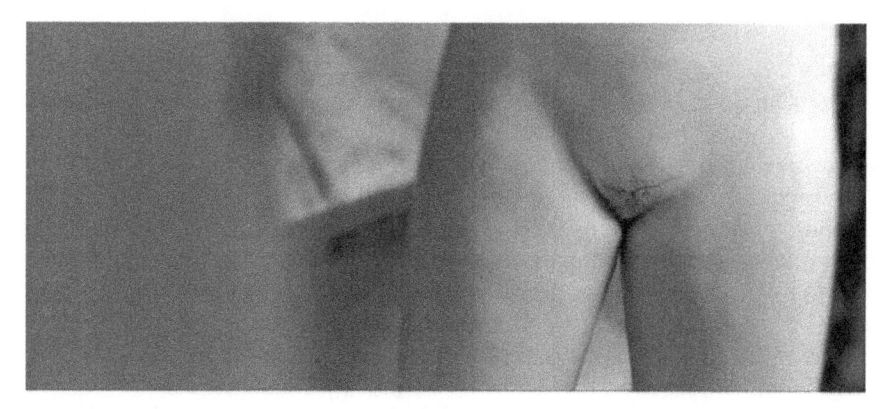

FIGURE 3.2 *Eli's (Lina Leandersson) scar in* Let the Right One In *(2008, Tomas Alfredson).* © EFTI, Sandrew Metronome Distribution Sverige AB, Filmpool Nord, 2008.

if I don't?" Eli then enters uninvited, and when blood streams from all over her body, Oskar screams: "No! You *can* come in." She looks him in the eye and whispers: "Dear Oskar, be me for a little while." The image dissolves to indicate Oskar shares Eli's memories. In the novel, where Eli kisses Oskar on the mouth, Oskar sees the castration and impalement: "Cold fingers grasp Oskar's [Eli's] penis, pulling on it . . . Then the pain. A red-hot iron forced into his groin, gliding up through his stomach, his chest corroded by a cylinder of fire that passes right through his body, and he screams, screams so his eyes are filled with tears and his body burns."[46]

In *Let the Right One In*, Eli showers, and Oskar gives her one of his mother's dresses to wear instead of her blood-soaked clothes. When he spies on her, he sees the scar on her groin. The image is quickly gone and we barely have time to think about genitals (should here be a vagina or a penis?). The camera centers on the scar, and I think the film invites us to think about this scar rather than genitals. The scar is a sign that flesh has been opened. It was once a wound, and can be read as a cut, an opening, a passage, and a crossing of boundaries and borders.

I want to discuss the scar as metaphor of passage and borders. In "Parallel Worlds of Possible Meetings in *Let the Right One In*" (2011) Norwegian film scholar Anne Gjelsvik and Danish film scholars Henriette Thune and Jørgen Bruhn discuss how windows are used as metaphor of passage and change. We first see Oskar as a ghostly reflection in a window. Then he looks down at a taxi that brings Eli and Håkan to the house. Later, Eli enters through Oskar's window, and she also visits Håkan through the window at the hospital. The window can be read as physical and figurative, it separates yet is transparent, it reflects like a mirror, but can also serve as passage.[47] To cross a threshold can be a passage into a new, parallel world.

I think the scar, too, functions as metaphor. A scar invokes death and mortality, the groin is next to our genitals, and our skin is a sensuous border between inside and outside. The living-dead vampire is a border-crossing monster. Eli is both human and vampire, both twelve years old and two centuries old, and the vampire moves between male and female bodies. In the novel, Eli becomes the boy Elias, but in *Let the Right One In*, Eli's gender is ambiguous. The vampire is, literally, without male or female genitals.

I may push the scar as metaphor too far, but I see the scar as an opening of the body that is an invitation to "enter" and "be" Eli. We are invited to cross the border of the body. Writing in the area of border studies, German media scholar Holger Pötzsch discusses borders as geographical (national) and epistemological (separating "me" from "other"). Borders mark a nation and identify foreign and potentially threatening nations. To draw a border is to construct a "me" and an "enemy." A border keeps something *in* as well as something *out*. A border can be questioned, crossed, and opened through gaps, cuts, and ruptures. The rupture opens "a liminal space" and "from it new meanings and alternative discourses might emerge."[48] Pötzsch says borders can be made visible, questioned, crossed, and shifted.

In the former chapter, I discussed the child in film as a metaphor of fear and hope. In her analysis of *Pan's Labyrinth*, Mackey uses the concept of *border pedagogy*. This concept connects geography with pedagogy, and understands "border," "child," and "pedagogy" figuratively and literally in today's global fear of migrating children in a world with "mass migration, unstable borders, and extreme global inequality."[49] A child signifies hope: "Paradoxically, despite the fact that many of the world's youth are essentially abandoned to the neoliberal world order – whether through poverty, disease, economic politics or war – children also act as a symbolic referent of the future, a contradiction which brings to the fore fundamental questions about the nature of ethical responsibility and the possibility of hope."[50]

The scar signals that Eli is a border-crossing figure, straddling positions as girl and boy, human and vampire, moral agent and moral patient, a traveler in time. In the last scene, Oskar is in a train with open doors, the windows are open, and we see a bright winter landscape. With Eli in a trunk by his feet, bullied Oskar has become a migrant child. Eli has drawn Oskar into her world of passage. Society should enable citizens "to be border-crossers capable of engaging, learning from, understanding, and being tolerant of and responsible to matters of difference and otherness."[51] Looking out of the windows we see an "ethical horizon."[52] Hope for a better future.

Conclusion

I began the chapter by asking what it means to "be" Eli. For Oskar, it means to become a moral agent, recover self-esteem, and see himself with love. In the novel Oskar accepts the boy Eli: "And the person in his arms was ... Eli. *A boy. My friend. Yes.*"[53] He experiences love when Eli kisses him after the vampire has killed the bullies: "For a few seconds Oskar saw through Eli's eyes. And what he saw was ... himself. Only much better, more handsome, stronger than what he thought of himself. Seen with love. For a few seconds."[54]

Eli is a mirror of what Oskar has the potential to be. However, if we ask what it means to be Eli across the three texts, there are three possibilities. I have focused on *Let the Right One In* and used my viewing experience to read Eli as an invitation to do imaginary play. Now, I read the book when it was published and so when I saw Alfredson's film, I knew Eli was a boy and that *Romeo and Juliet* was a reference. Thus, I added this information to my viewing experience. However, talking to people, I discovered they did not notice the scar or the Shakespeare quote. I think this means the film leaves Eli open to interpretations. Thus, in the novel Eli is a boy, and in the American remake Abby is a girl, however, in *Let the Right One In* Eli can be read as either girl or boy and has no genitals making her/him a mysterious and open being.

With Eli borders are fuzzy. In the novel Eli is two centuries old, but in the two adaptations we only know she is older than twelve, and in *Let Me In* we see a photograph of her and the assistant when he was twelve. Is Eli mentally a child or an adult? Eli defies dichotomies of nature versus civilization, child versus adult, love versus friendship, agency versus patiency, and, most vexing of all, female versus male.

In Chapter 2 I mentioned Mackey's analysis of children in *Babel*, *Pan's Labyrinth*, and *Children of Men*, who she reads as signs of public policy. The children in *Let the Right One In* are not among Mackey's examples, and here empathy serves private vengeance. Yet the four films share a focus on border and change. In her discussion of borders, Mackey draws on Henry Giroux's concept of "border pedagogy" which is "the fundamentally ethical project of education, in the broadest sense [which] consists in recognizing this unfinishedness and of intervening in the world in order to change it. Border pedagogy is a crucial element in the forging of alliances across literal and figurative borders."[55] *Let the Right One In* is complimentary to *Pan's Labyrinth*. Like Ofelia, Eli is a migrant child, but unlike Ofelia, Eli is a killer and a survivor. Ofelia's death symbolizes public political and emotional powers, but Eli represents the individual's right to agency, pride, and self-esteem.

Pulling together the piggy game, the love story, and vengeance, we can compare opening and closing scenes in *Let the Right One In*. The opening has Oskar behind a window as snow falls at night, and the ending puts him on a train with open windows, open doors, it is day, and Eli is with him. To be Eli means to form alliances across borders and across old dichotomies. To be Eli is a journey that dissolves our conventional dichotomies about human nature. Folded into a love story is a story which re-inscribes the bio-logic of vengeance and re-authors gender.

Teen & Emerging Adult

4

"She Made a Choice":

Werewolf Affordances and Female Character Development

Every time someone jokes about a man "marking his territory" with urine, or discusses the "pack mentality" of gangs, or refers to a seducer or rapist as a "sexual predator," we see an instance of how our culture has internalized the man-wolf analogy.
HEATHER SCHELL, "The Big Bad Wolf" (2007)

It was not until *Bitten* (2014–2016, Space) and *Hemlock Grove* (2013–2015, Netflix) that the female werewolf caught my attention. In *Bitten*, werewolf Elena tells a friend, "it's time to come up with new rules. If we don't change, the pack, all of us, we're gonna die off." "Maybe you should be alpha," he replies. And in *Hemlock Grove*, slight teenager Christina at the end of season one is revealed as *vargulf*, a crazy werewolf. But she isn't crazy, she tells Peter. "She made a choice. She went down the hole," Christina says, referring to herself in third person. Christina transformed by drinking water from a werewolf's paw print. She wanted to be an author, but needed Character and Material. In other words, she needed character development.

When I was a child, werewolves were men. On the television I watched *Werewolf of London* (1935, Stuart Walker) and *The Wolf Man* (1941, George Waggner), and I recall going to the cinema to see Jack Nicholson seduce Michelle Pfeiffer in *Wolf* (1994, Mike Nichols). There were, of course, female werewolves, however, *She-Wolf of London* (1946, Jean Yarbrough) was not part of the Danish television schedule, and independent films like *The Curse* (1999, Jacqueline Garry) and *Wolf Girl* (2001, Thom Fitzgerald) did not premiere at Danish cinemas. Nor do I recall a female werewolf at my video rental. No, most werewolves were men who suffered lycanthropy as a curse. Then, as film scholar Heather Schell (2007) points out, in the 1990s, the representation of lycanthropy changed from tragedy to makeover: "Unleashing the hero's inner beast has finally made a man out of him."[1]

In this chapter, we ask what happens when the werewolf is female.[2] With male protagonists, the story usually follows the horror narrative I call identity horror in Chapter 1, with the hero struggling to master his new instincts. For female protagonists, however, a werewolf story offers different material. Here, lycanthropy is not a curse, but a blessing, because it liberates her from gender. Lycanthropy takes a woman into a territory with predator aggression, a new life she will embrace. The werewolf is for female protagonists both identity horror and social horror, because the new body has two sets of senses and two sets of behaviors. A werewolf, thus, means more opportunities for change.

To explore this change I use James J. Gibson's ecological theory of *affordances*, which is about how we engage with the environment with our bodies, and I draw from French philosopher Christine Malabou's ideas about change and trauma. Malabou calls traumatic change *existential explosive plasticity*. We will look at four texts: British mini-series *Wilderness* (1996), Canadian independent film *Ginger Snaps* (2000, John Fawcett), horror-fantasy television show *Hemlock Grove*, and Canadian drama-fantasy television show *Bitten*.

Lycanthropy

Lycanthropy means the transformation of man into wolf and is from Greek *lukos* (wolf) and *anthropia* (human being, man). In *Metamorphoses*, Ovid tells the myth of how Zeus turned King Lycaon into a wolf, because Lycaon served Zeus human flesh for dinner. In the medieval age, lycanthropy was believed a real phenomenon, where a person could turn into a wolf, but also "a mental disease" where lycanthropy was "a form of madness or melancholy."[3] Then, in the fifteenth century, the werewolf became associated with the Devil, and in the seventeenth century it became a fictional being. However, superstition continued well into the nineteenth century, and the talking wolf in Charles Perrault's fairy tale "Little Red Riding Hood" from 1697 is but a century from the conviction of Jacques Roulet in 1598 of lycanthropy.[4]

With the werewolf's change from a believed real being to a monster in fiction, came also a change in sex. The lycanthrope crimes of "bloodthirstiness, cruelty, shapeshifting and cannibalism," recorded in Sabine Baring-Gould's *The Book of Werewolves* (1865) were committed as often by women as by men.[5] Thus, Thievenne Paget, "a witch of the most unmistakable character, was also frequently changed into a she-wolf, according to her own confession

... slaying cattle, and falling on and devouring children."⁶ Both Paget and the above-mentioned Roulet ate children.⁷

It is in the late nineteenth and early twentieth century that the werewolf becomes a primarily male monster. At this time, its behavior changes from eating people, which we remember is the predatory aggression in survival horror, to attacking and killing people (that is, without eating them). Thus, predatory aggression transforms into identity horror, with the victim of lycanthropy becoming a changed person with a different personality, and aggression becomes angry aggression, with the werewolf attacking people, and its aggression is now also mate-related aggression and sexual horror, since its victims are women. Australian film scholar Chantal Bourgault du Coudray says in *The Curse of the Werewolf* (2006) that "Gothic monstrosity in the twentieth century 'has become Gothic masculinity and fear is coded as the female response to masculine desire.'"⁸

There is no single origin text for the werewolf as there is for its fellow monsters Dracula, Dr. Jekyll, and Frankenstein's monster. It is created from multiple sources, that contribute different elements, like wolfsbane (the poisonous flower *aconitum*), a full moon, the hereditary curse, the contagious bite, or the silver bullets. The werewolf's nature is supernatural, but not set in stone. Each text can interpret what it means to be a werewolf.

Werewolf Affordances

In Chapter 1, I mentioned my talk about the female werewolf. A main point in this talk was that where the hero, traditionally, suffers lycanthropy as a curse, as in *The Wolfman* (2012, Joe Johnston), the horror heroine welcomes her change. She is only too happy to finally be able to defend herself with claws and fangs, and if her new body can be a problem, it is nonetheless an improvement. As a werewolf, she is no longer "just" a woman but now has two bodies, two sets of senses, and two sets of responses.

One could read the werewolf as a case of split personality; however, I want to focus on the predator body, and ask what being a werewolf can mean to a heroine. How does a werewolf body facilitate change, agency, and feminist self-development? For this discussion, I turn to ecological psychology and the theory of affordances. Ecological psychology thinks behavior is determined by the individual's interaction with the environment. Thus, where psychoanalysis focuses on mental worlds, ecological psychology looks at behavior. In "The Theory of Affordances" (1977) Gibson coined "affordances" to describe how an individual uses an object: "[t]*he affordance of anything is a specific combination of the properties of its substance and its surfaces taken with reference to an animal*" (emphasis in original).⁹ An affordance is not "in" the individual or "in" the object, it arises from what we *do* with an object. An affordance is the realization of possibilities.

All objects afford something, and individuals interact with objects depending on their physical bodies, and depending on what they can see. For example, air is breathable to mammals, but not to fish, and a cliff is fall-off-able to most species, but not to birds. Also, animals who see well in the dark can hunt, but the night does not afford good hunting for predators without night vision. And, to take vision a step further, to an experienced user, a touch-screen phone affords dialing a phone number, however, users of the old phones might not know how to realize this affordance, but must first see and learn it.

Affordances, thus, are the *uses* we can make of the environment, some simple and some advanced. All animals, in which Gibson include humans, use the environment according to abilities:

> ... the objects of the environment afford activities like manipulation and tool using. The substances of the environment, some of them, afford eating and drinking. The events of the environment afford being frozen, as in a blizzard, or burned, as in a forest fire. The other animals of the environment afford, above all, a rich and complex set of interactions, sexual, predatory, nurturing, fighting, play, cooperating, and communicating ...[10]

The theory of affordances is helpful, because it describes behavior as realized by our actions. Like animals, we realize affordances as instinctively as we breathe. We don't *think* about how we walk, unless we fear the ice under our feet might break. Most of the time, we take our environment for granted. Gibson underlines that we do not discover affordances with the mind, but with the body, because "perception of the environment is inseparable from proprioception of one's own body – that egoreception and exteroception are reciprocal ... A man can bite into an apple but not a rock; he can get a grip on a handle but not on a wall ... He measures these features of the environment by the standard of his body."[11]

The protagonist's shift from human to werewolf means a shift from a human body with human senses to a new predator body. The werewolf is interpreted in different ways—it can be a wolf-human, a monster, or a wolf—but the point is that *the protagonist has a new way to interact with the world and realize affordances.* For the hero, this means a change from an anthropocentric (human-centric) world view to a non-anthropocentric world view. However, to the horror heroine, it also means a change to a world no longer restricted by gender. In contrast to female vampires, you cannot tell the sex of a werewolf (at least not in our four texts).

The werewolf is a new way to sense and feel, a new way to act in the world, and a new way to interact with surroundings. With fangs comes the question of ethics: What will the werewolf do with her instincts? In ecological terms, a *habitat* is where an animal lives and a *niche* is how it lives.[12] A recurring theme in werewolf fiction is coexistence with humans. To find a habitat, the werewolf must be able to master its predator instincts. If not, it will be hunted and killed. If, on the other hand, it can control itself, it stands the chance to survive in a human habitat. And, if the werewolf can master her instincts, she can be more than a woman. With two bodies comes two sets of senses, two ways to interact with the world, and twice the affordances.

Wilderness: Wolf as Zen Master

My favorite scene in British mini-series *Wilderness* (1996, Ben Bolt) is when psychoanalyst Luther hypnotizes his patient, who claims she is a werewolf. He insists she must take a risk, if she wants the therapy to progress. You won't believe me, Alice answers. "Try me." When she transforms from beautiful young woman to a wolf with fangs and fur, he reacts with denial. This did *not* happen.

Wilderness is the only text in this book from before the millennium, and I include it, because I think it is ahead of its time in the story of lycanthropy as female self-development. The mini-series combines identity horror with social horror in the story of Alice who is trying to change, so she can fit her society. Alice (Amanda Ooms) is a 31-year-old university librarian, who locks herself in the basement every full moon. She is seeing a psychoanalyst because she wants "to be able to have a proper relationship" with a man. Alice describes being wolf as pleasant: "It just felt right. The woods were calling me and I had to go ... next thing I knew I woke up naked in the woods. I didn't know what had happened exactly. But for the first time I remember I felt satisfied." We share a thirteen-year-old Alice's wolf POV as she kills a rabbit. The young Alice liked hunting. But as an adult working in the city, she cannot find a niche for her wolf. "I used to love it when she ran wild," she tells Luther (Michael Kitchen), "now I hate it. I hate having to lock her up and pace around in that bare room until she is exhausted. Piss in corners. Shit on newspapers. But I can't see any other solution. She is not compatible with civilized society."

Werewolf Alice turns into an ordinary gray wolf, who likes ordinary wolf things like hunting. Her affordances are those of a wolf: Heightened predator senses and the ability to sense dishonesty. And the biggest problem with society is dishonesty. Alice meets and dates the biologist Dan (Owen Teale), and she wants to show him her true self, the wolf. "It's you, you don't want her. You're stopping her," she cries, when he interrupts her shifting. Later, on a visit to her parent's farm, she asks her father, if he knew about her nature? "I was frightened," he says. "I'm sorry, I don't wanna talk about it." Luther, Dan, and Alice's father represent male control, conformity, repression, and lies. "Don't you ever lie to me," she warns Dan, "because if you do, I'll kill you." After Dan cheats on her with his ex-wife, Alice has

FIGURE 4.1 *Werewolf Alice (Amanda Ooms) dreams that she is caged and about to be operated on in Ben Bolt's British three-part mini-series* Wilderness *(1996).* © *Red Rooster Film & Television Entertainment and Carlton Television, 1996.*

nightmares she is in a cage and surrounded by doctors about to perform surgery.

The wolf also offers the affordance of self-defense. As a teenager, Alice was assaulted by a rapist who the wolf killed. "I hardly think that what Dan needs is a girl who howls at the moon and eats dog food," Dan's ex-wife taunts Alice. "I am not sick, but I am very dangerous," Alice retaliates. With lycanthropy comes angry aggression and when Luther assaults Alice, she transforms on the couch to defend herself against yet another sexual assault. Alice does not so much master her lycanthropy as manage it so that she can survive in a human habitat. This is not a niche. She must lock herself in the basement, buy meat to satisfy her appetite, and pick up men from bars to satisfy sexual desire. Alice has learnt to control shifts with self-hypnosis, but she cannot find freedom and honesty.

The mini-series combines fantasy and horror, but the novel from which it is adapted is a paranormal romance. In Dennis Danvers' *Wilderness* (1992), the lover quits his job and leaves the ex-wife and moves with Alice to a national park with "park visitors hoping to hear wolves howl to them from a wilderness beneath the slender crescent of a new moon."[13] Written in 1992, the novel is part of an ecological turn that took place during the 1980s, where the wolf changes from being seen as evil predator to become a symbol of nature and eco-harmony. The mini-series rejects this romance.

"I understand. You want the wilderness. I want that too," Dan says. Alice corrects him: "It's not the same. I *am* the wilderness." And in the mini-series, Dan is a man and a liar.

Chantal Bourgault du Coudray argues that horror and fantasy are two genres with different views of monstrosity. Horror has an anthropomorphic world view, where monsters must be killed, and fantasy has a non-anthropomorphic world view, where humans and supernatural beings can coexist.[14] *Wilderness* lands somewhere between these views: Alice is not killed, but she moves to a wildlife reservation because she cannot find a niche in civilization.

Where does this leave feminist agency? On the one hand, lycanthropy is empowering because transformations provide Alice with fangs, claws, and the ability to defend herself. On the other hand, the shifts draw from stereotypical ideas of woman as sensual, sick, and hysteric, when Alice lies down naked and shakes in self-induced spasms.

Alice's struggle with the gender stereotype marks the beginning of a new gender script. In the 1990s, there were debates over women's relation to nature, both to her innate nature and to the world. Works like Clarissa Pinkola Estes's *Women Who Run With the Wolves* (1992) linked ecology to ideas of women as Goddess and a Wild Woman. As part of a biocultural

FIGURE 4.2 *Alice (Amanda Ooms) retreats into a wildlife reservation where she with smooth CGI transforms from woman. . . .* Wilderness *(1996). © Red Rooster Film & Television Entertainment and Carlton Television, 1996.*

FIGURE 4.3 ... *and into wolf.* Wilderness *(1996). © Red Rooster Film & Television Entertainment and Carlton Television, 1996.*

response, gender scholar Mary Zeiss Stange in *Woman the Hunter* (1997), argued the political right and feminist left both had essentialist ideas about women's nature. If the right uses the Man the Hunter story which we discussed earlier, radical ecofeminism thinks a woman is closer to nature than a man. Both views, says Stange, are wrong.[15] Hunting is about killing, and hunters, among which Stange counts wolves and humans, are both male and female. A predator is beyond gender.

The theme of honesty in *Wilderness* is interesting. We recall that animals cannot meta-think and cannot lie.[16] The lover's bed and the psychoanalyst's couch promise care and self-development, yet are spaces of cheating. To be a werewolf affords Alice to sense deceit and honesty. Honesty is also what psychologist and ethologist C. J. Rogers, who lives with wolves in a research sanctuary, describes. Wolves smell emotions, and Rogers must be honest, so she does not bring bad emotions to the pack:

> To me, all these wolves are Zen masters in disguise because of how they've changed me. I'm the apprentice. They can smell emotions. So if you don't want to bring bad vibes into the enclosures, you have to be aware of the state of yourself without the ego. This is all part of earning their trust and respect. And once you have that, then comes the rare honor of an intimacy that gives you a sensitivity to them that is almost like a special sensory perception.[17]

Wilderness gives us the wolf as Zen master, and wolf instincts as a "special sensory perception." Alice's withdrawal to a wildlife reservation, however, is a short-term solution.[18] If a werewolf is to survive, it must adapt *in* human society. Evofeminism is not about hiding but about realizing affordances in response to the world and making a niche, either by adapting to the environment or by changing the world.

Ginger Snaps: Menarche as Mayhem

If Alice had trouble finding a niche, so, too, do this chapter's two teenage heroines, Ginger and Christina. Both refuse to perform society's conventional gender scripts and both use their werewolf bodies in ways that make coexistence with humans impossible. In this section, we first turn to sixteen-year-old Ginger in the Canadian independent film *Ginger Snaps* (2000, John Fawcett).

Just before she is attacked by a werewolf on a full moon, Ginger (Katharine Isabelle) has her first period. "I just got the curse," she laments to her sister Brigitte (Emily Perkins).[19] Ginger is ashamed of her "condition," but when PMS symptoms and lycanthrope instincts coalesce to a "fireworks" of sensations, she welcomes the "curse." "How do you feel?" Brigitte asks when inserting a silver belly piercing into her sister's navel. Ginger smiles: "Wicked."

The plot is about social outcasts Ginger and her younger sister Brigitte. In the opening scene, they stage their own deaths in Cindy Sherman-style photos for a high school project, using fake blood, butcher knives, nooses, even prosthetics. They hate their suburban lives and find their feminist mother embarrassing when she praises sexual openness. After Ginger is bitten, she turns into a teen rebel. She dates the school's bad body, Jason, beats up Trina, the local bitch, and smokes pot. The pot-seller Sam (Kris Lemche) tries to help Brigitte make a cure, but when Ginger goes on a murder rampage, Brigitte has to kill her sister.

Ginger Snaps is co-written by director Fawcett and feminist scriptwriter Karen Walton, and is explicitly feminist in its reversal of gender scripts. The first hour depicts Ginger's bleeding as a black comedy, and the last half hour is a more conventional tale of horror. By linking the werewolf curse to menstruation, *Ginger Snaps* offers ordinary menarche as extraordinary monstrous mayhem, both beyond the heroine's control.[20] "Ginger, what's going on, something is wrong, like, more than you being just ... female," Brigitte asks, when Ginger has locked herself in the toilet at school. Yes, what is going on? The sisters consult the school nurse. "I am sure it seems like a lot of blood. It's a period. Expected every 28 days give and take for the next thirty years." Ginger asks about her new hair growth and the pains? "It comes with the territory."

FIGURE 4.4 *Sixteen-year-old Ginger (Katharine Isabelle) gets her first period after being bitten by a werewolf in* Ginger Snaps *(2000, John Fawcett).* © *Copperheart Entertainment, Water Pictures, Motion International, 2000.*

FIGURE 4.5 *The social outcast Ginger (Katharine Isabelle) becomes assertive, sexy, and self-assured after being bitten.* Ginger Snaps *(2000, John Fawcett).* © *Copperheart Entertainment, Water Pictures, Motion International, 2000.*

In *The Monstrous-Feminine*, Creed argues menstrual blood means horror, and the female teenage body is "a playground for bodily wastes ... [a] stereotype of feminine evil – beautiful on the outside/corrupt within..."[21] *Ginger Snaps* humorously plays with Creed's notion of female teen horror, self-consciously reversing menarche into a self-development embraced as "'a symbol of joyful transgression, dangerous new perspectives, revolt against societal norms ... and empowerment for the [conventionally] powerless (woman)'" [sic].[22] Part of what the school nurse called "the territory" is a small wiggly tail, gray streaks in Ginger's hair, the strong smell of being in heat, razor-sharp nails, and pointed teeth. Together, menarche and lycanthropy transform the social outsider into a self-confident young woman, who aggressively reverses gender scripts:

JASON [in his car]: Just lie back and relax.
GINGER: *You* lie back and relax.
JASON: Who's the guy?
GINGER: Who's the guy? Who's the fucking guy here? [Ginger bites and rapes him]

Menarche: Disease and Shame

Jane M. Ussher, a professor of women's health psychology, in a chapter in *Managing the Monstrous Feminine* (2006) discusses the menstruating body. The symptoms of menarche were called Premenstrual Tension in 1931, then changed to Premenstrual Syndrome in 1953,[23] next called Late Luteal Phase Dysphoric Disorder in 1987, and, finally, labeled Premenstrual Dysphoric Disorder in 2000. In short, modern society sees menstruation as a female disease registered with more than 150 symptoms, among which are "feeling sad, tearful, irritable, angry; marked anxiety, tension, feelings of being 'on edge' ... overeating or specific food-cravings..."[24] Most of these fit the werewolf just as well as the menstruating woman.

Menstruation is not only seen as a disease, it is also considered shameful, and Young thinks this view still exists in our society: "It seems apt, then, in this normatively masculine, supposedly gender-egalitarian society, to say that the menstruating woman is queer. As with other queers, the price of a woman's acceptance as normal is that she stay in the closet as a menstruator."[25] Before she turns into a werewolf, Ginger is petrified with shame when she shops for tampons in the grocery store and bumps into Jason. This shame underlines how women, in Beauvoir's words, are "affirming and denying themselves as women, split and alienated."[26] But when Brigitte locks Ginger, who has started to turn wild and rebellious, in the toilet at their house, she claws her way out. Ginger is *not* staying in the closet.

Ginger's transformation is played out as a reversal of the gender stereotype. The reversal is, on the one hand, a feminist critique but, on the other hand, also a turn from being abused to becoming the abuser. Thus, Jason was bullying the sisters, and Ginger gets even by raping him. "What's *that*? Her egg?" his friends laugh, when they see bruises on his face and blood on his pants. Ginger also warned that if Trina pushed Brigitte, Ginger would beat her. When Trina pushes, Ginger kills Trina. And Ginger is jealous that Sam becomes friends with Brigitte. "If he rapes you, don't come crying," she says. Such reversal is fun, but to be an abuser is not adaptive. Instead of becoming a moral agent, like Oskar in *Let the Right One In*, Ginger becomes an immoral agent, who rapes, beats, and kills people for revenge and for fun, not in self-defense.

Still, there is a feminist message of empowerment and independence. When Ginger goes to the high school dance, her posture is the opposite of her shameful figure at the grocery shop. The new Ginger has silver streaks in her hair, is self-confident, shows cleavage, and makes the boys whistle. Female werewolves are "women who'd rather howl than bleed at the moon,"[27] and Ginger conquers the space of agency (and misbehavior) until now occupied by bad boy Jason and bitch Trina. Ginger describes her change as intoxicating and erotic, "like touching yourself. You know every move . . . it's fireworks, supernovas. I'm a goddamn force of nature."

But the feminist message is ambivalent. On the one hand, feminist scholars found in the film "an awakening of tremendously powerful notions of self, sexuality, and female power . . . that refuse to be sublimated or redefined to fit the conventional expectations for female behaviour."[28] But, on the other hand, where to go after the transformation? Ginger doesn't want a cure. "You think I wanna go back to being nobody?" The film knowingly nods at a failed second wave feminism in the characters of Ginger's mother and the nurse who are part of a suburbia that, in bell hooks' words, supports "mainstream white supremacist capitalist patriarchy."[29] The female werewolf revolts, but her revolt doesn't lead anywhere. Male teen werewolves join a sports team and help their community in *Teen Wolf* (1985, Rod Daniel) and *Teen Wolf* (MTV, 2011–), but Ginger's werewolf causes mayhem.

Hemlock Grove: A Crazy Vargulf

I hasten to admit that in *Hemlock Grove* (2013–2015, Netflix), a female werewolf still cannot adapt to a human habitat. Like Ginger, werewolf Christina is on a frenzied murder-trip, and like Ginger, she is killed by a female teen. *Hemlock Grove* offers no recipe for an evofeminist change that will render the gender stereotype obsolete. Instead, I have chosen this little-known show because of its original take on the female werewolf.

Fourteen-year-old Christina (Freya Tingley) is not protagonist, but a side character. The protagonist is seventeen-year-old werewolf Peter Rumancek (Landon Liboiron), and around him we find unusual individuals and supernatural creatures. There is his friend Roman Godfrey (Bill Skarsgård), who turns out to be *upir*, a vampire; Christina is a vargulf, a crazy werewolf; Roman's mother Olivia is a widow and an upir; Roman's deformed sister Shelley is a radiant monster; Peter's cousin Destiny is a bisexual fortune-teller; and Dr. Clementine Chasseur (Kandyse McClure), is a former elite soldier turned werewolf hunter sent by the Order of the Dragon, a secret Catholic order.

The plot concerns a serial killer on the loose in small-town Hemlock Grove. The show combines horror with thriller and fantasy, and it keeps us in suspense not only about *who* the killer is, but also *what*—human, werewolf, vampire, or something else? The show is based on Brian McGreevy's 2012 novel, and because I had not read the novel, I was flabbergasted to learn Christina was the killer. She made me re-think my assumptions about gender and age. Christina is played by slight and innocent-looking actress Tingley, who is eighteen, but looks younger than her character.

The novel focuses on Peter, but in the show, female characters take center stage. Here, the story starts with Peter and his mother moving into a trailer outside Hemlock Grove. Roman and Christina seek Peter's friendship, Roman because he is bored, Christina because she needs Material to become a great writer. The Godfrey family owns The Godfrey Institute, a biotech

FIGURE 4.6 *Young and insecure Christina (Freya Tingley) with her friends, the sexually experienced twins.* Hemlock Grove: Season 1, Episode 2 ("The Angel"). © Netflix, 2014.

research facility that secretly performs strange experiments. Peter and Roman are both fatherless and watched over by protective mothers Lynda (Lili Taylor) and Olivia (Famke Janssen). Peter falls in love with Letha, Roman's cousin, who says she was made pregnant by an angel (the angel turns out to be Roman). And in the end, Letha gives birth to Roman's offspring.

Like *Ginger Snaps*, *Hemlock Grove* is self-conscious horror. It is less "about" monsters than about play with horror tropes. That is, the point or "message" is not political change or a critique of patriarchy; the point is to play with individuals, tear identity apart, and put it back in unexpected form. Like art, *Hemlock Grove* is creative play, and as such it belongs to horror's fourth narrative, which is creative play. In terms of horror's basic narratives, *Hemlock Grove* combines identity horror with social horror, because it is about altered identities and teens trying to fit into their society as their bodies and minds transform in fantastic ways. However, *Hemlock Grove* is, above all, about having fun, and we feel curious and intrigued, rather than terrified and anxious.

Fantastic Transformations

It is well-known that inside a timid person hides a monster and that the monster fulfills the person's character. So, too, with the werewolf, who functions as character development. *Hemlock Grove* was marketed with Eli Roth, director of torture porn films *Hostel* and *Hostel II*, as producer and director. Thus, the experienced horror viewer would expect visceral transformation scenes, and Peter's transformation in "The Angel" (1.02) is impressive. Roman watches at claws push from Peter's fingers, human eyes pop out of sockets to give way to yellow lupine eyes, teeth fall out as fangs erupt, mouth and face tear with wet sounds and a snout pushes forth. "You've gotta be fucking kiddin' me," Roman says in awe. However, I was more impressed, not least surprised, by the transformations involving female characters. One is the flashback in "Hello, Handsome" (1.05) where Dr. Chasseur is in a prison cell with a heavily pregnant woman. At the full moon, the woman turns and Dr. Chasseur hacks her to death with a machete. "It's better this way ... for both ... of you," she pants. I was more surprised by Dr. Chasseur's turn than the woman's.

And then there is Christina's transformation in "Children of the Night" (1.12). Peter, Roman, and Letha are hiding in a church, because the town believes Peter is the serial killer. The teenagers have brought along Christina, who is traumatized after finding a victim in the woods. Her hair has developed gray streaks and turned gray in the earlier episode. In the church, Christina confesses to be the vargulf. She turned herself because she wanted to have Character. As Christina now shifts into wolf, she describes the shift:

"I can feel it comin' cause I'm getting wet. Ooh. So, this is what it must feel like to come." Christina's face tears with wet sounds as a huge snout pushes from her small mouth with a deep growl. Christina is a tiny, skinny, and flat-chested teen, but she turns into a huge white wolf, that gobbles down its human remains and then attacks and kills Peter.

The surprise works due to a clever use of the gender stereotype and the meta-narrative. We expect a show with a male protagonist to feature *his* change, and we expect a story with a supernatural triangle of werewolf, human, and vampire (Peter, Leetha, Roman) to end with romance. However, *Hemlock Grove* is not a romance. Letha dies at the end of season one and Christina's revelation as vargulf is the peak of the season.

Hemlock Grove is about change and self-development. It is also about sex, but where sex is the natural expression of a woman/werewolf's libido in *Wilderness* and *Ginger Snaps*, here, sex is interwoven with social scripts and anxiety, manipulation, social rank, and trauma. All female characters, except Christina, have sex. Letha was impregnated by Roman, Olivia seduces men, fortune-teller Destiny sleeps with her clients, and so on. Let us recall horror's ping-pong of sensations. Ndalianis says about the paranormal romance in horror that it is "about grasping and giving voice to the sensory and emotional expression of female desire. Horror-paranormal romance, in particular, turns to its heritage – classic romance, contemporary romance, Gothic horror, contemporary horror – and mashes up its sources. The final result is a new form of romance fiction that explicitly explores questions of

FIGURE 4.7 *Christina's (Freya Tingley) face graphic and visceral transformation into a werewolf in* Hemlock Grove: *Season 1, Episode 12 ("Children of the Night").* © *Netflix, 2014.*

FIGURE 4.8 *Petite teenager Christina (Freya Tingley) becomes a huge white werewolf.* Hemlock Grove: Season 1, Episode 12 ("Children of the Night"). © Netflix, 2014.

desire, eroticism, and love through the lens of horror."[30] Ndalianis is talking about *True Blood*, a show that also has a serial-killer plot in its first season.

Like *True Blood*, *Hemlock Grove* mashes up paranormal romance with horror and thriller, but it does so differently. In *True Blood*, *Vampire Diaries*, and *Twilight*, sex revolves around questions of romance, and these texts play with dark eroticism. Vampire sex, explicitly or implicitly, usually plays with perversion. Werewolf fiction also plays with sex, however, here the monster body (that is, the non-human part of the werewolf) is less about sexual desire than physical change. A werewolf's body is used to make us engage with its animal senses and instincts, rather than with its sexual appetite. This is a difference between vampires and werewolves: Vampires engage in sex *as* vampires, but werewolves rarely have sex *as* wolves.

It seems obvious to read *Hemlock Grove* as a coming-of-age story, however, the show play with character development has little to do with development in Erikson's sense, as climbing *up* the life stages. Erikson's chart is usually depicted as a scale going up, like stairs. In his research, play scholar Henricks writes about adult play and suggests we "use ideas of a de-centered world, change, randomness, particularity, cultural and social diversity, conflict, and ambiguity," and that playfulness can be "the most appropriate response to contemporary circumstances."[31] For Henricks, play does not lead "up." Play is, instead, about changing and enlarging our self. Clinical psychologist and play scholar Terry Marks-Tarlow theorizes a nonlinear self, a "fractal self"[32] that, once we have passed childhood, can transform in nonlinear fashion, evolve and change, but not necessarily as a journey up through life stages. Marks-Tarlow suggests instead chaos systems to theorize the logic of *unpredictable change* through play: Play with one's self is sensitive to outset situations, but, like chaos, it is nonlinear and complex.

Returning to *Hemlock Grove*, characters transform in fantastic and unpredictable ways that break with conventions of genre and gender. French philosopher Christine Malabou in her work theorizes change in the individual, a type of change she calls "existential explosive plasticity."[33] This is the change after a sudden injury, shock, or trauma, where you might lose a limb, become depressed, or traumatized. Medical science uses "plasticity" about positive and expected change, but Malabou uses it also about negative change: "As a result of serious trauma, or sometimes for no reason at all, the path splits and a new, unprecedented persona comes to live with the former person, and eventually takes up all the room."[34] Destructive plasticity is "the phenomenon of pathological plasticity, a plasticity that does not repair, a plasticity without recompense or scar, one that cuts the thread of life in two or more segments that no longer meet, nevertheless has its own phenomenology that demands articulation."[35] I suggest that when a character changes into a monster, it is an example of Malabou's destructive plasticity. In contrast to a fairy-tale frog, which retains a positive state of a prince, horror changes both form and essence. Once bitten, the individual *is* traumatized.

The show hints Christina is traumatized by her parent's divorce. She often sleeps over at her friend's house, the twins Alexa and Alyssa, who are the sheriff's daughters. They are her age, but lost their virginity last summer and now tease Christina, "she still blushes at the word *menses*." In the novel, Christina buys condoms and plans to lose her virginity, and the reader is led to believe sex will be Christina's Material. Thus, both the novel and the show hides Christina's transformation into a werewolf and her murders. We think Christina's story is the conventional coming-of-age story.

However, Christina *refuses* the sexual scripts society offers young women. She kills sexually active women—Brooke, Lisa, Jennifer, Alexa, and Alyssa—in protest to what is expected of her. She does *not* want to become like the twins. Christina tells Peter: "All their dirty little stories, all the things they did, those fucking cunts. All the things they expected of her but filled her with so much fear she couldn't even dream about them," (1.12). At the prom, the twins say, "we are hot," and call a girl on the stairs "a slutty heavy"[36] (1.02). But Christina wants neither to be "hot" or "slut." Although the show has a coming-of-age story, it is not *about* coming-of-age. Instead, the show uses black humor to self-consciously play with tropes of sex, knowledge, and lost innocence. At the prom, Peter sets a python snake free in the corridors (a hint at the snake in the garden of Eden), which causes the headmaster to promptly end festivities and stops Christina's flirting with Tyler.

Explosive Plasticity as Character Development

Malabou describes existential explosive plasticity as a process that turns people into a new species:

> ... what was striking was that once the metamorphosis took place, however explicable its causes (unemployment, relational difficulties, illness), its effects were absolutely unexpected ... these people became strangers to themselves because they could not flee. It was not, or not just, that they were broken, wracked with sorrow or misfortune; it was the fact that they became new people, others, re-engendered, belonging to a different species.[37]

Christina's transformation is self-chosen explosive plasticity, her embracement of trauma as change. Christina *does* achieve Character Development. She is no longer the old timid Christina.

We recall du Coudray's suggestion that fantasy and horror have, respectively, a non-anthropocentric and an anthropocentric world view, which means in fantasy, fantastic beings can survive, and in horror, they must be killed. *Hemlock Grove* is a mash-up of the two genres, and thus draws from both world views. This makes the outcome of the play with tropes unpredictable. My focus has been Christina, the mad virgin-werewolf, but there are other extraordinary female figures I do not have the space here to analyse. For example, lesbian werewolf hunter Dr. Chasseur, bisexual Destiny, and Olivia, whose arrogance and costumes pay homage to Sacher-Masoch's *Venus in Furs*. At one point, Lynda and Olivia share thoughts about men: "You really have to wonder. I mean, what would a man provide anyway," says Lynda to which Olivia replies, "sometimes it's just nice having them around. Nice but incredibly stupid. Utterly useless" "What Peter Can Live Without" (1.09).

Such dialogue may sound like feminism, however, it is a play with feminism as a discourse, like the show is playing with horror tropes. Female monsters are stranger than usual, however, women do not fare well. Christine's victims are female, and it is dangerous to be a deviant female. Peter tells Letha one of his relatives once caught a fairy who died in her glass cage. "Noone can fucking live like that," he says (1.09). So, where does this leave an evofeminist body politics? The answer is in an ambiguous in between. On the one hand, there is possibility for character development, yet, on the other hand, the changed heroine cannot find a niche. In Chapter 2, Ofelia sacrificed herself, in Chapter 3 Eli is a migrant child, and in this chapter Ginger is killed by her sister.

Hemlock Grove is a confusing balancing act between creative play and expulsion. Where *Ginger Snaps* distanced its protagonist from second wave feminism, here, all the female characters are post-second wave. They reject patriarchy and do not accept scripts as "house wife" or "school nurse." They are man-eaters (Olivia), werewolf-hunters (Dr. Chasseur), and teen-vargulfs. They are *not* willing co-players in a man's world. Yet neither are they independent of it. While they act with independence, they nonetheless use scripts of seduction. In her discussion of postfeminism, Negra critiques "the turn toward conspicuous consumption of elite beauty products, and the routinization of cosmetic surgery and implants," because these things turn a woman into "a self-surveilling subject ... driven by status anxiety."[38] If we look at the relation between women and monstrous bodies, we might find a liberating change in the werewolf body. In vampire fiction, the female protagonist's body is often upgraded and embellished. Thus, Bella gets eternal youth and unlimited powers in *The Twilight Saga: Breaking Dawn – Part 2* (2012, Bill Condon). A werewolf, instead, gets fur and fangs, an appetite for meat, and instincts to hunt. When it is changed, it doesn't wear makeup or an evening dress.

We can see the werewolf transformation as an explosive plasticity that transforms the heroine into a new species with a new form and essence. Alice looks back in nostalgia for love, and Ginger reversed gender scripts, but Christina takes a different road. She does not reverse gender scripts, but refuses them altogether. This werewolf is indeed a strange creature, and rather than be a psychological and "whole" character, she is a monster trope to be played with, picked apart, and put together. In a discussion of third wave feminism, Shelley Budgeon says it "express[es] new amalgamations of contradictory feminine subjectivities ... expressed through acts of cultural production and consumption that seek to run counter to and subvert dominant representations of femininity yet often draw upon the products of popular culture as resources."[39] The female werewolf in *Hemlock Grove* points to the "increased levels of insecurity" and "state of uncertainty" of late modern society.[40]

Deep Ecology

There is an unresolved tension regarding lycanthropy and gender. Is Christina a vargulf *because* she rebels against gender and kills sexually active women? The show presents Peter's werewolf as a peaceful being seeking coexistence with other species. Thus, Peter learnt from a werewolf uncle that,

> ... the right way to be a wolf, not brain surgery but impossible to understate the importance: Don't hunt when you're not hungry; when you do hunt, go for the flank, thus avoiding antlers in front and hooves in the rear; and when you are filled with the song of the universe, the

breathing spirit that passes through and unites all things, throw your head back and close your eyes and join in.[41]

The subtitle of McGreevy's novel, *The Wise Wolf*, indicates that a werewolf is wise, perhaps wiser than humans. And when Roman in the show asks, if Peter ever attacked a human, Peter replies he never had reason to.

Hemlock Grove depicts the werewolf as a being that belongs in nature with humans. It is not a monster, but a species. Thus, the show has what environmentalist Gary Snyder calls a "post-human humanism,"[42] a world view where humans are not a master species with the right to rule other species. Snyder outlines three views of nature: First, a view where "the wild has a wind of hip, renewable virginity" and humans can use nature for leisure activity; next, there is "the naivete of the pristine preservationists" who want to keep nature separate and pure; and, third, there is "the view that holds the whole phenomenal world to be our own matrix – a locus of its own kind of consciousness ... I am describing, rather poorly, what I think of as a third way, one which is not caught up in the dualisms of body/mind, spirit/matter, or culture/nature."[43]

From a post-human humanistic view, all species inhabit the same world. What, then, are the rules for coexistence? Norwegian philosopher Arne Næss has coined the expression *ecosophy*, which is "a philosophy of ecological harmony or equilibrium. A philosophy as a kind of *sofia* wisdom, is openly normative, it contains *both* norms, rules, postulates, value priority announcements *and* hypotheses concerning the state of affairs in our universe."[44] As mentioned, during the 1980s, the wolf changed status from a feared monster to a symbol of nature. In 1987, Næss defended the wolf's right to live in Norway, where a pack of five to ten wolves caused a debate. In a country with 3.2 million sheep and 4.1 million humans, the Norwegians wanted to kill the wolf because it fed on their sheep.[45] Næss sided with the wolves and argued that they killed very few sheep and that the humans had invaded the wolves' territory. The wolves lost and were shot. The wolf would later return in Norway, and today it eats its share of the sheep, and it is yearly negotiated how many wolves must be shot to keep numbers low (in Denmark, too, the wolf has returned after being extinct for two hundred years).

You may ask why real wolves are relevant in a discussion of gender and werewolves? If we locate a body politics in our werewolf texts, then my point is that the viewer's engagement with the werewolf can create a shift in perspective. Young points out the body is individually felt, as well as socially structured. Looking at the werewolf from an ecological perspective, it relieves the protagonist of the gendered body, the socially structured body. Instead, she has a wolf body, a predator body. Bourgault du Coudray thinks the werewolf is basis for "the positive experience of feminine embodiment" and that it offers "the project of selfhood ... indissolubly linked to nature."⁴⁶ The werewolf "is an integral component of a greater whole, or positioned within a more panoramic or epic context."⁴⁷ What Bourgault du Coudray calls an "epic context" is what ecological philosophy calls a post-human world, a world beyond a dualism of civilization versus wilderness.

Hemlock Grove is a playful and ironic text, and it does not provide an answer or a single point of view from where we can look at gender and the female werewolf. But I want to indicate two perspectives, or points of interrogation. First, at character level, Christina's reaction to coming-of-age raises the question: How should women perform gender? Are you a virgin, a slut, a seductress, or a monster? Can a woman ever get out of her glass cage? And, from a wider and ecological perspective, Christina's self-induced change is an example of how explosive plasticity can take a woman out of the gender stereotype and out of the meta-narrative. However, if one can escape the dichotomies of gender, one cannot escape the laws of nature. Thus, humans and werewolves both have the right to exist, but a vargulf doesn't, because it puts the other supernatural beings at risk of being discovered and killed, like the Norwegian wolves.

Bitten: The Neofeminist Wolf

I want to end with drama-fantasy show *Bitten* (2014–2016, Space) about 24-year-old werewolf Elena. When I watched this show, I was struck by how Elena (Laura Vandervoort) balances her werewolf nature with a career, a boyfriend, a big city life, and loyalty to her pack. She neither locks herself in a basement on a full moon nor revolts against civilization.

The show is based on Kelley Armstrong's urban supernatural romance *Bitten* (2001). It downplays romance and fantasy for realist drama. I shall be concerned only with the television show. In season one, Elena is an art photographer and has just moved in with her boyfriend Philip in Toronto. When a murder is committed by a werewolf, her alpha, Jeremy Danvers (Greg Bryk), summons her back to Stonehaven to help him investigate. Elena was turned four years previously by ex-boyfriend Clayton (Greyston Holt), and ended their relationship because Clay turned her without her consent. Jeremy and Clay live in Stonehaven, a mansion in Bear Valley, New York.

In this universe, the female werewolf is unique and Elena the only existing one. Werewolves live in packs, and in season one, alpha werewolf Santos schemes to kidnap Elena and take over Jeremy's pack. "I am the bitch that he wants," she says in "Bitten" (1.05). The end of season one reveals that Jeremy's father, James, is the mastermind behind the attacks. James plans to use Elena to breed a pure wolf line with a wolf mother and wolf fathers.

FIGURE 4.9 *The beautiful young werewolf Elena (Laura Vandervoort) is a supernatural SYF (single young female) in Canadian show* Bitten: *Season 1, Episode 1 ("Summons").* © *Entertainment One, Hoodwink Entertainment, No Equal Entertainment, 2014.*

Sex and the Single Werewolf

Before Elena shifts, she undresses, meticulously folds her clothes, and removes jewelry. I never saw a male werewolf put that care into clothes. This tells us Elena is what magazine editor Kay S. Hymowitz in "The New Girl Order" (2007) calls a SYF, a single young female, who wants to live life to the fullest.[48] With twent-four years, Elena is young adult, a life phase psychology defines as between twenty and forty (adult is between forty and sixty-five). The young adult age phase is popular with television production companies, because a cast appeals to both an adolescent audience, who prefers protagonists older than themselves, and to the young adult audience.[49] Also, when it comes to plot, a young adult character is old enough to have sex. The casting of Vandermort, who was twenty-nine in the first season, underlines the emphasis on adult.

Unlike our earlier female werewolves, Elena has roots in well-established female fantasy territory. Armstrong's novel was the first in her book series *Women of the Otherworld* (2001–2012), and is contemporary with *The Sookie Stackhouse Novels* (2001–2013) and the *Twilight* books (2005–2008), both by women authors.[50] Elena, at the outset of the show, looks like the typical postfeminist heroine, balancing multiple social roles and identities and always well-dressed with perfect makeup. She fits a postfeminist discourse of "female achievement, encouraging women to embark on projects of individualized self-definition and privatized self-expression exemplified in the celebration of lifestyle and consumption choices."[51] I will discuss her as a neofeminist rather than postfeminist heroine, however, these feminisms do not exclude one another, but intersect and overlap. The important difference between, on the one hand, third wave feminism, and, on the other hand, postfeminism and neofeminism, is that third wave feminism is an extension of second wave feminism and has political goals. The latter two are neoliberal attitudes and lifestyles, and aim at individual, not political, change.

Recently, British film scholar Martin Fradley (2013) wrote about contemporary teen horror that it is "a knowingly *post*feminist terrain" that invokes "the 'spectre of feminism.'"[52] Contemporary horror looks *back* at feminism and as "a counterpoint to the broad critical emphasis on the supposed failings of the genre," Fradley wants to "interpret teen horror *on its own terms*" (emphasis in original).[53] By "its own terms" Fradley means we must acknowledge texts as historical situated. Now, as I have said before, my aim is not to make a normative claim about one version of feminism being better or more liberating than another, but to use any kind of feminism if it helps a feminist goal of equality. So, inspired by Fradley, I speculate contemporary horror is haunted not only by a specter of 1970s' second wave feminism (like *Ginger Snaps*), but potentially also by specters of 1980s' ecofeminism and 1990s' postfeminism. Contemporary horror might even be haunted by the specter of third wave feminism, a wave some say is today succeeded by fourth wave feminism, which is defined as the feminist users of new social media.[54] Haunting, however, requires a thing to be put to rest for its specter to rise, and a third wave is still alive, even if a fourth wave exists too. However, I shall put specters and waves aside, since none of the horror heroines I discuss in this book are situated in a fourth wave.

To get back to Fradley, I want to discuss my horror text *Bitten* on "its own terms." And where Armstrong's novel from 2001 was situated in an optimistic postfeminist climate, the show *Bitten*, from 2013, is created in a post–9/11 culture, where postfeminism is seen as (now only) neoliberal and (therefore) not empowering. As said, my project is not normative, but explorative. So, rather than discard *Bitten* because protagonist Elena is beautiful, sexy, and fashionable, like the (now rejected) typical postfeminist heroine, we will ask what affordances she offers the audience as werewolf.

As said, Elena always finds the right outfit for the occasion, whether it is a dress for a cocktail party, gym clothes for exercising, or boots and carry-on bags for traveling. We shall link her to what New Zealand film scholar Hilary Radner in *Neo-Feminist Cinema* (2011) calls *neofeminism*. "Neofeminism," coined in the 1970s as a critique of second wave feminism, embraces the things that second wave feminists supposedly reject: (heteronormative) sex, makeup, fashion, shopping, dating, capitalism, men, patriarchy. Radner traces neofeminism to the 1930s and 1930s' discourses in the US about the so-called Modern Girl and New Girl. In the early twentieth century, America encouraged women to work and shop, and this is when it became acceptable to be a single woman.

Radner explores neofeminist heroines, and examples include *Pretty Woman* (1990), *Maid in Manhattan* (2002), and *Sex and the City* (2008). She examines comedies and dramas, however, her neofeminist heroine also fits my purpose. The neofeminist heroine has four characteristics: First, her "girlishness" is not about age, but signifies a process of becoming. It is the attitude of makeovers, do-overs, and change. Second, she is a "can-do" woman who can handle herself and is a striver and an achiever. She doesn't wait for a prince to save her. Third, she is a "have-it-all" who works hard. She does not want to settle down, but wants to move on. Finally, she doesn't dream of a nuclear family, but has a social network of friends where a boyfriend is optional.

Radner takes her cue from Helen Gurley Brown, the author of the instructional guide *Sex and the Single Girl* (1962). Brown's single girl is independent, educated, has a career, is financially wise, keeps fit, and is above all a consumer. "The Single woman, far from being a creature to be pitied and patronized, is emerging as the newest glamour girl of our times."[55] In 2007, this single girl has evolved into Hymowitz's SYF, living in the New Girl Order. "SYFs bring ambition, energy, and innovation to the economy, both local and global ... [the SYF] represents a dramatic advance in personal freedom and wealth."[56]

Neofeminism is about independence, consumption, and moving up. A single girl can manage without men, but Brown warns she "need[s] to look glamorous every minute."[57] Thus, neofeminism shares with postfeminism a concern with self as consumption, however, also with self as development and self-work. The neofeminist individual is, like the postfeminist woman, "flexible, individualized, resilient, self driven and self made and [someone] who easily follows nonlinear trajectories to fulfilment and success."[58]

Mastering Change and Desire

"Self control is everything," alpha Jeremy repeatedly tells the pack in "Vengeance" (1:09). Like the neofeminist heroine, Elena learns to handle herself so she can move ahead in the world. She refuses to fall victim to her "condition." *She* wants to be in control, and if self-control requires hard work, she puts in the effort.

Season one starts with an unwanted shift, where Elena must leave Philip to run into a back alley, where she takes off her sequined evening dress, black leather jacket, and removes her necklace. Logan later explains she cannot just avoid her shifts. She must transform once a week, or she loses control over her body. Therefore, like Alice, Elena practices shifts to gain mastery over her body. When Jeremy's pack is being attacked by Santos' group, Elena panics, and the panic triggers a shift. We see her fingers, with nail polish, elongate into claws, and her vision turns lupine. She then wills the shift to stop. When Jeremy and Clay hear about this, they are impressed: "I've never heard of that happening before. Once a full change is triggered it's impossible to reverse it," says Jeremy. And Clay asks, "how did you do it?" Elena says, "I don't know. It just happened." But it did not "just happen." Elena practiced hard to gain mastery of her body.

The werewolf shift is visualized with smooth CGI morphing of new bones rippling under the human frame, fur grows, limbs elongate, a snout appears, and teeth become fangs. In our earlier texts, werewolf affordances were about a sensuous engagement with nature, and about the pleasures of predatory aggression (hunting) and angry aggression (self-defense). In *Bitten*, Elena's werewolf affordances include the pleasures of hunting, however, more to the point are two somewhat different traits, the first that a werewolf is fearless, and the second that it is powerful and aggressive. The werewolves in *Bitten* look like ordinary wolves, only stronger, bigger, and without fear (this is in contrast to real wolves, who are afraid of humans and have fear). The werewolf's lack of fear carries into its human form. Thus, when Elena meets her childhood molester Victor Olson (Patrick Garrow) in Toronto, she is not afraid of him anymore. And when a guy makes a move on her in a bar, she pins him to the floor, making her companion comment in "Summons", "what was *that*? Usually there's only one reason a woman knows that kind of self-defense" (1.01).

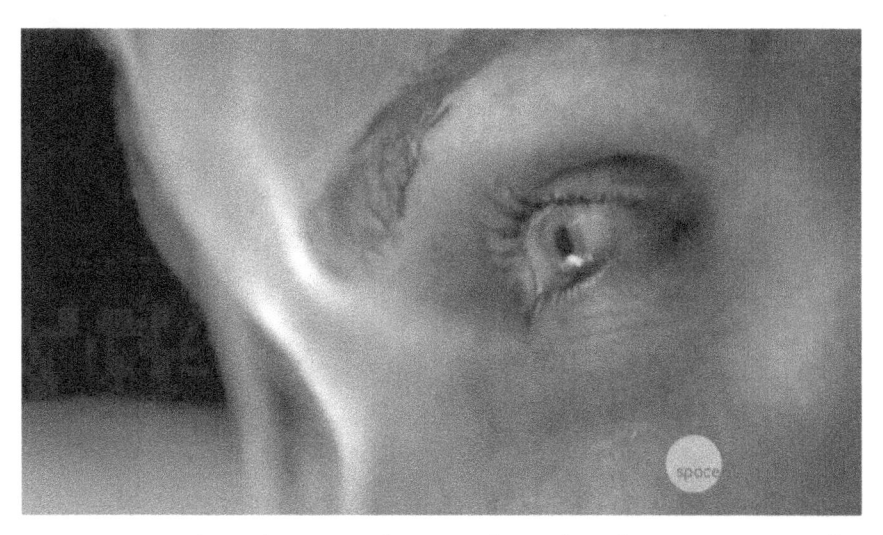

FIGURE 4.10 *Elena's (Laura Vandervoort) change from human into werewolf is rendered in smooth CGI.* Bitten: *Season 1, Episode 5 ("Bitten"). © Entertainment One, Hoodwink Entertainment, No Equal Entertainment, 2014.*

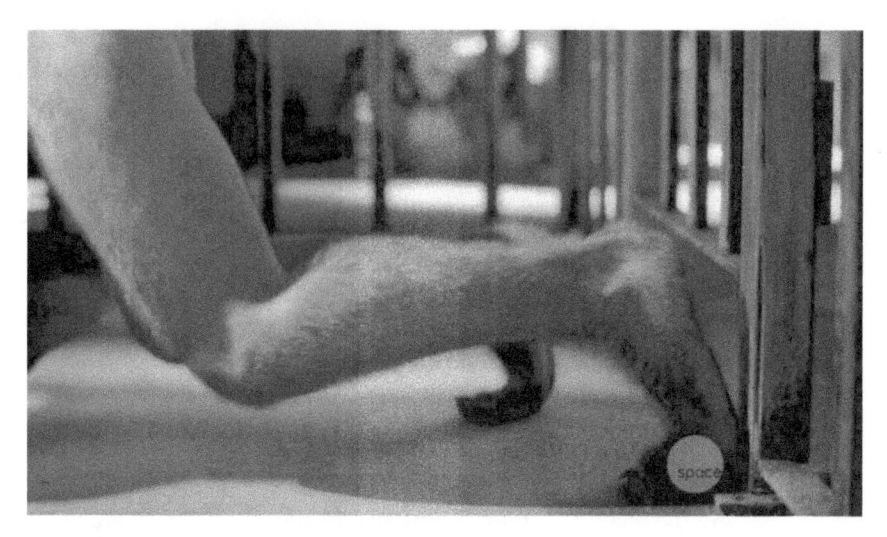

FIGURE 4.11 *Elena's (Laura Vandervoort) limbs slowly elongate into wolf limbs. Bitten: Season 1, Episode 5 ("Bitten").* © *Entertainment One, Hoodwink Entertainment, No Equal Entertainment, 2014.*

FIGURE 4.12 *The transition from human to wolf in Bitten has no blood or gore as in* Hemlock Grove. Bitten: *Season 1, Episode 5 ("Bitten").* © *Entertainment One, Hoodwink Entertainment, No Equal Entertainment, 2014.*

And the second werewolf trait, or characteristic, is that it can defend itself. This aggression combines the three basic aggressions, both predator, territorial, and angry aggression. And with practice, Elena learns to master the wolf instincts. In the words of Kahneman, she learns to switch from wolf instincts, which are now part of her System 1, to System 2, the control of behavior, our meta-reflection and meta-thinking. Using System 2, Elena no longer must turn into a wolf to use her wolf affordances. She can now break a guy's wrist when he threatens her (1.08), hide a dead body (1.05), defend a boyfriend (1.11), torture (1.12), rip a man's heart out with bare hands (1.02 and 1.13), and elongate a single nail to serve her as a weapon (1.12). These affordances are part biology, part achieved through Elena's hard work to harness *both sets of instincts* in her werewolf body. Hard work, thus, enables her to master aggression and channel it to get ahead in the New Girl Order, a world where she, in season three, becomes alpha.

One of Brown's tenets was the single girl's right to sex, be it with married men (infidelity was *his* problem) or dating several men simultaneously. Sex, like breathing and makeup, is a right and should be a pleasure. This neofeminist view of pleasure echoes a postfeminist view of sex. And where our former heroines had traumatic relations to men—Alice picked up random men in bars to satisfy her appetite, Ginger raped men, and Christina was terrified of sex—Elena can control and master desire, like she learnt to manage aggression. Elena enjoys sex, she chooses boyfriends, and she chooses when to cheat (unlike Alice, Elena does the cheating) or when to leave one boyfriend for another.

In *Bitten*, sex is not joyously transgressive as in *True Blood*, nor safely heteronormative as in *Vampire Diaries*. It is, instead, neoliberal sex, meaning as long as it is consensual, most sexual scripts are acceptable. Thus, bisexual werewolf Nick apologizes to "Mr. and Mrs. Smith" for leaving a threesome (1.01). For Elena, sex also has a special meaning, because she was victim of child abuse. To have sex, and feel excitement and lust, means overcoming trauma. For Elena, sex is positive and healing, it is a natural instinct, and to give in to sexual desire means becoming a balanced person with more self-esteem.

The Evofeminist Werewolf

Let us recall Henricks description of the self as a wide sense of self which has five dimensions: Body, mind, community (our social selves), possessions (our belongings), and our self is, finally, situated in a world (culture). Thus, one's home and community are part of the wide self. Radner also discusses home as part of a neofeminist self: "This expansion of the self to its surroundings mimics the evolution of makeover culture extending through the various parts of the body to the body's environment as the required arenas of cultivation . . ."[59] The expansion of self to surroundings is both a natural behavior and a culturally learnt behavior. In nature, a species must turn nature into a niche, however, humans also want the environment to mirror our self-building and self-work. In one perspective, this can be rejected as capitalist consumption, yet, in another perspective it can also be embraced as creative play.

Alice, Ginger, and Christina could not control instincts, master shifts, or find a niche. They could not interact with a community, had no werewolf friends, and could not expand their self to a home in a community. A wide sense of self is not only about "me," but also about "us." Elena has a home with Philip in the big city apartment, and she also has a home in Stonehaven, where she has her own room with romantic tapestry and a chic wooden closet. Her self is not an isolated mental construct, but formed in interaction with others. The wide sense of self include surroundings, and to do self-work, in this perspective, means to engage with others. Henricks says, "play is an exploration of powers and predicaments. We play to find out what we can – and cannot – do and to see if we can extend our capabilities."[60] Thus, rather than be hyper-aggressive like Ginger and Christina, it is adaptive to play with others.

Elena is, like the neofeminist protagonist and Brown's single girl, a learner. Brown, writing in 1962, says the single girl "supports herself. She has had to sharpen her personality and mental resources to a glitter in order to survive in a competitive world and the sharpening looks good. Economically she is a dream. She is not a parasite, a dependent, a scrounger, a sponge or a bum. She is a giver, not a taker, a winner and not a loser."[61] Elena, too, is a giver. She is the best hunter, a better strategist than Jeremy, can talk her way out of a cage, and understands humans better than Logan, who is a psychotherapist. Hymowitz calls the SYF "a triumph of planetary feminism" because she contributes to the global economy with knowledge, flexibility, and consumption.[62] Elena, too, contributes. In season one, she leads the defense against Santos' group, and in season three she becomes alpha and in "Rule of Anger" says, "none of us are worth saving unless we are all worth saving" (3.06). Radner ultimately sees neofeminism as negative, because it puts "self-cultivation and individual fulfillment" over a community.[63] However, Elena uses her hard-earned self-development to help her pack. She puts herself in service of the group and in season three she introduces the werewolves to human society, trying to make a niche in the open, instead of hiding.

I opened the chapter with Schell, who says lycanthropy makes "a man" out of the hero. Lycanthropy works differently for the heroine. It functions as Malabou's explosive plasticity, which transforms the body not into that of "man," but into a new species. The werewolf self can expand senses and affordances, and we recall that Csikszentmihalyi thinks "a psychologically androgynous person in effect doubles his or her repertoire of responses and can interact with the world in terms of a much richer and varied spectrum of opportunities."⁶⁴ The bitch werewolf has moved up in the world, from basement to alpha. I leave it open if her body is feminist or not. From a second wave feminist perspective, fashionable Elena might not be a politically correct answer. But from a neofeminist perspective, she signals choice, agency, and change. And from a third wave feminist perspective, which is open to multiple and contradictory discourses, Elena uses self-work to serve the group. Last, from an evofeminist perspective, the werewolf body combines neoliberal self-work with postfeminist plurality, and neofeminist ambition with commitment to a community. From an evofeminist perspective, lycanthropy is a change which, like trauma, "frees up the possibility of another story."⁶⁵

5

Lust, Trust, and Educational Torture:

The Vampire Diaries

> CAROLINE: Dad, I'm okay. I've learned to adapt. I don't need to be fixed.
>
> *The Vampire Diaries*, "The End of the Affair" (3.03)

Caroline in *The Vampire Diaries* (2009–2017, CW) starts as a dumb blonde who performs life from a me-me-me script.[1] When Damon asks her to help her friends with cleaning after dinner, Caroline says, "Does it *look* like I do dishes?" Caroline (Candice Accola) is vain, selfish, shallow, and manipulates people. But then events happen that make her change and be more emphatic. And after she is turned into a vampire, she learns to be trustworthy, a loyal friend, and a robust and resilient person.

Caroline's story of change and self-development is an example of what I call social horror, which is the basic narrative about learning to fit into a group and live in society. I base the social narrative on what Nell calls territorial aggression, which is aggression used to compete for a mate, fight for territory, or secure a place in a social hierarchy.[2] Predatory aggression, we recall, is about feeding, and angry aggression about self-defense. Social horror is not about eating or self-defense, but about acquiring social skills for our everyday life with family and friends.

In contrast to Ofelia and Oskar, Caroline's challenge is not to confront evil people or bullies. Nor is her challenge to express her full personality, like Alice, or rebel against a repressive gender script, like Ginger. Rather, Caroline's challenge is to learn to become emphatic and trustworthy, a person who is welcome in a group. Caroline starts to deal with her insecurities in the first season, but it is when she becomes a vampire that radical self-development happens. With vampire nature comes bloodlust and her friends will only allow her to live as vampire if she learns to control herself. This is not just a matter of bloodlust. No, Caroline must learn to *respect* other people.

For animals, territorial aggression serves mating and social life. In Chapter 1, I mentioned that play scholars think play fighting serves males' competition for females' attention, the so-called sexual selection theory. This theory argues that males play fight, so they can win a mate. In this chapter, I return to sexual selection theory and I argue three things. First, although play scholars believe play fighting is about boys impressing girls, I think today's sexual scripts offer other stories. Thus, we will see that *Vampire Diaries* has *two* sexual strategies, one a romance with Elena and vampire brothers Stefan and Damon, the other serial dating, which is what other characters do. Second, related to sex are issues of trust. Although the show is called paranormal romance, I think audiences engage with Caroline, who becomes a central character and is the series' protagonist from season six, because of her story of self-work and self-development. Third, finally, I argue that although *Vampire Diaries* is considered a teen show, it appeals to a broader age group. Today, where serial monogamy has replaced everlasting love, and we develop our self not just as part of growing up, but in every phase of our lives, serial dating and self-work is relevant to all age phases.

I focus on sexual emotions and trust, because love and trust are needed to become a caring and trustworthy person. In *Vampire Diaries*, love and trust connect to pain in unorthodox ways, one of which is torture, which we find in season three, where Caroline's father tortures her, because he wants to cure her of vampirism. I shall first look at sexual selection theory and genre. The chapter, then, analyses Caroline in relation to the sexual emotions. Next, I look at how Caroline learns to trust and becomes trustworthy. The chapter closes with a discussion of *Vampire Diaries* as more than a teen text, where Caroline's self-development appeals to what psychologist Jeffrey Jensen Arnett calls emerging adults, who are in a phase after adolescence but before commitment to children or marriage.

Sexual Selection Theory Revisited

Let us return to the link between play fighting and play. Play fighting in animals involves pain. This is physical pain of being scratched, pushed, bitten, and so on. When animals fight for fun, they learn that pain is part of play. Also mental pain, which is the pain of insecurity—did you mean to hurt me or was this just fun? Animals, like humans, have bullies and aggressive players too. And we recall that play fighting helps develop a range of skills for future situations, skills believed beneficial for sex, hunting, vigorous activities, and dominance. Later in life, a play fighting animal is better at wooing, hunting, and climbing the social ladder.

When play scholars combine play fighting in animals with R&T play in humans, they use sexual selection theory to argue that males play fight *more* than females, because males need to be aggressive to compete for the attention of the females. In "The Development and Function of Rough-and-Tumble Play in Childhood and Adolescence: A Sexual Selection Theory Perspective," psychologist Anthony D. Pellegrini says: "As dominance is not an end onto itself, boys' dominance status is related to dating popularity with females."[3] Such discussions of R&T play are often highly gendered and suggest boys are innately more aggressive, more active, and play differently than girls. Boys learn dominance and to be actively engaged in the world, girls learn to nurture and stay home with the family. "In short, leadership and competitive roles typify male groups and facility in these roles is related to their group status."[4]

Yet, I repeat my earlier reservations about sexual selection theory as an explanation of more R&T play in human males, including horror as mental play fighting. First, in predator species, males and females are equally good at using aggression for hunting, fighting, and self-defense. Second, in many mammal species, males are not out hunting while females stay home with offspring. Such behavior in humans is socially learned, and sexual selection theory may be a social script and not innate behavior. Third, play continues past the age of mating, both in mammals and in humans. Thus, play fighting is about *more* than competition for females. It is about practicing skills, that are beneficial across the age phases, perhaps across all age phases.[5] Now, I agree that sex, sexual emotions, and mating are part of the aggression in play fighting, but I don't think they are the single cause, and I don't think they explain only male aggression in mating. Rather, sex is one of the situations, which play fighting prepares players for, both male and female players.

So, before we move on, we will question two assumptions underlying research in human R&T play. First, that only children and adolescents play fight. But adults play fight too which is evident if we look at sports. And, second, that boys play fight more than girls. From an epigenetic perspective, it would make little sense if females were less able to hunt, fight, or protect offspring against predators. Instead, I suggest play fighting is adaptive for both sexes and at all ages. Today, where human life offers more changes than before in history with modern technology, an increasingly global culture, and a flexible late modern identity, play fighting is functional at every life stage, even old age. In humans, it is difficult to test if one sex play fights more than the other, since we are socialized into gender roles from birth. Thus, I suggest gender differences in play fighting belong to the meta-narrative and are not innate.

If it is assumed adolescent males play fight to win females, another widespread assumption is that adolescence is the life phase where we experiment most. Arnett, researching the phase between adolescence and commitment in marriage, calls this emerging adulthood and says it is more experimental than adolescence. We return to emerging adulthood at the end of the chapter. Here, I want to briefly introduce Erikson's view of adolescence as the phase where we experiment with different social roles, and where we learn about inner and external values, thus moving from a flexible adolescence into "fixed" adulthood. Erikson calls the conflict at this stage "identity confusion," and says society "permits some special leeway in the form of a moratorium devoted to 'sprees' or extended periods of experimental and yet prescribed ways of 'being different' ...."[6] Fiction is one such moratorium, and we can see horror as a dark stage, where we can play with being a vampire and going on a killing spree. Erikson thinks the basic conflict in adolescence is identity versus identity confusion, and trust versus mistrust, and that the aim of this stage is to prepare for adulthood, for family, and "to make of two persons a pair, and out of pairs, promising affiliations in productive and procreative life."[7] The "lesson" of adolescence is to meet the requirements of adulthood, that is, make a family, and be able to care and be compassionate.

The texts we have discussed so far were produced with an adult audience in mind, at least eighteen years old. *The Vampire Diaries*, in contrast, is aimed at teenagers and adults. CW's show is based on L. J. Smith's book series, which began with four books written between 1991–1992. The television show, which I am concerned with in this chapter, aired in 2009 and finished with an eighth season in 2017.[8] The initial young adult book series was a paranormal romance between Elena and vampire Stefan, like later paranormal romance book series *The Southern Vampire Mysteries* (Charlaine Harris' books 2001–2013, the HBO show *True Blood* 2008–2014) and *Twilight* (Stephenie Meyer's books 2005–2008, film series 2008–2012).

In the adaptation from book series to television show there is both a change in genre and a change in age. What was a young adult supernatural romance aimed at teenagers, is adapted into a horror-teen-show aimed at both adolescents and young adult viewers. Rebecca Williams in "Unlocking *The Vampire Diaries*: Genre, Authorship, and Quality in Teen TV Horror" (2013) calls *Vampire Diaries* "a resolutely teen text"[9] whose supernatural elements are "metaphors for the anxieties of adolescence and young adulthood" and whose "storyline plays out through discourses of alienation, misunderstanding, and distrust that are likely to resonate with teen viewers."[10] Williams situates *Vampire Diaries* as a middle ground between *True Blood*[11] and *Twilight*, "both horror and a teen drama, drawing on tropes from the horror genre and combining them with young adult issues such as parental tensions or romantic relationships."[12] Critics and reviewers agree the show carved out ground between *Twilight* and *True Blood*: "*Vampire Diaries* feels more edgy than *Twilight*. It's not as graphic and menacing as HBO's *True Blood*, a similar work, but the tension here is lethal, not just romantic ... By staking turf between *True Blood* and *Twilight*, *The Vampire Diaries* hopes it has found the promised land."[13]

In the book series, the love story with Elena and vampire brothers Stefan and Damon is central. But in CW's show, side characters get more space. And where the book series had one romance, the adaptation has two stories; one is romance (Elena's story), the other is serial dating. The two stories, or sexual strategies, end differently. Romance ends with Elena dating Stefan until season four, then dating Damon until her death in season six, and the second strategy, serial dating, ends with Caroline marrying Stefan after having had multiple boyfriends. The adaptation from novel to show expands genre from romance to *both* romance *and* drama. This can be seen as a strategy to expand a potential audience from the teen readers of the young adult book series, to an audience that would include that of *Twilight* as well as that of *True Blood*. The strategy proved successful, with audiences today ready for mainstream paranormal horror.[14]

The aim of paranormal romance and drama are different. Paranormal romance is a hybrid genre that draws from romance, Gothic, horror, fantasy, and crime, to name but a few.[15] Paranormal romance features love between a supernatural man and a young human woman. It combines traditional romance—"the *meeting* between the heroine and hero; an account of their *attraction* for each other [and] the *barrier* between them"[16]—with a supernatural lover, who is "'a glamorous outsider' who holds the promises of literally changing lives ... [and] has the ability to ensure that love will be everlasting."[17] Paranormal romance is about eternal love.

Drama, in contrast, is concerned with life changes and character development, as we remember with Christina (who has read Aristotle's *Poetics* in her drama class).[18] Drama characters can be superior to us (as in Aristotle's definition of the tragedy) or equal to us (as in his definition of the epos), and the topic is serious (in contrast to the comedy). Thus, according to drama genre conventions, each season of *The Vampire Diaries* has a new villain, a new mystery, a new quest, and characters who change or die. The show oscillates between *drama* with theme of personal development, *teen drama* with themes of dating, friendship, and growing up, it has *soap elements* like the small-town community of Mystic Falls, and it is of course a *horror drama* with murders, monsters, and torture.

Serial dating is, as Hymowitz phrases it in "The New Girl Order" (2007), not about finding Mr. Right. Instead, Mr. Right For Now will do just fine, because a SYF is concerned with changing and moving. In the New Girl Order, lovers may not last but friends are the new family, and if a girl is to have a social life (which can include a boyfriend) she needs empathy, to be trustworthy, and able to manage herself.

Caroline: Stupid and Shallow

The first episode introduces romance, when Stefan returns to his birth town Mystic Falls and says in voice-over, "I shouldn't have come home. I know the risk. But *I have to know her.*" The risk is if someone recognizes seventeen-year-old Stefan as a 171-year-old vampire. When he walks down the corridors at high school, Elena, Bonnie, and Caroline are mesmerized. Bonnie begs, "please be hot."

Stefan returns to meet Elena, who is the doppelgänger of Katherine (both Elena and Katherine are played by Dubrov). Back in 1864, Stefan and his 23-year-old brother Damon were turned by the beautiful and manipulative vampire Katherine. After Stefan returns, Damon returns too, and a new love triangle begins. Stefan is the gentleman hero and Damon the cynical antihero, who kills as he pleases.

Where Elena is the conventional good and compassionate romance heroine, Caroline is the conventional shallow blonde. She embraces Elena at school, asking how Elena feels after her parents' tragic death this summer, then waltzes down the corridor with a wide smile. The viewer understands Caroline feigns concern, and Elena and Bonnie look at each another. Elena says, "no comment" ("Pilot," 1.01). And despite Elena having fallen for Stefan, Caroline tries to snatch him. "Have you been down to the falls yet? Because they are really cool at night and I can show you. If you want." But Stefan rejects her offer. "Caroline, you and me. It's not gonna happen. Sorry."

Stefan choses Elena, and episode one lets Elena go to sleep with dreams of Stefan, while a drunk and devastated Caroline sobs her heart out to Bonnie:

> CAROLINE: Why didn't he go for *me*? How come the guys I want never want me? I'm inappropriate, always say the wrong thing. And Elena always says the right thing. She doesn't even try. And he just picks her. And she's always the one that everyone picks. For everything. And I try *so hard* and I'm never the one.
> BONNIE: It's not a competition, Caroline.
> CAROLINE: Yeah, it is.

Sexual selection theory speculates that the female chooses the male with the best genes. To decide who has the best genes, she selects the strongest or most outstanding male. An example of an outstanding male is the peacock with its large tail, which seems maladaptive because it obstructs flying, but serves to attract peahens. Feminist biologist Marlene Zuk says "males are expected to compete among themselves for access to females, and females are expected to be choosy, and to mate with the best possible male they can."[19] Peahens are choosy and do in fact prefer the peacocks with most eyespots on tail feathers. Zuk says, "modern biologists accept female choice as an important part of sexual selection."[20] According to sexual selection theory, males compete with each other, and must prove worthiness through courtship. This male competition is played out between brothers Stefan and Damon to be chosen by Elena.

But Caroline's story is not romance. Boys don't compete for her attention, instead she is desperate to get theirs. And she is not coy. Elena doesn't have sex with Stefan until episode ten, but Caroline has sex with Damon on the night they meet. In fact, Caroline seems to have very few qualities. At a dinner with her friends and the newcomers, Stefan and Damon, Caroline says Elena "used to be so much fun" before her parents died ("Friday Night Bites," 1.03). Later, Damon tells Caroline what everyone thinks: "You are the only stupid thing here. And shallow. And useless" ("162 Candles," 1.08). When Caroline asks if Matt (Zach Roerig) also thinks her shallow, he responds, "Is that a true question?" "I don't mean to be. I wanna be deep." "No offence, Caroline, but deep is not your thing." (1.08).

If we look deeper, however, Caroline is a neglected teen with low self-esteem who "believes she will never find a fairy-tale kind of romantic love."[21] Caroline is not clever like Bonnie or popular like Elena. She is the only child of a single mother, who works as the town's sheriff, and her father left them for another man. Caroline is no romance heroine; she is instead "the voice of normality" and "a mean girl who isn't mean, a shallow girl who wants things so deeply it hurts, and the voice on the show of every girl who's been treated badly, dismissed, or told a million times over that she's just not good enough – for a boy, for her friends, for her parents, or any of all of the above."[22]

When a handsome stranger flirts with her, Caroline stops sobbing to Bonnie and smiles. And while Elena falls in love, Caroline is charmed by Damon who will abuse and rape her.

The Sexual Emotions

Lust and love are part of our social emotions and part of social horror. In line with my biocultural approach I will examine sex and love from an emotions perspective, instead of from a psychoanalytic perspective. Sex is usually seen as a drive,[23] however, Frijda analyses it as an emotion, or more precisely, as one of eight emotions that all serve mating: "being attracted; being charmed; being in love; sexual excitement; sexual desire; lust; sexual enjoyment ... [and] love."[24] Out of these eight emotions, lust and love are often confused with each other, for example when Caroline, on hearing about Elena's night with Stefan, says, "You and Stefan *talked* all night? There was no sloppy first kiss or touchy-feely of any kind? ... What is it with the blockage? Just jump his bones off! Okay, it's easy: Boy likes girl,

girl likes boy. Sex!" ("The Night of the Comet," 1.02). To Elena, a date is for falling in love, and for Caroline it means sex.

Rather than see romance and serial dating as opposed stories, we will see them as strategies to handle the question of passing on genes. The first three—attraction, charm, falling in love—serve to bring two individuals together. The next four—excitement, desire, lust, and enjoyment—are carnal and serve to make individuals want to have sex. The last emotion, love, is complex and involves three behavioral systems, which Frijda says are "*attachment, caregiving*, and *sex*."[25] Love *attaches* you to someone for a long period, it makes you have *sex* repeatedly, and it makes you want to *care* for offspring. Love is found in many species such as geese, elephants, and humans.

Let us take a look at the sexual emotions in *Vampire Diaries*. Bonnie, Elena, and Caroline are attracted to Stefan. Attraction, says Frijda, is "almost like the reflex-like turning of the head"[26] when you see someone attractive pass by. It is "often a small and fleeting emotion. One just notices attractiveness like one notices a smell. Yet it is an emotion."[27] We are instinctively attracted to good-looking people (which, if you are a peacock, means having many eyespots). This is why every character in the paranormal romance is hot, whether they are good or evil. They all serve as eye candy. Being charmed and falling in love serve to lock on to a target. "Being charmed consists of appraising someone as a person who fits interaction with intimate and erotic implications," says Frijda, "[o]ne is charmed in the original sense of that word: one becomes subject to a spell."[28] To charm means flirting which can lead to falling in love. In animals, it is seen in courtship where males impress females with fluttering feathers and displays of beauty. Charming can be done with a glance. "Eye-play initiates flirting, and mutual eye-play seals it," says Frijda. "It can be understood as an expression of interest, but softened, toned down, to take away the threatening aspect that looking-at may have."[29] Stefan charms Elena and Damon charms Caroline. Stefan uses natural charm, and it is unclear if Damon compels Caroline with the vampire's mind control or uses natural charm too.

Stefan wants love, but Damon is using Caroline to close to Elena. However, Caroline also uses people to climb the social hierarchy. In the third episode, Caroline exits Damon's convertible and brags to her friends, "I got the other brother!" To Caroline, life is a competition. After dinner, when Damon wants a word with Stefan and asks if she will go with the dishes, Damon asks, "For me?" "Umm, I don't think so," Caroline replies, clearly immune to natural charm. *Then* Damon compels her (1.03).

The first three sexual emotions—attraction, charm, falling in love—serve to bring people together. The next four—desire, excitement, lust, and enjoyment—are carnal emotions that stimulate sex. It is an old convention in vampire fiction to mix the hunger drive and sex drive, as Stefan does when he explains to the newly-turned Vicki that her bloodlust is "hunger, blood, lust, it all blurs into one urge," but admonishes, "your choice defines who you are" ("Haunted," 1.07). Stefan is a humanized vampire who feeds on animal blood, so he doesn't have to kill, while Damon feeds on women and don't care about human lives. Frijda says the carnal emotions are distinct: *desire* is a feeling of readiness for sex ("being horny"); *excitement* is automatic and physical (erection or genital lubrication) and can happen with and without desire; sexual *enjoyment* can happen during and after intercourse; and *lust*, finally, is "the appraisal of someone as *my* sexual target ... in lust, the body comes into awareness as a body-to-be-touched, an instrument of penetration or of receiving penetration. It hums of it and aches for it."[30]

While love is a long-lasting and complex emotion, lust stimulates our senses, prepares for sex, and interacts with excitement and desire. Lust is when Stefan must control his vamp face when he makes out with Elena, and when Damon sniffs a pillow with Caroline's blood and flings himself at her with bloodshot eyes.

Abuse and Self-Confidence

Although the word "rape" is not spoken, there is a rape story in Damon's abuse of Caroline. When she wakes up in "Friday Night Bites" and tries to leave her bedroom, Damon blocks the door, and when she cries "please, don't, get away from me," he pushes her into bed. Later in the episode, Stefan says, "They are people, Damon. She is not a puppet. She doesn't exist for your amusement or for you to feed on whenever you want to." "Sure she does," Damon replies. In "Family Ties" (1.04) Damon takes Caroline to the Founder's Park Dance to use her to distract Stefan. Here, Elena notices bruises and bite marks on Caroline's neck and shoulder. "Did somebody hurt you?" "No, it's nothing, it's just ... Damon would kill me." "That is *not* nothing," says Elena, "did Damon hurt you?" "No, of course not, just leave me alone," says Caroline. Elena seeks out Damon: "There is something seriously wrong with you. You stay away from Caroline, or I will go straight to her mother, the sheriff," and she tells Stefan, "there are bruises all over Caroline's body, bite marks, and he has her all confused and messed up in the head." When Stefan tells Elena, he is handling it, she is furious: "Stefan, you should be having him arrested" (1.04).

Genre is crucial to our assessment of Damon's assaults. If this was a realist genre like the detective film or thriller, we would agree to take legal action, but because it is horror, we know the authority cannot settle scores. Horror is not about law, it is about the individual learning to manage aggression, so *you* can handle situations. At this point, Caroline is the old, self-absorbed and insecure Caroline incapable of saving herself. When Damon can't use her, he tries to kill Caroline. But Stefan has given Caroline a drink with vervain, a plant poisonous to vampires, and saves her.

Stefan compels Caroline to forget, and during the first season both Caroline and Damon learn empathy. Caroline starts dating Matt, and Damon changes from villain to antihero. After Caroline has a car accident, the rape story finds closure. To save her, Damon has given Caroline his blood. Vampire blood heals humans, but the evil Katherine murders Caroline, who awakens as a vampire. And now she remembers earlier events.

CAROLINE: I remember.
DAMON: What do you remember?
CAROLINE: I remember how you manipulated me, you pushed me around, abused me, erased my memories, fed on me.
DAMON: You're crazy.
CAROLINE: The memories have been coming back. In pieces.
DAMON: You can't remember. It's impossible. I mean, unless you're ... you're becoming a ...

Old Caroline wore clothes that made her appear soft and vulnerable and look like a sexual target. The new Caroline wears skinny black pants, a short leather jacket, has dark makeup, and a self-assured attitude. She smiles and flings Damon to the ground, a spectacle of postfeminist independence.

FIGURE 5.1 *Caroline (Candice Accola) can fling rapist Damon to the ground, now that she is no longer a weak human but a strong and an assertive vampire.* The Vampire Diaries: *Season 2, Episode 2 ("Brave New World").* © *Alloy Entertainment, Bonanza Productions, Warner Bros. Television, 2010.*

Managing Lust and Love

When we compare romance and serial dating, I find Caroline a more interesting character than Elena. Where Elena already is at journey's end from the outset, since she *is* beautiful, good, and popular, Caroline sets out on a journey of self-development and learning to be "deep." She is not searching for Mr. Right, but for self-management.

Vampire Diaries has, like *Ginger Snaps*, a humorous approach to the monstrous female body. Caroline seems more concerned with new veins in her pretty face than with the fact that she might be dead. Bloodlust is visible on the vampire's face with pulsating veins, bloodshot eyes, and protruding fangs, and for vain Caroline, it is worse to have one's looks ruined than be undead. We can recall Brown's admonishment to the single girl that she must *always* look glamorous. Caroline cries when she in "The Return" sees veins and fangs in the mirror (2.01). Later, unable to control her bloodlust when she hugs Matt, she runs away in shame. Damon is about to kill Caroline, because she cannot control her vampire body. "Why does this keep happening to my face? I'm hideous!" she cries. Stefan shows Caroline to breathe slowly and says, "look at my face." He makes blood run to his face, then wills it away. "When you feel the blood rushing you tell yourself that you are gonna get through this, that you are strong enough, yes, no matter how good it feels to give yourself over to it, you fight it off, you bury it. Watch me. It's the only way you're gonna survive this thing" (2.02).

The enhanced vampire senses and appetites demand that Caroline manage the sexual emotions, both lust and love and excitement and desire, so she can kiss a boyfriend without showing her vampire face. This is evofeminist management of sex: To be able to choose which emotions to show and which to hide, not to lie as such but to prepare for unexpected reactions.

With such self-control, *Vampire Diaries* takes a different route than *Twilight* and *True Blood*. Where Bella practices abstinence before marriage, and vampires in *True Blood* enjoy spanking sessions in sex clubs, *Diaries* holds out a fine line of emotional management, a balancing rope from which characters might fall but then climb back up on. Separating good from bad characters is that good characters have one love interest at a time, while bad characters use the sexual emotions to manipulate others. Critics saw *Vampire Diaries* as occupying the middle ground between teen abstinence and crazy kinkiness, a ground that reserves kinkiness for irony. "Look, dungeon boy, I am done being your little slave girl" Caroline tells Damon (1.08) and compels her first victim to say, "my husband likes to get kinky" (2.02) to explain the bite marks on the victim's neck.

The lesson in serial dating is that a woman must learn to manage attraction, charm, falling in love, excitement, and lust, or she risks falling

FIGURE 5.2 *Vampire Caroline (Candice Accola) cries, when she sees her new fangs in the mirror.* The Vampire Diaries: *Season 2, Episode 1 ("The Return")*. © Alloy Entertainment, Bonanza Productions, Warner Bros. Television, 2010.

prey to a sexual predator such as Damon. The adaptive response to sex and mating is not romantic love (which I am not pursuing here), but serial dating. The latter allows for things to be complex, and then learn from experience. After Damon, Caroline takes it slow with the next boyfriend, Matt. They break up as friends, after which Caroline dates werewolf Tyler in season three, and is involved with Klaus in season five. In season six, Caroline finally dates Stefan, who rejected her in first episode. And in season seven she parents children, magically giving birth to babies belonging to a murdered witch, and considers marriage to a man she doesn't love to give them a stable home.

Let me return to the sexual selection theory, which is used to link play fighting with males competing for females. When we understand horror as a dark stage that offers mental play fighting, we can view its emotional engagement from multiple perspectives. One is character perspective, where we engage with characters' emotions, experiences, and situations. Here, *Vampire Diaries* has two sexual strategies, romance and serial dating. From Caroline's perspective, hers is a story of learning to manage sexual emotions. She should not look for a Mr. Right, as in a romance story, but learn to understand her sexual emotions, so she is not fooled by a sexual predator and doesn't perform a manipulative sexual script herself. Her vampire body is not abject as in Creed's reading, nor is it glamorous as in *Twilight*, but is instead a body that brings change. Like the werewolf in the previous chapter I read as Malabou's explosive plasticity, a vampire, too, offers unexpected self-work. From a character perspective, *The Vampire Diaries* turns sexual selection theory inside out. Sexual selection does not have males competing over females, as in the love triangles in *Twilight* and *True Blood*, but has Caroline learning to maneuver social situations and manage the sexual emotions, which include both lust and love.

From a wider genre perspective, it is reductive and highly misleading to read horror as being "about" sexual selection. As I have argued, horror is edgework, and the edge is anywhere we face challenging emotions and situations. Thus, in social horror, the edge can be in everyday interaction with friends and family. From a genre perspective, the dark stage practices the management of emotions, not only specific emotions like sex or fear or disgust, but all emotions. And as I researched the sexual emotions, it struck me that two of these, love and falling in love, involve trust. Trust is rarely analysed in horror, yet once I started thinking about trust, I noticed that characters talk more about trust than any other emotion. Caroline's self-development, I discovered, has plenty of trust issues, and it is to those we now turn.

Trust, Pain, and Play

Trust is a study in its own right,[31] and my goal is not to analyse trust as such but, more specifically, to see how *Vampire Diaries* teaches Caroline to find trust and become trustworthy, like she learns to manage sexual emotions. Trust is a central theme in the show and it is interwoven with pain and deceit. We shall look at situations of trust between Caroline and her friends (2.03), with Caroline's mother Liz, with the werewolf Tyler (2.13), and with her father Bill (3.03).

I was unaware of the link between pain and trust until Caroline in season three is tortured by her father (Jack Coleman), who is a vampire hunter and wants to cure her bloodlust (3.03, "The End of the Affair"). She is rescued by her mother and boyfriend, and she forgives her father because she realizes he is doing this, because he loves her. She continues to trust him, and in "Bringing Out the Dead" (3.13) he dies trying to help her. Thus, the viewer understands that pain is not opposed to trust, rather, it is *part of* trust. We recall that play fighting calls for both pain and trust. I trust you won't hurt me more than necessary, and I accept pain in our mutual pushing, pulling, biting, and kicking, because I trust you to stop if I ask you to. Trust is thus fundamental to play fighting, where the aim is to push the individual's point of "too much" a bit further. A function of play fighting is to learn resilience and robustness, and it is highly adaptive to be able to endure pain.

But what is trust? Philosopher Annette Baier in "Trust and Antitrust" (1986) explains that trust is, to begin with, an innate emotion and starts with a child's trust of the goodwill of its parents:

FIGURE 5.3 *Caroline (Candice Accola) is tortured by her father who wants to "fix" her vampirism through conditioning with pain.* The Vampire Diaries: Season 3, Episode 3 ("The End of the Affair"). © Alloy Entertainment, Bonanza Productions, Warner Bros. Television, 2011.

> Some degree of innate, if selective, trust seems a necessary element in any surviving creature whose first nourishment (if it is not exposed) comes from another, and this innate but fragile trust could serve as the explanation both of the possibility of other forms of trust and of their fragility ... Trust is much easier to maintain than it is to get started and is never hard to destroy. Unless some form of it were innate and unless that form could pave the way for new forms, it would appear a miracle that trust ever occurs.[32]

Baier, thus, says basic trust is innate and is the first version of trust. It exists in a climate of good will and hope, and it springs from the assumption that the intention of the other is to do good. Later "cool" and contractual versions of trust builds on this innate and basic trust. Continuing Baier's discussion, Lawrence C. Becker in "Trust as Noncognitive Security about Motives" (1996) discusses "trust as an attitude" where we have "a sense of security about other people's benevolence, conscientiousness, and reciprocity."[33] Becker divides trust into three kinds: credulity, reliance, and security. The first is when we believe in someone (for example that they tell the truth), the second is when we rely on other people's competence (that the mechanic will repair your car), and the last is feeling secure about someone (that a caretaker won't abuse your child). Becker thinks that the last kind of trust, feeling secure, originates in the child's basic trust and forms the basis of trust later developing into different kinds of trust.

Let us turn to Caroline. When she becomes a vampire, all her emotions become enhanced and intensified. "When one becomes a vampire all your natural behavior becomes magnified," Stefan tells her. Stefan and Damon both have magical rings, that allow them to walk in daylight. However, the witch Bonnie will only make such a magical ring for Caroline, if Caroline learns to control her bloodlust. And the newborn vampire Caroline is to begin with still the old, insecure Caroline, only now with vampire powers. "So, you're saying I'm an insecure control freak on crack?" Caroline concludes. When she learns to control her bloodlust, Bonnie makes her a ring. However, the road to control one's behavior requires not only control over appetite and sex, but takes Caroline through the territory of trust.

Friends and a Climate of Trust

Because she is insecure and has low self-esteem, Caroline can be selfish and even lie to her friends. She has lost the innate trust of the child. But Baier says trust can be cultivated in "climates of trust affecting the possibilities for individual trust relationships."[34] One such climate is friendship.

Caroline's transformation into vampire enhanced those earlier mentioned insecurities that made her feel inferior. In season one, when she dated Matt (Elena's ex-boyfriend), she told Elena: "Matt is always gonna be in love with you and I am always gonna be the backup ... I am Matt's Elena-backup. I am your Bonnie-backup ... you don't get it. Why would you? You're everyone's first choice" ("There Goes the Neighborhood," 1.16). Caroline feels she is no one's first choice. She is the backup, the person you turn to when your best friend is unavailable. Her low self-esteem makes Caroline lack self-trust, and makes her weak and easy to manipulate. In season two, the evil Katherine uses Caroline in her schemes to bring back old vampires that have been buried. Katherine threatens Caroline to help her, and makes Caroline spy on her friends and report back to Katherine. "Let's not forget I killed you once and I can do it again."

Caroline now becomes manipulative and negative with her friends, instead of being supportive and helpful. "What is the ration of success for a vampire-human couple? I guess nil," she tells Elena. "Where is this coming from?" Elena asks. "I am just trying to be your friend." "Well do me a favor and stop trying" ("Memory Lane," 2.04). The friends guess that Katherine is behind Caroline's strange behavior, and they start to keep information from her and lie to her. However, Caroline then instinctively acts to save her friends. In "Kill or Be Killed" (2.05), while she is in the woods with Elena, she discovers Stefan and Damon are about to be killed by the town's vampire squad, led by Caroline's mother Liz. Caroline saves the brothers. In the evening she confesses her deceit. "I can't go home," Caroline cries, because she is scared Katherine will kill her. Elena says, "I have been so mad at you. But then I tried to put myself in your position. So I could understand why you would do this to me and to Stefan, because he's been such a friend to you."

Sitting in a couch in front of a fireplace, the friends embrace. Caroline has finally found the courage to help her friends and stand up to Katherine. And her friends were patient, and waited for her to find this courage. Thus, they will defeat Katherine, an older and stronger vampire, by creating and sharing Baier's climate of trust. In other shows—*Mean Girls* (2004, Mark Waters), *Gossip Girl* (2007–2012, CW), or *Pretty Little Liars* (2010–, ABC)—friendship is more conflicted, however, in *Vampire Diaries*, friendship is supportive, honest, and with deeper affects than family. The circle of friends is, in fact, far more fantastic than the supernatural forces.

Restoring Trust

Interwoven with Caroline's deceit of her friends, is the story of trust issues with her mother, Liz (Marguerite MacIntyre), who she blames for making her father leave them. When Liz asks, if Caroline has boy troubles, Caroline says, "If I want to talk about boys, I'll call dad. At least he's successfully dating one" ("You're Undead to Me," 1.05). And when Liz tries to care for her, Caroline snaps, "You're gonna pretend to be a mother?" Even Damon notices her acid remarks. "Why are you being such a bitch to your mum?"

When Caroline saved Stefan and Damon from the vampire hunters, she revealed to her mother that she was a vampire. Caroline has kept her new nature hidden until now. Liz at first rejects her vampire daughter. Damon and Stefan have locked Liz in the basement, waiting for the vervain Liz has taken to protect from vampire attack, to wear off, so they can compel her to forget everything. Caroline visits her mother in the basement cell, and these visits become the start of a new relationship between mother and daughter built on trust. "You don't have to kill?" Liz asks. "I want to. It's my basic nature now. But on a healthy diet I can control it." At the next visit, Liz looks at her daughter: "It's just that you've become this person . . . this strong, this confident person . . . You don't have to compel me. I will keep your secrets." Caroline recovers the love she had for her mother, and lets go of her blame and anger. "Mum, we never talked like this, ever, and today meant *so much* to me. I know I can trust you." However, to keep her vampire friends safe, Caroline still must compel her mother to forget everything, including this intimate moment between mother and daughter. "You will remember you got sick with the flu . . . you got better and then your selfish little daughter, who loves you no matter what, went right back to ignoring you, and all was right in the world."

Who Do You Trust?

It sounds simple to trust, however, *Vampire Diaries* shows that social life has situations where one must choose who to trust.

When Caroline discovers Tyler (Michael Trevino) is a werewolf (this is when his father dies and Tyler inherits the "curse"), she helps him adjust. She tells him she is a vampire, but she doesn't tell him about the other vampires in Mystic Falls, because vampires and werewolves are not on good terms and a bite from a werewolf will kill a vampire. Then Tyler's relatives, a pack of werewolves, kidnap Caroline. "You just stood there when they were going to kill us, you didn't *do* anything!" ("Daddy Issues," 2.13). "I don't know who to trust. You lied to me." Caroline is furious: "I lied to protect my friends. I lied to protect you." Tyler didn't know if he should side with his species, the werewolves, or his friends, the vampires. Caroline makes priorities clear: "You help your *friend*, that's what you do." Tyler was, like the old Caroline, untrustworthy. "It's too late, because we're not friends anymore," she tells Tyler. Caroline had shown Tyler trust and he repaid this by not helping her in return. However, Caroline learned about trust when her friends forgave her and created a climate of trust, and Caroline, too, will forgive Tyler and let him into the climate of trust. This is what friends do.

After Caroline is rescued, Stefan brings Elena and Bonnie over for a sleepover like in the old days. The image of three seventeen-year-old girls hugging, one a vampire, one a witch, and one human, and the vampire-hero-boyfriend watching, underlines how *Vampire Diaries* harnesses trust around today's new affective family, friends. "Trust of this sort [noncognitive] is not only a way of handling uncertainty; it is also a way of being, a way of going, in uncertain or certain terrain. It is one of many possible general structures of concrete motivation, attitude, affect, and emotion."[35] By putting friends before herself, Caroline becomes a caring person. She also transforms from moral patient into a moral agent. And she learns to accept risk and pain. Bernd Lahno in "On the Emotional Character of Trust" (2001) points out that trust means we accept risk and vulnerability:

> Risk is generally held to be a central characteristic of trustful interaction. In a trust situation, one person allows another to exercise a certain amount of control over matters that are of some importance to him. A trusting person is vulnerable. She is open to harm caused by the actions of the person being trusted; and, in trusting she intentionally accepts being vulnerable in this way.[36]

A trusting person is vulnerable. When we trust, defenses are down, and to be trustworthy we need inner strength so we don't fall apart when events go against us. A trustworthy person must be empathic but also robust. The old

Caroline was afraid, but the new Caroline risks her life. And where the old Caroline couldn't master pain, the new one can endure being shot with wooden bullets, sprayed with vervain, and calmly face the prospect of being tortured to death. "I'm not girlie little Caroline anymore. I can handle myself," she tells Stefan, after he rescues her from the werewolves (2.13).

Trust, Educational Torture, and Change

By having *a trusting attitude*, says Bernd Lahno, trust becomes more than an emotion; it becomes part of a situation. For example, we trust other people can learn and change, *even if the quality we hope for is not there yet*. This is what happens between parents and children, teachers and pupils, or between friends helping each other. Stefan trusts that Caroline can learn to control her bloodlust, and Caroline trusts Tyler can learn to control his transitions. We trust there is a "good core" in the other person: "There is some fundamental form of trust involved here, namely trust in the responsiveness and malleability of the pupil, trust in his good core and his capability to develop his person favorably if assisted in suitable ways. This sort of trust is at the heart of any genuine educational enterprise. It requires *a positive sympathetic attitude* toward the pupil as an evolving person" (added emphasis).[37]

It is, of course, a common situation in horror that the heroine is deceived by someone *pretending* to be trustworthy, like a serial killer. Trust is often invoked in horror as its lack, untrustworthiness, or when *not* to trust. However, in Caroline's story the point is to learn trust. And I want to discuss a final example of trust, which I call educational torture. It is when someone tortures another, not to be cruel, but to achieve a positive change in the victim. Thus, the torturer has goodwill towards the victim and trusts the pain inflicted will lead to a positive change. We find an example in season three, where Caroline is tortured by her father.

In season two, Caroline has begun to change and feel more trust. She has shared her vampire secret with her mother, and she dates Tyler, even if a bite from a werewolf would kill her. In "The Birthday" (3.01) Caroline sleeps with Tyler, but as Caroline leaves his house, Tyler's mother Carol shoots her with vervain. Carol is, like Liz, part of the town's group of vampire hunters. Carol knows about vampires, but not about the werewolves. Carol tells Tyler that Caroline is "a prostitute" and "you can't be with her. She's a monster." Then Tyler makes her watch him transition into werewolf and when she understands that her son is a monster too, Carol phones Bill, whom she has handed Caroline over to. "Don't feel guilty," Bill (Jack Coleman) tells her in "The Hybrid," "they're not human. They're monsters" (3.02).

In "The End of the Affair", Bill has Caroline strapped in a steel chair in a dungeon room equipped with vervain in the ventilation system and an opening in the roof to let sun in. He wants to "fix" her with pain. "I am conditioning you to associate vampirism with pain. In time, the thought of human blood will make you repress your vampire instincts completely." Without her magic ring, Caroline's wounds don't heal. "Please stop, I won't hurt anyone, I swear. I can handle the urge," she begs. The show playfully uses the torture porn trope of a dark torture room and a blonde female victim in a chair, like Whitney in *Hostel 2*, who dies begging for mercy. However, Bill is not a perverted sadist, he is a loving father who wants what he thinks is best for his daughter. "Daddy, you can't change who I am." "Yes, I can."

When Liz saves Caroline, she tells Bill, "that's our daughter in there. She looks up to you and loves you." "Then she'll trust me to do the right thing," he responds, "not because she is a monster, but because we love her." Bill's motive is educational, to change his daughter for her own good. He assumes she trusts him. Yet, the two don't share the vision of what is best for Caroline. Caroline has learnt to be a good person from her friends, and her mother has come to respect and accept the new Caroline. The new Caroline is strong enough not to fall apart under torture. In fact, it only makes her stronger. In time, Bill will change and learn to see the world from Caroline's perspective. What is intriguing about the torture is that everyone sees it as excusable because it is done in good faith. In the evening Liz comforts Caroline:

LIZ: Honey, your dad ... all our families, we have beliefs that have been passed on in generations and we were taught never to stray from them.
CAROLINE: You did.
LIZ: *You* taught me to look at things in a different way.
CAROLINE: I just thought he [her father] was the one who got me.
LIZ: He did.
CAROLINE: Mum. Thanks for believing in me.

On one level, the acceptance of torture is, of course, problematic. It is acceptable to torture a person if it is done in good faith to achieve a positive change in the victim. Thus, the show repeatedly uses pain for emotional education, which returns us to the question of horror as mental play fighting. Bill tortures his daughter to condition her to repress her bloodlust. Caroline forgives him because his motive is to make her change. Torture functions, like in the action movie, to test stamina and make the victim stronger.[38] The action hero proves his masculinity by enduring pain, and Caroline, similarly, shows her strength by enduring pain.

Season three has several scenes with educational torture. Thus, Stefan's vampire friend Lexi in "Ghost World" (3.07) teaches Elena how to use torture to make Stefan flip his humanity switch back on, so he will stop being evil and return to his old humanized vampire self. And Caroline in

"The Ties That Bind" (3.12) asks Bill for help to release Tyler from the sire bond binding him to Klaus. To be released, Tyler must learn to transition at his own will. However, transitions are painful, and the only way to be released from the sire bond, is to bear the pain willingly. When Tyler complains the pain is unbearable, Bill says, "You asked for my help. This is the only way. How badly do you want it?" And when Caroline can't watch Tyler in pain, Tyler and Bill tell her to leave if she "can't handle it." Pain hurts but makes a person stronger. The ability to endure pain sets you free, like Tyler is freed from his sire bond (3.13). And as long as intentions are good, torture is excusable. Bill, Lexi, and Elena torture loved ones, because they want to make them more humane and less monstrous.

The idea that pain is educational ties into play fighting. If it doesn't hurt, you are not play fighting properly. And Caroline forgives her father, and in "Bringing Out the Dead" says, "You're the strongest person I know." Before Bill dies, he acknowledges his daughter's self-development: "I love you. You're strong. You're beautiful. You're good. And even after everything that has happened to you, you are exactly who your mother and I hoped you'd grow up to be."

The Doubling of Choices

Although the show was called "a resolutely teen text," it was popular with adult viewers too. *Vampire Diaries* outlived the *Twilight* film series and the *True Blood* television show, it was the most watched show on the CW network channel in its first four seasons, and it was the second most popular show with women between eighteen and thirty-four.[39] Also, the teen characters were played by adult actors:[40] Accola playing seventeen-year-old Caroline was twenty-two, Dobrev playing seventeen-year-old Elena was twenty, Wesley playing eighteen-year-old Stefan was twenty-seven, Somerhalder playing 25-year-old Damon was thirty-one, and Steven R. McQueen playing Elena's fifteen-year-old brother Jeremy was twenty-one.[41]

One explanation for the show's success might be the two narratives I have outlined, romance and serial dating. The latter is a story about learning to change so one can adapt to a group and to society. Also, Caroline's development from vain and shallow to become empathic, trustworthy, and robust, appeals not only to teens or fans of paranormal romance. In her discussion of *Vampire Diaries*, Ann Thurber points to the use of doublings: There are two vampire brothers, Elena is Kathrine's doppelgänger, and at one point, Damon reads the *Twilight* novel and says he prefers Anne Rice (author of *Interview With the Vampire*), thus creating a textual doubling.[42] To these we will add two sexual narratives, romance and serial dating. Thurber reads these doublings as a doubling of choices. Comparing strong and evil Katherine to the weaker but good Elena, Thurber asks, "is it possible that these conflicts are not conflicts at all, but merely a portrayal of women who can be both one way and another simultaneously," and concludes "Elena and Katherine must represent choices and agency."[43] Thus, rather than read the doubling of choices as a strategy to reach teen as well as young adult audiences, we can understand the doublings as, simply, a multiplication of choices and possibilities for emotional engagement. We are not limited to a single protagonist or a single plot, but have multiple options.

I want to return to the meaning of "teen text." Adolescence is conventionally viewed as a liminal phase, where the adolescent moves from one life stage to another. However, *every* life stage is liminal in the sense of changing from one phase to another. Erikson links each life phase to a psychological development, which he calls a crisis. The crisis in adolescence is a lack of shared values and experiments with identity.[44] This behavior—experimenting with identity, life styles, and values—is today the life style of what Arnett calls "emerging adults." Emerging adulthood is the phase from being legal adult (in most countries at the age of eighteen) and commitments like marriage or children. Since Erikson formulated his theory, the median age of marriage has risen from twenty-one for women and twenty-three for men in the US in 1970, to twenty-seven and twenty-nine for women and men in the US in 2013.[45] In 1970, thus, individuals went almost directly from adolescence to marriage. Today, however, marriage and parenthood come more than a decade after adolescence, and in Denmark the median age of marriage in 2014 was thirty-two for women and thirty-four for men. Today, emerging adulthood is about fifteen years in most Western countries.

It is said we experiment as teenagers, however, Arnett says we experiment more in emerging adulthood. There are "three main areas of identity exploration: love, work, and world views."[46] When asked in surveys, emerging adults answer they don't feel like adults; they feel they are learning to become adults. They are learning "*individualistic qualities of character*" and "*accepting responsibilities for one's self* and *making independent decisions*" (emphasis in original).[47] Emerging adulthood is where we try out possibilities. "Emerging adulthood is very much a transitional period leading to adulthood, and different emerging adults reach adulthood at different points ... this heterogeneity makes emerging adulthood an especially rich, complex, dynamic period of life to study."[48] The experiments with identity we think of as typical of the teenager, is today characteristic of later life phases too. What Erikson saw as an identity crisis is, perhaps, not a crisis, but an openness to change, a readiness for self-development. This reminds us of the SYF from the previous chapter.[49] The SYF is a single young female who prefers friends to a nuclear family, and Mr. Right For Now to a Mr. Right. Caroline can, like werewolf Elena in *Bitten,* be a SYF.

As said, we think of adolescence as "liminal," however, liminality can have a wider meaning. Liminality comes from Latin, *limen*, "threshold." In myth, liminal beings cross thresholds and borders, like the centaur Chiron, who is half man and half horse, or the vampire, who is both dead and alive. In this sense, liminality is not a phase, but a state of transgression. Erikson thought the crisis in adolescence is to become a "numinous adult" who can care and be a role model.[50] To care and become trustworthy is what Caroline learns, however, I think these themes appeal to adults too. Perhaps to all ages. Erikson thinks values and identity become "fixed" and stable when we are adult, however, it may be adaptive that they stay flexible. To learn to manage one's emotions, both the sexual emotions and the emotion of trust, provides self-esteem, agency, and the freedom to make choices.

Adult

6

Disgust and Self-Injury:

In My Skin, Martyrs, Black Swan

I remember feeling extreme disgust when I saw the psychological drama *In My Skin* (*Dans ma peau*, 2002, Marina de Van). It is the story of thirty-year-old Esther who after an accident starts to self-injure, cuts pieces out of her skin, and eventually rents a hotel room to feast on her own flesh. I presented a draft of this chapter at an annual conference I often attend and, two years later, a German colleague approached me and said she vividly remembered my presentation and asked how I could *stand* working with such material? Truth is, I find *In My Skin* as troubling as my colleague. So, how can I claim it is good to be extremely disgusted?

Until now, I have argued that horror's dark stage provides emotional engagement where we feel challenging emotions, face difficult situations, practice predator affordances, and can learn agency and empathy. In short, that when we play with fear, we grow stronger, braver, and wiser. My texts so far have been "nice" horror, in the sense that they are mainstream viewing. In this chapter, however, we enter darker territory. In fact, it is fair to warn that we are about to descend a pitch-black hole, from which there is no coming back up. This time, our heroines will not survive. Yet, even in the extreme section of the dark stage, where viewers want to break game and leave, my argument is the same: There *are* benefits, even to the extremely unpleasant experience of watching *In My Skin*. I couldn't forget the film, and when I saw Pascal Laugier's torture drama *Martyrs* (2008) and Darren Aronofsky's psychological drama *Black Swan* (2010), the three films sparked flames of ignition.

All three use self-injury, and all three work with the emotion of disgust. While they share elements, they are also different. *In My Skin* and *Martyrs* belong to the New French Extremity, while *Black Swan* is a mainstream Hollywood drama. *In My Skin* is the story of career-woman Esther, who becomes obsessed with her body and abandons ambitions at work to surrender to self-injuring. *Martyrs* is the story of Lucie, a child victim of torture, and Anna, her friend. After Lucie kills her tormentors and commits suicide, the people responsible for Lucie's torture capture Anna and torture her to death. Finally, in *Black Swan* the ballet dancer Nina returns to a habit of scratching when she becomes the new ballerina and lead dancer in "Swan Lake." Her role, the Swan Queen, commits suicide, and so, too, does Nina.

As said, this is extremely unpleasant territory and protagonists do not survive. So, to return to my colleague's question, why enter? After analyzing heroines who were children, adolescent, and young adult, we in this chapter enter the life phase of adulthood. Erikson says the existential crisis in adulthood is to become a numinous adult, who can care for and love other people, can create a family, and can contribute to society. If this crisis isn't solved, the individual will feel isolated, reject society's norms, and be caught in "a regressive and hostile reliving of the identity conflict."[1] We shall see that the self-injuring heroines fit this description of what happens, if you cannot solve the crisis of adulthood. Unable to fit society's gender script and unable to follow the meta-narrative, they turn to self-injury.

The films offer viewers an emotional engagement, that film and game scholars describe as a *feel-bad* experience and as *extreme play*.[2] Yes, our experience will be extremely unpleasant. And yet, as said, there are benefits. By taking the plunge, we do what Malabou calls to "accidentialize" oneself. It is to accept a violent change, a trauma, knowing you will become a different person. By exposing ourselves to extreme emotions, which in this chapter is the emotion of disgust, we become less disgust sensitive and less afraid. By exposing ourselves to the darkest of darkness, by accidentializing ourselves, we acquire the emotional resilience the protagonists lack. We grow new neuronal synapses that make us adapt to the strains of society, without having to cut our skin or eat our flesh.

I start the chapter by outlining three contexts for understanding extreme emotions, namely disgust, French Extremity, and self-injury. Next, I discuss disgust and self-injury in *In My Skin, Martyrs,* and *Black Swan,* asking what emotional engagements the films offer and how we can interpret these extreme experiences.

Brace yourself. We are going down a dark rabbit hole.

Disgust

While the auto-cannibalism of *Inside My Skin* is extreme, *Black Swan* uses disgust with more restraints, yet to equal effects. The film is aesthetically beautiful, but has brief scenes of shocking self-injury. One is when Nina washes her hands in the bathroom, after she has been announced as the new ballerina at a grand gala. She inspects a left middle finger which has a nail root. She rubs her skin, grabs a firm hold of a skin edge, and slowly pulls a

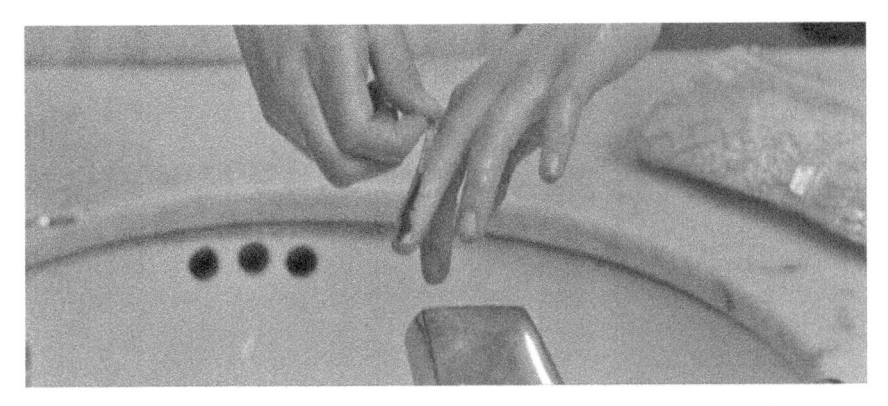

FIGURE 6.1 *Nina (Natalie Portman) pulls the skin off her finger in* Black Swan, *a self-injury that takes place in her imagination.* Black Swan *(2010, Darren Aronofsky). © Fox Searchlight Pictures, Cross Creek Pictures, Protozoa Pictures, 2010.*

FIGURE 6.2 *Nina (Natalie Portman) cringes and makes a universal "disgust face" when she self-injures.* Black Swan *(2010, Darren Aronofsky). © Fox Searchlight Pictures, Cross Creek Pictures, Protozoa Pictures, 2010.*

two-inch long strip of skin from the finger, while she grimaces in disgust and pain. The camera cuts from a close-up of her face to close-up of the finger, then back to her face. Even now, putting the scene into words, I cringe from the memory.

To cringe is a universal response, and disgust is one of our six basic emotions. It is an aversive emotion that serves to protect us against corrupt foods and contagious things. It has a facial expression called *the gape face* where we wrinkle our nose to block foul smell, open our mouth to vomit, and pull back in revulsion. Even people born blind have a gape face. fMRI images show disgust is active in the anterior insular cortex of the brain, a section that processes smell and taste and is called the gustatory cortex. Fear and anger are associated with the amygdala and trigger a fight-or-flight response that make us act. Disgust, in contrast, slows the heartbeat and causes revulsion.[3] We don't think about how to respond, because there is only a single response, *disgust*.

Although it is a basic emotion, it is unique to humans. Philosopher Rachel Herz in *That's Disgusting* says, "[e]ven chimps and gorillas that appear to share all our other basic emotions do not exhibit facial expressions or behaviors that anthropologists equate to disgust in humans . . . animals will react to foods that taste bitter and steer clear of foods that have made them sick in the past, but they do not experience emotional disgust."[4] While disgust is found in all cultures, and even blind people have a gape face, it nonetheless seems disgust must be learnt. The study of feral children shows that they, like animals, do not know disgust.

Disgust is a vast topic, but to summarize, scientists distinguish between *core disgust* and *moral disgust*. Core disgust is the same across cultures, while what is morally disgusting differs from one culture to another. Psychologists Jonathan Haidt, Clark McCauley, and Paul Rozin (1994) have analysed which objects people find disgusting, and found seven categories: Certain foods; body products; certain animals; sex; wounds (which they call "body envelope violations"); death; and hygiene. The first three—food, body products, and "those animals that are associated with spoiled food or body products, e.g., cockroaches, rats, flies"[5]—belong to core disgust, but the other four are learnt from one's culture. Haidt et al. speculate core disgust evolved into "a broader form of disgust we call *animal-reminder disgust*" (emphasis in original).[6] Animal-reminder disgust reminds us that we are animals: We eat, excrete, have sex, bleed if we are cut, and our body will decompose and die. They call this "the terror management theory," because things that remind us of our animal nature are terrifying, and disgust protects us from our terror.[7] For example, an animal would not react with disgust to a wound, but Nina's face shows she is disgusted by the wound on her finger. Not because it hurts, but because wounds "are direct reminders of the fragility and animality of our bodies."[8]

Why did we develop disgust, if animals live without this emotion? Evolutionary theory suggests core disgust evolved into moral disgust, because it can protect us against a wide range of things that are dangerous to us in our culture. Through cultural co-option, the response of aversion to what can harm our body is transported into what can harm us socially. Where core disgust serves to keep us in physical health, moral disgust serves to avoid moral corruption and its function is to detect a breach on society's moral boundaries.

Core disgust is about health, and moral disgust about social behavior. Hygiene researchers Valerie Curtis and Adam Biran (2001) say moral disgust teaches us "aversion to social parasites" and that "avoidance of the perpetrator is a helpful reaction, one which may also serve to punish and ostracize the parasite."[9] In their study, people reported that "certain categories of 'other people' [and] violations of morality or social norms" were disgusting.[10] Other people may not pose a physical danger, but if they reject our social values, such people are a moral threat. Now, returning to Nina and the self-injurer, wounds trigger disgust according to the animal-reminder theory, and for a woman to self-injure is even more disgusting, because she rejects the sanctity of female beauty. *She* is morally disgusting.

Horror offers plenty of simple core disgust in the form of rotten zombies, slimy aliens, and dirty torture dungeons, however, in this chapter disgust is moral and complex. According to Hungarian philosopher Aurel Kolnai, disgust "is at work in creating and sustaining our social and cultural reality. It helps us to grasp hierarchies of value to cope with morally sensitive situations, and to maintain cultural order."[11] Disgust teaches good and bad behavior. What is good and bad varies from culture to culture, and the more complex society is, the more complex are its rules of disgust. "We have to learn what is disgusting," says Herz.[12]

So, we will bear in mind not only the wound on Nina's finger is disgusting, but she is too, because she inflicts the wound on herself. The protagonists in this chapter are morally disgusting, which is a further reason these films feel so extremely unpleasant.

New French Extremity

The second context is New French Extremity, of which *In My Skin* and *Martyrs* are part. New French Extremity was coined by the Canadian art critic James Quandt in 2004 to describe a group of French films that included drama, horror, and the thriller. French Extremity starts in 1991 with Gaspar Noé's *Carne*, and includes *Irreversible* (*Irréversible*, 2001, Noé), *Trouble Every Day* (2001, Claire Denis), *In My Skin*, *Frontière(s)* (2007, Xavier Gens), and *Martyrs*. These films share three elements: A theme of *flesh* which involves torture, transgressive sex, and cannibalism; *extreme emotions* of disgust, terror, and pain; and shock aesthetics to make the audience's emotional dialogue *unpleasant*, which is why the development is also called *cinéma du corps* (Palmer, 2006), "cinema of sensation," and *cinéma brut* (Palmer, 2011).[13]

New French Extremity, thus, wants the audience to experience extremely unpleasant sensations and emotions, it is a cinema "determined to break every taboo, to wade in rivers of viscera and spumes of sperm, to fill each frame with flesh, nubile or gnarled, and subject it to all manner of penetration, mutilation, and defilement ..."[14] Tanya Horeck and Tina Kendell (2011) describe the movement as an "embodied dialogue that takes place between film, spectator and context, and which has to be sensed before it can be understood."[15] Quandt rejects the movement as "absurd, false, and self-important ... a failure of both imagination and morality [and] a narcissistic response to the collapse of ideology."[16]

The directors replied, that their films were a "terrorist attack" to "rape the spectator into independence."[17] This is a well-known avant-garde strategy with the idea, that unpleasant art can make us question society's norms. We return to this strategy in the discussion of *In My Skin*. Central here is the intention to touch and upset the viewer. And many viewers did feel violated and assaulted, and left cinemas. Reviewer David Edelstein (2006), who coined "torture porn," included French Extremity in his discussion of torture in American and European film. Edelstein wrote about the eight-minute-long rape scene in *Irreversible*: "For a while I stared at the EXIT sign, then closed my eyes, plugged my ears, and chanted an old mantra. I didn't understand why I had to be tortured, too. I didn't want to identify with the victim *or* the victimizer."[18] *Irreversible*, like *In My Skin*, is beautiful and brutal art cinema that raise complex questions to do with identity and ethics. Quandt and Edelstein, however, suspected these extreme viewer experiences could harm us. "Fear supplants empathy and makes us all potential torturers, doesn't it?"[19]

While these films undoubtedly are unpleasant, the intention is not to turn audiences into torturers, but, in contrast, to make us feel, reflect, and see with new eyes.

Self-Injury

The last context, before we turn to Esther, Lucie, and Nina, is the female self-injurer. In medical terms, she is "someone who repeatedly has inflicted superficial injuries or mutilations to herself without suicidal intentions," and her act is "understood as a response to an increasing feeling of inner tension which is brought to an end by the injury."[20] Scientific discourse oscillates between seeing self-injury as a meaningful reaction to psychic pain or seeing patients as "manipulative" and using "emotional blackmail" because they "need to be in the spotlight," says doctor and developmental psychologist Sarah Naomi Shaw.[21] Clinicians report that self-injury is extremely upsetting: "Of all disturbing behaviors, self-mutilation is the most difficult for clinicians to understand ... the typical clinician ... is often left feeling some combination of helpless, horrified, guilty, furious, betrayed, disgusted, and sad."[22] Feminists point out that the popular image of the self-injurer as a young female "delicate cutter" (with surface wounds) ignores that almost half are men, and depicts self-injury as almost synonymous with the stereotypical definition of femininity as masochistic, soft, superficial, and weak.

Self-injury is also an active communication with and on the body. Swedish art historian Hans T. Sternudd has analysed 6,000 images of self-injury on the Internet as semiotic messages. Most images are close-ups of skin. A quarter of these has words like "FUCK OFF," "I HATE U/ME," and "FTW." "The skin becomes the arena on which discourse is formulated," says Sternudd, and "anger is not the expression of a passive victim; it comes from somebody that is putting up a fight."[23] The scars manifest the psychic pain that marks the cutter as different: "Cutting is separating the body from the body of others . . . it pushes people away," and to "deliberately cut and thereby often permanently disfigure the skin is also a very strong rejection of the hegemonic ideals of beauty (especially for young women)."[24] The self-injurers on the Internet are not passive. They communicate. On blogs, self-injurers report being conflicted about feeling proud and ashamed of their scars. They want "to be for real, to be authentic."[25]

In My Skin: Fascinating Flesh

The films in this chapter are concerned with questions of self, identity, and existential discomfort, and belong to identity horror. Where texts, until now, had monsters and external threats, two of our films here have no external danger. The danger is inner tension and self-inflicted injury. The core aggression of identity horror is angry aggression, self-defense. And when attack comes from within, self-defense becomes, paradoxically and difficult to understand, self-destructive.

Such paradox is at the heart of *In My Skin*, which opens with a piano soundtrack and beautifully composed split-screen images of a big city. The camera zooms from skyscrapers to an apartment with Esther (de Van) who is without a steady job. "I want to live in luxury," she jokingly tells her boyfriend Vincent (Laurent Lucas). Her friend Sandrine (Léa Drucker) takes her to a party where Esther accidentally injures her leg, but flirts and drinks before she sees a doctor. "Does this leg really belong to you," he wonders, "can't you feel the pain?" Flirting lands her a job at Sandrine's work.

Esther advances to Junior Project Leader, superseding Sandrine who has been there five years. And now Esther suddenly turns cold towards her friend. At a business dinner Esther dissociates her arm from her body and sees it lying, cut off, on the dinner table. She stabs her arm with a fork to feel if it is still there, and after the dinner she rents a hotel room where she cuts and eats her skin. She covers up the self-injury by faking a car accident. Vincent wants them to move in together, but after a discussion over where Esther's wounds come from, she again rents a room and self-injures. The film's final image turns dizzyingly round, and zooms from a close-up of Esther's mutilated face to an image of an unmoving woman.

De Van offers no background and no explications. Esther says, she can't feel her wounds, but when Vincent touches her lightly, she jumps. "How is this possible?" he wants to know. "You are always looking for meanings," she rejects him. Sandrine, too, is concerned at first, "you should go see a doctor, get some pills." The doctor, after dressing the wound, tests for abnormal insensitivity, but nothing is wrong. The viewer knows nothing about Esther, yet we are intimate observers of her injuries and perfectionism: "At three words an hour that will take forever," Vincent comments on her typing. We also see how she manipulates people by flirting, exploiting friends, and lying to Vincent. Esther's manipulation is mirrored by the film's aesthetic manipulation in cleverly composed images. Into ordinary situations, such as credit card withdrawals, are inserted pieces of skin (for example pieces of skin next to the credit cards in Esther's purse) to remind us of the breaches on her body.

Instead of explaining Esther's psychology, the film takes us to her body. What starts as a story about an ambitious career woman ends as a split-screen image of a bloody body, mirroring the split-screen images from the start. De Van wants the audience to feel Esther's sensations. The camera meticulously registers her facial expressions as she self-injures. When she discovers her first leg wound, she delicately fingers the flesh and, although she does not seem to be in pain, instinctively reacts with disgust. The actor's face shifts from strong to light disgust, then pain, curiosity, and, last, an empty stare. The wound has been "emptied" of emotions.

During work hours, Esther goes to the basement to self-injure. Her office has a view of a clear blue sky, but the basement wraps her body in soft darkness. She takes off her pants and squats, her body lit in chiaroscuro, like Rembrandt's 1632 painting "The Anatomy Lesson." Like Rembrandt's painting, the image shows the examination of a body. Esther jabs a metal

FIGURE 6.3 *Esther (Marina de Van) self-injures in the basement, a scene which is beautifully composed and lit in chiaroscuro.* In My Skin *(Dans ma peau, 2002, Marina de Van).* © *Lazennec & Associés, Canal+, Centre National de la Cinématographie (CNC), 2002.*

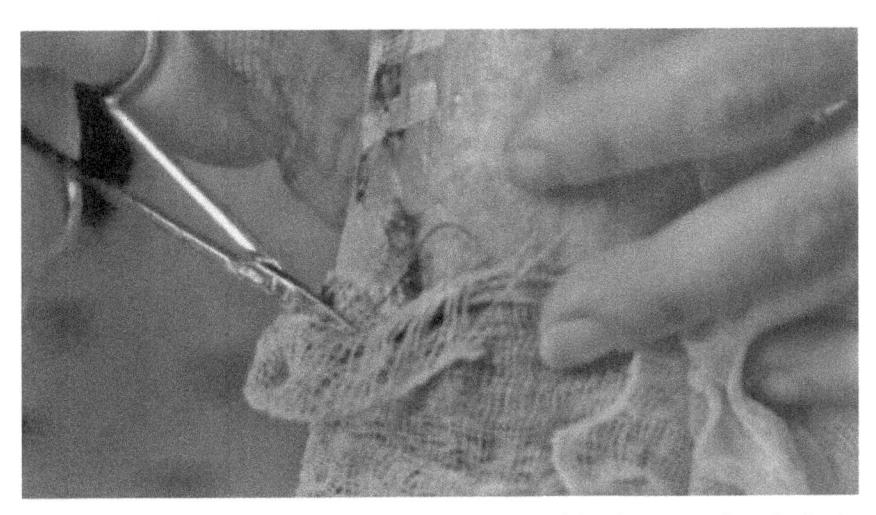

FIGURE 6.4 *Esther (Marina de Van) is fascinated by her wounds, which she examines and reopens.* In My Skin *(Dans ma peau, 2002, Marina de Van).* © *Lazennec & Associés, Canal+, Centre National de la Cinématographie (CNC), 2002.*

piece into old wounds and digs new wounds in her leg, tearing skin with a loud sound. This is extremely disgusting, but beautifully rendered. Emotions of disgust, pain, and ecstasy flicker across Esther's face as she gazes upwards, like Jeanne in C. T. Dreyer's *The Passion of Joan of Arc* (*La Passion de Jeanne d'Arc*, 1928).

Cut N Slash Transgression

Without explanations, we watch Esther's actions and ask why? She fingers wound edges, tears off gauze with puss and viscera sticking to fabric, rips open flesh, and with a pen draws a square on her skin which she cuts out, about two-and-a-half-inch wide. We read such scenes affectively, feeling but not understanding actions, and I found them nauseating, like my German colleague.

Esther hands her skin square, which she keeps in a makeup container, to the pharmacist. She asks how she can preserve the skin "smooth and soft." The visit transgresses the usual visit to the pharmacy, where people don't talk about their cut-out skin pieces. Such scenes have a surrealist ring, like Esther trying to have a conversation at the business dinner, while hallucinating her cut-off arm on the table. We may be too disgusted to notice aesthetic beauty, yet it is in the chiaroscuro lighting, in Esther's body dressed in delicate fabrics and soft colors to match her brown eyes and auburn hair, in her jewelry glimmering like the metal object she uses to cut skin. We can read the self-injuries as the "inner tension" of the cutter. Thus, tension would signify anxiety about social expectations at work, with friends, with Vincent, pressure to become a numinous adult who cares and contributes to society by creating something worthwhile.

However, *In My Skin* wants us to *feel* the self-injury and be voyeurs of intimate moments. In interviews de Van said her film did not have a feminist agenda but was "corporeal and not gender-specific."[26] It was based on a childhood leg injury with a "limb left horrifically wounded, the rough edge of a snapped bone protruding through its flesh and skin."[27] The scars became objects of curiosity and "my friends and I amused ourselves by sticking them with needles, because my skin had become numb here. I felt proud, but at the same time this insensitivity was frightening."[28] De Van doesn't want the viewer's sympathy, but she wants our full attention. She is a graduate of the prestigious Parisian film school la Fémis and was the muse of François Ozon, a central director in New French Extremity, and had starred in his *See the Sea* (*Regarde la mer*, 1997) and *Sitcom* (1998) and co-written several of his films. *In My Skin* is her debut film which she meticulously prepared for. She used an acting coach "to dissect her mannerisms, sustain her performance and re-interpret for her the physical nuances of the script [to portray] Esther in a kind of narcotized withdrawal that . . . does not seek sympathy from the viewer."[29] Esther's facial expressions should not explain, but merely reflect, feeling states arrived at through self-harm.

Yet, there is of course a meaning in such feeling states and self-injury. In "'Cut N Slash': Remodeling the 'Freakish' Female Form" literary scholar Inga Bryden (2008) discusses women's body modification. Bryden points to the metaphor of the body as house and the "cultural policing" of its borders to keep separate inner from outer. To breach borders creates ambiguity and "where the body's surface is marked by cuts and gaps becomes culturally-sensitive territory . . ."[30] The body as house is about "private and public property . . . the space of the subject and the space of the social. Trespass, contamination, and the erasure of materiality are the threats presented to the enclosed world."[31] The female freak challenges such boundaries. Where "normal" women police and uphold their body borders, the freak breaks them. And as Shaw and Sternudd note, a woman's self-injury rejects the West's ideal of female beauty. If the female body is a house whose interior is private, her exterior—that is, her skin—is public. To disfigure your face, the site par excellence of beauty and identity, is a radical rejection.

Self-injury confounds borders separating inner from outer, private from public, animal (visceral) from human (the culturally scripted body). It is disgusting because it breaches physical borders and reminds us of our animal nature. A woman's skin is *supposed* to be policed and kept in place. Esther's self-injury disgusts us because it violates social norms. It is provocatively deliberate with scars on her leg forming a symmetrical pattern. Sternudd suggests symmetric patterns are male strategies to master female flesh.

Cognitive psychologists like Baron-Cohen also think mathematics and symmetrical patterns are typical of the male brain, however, I am unsure about such a gendered reading. Esther's cuts may simply be strategies, neither male nor female, just strategies of revolt.

But revolt against what precisely? *In My Skin* refuses to present Esther as "sick." It makes us witness and share her feeling states in an emotional dialogue where we experience disgust, curiosity, fascination, excitement, pleasure, ecstasy, divine revelation, and dissociation, all inappropriate responses to self-inflicted wounds. The self-injury gradually dissolves Esther's identity and she becomes other, strange, empty. Yet she remains an enigma, and if self-injury feels disgusting, we recognize it as honest communication. But what is it *about*?

A New Ethics of Viewing

Norwegian film scholar Asbjørn Grønstad (2006) suggests French Extremity wants to show what is unsayable and unwatchable. Grønstad is discussing Catherine Breillat, another director in New French Extremity, whose investigations of women and sex in *Romance* (1999) and *Anatomy of Hell* (2004) caused walk-outs at cinemas, as did also *In My Skin*. Breillat said *Anatomy* "is about showing what is unwatchable," and rejected a Freudian interpretation: "To me Freud is the protector of bourgeois society: he assuages the symptoms so that society can continue unchanged."[32] Instead of supporting a bourgeois Freudian world view, New French Extremity calls for a "new ethics of viewing" which is an "optics of corporeal revulsion" employing a "conflict between the scopic and the tactile."[33] Tim Palmer, discussing *In My Skin*, says de Van wanted to "privilege eye and mind . . . to enter into [Esther's] perceptions and emotions to create a deeper association with her intimate and sensorial experience."[34]

But because sensations are so extreme, they also pull a viewer *out* of the emotional engagement, asking why this extremity? In his discussion of why spectators identify with morally bad characters in *The Silence of the Lambs* (1991, Jonathan Demme) and *Pulp Fiction* (1994, Quentin Tarantino), British film scholar Murray Smith (1999) turns to the Aestheticist and Decadent movement in the late nineteenth century and the works of Wilde, Baudelaire, and Poe. Murray says, "what is being repudiated by these Decadent or 'Baudelairean' films is not morality per se, but *moralism*."[35] The goal of a decadent provocateur is to reject the norms of society and encourage the individual's own imagination and expression:

> Aestheticism and Decadence underline the distinction between representation and reality, maximizing the space for the knowing play of imagination . . . Again Wilde is illuminating: "What is termed Sin is an

element of progress ... Through its intensified individualism it saves us from monotony of type. In its rejection of the current notions about morality, it is one with the highest ethics." In essence, this is a Romantic moral attitude in which the highest good is self-expression and self-realization through fearless experimentation ...[36]

In a Romantic view, sin rejects "monotony of type" and celebrates revolt and the individual. Following Smith's argument, *In My Skin* can be seen as Decadent and Esther's self-injury as a revolt against society's expectations that she be a career woman and a girlfriend. Yet, it is still difficult to understand. She has a male boss, who might represent "patriarchy," however, de Van rejects a gendered reading, and around Esther are friends and a boyfriend who she pushes away.

In contrast to earlier protagonists, who wanted friends in their social life, Esther rejects company. Her rejection is different than that of an adolescent. It is an adult's rejection of society, a refusal to be a numinous role model, a refusal to care about others. Esther cares about the skin square she keeps inside her bra, directly on her chest. She locks the door of her hotel room from the inside and leaves viewers no key, disgusted and bewildered, forced to find our own in to the film.

Martyrs: Third Wave French Extremity

Turning to *Martyrs*, emotions turn more extreme and the viewer's emotional dialogue still difficult to understand. If *In My Skin* is hard to watch, so, too, is *Martyrs*. New French Extremity started with *Carne* in 1991, *In My Skin* belongs to a second wave of the movement, and Pascal Laugier's *Martyrs* from 2008 to a third wave where films are conscious about their transgressive character. After his debut film, *House of Voices* (*Saint Ange*, 2004), writer-director Laugier was invited by a French company to make a film in the style of the popular American torture porn film. Thus, *Martyrs* is a successful commercial product sold to more than forty countries. And while it's strategy still is to "rape" a viewer with extreme emotions, *Martyrs* is also a meta-film about the viewer experience. It asks how much displeasure and violence *we* are willing to accept. It is identity horror, because the plot is concerned with attacks on the protagonist, and it is creative horror, because a viewer must do a lot of cognitive work to make sense of events, piecing together how and why.

Martyrs opens with a child (Jessie Pham) escaping from an abandoned factory, where she was held captive and tortured. Lucie grows up in an institution and becomes friends with Anna. At night, we see a monster attacking Lucie. The story then jumps fifteen years forward to a family in a villa. While the father has breakfast with the children—the son is eighteen, the daughter a few years younger—the mother finds a white mouse stuck in a water pipe in the garden. When she drops the rodent on the kitchen table, the doorbell rings. Lucie (Mylène Jampanoï) shoots the father in the doorway, the mother in the hall, the children in the kitchen and the bedroom. Lucie calls Anna, and while she waits for Anna to arrive, the monster, a naked and disgusting woman with pulsing veins and gray complexion, attacks. Anna (Morjana Alaoui) stitches up Lucie's wounds. The mother is not quite dead, but when Anna tries to save her, Lucie bashes the woman's head in with a hammer. "Why would you want to save her after what she did to me?" Then the monster attacks again. A reverse-shot, however, shows that there is no monster. Lucie is a self-injurer and the monster is in her imagination. "You never believed me. You think I'm crazy, like the doctors," Lucie says to Anna before she shoots and kills herself.

The story then takes a surprising turn. Anna finds a hidden entrance to a torture facility in the basement of the villa, where there is a victim, Sarah (Isabelle Chasse). Anna tries to stop Sarah self-injuring, when a crew arrives and promptly executes Sarah. Their leader, an old lady called Mademoiselle (Catherine Bégin), explains that they experiment with pain to see into the next world. The people chain Anna and beat her for weeks until she is delirious. They then cut the skin from her body, leaving only the skin on her face, and invite guests to celebrate Anna's "revelations" about the next world. However, when the Mademoiselle hears Anna's last words, the old lady commits suicide. The film ends with a text explaining "martyrs" is from Greek and means "witness."

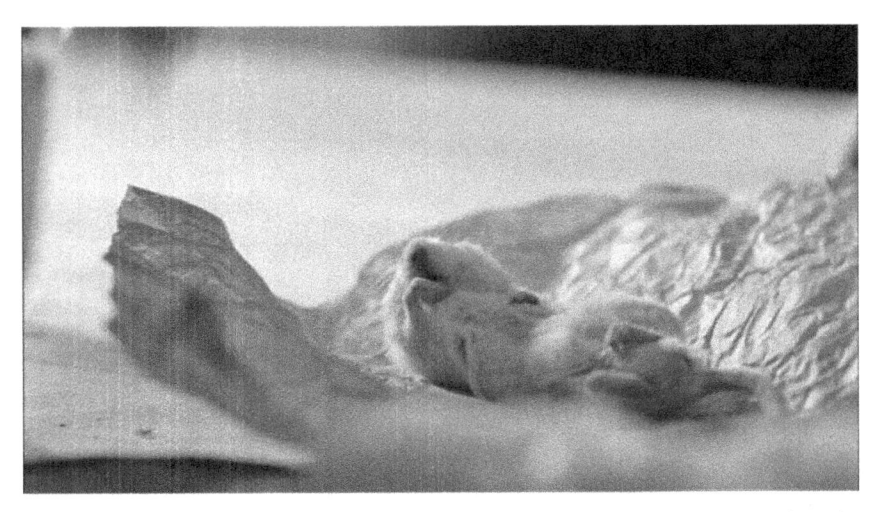

FIGURE 6.5 *The mother in the nuclear family finds a little white mouse stuck in the drain in the garden. A meta-reflexive comment on nasty experiments.* Martyrs *(2008, Pascal Laugier).* © *Canal Horizons, Canal+, CinéCinéma, 2008.*

Martyrs, thus, is about pain, about watching pain, and about the viewer experience. Like Edelstein, most people find it morally disgusting to be entertained by pain. It is "bad" to "enjoy" pain, and Nell uses horror films as example of how spectators take cruel pleasure from violence. However, it is misleading to describe the viewing experience of the pain and violence in this chapter's films as "pleasure." Instead, we will remember that play fighting has fun and pain, and pain is part of fun. The pain in play fighting is pain, and animals stop play fighting if they are in too much pain (like people leave the cinema if a film is too unpleasant to watch). Pain is *not* pleasure, but part of fighting for fun. Now, horror films can realize the events of a plot in many ways. However, in this context, I suggest that instead of calling pain "fun" or "cruel," "acceptable" or "immoral," we shall say pain can be mixed with other emotions, like black humor in *Hostel 2*.

Returning to *Martyrs,* the film is self-conscious about the use of pain and of playing with genre expectations. At my first viewing, I expected a realist torture porn film like *Saw* (2004, James Wan) and *Wolf Creek* (2005, Greg McLean). The film's poster and tagline suggest a realist torture porn film. But then, to my surprise, the torture-escape-revenge plot is over after only twenty minutes. Like Hitchcock effectively did in *Psycho*, the film shifts the viewer's engagement from one protagonist to another. And because a new protagonist usually survives, we expect Anna will too. Instead, *Martyrs* plays with pain and genre expectations, which causes confusion. Is there a monster or not? Who is the Mademoiselle? Will Anna escape the torture room? What is going on in this plot?

When Self-Injury is Comforting

Martyrs orchestrates pain at multiple levels, as the within-fiction pain of characters, and as the viewer's emotional experience of watching within-fiction pain. The levels interact. As we try to make sense of characters' sensations and actions, we simultaneously try to make sense of our own emotional experience and response. And the more confusing events are, the more we alternate between our System 1, the instinctive system, to System 2, analyzing and evaluating events before we choose how to interpret and react to events.

In the first twenty minutes, as said, the film "explains" the monster as Lucie's hallucination and her way to cope with trauma of capture and torture. Thus, where *In My Skin* formulates no reason why Esther self-injures, *Martyrs* says Lucie self-injures in response to childhood trauma. The disgusting monster keeps the trauma from overwhelming the adult Lucie. Rather than the full pain of trauma, she has the pain of self-injury. Now, it is beyond the scope of my discussion to go further into self-injury, which I will see as the three films' use of self-injury as an individual's response, or reaction, to society. I mentioned that science finds self-injury upsetting and perplexing. It is not at all clear what is going on. So, let us look closer at self-injury, which society regards as sick and disgusting.

We assume it is painful to self-injure, however, self-injurers say it takes away psychic pain and provides comfort. Thus, in a study of 240 female self-mutilators, psychologists A. R. Favazza and K. Conterio (1989) asked why the women harmed themselves. Responses showed that self-injuring "helps subjects to control their mind when it is racing (72%), to feel relaxed (65%), to feel less depressed (58%), to feel real again (55%), and to feel less lonely (47%)."[37] Only ten percent feel great pain and "23% report moderate, 38% little, and 29% no pain."[38] Self-injury makes psychic pain go away and comforts the individual. Similar effects are seen in animals, where ethologists report that animals can self-harm in response to isolation, trauma, and long-term captivity. Birds hack off feathers, and mammals lick skin until the flesh is gone or bite themselves to the bone in excessive self-grooming. Grooming relaxes the body by lowering the pulse and reducing anxiety, which is why animals and humans want to be comforted. When no one comforts us, we comfort ourselves. The excessive self-grooming in animals can be regarded as analogous to self-injury in humans. Both exchange one kind of pain—being caged or being traumatized—with physical self-injury. Excessive grooming and Lucie's self-injuries feel better than the alternative, the psychic pain of a social context or situation.

If we look at the social context of pain, the film moves from core disgust to moral disgust. At first, Lucie's torture and pain are represented with images of core disgust in the dirty factory, the monster with an abject body, and Sarah too looks abject with her tortured body. As said earlier, we avoid disgusting things, and we want to avoid dirty places and abject bodies. But Anna is in a fashionable, middle-class villa, and the torture basement fitted like a hospital. Things are "clean" and bourgeois, yet, here is pain and torture and a behavior which is morally disgusting. I suggest the Mademoiselle and her people, who look bourgeois, and use a nuclear family to torture women, represent a viewer's bourgeois values: villa, nuclear family, breakfast, things we welcome and do not find disgusting. Yet they do disgusting things that are unwatchable, and we are forced to use System 2 to reevaluate what we see.

The White Mouse

The scene where Anna is chained and beaten in the basement lasts eighteen minutes. Now, why do we want to watch this? The dead white mouse hints at an answer. Like a lab mouse, we are subject to an experiment. An experiment in pain and disgust. But unlike lab mice the viewer can leave any time. Horror is, after all, play.

Martyrs is what Thomas Elsaesser and Malte Hagener (2010) calls a mind-game film. This is a film that "draws attention to the fact that there might exist another level of reflexivity, less in the sense of the mirror or a *mise-en-abyme* construction and more as pure brain activity ..."[39] This "pure brain activity" is not the Romantic revolt, Smith discusses. It is rather a cognitive point of view, a deliberate and meta-reflexive shift from playing a game to looking at the game itself to understand what it means to play this game. In this meta-reflexive position, you can shift between perspectives and, for example, think about the rules and if you want to play at all. Let us look at the torture. Anna's torture begins when she discovers the hidden entrance to the torture facility and descends to the basement, like Alice going down the rabbit hole. Anne had until now thought Lucie killed a random family, but now she finds a state-of-the-art torture facility with a hospital theater, and a corridor with photographs of people in pain.

The Mademoiselle explains about victims and martyrs: "It's so easy to create a victim, young lady, so easy. You lock someone in a dark room. They begin to suffer. You feed that suffering, methodically, systematically, and coldly. And make it last." Her project is to create martyrs who "see" beyond the pain. "People no longer envisage suffering, young lady. That's how the world is. There is nothing but victims left. Martyrs are very rare." To become a martyr, Anna must be traumatized and tortured so she can hear voices. She is then taken to the hospital theater and her skin is removed. Her torture is also painful to the audience. I remember teaching at the University of Nuuk in Greenland where I was asked to select a horror film for a film club. I chose *Martyrs*, which I was writing about at the time, and the film caused several people to leave. French Extremity is notorious for this effect, and I felt guilty about inflicting the pain of watching on people, who were not at all prepared for such an extreme experience.

Again, why do we watch? In the story, the Mademoiselle talks about visions beyond the ordinary world, and she shows Anna photographs of victims, authentic photographs. One photograph from 1910 is of Chinese Lingchi torture, the so-called hundred cuts torture, and the literate viewer might recognize it as an image French philosopher Georges Bataille used in *Tears of Eros* (1961) to discuss dark eroticism.[40] The image shows a woman tortured at the stake in public with her breasts cut off and an upwards gaze, like Jeanne's gaze in *The Passion of Joan of Arc*. Another hint at French philosophy is that the Mademoiselle looks precisely like Simone de Beauvoir. So, Bataille and Beauvoir are "clues" in a New French Extremity film, clues used to ask if the viewer really wants to watch abused women and disgusting torture?

A mind-game film invites "pure brain activity," but what does this mean in the case of *Martyrs*? Should we "use" Bataille's eroticism and Beauvoir's feminism to debate misogyny? Is this, then, the "deeper" meaning of the film? Critics were divided if the New French Extremity elevated "the extreme into a sublime value" or was "merely basely violent."[41] In an article from 2011, Quandt discarded the films as nonsense and "philosophical affectations."[42]

The Feel-Bad Experience

Before leaving *Martyrs*, I want to add some further thoughts on the viewing experience. I cannot say if a viewer might "enjoy" the film, however, in my experience it was a traumatic and unpleasant viewing experience. So, why did I watch?

In an analysis of Lars von Trier's film *Dogville*, (2003) literary scholar Nikolaj Lübecker (2013) discusses what he calls a *feel-bad* experience. A film can make us feel bad, when opposite aesthetics are at work simultaneously. Lübecker draws on Antonin Artaud's theory of Theatre of Cruelty (pain as entertainment) and on Brechtian *Verfremdung* (affective immersion and cognitive distance to events). On the one hand, we experience an immersion in the film's painful elements and, on the other hand, we distance ourselves critically and cognitively from the very same events. Lübecker says, "these two aesthetics arrest each other,"[43] and put a deadlock on catharsis which is denied. In *Dogville,* this means the film's ending makes us feel bad and, "this results in a tension which aims to engage the spectator in ethical reflections."[44] Thus, Lübecker argues the feel-bad experience forces the viewer to reflect on ethics.

In another discussion of viewer experience, William Brown (2013) points to similar reflections. Lübecker suggests we experience tension between affective immersion and cognitive reflection, and this is conflicted pleasure. Brown, instead, analyses his viewer experience in *The Great Ecstasy of Robert Carmichael* (2005, Thomas Clay) as pure displeasure:

> ... it is a deeply unpleasurable looking, one that I am characterizing as revulsion. And revulsion encourages an ethical engagement with the film, because, by virtue of our watching the scene despite our lack of pleasure, we must ask why we are watching ... What I want to emphasize is that while I do not always *like* what I see, I do not turn away ... That is, I persist not out of a sense of viewing pleasure, but out of a sense of viewing displeasure that is far removed from the paradoxes of horror as a genre.[45]

Conflicted pleasure and pure displeasure are valid responses. Personally, I felt curious about the plot but disgusted about events. However, I disagree with Brown that viewing displeasure is "far removed" from the paradox of horror. From a play perspective, this is not a paradox, but the ambivalence of play fighting. It is when play is too painful, too much, and we go over the edge and fall into our trauma zone. When we play fight, that is the risk we take.

Black Swan: A "Delicate Cutter"

The three films of this chapter were international successes. *In My Skin* launched the career of de Van, who directed *Don't Look Back* (*Ne te retourne pas*, 2009) and *Dark Touch* (2013). *Martyrs* was exported to forty countries, remade in an American version (2015, Kevin and Michael Goetz), and made Laugier a horror auteur with *The Tall Man* (2012) and *Incident in a Ghost Land* (2018). But most successful was *Black Swan* with a budget of thirteen million dollars and a return of 330 million dollars. Natalie Portman won an Oscar and a Golden Globe for best actress, and the film was Oscar nominated for best picture, direction, cinematography, and film editing. There are surely many reasons for this success, but one is beyond doubt the portrayal of a protagonist who is a beautiful and gifted young ballet dancer, yet insecure, guilt-ridden, over-ambitious, a perfectionist, and a self-injurer. Nina perfectly captures society's stereotypical image of the female self-injurer.

Black Swan is a psychological drama which turns increasingly uncanny and horrific as Nina (Portman) becomes delusional and, ultimately, commits suicide. It is the story of a young woman plagued by performance anxiety, sexual repression, and guilt towards her mother. Nina is a dancer in a New York ballet ensemble and lives with her mother Erica (Barbara Hershey), although she is in her mid-twenties (actress Portman was twenty-nine). Nina gets the lead part in Tchaikovsky's Swan Lake, which ballet master Thomas (Vincent Cassel) wants to do in a new version—"we strip it down, make it visceral and real"—where Nina must dance both the White Queen and Black Swan. Her technique is perfect, but Thomas wants her to release the "dark energy" for the Black Swan. "The only person standing in your way is *you*," says Thomas, "lose yourself!" Realizing she is a virgin, he gives her a home assignment to touch herself. The pressure makes Nina return to an old habit of scratching, and she hallucinates encounters with her own doppelgänger and with others, and sees people reflected in windows, mirrors, corridors, and her dreams. She fears a talented new dancer, Lily (Mila Kunis), wants her part. As a premiere draws close, Nina fantasizes about self-injuries and having sex with Lily, and on the premiere evening Nina thinks she murders Lily when she instead plunges a mirror glass piece into her own abdomen. With her mother in the audience, and Thomas watching in the aisle, Nina hallucinates being covered in black swan feathers while dancing. "Why did you do it?" Thomas asks. "I felt it. Perfect. It was perfect," are Nina's last words.

As mentioned, despite almost half of self-injurers are male, society's preferred image of a self-injurer is a young woman. Barbara Jane Brickman (2004) describes the stereotypical self-injurer as a "young, attractive, even talented, and on the surface socially adept woman who generally appears 'normal' except when periodically overwhelmed by inner emotional tension."[46] When it comes to sex, she is "unmarried [and] ... either promiscuous or overly afraid of sex, and unable to relate successfully with others."[47] Nina fits this stereotype, and her self-injury fits science's view of male and female self-injury, which is described as, respectively, "coarse" and "delicate." Men "tended to strike themselves violently, causing much bruising," while women "either scratched, picked or dug at their skin, often causing bleeding."[48] The science literature divides cutters into "'coarse' cutters who cut deeply ... and 'delicate' cutters who make repeated, superficial, 'carefully designed incisions.'"[49] Nina is such a "delicate cutter," scratching her body.

The word "delicate" is significant. Brickman points out that the "delicate cutter" with a sick history of bulimia, anorexia, depression, and borderline personality disorder—disorders Nina suffers too—fits the Western myth of femininity and that "cutting is performed by females because femininity and cutting are nearly identical."[50] Our culture superimposes femininity over self-injury, a move that highlights young and female flesh instead of old or male flesh, and focuses on delicate cutting while ignoring coarse injury. If we return to Bryden and the policing of body borders, Western culture sees the female body as chaos to be mastered, and mastering as a male activity. Thus, "men do not think of themselves as cases to be opened up. Instead they open up a woman as a substitute for self-knowledge."[51]

What, then, does it mean to "open up" the female self-injurer's body? For de Van, the project is to make viewers ask *why* Esther behaves the way she does. For Laugier, the project is meta-reflective and not about the female self-injurer, but about the viewing experience. And for director Aronofsky, who hired three male play writers to write his plot idea into a screenplay, the project is to explore, critique, but also perpetuate a certain kind of identity, which is defined by striving, being perfect, and the beauty myth.

Ordinary Disgust

While *In My Skin* and *Martyrs* have implausible plots with extremely disgusting scenes, Nina's self-injuries reflect everyday behavior all audiences can relate to, because it is what everyone does: Pulling at a nail root, nervous scratching, biting fingernails, and so on. We know such sensations from our own bodies, and because they are ordinary and real, we at first think Nina's sensations are real too. I already mentioned Nina pulling the two-inch-long piece of skin from her finger in the bathroom. For me, this was a stinging yuck experience with the entire affect program of disgust kicking in. When I watched the film with my seventeen-year-old daughter, she told me the girls in her class found this scene the most disgusting in the film. Yet the act of pulling at a nail root is ordinary disgust compared to eating one's flesh or being tortured to death.

Brief scenes of self-injury, that look like ordinary body policing, becomes a pattern in the fabric of the psychological drama. When the camera reveals that there is no nail root and no wound on her finger, we understand there is a discrepancy between what Nina sees and what is real. The later self-injury scenes function similarly: Nina finds a small anomaly on her body—a rash, that her toes stick together—and she pulls or scratches with the camera cutting between close-up of her body and close-up of her gape face. After the nail root, we experience what Hanich calls *disgust anticipation*, which means we feel a small degree of disgust in anticipation that something disgusting will happen. Thus, when Nina examines her body, the viewer feels slightly disgusted. Thus, we experience what it feels like to have a perfect body, yet constantly police its borders because the body may anytime become "opened" and become disgusting.

Nina's self-injury, at a first look, looks deceptively like the ordinary work women do when they police their bodies. Here is no need for a psychiatrist, Nina is just being too vigilant. Her policing is understandable, yet too much, which is why the mother reproaches Nina, "you have been scratching yourself, you still have that disgusting old habit. Jesus Christ, I thought you were done with this, Nina ... I'll dig out that expensive cover-up, we still have some."

"To Beauty"

Nina's self-injury is about beauty and perfection, and about tooth and nail competition. Let us return to the gala when Nina is in the bathroom. This is after Thomas gave a speech saying goodbye to the old ballerina, Beth (Winona Ryder), and welcome to a new, Nina: "As we all know, every great career has to come to an end. But as we bid adieu to one star, we welcome another ... The exquisite Nina Sayers. You'll soon have the pleasure of seeing her perform, but right now, let's raise a glass. To all of us, to Beth, to Nina, to beauty." Beth is furious. "He always said you were such a frigid little girl, did you suck his cock?" Nina responds, "not all of us have to." Later that night Beth walks in front of a car and destroys her discarded body.

Washing one's hands is a way to "cleanse" oneself of guilt, and Nina's self-injury is presented as a result of the pressure to be perfect and guilt about taking another's place. Self-injury is also an act of revolt because it lessens beauty and the value of a female body. "What is not culturally tolerable is for women to objectify and destroy their own bodies in ways that do not serve western aesthetics," says Shaw. "To wear the scars of self-injury ... is to make oneself ugly in this culture and to violate sacred beauty standards for women."[52] While Nina works hard at her technique, she simultaneously "destroys" the beauty Thomas toasted to.

Black Swan depicts hard work and practice as necessary to be a good dancer. But it takes more to be *perfect*. During training Thomas scolds Nina, "you shouldn't be whining in the first place. You could be brilliant. But you are a coward." When she says, she is sorry, he explodes: "Stop being so fucking *weak*!" To be perfect requires a *sacrifice*. After Beth's accident, Thomas tells Nina: "I am almost sure she did it on purpose. Because everything Beth does come from within. From some dark impulse. I guess that's what makes her so thrilling to watch, so dangerous. Even perfect at times." Perfection comes from a "dark impulse." The film doesn't naively share Thomas' idea of perfection as a mysterious impulse, but it nonetheless shows Nina's search for perfection *as* dark impulse, her dance on the brink of death when she commits suicide on the stage.

Unlike the other two films, *Black Swan* blames the mother for Nina's pathological behavior, showing Erica to pass on her own struggle to embody female perfection to the daughter. Erica gave up a career as ballet dancer to have Nina. Or did she? "You were 28," says Nina, hinting Erica was past the age of success. Erica is presented as depressed, over-protective, and smothering. She undresses Nina, cuts her fingernails, and treats her like a child. When Nina gets the role, Erica buys a cake. Nina protests her piece is too big and Erica is about to throw the cake out. "Don't! I'm sorry," says Nina. "I'm just so proud of you," says Erica and extends a hand with filling on the tip of a finger. "Mmmm," says Nina and licks her mother's finger, although she looks disgusted. You can lick a lover's finger or a child's finger, but a young woman cannot lick her mother's finger. It is inappropriate and morally disgusting.

Black Swan is ambivalent in its critique of the beauty myth. On one hand, the scene where Nina transforms into the Black Swan, all feathers and fluttering wings, is the film's visual climax and an extraordinarily beautiful scene. On the other hand, the sacrifice to embody the beauty myth and its perfection, is presented as leading to self-injury and, ultimately, suicide. Beth gave everything to be Thomas' "little princess" and ended broken. Now, as Nina says, "it is *my* turn." And she ends dead.

The Magic Circle and the Moral Circle

Let us return to the question my German colleague asked, why we should watch extremely disgusting horror. In Chapter 1, I mention sociologist Margee Kerr who explains people self-scare because they feel stronger and more confident after visits to extreme haunts.[53] Basically, *overcoming* your fears makes you less fearful. The same dynamic is the core of *disgust exposure therapy*, which is when people become less disgust sensitive by exposing themselves to disgusting objects. "Clinically, exposure therapy is done in gradual steps of learning how to relax, confront, and accept your terrorizing-repulsive trigger."[54] By slowly exposing oneself to disgust, you learn to stay in your response emotion of terror-repulsion, and control your instinct to pull back from the disgusting object. You become less disgust sensitive. Such exposure is the appeal of texts that heap disgusting things upon the viewer, like *Hostel* and *The Human Centipede* (2009, Tom Six), or reality shows like *Fear Factory*. Basically, their challenge is how much we can stomach, before we must break game.

Why, you may ask, is this relevant to women? Is there a feminist perspective on disgust and gender? Yes, I think there is. Social experiments show women are more disgust sensitive than men. Haidt, McCauley and Rozin say, "gender was the most powerful predictor" of disgust and that "the best demographic predictor of disgust sensitivity in our data was gender. Women scored significantly higher than men in each of our five samples."[55] Women are more easily disgusted than men are. There is no innate reason for this difference. We can speculate that society expects men to be more emotional robust than it expects women to be, and that men, therefore, self-disgust more than women, and so become less disgust sensitive. Social expectations about gender and disgust could explain why men watch disgusting horror films, that women avoid. As my approach is textual analysis and not qualitative data, I can only speculate if our socially constructed gender roles explain the difference in men and women's taste and choice in horror films.

The downside to women's higher disgust sensitivity is that we are more fearful than men: "Highly disgust sensitive people [are] guarding themselves from external threats: they are more anxious, more afraid of death, and less likely to seek out adventure and new experiences. Disgust appears to make people cautious not only about what they put into their mouths, but about what they do with their bodies."[56] To be *more* disgust sensitive than men means women are also *more* anxious. It is my experience that women dislike films with extreme disgust more than do men—at least, this is what I have heard people say.

I must underline, I am not saying men like being disgusted any more than women do. Rather, the point is that disgust is part of the meta-narrative of how men and women are, and how they ought to behave. When men practice to master extreme emotions, this is challenging, and perhaps it is equally challenging for men and women. I recently discovered research in games, that take players to the same dark place *In My Skin* and *Martyrs* takes viewers. Cindy Poromba (2007) discusses what she calls forbidden games or *brink games* that blur borders between game and life, playing and not playing, and take players to the brink of the magic circle. When we are inside the magic circle, we play, and when things turn too painful, play stops. But in brink games "the second-order reality nature of the game [that it is 'just a game']... makes possible a full-scale enactment of that which you might never dare if this was for 'real.'"[57] Poromba defines "brink" as "any extreme edge" or as a "critical point, esp. of a situation or state beyond which success or catastrophe occurs."[58] Thus, like when we do extreme edgework, the brink is where a player can touch trauma or fall into the trauma zone.

In a similar discussion of what he calls *rough games*, game scholar Markus Montola (2010) asked the players of the freeform role-playing games *Gang Rape* (2010) and *The Journey* (2010), about why they play these games where they enact taboo behavior of, respectively, gang rape and survival cannibalism. The players, who could choose between being rapist, cannibal, or victim, reported feeling "brainfucked" and shaking and crying. Montola calls this *the positive negative experience* because it is "unpleasant on a momentary and superficial level, but rewarding through experiences of learning, insight and accomplishment."[59] A player, who played the role of a rape victim, explained, "[I want to play] everything that transcends your body and will be a lasting memory. Not just a game, but will actually become something more." And a player, who played a rapist, said, "I want to get better at being with people. And I think a part of that is sort of also experiencing yourself better. In the terms of like discovering your limitations and where you can't go. And I also want to push myself."[60]

Conclusion

When we play a brink game or a rough game, or watch an extremely disgusting film, we push ourselves in the hope that, after a limited time where we are "brainfucked" and experience highly unpleasant emotions, we will be rewarded. The reward is our learning experience on the dark stage which sends us into the "dark parts of our minds."[61] This is not trying on emotions, like one trying on clothes and taking them off. We change.

As said, moral disgust functions to define moral behavior. Psychologists Gary Sherman and Jonathan Haidt (2011) say we do not mentalize people, if we find them disgusting, but instead treat them as objects. "To be deemed 'disgusting' and the object of revulsion, therefore, is to be imbued with negative social value, to be denied full mental life, and in extreme cases to be pushed beyond the protection of the moral circle."[62] To draw a moral line is not only a cultural, but also a gendered act.

There is not a single feminist meaning in the three films. By withholding explanation, *In My Skin* challenges a viewer to find one herself, and although de Van denied her film was about gender, I disagree. *In My Skin* challenges our beauty myth and the gender script. *Martyrs,* on the other hand, repeats the gender stereotype and is interesting because of its use of self-injury and an original plot structure, not because it challenged the gender script. *Black Swan*, finally, is ambivalent about female identity and beauty. It celebrates and exposes in one and the same gesture of death and delusion, when Nina commits suicide during her performance. Yet, together, the three films tell a story of disgust and self-injury as women's response to the meta-narrative. And here we find a single evofeminist meaning: When we watch, we widen our moral circle, we become less disgust sensitive, and we become less anxious.

7

The Maternal Myth:

Birth, Breastfeeding, Mothering

The maternal instinct, as a behavior that arises absolute and predetermined from its primordial genetic roots, is a myth.
MARLENE ZUK, *Sexual Selections*[1]

After having looked at child protagonists, adolescent werewolves and vampires, and young adult self-injurers, we arrive at the mother, a social role which belongs to adulthood. As we shall see, it is not easy to be a good mother. A review of Jennifer Kent's Australian indie ghost movie *The Babadook* (2014), about single mother Amelia and her six-year-old son Sam, described the film as, "[m]otherhood as demonic curse. A masterwork of darkness and shadow. Essie Davis is a force of mad nature."[2] Amelia (Essie Davis) struggles with grief after her husband's death. When she is possessed by a mysterious entity called the Babadook, she turns abusive and tries to kill her son. No, this is *not* how you should be a mother.

The mother is an old trope in horror and has since *Psycho* (1960, Alfred Hitchcock) been used to blame women for sons becoming serial killers. Also, Creed's analysis in *The Monstrous-Feminine* (1993) about the abject maternal and the castrating mother in films like *Alien* (1979, Ridley Scott) and *The Brood* (1979, David Cronenberg) explained the mother in horror as a representation of male fears about women's fecund bodies. In this view, maternal horror is not about real mothers, but about male fears. However, taking our cue from bioculturalism, we shall examine the mother in horror as a character that represents *real* mothers and motherhood.

To say the mother in horror is real is, however, misleading. What I mean is that she is an example of the mother script, which, like all scripts, is socially constructed. The mother script is a subscript of the gender script, and this is one of the basic scripts underlying almost all our scripts. The idea of the maternal is, like the idea of being a girl or a boy, woven into the fabric of everything we do. So, to be crystal clear, the mothers in this chapter are scripts. Scripts come from society, they become imaginary when we internalize them, and we embody them as we live. The mother in horror is both real and an example of society's Maternal Myth.

The chapter starts with a discussion of the mother script. The chapter then examines three films with a pregnant woman, a postnatal mother, and a single mother with a young son. In French Extremity film *Inside* (2007, Alexandre Bustillo and Julien Maury) I discuss terror and an attack on the pregnant body. In horror film *Grace* (2009, Paul Solet) disgust is used to expose conventional motherhood as sick. Australian ghost film *The Babadook*, finally, rejects both the good and the bad mother, and instead use wild, deep, and dark play to write a new mother script.[3] The films belong primarily to identity horror, because they are concerned with threats to the protagonists' life, body, or self.

Mother: The Good, the Bad, and the Real

Because the mother script is part of the gender script, it feels so natural. It is almost impossible to see, that when we talk of "the mother," we are dealing with a script and not an innate essence.

Sarah Arnold in *Maternal Horror Film* (2013) analyses the good and the bad mother in horror, and says both originate from an idealized or essential motherhood, by which she means Western discourses of motherhood. But Arnold also finds in contemporary horror a struggle "to find an alternative space or voice for the mother outside traditional modes of representation." She thinks some horror films "demonstrate the problem of maternal representation, namely, how to separate essential motherhood from biological motherhood."[4] Drawing on film scholar E. Ann Kaplan, Arnold outlines two mothers, the good mother and the bad mother. The good mother is "all-nurturing and self-abnegating, the 'Angel of the House,'" while the bad mother is selfish and "sadistic, hurtful, and jealous, she refuses the self-abnegating role, demanding her own life."[5] Both are found in patriarchy, the first as dutiful wife who serves children and husband, the second serves herself, which is why she is evil. Theorizing the mother in horror, Arnold also draws from the melodrama, where a mother is linked to self-sacrifice.

Good and bad mothers are thus *both* written into society's mother script. As Ussher says, "society tells us that motherhood is natural and blissful. The beatific Madonna adorns church frescos. Smiling sun-kissed supermodels hold their babies in a modern mimicry of the ancient motif."[6] It is seen as unnatural for women *not* to bear children, which turns stepmothers, adoptive mothers, and women who are not mothers into "failed" women. In a time where almost half of marriages in the West end in divorce, representations of children remain linked to a nuclear family: "From childhood, fairy tales tell us that romance and love – followed by the 'happy ever after' of marriage and motherhood – are our route to happiness and fulfillment."[7]

Arnold doesn't use scripts, but talks instead of *essentialized* or *idealized* motherhood, which is the ideological formation that "marks the culmination of a range of maternal discourses (historical, scientific, religious) all of which produce images and representations of idealized motherhood. It establishes mothering as an exercise in self-sacrifice, which is in turn an inevitable consequence of biology."[8] Like the meta-narrative of gender, essential motherhood is a meta-narrative of motherhood. Essential motherhood is intrinsically ambivalent because the higher the pedestal, the further a woman falls when she fails to climb it. Film scholar Linda Williams says of such ambivalence: "The device of devaluing and debasing the figure of the mother while sanctifying the institution of motherhood is typical of 'the woman's film' in general and the sub-genre of the maternal melodrama in particular."[9]

The maternal body is also a contested figure in our medical science. In *Managing the Monstrous Feminine*, Ussher analyses women's relations to their bodies. She argues, "it is when women become mothers that regulation of the monstrous feminine [the female body] moves into the sphere of pathology."[10] Society scrutinizes the mother with an all-controlling "medicalised gynaecological-obstretic gaze."[11] In this gaze, the maternal body is not natural, but sick, and needs medication and surveillance to be put back in its place. For example, says Ussher, the lack of sleep mothers experience would make anyone irritable and, if experienced over a longer period, cause pathological reactions. Lack of sleep, however, is seen as a symptom, and not as a cause, of postnatal depression.

From a medical perspective, the female body is associated with mental and physical weakness, the abject, the monstrous, and crossing boundaries of animal-human behavior. In this view, a woman is "reduced" to an animal state when she becomes a mother, a state considered primitive, dangerous, and abject (we recall from Chapter 6 that the body's animal status causes disgust and terror). It is this view of the maternal body, that Ussher wants women to reject. The fecund body is "simply a part of who we are as women – at times an irritation ... at times a site of vulnerability, but also a site of creativity, energy, and power. Making more space within theory, research and the popular imagination for *these* experiences of fecundity will reveal the monstrous feminine for what it is: a figment of a misogynistic imagination."[12] In short, there is nothing monstrous about women's bodies, not even when they are mothers.

Feminist works like Creed's *The Monstrous-Feminine* and Ussher's *Managing the Monstrous Feminine* expose the misogyny in society's mother script. In the area of crime, however, forensic psychologists Helen Gavin and

Theresa Porter in *Female Aggression* (2015) wants us to consider that women, like men, can be aggressive and violent. Gavin and Porter say the female sex offender is under-represented in crime statistics because she violates our mother script. "One myth about women," says Porter (2010), "underlies many other women myths; the Maternal Instinct. We maintain the myth that women are inherently loving towards children by virtue of the fact that we carried them in our wombs, which also appears to make children into mere extensions of women. Women are defined by their relationship with motherhood and are presumed to have a special, desexualized relationship with children."[13] It is incomprehensible to us that a mother could violate the Maternal Myth. "If a woman steps outside the prescribed sexual scripts, society translates her behaviour into less threatening terms. She must be mentally ill or a man made her do it, or it wasn't really sexual abuse. It's a way of maintaining the boundaries of 'womanhood.'"[14] Gavin and Porter point out society's explanations to why a woman may molest children—she is sick (pathological), a witch (evil), or a man made her do it (weak)—serve to keep her in the mother script, now in the role of bad instead of good mother. Their point is that like men commit violent crimes for many reasons, so, too, do women. But when an offender is a woman and a mother, the reason is that she is a bad mother.

Why women commit crimes is beyond my inquiry and I leave such a question to others. Our aim is to examine the mother script in contemporary horror and see if it can open a space beyond essential motherhood. Writer-director Kent said that with *The Babadook* she wanted to show the struggle to live up to the ideals of essential motherhood: "I remember a writer friend of mine burst into tears after one scene, and she told me, 'Oh my God, all the times I've lost my temper or been impatient – that scene made me realize how *big* I look to my little kids.' That's the kind of thing I really wanted to address in the film."[15]

Let us now meet Sarah, Madeline, and Amelia.

Inside: "Completely Unwatchable"

Inside (*À l'intérieur*, 2007) mounts a full-frontal attack on the most sanctified object in the West, the pregnant body.[16] It is the feature debut by French directors Alexandre Bustillo and Julien Maury, who also wrote the story. It starts with a car accident, which leaves five-month-pregnant Sarah (Alysson Paradis) alive and her husband dead. We then jump to the day before the planned caesarian delivery at a hospital, where Sarah is examined by a doctor who declares from ultrasound images that her daughter is fine. It is Christmas, but Sarah rejects offers from her sister, her mother, and her boss to spend the holiday with them. During the evening a woman rings Sarah's doorbell and asks to borrow the phone. Sarah declines, and The Woman

THE MATERNAL MYTH 181

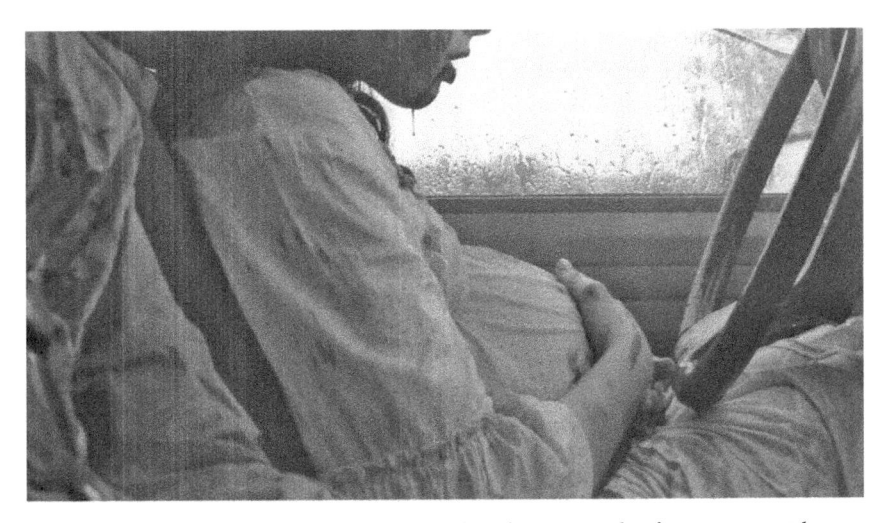

FIGURE 7.1 *Sarah (Alysson Paradis) holding her stomach after a car accident in French extremity film* Inside *(À L'intérieur, 2007, Alexandre Bustillo and Julien Maury).* © *La Fabrique de Films, BR Films, Canal+, 2007.*

(played by Béatrice Dalle, credited as *La femme*, The Woman) threatens her. Sarah calls the police, who come to the house and promise to return later. The Woman enters the house when Sarah is asleep and attacks her with scissors. Sarah escapes and barricades herself in the bathroom. Sarah's boss later comes to the house, her mother shows up, and three policemen, with an immigrant arrested in city riots, also return to her house. They are killed with knitting needles, scissors, and a gun. The Woman reveals she was the pregnant driver of the other car. Having lost her baby in the accident, she now wants Sarah's child. Sarah attacks The Woman with a piece of mirror glass, a knitting needle, and a home-made spear, even sets her on fire, but is defeated. On the stairs, The Woman cuts up Sarah's belly and removes the fetus, the last image framing her in Sarah's rocking chair holding the infant.

We recall from previous chapter that a feature of French Extremity is that films are unwatchable. *Inside* is among a handful of films I found extremely difficult to watch. In the Introduction I shared how my husband left the living room when The Woman attacked Sarah's belly. And it was when I showed a clip from *Inside* that a professor in my audience exclaimed, "I am *never* gonna watch this movie." Afterwards, she told me she felt assaulted by the clip. However, if *Inside* is almost unwatchable, it is not without merits. A comment on IMDB says:

> The film starts out incredibly bleak and depressing in the first 20 minutes. Then it turns shocking really quickly. Then it goes from shocking to cruel, to immoral, to extreme, to nearly unwatchable, and then finally completely

unwatchable. About 30 minutes in, I had to pause it and collect my thoughts. I couldn't believe what I was watching ... It is an uncommonly effective piece of film-making. It is one of the most depraved films I have ever watched.[17]

The IMDB writer concludes that although he finds the film "completely unwatchable," it is "one of the greatest French horror films ever made." Many IMDB comments, both by men and women (judging from pen names), agree. A male viewer says it is, "in its own twisted way, the ultimate chick flick. The two women in this film that battle it out are two of the greatest female characters I have seen in a horror film," and he thinks Sarah "TRULY kicks a lot of ass."[18] Female viewers agreed, one identifying with both The Woman—"Beatrice Dalle! Her performance was one I'll never forget"—and Sarah: "Alysson Paradis made for a vulnerable heroine that I sympathized with. I felt her agony and her fear. I was rooting for her the entire way!"[19]

Terror and a Real Maternal Body

One can experience many emotions during a horror film, and watching *Inside*, my salient emotion was terror. I was terrified The Woman would cut up Sarah's belly, which is what happened at the end. The maternal body is often interpreted as symbolic in horror, however, we shall explore terror and the thought of a threat to a real pregnant body.

FIGURE 7.2 *The Woman (Béatrice Dalle) attacks Sarah's (Alysson Paradis) stomach with scissors.* Inside (À L'intérieur, 2007, Alexandre Bustillo and Julien Maury). © *La Fabrique de Films, BR Films, Canal+, 2007.*

My worst (one could say best) scene in *Inside* is The Woman's first attack on Sarah in her sleep. The Woman has entered her bedroom, and then goes to find scissors and antiseptic water in the bathroom, and returns to Sarah's bed, slowly removing her dress and displaying the belly. The Woman tracks the scissors slowly to the top of the belly, then settles the scissors' tip in the navel. And then she jabs it into the flesh. At this point, my anticipatory fear exploded into full terror, Sarah awakens, and the image cuts between the scissors, Sarah's face, and an intravenous close-up of the fetus' face, and on the soundtrack we hear loud sounds and the fetus' heartbeat.

Terror is one of Hanich's five categories of fear (the other are dread, shock, suggested horror, and direct horror):

> The crucial prerequisite of terror is the fact that *we* know the nature of the threat ... as a consequence, the scene frightens us because the approaching threat relentlessly urges us to fear with or for the character *and* to fearfully anticipate a negative ending for ourselves: the confrontation of a scene of horror ... terror is an anticipatory type of cinematic fear in which we both feel *for the endangered character* and fearfully expect a threatening outcome that promises to be horrifying – though not shocking! – to *us*.[20]

Terror is what we feel when there is a real, imminent, and unavoidable threat to our life. I was never afraid of vampires or zombies, but since I learnt in school about soldiers committing crimes against civilians during war, among which crimes was to cut up pregnant women's bellies and pull out fetuses, I have been haunted by this. When I was pregnant, I had nightmares that someone might attack *my* belly.

If we look at the scissors scene, danger (The Woman) is visible to the viewer, the threat (scissors) is lethal and overt, and the outcome likely negative since Sarah is asleep and pregnant. This is prototypical terror, where an attack feeds directly into the viewer's instinctive fight-or-flight reactions—wake up! defend yourself! run!—and we anticipate a negative outcome. Terror is different from dread and horror. Dread is quiet and slow and "lasts until it gives way to shock or horror,"[21] and the threat is vague. Horror is overwhelming, mortifying, and immobilizing, and we surrender to horror. Terror, in contrast to dread and horror, is real, clear, and activating. It is represented in loud, accelerated, and agitated *mise-en-scène*. The "*hampered-escape scene*" and "*in-the-nick-of-time scenario*"[22] are classic ways to create a sense of terror, as when Sarah is *almost* stabbed to death. In terror, we do not stop to ask questions of why. Terror is here and now, it has realistic sensations and stimuli.

In Chapter 1 I mentioned Lazarus' division of fear into fright and anxiety. Fright fits our definition of terror while anxiety is existential, like Kierkegaard's *angst*. Terror is, like fright, a sudden threat and does not invite deeper reflection: "Because the appearance of danger is sudden, it is difficult to develop expectations about what will happen in a frightening encounter."[23] Terror, thus, is not existential and is not related to aesthetics or to the symbolic. When we feel terror, we react to a real threat, here and now, to what we think is a real person.

Now, as said, earlier theories of the maternal body in horror has read it as symbolic. To Creed, thus, the maternal body is per se monstrous. In her analysis of *Aliens* (1986, James Cameron), protagonist Ripley and her opponent, the Alien, are both mothers. Creed argues, "Mother Alien represents Ripley's other self, that is, *woman's*, alien, inner, mysterious powers of reproduction . . . the female reproductive/mothering capacity *per se*, which is deemed monstrous, horrifying, abject."[24] From a psychoanalytical perspective, Ripley and the Alien are both good Mothers, trying to protect their offspring, and Creed argues that both represent male fears of the maternal. In my reading of *Inside*, however, terror is not evoked by the maternal body, but by our perception of a threat to this body.

I want to underline that our emotional engagement is with Sarah as a *real* person with a *real* body. Most pregnancies in horror involve aliens, demons, computers, and fantastic scenarios. For example, the films in lists like "10 Most Disturbing Movie Pregnancies" are all fantastic.[25] However, Sarah's body is not fantastic, but physical and human, the object of car crashes, of soon-to-be surgery, and of caresses: We first see her pregnant body in a car crash, bleeding, and later in the hospital in an ultrasound machine, and we also see how Sarah imagines her husband's hands caressing her belly. We recall from Haidt, McCauley, and Rozin that breaches on the body stir disgust and terror. However, when the body is furthermore pregnant, a breach evokes both the body script (disgust) and the mother script. And in the West, a pregnant body is linked to the good mother, the Madonna, and the miracle of life. A breach violates our script of the pregnant body as sacrosanct. Sarah and her belly are attacked not only by The Woman, but also, in later chaotic fights, by a blinded policeman who beats Sarah's stomach with his baton which makes water and blood gush out and causes labor to start.

These attacks are not just terrifying, they are so upsetting that they are almost unwatchable. The shocking scene is not a maternal (horrifying) body, but the attack on a maternal body. And in this case, I don't think unwatchability has a philosophical meaning, as Grønstad argues it does in French Extremity film: "The unwatchability of the films by someone like Noé, Haneke or Breillat lies not so much on an experiential level as on a philosophical one . . . [the films] are really preoccupied with deeply humanist issues even as they at times seem disturbingly misanthropic."[26] However, *Inside* doesn't want us to question ethics. It wants us to witness a terrifying attack on a pregnant body. When I met the two French directors at a Danish horror film festival in 2011, I asked why they had chosen a pregnant body as site of violence. They responded they had chosen a pregnant body, because they thought this would be the most terrifying thing for an audience to watch.

Who is the Good Mother?

It seems obvious to read The Woman as evil and Sarah as a good mother, however, *Inside* complicates such a reading.

First, beautiful Sarah is reduced to a bloody pulp during the night. The meta-narrative says a woman must keep control over body perimeters. Ussher says, "the reproductive body is positioned as the depository of all that is transgressive and dangerous, all that is outside the boundaries of what a good woman should be – an enemy to be contained and controlled."[27] As the ordeal progresses, Sarah's body leaks blood and water and is reduced to its animal nature as flesh and prey. We are disgusted by the blood and viscera inside us (our animal nature) and by the violation of the mother script (provoking moral disgust and terror). Sarah tries her best to uphold body perimeters, even covers a hole in her throat gushing with blood, with Duct Tape and crafts a spear from her kitchen inventory.

But also ethical issues complicate the view that Sarah is good and The Woman evil. It turns out The Woman was the driver in the other car in the car accident, and that she, like Sarah, was pregnant and lost her child. When the women fight, and Sarah has the opportunity to kill The Woman, the film shows a flashback of The Woman in her car, elegantly dressed and, like Sarah, caressing her belly. We also learn Sarah, who was driving, was at fault. "They told me there were no survivors," Sarah says. We get no further background but can hypothesize from The Woman's elegant appearance in the flashback, that she might be a career woman, perhaps single. From an evolutionary perspective, The Woman is a mother claiming what she believes is hers, a baby.

From The Woman's point of view, *she* is the good mother and this is a legitimate fight. Let me finish our discussion of *Inside* by linking the fight between two women over a fetus, to real crime. I thought *Inside* was pure fiction, however, the day after watching the film, I read in a Danish newspaper about a wombraider crime in the US. I had probably not noticed this news article if *Inside* was not still fresh in my memory. The term "wombraider," coined as a pun on *Lara Croft: Tomb Raider* (2001, Simon West), was new to me. Wombraiding is the crime of taking a fetus from a woman's body and kidnapping it. The first such crime was reported in 1987, in 2005 there had been nine cases, and in 2015 there had been seventeen reported cases in the US. In three, the mother survived. The crimes were all committed by women, were premeditated, and the offender usually befriended the victim or lured her with promise of baby clothes or gifts.

FIGURE 7.3 *The Woman (Béatrice Dalle) cuts Sarah's (Alysson Paradis) baby from her stomach on the stairs in Sarah's house.* Inside *(À L'intérieur,* 2007, Alexandre Bustillo and Julien Maury). © La Fabrique de Films, BR Films, Canal+, 2007.

The premeditation rules out psychosis, says Lieutenant-Commander Vernon J. Geberth in "Homicides Involving the Theft of a Fetus From a Pregnant Victim," and notes that the perpetrators were obsessed with having a baby: They faked pregnancies and convinced partners, family, and friends by gaining weight, dressing in maternity clothing, setting up nurseries, going to hospitals, and showing sonograms of a fetus.[28] Crime researchers say there are several motives, one being "to sustain a relationship with a male partner by providing them with a child," another to "become a mother by proxy by acting out a fantasy of them delivering a baby," and finally the obsession to have a baby. Thus, in a 2015 case, a 34-year-old woman lured the victim to her home and cut the infant from her stomach. The perpetrator was the mother of three, and had shown her teenage daughters ultrasound photos of a son. She was described as a "fine parent" and trained as a nurse's aid. Yet she cut the fetus out with "a knife and a broken glass" and surgeons "told police that whoever cut the woman had to have researched cesarean births, given the accuracy of the incision."[29] In a case from 1987, the offender also had surgical instruments and medical books at home, but took the victim to an isolated place and cut the fetus out with car keys because her husband was home at the time of kidnapping.

The wombraider crimes were meticulously planned and carried out with knives, broken glass, car keys, baseball bats, and shotguns. The tone in crime writings and media reports echoes Porter's point that society reads the perpetrator from a bad mother script. They are called "brutal and *savage* crimes ... [with] *bizarre* replication of a cesarean section procedure," the offenders demonstrate "*depravity* and *evil*," and "these crimes are *unimaginably evil*" (added emphasis).³⁰ Reports describe the behavior as deviant, sick, savage, and "unimaginably evil." But there is another perspective. The motive for the wombraider crimes was desire for a baby. These are women wanting what belongs to another woman. These are women's stories of crimes with female offenders and female victims. In horror cinema, attacks on a pregnant body are almost always motivated by male interests: In *Demon Seed* (1977, Donald Cammell) a computer, programmed by a male scientist, rapes the scientist's wife; in *Rosemary's Baby* (1968, Roman Polanski) a husband sells his wife's baby to the Devil; and in the *Alien* series the patriarchal Company wants to use Ripley's body to secure the Alien as a weapon. *Inside*, in contrast, is female terrain with female interests. The attack is carried out with unflinching aggression and while it is revulsive, we understand the motive: The Woman lost her baby.

The "completely unwatchable" scene, which the IMDB comment mentioned, is when The Woman cuts the fetus out with the scissors, showing the body breach in close-up and with a flood of blood running down stairs. It is savage but not unimaginably evil. We can in fact, as another IMDB comment said, see *Inside* as "the ultimate chick flick" with an attacker set on her threat, and the victim using angry aggression to defend herself. The pregnant body is no longer a male territory with male fears. It has become a woman's battlefield.

Grace: "It's All About Maintaining Your Diet"

Where *Inside* gave us an attack on a pregnant heroine, Paul Solet's debut *Grace* (2009) takes us to the postnatal period with breastfeeding and postpartum depression. And where *Inside* has a villain character, The Woman, the threat is not a person in *Grace*. The threat is the mother script, and an attack therefore more difficult to protect oneself against.

If we remember Henricks' extended self (2014, 2015), this self extends into five circles: body, mind, possessions, our social self (community), and cultural self (culture). An attack on either of these circles is part of the identity horror narrative. Thus, *Inside* belongs to identity horror, because its home-invasion plot is an attack on Sarah and results in self-defense, in angry aggression. *Black Swan,* too, uses the identity horror narrative, because Nina is attacked, albeit the attacks are in her imagination. Here, the viewer sees the imagined figures of Lily and Nina's doppelgänger. Underlying identity horror can, of course, be a social horror narrative too. Thus, *Black Swan* faults society and Nina's mother with her self-injuring and schizophrenia. Where *Inside* and *Black Swan* use home-invasion and pathology to tell stories of attacks on the self, *Grace* uses supernatural elements. Thus, there is no villain like The Woman, but instead supernatural

FIGURE 7.4 *Madeline (Jordan Ladd) prepares a bottle with cow blood for her baby Grace.* Grace *(2009, Paul Solet).* © *Ariescope Pictures, Dark Eye Entertainment, Leoma Entertainment, 2009.*

elements of an undead baby with a hunger for blood. These supernatural elements, however, are not the "cause" of Madeline's trouble, but merely, like all other elements in her world, part of the mother script which is the threat. In *Grace*, the attack is not from a single place or carried out by a single character; attacks are on *all* the fives circles, or we can say the attack *comes from* all five dimensions of Madeline's self. This is because the mother script exists both externally, in society, and is internalized inside Madeline.

The film's poster has a nursing bottle with blood and a fly crawling on the teat and sets up the theme of motherhood as "sick" behavior. "You don't understand. She's special. She needs special food," Madeline (Jordan Ladd) explains when Dr. Sohn (Malcolm Stewart) comes to her house. When he intrudes, she next feeds his blood to Grace, hoping a change from animal to human blood will stop her baby's crankiness.

The film is about "sick" motherhood. In the start of the film, the pregnant Madeline and her husband Michael (Stephen Park) have his parents over for dinner. Mother-in-law Vivian (Gabrielle Rose) is a judge and talks about a case: "This woman *starved* her baby to death feeding it wheat grass. It's lucky she had a jury trial. I'd have *locked her up*." The film's very first scene is when Madeline has sex with Michael and conceives. Madeline is vegan, and Vivian disapproves of this as well as of Madeline's choice to give birth at a midwife's clinic instead of at a hospital. When Michael dies in a car accident that also kills the eight-month-old fetus, Madeline must carry it to term. After birth she, miraculously, wills the dead baby back to life. Grace, however, wants blood. When Madeline's nipples bleed, she buys ecological meat—"kinder kills and cleaner cut, no antibiotics"—but Grace needs *human* blood. When Vivian sends Dr. Sohn to check on Madeline, Madeline kills him. Vivian then visits Madeline and the women kill each other. The midwife Patricia (Samantha Ferris) finally comes to the house and takes Grace. In the last scene, Patricia and her assistant Shelly (Kate Herriot) travel in a mobile home. Shelly looks pale. "It's all about maintaining your diet," Patricia tells her. "There's something more," Shelly replies. "She's teething." In a shock image, the baby reaches out for Shelly's half-eaten breast.

Milk: "A Whole New Level of Freaky"

Grace cleverly weaves the theme of sick motherhood with natural and supernatural elements—breastfeeding and an undead baby—using threads of core disgust and moral disgust.[31] What should be "natural" nursing turns horrible. The tone is realist with a minimalist aesthetic, and the tempo slow. "It's that low-key, realist framing that takes the movie's macabre events to a whole new level of freaky," a reviewer observed.[32] "Ready for a snack?" Madeline asks Grace and offers the child her milk-filled breast.

Through the element of *milk*, the film links different sets of associations and behaviors. There is animal milk and human milk, the first used in human food culture and the other part of our nature. Through milk, the film also blends innate behavior with learned cultural behavior. The colloquial word for mother, mama, comes from mammary glands which produce milk in mammals. Milk production and breastfeeding is in our biology, but nursing and caring must be learned. Experiments show that if primates are raised in isolation, they are unable to mother offspring. Humans, like primates, learn how to be mothers. Madeline is a first-time mother and she must learn how to mother her baby. However, she has no positive role model to emulate and instead learns from scripts around her, like the documentaries on Animal Channel. "Animal Channel, I'm hooked, it's like a vegan horror movie," she tells Patricia. A program about cows is called "Over-Milking Causes Anemia," a condition Dr. Sohn diagnoses Madeline with after the birth. Another program shows a cat nursing its kittens. Between the "bad" milking in the food industry and the "good" nursing with the pet cat, *Grace* inserts human breastfeeding. However, after the first weeks, Grace vomits up breast milk and wants blood. "Okay, mommy needs a break! Ah," Madeline cries in pain.

Through milk, the film ties core disgust to moral disgust. We recall that core disgust serves to warn against diseases and corrupt foods, and the later socially learned moral disgust serves to warn us against "corrupt" behavior and "corrupt" people. However, society is complex and moral disgust is multilayered and not at all straightforward. It might be easy to see flies on decayed meat, but difficult to "see" morally healthy or sick behavior in humans. The mother script should point out "right" behavior, however, motherhood is a minefield of demands and anxieties. Madeline does her best to master disgust by controlling her foods. Madeline is vegan, yet cooks her husband's steak even if she is disgusted by meat. And veganism is to care about life, right? But the film links veganism to Madeline's repression of her own nature, which includes her rejection of being homosexual. Madeline and the midwife Patricia were lovers when they were students at the university, and they still have feelings. However, Madeline chose a heterosexual and bourgeois lifestyle and became a housewife instead of having a job and a homosexual partner.

Milk and meat meet in Michael's meals, and Madeline tries to control him, like she controls everything else. Michael has milk with his steak, and Madeline tells him to wipe his mouth. Milk in the corner of one's mouth is disgusting—and then there is the whole implied perversity of a man having milk with his steak, especially soya milk, which is not even real milk, but a vegan substitute for the real thing.

Perversion is tied to milk, which here is the key symbol for a sick mother script. Grace buys ecological meat and blends it wearing rubber gloves. But Grace vomits up the animal blood and flies begin buzzing around her cradle. Images of the transgression and mixing of milk/mother and meat/dinner are more disgusting and disturbing than a vampire sucking blood, because they violate the mother script. Another problem is Vivian. She thinks Madeline is unfit to mother and plans to take custody of her grandchild. She makes her husband nuzzle her breasts to stimulate her milk production. Vivian finds the old breast pump from when she breastfed Michael, and in front of the mirror she pumps milk from her breasts. Vivian looks too old to produce milk (actor Rose is fifty-five). A third milk problem is Dr. Sohn and his desire for breast milk. When Vivian asks him to visit Madeline to document child neglect, he says, "maybe there's something you could do for me too. I got myself into a little 'trouble'." When he visits Madeline, who is on the verge of breakdown from lack of sleep and anemia, he brings his private breast pump made of brass, leather and glass, and makes a "proper examination" which is "slightly intrusive." As he pumps Madeline's milk, drops of milk run down his fingers, and the camera zooms in on his eager face.

Mother Discourses

As said, *Grace* interweaves a maternal body with the mother script. Although Madeline's baby has "special needs," her experience of breastfeeding is similar to what real mothers describe: "One women described it as a 'battle ground', others talked of pain and discomfort, or used metaphors of intrusion and devourment, feeling as if they were being 'sucked dry', by a baby who was a 'rotten sucking little leech.'"[33] The innate process of nursing is not always as idyllic as society's mother script tells. Real women experience pain and problems: "Breast-feeding became agony, but she was determined to persevere . . . The pain was so severe that she often cried throughout his feed."[34] Ussher says a maternal body produces children and leaks blood and milk, however, this is natural, not monstrous. Pain is, simply, part of the process and the idea that the maternal body is monstrous is a product of the mother script. Women should separate their bodies and pains from the meta-narrative of idealized motherhood. One way to do so is to find women who resist the self-disciplining society requires women to do and use them as role models. We should re-author our experiences of our body in our own words and write our own scripts.

Madeline can't do this. She cannot see essentialized motherhood, because she is desperately trying to perform it with her nursery and baby toys and breastfeeding. Madeline isolates herself instead of learning from other mothers, which makes it impossible for her to re-author the mother script. She phones Patricia for help, but because she is Patricia's ex-partner, the assistant Shelly, who is Patricia's new partner, is jealous and doesn't pass her calls.

The mother script is not one, but many discourses of motherhood. In *Motherhood and Representation* (1992) E. Ann Kaplan says the mother in Western culture developed over three phases: Rousseau's ideas of mother as caretaker created an *early modern mother* in the eighteenth century, Darwin and Freud's ideas established a *high-modernist mother* in the nineteenth and early twentieth century, and after second wave feminism and modern gene technology came a *postmodernist mother* who can create children without men. The three discourses coexist today: "It is not that the new discourses and their accompanying technologies sweep aside the old order of things, or found a totally new language: they enter into a culture already laden with older discourses, causing a general shake-up, disruption, dislocation – a scene of struggle of one discourse against another, with often bitter, hostile and violent results."[35]

We can read characters in *Grace* as competing mother discourses. The housewife Madeline represents an early modern mother. Vivian, the judge presiding over the dinner table with her son drinking soya milk, is a high-modernist mother (and a version of Norman Bates' mother). And Patricia, with her clinic, vegan cookies, and homosexual lover, is a postmodern mother. However, these discourses are all maladaptive and lead to abuse. Vivian wants to take custody of Grace, and Patricia and Shelly might look like some *Thelma & Louise* (1991, Ridley Scott) revolt against patriarchy, but their relationship is an abusive one.[36] Patricia is using Shelly's body.

Society's script is impossible to perform, and Madeline can't write a new mother script because she has no positive role models. "She's sick. Whatever you had with her is over," Shelly warns Patricia, and Vivian tells Richard, "I do not want this woman raising my granddaughter." They are right, Madeline *is* sick. Like the woman in Vivian's case, she feeds her daughter a "wrong" diet. But what can she do, when given the "wrong" material in the first place? *Grace* does not write a new mother script, but it exposes the existing script as disgusting and sick. Women want to be perfect, however, the ambition to perform idealized motherhood kills Madeline.

The Babadook: "This Monster Thing"

SAM: I just want you to be happy.
AMELIA [mimicking in a sneering tone]: "I just want you to be happy." Sometimes I just want to smash your head against the brick wall until your fucking brains pop out.
SAM: You are not my mother.

The Babadook (2014)

In Jennifer Kent's Australian indie ghost movie *The Babadook*, single mother Amelia (Essie Davis) turns into an abusive mother who tries to kill her six-year-old son, Sam (Noah Wiseman). It is open if she is possessed by a ghost or deranged. However, rather than explore this fantastic uncertainty, I find it interesting how the film uses play to make the heroine write her own mother script. Sarah and Madeline died, but Amelia survives, perhaps because Sam teaches her what play scholar Sutton-Smith calls wild, deep, and dark play. Sam is obsessed with monsters and magic. At the film's start, he demonstrates to Amelia one of his home-made weapons and smashes a window. He then does magic, wearing a golden cape, and waves hands in front of her, "look at me, look at me, it only works if you *look at me*." He produces a bouquet of plastic flowers, but Amelia is tired. "This monster thing's gotta stop," she says. "Why can't you just be normal?"

FIGURE 7.5 *Wild, deep, and dark play between mother Amelia (Essie Davis) and her son Sam (Noah Wiseman) in* The Babadook *(2014, Jennifer Kent). © Screen Australia, Causeway Film, South Australian Film Corporation, 2014.*

She became a widow when her husband Oskar died in a car accident on the way to the hospital to give birth. With Sam's birthday approaching, she is reminded of the loss. They have until now held Sam's birthday with his cousin Ruby at her sister Claire's house. But this year Ruby wants a princess birthday. Sam's monster play is becoming a problem at school, and Amelia takes him out of school. At the start of the film, Amelia and Sam read a pop-up book, *Mister Babadook*, about a monster in a closet. Sam tries to keep the monster away, but when the Babadook possesses Amelia, he takes command of the game and captures his mother in the basement.

Amelia represses loss and anxieties, and is emotionally distant. Sam sleeps in her bed, because he is afraid of monsters, and she moves to the edge to avoid the touch of his body. When he hugs her, she hisses, "*don't do that.*" "It's time you move on," Claire (Hayley McElhinney) tells her. "I *have* moved on," says Amelia, "I don't mention him. I don't talk about him." But the loss haunts Amelia. She keeps Oskar's affects in the basement where Sam finds them and places his father's clothes on a hanger, in a shape similar to the Babadook. The basement is also where Sam makes weapons and keeps stuff he buys on the Internet, such as DVDs about magic. "Life is not always what it seems," the magician warns from the television screen.

Sam doesn't repress loss. "My father is in the cemetery, he got killed driving my mom to the hospital to have me," he tells strangers at the supermarket. His infatuation with monsters and magic is not acting out, it is healthy and healing. Kent said about her film: "For me, *The Babadook* is a film about a woman waking up from a long, metaphorical sleep and finding that she has the power to protect herself and her son. I think we all have to face our own darkness, whatever that entails. Beyond genre and beyond being scary, that's the most important thing in the film – facing our shadow side."[37]

Identity horror raises questions of self and sanity. In *The Babadook*, identity horror is combined with the fourth narrative, creative horror, where a text self-consciously plays with its own conventions. In *The Babadook*, play is used as meta-play to coach our protagonist and to teach her adaptive behavior. Through play, she learns to face her trauma.

Meta-Play

I have until now used play about how a viewer interacts with fiction. My argument is that we use horror as mental play fighting, and that when we engage emotionally with the fiction, we enter a magic circle of play. In this circle, events are both real and not-real, like play is both real and play, that is, events are half–real.

I now want to extend my use of play. We can call the viewer's engagement with the fiction for *play-with-fiction*. In Apter's terminology, it means we do edgework using the protective frames he calls detachment frames. This is when we know events are fiction, and that we are not in real danger. A second use of play is when we see play represented in the fiction, like Oskar who plays chess with his father and offers Eli his Rubik's cube in *Let the Right One In*. We can call this *play-within-fiction*. We have all been children, so we all understand what play is, whether it is child's play or adult games. And then there is a third use of play. For example, in *House of Voices* (*Saint Ange*, 2004, Pascal Laugier) and *The Orphanage* (*El orfanato*, 2007, Juan Antonio Bayona), where ghost children teach mothers to play. And in *Mama* (2013, Andrés Muschietti), two girls play with a ghost mother and a foster mother. In these stories, play is taken to a level where it is instructional, coaching characters and viewers *how* to play. In these cases, we are meant to reflect on the function of play as a way to engage with the world, as Ofelia uses play to relate to her world. We can call this third sense *play coaching* or *meta-play*. It is when play provides an alternative take on reality and becomes creative, communicative, engaging. This is Henrick's theory of play as self-work.[38]

My idea of play coaching and meta-play is inspired by the concepts of meta-emotions and emotion coaching in a study by psychologists Carole Hooven, John Mordechai Gottman, and Lynn Fainsilber Katz of how parents handle their own emotions when they raise their children. The psychologists examined children at the age of five and again at the age of eight and asked parents about their

> ... feelings about their own emotions, and their attitudes, and responses to their children's anger and sadness ... Two meta-emotion variables were studied for each parent, awareness of the parent's own sadness, and parental "coaching" of the child's anger. We termed the high end of these variables an "emotion coaching" (EC) meta-emotion structure ... EC-type of parents ... were less negative and more positive during parent-child interaction. Their children showed less evidence of physiological stress, greater ability to focus attention, and had less negative play with their best friends.[39]

The researchers looked at *awareness* of one's emotions and at *coaching*, the ability to teach another person to manage emotions. Children with parents who did emotion coaching were less aggressive and did better in school than those who had no coaching. So, clearly, it is adaptive for children when a mother is aware of her emotions.

I am after this ability to reflect and coach. The prefix *meta* is often used to indicate the ability to distance one from oneself and look at a situation from an outside frame, like when you step out of a game to reflect at higher level if you should change strategy, change the rules, or play a different game. The above study defined meta-emotion structure as "the parents' awareness of specific emotions, their awareness and acceptance of these emotions in their child, and their coaching of the emotion in their child. Coaching refers to talking to the child about the emotion, the conditions that elicited it, and strategies for coping with it."[40]

I use meta-play and play coaching about awareness of how to play. However, in our example, *The Babadook,* it is not an adult coaching a child. Instead, Sam is coaching his mother.

Princess Play and Monster Play

When they read for the night, Sam chooses a new book, *Mister Babadook,* about a monster. The text says: "If you're a really clever one and you know what it is to see, then you can make friends with a special one, a friend of you and me." But Amelia doesn't want to "see," she puts the book away and reads a princess fairy tale instead. Sam, however, doesn't want to hear about princesses. He wants to slay monsters.

The film contrasts monsters with princesses, and Sam's play with Ruby's play. The sisters meet at a playground to discuss the birthdays which are usually held together on Ruby's birthday and at Claire's house. "Don't play there, it's wet," Claire tells Ruby, who is nicely dressed and holds a plush bunny. Meanwhile, Sam battles an imaginary monster. "Mom, I'm gonna *smash* its head," he yells and climbs on top of the swing instead of sitting in the swing. His wild play is stressing Amelia, who is developing tics.

Amelia's refusal to face monsters and loss creates tics and anxiety. Lazarus in *Emotion and Adaptation* (1991) says avoidance and repression are ineffective ways to handle anxiety. "Clinicians often assume that both are dangerous, especially suppression or denial of anxiety. They are said, for example, to result in so-called posttraumatic stress disorders in which dysfunction may not be evident during the period of acute stress but may appear at a later time."[41] Oskar's death is the origin of Amelia's trauma and Sam's birthday has become the trigger. Amelia wants to forget, but Sam *wants* a birthday. "I *hate you,* she won't let me have a birthday and she won't let me have a *dad,*" he yells to a co-worker, who visits Amelia. His monster play is clearly a child responding to a mother in crisis. The school confiscates his home-made crossbow. "The boy has significant behavioral problems," the school warns and wants to hire a person to monitor him. Amelia instead takes Sam out of school.

Amelia and Sam give Ruby a Barbie doll, which she already has. Sam builds his own toys, thus there is no danger of duplicates. Barbie belongs to a commercial play culture, like the clown Claire has hired to entertain the children, and the mothers wear perfect makeup and chic clothes and look like big-scale Barbies. They share the problem of how one is to find time to go to the gym *and* do volunteer work with disadvantaged women. "That's a

FIGURE 7.6 *Amelia's sister Claire (Hayley McElhinney) and her friends performing motherhood as Perfect Mothers at the princess play birthday.* The Babadook *(2014, Jennifer Kent).* © *Screen Australia, Causeway Film, South Australian Film Corporation, 2014.*

real shame," says Amelia, "you must have *so much* to talk about with those disadvantaged women." Amelia has dark rings under her eyes from lack of sleep due to her problems with the Babadook.

The mothers perform the mother script as retro–1950s momism, a modern woman's choice to be a stay-at-home mom who serves her family with "intensive" mothering. In *The Mommy Myth* (2004) Susan J. Douglas and Meredith Michaels write: "The mythology of the new momism now insinuates that, when all is said and done, the enlightened mother chooses to stay home with the kids." Momism is "promoted through the toys and myriad other products sold to us and our kids."[42] The good mother takes her child to the fast-food diner for a nice time, and after Amelia shouts, "if you are that hungry why don't you go and *eat shit*," she feels guilty and takes Sam to the diner. But the girls in the adjacent booth yell and fight, and on the way home, the Babadook is in the car and Amelia has an accident. Momism and the commercial children's culture is presented as shallow and nasty. When Ruby finds Sam hiding in her play house, she says, "this is *my* tea house you are not allowed in here," and, "you're not even good enough to have a dad. Everyone else has one and you don't. Your dad died so he doesn't have to be with you." Sam pushes Ruby from the play house, and after this, Claire throws Sam and Amelia out of the princess birthday. Sam's pushing was self-defense, but Claire's rejection shows she doesn't care about wild play or about a sister haunted by a monster.

Amelia tries to make the Babadook disappear by suppressing her anxiety even harder, however, the book returns on her doorstep, glued together and with a new ending: "I'll make you a bet, the more you deny, the stronger I get." The last pages show Amelia strangling the dog, strangling Sam, and then cutting her own throat with a knife. She burns *Mister Babadook* and feeds Sam tranquilizers. "Will this keep the Babadook away?" he asks. Of course not.

Wild, Deep, and Dark Play

Sam's monster play is what Sutton-Smith calls "deep" and "wild" play: "Paradoxically children, who are supposed to be the players among us, are allowed much less freedom for irrational, wild, dark, or deep play in Western culture than are adults, who are thought not to play at all. Studies of child fantasy are largely about the control, domestication, and direction of childhood."[43]

The film presents monster play as wild, deep, and dark. It is *wild* in the sense that it cannot be controlled by adults, although teachers, social workers, and Claire, try to stop Sam's monster play. It is *deep* in the sense that it will take Sam and Amelia back to trauma. Play can, as play researcher Greta Fein says, "bring to the surface deep feelings and anxieties. When we engage in socio-dramas, we create scenarios that place our general life concerns into altered formats where we can confront the issues involved and turn them into positive experiences."[44] And monster play, finally, is *dark* in the sense that it can take players *over* the edge, from the danger zone into the trauma zone where actions can harm players.

One of Sutton-Smith's rhetorics of play I mention in Chapter 1 is *child phantasmagoria*, which is when children fantasize make-believe worlds. For example, when a father's clothes become a monster hiding under the bed. Sutton-Smith says adults often ignore child phantasmagorical play because we cannot control it and that "there is much ambiguity in the adult-child relationship about fantasy. At the same time, imaginative activity is itself often extremely ambiguous as to what it expresses, what it conceals, and what on earth it means."[45] Children use phantasmagorical play to engage with their world and surroundings: "It takes the world apart in a way that suits their own emotional responses to it. As such, their play is a deconstruction of the world in which they live."[46] Adults prefer to understand children's play as developmental, and serving a specific learning process that advances the child from childhood to adulthood. For example, Barbie play prepares a little girl for an adult female world. But the child's phantasmagoria engages the world on the child's own terms. Phantasmagorical play does not use rented clowns. It uses old stuff found in boxes in the basement and takes no directions from adults. It is not linear, leading to well-defined social roles like Barbie in her doll house. Monster play—phantasmagorical play—is explorative, creative, painful, and destructive. It leaves bruises and smashed windows and allow players to fall from swings. It is self-work, and it is on its own terms, unscripted.

It is well-known in horror that play will open a door to traumas. Thus, in *The Orphanage*, play between son and mother leads to the son finding documents revealing he is adopted and has Aids, and play leads the mother to find the son's body in the basement. Here, play "opens" a problem but doesn't "solve" it, rather it provides an answer and thus puts questions to rest. In *The Babadook*, however, play is presented as meta-play and self-healing. Monster play brings out the bad mother in Amelia. The possession can be read fantastically or literally, the last as a mother turning abusive. Such an interpretation is underlined by news on the television about a mother who killed her child, "who just turned seven today." Amelia medicates Sam against his will: "I am the parent and you are the child, so *take the pill!*" The hungry Sam begs Amelia, who lies apathetically in bed, for food. He tries to call aunt Claire, but Amelia has cut the phone cord. And when Sam pees his pants in terror, Amelia says, "You little pig. Six years old and you're still wetting yourself."

Monster play is challenging and terrifying, but also a journey to the origin of the trauma. When Sam can't reach the outside world, he confronts his mother in play. "Sorry, mommy," he says as he hacks a knife into her thigh. Having just killed the dog, she is trying to kill him. He runs down to the basement and traps her with his booby traps. When she wakes up, her hands and feet are tied like Gulliver captured by the Lilliputs. "I know you don't love me. The Babadook won't let you. But I love you, mom. And I always will," Sam tells her. She gets a hand free and grabs him by the throat and tries to strangle him, but even then, he caresses her chin. Sam shows his mother he sees *both* her *and* the Babadook, both reality *and* play. The film is aware of the tropes of "evil child" and "monstrous mother." However, it is not a story about evil children or monstrous mothers, but about how to re-author the mother script by playing *together*.

Sam uses monster play to deal with his mother's crisis and he uses play coaching to teach her how to play. "Don't let it in, don't let it in," he warns and later, when she wants him to put his weapons away, yells "do you want to die?" And when Amelia is possessed, he tells her, "you have to let it out."

At one point, *The Babadook* has a frame that shows a possessed Amelia searching for Sam, who is hiding in a closet on her right. This frame echoes a similar scene in *The Shining* (1980, Stanley Kubrick), where the possessed father is looking for his son, who hides too. However, *The Babadook* is not about a father or supernatural evil. It is, as Amanda Howell (2017) points out, "a vision of maternal monstrosity that evades simple oppositions between good mothers and bad ones."[47] Maternal horror often kills the mother, as in *House of Voices*, *The Orphanage*, *Goodnight Mommy* (*Ich seh, ich see*, 2014, Severin Fiala and Veronika Franz), *Inside*, and *Grace*. But *The Babadook* instead uses meta-play to enter deep and dark play. "You are not my mother," Sam tells Amelia while caressing her. Meta-play foregrounds the management of different frames, reality *and* play, like meta-emotions

FIGURE 7.7 Sam (Noah Wiseman) teaches his mother to play The-Babadook-Game and hugs Amelia (Essie Davis) who is trying to kill him. The Babadook (2014, Jennifer Kent). © Screen Australia, Causeway Film, South Australian Film Corporation, 2014.

foreground managing emotions. By showing Amelia his ability to master fear, Sam is coaching her to master her anxiety. "I will *always* take care of you," he promises.

The haunted house is another horror trope. "In the gothic tradition, domestic spaces are used to dramatize hidden secrets, repressed desires, fears, alternative identities, other selves. In the emphasis on cellars, attics, lives lived behind barred windows, secrets hidden in locked rooms – often at the end of seemingly endless corridors, we are given a three-dimensional modeling of the uncertainties that threaten domestic happiness and security."[48] Again, many haunted houses become cemeteries, but not this time. Sam turns his home into a magic circle of play. The house is terrifying, haunted, but also a play space. When Amelia locks the doors and cuts the telephone cord, Sam uses his home-made weapons and booby traps to save them both.

Phantasmagorical play is free play. You don't "win" make-believe games, instead you immerse yourself in a play world and experience playing. Make-believe play is used as self-healing by children, and psychologists use it for play therapy. It is "a free-floating, interpretive activity in which players improvise meanings in response to circumstances."[49] Play therapy is, to my knowledge, not used for adult patients. But we can speculate that adults use play, like children, as self-work and self-healing. About risk sports, sports sociologists say players use dangerous edgework to change their social conditions and to face risk "as part of the process of (re)constructing, shoring up, and/or challenging these conditions."[50] In horror made for an adult audience, like *The Babadook*, children use play to face monsters. We can compare this play-within-fiction to mental edgework, and when the fiction furthermore uses play to coach adult characters, it is meta-play and play coaching. Again, I will underline that since these fictions are not made for child audiences, but adult audiences, the use of children's phantasmagorical play is to teach *adult audiences* to play with fear.

Amelia has dodged her emotional responsibility to be a *real* mother to Sam. As a review said, *The Babadook* voices "that nagging sense that you're failing miserably at the job of raising a child. Worse still are those moments when you find yourself wondering whether you even like, let alone love, that child in the first place."[51] Amelia is struggling with *how* to be a mother. She is too consumed by her trauma and the resulting anxiety to write her own script, and she rejects the mother script handed her by society, represented by Claire and Claire's friends, and by the school. From trying to be a "good mother," Madeline has become a "bad mother." It is as if every version of the mother script fails. Gavin and Porter warn that "the majority of research shows that, rather than motherhood decreasing a woman's antisocial behaviour, motherhood can become a forum for it."[52] The answer is not to try harder to be a good mother. The answer is *to see a different way* to be a mother. If you want to write your own script, you must be able to step back and see that script from a distance. This means using System 2, so you can choose between options and responses. Amelia must learn not to avoid what is unpleasant, but face it, so she can see new ways of being a mother.

To be released from trauma, you must face it, and to slay a monster, you must face that too. Sam shows his mother how to slay a monster from inside the magic play circle. When the Babadook returns, Amelia shouts, "you are nothing, you are trespassing in *my* house. If you touch my son again, *I'll fucking kill you*." She traps it in the basement, and for the first time they celebrate Sam's birthday on the day. There is no rented clown, Sam performs magic, and she hugs him intimately. When social workers pay a surprise visit, she is proud of Sam's candidness: "He speaks his mind just like his father." In the garden, they collect rain worms—symbols of death, rebirth, and growth—which Amelia feeds to the Babadook in the basement. "Am I gonna see it?" Sam asks. "Maybe one day when you're bigger." Amelia has learnt to balance play *and* reality so she can write her own mother script.

It may be a stretch, but I think the film offers the viewer a parallel position, where we juggle multiple frames. It does so by playing with genre texts and textualities. Polish film scholar Justyna Hanna Budzik points to the clever use of Méliès' silent films, that play on Amelia's television where "we watch several [of] Méliès' works: *Éclipse du soleil en pleine lune*, 1907; *Livre magique*, 1900; Dislocation mystérieuse, 1901; *Faust aux enferes*, 1903 . . ." The purpose of these silent films "is to show trick-based attractions and such as metamorphosis, dissolving images, appearances and disappearances, substitutions."[53] This is a meta-reflective use of old materiality, with the pop-up book, Méliès' silent films, Sam's home-made weapons from odd pieces of wood, and the design of the Babadook, played by an actor and visualized

FIGURE 7.8 Amelia (Essie Davis) intimately hugs seven-year-old Sam (Noah Wiseman) at his first birthday party held on the day of his birthday. The Babadook (2014, Jennifer Kent). © Screen Australia, Causeway Film, South Australian Film Corporation, 2014.

with stop-motion and cut editing instead of CGI. The film's monster design also alludes to fantastic texts, for example *The Cabinet of Dr. Caligari* (*Das Cabinet des Dr. Caligari*, 1920, Fritz Lang).

Like the Babadook is trapped in the basement, and not gone, the film ends with a reminder of what Amelia did to Sam. "It's pretty much better, mom," Sam says about the bruises around his neck. Hopefully, there will be no bruises in the future, because Amelia has learnt to control emotions and play, and can now juggle multiple frames, and write a script in her own words.

Conclusion

Meta-play and play coaching can help us step back and look at society's script of idealized motherhood. Ussher recommends that women should "stop trying so hard to be good, and take time for ourselves," and says, "women who are able to accept themselves and their children for who they are, and who do not experience a conflict between their expectations and experience of motherhood, are less likely to experience depression postnatally."[54]

Play can take us beyond society's mother stereotype. If we reject the Maternal Myth, we see that the mother script is a social script, and that the good mother and the bad mother are both characters from this script. If we step back, we can reject it and stop internalizing it. We can accept that we are imperfect, and our bodies not monstrous. Failure is part of play, and in wild, deep, and dark play we do edgework, that takes us into the unknown.

We must accept fear and pain as part of life. *How* we re-author the mother script is up to us. On horror's dark stage, we are invited to play a make-believe game, where we can face our own Babadooks.

Middle Age

8

Home and Road:

Carol's Change in *The Walking Dead*

> *We are, not what we are, but what we make of ourselves.*
> ANTHONY GIDDENS, *Modernity and Self-Identity*[1]

When Rick kicked Carol out of his group in AMC's zombie television series *The Walking Dead* (2010–), my son was furious. "Nooooo," he yelled, "Rick *can't* do that. Not Carol! She's such a great character!" My son and I had become fond of Carol, a battered housewife who grew strong and independent over the seasons. In season four she decides to kill two sick people in the group, so they won't infect the others. When Rick learns this, he casts her out. "I stepped up. I had to do something," Carol (Melissa McBride) protests. "No, you didn't," says Rick. But he is wrong. And, luckily, Carol will step up again later and save the group.

In this chapter, we arrive at middle adulthood. In Erikson's theory, adulthood is from twenty until sixty-five, and is divided into young adulthood from twenty to forty-five and middle adulthood, middle age, from forty-five to sixty-five.[2] In young adulthood we find a partner, form a family, and pursue a career. In middle adulthood we become what Erikson calls "numinous" role models with "true authority" who can guide the young with our "ethics, law, and insight."[3] Until recently, horror heroines were adolescent or young adult. Thus, none of Clover's final girls were older than thirty. This is because the middle-age woman is a negative stereotype, *more* negative than the gender stereotype. Sylvia Henneberg in "Moms Do Badly, But Grandmas Do Worse" (2010) say middle-age and old women fare badly in fairy tales, where they are cast as evil witch, self-sacrificing mother, or ineffectual old crone, and killed.[4] But, as you will see in this chapter, things are changing. What film theorist Jason Mittell calls "complex television" has opened a door to new stories, and a surprising result is that audiences welcome a middle-age horror heroine.[5]

I am aware zombies beg us to look at disgust, however, I did that in Chapter 6. Instead, I will explore Carol's change in season four and discuss choice and freedom. She is an example of Steele's incremental narrative, which is when we tell ourselves that we can expand our knowledge and we are able to learn and change. Carol was written to die in season three, however, she became so popular with fans that she instead became female protagonist in seasons four and five, which is when *The Walking Dead* became the most watched drama series in US cable history.[6] Rick thinks *he* is leader, however, season four ends with him and the group lined up to be slaughtered. They are saved by Carol, who after being on the road has become even more awesome. "What are you gonna do?" Tyreese asks Carol. "I'm gonna kill people," she calmly responds.

With Carol, the negative gender script is subverted into a strong, independent, and off-script protagonist. Erikson says an adult is "a judge of evil and a transmitter of ideal values."[7] In post-apocalyptic survival horror, it is crucial to be a judge of evil. If not, you can be eaten by zombies or evil people. To survive requires not only that you can kill, but also that you know *when* and *who* to kill. It involves ethical questions of choice.

The chapter first compares Carol in the graphic novel to Carol in AMC's show and introduces the concept of change. I then examine the tropes of "home" and "road," one conventionally linked to women and one to men, and ask how they are used to develop Carol as a character. Last, I return to her choices to kill, and look at self-growth, freedom, and ethics. A post-apocalyptic world is not much different from ours, and Carol's change makes her an attractive character. So attractive, in fact, that she is an excellent example of evofeminism; Carol shows how to subvert negative stereotype by learning, changing, stepping up, and claiming the freedom to make our own choices.

Graphic-Novel Carol and Television Carol

As said, in season four a badass Carol with a silver-pixie haircut, becomes a primary character along with leader Rick (Andrew Lincoln), crossbow-shooting Daryl (Norman Reedus), samurai warrior Michonne (Danai Gurira), and lovers Glenn (Steven Yeun) and Maggie (Lauren Cohan). But this is not where Carol began. The show is adapted from comic book series *The Walking Dead*, created in 2003 by writer Robert Kirkman and artist Tony Moore.[8] Comic-book Carol is one of the survivors in a camp outside Atlanta where Rick finds his wife Lori and son Carl in issue 2. Her husband commits suicide shortly after the apocalypse and she is alone with an eight-year-old daughter, Sophia. Carol is twenty-four, an insecure and needy character, who befriends Lori to feel safe. She has a romantic relationship with Tyreese, who cheats on her with Michonne, who is a strong female character in both the graphic novels and the show. Michonne with her samurai sword is a popular female action hero who I do not have the space to explore here. In the show there is no sexual relationship between Tyreese and Carol, or between Tyreese and Michonne. Graphic-novel Carol tries to match Michonne's sexual services but disgusted by her sexual acts, she breaks up with Tyreese, and suggests to Lori that the three of them—Lori, Rick, and Carol—form a polygamous relationship. When Lori rejects this, Carol commits suicide in issue 41 and her daughter dies in issue 132, twelve years old. To a fan's question of why all this "crazy shit" happens to Carol, writer Kirkman replied: "I just wanted to show how stressful life . . . actually is and how crazy it can make weaker people. Carol was a pretty weak, dependent person. Things wouldn't work out for people like her in this world."[9]

So, where graphic-novel Carol is a young adult who was a teen mother, television Carol appears to be in her forties or fifties. In season one, television Carol is the submissive and battered wife of Ed, her lazy and aggressive husband, and they have the eight-year-old Sophia. "We're just fine," Carol tells Shane (Joe Bernthal) in "Tell it to the Frogs" (1.03). Shane is leader of the camp until Rick arrives, and when Shane sees Ed hit Carol, Shane beats Ed savagely: "You put your hands to your wife, your little girl, or anyone else in this camp, I will not stop, do you hear me? I'll beat you to death, Ed."

There is no need to beat Ed to death because he is killed by zombies in "Wildfire" (1.04), and Carol puts an ax to his head to prevent him from returning as a zombie. Her strikes with the ax impress Daryl, and what begins as sad swings with the ax turns into the satisfaction of returning the blows of the past. This is where the bond between Carol and Daryl starts, both characters having suffered beatings, one by a husband and Daryl by his father. The graphic novel has no abusive husband, but a young woman breaking under the pressure of survival, and Daryl exists only in the AMC show. The show, thus, tells Carol's story not as breaking, but the opposite, changing and growing stronger.

In season two, Sophia disappears and returns as a zombie to be shot by Rick in "Pretty Much Dead Already" (2.07), and although Carol is depressed the entire season, she learns to handle a knife and a machine gun in season three, where the group settles down in a federal prison. Carol is now a strong and compassionate character who teaches the children self-defense. "You ain't like you were back in the camp, a little mouse running around, scared of her own shadow," says Merle (Michael Rooker) while Carol loads bullets into chambers. "It wasn't my shadow, it was my husbands," she replies. "Well, you don't seem scared of nothing anymore" ("This Sorrowful

Life," 3.15). True. When a lethal virus breaks out in the prison, she kills two sick people to protect the group. "It's about facing reality," she later explains to Rick in "Indifference" (4.04).

Change

The theme in season four is change. After Carol is cast out, the prison is overrun and Rick's group flee and people are scattered over a vast area in small groups or alone. Because Carol has kept close to the prison to keep an eye on the children, she quickly finds Tyreese who has fled into the woods with Rick's infant baby Judith and sisters Mika (Kyla Kenedy) and Lizzie (Brighton Sharbino), who are about ten and twelve.

Tyreese is traumatized and unable to kill, even zombies. Thus, Carol saves him and the children from the zombies in the woods. Carol, once a terrorized housewife, has learnt to kill. But the others are "stuck" in maladaptive scripts. Tyreese is traumatized, the unstable Lizzie thinks the zombies are her friends, and Mika says she can outrun the zombies and don't need to kill them. "You will have to change, everyone will. Things don't just 'work out,'" Carol explains to Mika as they follow a railroad track they hope will take them to a safe place ("The Grove," 4.14).

To change means you must switch from System 1 to System 2 and overrule your instincts and your old behavior. It means you must reevaluate ethics about who and when to kill, if you want to survive in a hostile environment. This is not the old America. Returning to Steele and his incremental narrative, we can create change by telling ourselves a positive narrative. What Steele calls the *fixed narrative* says our learning abilities and skills are limited, and that "you either have it or you don't." Reversely, an incremental narrative tells people that they can learn and it provides "information that enables a more accurate and hopeful personal narrative," a narrative which "can put [people's] achievement on very different trajectories."[10] A fixed narrative limits people and makes them underperform. An incremental narrative tells you that even if you feel, you cannot change, you *can* learn and change. Change is, like any other skill, something you can learn. And in a zombie apocalypse you *must* change.

Today, change is invested with commodified discourses of personal growth, an individual flexibility intertwined with professional flexibility, and the obligation that you must change to remain attractive as a labor force and as a romantic partner. However, I will view change in an evolutionary perspective, as part of what we can learn when we play. I am here thinking of the viewer as playing with fiction, and as playing on horror's dark stage. This play changes the player and involves our self. Play scholar Henricks says, "[e]xperiencing self means positioning oneself in the world, but those positions reflect the changing capabilities and intentions of the

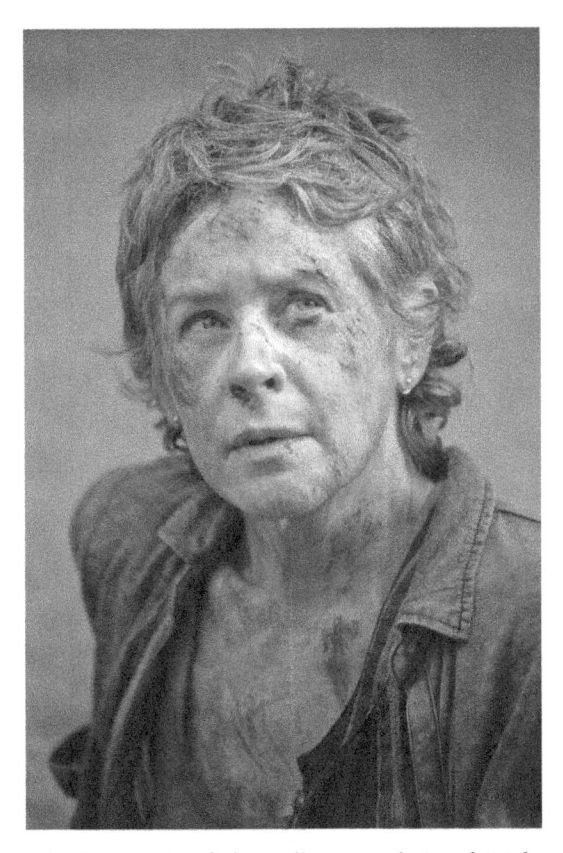

FIGURE 8.1 *In the first season of* The Walking Dead, *Carol (Melissa McBride) is a battered housewife. Her abusive husband dies in season one, she loses her daughter in season two, and in season three she becomes an able survivor.* © *American Movie Classics (AMC), Circle of Confusion, Valhalla Motion Pictures, 2010. Courtesy Gene Page/AMC.*

otherness as well as one's own powers and desires."[11] When we play with fiction, we invest ourselves in characters, and in this chapter we will invest ourselves in Carol. Our emotional dialogue will make us share her emotions, her dilemmas, and her choices. This is where play offers a "process of 'existential testing' [which] creates the possibility for favored strategies, schemas, or life lessons."[12]

A dilemma we shall meet is how to respond to the world in an adaptive yet also ethical way. To survive, Carol responds to the world *as it is*, not as it was in the past or as we think it ought to be in the future. This choice should not exclude hope nor equate survival with cynicism. Yet, sometimes it is challenging to act in a way where you can "live with yourself," as Eugene puts it when he mans up to be brave ("Us," 4.15). In season seven, Eugene will act like a coward to survive. Survival is not simple. However, it is dead certain that you do not survive, if you use outdated scripts and schemas, of which "home" is one. This is where we now turn.

House and Home

Home is conventionally linked to women, and Carol is linked to a bourgeois home. In the graphic novels, Carol used to sell Tupperware and was a happy housewife, and she is eager to try a washing detergent Glenn returns with from a scavenger trip into Atlanta. The show introduces Carol as a housewife who has lost her home in the apocalypse. She wears feminine blouses and irons clothes and is no hunter like Daryl, explorer like Glenn, or fighter like Michonne. But her mindset and clothes change in season three, where she learns to fire a machine gun and wears work pants with pockets, earth-colored blouses, a unisex-jacket, and in season four gets a leather belt to hold her iconic knuckle knife. She has come a long way from Tupperware.

A home is more than a house. It is invested with dreams. I don't know if other species share the sentiments that make us decorate a home with wallpaper, buy expensive furniture, and frame family photographs. I know little about the relation between animals and their homes, but I know they can build beautiful and elaborate living spaces. The male bowerbird, for example, builds a colorful nest to attract a mate. But are animals' homes invested with dreams like ours? I think not. And I am here not interested in habitat, or in the bricks and concrete of a house, but in the scripts we use to make a home. The *dreams* invested in home. Only humans have family pictures, and only humans could take framed pictures of the former inhabitants of our new house out to the forest to use for target practice, as Sasha does in "Forget" (5.13). She must remove traces of the former inhabitants before her new house can become her home. A house is where you live, but a home is where you build and restore your "self." And in this chapter, we are after self-development and change.

In a chapter called "House and Home," Young observes that, "[t]he rooms in house magazines are nearly always empty of people, thus enabling us to step inside their space."[13] The homes are empty, so we can picture our own bodies and our own selves in them, and in Young's view a home "carries critical liberating potential because it expresses uniquely human values."[14] It is this "uniquely human" I am after. "Home" is a cultural script and like the schema and stereotype, it is gendered. Young draws on Heidegger's discussion of dwelling as consisting of building and restoration. Heidegger reasons that men build and women restore. Not surprisingly, it is highly valued to build and connected to work, and it is lowly valued to restore and connected to cyclical labor. Now, Young wants to raise our regard for restoration and see restoration and maintenance of a home as building too. Feminists, however, are suspicious of home as a site of a feminist identity because, they argue (and I agree), our cultural script of "home" positions man as builder and woman as material. Thus, a woman is not in a home or has a home; she *is* the home.

In Western culture, an important part of the script for women slash home is the "angel in the house," a Victorian stereotype that is from Coventry Patmore's poem "The Angel in the House" (1854) written to his wife: "Man must be pleased; but/ him to please/ Is woman's pleasure; down the gulf/ Of his condoled necessities/ She casts her best, she flings herself." Patmore's angelic wife, his ideal woman,

> ... was the one near to God, the pious one who kept the family on the Christian path. In secular terms the angel provided the home environment that promoted her husband's and children's well-being in the world; she also provided a haven from its worst pressures through her sound household management and sweetness of temperament. The latter meaning suggests the angel's domesticity, unworldliness, asexuality, innocence, even helplessness in matters outside the domestic sphere.[15]

The trope of home has an angel in the house, an angel who belongs to the momism we discussed in the previous chapter. Let us now take the angel and Young's discussion of home into *The Walking Dead*.

Home Is Where You Die

The houses empty after the zombie apocalypse, like those in the home magazines, allow us to picture ourselves in them. When characters find what they think can be a suitable house, they clear out zombies and evaluate pros and cons. Defendable? Comfortable? Inconspicuous? Near food?

Carol promises to escort Tyreese and the children to Terminus, a place they have read about on posters, and which they hope is safe. She has not told Tyreese that she killed the two sick people in their group, or that Rick cast her out. And Rick didn't say anything to the others. Only Rick and Carol knew how she stepped up and was cast out. In "The Grove" Carol and Tyreese find a house in a grove, a cozy house with a porch, a garden, an old-style kitchen with a functional gas stove, an armchair in the living room with a fireplace, and roses out front. "We could stay here," says Tyreese, "we need not go to Terminus now." Mika finds a doll in the house and is ecstatic, "I'm gonna name her Giselda Gundersen." And Lizzie, who is psychologically unstable, seems to get better and understand that zombies are not friends to play with, but monsters you must kill. Carol even bakes pecan cakes. But then, returning home from a hunt, tragedy awaits: Lizzie has killed Mika and is waiting for her to return as a friend, a zombie sister.

Carol kills Mika again so she doesn't return as zombie, and Carol takes Lizzie out back and shoots her.

The pecan cakes symbolize the angel's sweetness. "I'm not used to this," Tyreese says, "being in a living room, in a house." He is overwhelmed: Mika plays with her doll, Lizzie solves a jigsaw puzzle, and Carol cracks nuts. But a home is not merely a beautiful space where you rest and live. It is also a barrier to keep others out. A home is about inclusion and exclusion: "Longing for home is the effort to retreat into a said unified identity at the expense of those projected and excluded as Other."[16] The borders of a home are meant to keep you safe. But in a post-apocalyptic world, where children carry rifles and hunting knives, borders have dissolved.

They cleansed the house of zombies and Mika killed her first walker. But a zombie world requires a constant vigilante mind. To let your guard down even a moment can bring death. "It's ugly and it's scary and it does change you. But that's how we get to be here, that's the cost, that's growing up now," Carol tells Lizzie. Lizzie must understand that zombies are *not* friends, and Mika learn to kill not just zombies but also people. When Carol made the house a home, she let her guard down. Carol and Tyreese can keep out zombies, but the sentimental script of "home" as angelic haven makes them forget the enemy within, Lizzie's illness. Carol is charmed by the idea of being an angel in the house. But this world no longer has homes or angels.

"The Grove" subverts the trope of home as a haven, where an evil world can be excluded, and you can nurse a sick mind back to being sound, that is, where you can do the restoration, Young praises. The trope is so appealing Carol forgets herself, and performs the script of the angel. It is, however, an outdated script. Before they find the house, Carol tells Mika she "will have to toughen up." At the sight of the house, Mika happily exclaims, "my mum used to say everything works out the way it's supposed to." When Carol takes Lizzie out behind the house, Lizzie sobs: "I'm sorry. You're mad at me." Carol repeats Mika's words: "Everything works out the way it's supposed to. Just look at the flowers." Then she shoots Lizzie in the back of the head.

We know home magazines offer illusions, yet we buy them. The lesson of *The Walking Dead* is that "home" and "angel" may live in characters' minds, but the old scripts are lethal. Young wants us to re-think gender and home, and she draws from philosopher Hannah Arendt a distinction between work and labor as respectively producing objects (work) and being cyclical (like household care). In such a dichotomy, men are the builders and women restore and do maintenance labor and serve the family and preserve the home. Young wants to see the female subject as fluid, her home as changing, and her work on/in home as both labor and work, both making and changing her home and her identity. Young mentions other kinds of homes that are open to a community, like churches and communal spaces. However, after the apocalypse, all versions of home are lethal, private houses as well as communal spaces. Every season has a safe place which is overrun: In season one it is the Center for Disease Control in Atlanta; season two has Hershel's farm; season three the fortified town Woodbury and the prison; season four has Terminus, a train maintenance facility run by cannibals; season five has Father Gabriel's church and the Grady Memorial Hospital; and season six has the gated city Alexandria.

A home cannot keep you safe, because after the apocalypse, a house is just a house and the sacrosanct home with the angel a dream. Carol had cared for Mika and Lizzie since season three, but she lost the children because she performed an outdated script.

Alexandria

At the end of season five, Rick's group is invited into Alexandria, an exclusive gated community. Alexandria shares its name with Egypt's Alexandria, a city that once housed the world's biggest library and one of the Seven

FIGURE 8.2 *At the end of season five the group is invited into the gated community Alexandria. In season six Carol (Melissa McBride) masquerades as a lost housewife who in Alexandria has found a new "home" where she bakes cookies.* The Walking Dead. © *American Movie Classics (AMC), Circle of Confusion, Valhalla Motion Pictures, 2012. Courtesy Frank Ockenfels 3/AMC.*

Wonders of the Ancient world, the 449 ft. tall Lighthouse of Alexandria. In this city echoing past wisdom and wonders, citizens are now inept at defending themselves, which is why they invite Rick's able group. The leader, former senator Deanna, interviews them individually on camera in "Remember." Carol hides her abilities as a hunter and killer and pretends she is an Angel who lost her House and just wants to bake cookies. Carol has changed outdoor clothes for an ironed shirt and a blouse with flowers. In the mansion with leather-bound books and Chesterfield couches, Carol smiles to the camera: "I did laundry, gardened, um. Always had dinner on the table for Ed when he came home. Um. I miss that stupid, wonderful man every day. You know, I really didn't have much to offer this group [Rick's group], so I think I just sort of became their den mother. And they've been nice enough to protect me" (5.12).

Carol is beyond subversion, this is re-authoring. From battered housewife to zombie killer she is now a sly liar, who uses the angel of the house trope as decoy to break into the pantry, where chocolate and weapons are stored. The group surrendered weapons on entering Alexandria, but they don't want to "become soft" and thus steal guns for secret target practice. When the boy Sam finds Carol stealing weapons, she threatens him:

> CAROL: You can never tell anyone, especially your mum. Because if you do, one morning you wake up and you won't be in your bed.
> SAM: Where will I be?
> CAROL: You'll be outside the walls. Far, far away and tied to a tree and you'll scream and scream because you'll be so afraid. And no one will come to help because no one will hear you. Well, something will hear you. The monsters will come ... And they will tear you apart and eat you all up while you're still alive. All while you can still feel it. Then afterwards noone will ever know what happened to you. Or, you can promise not to ever tell anyone what you saw here and then nothing will happen and you'll get cookies ("Spend," 5.14).

After the 2008 economic recession, feminists were disappointed with media representations of women. Carol, however, is just that off-script femininity that Negra called for in 2009. Her homemaker figure is a masquerade that will out-perform and outlive Deanna and poor, terrified Sam.

The Chronotope of the Road

In season one, Carol loses a wife-beating husband, and in season two she loses a daughter. In season three she learns to hunt and shoot and kill, and in season four she is ready for her next test, the road. Rick and Carol had driven to a small town to search for supplies, which is where

Rick leaves Carol with a car. "You're not that woman who's too scared to be alone. Not anymore. You're gonna start over, find others, people who don't know. And you're gonna survive out here." If "home" is by convention a female space, "road" is by convention a male trope which invokes rebellion, mobility, journey, promise, exploration, and psychological change.

Russian literary scholar Mikhail Bakhtin used the term "chronotope," combining Greek *chronos* (time) and *topos* (space), to discuss the road in Western narratives. Bakhtin's chronotope is both a physical time/place and a metaphor: "In the literary artistic chronotope, spatial and temporal indicators are fused into one carefully thought-out, concrete whole. Time, as it were, thickens, takes on flesh, becomes artistically visible; likewise, space becomes charged and responsive to the movements of time, plot and history. This intersection of axes and fusion of indicators characterizes the artistic chronotope."[17] In literature, a reader must picture the road in her mind. In *The Walking Dead*, roads are visualized as the cracked highways leading into Atlanta, country roads in rural landscapes, dirt roads through small towns, or railroad tracks in the woods promising a "way out." These roads are invested with time and space, a historical America gone awry, and concrete space, *this* highway bridge in Atlanta where Carol and Daryl try to escape in a car from walkers. The road, says Bakhtin, offers chance encounters with strangers and can transport characters to unpredictable places and turn a plot in new directions.

We know American roads from the road movie. *Easy Rider* (1969) rejected the middle-class home and celebrates male buddies traveling across the continent in a revolt against a consumerist, late modern America.[18] This type of road symbolizes counter culture and identity work and to travel is both a physical journey—taking the straight road, being lost, making a U-turn, being trapped in a dead-end place—and a psychological journey. Furthermore, in the travel narrative, with the novel *Utopia* (1516) as paradigmatic example, we find the search for a Promised Land where you can be "free" and society is "better" than the one we live in. Thus, from travel literature to the road movie, roads are invested with chance, adventure, revolt, personal development, change, and utopias.

The travel narrative and the road used to be a male space with a "male hero on the road of discovery ... a highly gendered space ... [about] the male flight from domesticity ... linking man, machine, and mobility."[19] But since *Thelma & Louise*, roads are also traveled by women as "an escape from the patriarchal law of domestic servitude and economic dependence," yet fraught with a sentimental longing for what was "lost," namely home as peaceful sanctuary. "Somehow, time is out of joint and the characters are out of place; consequently, their projected destination is one where they hope to find a home (also within themselves), some illusionary place where space-time relations are perceived to be still unharmed. Mobility is conceived of as a journey back to, not from, home."[20]

FIGURE 8.3 *Carol (Melissa McBride) travels the post-apocalyptic road with her friend and fellow survivor Daryl (Norman Reedus).* The Walking Dead. © *American Movie Classics (AMC), Circle of Confusion, Valhalla Motion Pictures, 2011. Courtesy Frank Ockenfels 3/AMC.*

Rick kicked Carol out on the road, a place she masters so well that weeks later she can save Tyreese. After losing Lizzie and Mika, they return to the railroad track which posters say lead to a sanctuary called "Terminus." But like "home" turned out to be a lethal trope, "road" too is a dangerous script.

The End of the Road

Like home magazines, post-apocalyptic roads invite us to picture ourselves in the empty roads, ambiguously invested with nostalgic memories of past roads and homes and traumatic memories of their recent destruction. Characters cling to the hope that roads—*these* railroad tracks—might lead back to "home" or perhaps even a Utopia (a better place). However, after the apocalypse, roads are extremely dangerous spaces as we see in post-apocalypse road movies *The Road* (2006 novel by Cormac McCarthy, film

2009 by John Hillcoat), *Carriers* (2009, David and Àlex Pastor), and *The Book of Eli* (2010, Albert and Allen Hughes).

The railroad tracks lead to Terminus, a brick building and facility for train maintenance. Already in the episode "Isolation" (4.03), Michonne and Daryl hear a radio broadcast promising sanctuary long before the prison is overrun in "Too Far Gone" (4.08). After Rick casts Carol out (4.04), we don't see her until she saves Tyreese and the children much later ("After," 4.09). When the group is scattered in the mid-season finale and everyone is on the run, characters encounter posters and signs along railroad tracks that point to a place called "Terminus": "Sanctuary for all. Community for all. Those who arrive survive." There are maps showing how to find Terminus. The survivors follow the signs and Maggie even writes on posters so Glenn can find her. Glenn brings Abraham's group.

They all hope Terminus is the sanctuary signs promise. But it is, like the house in the grove, a Dead End. It turns out to be a cannibal slaughterhouse, and the railroad tracks leading to the red brick buildings bring to mind Auschwitz-Birkenau, the infamous Nazi extermination camp which also had railroad tracks leading into the part of the camp with gas chambers for extermination. When Carol searches the buildings to find her captured friends in "No Sanctuary" (5.01), she sees piles of weapons and items stolen from slaughtered victims, piles that echo the heaps of stolen items in Nazi camps. The cannibals' friendly demeanor fools everyone. First, Maggie and her group walk through the gates. And although Rick and his group are suspicious in "Us", and bury a bag with weapons before they climb the fence, they, too, are fooled by smiling leader Mary (Denise Crosby) and her adult son, Gareth (Andrew J. West). Because they hope for a home and sanctuary, they put down their defenses.

Carol and Tyreese with infant Judith are nearing Terminus, when they hear distant gunfire. They leave the railroad and take a small track east. Daryl has taught Carol to hunt in silence, which is why she can surprise Martin, one of the cannibals talking to his friends over a walkie-talkie. Carol captures and disarms the cannibal, takes his M16A4 assault rifle, and smears herself in walker's rotten guts so she can blend in without being attacked by walkers. When Carol hits Terminus, a one-woman army, she finds her friends lined up at a metal tub with their hands tied behind their backs, ready to be slaughtered like cattle. In a face-off between Carol and Mary, Mary explains why her group became cannibals: Initially the place *was* a sanctuary, and they had put signs for people to find Terminus. However, evil people came and killed and raped, and when Mary's group took back the place they decided, "you're the butcher or you're the cattle."

Mary compares herself to Carol. "You could have been one of us," Mary (Denise Crosby) cries, as Carol shoots her. They were both traumatized and suffered loss. Mary lost family and friends, and she assumes Carol lost family too. However, Carol reacts differently. "You could have listened to what the world is telling you," Mary tells her. "You lead people here and you take what they have and you kill them?" Carol asks, leaving Mary to the walkers.

The post-apocalyptic road is a more complex script than home is. Where home is useless, the road combines several scripts, some useless and others still useful. The road can still take characters through landscapes and lead to encounters with strangers and new opportunities. Thus, it can be a psychological journey, a test of character, and develop one's self into a stronger person. However, it holds no promise of Utopia and strangers can be friends or killers. The post-apocalyptic road movie still has light at the end of the tunnel in *The Road* and *The Book of Eli*, where children and the Bible promise future sanctuaries. *The Walking Dead* offers no such hope. Children die, the Bible is just a book, Alexandria falls in season five, and the road can mean self-development but also bring death.

But if there are no homes left, the road is still ours to travel and prompt ourselves the question if we will be butcher or cattle, or if there are other options.

Stepping Up

As said, I find Carol intriguing. She is a battered housewife who turns into a child-killer and a road-warrior, a pragmatic horror heroine who can retire the useless home trope and re-author the dangerous yet transformative road script. Rather than nurture nostalgia for lost dreams, she develops the emotional stamina necessary to survive in a zombie world and she learns to switch to System 2. She liked Karen and David, the people she kills so they won't infect others. She stepped up. In the next sections I discuss what is required to survive and how Carol reasons about killing, but in this section I want to first relate her change to the self-growth that became popular in the 1990s.

British sociologist Anthony Giddens argues that late modernity expects us to be reflexive and strategically plan our lives and choose which lifestyle we want. "What to do? How to act? Who to be? These are focal questions for everyone living in circumstances of late modernity – and ones which, on some level or another, all of us answer, either discursively or through day-to-day social behavior."[21] These questions are relevant in the West, where most nations are democratic and have welfare systems and free education. In Chapter 5 I discussed emerging adulthood, where we experiment before making lasting commitments. This phase between adolescence and commitment is growing longer in high-modernist countries as we postpone having children. To choose a lifestyle is, like emerging adulthood, a privilege in rich societies. Now, within the fiction, Carol's change of course does not spring from free choice, however, for the viewer her change illustrates how

FIGURE 8.4 *In seasons four and five Carol (Melissa McBride) becomes a road warrior, an experienced killer, and the group's savior.* The Walking Dead. © American Movie Classics (AMC), Circle of Confusion, Valhalla Motion Pictures, 2014. Courtesy Gene Page/AMC.

an individual can learn to change, thus reflecting our life situation. We do not face zombies, but we face a world with other challenges.

To return to choice and change, Giddens takes his point of departure from the self-therapy literature that tells the reader she must "take charge of time" and not "cling to the past" but accept the risk of wrong choices because "this clutching at security can be very discouraging to interpersonal relationships, and will impede your own self-growth."[22] The self is "a reflexive project for which the individual is responsible ..."[23] Thus, if you want to fashion a new self you must accept risks:

> The individual has to *confront novel hazards* as a necessary part of *breaking away from established patterns of behavior* – including the risk

that *things could possibly get worse* than they were before... Negotiating a significant transition in life, leaving home... moving between different areas or routines, confronting illness, beginning therapy – all mean running consciously entertained risks in order to grasp *the new opportunities which personal crises open up* ... such transitions are drawn into, and surmounted by means of, the *reflexively mobilised trajectory of self-actualisation* (added emphasis).[24]

Butcher or cattle? Or, as the tagline goes in season five, will you "hunt or be hunted"? A difference between survival horror and identity horror is that protagonists in identity horror usually do not see danger coming, and are slow to realize what choices to make if they are to survive. They are attacked by forces they hardly understand—a psycho or their own mind—and often die. In survival horror, the situation is simple—are you dinner?—and it is also simple to assess the danger. It may not be easy to learn what it takes to survive, but protagonists in survival horror stand a better statistical chance of survival than those in identity horror. Now, Giddens' reflexive individual is a person who chooses "how to act" and "who to be," the latter which "concerns the very core of self-identity, its making and remaking."[25]

We can read the neo-primitive world of *The Walking Dead* as an example of our late modern society, which Giddens calls post-traditionalist. We no longer follow traditions but make free choices. It is not entirely clear which skills are required after a zombie apocalypse, but it is crystal clear that life is a stream of dangerous and unpredictable events, and hard decisions require what military psychologists call *battle mind*, which is the ability to make quick and "cold" decisions under life-and-death circumstances.[26] When Rick casts Carol out, she says, "I thought you were done making decisions for everyone." Why can only Rick make decisions on behalf of the group? "I could have pretended that everything was gonna be fine," she says, "but I didn't. I did something. I stepped up. I had to do something."

When Carol "steps up," she challenges Rick's leadership. In season three Rick lost his wife and became a weak and occasionally delusional leader. In season four he makes only wrong decisions, and the season ends with Rick and his group lined up to be slaughtered by the cannibals. Thus, it appears a blessing that Carol "stepped up," because she saves the group in the first episode of season five when she single-handedly attacks Terminus. Her personal journey is one long personal crisis to which she reacts with learning from mistakes and adapting to the hostile environment.

"You Have to Change"

At the end of season seven, Rick, Carol, and Daryl are the sole survivors from the first season. And since Carol in "No Sanctuary" saves Rick and the entire group, we can say she represents what it takes to survive in a hostile world: *the ability to change.*

Carol told Mika that "you're little and you're sweet and those are two things that can get you killed. Can you change that? Toughen up?" "I don't need to toughen up, I can run, I'm good at that," Mika responded. Carol corrects her: "No! My daughter ran. And it wasn't enough. It's why I taught the kids at the prison to do more than that . . . sooner or later you'll have to do it [kill people] or you'll die. So you're gonna change the way you think about it. You have to change, everyone does now." As the episode ends—after Lizzie has killed her sister Mika, and Carol has shot the dead Mika and killed Lizzie—Carol in voice-over recalls telling Mika, "You can't win. You fight and you fight it, and you don't give up. And then one day you just . . . change. You'll change" (4.14).[27]

In its purest form, survival horror is when you become prey. Films like *Predator* and *Stake Land* demonstrate that: You cannot reason with a lion if it chooses you for dinner, neither can you reason with the aggressor in survival horror. Zombies are beyond reasoning and so, too, are the Governor, the cannibals, the Claimers, and Negan and his Saviors, all the predators in *The Walking Dead*. As Carol explained, it is not enough to run, because the predator will find you. It is fine to be able to read maps, track game, hunt and kill, hard-wire cars, scavenge, and so on, as these are handy tools in a survival tool box. But the best tool of them all is the ability to change.

In survival horror, change means you must learn to kill, and also know *when* and *who* to kill. Sometimes you must kill when you don't want to. How do you know who to kill? Not all killing is instinctive self-defense. Creativity researcher Csikszentmihalyi differentiates between two types of knowledge, one he calls *fluid knowledge*, which is when we solve tasks that involve System 1 (remembering strings of numbers, recognizing patterns, drawing inference from logical relationships), and another he calls *crystallized knowledge*. This latter is learnt and "involves making sensible judgments, recognizing similarities across different categories, using induction and logic reasoning. These abilities depend more on reflection than quick reaction . . ."[28] With crystallized knowledge you are using System 2. It takes practice.

Carol says everyone must change. We recall from Chapter 1 how Gazzaniga says our ability to generate a self is performed by an interpreter module, which generates ad hoc explanations to situations. Our left-brain interpreter module is not governed by a "self," but produces interpretations, stories where we see ourselves as subjects with agency, and those interpretations are what we think of as our self. The human brain is unique in its flexibility. You *can* change from abused wife to someone stepping up. It takes time, but if you keep fighting, someday you will be a different person.

In late modernity, says Henricks, adults play to realize and test and change their selves, and "play represents a special process of self-construction and evaluation, one that celebrates the role of agency in human affairs."[29] Within the fiction Carol is of course not playing, however, the fiction is playing with Carol. We engage emotionally with Carol and with her change from victim to victor, from moral patient to moral agent, and we salute her challenge of Rick's leadership and agree with her choice to kill not only zombies and predators, and we even accept her decision to kill friends who are potential dangers.

Two Kinds of Freedom

When she kills without asking Rick for permission, Carol claims freedom to act. She also claims the freedom to choose between alternatives (should the sick be isolated or killed). In this section I want to ask what it means to be free to make such choices.

Freedom is a philosophical concept, but I will deal with it as an *emotional experience*. For example, when Carol kills Lizzie, I felt sad and frustrated, but when she killed the cannibals I felt uplifted and relieved, excited and even exhilarated. Go, Carol, go, an inner voice shouted. And when we in flashback see Carol killing Karen and David, I felt surprised, shocked, but rather than be revolted I felt impressed. In all three situations Carol exercised *free will* and made *a choice*.

In "Emotions and the Psychology of Freedom" (1994) cognitive psychologist George Mandler discusses freedom, which is not an emotion per se, but an emotional experience of a situation. Mandler links the experience of freedom and unfreedom to the removal or setting of hurdles and constraints to the individual's ability to act. Thus, our experience of changes to our ability to act makes us feel free or unfree, and the more sudden the changes are, the stronger is our sense of freedom or unfreedom. Mandler links freedom to "detection of discrepancies," an ability to assess changes in our situation. This difference detector "informs the organism that the situation it is in is different than expected, that the world has changed, that new ways of dealing with it need to be developed, and that preparation for further action is needed."[30] Thus, the ability to respond to discrepancies leads to new ways of perceiving our world and coping with changes. Mandler says we respond to changes in our environment with *assimilation* (accepting changes) or *accommodation* (changing ourselves). Accommodation requires,

> ... the change of existing mental structures in order to deal with new events and changing conditions ... The positive evaluation of the novel derives in part from the satisfaction of dealing with the unknown, the sense of completing and the feeling of achievement when new situations are mastered and brought under our control ... In the absence of value systems that favor dealing with new situations, they usually will be seen

as somewhat disturbing and anxiety arousing ... Discrepancies are not only indicative of novelty, they also, by the very act of accommodation, *create new ways of seeing the world, new ways of perceiving and thinking* (added emphasis).[31]

When Carol talks of change, she means we must learn new ways of "perceiving and thinking." Mandler discusses two kinds of freedoms. The first is innate, it is "doing what one desires" in the liberal tradition of John Stuart Mill. It is an egocentric emotion and takes pleasure in *me* being able to do what *I* want. Mandler calls this freedom natural because it is physical and instinctive. It is our relief when a restraint is removed, such as the freedom to leave a prison cell, or the freedom to eat if you were starving. The second kind of freedom is to be able to make the choice to do what feels good and right. This freedom is socially constructed and such choice falls within the virtue ethics of Aristotle. It is the freedom to do what is perceived as good for your society or your group. Martin Luther King's "free at last" meant the freedom for African Americans to be equal to white Americans. This freedom is more complex than the first, and involves a sense of present and future, of what we hope for and what might be the consequences of our actions. Greek philosopher Epictetus said that "freedom is not acquired by satisfying yourself with what you desire, but by destroying your desire," and Rousseau observed, "obedience to a law which we prescribe to ourselves is liberty."[32] In this sense *freedom is the ability to choose to do what feels right.* When Tyreese is unable to kill walkers and humans, Carol takes over. Tyreese is traumatized and unfree, but Carol is free to make the choice to kill if she thinks there is reason to do so.

Let us take an ethological detour. The problem in post-apocalyptic fiction is to know what is good and right when civilization has crumbled and people no longer agree on the rules. Are we to revert to a primitive "nature red in tooth and claw" state? Bekoff and Pierce in *Wild Justice* say all social animals have rules about behavior, and such rules are part innate, part learned. If animals break social rules they are punished by the group. What is "good" moral behavior is specific to each species; dogs have dog-rules, mice have mice-rules, lions have lion-rules, and humans have human-rules. Yet Bekoff and Pierce say across social animals there are universal normative elements: "Moral behavior is other-regarding and prosocial; it is behavior that promotes harmonious coexistence by avoiding harm to others and providing others with help. Norms of behavior that regulate social interactions are found in humans and animals alike. And these norms seem to be universal."[33] Such rules look like the so-called Golden Rule: Treat others like you want to be treated.[34]

Humans have more advanced cognitive abilities than other animals, which provide us with more options. We can think up imaginary scenarios and make alternative routes rather than take those that are hard-wired or learnt, and we can write individual scripts in addition to those society hands us. In short, where animal morality is biological and universal, ethics is an exclusively human concept, and it is abstract, situational, and agreed on by individuals.[35] One society may have slavery and another not, one society may stone women as punishment for infidelity and another not, one nation may exterminate Jews like Nazi Germany and another not.

Eudaimonia

Balancing morals and ethics is only a problem for humans. Animals have morality, not ethics. But humans can create different societies with different ethics, which is what we find in *The Walking Dead*. Do you want to join the cannibals, the Claimers, or Rick's group? What kind of late-modernist "self" have you fashioned, what do *you* think is good and right (freedom of choice), what society do you want to belong to (choice of ethics), and how do you want life to be in the new world?

Let us make a brief philosophical detour. Please bear with me. In survival horror, survival means killing, which raises questions of moral behavior, freedom, free will, and the individual's ability to change and make choices. What is good for *your* survival? Is survival linked to belonging to a group? What, then, is good for the group? Now, in philosophy we find three moral schools: In *deontology* (Greek *deon* means duty) you follow the rules, for instance, Christianity's ten commandments. In *consequentialism* you assess an outcome and choose that which provides maximum good for your group. And in *virtue ethics* you weigh virtue (*arete*) with moral wisdom (*phronesis*) to achieve happiness or "human flourishing" (*eudaimonia—eu* [good] and *daimon* [spirit]). The latter, *eudaimonia* or virtue ethics, has been a constant matter of disagreement. Aristotle, for example, believed one could be virtuous and live a good life, while the cynics and stoics believed that to have virtue you had to forsake the good life, because it was a distraction.

My focus in this chapter is not ethics and I leave further discussions of values to others. My interest is Carol's change, which I think makes her a survivor and an attractive character to the audience. I raise the philosophical issue because I think her change involves moral reasoning. Let us look at three situations where she kills. First, she kills the cannibals, which I felt was good, because they violated universal rules. They killed their own species when they didn't have to and thus broke the Golden Rule, and what Bekoff and Pierce call universal prosocial behavior in social animals. We can say Carol's killing is *deontologism*. If you break the rules, you must pay, a view every viewer can understand, because it is innate. The second situation is when she kills Karen and David, and justifies the killing with saving others from being infected. This would be *consequentialism*, doing what is unpleasant for the greater good. Last, then, is when Carol kills Lizzie.

The image of a crying Carol shooting Lizzie tells us Carol is highly conflicted. Back in season two, when Rick shot her zombie daughter Sophia, Carol was hysterical and Daryl had to hold her back with force. Now, Carol is pulling the trigger to kill a child. This is *virtue ethics*, where Carol weighs pros and cons to find what is necessary to achieve "human flourishing." It is unethical to kill, especially a child, yet it is necessary because this particular child is sick and dangerous. Carol is conflicted between the instinct to protect Lizzie and the decision to kill Lizzie. Such conflict and the sanctity of a child's life presents a dilemma. In animal society, mothers are not conflicted about killing offspring if it is necessary for survival. Thus, Zuk writes about kangaroos whose pouch closes to the young joey if conditions are harsh: "If they are still too young to survive without their mother's milk, they starve and die. No conscious decision, no heartbreaking dilemma, is required; mothers that did this and survived to reproduce at another time were more likely to pass their genes on than mothers that tried to keep their

FIGURE 8.5 *Carol from* The Walking Dead *as a McFarlane action figure.* © McFarlane Toys, *The Walking Dead TV Series 6, 5 in Action Figure, Carol Peletier.*

FIGURE 8.6 *Carol from* The Walking Dead *as a POP! vinyl figure.*
© POP! vinyl by Funko.

young alive as well as themselves, and lost the battle."[36] In the animal world mothers will kill offspring when circumstances call for it, because the aim is "not to take care of the helpless but to maximize one's reproductive success."[37] Those mothers are not conflicted and they don't cry.

To survive in a hostile environment requires a calm mind that stays focused under pressure. Such a mind requires self-esteem. If you have low self-esteem you will be afraid and make choices based on fear, and if you have too high self-esteem you will favor yourself and your group and become cruel and arrogant like Negan in season seven. Carol changes from someone who made choices based on fear to become someone who makes choices based on compassion and reasoning, someone who has the self-confidence to make unpleasant decisions. We see this in Carol's comments "it's about facing reality," "you do what you have to," and "I'm gonna kill people." Psychologists Jonathon D. Brown and Margaret A. Marshall (2001) say the biggest difference between people with high and low self-esteem is not their feelings when they fail, but how they handle failure. People high in self-esteem "possess the ability to respond to failure in ways that ensure that these feelings [to feel better about themselves] remain. In our judgment, it is this capacity, rather than the feelings themselves, that is most critical to understanding the nature of self-esteem."[38] People with self-esteem, for example, compensate for failure in one area by reminding themselves of their abilities in other areas.

I don't have space to explore self-esteem, self-confidence, and freedom further, but my point is that these "deep" concepts tie in with challenging emotions and crystallized knowledge, and are necessary for survival. The survival scenarios in *The Walking Dead* constantly involve dilemmas. During season four, when Carol was cast out, is when she changed the most. She already knew how to handle a knife and a gun, but on the road, she learnt virtue ethics and became ready to lead the group as Rick's equal. This was also the time when her character became available as an action figurine complete with her iconic knuckle knife and badass demeanor.

Surviving Middle Age

As I said at the start of the chapter, until recently, middle-age women were cast as stereotypes of evil witch, inefficient crone, or self-sacrificing mother, and destined to die. However, things are changing and Carol is part of an increasing use of more positive middle-age female characters in television series. Other examples are Olivia in *Hemlock Grove*, Angela in *The Exorcist* (2016–), and Jessica Lange's characters Constance, Sister Jude, and Fiona in the first three seasons of *American Horror Story*. Let us end the chapter by reflecting on why Carol didn't die as originally scripted.

Writer Robert Kirkman credits McBride's acting for the choice to keep Carol alive. "Carol, in the comic, was an attempt at showing someone who just crumbles . . . for the show, we did a little bit of that, but from the get go, we were trying to do something different with television Carol. And Melissa was a huge part of that. She was too capable of an actress and had too much of a presence."[39] Fans, however, say they like Carol's ordinariness: "Why is Carol such a unique female character? Because she doesn't look like the stereotypical bombshell babe with her boobs hanging out and her makeup and hair all done up right, she gets better and better as a character as the story progresses."[40] In addition to McBride's acting, I suggest Carol's change from a weak and dependent person to a strong and independent person makes the character attractive, even sexy and romantic. I have focused on her relation to home and road. An element I have not examined is Carol's relationship to Daryl (Norman Reedus), a rebellious motorcycle-riding hunter in Rick's group who exists only in the television show. The age difference between actors Reedus and McBride is four years, however, with her gray hair Carol appears older than Daryl who has unkempt hair and a rebellious attitude. And in a culture where ageism is part of gender stereotyping, it is interesting that when fans pair Carol and Daryl—the so-called Carylers—they depict the age difference as bigger than four years. Thus, fan art portrays Daryl and Carol as Beauty with a younger Beast, or Jane with a younger Tarzan.

We can speculate Carol's popularity with fans of the show added to the decision to keep Carol and kill another character instead. "In the original draft of that script ["The Killer Within" 3.04], Melissa McBride's character

FIGURE 8.7 *Carol (Melissa McBride) leading fellow female survivors in season eight of* The Walking Dead. © *American Movie Classics (AMC), Circle of Confusion, Valhalla Motion Pictures, 2014. Courtesy Alan Clarke/AMC.*

(Carol) was supposed to die. Iron-E (T-Dog) wasn't going to die, it was going to be Carol. And there are times when one of the producers has to make that sad call and say, listen, I have some bad news for you . . . Because, by the time they get to episode six, you know what, we changed that a little bit and Carol's going to live now and T-Dog's going to die."[41] Actors Reedus and McBride were asked about fans' speculations acknowledged the pairing. "It's more interesting to see these two damaged people gravitate to each other, needing each other's friendship," Reedus commented, and McBride suggested the characters were, in an emotional sense, a couple. "Look at it this way, they already are, just by virtue of wanting something like the kiss or whatever . . . but I think people don't see it that way 'til there's a physical confirmation."[42]

Carol is an example of what until recently was believed impossible: That we can re-author the negative middle-age stereotype into a strong and compassionate character, who has the courage to step up, the willpower to change, claims freedom and independence and agency, wears unisex clothes, isn't botoxed or surgically altered, has gray hair and no makeup, *and* is attractive and sexy and is embraced by the audience.

9

Age Anxiety and Chills:

Jessica Lange and *American Horror Story*

> *So, the first step toward a more creative life is the cultivation of curiosity and interest.*
> MIHALY CSIKSZENTMIHALYI , *Creativity*[1]

When I set out writing this book, there were no middle-age horror heroines, except in old "hagsploitation" from the 1960s.[2] Since then, things have changed. In the previous chapter, I examined Carol in *The Walking Dead* and this chapter is dedicated to Jessica Lange, the star of horror television series, *American Horror Story* (2011–, FX). Seasons one and two were well received, but when Lange took over the show in seasons three and four, reviewers raved. *Los Angeles Times* wrote about season three, "There will be blood, and monsters, power plays and many horrible things going bump in the night. More important, most important, there will be Jessica Lange."[3] And about season four *The Guardian* wrote, "Jessica Lange is again some kind of Emmy-attracting whirlwind."[4]

In season one, Lange plays a side character, but she plays a primary character in season two, and in seasons three and four plays all-dominating protagonists around whom other characters' stories revolve. In season three, "Coven" (2013), Lange is the age-anxious witch Fiona, and in season four, "Freak Show" (2014), she plays Elsa, a German ex-dominatrix and owner of a freak circus in Florida in 1952. The show has a burlesque tone, so fans were prepared for surprise. However, the first episode in the fourth season made my jaw drop. Here, Elsa sings in her circus on opening night, wearing an ill-fitting blue suit and smeary makeup—and performs David Bowie's

"Life on Mars." Elsa's thin, yet deeply moving voice and Lange's intense performance sent chills down my back. Why did she sing a 1971 Bowie song in a 2014 horror show set in 1952? Why was I moved and felt chills, when I am not even a Bowie fan?

Until now, we have held the horror heroine up to her life stage. According to Erikson, each life stage has its own aims and conflicts. In young adulthood, the aim is to form relationships, build a family, make a career. In middle adulthood, the aim is to be generative and contribute to society. Caroline changed from shallow teen to empathic young adult, and Carol becomes a brave and numinous adult. However, Fiona and Elsa are selfish. They just want to turn back time and go back to be young again. *American Horror Story (AHS)* is not about character development, but prioritizes surprise over plot, giving viewers a puzzle to play with rather than a story to follow. The show's trademark is to use and break conventions. Fiona and Elsa are appealing *because* they reject conventional scripts and the gender stereotype.

The anthology series was created by Brad Falchuk and Ryan Murphy with a recurring ensemble cast of actors and a different story in each season. Season one, "Murder House," is a present-day haunted house story; season two, "Asylum," is set in 1964 in an asylum for the criminally insane; the third season, "Coven," deals with witches in present-day New Orleans; and the fourth season, "Freak Show," follows Elsa's freak circus in 1952. Each season has new stories and characters, and the aim is to offer something novel and different. For example, the second season has a Nazi doctor experimenting on patients, a serial killer, *and* aliens.

As said, things are changing. A middle-age horror heroine, once unheard of, becomes common and even older. Carol is mid-forties in *The Walking Dead*, Famke Janssen, playing Olivia in *Hemlock Grove*, turned fifty in season two, Geena Davis starring in *The Exorcist* (2016–) is sixty, and Jessica Lange is mid-sixties in seasons three and four of *AHS*. But middle age no longer prevents horror stardom and among the accolades for Lange's performances in *AHS* are two Emmys, a Golden Globe, a Critics Choice Television Award, a Screen Actors Guild Award, and a Satellite Award. Whirlwind indeed.

In contrast to other middle-age protagonists, Lange's characters draw attention to age as a negative script for the middle-age woman. Fiona refuses to age, and Elsa is afraid she is too old to be a star. Seasons three and four approach the theme of age and ageism in different ways. "Coven" pits Fiona against a group of millennial witches, thus starting a generation war, and "Freak Show," plays with intertextual puzzle pieces to generate surprise and chills. In the first part of the chapter we will explore the emotion of *interest*, which is central to Elsa's character.[5] Interest is an epistemological emotion to do with curiosity, novelty, and learning. I then discuss age anxiety in season three, and interest and chills in season four. We will see that although Fiona and Elsa are selfish, their critique of the middle-age script is exceptional in our culture obsessed with youth. Their refusal to submit to conventions and instead write their own scripts is highly appealing to an evofeminist viewer.

The Emotion of Interest

Play with genre conventions is the core of the show and makes *AHS* creative horror, which is the narrative where the salient theme is the play-with-play function. The three basic narratives—predator horror, social horror, and identity horror—are driven by the three types of aggression linked to hunting, competition, and self-defense. Creative horror is not driven by aggression, because the narrative is concerned with voluntary play with challenging and dangerous edgework. Thus, we recall our discussion of meta-play in Chapter 7. Talking of *The Babadook* I defined the film's use of play as coaching characters in *how* to play. In *AHS*, the meta function is different; it is to draw a viewer's attention to multiple viewer positions and layers of meaning in the fiction, to the text's play with tropes, scripts, and stereotypes. If the three basic horror narratives have inherent rules, creative horror is concerned with exploring rules, with questioning, undoing, redoing, and changing the rules.

An example of meta-play is Twisty the Clown, a character in "Freak Show" who wears an uncanny half-face mask with a grinning mouth over his clown-painted face. When he approaches a victim, she freezes to contemplate the weirdness of a mask over a mask, and Twisty can kill her, unhindered. She is so taken by surprise, she forgets to run (4.01). We see a similar multi-masking when Elsa sings Bowie: Her makeup and costume mimics Bowie's makeup and costume in the 1973 song video,[6] and Bowie's makeup is an exaggerated version of a woman's makeup and his face can be interpreted as a mask of femininity. Elsa's white-painted face is that of an aging female performer, both Elsa *and* Lange, wearing Bowie's face wearing a woman's face. No wonder Elsa's song made my jaw drop; my brain exploded in new neuronal synaptic connections seeking explanations to what was happening.

Creativity is linked to the emotion of interest. Social animals are naturally interested in new and complex things. In *Exploring the Psychology of Interest* (2006) psychologist Paul J. Silvia says interest has an action goal, cognitive content, and a physical component. And, just to be clear, *interest* and *curiosity* is the same emotional state. Interest is "associated with curiosity, exploration, and information seeking," and its aim is "the cultivation of knowledge and competence."[7] It is a "cold" emotion that make us stop and think. The drive to explore and learn new things—affiliated to the ability to change we discussed with Carol—makes us better equipped to survive. Some define interest as a drive, rather than as an emotion. Thus, neuroscientists Habibi and Damasio (2014) see interest as the drive of exploration, however, the function of exploration is the same as that of interest.[8]

The physical response to an interesting object has several phases. We *notice* a new object and raise our eyelids, then *wonder* and tilt our head and move closer; we become *curious* about details, our curiosity turns into *fascination*, we feel *amazement* and our jaw drops, and, finally, amazement can become *ecstasy* and make us forget everything else.[9] Thus, interest has a facial expression, draws us close, and demands attention, time, and effort. You simply cannot let go of an interesting object. Reviewers wrote, "[t]he online recappers at the A.V. Club gave it a D while claiming they couldn't stop watching it,"[10] and "I laughed and gasped. The show may be ridiculous, but the humiliation and panic feel real. And there's something to be said for surprise."[11]

German psychologist Klaus Scherer (2001) explains that new things call for a so-called *novelty check*: "A novelty check would thus include a family of appraisals, such as whether people appraise something as new, ambiguous, complex, obscure, uncertain, mysterious, contradictory, unexpected, or otherwise not understood. People probably experience the output of this appraisal as a disruption in processing and a subjective feeling of uncertainty."[12] Psychologists talk of *information gaps*, which is when an object makes us realize we need new information to understand it. So, an interesting object presents us with an "information conflict" which "refers to the competing information relative to identifying, labeling, remembering, categorizing, and otherwise encoding the stimulus."[13] What *is* this novel thing about?

We experience an interesting object in two phases, or with two appraisals: We first appraise the novelty and complexity of the object and next appraise our ability to cope with the object. The higher we estimate our ability to understand, the more time and effort we are willing to spend with the interesting object. Novelty must therefore be within our reach of understanding, if we are to find it interesting. This is why people find paintings with titles more interesting than those without titles; the titles make paintings easier to understand.

It involves energy to engage with interesting things, which is why interest has a neurochemical reward system with so-called "wanting" and "liking" sensations. Our desire for new information ("wanting" sensations) anticipates reward in the form of relief (filling the information gap), and when we understand what has made us curious, we feel pleasure ("liking" sensations).[14] These sensations make us stay focused on an interesting object until we have filled our information gap. The effort we are willing to dedicate to interesting things is virtually unlimited. For instance, interest made me write this chapter about Lange's characters and interest can make an author work for years on a book without certainty it will be finished.

Interest is about novelty, complexity, and filling the information gap. I return to the emotion of interest later, when I discuss Elsa. An aged female face does not usually capture our interest. As Danish media scholar Anne Jerslev (2017) points out, the elderly female face is a ghostly thing in a culture where the ideal is "never to visibly age at all."[15] Yet, Jerslev points to recent uses of middle-age and old women in fashion advertising, where a woman can be cool and edgy if she is a celebrity. Hollywood star Jessica Lange is a celebrity, and her characters Fiona and Elsa share the fear, that is the greatest cause of anxiety in women in the West: Aging.

Fiona, Supreme Witch

"Coven" is about age anxiety and the failure to be a good mother. The season ends with sending its heroine to hell, however, it first overturns the conventional script of a middle-age witch and an innocent stepdaughter.

Age is addressed head on in "Bitchcraft" (3.01) where Fiona Goode (Lange) meets with chief researcher David (Ian Anthony Dale) at a pharmaceutical laboratory. Fiona's late husband funded David's research, and she now wants the youth serum. David shows her a video of an old monkey, "the equivalent of a human female in her late eighties," who after it is injected with his serum jumps around.

FIONA: I'll have what she's having.
DAVID: And you will. It should be ready for human trials in two years' time.
FIONA: This afternoon. Preferably in the next half hour. I have a dinner engagement. [David refuses]
FIONA: I've made you rich and soon-to-be-famous. I want that medicine. I paid for it. And I want it now!
DAVID: Fiona. You are a very beautiful woman. But if you're just looking for something cosmetic I can recommend a plastic surgeon.
FIONA: What I *need* is an infusion of vitality. Of youth. I want that drug, David, and I want it now.

In the next scene, Fiona calls David to her home. The infusions Fiona has been taking for weeks don't work. While she waits for him, she snorts coke, chain-smokes, and dances to psychedelic music in her New York apartment. Like the evil queen in *Snow White*, she looks in the mirror and can tell she is not "the fairest of them all." When David says he cannot help and quits his job, Fiona kisses him. The kiss sucks life out of him and she tosses aside his shriveled body. Fiona may be aging, but she will *not* go quietly into the night.

Ageism

Age anxiety is a theme with all Lange's characters. Constance in "Murder House" has two adult children and a young lover, whom she kills when he leaves her for a young woman, and in "Asylum" Sister Jude abuses young patients. Constance and Jude appear to be in their fifties. In "Coven" age is the central theme of the season, and Fiona seems to share Lange's actual age, the actress being mid-sixties in 2014. Instead of making Lange appear younger, as in earlier seasons, the camera now provides unsparing close-ups of the wrinkles on her face.

Fiona is a Supreme, the most powerful witch in a generation. When a new Supreme is born, she kills the old Supreme. The Supreme is supposed to lead her Coven, however, Fiona has neglected this duty and enjoyed a human life with three husbands. Fiona's daughter, Cordelia (Sarah Paulson), has instead taken care of witch affairs and founded a witches' school in New Orleans, the Miss Robichaux's Academy for Exceptional Young Ladies. When David's serum doesn't work, Fiona returns to New Orleans to resume leadership of the Coven. She thinks a new Supreme is draining her powers. The plan is to find and kill this new Supreme before she can kill Fiona. Interwoven with Fiona's scheme are other storylines mirroring Fiona's age anxiety. There is the head of the voodoo community, high priestess Marie Laveau (Angela Bassett), who knows a youth spell; Fiona resurrects the nineteenth-century serial killer Madame Delphine LaLaurie (Kathy Bates), who was obsessed with youth; and there is, finally, middle-age mother Alicia who is a sexual molester.

"Coven" pits the middle-age women against a younger generation. "Why don't you just die?" Cordelia greets her mother in episode one, and in episode thirteen tells Fiona, "You were the monster in every one of my closets." They have a strained relationship. In the penultimate episode, "Go to Hell" (3.12), Fiona stages her own death to learn the identity of the new Supreme. Thinking Fiona is dead, the young witches go through the tests of The Seven Wonders to find the Supreme, who turns out to be Cordelia. What now? Kill your own daughter? What is a woman to do, when her daughter takes her powers?

In the previous chapter I mentioned Henneberg's study of mothers and grandmothers, who are cast as evil crone, self-sacrificing mother, or ineffectual nanny in the fairy tale.[16] The witch is an evil crone, and Fiona's ironic surname Goode underlines the kinship with fairy-tale villains Maleficent (*Sleeping Beauty*) and Cruella De Vil (*101 Dalmatians*), who are obsessed with youth. The witch represents "the idea that as women grow old, they also grow evil and that any power they have will naturally be put to ill use."[17] The middle-age and old female fairy-tale characters are shrouded in ageism or, in sociologist Susan Pickard's words, viewed with a discriminating "age gaze."[18] Ageism is a stigmatizing process, which tells women they ought to "'naturally' withdraw from their social roles so as to make their ultimate disappearance – death – less difficult for the smooth functioning of society."[19] Ageism equates aging with decline and portrays the aging woman as a burden or a danger. Society expects her to withdraw, so her children can take over. To die is, literally, what is expected of Fiona.

When Cordelia is Supreme, Fiona turns very old, older than David's monkey. She now looks ninety years old. Psychologists divide old age into "young-old (65–74), middle-old (75–84), and oldest-old (85+)."[20] Oldest-old is also called "deep old age," a metaphor that depicts aging as an abyss.[21] To age is to fall into the abyss of death. Susan M. Behuniak in "The Living Dead? The Construction of People With Alzheimer's Disease as Zombies" (2011) says society constructs aging as dying. Society's gender script stipulates that, as Jerslev says, "youth is good, desirable, and beautiful; old age is bad, repulsive, and ugly."[22] Whereas men have two faces, that of a boy and a man, a woman has one, that of a girl. When that face ages, beauty disappears, and a woman's "looks" disappears. Erikson suggests an alternative discourse, that we become wise with age and that experience shows in the wrinkles on our face. This would be a "facial archive,"[23] a sign that time passed and we have changed.

This physical process is written into society's middle-age script. Behuniak says we construe age through a triangular process of available scripts, our individual speech acts, and "the person's contribution to the storyline": "This triangle reveals the limited nature of the person's real choices, the social meaning of every act, and how narratives tend to follow an established script."[24] The age script says growing old is to fall into the abyss: "This system then frames the stage of old age within an ontology of decline and inferiority that is 'given' or 'natural' to the 'human condition.'"[25] Aging patients are placed in "malignant positions" where instead of receiving recognition of their individuality, they experience "treachery, disempowerment, infantilisation, intimidation, labeling, stigmatization, outpacing, invalidation, banishment, objectification, ignoring, imposition, withholding, accusation, disruption, mockery, and disparagement."[26]

No wonder women are anxious about aging.

Millennials and WAGs

At first glance Fiona fits the script of the evil witch who refuses to grow old and ought to die. However, *AHS* pits Fiona against a generation of witches, who are as narcissistic and murderous as she is. They are entitled millennials.

"I am a millennial. Generation Y. Born between the birth of AIDS and 9/11, give or take. They call us the global generation," says the witch Madison (Emma Roberts) in a monologue in "The Dead" (3.07). "We are known for our entitlement and narcissism . . . I can't feel anything. We think that pain is the worst feeling. It isn't. How could anything be worse than this eternal silence inside of me."[27] Madison has bulimia, is a self-injurer, and was gang raped in high school. She wants attention and worked as an actress before she came to the school. When Madison and Zoe (Taissa Farmiga) are out on a girl's night in "Bitchcraft," Madison is gang raped again, now by a team of young athletes who drug her. Zoe gets her out of the club, and Madison gets even by using her powers to crash the bus and kill the athletes.

However, we are not meant to feel sorry for the millennials, but to understand their pain and rage. Although the storyline faults society, the show also presents Madison as ungrateful and unsympathetic. Fiona kills Madison in episode three, but another witch, Misty (Lily Rabe) brings Madison back from the dead. However, the ungrateful Madison kills Misty when she thinks Misty is the Supreme. Madison also takes a resurrected Kyle (Evan Peters) from Zoe and uses him as her boy toy. Madison is nothing like the compassionate stepdaughter in *Snow White*. The millennium witches scheme and lie, betray friends, and commit murder.

Next to Madison, Fiona becomes less evil. When Fiona invites Madison to a bar, Madison flirts with men and makes Fiona feel old, which is the cruelest of things young can do to older women. Thus, we have little regrets when Fiona kills Madison. Looking at the dead witch bleeding on a rug, Fiona lights a cigarette: "This coven doesn't need a new Supreme, it needs a new rug" ("The Replacements," 3.03). Lange serves Fiona's one-liners with such glee, one can't help but take her side. And reviewers, too, singled out Lange's performance: "Goode is the kind of creation that an actress like Lange eats alive. She's an over-the-top, aging celebrity Queen with the ability to suck your soul out . . . Lange chews the scenery in ways that only she can, stealing focus every time she's on screen, and I don't mean that as a negative. It fits her part here. She's the most important person in the room every time."[28]

Fiona may be middle-age and loose in terms of age, but she is far wittier than the millennials. She also dresses more sexy and classy. She wears elegant dresses, high heels, gloves, sunglasses, and looks as if she stepped from the pages of a fashion magazine. This battle of style is humorously played out in "Bitchcraft," where Fiona takes the witches for a walk in New Orleans. They were asked to wear black and look as if dressed for Halloween, whereas Fiona, as always, is elegant.

The issue of what to wear is important. In an analysis of actress Judi Dench, who plays M in the James Bond film series, Eva Krainitzki argues Dench subverts the "master narrative of old age as decline" because 61-year-old Dench plays a younger character. Dench retired from the role as M in 2012 when Dench was seventy-eight.[29] The media praised Dench as a WAG (women aging gracefully), a term that underlines the attention society pays to women's performance of age.[30] In a linear and normative notion of time

FIGURE 9.1 *The Supreme Witch Fiona Goode (Jessica Lange) takes the young witches for a walk in New Orleans.* American Horror Story: Season 3, Episode 1 ("Bitchcraft"). © Brad Falchuk Teley-Vision, Ryan Murphy Productions, 20th Century Fox Television, 2013.

and age, the aging woman becomes increasingly problematic and is expected to withdraw and die, which M/Dench did after *Skyfall* (2012, Sam Mendes). Krainitzki points out the risks and possible scandal if a woman should break the age/gender scheme: "[N]ot acting one's age, for instance, is not only inappropriate but dangerous, exposing the female subject, especially, to ridicule, contempt, pity, and scorn – the scandal of anachronism."[31]

The way Lange plays Fiona is different than how Dench plays M. Dench was discussed as appearing strong, masculine, and butch, and M is not concerned with appearing young or being sexy. Lange, in contrast, plays Fiona as an aging SYF. The SYF, we recall from werewolf Elena, is a single young female in the New Girl Order.[32] She is girlish, single, fiercely independent, and enjoys sex. Fiona invokes the "scandal of anachronism" by dressing (too) sexy for her age and wanting to have sex, and she is here different from M. Where Dench was praised in articles on the Internet as a WAG, comments found the term demeaning. "Why do women have to age gracefully? Since when does graceful = a downward slide from sexy? And why should any woman give a toss what anyone else thinks about how she dresses? If we are still hyper-sensitive like a 15-year-old girl then what's the point to anything? Men don't have this rubbish to put up with."[33] Another comment said, "Who makes these rules??? So basically after 40 you better dress like you're told otherwise you will be an outcast?? I for one will not take any notice. I like jeans and t shirts, and I will get a tattoo."[34]

Where Dench/M ages gracefully and is not sexually active, Fiona, in contrast, wants to stay in power *and* be young and sexy. Fiona acknowledges being a bad mother and a lousy wife to her one-night-stand, The Axeman. This was a deliberate choice. Yes, Fiona *is* self-centered, and she rejects the middle-age woman script and the meta-narrative that says beauty is youth, and when a woman ages, she becomes invisible, dies, or should at least age gracefully. Comparing M and Fiona, the latter does not subvert the age script, because Fiona desires what is the "message" of that negative script, namely that only the young are attractive. However, *AHS* re-authors the age gaze by making Fiona a complex character whose desires the audience can relate to. She may not be sympathetic, yet we can sympathize with her.

The Bad Mother

Henneberg observes boys can learn from fathers but girls can't learn anything from mothers. Instead "the dead mother plot" kills off the mother so the heroine can develop a new self, as happens in *Snow White*, *Cinderella*, and *Frozen* (2013, Chris Buck and Jennifer Lee). A mother must die, regardless if she is good or bad, to make room for the next generation.

"Coven" kills all three mothers, however, it positions Fiona in a mother script with more possibilities than merely "good" or "bad" mothering. We don't know how bad a mother Fiona has been to Cordelia, the show does not elaborate on the issue. But the season starts with Cordelia's accusations and also closes with her. When Cordelia becomes Supreme, Fiona returns as a deep-old witch with spotted and wrinkled skin, but still fashionably dressed in a black, tight dress and wearing high-heeled shoes. She may have fallen into the abyss, but is still cool. In "The Seven Wonders" Fiona must choose between killing her daughter to get back her powers, or die.

> FIONA: You took my power the moment I gave birth to you. When a woman becomes a mother she can't help but see her mortality in the cherubic little face. Everytime I looked at you I saw my own death.
> CORDELIA: And all that time I thought you just didn't like me.
> FIONA: It was nothing personal, darling. I loved you plenty though. In just my own way. Which I'll admit had its limitations. Your fault was you were always looking for another version of motherhood. I can feel the power vibrating of off you. It feels good, doesn't it? Its mine, you know ... I have to die for you to truly live (3.13).

As said, Fiona is not the only bad mother. She is contrasted with serial killer Madame Delphine LaLaurie (Bates) and sexual molester Alicia (Mare

Winningham). Delphine was a white slave owner who tortured slaves and murdered her two daughters in 1830s New Orleans.[35] Like the infamous Hungarian aristocrat Elizabeth Báthory, Delphine killed female servants and used their blood in an attempt to stay young. Voodoo priestess LaVeau damned Delphine with eternal life and buried her alive, because Delphine tortured LaVeau's lover. In her search for youth, Fiona digs up Delphine and sets her to work as a maid in the coven. When Delphine's daughters return as zombies in "Burn, Witch, Burn" (3.05) and are killed a second time, the repentant Delphine says, "they deserved a better mother than I could ever be." "I know the feeling," says Fiona.

The other bad mother is Alicia, an aging, pot-smoking, and working-class hippie. While Madison was gang raped, one of the young men, Kyle, was talking to Zoe and didn't know about the rape. After the bus crash, Zoe goes to the morgue and retrieves Kyle's body parts and asks Misty to resurrect him. Zoe then returns Kyle to his mother (3.03). Zoe assumes she will be nice and caring, but Alicia is a sexual molester. Forensic psychologist Theresa Porter says society often ignores the female sexual molester. "The issue of female child molesters is generally so discomforting that any discussion on the topic results in multiple digressions and diversions. The most common is the idea that any woman who does this 'must' be mentally ill."[36] I discussed the mother stereotype in Chapter 7, and Delphine, Alicia, or Fiona are not portrayed as mentally sick, but sane. Porter argues our scripts prevent us from seeing that women commit the same crimes as men. "We maintain the myth that women are inherently loving towards children by virtue of the fact that we carried them in our wombs . . . We need to view women as people, not just mythical mothers but as full persons with the agency to exhibit a vast variety of behaviours. And some of those behaviours are monstrous."[37] The resurrected Kyle is mute and brain deficient, but when Zoe leaves him with Alicia, his first post-mortem word is "*no.*" Kyle stabs his mother to death and Zoe takes him back to the coven.

Sandwiched between Delphine and Alicia, the bad mother Fiona fares better.[38] She may not be a good mother, but we believe her when she says she loved Cordelia. When Fiona is in the hospital to visit Cordelia, she also resurrects a dead infant to a grieving mother. She has a heart. The mother script has more nuances to motherhood than good or bad, and Fiona accepts Cordelia as Supreme and dies in her arms. But apparently, it is too late, because Fiona wakes up in hell.

Sex, Love, and Hell

Fiona's line, "I'll have what she's having," in episode one is from *When Harry Met Sally* . . . (1989, Rob Reiner), where Sally fakes an orgasm in a restaurant, and a middle-age woman at a neighboring table asks for what Sally is having.

The scene illustrates not just that women know how to "perform" sex but also that they, apparently, lose sexual vitality at middle age.

Sex is a key part in Lange's early star persona in Hollywood, where she debuted as a blonde damsel-in-distress in *King Kong* (1976) and later was femme fatale in *The Postman Always Rings Twice* (1981) and romantic lead in *Tootsie* (1982). Sex is integral to her *AHS* characters, but here interwoven with a violation of an age script which says middle-age women are not supposed to be sexually active. However, Lange's characters have sexual appetites: Constance keeps a lover half her age, Sister Jude hides lingerie and fantasizes about the Monsignor, Fiona had three husbands and picks up men in bars, and Elsa was a dominatrix in pre-war Berlin and has a freak as her lover.

The age script says middle-age women lose sexual drive, however, Fiona's demand for an "infusion of youth" is not because she needs to refuel her sex drive but because she looks old. Her sex drive is intact and takes her to a jazz club in "The Dead" (3.07) where she picks up a saxophone player. The musician is The Axeman (Danny Huston), who was once a serial killer in New Orleans. After his death he became a ghost, and when the young witches dabbled with spells, they accidentally raise him from the dead. Now this middle-age serial killer invites Fiona home for a drink, the original tenant murdered and stashed in the bathroom.

"Love transforms," he tells her, wanting more than an affair. "Come on, you don't believe in love," Fiona tells him. "Okay, let's table love then. How about sex? Good, old-fashioned, great sex?" They then have sex, visualized in red-tinted images and accompanied by an up-beat jazz soundtrack. Fiona prepares to leave: "It was a charming evening, but that dead body in your bathtub is going to start putting off some very noxious odors soon." The Axeman then confesses he has been in love with Fiona since she was eight and has followed her as a ghost, protecting and helping her. Fiona is angry and upset, and thinks he has been stalking her. The Axeman says Fiona is afraid of love and explains he wants to help. "So, what was this, some mercy lay?" she shouts.

She doesn't care if he loves her, she just wants sex. Fiona later uses The Axeman in her scheme to find the Supreme. She pretends she is in love and whispers "I promise you the world" (3.13). But her manipulation of The Axeman, who has real feelings for her, backfires. After dying, she wakes up in an idyllic farmhouse with The Axeman as her adoring, and sexually demanding, husband. This time, when she slaps him, he slaps her back. The scene turns the stereotypical image of a happy aging couple upside down. This is not heaven, but hell.

Truth be told, I find it unfair. Fiona did after all accept death, and whether we sympathize or not with her desire to look young, have sex, do coke, be in power and be independent, those are common desires in the West. If Fiona deserves to go to hell, many of us do too. However, "deep" meanings are not the point with *AHS*, the aim instead is to playfully turn scripts upside down and surprise us. Perhaps Fiona is not punished for violating the age script, but for using people. The season ends with Cordelia greeting a crowd of new witches: "I look at your faces, all of them beautiful, all of them perfect. I know that together, we can do more than survive. It's *our* time to thrive."

"Coven" salutes sisterhood across ages rather than take sides in the generation war. However, the season had a clear winner, namely actress Lange. After her role as age-anxious Fiona, Marc Jacobs chose Lange to be the face of his "Beauty" fragrance in February 2014, and she graced the November cover of *Elle*. Fiona may be dispatched to hell, but Lange showed that middle-age women are no longer invisible.

Freaks and Chills

As said, *AHS* excels in being playful, and season four is a potpourri of exhibits rather than a story. In episode one the bearded lady (Bathes) announces Elsa's performance: "Ladies and Gentlemen, direct from the cabarets of pre-war Berlin, the enchantress who holds sway over all of nature's mistakes, Elsa Mars!" There are only two people in the audience, Dandy and his mother Gloria (Frances Conroy). Dandy's eyes widen at the

FIGURE 9.2 *The middle-age woman as the ultimate freak: Jessica Lange plays Elsa Mars, who in 1952 performs David Bowie's song "Life on Mars" from 1971. American Horror Story: Season 4, Episode 1 ("Monsters Among Us"). © Brad Falchuk Teley-Vision, Ryan Murphy Productions, 20th Century Fox Television, 2014.*

sight of the freaks, especially the Siamese twins (Sarah Poulson). But he is bored with Elsa's performance, and when Gloria has no success in buying the twins for her son, she tells Elsa: "By far the most freakish thing of all tonight was your pathetic attempt at singing."

The freak is the theme in season four, "Freak Show" (2014), where Lange plays Elsa, the owner of a freak circus. "Freak" means to "change, distort" and in the sixteenth century it meant a "capricious notion."[39] In the eighteenth century a freak was an "unusual thing, [a] fancy," and in the nineteenth century it was used about the abnormal example of a species, *a freak of nature*. By then human freaks were exhibited in variety shows, where you could find natural freaks like bearded ladies, dwarfs, and albinos, and made freaks, people whose bodies had become capricious and unusual by design or accident, like the fat lady or tattooed woman or the strongman. Middle-age Elsa is the "biggest freak," as she calls herself in the last episode. She is a freak because she has lost both lower legs and wears prosthetics, but most of all because she dreams of becoming a star, thus violating society's middle-age script. It is the second sense, her violation of the age script, which makes her the "biggest freak" and an intriguing and subversive horror heroine.

When I saw Elsa perform Bowie's song I experienced the strangest mixture of emotions: Amazement, surprise, shock, embarrassment (on Elsa's behalf), and I also felt chills and was intensely moved. I went back to see the scene several times. Like the deadlock of opposite emotional states Lübecker described in his feel-bad viewer experience, where he was immersed and distanced, my emotional state was somewhat similar, just with different emotions.[40] To be moved and feel chills, two distinct states, are two emotional and physical states, while interest, as I explained, is an epistemological emotion that makes us stop and ask what is going on. So, I was deeply immersed while my brain exploded as it formed new neuronal connections trying to fill the information gap.

It did not take long to respond to interest and make a novelty check of the Bowie reference. A more interesting question is why I was moved and felt chills. Research explains that to be moved is a highly positive emotional state, even if we are moved by something sad. When we are moved, we reframe emotions to be not just sad, but positive *and* sad. The chills we get from sad art are different from the chills from fear.[41] Fear-induced chills feel unpleasant and lead to avoidance (run or fight), while chills from sad art feel sad but also positive and lead to approaching (like me repeating the Bowie scene).

Some time after watching "Freak Show" I experienced another musical chill, and I ask you to bear with me, because you may think this second chill has nothing to do with Elsa. But I think it has. I listened to the song "Let it Go" from Disney's animated *Frozen* (2013) on one of my long runs. Its inspirational message had lifted me up many times on long runs when I was tired: "The fears that once controlled me/ can't get to me at all!/ It's time to see what I can do/ To test the limits and break through/ No right, no wrong, no rules for me, I'm free." Then, suddenly, my mind connected the Elsa songs. Both are sung by freaks. Elsa in *Frozen* can command ice by the touch of her hand, and Elsa in *AHS* has lost her legs and wants to be a star. Both are misfits and, for both characters, their songs express a "true" self. This connection made me discover the ageism being cleverly exposed in *AHS*: Elsa in *Frozen* is in her early twenties, and "Let it Go" is performed by Idina Menzel, a professional singer with a beautiful vocal. Elsa in *AHS* is middle-age and Lange has a thin and rusty voice strained to its most.

And here is the ageism: We expect young Elsa to go ahead and realize her dreams, but middle-age Elsa performs the scandal of anachronism when she sings. How dare she dream she can be a star if society's gender script says she should be dead or invisible? Yet Lange did it again: She moved the audience with her performance. I was not the only one moved, Lange again stole the show and reviewers saluted her as "metaphorical ringleader" of *AHS*: "First things first – it's Jessica Lange's world, we all just live in it."[42]

Piecing Together Elsa Mars

As the title indicates, "Freak Show" is a compilation of freaks, oddities, and arresting moments, exhibited on the circus stage and on the viewer's television screen. I felt cognitive giddiness at all these pieces, like pieces in a pile on a table for a jigsaw puzzle. The freak is not a monster, in the sense that it does not generate fear as in Carroll's definition (the monster generates fear and curiosity). The freak is an aberration, a freak of nature, and generates curiosity due to its novelty, and thus calls for a novelty check. So, in this section we shall look at some of the pieces that are part of the full picture and ask where they are from.

First, the freaks in Fraulein Elsa's Cabinet of Curiosities, as the circus is called. Here we find a bearded lady who suffers from hypertrichosis (Bates), lobster boy Jimmy Darling (Evan Peters) who suffers from ectrodactyly, a couple of microcephalics (one of which is Pepper, a character from "Asylum," played by Naomi Grossman), a pituitary dwarf, a half lady, a tall lady, a tiny lady, in episode one Elsa adds Siamese twins Bette and Dot, in episode two the three-breasted hermaphrodite Desiree (Angela Bassett), and later a tattooed woman and a fat lady arrive. The end of episode one reveals that Elsa has prosthetic legs, her own legs amputated from under the knees. With the freak theme, a central puzzle piece is Tod Browning's *Freaks* from 1932. In *Freaks*, trapeze artist Cleopatra and her lover, strong man Hercules, scheme for Cleopatra to marry a rich dwarf in the circus, then poison him and inherit his money. When the freaks discover the plan, they castrate Hercules and cut off Cleopatra's legs, transforming her into a duck woman. Should an audience be unaware of this film, the freaks tell con man Spalding they are inspired by Browning before they turn Spalding into a duck man ("Show Stoppers," 4.12).

Browning used real freaks, and so does *AHS*: Ma Petite is played by the world's smallest woman, the 2,2 feet tall Indian Jyoti Amge; Meep is played by pituitary dwarf Ben Woolf; Legless Suzie is played by Rose Siggins suffering from the genetic disorder Sacral Agenesis; Paul the Illustrated Seal is played by British Mat Fraser suffering from congenital malformation of both arms; and Amazon Eve is played by 6,7 feet tall transgender model Erika Ervin.

Another piece is Elsa's Berlin past, a hint to German actress Marlene Dietrich. Dietrich was known for her deep voice, and reviewers noted this puzzle piece: "[Elsa] channels the future to sing David Bowie's 'Life on Mars' the way Dietrich sang 'Falling in Love Again' and it's nothing short of a sideshow aria."[43] The Bowie song is yet another piece, where song lyrics tell of "the freakiest show" (a reference to television) and a woman in pursuit of her "sunken dream." I already mentioned that Elsa is dressed like Bowie from 1973, in a blue suit and with psychedelic makeup. The freaks sing several songs, including Fiona Apple's "Criminal" and Lana Del Rey's "Gods and Monsters." Actor Paulson said these song scenes were "a nod to Baz Luhrmann, who creates these worlds that are so hyper-real and hyper-fantasy-based all smushed into one thing." Also, the songs were sung "by people who identified themselves as freaks."[44]

Next to *Freaks,* Dietrich, and Bowie, is a piece with the infamous Nazi sadist Ilsa from the women-in-prison film series *Ilsa, She-Wolf of the SS* from the 1970s.[45] A flashback in "Edward Mordrake Part 2" (4.04) shows how Elsa provided sex services in pre-war Berlin. She wears high, black boots and has a blond page, Ilsa's iconic outfit. In Berlin, her customers cut off her legs and leave her for dead. Later in the show, when Elsa is a television star in Hollywood, she services her producer husband as his dominatrix, again in boots and holding a whip. Finally, I think Elsa's namesake from *Frozen* is also a piece in the puzzle. *Frozen* might not be intentionally woven into the text, however, both are freaks who sing.

If we take a step back from our jigsaw puzzle, we find a middle-age female freak on a background with authentic freaks, nostalgia for past depravity, Dietrich, musical freaks, and exploitation fantasies. I am not sure there is a single image or theme keeping the pieces together, however, if there is, it is something with dreams and freaks. If you are a freak, or accused of being one, society casts you out. A freak must struggle hard to make a dream come true. Twisty (John Carroll Lynch), for example, was once a real clown but became crazy when wrongly accused of pedophile murder. Most of the freaks just dream about leading ordinary lives, but their "freakishness" makes them prey. Con man Spalding (Denis O'Hare) thus buys the freaks from Elsa, kills them, and sells them as stuffed oddities to The Museum of Morbid Curiosities.

The most freakish dream is Elsa's dream to become a star in the new television industry in Hollywood. She is late middle-age, and her dream appears crazy to everyone. But if we take another step back from the pieces, we will see the space around the puzzle, which provides yet a different picture.

Lange Doing Lange

In Chapter 6, I discussed *Martyrs* as a mind-game film that wants the audience to examine our reasons for watching violence. The argument I offer here is also a meta-position. The Elsa/Bowie scene has a surprising complexity, and novelty and complexity stir interest. When we are curious, we step back to fill the information gap. Now, in the Bowie scene and in several other scenes in "Freak Show," surprise doesn't revolve around violence or disgust, but around *performance*. And by using pieces external to the story, the show wants the television audience to step back and bring extratextual perspectives to their viewer experience.

In the penultimate episode Elsa sells the circus to Dandy, who runs amok and slaughters most of the freaks when they rebel against his incompetent leadership. Elsa, knowing the freaks might lose their home, went to Hollywood to pursue her dream. She marries a producer, and becomes his dominatrix, and gets her own television show. But she is bored, and she commits suicide by singing Bowie's "Heroes" on Halloween, a night it is rumored the ghost Edward Mordrake will take the freak who performs. But where Fiona is sent to hell, Elsa is sent to heaven to perform her Bowie act in eternity to a full house. Some fans thought this was an unfair reward:

> I don't quite get why Elsa deserves to go to heaven. Because she suffered in this life? I'm sorry, no. Let me break it down for you: Elsa is kind of an asshole. I do not like Elsa. She didn't do one nice thing. Any nice thing she did, like give the freaks a home, was for her own benefit. Without the freaks, would she have a stage to perform on? No. If she had no stage, how could she continue her delusion that she was a star? She couldn't. See, it's all about Elsa doing Elsa.[46]

From the perspective of fiction events, the fan is right. Why should Elsa go to heaven? But if we step back and view the season from a wider perspective, where we see both the fiction and the fiction frame, Lange in FX's television show we can watch on Netflix, then "Freak Show" is not about "Elsa doing Elsa" but about Lange doing Lange. As reviewers noted: "Granted, [Lange's] riffing on the same character each season (the singularly driven fading starlet), but the character's a doozie so it doesn't really matter. I'm not sold entirely on her accent ... but you can forgive her because She Is Lange."[47]

Already by season three, reviewers said *AHS* belonged to Lange, and with Lange doing Lange, we enter a meta-level of play.

We recall Carroll thinks *curiosity* and *fascination* are key to our attraction to horror: "Central to my approach has been the idea that the objects of horror are fundamentally linked with cognitive interests, most notably with curiosity."[48] Carroll thinks fear is the prize we pay for learning about the unknown: "[A]rt-horror is the price we are willing to pay for the revelation of that which is impossible and unknown, of that which violates our conceptual schema."[49] We are engaged in "processes of discovery, explanation, proof, hypothesis, confirmation, and so on."[50] In *AHS*, the viewer's cognitive work with filling information gaps differs from Carroll's examples. Where Carroll talks of supernatural monsters like werewolves and gooey slime, our "monster" is a middle-age woman giving a freak performance. And our fascination and curiosity is not mixed with fear, but with being moved and chills. I want to draw into focus the process of our play on horror's dark stage.

Let me remind you of meta-play and meta-emotions we discussed earlier. I took meta-play from the concept of meta-emotions, used in psychology of learning about parents who can manage their own emotions and who can coach their children to master their emotions.[51] We recognize here System 2 at work again, the ability to observe one's emotions and to observe one's cognitive processes. There is a meta-aspect in the Bowie scene, I haven't mentioned yet. There is not one, but three, Elsa: The first is Elsa performing on the stage, the second is a happy Elsa being showered in confetti (her fantasy about success), and then a sad Elsa dressed as The Sad Clown, sitting in the aisle and watching herself perform. The camera cuts between the them, one real Elsa and the other imaginary. The woman in Bowie' lyrics is a lost soul like Elsa, cast into a world of chaos and rejections.

Viewed in a within-fiction perspective, Elsa is an egoist. But viewed from a meta-perspective, Elsa tells a different story. She is not "pathetic," as Gloria puts it, because Elsa is going off-script and, as the chapter's opening quote by creativity scholar Csikszentmihalyi suggests, the show uses the emotion of interest to capture our attention so we can play and become more creative. *AHS* uses the middle-age script to twist the stereotype of middle-age woman into a performance so unusual that it demands interest and a novelty check.

I earlier said Bowie wore a mask of femininity in the 1973 music video. Lange wears several masks in her performance as Elsa: Lange as Elsa, Elsa as Bowie, Bowie as woman, Elsa as Sad Clown. All these faces and masks bring to memory British psychologist Joan Riviere's classical essay "Womanliness as Masquerade" (1929). Here, Riviere analyses a patient who uses feminine behavior to "mask" her intellectual ability when she had given a public talk to avert feared reactions from men in the audience. Riviere, famously, said there is no difference between womanliness as a masquerade and authentic womanliness. "The reader may now ask how I define womanliness or where I draw the line between genuine womanliness and the 'masquerade'. My suggestion is not, however, that there is any such difference: whether radical or superficial. They are the same thing."[52] In cognitive terminology, Riviere's "masquerade" is the script. And Lange's performance as Elsa who performs Bowie exposes our expectations about proper behavior as scripts.

The Void of Identity

As said, I believe the chills I felt, when I watched Elsa in *Frozen*, are relevant. You probably think this is a detour, because *Frozen* is a Disney animation fantasy film, and you may be right. Experimental studies show that fear and horror was never mentioned by respondents, when they were asked to name what emotions they felt when they were moved by a film.[53] But Carroll insists curiosity is key to horror and I was moved by Elsa to do this chapter, so please take the detour with me anyway.

You can feel a chill without being moved and you can be moved without feeling a chill. But if you are moved, you easily also feel chills. In their work on chills in films, Eugen Wassiliwizky, Valentin Wagner, and Thomas Jacobsen (2015) define being moved as "pleasure associated with representations of great life challenges and considerable suffering" for a character. We are moved by stories of people who struggle in life. Being moved holds opposite emotions; people describe it as highly pleasant even if it also feels sad:

> ... episodes of being moved are inherently self-rewarding, even when they involve readers – or onlookers – in intense negative emotions such as sadness, pity, or worry regarding the main character ... Importantly, feelings of being moved do not seem to counteract or compensate for negative emotions, but seem rather to integrate them into an overall pleasurable emotional episode.[54]

We are moved by characters' struggle with obstacles and we reframe a character's sadness and our own sadness as moving and therefore pleasant. We get a lump in the throat, tears in our eyes, and goosebumps. Cognitive psychology explains the appeal of moving pictures with social bonding; we are moved because characters do what is good for a group or for society.[55] You can be moved and cry tears of joy or tears of sadness. Now, at first look, it does not seem Elsa is doing anything good for society, yet, from a meta-perspective, she is struggling with the negative middle-age script, just being a guerilla warrior paving the way for future more positive scripts.

Like being moved, to feel chills is an extremely positive feeling. Neuroscientists Assal Habibi and Antonio Damasio (2014) say "music evokes a broad range of emotions and feelings" and that "music-related affects are accompanied by physiological and behavioral changes."[56] These changes are chemicals like "dopamine release in the nucleus accumbens," a region "involved in the process of experiencing highly pleasurable music."[57] In short, music chills are extremely pleasant. Habibi and Damasio say music serves homeostasis and complex social functions of bringing people together. They speculate music evolves from animal vocalizations and was co-opted into culture to be used to communicate and share emotions.[58] We are moved by music, and music is so deeply embodied that it is used in therapy to heal brain damages and make paralyzed limbs move again.[59]

I felt chills in the song scenes in *AHS* and *Frozen*, but they were different and I will describe them as respectively "cold" and "hot." When Elsa sang Bowie, my jaw dropped and I call this chill cold, because I stopped to make a novelty check. When Elsa in *Frozen* sang, I was moved, felt chill and had goosebumps, and cried, but I did not make a novelty check because I was not curious. The meaning of events, lyrics, and Elsa's magical abilities was obvious: "The fears that once controlled me/ can't get to me at all!/ It's time to see what I can do/ To test the limits and break through/ No right, no wrong, no rules for me I'm free!" My chill was "hot" because I was immersed in the fiction and not doing cognitive work. The chill in *Frozen* is the experience of freedom when Elsa releases her powers after holding them back for years. This is Mandler's natural freedom: no more obstacles! Elsa transforms into a beautiful queen, and she represents Henricks' self-realization through play.

Elsa does not turn into a queen until the end where she goes to heaven to be a star, surrounded by her family, the freaks. My chill with Elsa in *AHS* is, like being moved, composed of opposite emotions: I felt curious when Elsa went off-script, and sad and embarrassed when she was rejected as "freakish" and "pathetic," yet I also shared the uplifting joy when she fantasizes she is showered in confetti. Furthermore, the Bowie performance itself may be judged pleasant or unpleasant depending on one's taste in music. However, most of all, my chill is related to a recognition that Elsa is off-script, because she is late middle-age and past the time when you are supposed to pursue your dreams. She performs the scandal of anachronism.

As research shows, we are moved by character's life struggles with big obstacles and chills serve physical well-being and social bonding. So, on the one hand there is obstacles, and on the other hand the struggle to overcome. The chill I experienced is linked to my recognition that Elsa is off-script and so is Lange, and this is dangerous and brave and immensely inspiring. The obstacle is the middle-age script. We all want to pursue our dreams, no matter our age. Yet Elsa's performance is also somewhat grotesque, reminding us of the danger of going off-script, and of another uncanny-chilling performance when Baby Jane, played by Bette Davis, sings in the psychological horror movie *What Ever Happened to Baby Jane?* (1962,

Robert Aldrich).⁶⁰ Baby Jane is delusional, because she thinks she can be a Hollywood star even though she is middle-age. We might here recall another performance, when judge Simon Cowell in 2009 in British "X-Factor" asked a gray-haired 47-year-old participant, "What's the dream?" and she replied, "Elaine Paige."⁶¹ Cowell rolled his eyes, signaling this middle-age participant was ridiculous. How could she dream she could be Elaine Paige? The participant was Susan Boyle, whose audition with the song "I Dreamed a Dream" got more than 200 million views on YouTube, and who today is more famous than Paige.⁶²

Elsa is afraid she is too old to pursue her dreams. "Is it too late for me? Is it wrong?" she asks Ethel. Ethel assures her: "You're gonna become a household name, I know it" (4.01). Today, Lange's performance is available on iTunes and YouTube, and the official video has five million views while her other songs in *AHS* has between one and three million views. Philosopher Malabou defines plasticity as, "the relation that an individual entertains with what, on the one hand, attaches him originally to himself, to his proper form, and with what, on the other hand, allows him to launch himself into the void of all identity, to abandon all rigid and fixed determination."⁶³ What moved me and gave me chills was Elsa's fall into the void of all identity, her fall into the abyss of aging, into the accident of trauma which may change an individual and ignite neural repair. *AHS* returned Lange to Hollywood stardom and proved there is space for the middle-age horror heroine.

Old

10

Abyss and Peak:

The New Old Woman

With this chapter, we come to the old woman in horror. There may be old horror heroines who are protagonists, however, I have not met them.[1] We will therefore turn to two supportive characters from the Gothic-horror television show *Penny Dreadful* (2014–2016, Showtime/Sky), the witch Joan in season two and the alienist Dr. Seward in season three. Joan and Dr. Seward are played by American actor and singer Patti LuPone, who was sixty-six years old when she appeared on the show. Joan appears only in a single episode, yet that episode was rated highest of all episodes in the first two seasons, and her character was so popular, that the show's writer and creator, John Logan, wrote the new regular character Dr. Seward for LuPone.

Old age is Erikson's eighth life stage. Its virtue is wisdom, and its crisis, or conflict, is integrity versus despair. In old age, we share our knowledge with our community. Integrity comes from successful integration into our world and completion of conflicts of earlier life stages. Despair arises if we are not integrated and can't accept death. Erik Erikson thought old age was not a "real" stage because it did not lead to a new life phase.[2] His wife, Joan M. Erikson, who revised their co-authored *The Life Cycle Completed*, disagreed and added three chapters on a ninth stage, life in the late eighties and nineties. Old age is divided into young-old (65–75), middle-old (75–85), and old-old or deep-old (85+). It is often visualized as an abyss, the "deep" old age one "falls" into, but Joan uses the metaphor of a mountain hill from where we have an overview over life. A peak.

Old age is, like middle-age, a negative social script and contemporary horror continues to portray old women as monstrous, lethal, or repulsive: There is an evil witch in *Vvitch: A New-England Folktale* (2015, Robert Eggers), a psychopathic grandmother in *The Visit* (2015, M. Night Shyamalan), and an evil old female ghost in *Don't Knock Twice* (2016, Caradog W. James), and in all three films the old women kill children. So, I am not saying old women are no longer portrayed as monstrous. Rather, we will see that contemporary horror also produces positive representations of old women, and it is to these we turn.

Joan and Dr. Seward break with the gender script, the meta-narrative, and with the conventional stereotypes of witch and psychoanalyst. They are "active initiators"[3] who continue to learn and develop as they age, and Dr. Seward is also "cool" and "edgy," like the old women used in today's advertisement to sell luxury brands (Jerslev, 2017). Joan and Dr. Seward are mentors for the protagonist, Vanessa Ives (Eva Green), but if only side characters, they are psychologically complex and examples of what I call the New Old Woman. She is fashioned after the feminist New Woman in the late nineteenth century.

The chapter first introduces *Penny Dreadful* and actress LuPone, then presents the old woman as stereotype. Next, we will see how Joan re-authors the proverbial evil witch, and how the alienist Dr. Seward combines the archetype of Wise Woman with modern science. The New Old Woman is a promise of what is, hopefully, to come: New positive scripts for old age and an old heroine who is also a protagonist.

Penny Dreadful and Patti LuPone

"Viva Patti!" is the headline for a fan comment on IMDB to Patti LuPone's appearance as Dr. Seward in 2016. Her character in "The Nightcomers" in season two, the witch Joan, was burned at the end of the episode, but after emails between LuPone and the series' creator and playwright John Logan, Logan wrote the new regular character for the actress. Joan and Dr. Seward are relatives, and Dr. Seward is an American alienist from New York practicing in London in 1892[4] with Joan a British ancestor from generations back.

Ensemble series *Penny Dreadful* is a mash-up of British classic Gothic literature. It centers on a group of four people who battle supernatural forces in Victorian London: The witch Vanessa[5] (Green), explorer Sir Malcolm Murray (Timothy Dalton), American werewolf Ethan Chandler (Josh Hartnett), and Dr. Victor Frankenstein (Harry Treadaway). Around them are characters from British Gothic literature: Frankenstein's creatures John Clare (Rory Kinnear) and Lily (Billie Piper), decadent aristocrat Dorian Grey, Dr. Jekyll, and Dracula. Over the three seasons Vanessa seeks answers to what her powers are (it is hinted she is a reincarnation of the Egyptian goddess Amunet). In her youth, she seduced her best friend Mina's fiancée on the eve before their marriage, which led to social catastrophe: The marriage was cancelled, the Ive and Murray families broke off their friendship, Mina was abducted by a vampire, and Vanessa fell ill and was hospitalized at Dr. Banning's clinic for five months where Vanessa underwent treatments for "women's illness," that is, being a hysteric. Vanessa's parents died, and Malcolm's children and wife died too. In season one, the group searches for Mina. Vanessa is a medium who can enter the *demimonde*, a half-world where spirits and supernatural forces communicate with the living. In season two the group battles a witch coven, and in season three they face Dracula and stop an apocalypse.

Season two explores Vanessa's status as a witch, and "The Nightcomers" (2.03) is a stand-alone flashback story about how Vanessa was the apprentice to the witch Joan. Reviewers and fans singled out LuPone's acting and character. A fan wrote, "Played by American Theatre Hall of Fame Inductee Patti LuPone and she is outstanding giving us one of the best guest television performances you will see all year. The Cut-Wife is superbly written, a truly tragic individual she was banished from her coven after refusing to pledge her allegiance to the Devil."[6] When discussing season three, Logan singled out "The Nightcomers" as his favorite episode which brought together two strong women, Vanessa and Joan:

> We were working on "The Cut Wife" episode ["The Nightcomers"], and I saw the chemistry she had with Eva, the chemistry those characters had together. I knew that this season [season three], Vanessa was going to need to have a very strong ally in Dr. Seward ... It was partly about having an actress I really love in Dublin for six months, but also it was about giving Vanessa a strong ally this season ...[7]

Patti LuPone was nominated best guest actor in a drama series by Critics Choice Television Awards and by Gold Derby Awards for her role as Joan. LuPone is known for musicals and has won numerous awards for best actress in, among others, *Evita* (1980), *Les Misérables* (1985), and *Gypsy* (2008). She is also known as a dedicated actress who stops her performance on the stage if audiences use their cell phones.[8]

The Cut-Wife, as Joan is called because she performs abortions, resonated with fans. "After the episode last season where Patti LuPone's character was burned at the stake, people came up to me angry. They were so emotional about it," said Logan. In season three, Dr. Seward treats Vanessa for depression and when she realizes that the supernatural forces, Vanessa tells about, are real, Seward joins the group to battle Dracula. Fans noticed the "outstanding professionalism and precision of Patti LuPone as a new key character, Vanessa's alienist Dr. Seward. Last year LuPone gave one of the greatest TV performances I've ever seen, and it is stimulating to see the runners of this series having the good sense to bring her back in a different, recurring role."[9] In "A Blade of Grass" (3.04) Dr. Seward hypnotizes Vanessa to return her to Dr. Banning's clinic, so Vanessa can remember who their adversary is (she met the evil forces during her depression but cannot recall who they were). This episode is again a flashback with only three characters, the alienist, Vanessa, and the orderly at the clinic, played by Rory Kinnear (who also plays John Clare, Frankenstein's creature).

In interviews, Logan referred to Vanessa as, "Vanessa Ives, c'est moi," echoing Gustave Flaubert's famous words "Bovary, c'est moi"[10] about the protagonist in Flaubert's 1856 novel, *Madame Bovary*. And like Flaubert, Logan killed his artistic progeny. The show ends with Vanessa becoming Dracula's bride which sets off the apocalypse and calls for the group to kill her. *Penny Dreadful* thus reverses fairy-tale ends, where old women die and young heroines become queens. In *Penny Dreadful*, young Vanessa dies and old Dr. Seward lives.

The Old Woman

We recall that scripts and stereotypes, the elaborated form of the stereotype, are mental short cuts we use to orient ourselves in the world. Without them, we would be overwhelmed by the amount of data. Animals have instincts, and I leave it an open question if they have free will. However, we do. Scripts are social constructs, and if we take a step back, we can rewrite them, even if we have internalized them and use them to define ourselves in our self-scripts. Scripts and stereotypes are software. Some are positive and others are negative. The negative stereotypes limit us and suppress our performances. They are not helpful.

As said, the old woman stereotype and script is restrictive and negative. As we have earlier discussed, in children's fairy tales the "dead mother plot" kills the mother and makes the fairy-tale heroine an orphan. Henneberg explains that "the dead mother plot is a feminist necessity,"[11] because the heroine cannot learn anything from the mother, who is part of a patriarchal society. Henneberg says fairy-tale grandmothers fall into three stereotypes, "wicked old witch, the selfless godmother, or the demented hag."[12] If the old woman is presented as wise, "these elders give advice from an aloof position, far removed from the center of action ... this kind of retreat reflects and exacerbates the stigmatization of the old, no matter how sagacious they are."[13] The image of the old woman living isolated has "a simplistic equation between aging, withdrawal, and decline."[14] Thus, fairy tales represent old women as either wise and good, for example as a fairy godmother, or as cunning and evil, for example as a witch, both, however, isolated and living outside the community. The witch and the fairy godmother are the negative and positive version of one and the same, the old woman.

In myth there is also the figure of the *wise old woman,* who functions as mentor, guide, or helper to the heroine. The wise old woman stereotype is positive, but is isolated, childless, and without a family, like the old woman in the fairy tale. She can be a goddess, a witch, or a wise woman. Before the witch was demonized by the church, she was one among many individuals with supernatural abilities, such as necromancers, wizards, seers, and magicians.[15] Supernatural powers could be good or evil, but evil was not demonic.

Finally, when we shift focus from fairy tales and myths to modern society's master narrative of old age, this is "generally constructed negatively as a period of helplessness that implies physical vulnerability and dependency as well as meanness and bitterness."[16] Today, aging means decline, loss, becoming weak, fragile, infantilized, demented, and, ultimate, the discourse of aging is one of dying. Old age is an abyss. In such "chronometric measurement," time equals loss. And in the West, women are judged more harshly than men, because they face ageism and sexism. Men are judged by their career, women by their bodies. Women lose a sexually reproductive body, they lose status, and they lose youth. In a youth-obsessed era, women "lose" their face when they age in a beauty regime where youth equals beauty. Jerslev says women's looks are "not anchored in a sense of time as duration but frozen in a utopian eternal present."[17] Trying to keep up with today's beauty ideal is increasingly impossible as models in fashion magazines become younger. Finally, we recall how an "age gaze" constantly surveilles women, who risk the "scandal of anachronism" if they fail to act age appropriately.[18]

In the fairy tale, old women are supposed to die and make room for the heroine, or at least be invisible. But as old people are increasingly targeted as consumers, old women again become visible. Krainitzki says this creates "another set of assumptions in relation to a successfully aged female body, by enforcing and reproducing heteronormative youthfulness, in line with a youth-centered postfeminist cultural framework."[19] Today, not only young and middle-age women, but old women too, are expected to police and correct their faces and bodies with anti-age pharmaceuticals and plastic surgery. Against the ageism and sexism of old age scripts, feminists call for "alternative temporal experiences of old age."[20] That is, narratives with a positive old woman stereotype and script. We shall now see how Joan and Dr. Seward offer precisely that.

Joan: Witch and Wise Woman

"The Nightcomers" opens with Vanessa telling about when she learned to be a witch: "It all began several years ago and far from here. The moors of the West country. I went in search for answers to who I was, to a woman I came to know as the Cut-wife of Ballentree Moore. She was the first witch I ever met" (2.03). The story cuts to a backflash where Vanessa stands outside Joan's house with a dead, black tree behind her.

Joan combines a pre-Christian witch with the stereotype of the Wise Old Woman. She lives isolated on the moor, has gray unkempt hair, is rude, and

FIGURE 10.1 *Patti LuPone as the unruly witch Joan Clayton, who becomes mentor to Vanessa, the young witch and protagonist in* Penny Dreadful. Penny Dreadful: Season 2, Episode 3 *("The Nightcomers")*. © Sky/Showtime, 2015.

dressed in gray clothes, almost rags. She makes potions, performs abortions, and in the attic has a leather-bound book with dangerous spells, a book she will pass on to Vanessa. She fits the Wise Woman stereotype of having knowledge, but warns: "If you think you are touched by the demon, then you best walk out that door, because what I can give you for that is only knowledge you don't want, little girl." However, Vanessa seeks Joan's knowledge:

JOAN: You want to learn?
VANESSA: Yes.
JOAN: Everything?
VANESSA: Yes.
JOAN: You're not frightened?
VANESSA: No.
JOAN: Why do you want to learn the arts?
VANESSA: To find out what I am.
JOAN: And if the answer you don't' like?
VANESSA: Better to know.
JOAN: Not really.

From Joan's teaching, Vanessa learns witchcraft as a combination of knowledge and self-knowledge, the latter insight into Vanessa's own self. In the plot chronology, the apprenticeship is after Mina is abducted and before

Vanessa joins Malcolm in London. Vanessa is at this time supposedly late teen, however, there is no attempt at making the actress appear younger. While Green is mid-thirties, Vanessa seems to be in her twenties. Joan's age is also unspecified, but Cromwell gave her the house and land in 1644, which makes her at least three centuries old. Her hair is gray, she has wrinkles and hunches, and she looks in her seventies.

Joan functions as guide, mentor, and teacher. She shows Vanessa how to access her powers, which means reaching into oneself and connect with senses and instincts. "Feel, reach into yourself," she says, when she tests if Vanessa can feel where the scars on Joan's back are from. Joan is touching Vanessa's forehead with a bloodied thumb. When she teaches Vanessa to cast the Tarot cards, she slaps Vanessa furiously in the head and yells, "look at them," and says "believe." Asked to do an interpretation, Vanessa says the card "The Devil" signifies "evil." Joan responds, "You can do better!" Vanessa then reads "The Devil" as lover, desire, and longing. "That's more the feeling." The source of Vanessa's powers is in her senses and her faith. Joan also teaches abilities, like knowledge about herbs and how to make potions, to speak *verbis diablo*, the devil's tongue, and to snap a rabbit's neck to make a stew. Joan's teachings combine what Csikszentmihalyi calls *fluid* and *crystallized* abilities.[21] Fluid abilities are innate and the ability to, for example, "have quick reaction times, to compute fast and accurately."[22] This is when Vanessa "feels" in response to the world, like "feeling" the Tarot cards. Fluid abilities peaks in our late twenties. Crystallized intelligence is comparing learning across different categories, and it uses deliberate thinking and reasoning. "These abilities depend more on reflection than quick reaction, and they usually increase with time ... even in the ninth decade of life."[23] We here recognize Khaneman's System 2, the ability to stop and access fields of knowledge. Vanessa was born with the gift, while Joan learned witchcraft. But although Vanessa was born with her fluid abilities, she must learn from a teacher how to master them. Joan's character combines the witch and the Wise Woman stereotype, passing on her knowledge to Vanessa.

Joan has aged, because unlike Evelyn, she has not made a deal with the Devil, but remained a *good* witch. She warns Joan against speaking *verbis diablo*. "Only if all fails speak the devil's tongue but mark me girl, it's a seduction and before you blink twice it's all you can speak. And so does a daywalker become a nightwalker" (2.03). A nightwalker has sold her soul, like Evelyn (Helen McCrory), the season's villain who heads a witch coven that Joan once belonged to, centuries ago. "What do they seek?" Vanessa asks. "Power. Youth. Beauty. Love," says Joan. The coven comes to Joan's house to claim Vanessa. Evelyn serves the Devil in return for her youth. When Evelyn cannot enter Joan's house, she uses her powers to draw Joan out. The two witches have a face-off under the dead tree outside Joan's house:

EVELYN: You're so very old. Is your mind slipping a bit?
JOAN: And you are young as ever.
EVELYN: Yes. That's rather the point.
JOAN: Give up your soul for that, sure, so that you still live?
EVELYN: God, sister, how you speak. Like a talking potato. You never change. Of course except in every way that matters . . . Those bones are brittle. Do you really want this to be your last battle?
JOAN: It is the *only* battle.

Joan is older and weaker than Evelyn, but fearless. She shrugs off Evelyn's threats, "I'm an old woman. It gives spice to my last days." Csikszentmihalyi's research in creativity shows there are positive sides to aging: "The positive outcomes featured diminished anxiety over performance, being less driven, and exhibiting more courage, confidence, and risk taking."[24] When creative people age, they become less proficient in fluid abilities, but more proficient in crystallized abilities. They are wiser and have more confidence and courage. They can break with stereotypes and choose their own way. "I've not had a happy life. But it has been my life," says Joan.

The Witch in History

In the cultural imagination in the West, a witch can control the weather, kill crops, cause disease, kill and raise the dead, and tell the future. The extent of her magic depends on the intensity of her powers. In *Witchcraft and Folk Belief in the Age of Enlightenment Scotland, 1670–1740* (2016), Scottish historian Lizanne Henderson examines historical witch trials and witch beliefs. Between the fifteenth and eighteenth century, 100,000 women and men in Europe were accused of witchcraft and between 50,000 and 60,000 executed.[25] Before 1450, "witch" was used about practices such as charmer, diviner, sorcerer, magician, necromancer, and warlock. The *Bible*'s Witch of Endor (I Samuel 28:3–25) was, for example, a necromancer who had "divinatory powers and could raise the dead,"[26] and the passage "Thou shalt not suffer a witch to live" (Exodus 22:18) has *kashaph*, a Hebrew word that "carried the meaning of magician, sorcerer or diviner, but was not considered diabolical."[27]

Joan is a witch, but not a demonical one. She is the ancient sorcerer, or the later Wise Woman, and uses her powers and knowledge for the good. *Penny Dreadful* distributes the witch stereotype over four characters: The evil Evelyn, young Hecate (one of the coven's witches who escapes death and joins Ethan in America in season three), the good Joan, and Vanessa.

In our cultural imagination, and in popular culture, the witch has three ages. There is the old evil woman we know from fairy tales, a witch with "bad skin, crooked teeth, foul breath, a cackling laugh and a big nose that has a wart at the end of it."[28] Then there is the middle-age witch obsessed with youth, the witch we know from Disney films like *Snow White and the Seven Dwarfs* (1937, William Cottrell). Finally, there is the young or teenage witch who became popular in the 1990s, for example *Sabrina – The Teenage Witch* (1996–2003, ABC, WB).[29] Historical records, however, show that the women accused of being a witch were of all ages and not obsessed with youth. Of women accused of witchcraft in Scotland between 1670 and 1740, seventy-eight percent were married and only two percent single.[30] The typical woman accused of witchcraft was ordinary, middle class, any age, and accusations sprang from quotidian quarrels, "reflective predominantly of tensions between women."[31]

While the witch in history thus is not related to issues of youth, the witch in our popular culture is. She has sold her soul to the Devil because she is terrified of old age. The poster for *Vvitch* has the tagline, "Evil takes many forms," under the image of an old-old woman. Like Evelyn, that film's old witch sacrifices a baby to get back her younger, seductive form. When Vanessa in the season's last episode defeats the Devil in Evelyn's mansion, Evelyn screams "no" and takes a hand up to her face, which is aging to be old-old ("And They Were Enemies," 2.10). As Jerslev points out, a woman's face "loses its value when the process of ageing cannot be concealed by any means anymore."[32] According to the beauty myth, "old age is bad, repulsive, and ugly."[33] But Joan is not afraid of aging and hasn't sold her soul. She serves her community and helps women with abortions, even if they despise her and are ungrateful. A young woman, who Joan has performed an abortion on, is the one to shout accusations and to set Joan on fire.

Evelyn is the demonic witch who seduces men to gain power. She charms the local lord and persuades him to burn Joan. Joan picks her battles and missions and she accepts her aging face and death. Later, when the Devil tempts Vanessa, he manifests a nuclear family with Vanessa and Ethan as a married couple with children: "Let me show you what I can give you: to be free of pain. To be normal. To be loved by others. Is that not the aim of all human beings?" But it is not the aim of Joan or Vanessa. Joan refused the Devil and when Vanessa refuses to serve the local community after Joan's death, Joan says, "you selfish bitch, you will never have a happy life." Joan also tells Vanessa to "be true," two words echoed when Vanessa leaves Joan's house with the Tarot cards in her bag, and passes the dead tree, which again frames her. The black tree has the form of a gallows and it appears several times. Jung says about the tree as an archetype that

> ... the commonest associations to its meaning are growth, life, unfolding of form in a physical and spiritual sense, development, growth from below upwards and from above downwards, the maternal aspect (protection, shade, shelter, nourishing fruits, source of life, solidity, permanence, firm-rootedness, but also being "rooted to the spot"), old age, personality and finally death and rebirth.[34]

Jung's description also fits Joan's witch character. "The Nightcomers" ends with her words, "be true," which means one must be true *to oneself*. When you are on a journey to know yourself, you must stay the course even if there is a storm. Henderson links the witch trials to society's fear of women. The witch is an "independent adult woman who does not conform to the male idea of proper female behavior," because she is "assertive ... [and] does not nurture men or children, nor care for the weak" and "has the power of words – to defend herself or to curse."[35] In a patriarchal world, "the imagery of a rebellious, subversive woman must have seemed incredibly threatening to men and women alike."[36] Henderson reminds us that the rebellious witch script is modern, because the witch in historical records was not a rebel or a feminist.

Joan passes on her accumulated knowledge to the next generation, Vanessa. She rejected the Devil and did not become a nightcomer, like Evelyn, but a good witch instead. Joan, thus, re-authors the witch script from evil and age-anxious (like Fiona), to a Wise Old Woman and Witch, who is rude but takes responsibility for others, able and caring, wise and compassionate. She writes her own life scripts and follows her own path, even if it means an unhappy life.

Dr. Seward: Scientist and Survivor

The alienist Dr. Florence Seward is a female version of Dr. Seward in Stoker's *Dracula*. She is a scientist, but also caring and compassionate. Alienist is the Victorian term for a psychoanalyst. Dr. Seward is an American from New York and has moved to London where she has a praxis and a male secretary, Renfield (Samuel Barnett). In season three Dr. Seward treats Vanessa for depression and when she discovers the supernatural forces are real, she joins the group. Dr. Seward appears in eight of the season's nine episodes. In contrast to the unruly Joan, Seward is meticulously neat in a respectable dress and jacket, signaling money and upper middle class, has a short page, and takes care of her appearance. She looks young-old, around the actress' age, which is late-sixties. Like men at the time, Dr. Seward smokes and drinks. She is self-assured and in control of any situation. At Vanessa's first visit, Dr. Seward informs the client:

> Since I'm sure you're not familiar with alienism, I'll tell you how it works. If I accept your case, I insist on one-hour sessions every other day, no exceptions. Our sessions are strictly confidential, I don't talk about them and you can't, no exceptions. Given we are a new branch of science, there's no standard scale for fee so I charge ten shillings per session, as much as a visit to a half-way decent dentist. So, you can come see me or get your teeth fixed, your choice ("The Day Tennyson Died," 3.01).

Vanessa is surprised that the alienist looks exactly like Joan: "We've met before. I've met someone very like you. Joan Clayton was her name." Seward replies, "my family name was Clayton," but underlines her and Vanessa's relationship is professional: "I'm not your friend or your priest or your husband. I'm your doctor." At the end of the episode, Vanessa writes in her diary that "if my own immortal soul is lost, there remains something else: my self." Thus, Dr. Seward pulls Vanessa out of depression and back into a world as a moral agent with free will and a self. At the end of the session, Seward orders Vanessa to "do something that will make you happy," and in episode two, after Vanessa has told she is haunted by the Devil, the doctor cries after Vanessa closes the door. Clearly, Seward has a big heart.

In "Ageing and Cultural Stereotypes of Older Women" (1993) Jan Ginn and Sara Arber divide old women into "passive responders" and "active initiators." The latter are women who "had pursued many outside interests and activities, including employment in a satisfying job, [and who] were more likely to feel able to cope on their own, and to have a strong sense of independence."[37] With her professional praxis as alienist, which in 1891 is a "new branch of science" Dr. Seward is an active initiator. Furthermore, she records sessions with a phonograph, a machine with cylinders which allows her to listen to the confidential material (and which also allows Renfield to listen to the recordings and report to Dracula). The phonograph was invented in 1877 and cylinders in the 1880s, which makes the machine a fancy new piece of technology in 1892. Dr. Seward interprets Vanessa's

FIGURE 10.2 *Dr. Seward (Patti LuPone) comforts hypnotized Vanessa (Eva Green) inside Vanessa's memory of her stay at the Banning clinic.* Penny Dreadful: *Season 3, Episode 4 ("A Blade of Grass")*. © *Sky/Showtime, 2016.*

symptoms as those of a neurotic, however, unlike Dr. Banning who treated Vanessa with hydrotherapy, isolation, and trepanning, Seward uses words. Words can be recorded and replayed, and if used wisely, words can transport a patient back in time through hypnosis.

Dr. Seward thinks Vanessa is a neurotic who rebels against her social role in society, and she finds Vanessa conventional. To demonstrate she is not as naïve as the doctor thinks, Vanessa points out that Seward's motive for working is curiosity, not a need of money. "You don't need the ten shillings but you do need interesting people" (3.01). Unlike the medical doctors Frankenstein and Jekyll, who in season three submit patients to injections and electric shock, Dr. Seward uses cognitive science. And where Frankenstein wants to create new life, Seward wants, more modestly, "to cure" (3.01). The female alienist expands on Henneberg's old woman stereotypes, godmother, witch, and old crone. Contrary to the negative stereotyping of old people as evil and demented (as in *The Visit*), Dr. Seward is good and also shows that old people's brains continue to learn. As French neuroscientist Alain Prochaintz says, "every day new fibers are growing, synapses are becoming undone, and new ones are being formed. These changes in the neuronal ... landscape mark our capacity for adaptation, our capacity for learning and improvement, which continue until an advanced age, and in fact until death"[38]

The Wise Woman in the White Room

We can interpret the alienist as a modern version of the Wise Woman and Old Crone in myth. In "A Blade of Grass" Vanessa asks the doctor to hypnotize her, so she can return to the white room at Banning's clinic, a padded cell where she spent five months diagnosed with "women's disease" and was submitted to trepanning. Here she met Lucifer and Dracula, two fallen angels who haunt her, Lucifer for her soul and Dracula for her body.

Under hypnosis, Vanessa re-lives the depression. "It's not torture they're doing, it's science. It's meant to make you better," the nurse (Rory Kinnear) says to Vanessa, who refuses to eat. "It's meant to make me normal. Like all the other women you know. Compliant, obedient" (3.04). Dr. Seward appears in five scenes in the episode: At the start and end to guide Vanessa in and out of the hypnotic state, and three times as a helper when Vanessa manifests Seward inside her hypnotic state. In these scenes, Seward appears inside the cell and helps and comforts Vanessa:

VANESSA: I don't remember.
DR. SEWARD: Try!
VANESSA: I am!
DR. SEWARD: Try harder!

VANESSA [yelling]: Dr. Seward, Stop this session now!
DR. SEWARD: I can't Vanessa, I've been trying. You won't come out. You won't wake up. I burnt your hand with a cigarette, it didn't work. You've apparently gone into something called a fugue state ... It's a mental and physical break, a dissociation with your bodily functions, something like a coma.

Let us take a closer look at the Wise Woman/Old Crone archetype. Discussions of the wise woman draw on D. J. Conway's *Maiden, Mother, Crone* (1994) which argues that a Triple Goddess has been a primary deity for thirty thousand years. This work is, like the works in ecological theory about a Goddess, speculative. Its truth is, like that of the Man the Hunter and Woman the Gatherer stories I discussed in Chapter 1, impossible to verify because it is rooted in prehistory. We will, however, not be concerned with historical truth, but with the *idea* and thus *script* of the crone and wise woman. She "deals with death and the end of cycles ... [She] is winter, night, outer space, the abyss, menopause, advancement of age, wisdom, counsel, the gateway to death and reincarnation, and the Initiator into the deepest of Mysteries and prophesies."[39] The Wise Woman counsels and shares her wisdom, she initiates the process of self-development and knowledge, and she is the gateway keeper into "deep" knowledge. This role aptly describes Dr. Seward's relation to Vanessa.

Dr. Seward fits the Wise Woman archetype and expands it into a modern old woman stereotype. I want to point out two things about the knowledge Seward facilitates in Vanessa. In the negative version as evil witch, the old crone can hurt and kill and uses knowledge to serve herself. But in her positive version, which is the one we are after, the Wise Woman is about wisdom. I earlier mentioned *crystallized mental abilities*. These are to do with learning and make connections across fields of knowledge, and, in Kahneman's terms, they involve the combination of System 1 and System 2. Crystallized abilities require instinctive responses *and* deliberate reflections. This was what Joan taught Vanessa: To feel *and* think. Joan's last advice was: "Be true."

In his discussion of creativity and old age, Csikszentmihalyi draws on Erikson's life stages, which end with wisdom in old age. Summarizing Erikson, Csikszentmihalyi says, "if we live long enough and if we resolve all the earlier tasks of adulthood—such as developing a viable *identity*, a close and satisfying *intimacy*, and if we succeed in passing on our genes and our values through *generativity*—then there is a last remaining task that is essential for our full development as a human being. This consists in bringing together into a meaningful story our past and present ..." (emphasis in original).[40] According to Csikszentmihalyi and Erikson, the ideal old identity can "be summarized in the sentence 'I am what survives me,'" and in the words of one of Csikszentmihalyi's respondents, "being a good ancestor."[41]

In "Tracking the Archetype of the Wise Woman/Crone" (2005) Dorothy S. Becvar says the Wise Woman "provided guidance in the search for truth"[42] and her wisdom is knowledge that can be passed on to the next generations. We will separate knowledge from wisdom by defining the first as information one can use, like Frankenstein uses knowledge to build bodies, and wisdom as knowledge filtered through System 2 and thus having been through our deliberate evaluation—is this useful knowledge or not?—and valued in ethical terms of *how* to deal with knowledge. Beaver says the wise woman accepts the "responsibilities . . . to distill what had been learned into wisdom that could be shared."[43] Becvar also underlines that the Wise Woman is true to her values: "Corresponding with the mandate for a crone to be true to herself, perhaps most important to me is how I live my life, meaning the degree to which I act in integrity with myself."[44] Wisdom is more than knowledge, it is the essence distilled from living a life where you have worked through the themes of the life stages. To help Vanessa, who self-injures, refuses food, and is in suicidal despair, Dr. Seward taps into wisdom:

DR. SEWARD: My ancestor, the old woman. Joan Clayton. What would she say to you?
VANESSA: "Be true." [Vanessa crawls over to Dr. Seward and lies down and puts her head in Seward's lap].
DR. SEWARD: Be true. You will come out of it. When you're at the heart of your trauma. When you've found what you're here for. I'm not leaving you for anything in this world.
VANESSA: What do I do?
DR. SEWARD: Keep going. What happened next?

Seward guides Vanessa through her mental journey and helps Vanessa tap into Joan's lesson: To be true, think, and feel. Seward is guide and protector, Wise Woman and alienist. In "The Blessed Dark" (3.09) Seward uses hypnosis again, this time to access Renfield's mind to reveal the location of Dracula's lair. This use of hypnosis might strike a modern viewer as old-fashioned and fantastic, and in *Wilderness* hypnosis did not help werewolf Alice. However, in the Victorian era, hypnosis is a new science used by medical doctors and alienists to focus attention of the mind and alleviate pain and anxiety. Western doctors drew from the self-induced trance states in the East, where hypnosis had been used for medical purposes for millennia. Mesmerism, an early version of hypnotherapy, was investigated by French scientific commissions in 1784 and 1826. In 1892, a report from the commission by the British Medical Association confirmed that, "as a therapeutic agent hypnotism is frequently effective in relieving pain, procuring sleep, and alleviating many functional ailments [i.e., psychosomatic complaints and anxiety disorders.]"[45] In short, Seward's hypnosis is not fantastic. It is, like the phonograph, modern science.

Cool and Edgy

Dr. Seward is more than wise, she is also *cool*, a concept Jerslev uses to describe the recent trend in advertisement where old female celebrities are used to sell luxury brand goods. We recall from previous chapter how Lange was used by Marc Jacobs as face for his "Beauty" fragrance in 2014. LuPone, too, is a cool and acclaimed actress in musical and theater. She is known for walking down into theater audience to take cell phones out of their hands if they text during a performance. A 2016 interview calls LuPone "Patti Badass LuPone" and says, "There's absolutely no one like her. But isn't that what makes her a legend?"[46]

In an illuminative discussion of Joan Didion in an ad for fashion brand Céline, Jerslev argues Didion is featured not because she is an old woman, but because she is an old and cool celebrity writer. As mentioned earlier, to be old is doubly negative for women due to ageism and sexism. Age is "the unwatchable demon inside of us,"[47] which should remain hidden or be controlled with pharmaceuticals or surgery. The ideal is eternal youth. For example, when images of cover girls for *Vogue* are fed to computers with face-recognition software, the computer judges them to be between six and seven years old. Thus, ideal female beauty in the West is not middle-age or young or adolescence—it is the face of a girl. Women are not allowed to age, because our culture does not accept that time leaves the signs of lived life,

FIGURE 10.3 *Dr. Seward (Patti LuPone) is a Victorian alienist and a New Old Woman who smokes, drinks, and can shoot guns.* Penny Dreadful: *Season 3, Episode 2 ("Predators Far and Near"). © Photo: Jonathan Hession/Sky/Showtime, 2016.*

signs such as wrinkles and gray hair. Men "grow" old, but women "lose" their sex appeal and social status, and, most of all, they lose their "face," the site par excellence of identity.

A counter strategy against "effacement" and invisibility is coolness. Jerslev says, "cool is an attitude of detachment and aloofness that expresses a thought-out position on the edge. Cool is public appearance, an expression of individualism, detachment and a certain superiority."[48] Cool was once attributed to the young but is today adopted across generations. I find Jerslev's discussion of being "cool" and "edgy" highly relevant to our discussion of LuPone. Jerslev says "cool" is ambiguous, both inclusive—one wants to be looked at and noticed—yet also exclusive—the cool attitude is anti-mainstream, it is not avant-garde, yet it is "constituted in opposition to fashion."[49] If we use the scale of reaction to the stereotype (Table 1), a scale which spans from compliance to re-authoring, then to be cool is to revolt against stereotype. Cool signifies revolt, independence, self-containment. It may not be a full re-authoring because to be cool is to stand out, yet still be in a crowd. As leading actress in musicals and plays, LuPone is known to stand out. And her character, Florence Seward, has a rather cool dramatic past which we learn about in episode six, when she has drinks with Vanessa. "He would have killed me, but . . ." Vanessa: "You killed him first." Dr. Seward smiles: "With a cleaver from the kitchen. Trust me honey, when you kill your husband with a cleaver and then stand trial for it in New York city, you know what it is to be alone. I've tried not to rely on anyone since then."

To be cool is also to be edgy, on the edge between mainstream and the avant-garde, and edgy takes us back to horror as edgework. Dr. Seward is on the edge of what is an acceptable old female character, and her view of men resonates in another of the show's characters, Lily Frankenstein. Lily is on a quest to kill all men, and film scholar Stephanie Green (2017) in her analysis of Lily as a Gothic New Woman draws on the New Woman from the 1890s.

"The New Woman" was coined in 1894 by author Sarah Grande, and the term quickly caught on. The New Woman sought "education, independence and a role in public life," and she was both "enmeshed with the popular discourse of the 'new' and the cult of decadence with which Oscar Wilde . . . [was] associated."[50] A famous photo from 1896 by photographer Frances Benjamin Johnston, entitled "Self Portrait (as New Woman)," shows Johnston in Victorian dress, drinking and smoking a cigarette in front of a fireplace. The picture perhaps influenced Seward's appearance in *Penny Dreadful*, where she in the above scene smokes and drinks in front of a fireplace.

Penny Dreadful evokes late Victorian feminism and we see Suffragettes be arrested by the police in "Good and Evil Braided Be" (3.03). Watching this, Lily comments, "they think of equality. I think of mastering man." Lily doesn't want to vote but "to go to war" (3.03). The New Woman holds both sides, a demand for equality and a threat against men. Green connects the New Woman, a *fin de siècle* figure, to "monstrosity, modernity, sexuality," and points out that "[i]n *Penny Dreadful*, however, the New Woman is Gothic not simply because she is associated with destruction but because she is associated with unending change."[51]

In *Penny Dreadful,* Lily desires the violent change of revolution and is stopped by Dorian, Frankenstein, and Jekyll in union. Dr. Seward is an alternative to Lily. Dr. Seward, too, has proven able to defend herself with a cleaver, and she, too, can change from beaten wife to self-employed alienist. Dr. Seward does not possess Lily's youth, beauty, and supernatural immortality, she is a different character. She is the New Old Woman, an independent, lethal, professional, wise, and caring figure who straddles both sides of the New Woman, destruction and change.

The New Old Woman

In the analytical chapters, we have encountered women across the life phases; from the children Ofelia and Eli to teenage werewolves and emerging adult vampires, from adult and self-injuring women to mothers, and middle-age women in their late forties and sixties. Rather than deploy a single lens, my aim has been to parse out the various kinds of play horror invites us to experience on the dark stage. These experiences do not make up a single "learning" but invite us to join life's challenge of continuous learning to adapt to our environment as we change, and the environment changes too. Each life stage has new themes and conflicts, and horror has the unique ability to engage with what is challenging, unpleasant, unsolved, and traumatic. Horror is life's edgework, fascinating and terrifying. It can, like in "The Nightcomers" and "A Blade of Grass," be an experience of life as utterly bleak. But this is also growing stronger.

The old woman differs from previous heroines because she faces two threats. One is within the diegetic story (in *Penny Dreadful* it is the Devil and Dracula). And the other opponent is old age as dying. After all, Erikson is right when he says old age leads to death. Ultimately, it does. Our younger heroines are on a life's journey that is prematurely interrupted. As middle age nears old age, Lange's characters Fiona and Elsa are desperate to stop or turn back time.

Joan and Seward offer a new script for the negative old woman stereotype. I will discuss them as making up a single character, because Seward is written as Joan's ancestor. Joan/Seward makes no attempt to turn back time. "It is the *only* battle," Joan tells Evelyn, who in death loses her youth and her soul to the Devil. Joan, in contrast, has passed on her wisdom to Vanessa and set the younger woman's moral compass: Be true. Joan is a "good ancestor" and dies fighting the battle without remorse, complaints, no hell awaiting her, as it does Evelyn and Fiona. Whether in rags, or composed and elegant, Joan/Seward makes no attempt to police her body or hide wrinkles. She wears her face like her wits, razor-sharp and unapologetically. Jerslev, quoting V. Brown (2014), says the rebellious cool attitude is "principally against the past, against yesterday, and all those still stuck there."[52] Joan/Seward is not stuck with a young face from the past, but moves ahead to new times and new battles with her face an archive of lived life. Pretty cool.

The New Old Woman doesn't care about her face, she cares about others. She is cool and wise. Becvar outlines five guidelines for wisdom: "(1) acknowledging connectedness; 2) suspending judgment; (3) trusting the universe; (4) creating realities; and (5) walking a path with heart."[53] Such values are inspired by Zen Buddhism and the idea that it is more important to be connected with the universe and with others than it is to achieve the self-development and individualism we value in the West. The New Old Woman shows care by teaching and mentoring. She ignores conventions, stereotypes, rules, and restrictions. "I don't care about politeness," Seward tells Vanessa, "There are no manners here. If you want to scream like an animal you should. Or cry. Or yell. *There are no emotions unwelcome in this room*" (my emphasis, 3.01).

In the East, old age is valued for wisdom and elders are held in high esteem.[54] In the West, old age signals loss of youth and beauty and we demonize or ridicule the old woman. However, old age has recently become a contested and conflicted territory where old people are expected to continue to be consumers. Thus, Jerslev warns that the colonization of old age as an age of consumption makes demands on old people to age appropriately and look young, slim, fit, and act as if they are not really old. Social gerontologists suggest the appearance of a fourth age. The third age used to be old age, however, today the third age is for the able seniors, and it has "the values of choice, autonomy, self expression and pleasure." The fourth age is then for "an abject class" and signals decline. It is "a kind of black hole from which the light of agency becomes dimmed."[55] The "black hole" is the abyss.

Seward belongs to the third age as an able-minded and able-bodied young-old woman. She demonstrates what social studies show, "that the less completely a woman has conformed to the conventional ideal of domestic femininity, the more likely she is to age with pride and independence, maintaining a positive self-image."[56] Ginn says, "resistance, change, and a rebuilding of life-goals and identity is possible at any age."[57] I find it telling, that the viewers who rank "A Blade of Grass" highest on IMDB are women in the age group 45+. They rank the episode 9.7, while its median rank is 9.3. Women between eighteen and twenty-nine rank the episode 9.5, and women between thirty and forty-four rank it 9.4. Overall, women rank this episode higher than men.

Like Joan faces her executioners and Dr. Seward faces Dracula, audiences, too, face death on horror's dark stage. In *Penny Dreadful*, female audiences value this experience higher than male audiences. Women are not afraid to take the dark stage. We know struggle is part of life that will make us stronger, also if a struggle is embodied in old characters. Joan Erikson's last chapter is called "Gerotranscendence," which is what respondents describe as peace of mind in old-old age, "a new feeling of cosmic communion with the spirit of the universe, a redefinition of time, space, life and death, and a redefinition of the self."[58] The respondents' experience of old age is not as loss and abyss, but as climbing a mountain and being deeply involved, yet disinvolved, letting go of old conflicts and embracing the new, to live in the now and to share their knowledge. This last voyage requires the courage to face death, and Joan Erikson says, "there is no time for self-pity and weakening of purpose."[59] Ussher called for re-authoring the negative gender script. In her experience with women, they describe that to grow old and leave behind old myths felt liberating, exciting, and as a journey: "I really am excited to see what lies ahead because it might be a kind of power that I haven't known before – and it might be an authority that I never would have dreamed I could speak."[60]

The New Old Woman can be a witch and an alienist, and need no longer be an abject monster. She has changed to a moral agent. Ussher says, "women who are able to tolerate change, and who can recognise the sadness associated with these changes, but also allow for pleasure in being older in all of its forms, can escape the curse of the monstrous feminine, and avoid taking up a position of abjection personified."[61] Seward used a cleaver to start her journey to become a cool old woman. Viewers can use less radical means. We can instead learn to master fear on the dark stage of horror.

Exit

Playing the Ball Back to the Universe

The aim with *Mastering Fear* has been to explore horror as edgework and show how it can be a play experience. Horror is not nice princess play. It can be upsetting, revolting, disgusting, and traumatizing, and this is the value of entering the dark stage. When we play fight we learn to be resilient, strong, brave, more creative, less afraid, and willing to take chances in life.

Csikszentmihalyi notes that men and women are equally creative, but creative men have more traits we think of as female, and creative women have more traits we think of as male. Creative people are more androgynous, which gives them "a much richer and varied spectrum of opportunities."[1] These are benefits I want us to reap: To have as wide a range of options as possible to choose from so we can learn to master System 1 with our System 2. I am aware horror can be extremely unpleasant, but like Malabou's accidents and traumas, it facilitates new and until now unforeseen ways of being in the world. When animals play fight, they are not afraid. If they are, play automatically stops. But we can be afraid while we play, because we have the meta-emotional ability to self-scare. That is, we can choose to lose control and allow things to become "too much," because we know that albeit the fear is real, the situation is fiction and play.

Play happens in a magic circle where actions are real and not-real, and beyond ethics. Horror does, however, have a play ethic, which is to learn to master the art of falling. On the dark stage of horror, we can accidentialize ourselves without breaking bones. We can re-author our self-scripts after we have emotionally engaged with horror. And as complexity scholar John E. Mayfield says of the imaginary, "[t]his internal model world allows us to explore choices without actually moving any muscles. Whenever the imaginary outcomes are judged to be desirable, real actions can be motivated."[2] To describe how horror engagement is physically felt and experienced, and is not just some symbolic endeavor, I have used the biocultural approach which includes Gibson's affordances. Gibson coined "affordances" because he wanted to avoid "values," which conjured up the concept of meanings. Affordances do not have meanings; they are our actions when we are immersed with *this* body in *this* situation and in *this* world, whether imaginary or real. In the course of writing this book I have become convinced gender is in our mind and that the mind is a result of our emotions and feelings, our thoughts, and the environment. As Fines argues, gender *is* brain software and *can* be rewritten. Gender is a schema and we can re-author our schemas, because such flexibility is a cognitive ability that is in our genes.

As said, horror can be visceral and nauseating and can burn images into our minds we would rather have been without. This, however, is how we develop the self-confidence to play wild play and explore the unknown. In contrast to animals, we can take play to a meta-level where we can challenge knowledge. We can negotiate the gender stereotype and re-author scripts in our own words. A girl doesn't have to throw like a girl, she can learn to throw. Period. Restricting stereotypes can be unlearnt. All it takes is that we tell ourselves the incremental narrative that, yes, we *can* change. Austrian poet Rainer Maria Rilke in one of his poems wrote that if we catch a ball we have ourselves thrown into the air, "all is mere skill and petty gain," but if we catch the ball the universe throws us, then "from your hand issues the meteor and races towards its place in the heavens."[3]

I want us to play ball with the universe. When we catch the ball the universe throws us and play it back, we learn qualities that widen our spectrum of actions. Only when we leave our comfort zone can we do edgework and learn independence. By looking for other scripts than those offered by society, we can make individual choices. Finding courage to explore makes us flexible and creative. And when we practice using System 2 and master our fear, we gain agency. Choice, flexibility, and agency make it possible to choose our own path and author our own scripts. Such freedom is not a neoliberal free ride. Freedom carries a responsibility to be compassionate and care about others, Mandler's second freedom, to choose what is good *because* it is good.[4] The aim of edgework is not to walk the edge alone, but to share this newfound mastery of danger with a community. As we grow old, I hope we continue to play with horror and that we will pass on our wisdom to others and be good ancestors. This has been the intention with *Mastering Fear*.

APPENDIX 1

A Note on Age

I use the words "child," "adolescence," "teen," "adult," "young adult," "emerging adult," "adult," "middle age," and "old" throughout this book. Generally, I am concerned with scripts, stereotypes, and ideas rather than with real people. This is not a sociological study, but a study of fiction and the representation of fictional characters. However, the terms also relate to an ordinary use of language about ourselves and the world, a language which is often imprecise and draws from different discourses. For example, "young adult" means different things whether used in connection with Erikson's life stages or about young adult fiction. Therefore, this is a note on how I have defined these words for the purpose of the discussions in this book.

Child

One is a child until society considers you adult, after which you are legally responsible for your actions. In Denmark, the age of criminal responsibility is fourteen. You can vote at eighteen and are considered an adult at eighteen. However, I use "child" about an individual younger than a teenager. Thus, I use "child" for twelve-year-old Ofelia, but thirteen-year-old Christina I call a teenager or an adolescent.

Puberty

Puberty refers to the biological changes from child to adult, especially in regard to reproduction. The onset is menarche for girls and ejaculation for boys, for both sexes at the approximate age of twelve. Puberty is completed when the adult body has developed. Thus, the age period varies since reproduction is possible from the onset of menarche, but growth (for example in height) may not be finished until the early twenties. Mostly, puberty refers to the age from twelve to seventeen.

Adolescence

In my use of "adolescence" and "teenager" I rely on Waller who in *Constructing Adolescence in Fantastic Realism* discusses the terms as socially constructed.[1] Adolescence is both the biological process of puberty and psychological, social, and cultural changes. It is a phase of physical and mental transformation and considered more liminal and developmental than other life stages. Waller says the notion of adolescence as a phase originates from the turn of the nineteenth century. Before that, one transitioned directly from childhood into adulthood. In terms of age, adolescence is simultaneous with the teenage years, thirteen to nineteen. However, as Wikipedia says, "age provides only a rough marker of adolescence, and scholars have found it difficult to agree upon a precise definition of adolescence."[2] Waller points out adolescence is less clearly defined than childhood and adulthood: "[A]dolescence does not clearly refer to ideas of innocence, origin or moral security, and it is located, not merely as 'other' to adulthood, but also as 'other' to childhood. It is a liminal space onto which a distinct dichotomy of desires or fears cannot easily be projected."[3]

Teenager

The term teenager "is predominantly a cultural one" and linked to consumption. It originates in the Cold War period in the US and was used about young people as consumers. Thus, in 1957 the Young Adult Services Division of the American Library Association was established, acknowledging young adult fiction aimed at teenagers. I use the term teen to refer to a character who is between thirteen and nineteen.

Adult

In Erikson's terminology, adulthood is, strictly speaking, from legal adulthood and until old age, that is, from eighteen to sixty-five. He divides adulthood into young adult (approximately from twenty to forty) and middle age (approximately from forty to sixty-five). I use adult about characters who are between eighteen and sixty-five.

Young Adult

There are at least two common uses. First, in psychology and sociology in general, a young adult is someone in the first half of adulthood, which is between twenty and forty, and this is where Erikson thinks we pursue a career and make a family and learn love, care and compassion. In the second sense, "young adult" is used to categorize products such as literature, film and television shows aimed at young audiences. In US literature, young adult fiction is considered for readers between twelve and eighteen, and in the UK young adult fiction is considered for readers between twelve and sixteen.[4] I follow *The Diagnostic and Statistical Manual of Mental Disorders*, American Psychiatric Association, which in Edition IV (1994) defines young adulthood as between twenty and forty-five, and middle age as between forty-five and sixty-five.

Emerging Adult

The behavior Erikson calls adolescent—experimenting with identity and life style—is today the life style of what psychologist Jeffrey Arnett has coined "emerging adults."[5] Emerging adulthood is the period between adolescence and marriage or children. In 1970, the median age of marriage was twenty-one for women and twenty-three for men in the US, making the transition from teen girl to adult a single step. In 2013, the median age of marriage was twenty-seven for women and twenty-nine for men. In Denmark, the median age of marriage in 2014 was thirty-two for women and thirty-four for men.[6] I use emerging adult about characters between eighteen and early thirties, and the term indicates a liminal mentality open to change and experimenting with identity and life style like the adolescent. Arnett notes that the emerging adults experiment more than adolescents, because they have the money and legal age to be able to do so.

Middle Age

I follow *The Diagnostic and Statistical Manual of Mental Disorders*, American Psychiatric Association, which in Edition IV (1994) defines middle age as between forty-five and sixty-five.[7]

Old Age

I follow Erikson and *The Diagnostic and Statistical Manual of Mental Disorders*, both of which define old as after sixty-five. Gerontology divides old age into young-old (65–75), middle-old (75–85), and old-old (85+). Sociologists call old age the "third age" after childhood and adulthood, and today also talk of a fourth age. The third age would then be the old people who can still be consumers, and fourth age reserved for old people unable to care for themselves and perform the consumer script.[8]

APPENDIX 2

TABLE 3 *Horror, Age, and Learning*

AUDIENCE'S AGE	CHARACTER'S AGE	ABILITIES	GENDER STEREOTYPE	SOCIAL SPACE	EMOTIONS
Adult	Child (0–12)	• Learning aggression • False beliefs • Stamina *Identity and social horror*	Learn	Family Dependence	Fear Disgust Love Vengeance
Teen/Adult	Teen and Emerging Adult (13–early 30s)	• Manage emotions • Identity confusion • Sensorimotor skills • Sexual emotions • Social skills *Social horror*	Negotiate	Friends Inter- dependence	Freedom Love Lust Trust
Adult	Young Adult (20–45)	• Manage aggression • Mating • Social rank • Care *Identity horror*	Struggle	New family Alienation	Anxiety Disgust Pain Despair
Adult	Middle age (45–65)	• Experimentation • Creativity • Social rank • Self-management *Survival and social horror*	Subvert, Re-Author	Community Emerging independence	Self-esteem Freedom Interest
Adult	Old (65+)	• Wisdom • Mentor • Self-reliance *Social horror*	Re-Author	Society Independence	Freedom Pride Helpfulness

NOTES

Introduction

1 For two different views of *Hostel: Part II* see Murray (2008) and Schubart (2008).

2 Karl R. Popper, "On the Theory of the Objective Mind," Chapter 4 in *Objective Knowledge: An Evolutionary Approach* (Oxford: Oxford University Press, 1973), 153–190.

3 For a discussion of emotions and horror, see Rikke Schubart, "Monstrous Appetites and Positive Emotions in *True Blood*, *The Vampire Diaries* and *The Walking Dead*" in *Projections: The Journal for Movies and Mind 7*, Special Topic: Entertaining Violence, ed. Dirk Eitzen, no. 1 (2013): 43–63.

4 For a discussion of the use of anecdotes (also called narrative ethology) in comparative biology see Marc Bekoff and Jessica Pierce, *Wild Justice: The Moral Lives of Animals* (Chicago: University of Chicago Press, 2009), 36–37.

5 For reception studies, see Joanne Cantor and Mary Beth Oliver, "Developmental Differences in Responses to Horror," in ed. Stephen Prince, *The Horror Film* (New Brunswick: Rutgers University Press, 2004), 224–241; Mary Beth Oliver and Meghan Sanders, "The Appeal of Horror and Suspense," also in *The Horror Film*, 242–259; Janet Staiger, *Perverse Spectators: The Practices of Film Reception* (New York: New York University Press, 2000); and Janet Staiger, *Media Reception Studies* (New York: New York University Press, 2005). Social psychologists and media scholars who do social experiments with test subjects cannot, due to ethical reasons, submit subjects to genuinely traumatizing horror scenes. Instead they use less anxiety-raising scenes, for instance from television series *Dexter*. It is different with cultural amusements such as haunted houses. For a sociological analysis of extreme haunts (extreme is when actors in a haunted house interact with visitors, for instance by grabbing them, tying them to torture chairs, and locking them in coffins) and other self-scares, see Margee Kerr, *Scream: Chilling Adventures in the Science of Fear* (New York: Public Affairs, 2015), Kindle edition.

6 It has been argued postfeminism has no politics. My evofeminism is planted in humanism and ecological philosophy, two ideas which in Denmark are represented by the political party The Alternative [Alternativet] that focuses "on serious sustainable transition, a new political culture and the entrepreneurial

creative power of society and individuals." The Alternative seeks global answers to questions about welfare and well-being, migration, and pollution. Website available online: https://en.alternativet.dk/alternative/ (accessed September 6, 2016).

7 Torben Grodal, *Embodied Visions: Evolution, Emotion, Culture, and Film* (New York: Oxford University Press, 2009), 4.

8 Popper, *Objective Knowledge*, 186.

9 For the use of psychosemiotics and feminism in the analysis of horror, see Linda Williams, "When the Woman Looks" (original 1983) in *The Dread of Difference: Gender and the Horror Film*, ed. Barry Keith Grant (Austin: University of Texas Press, 1996), 15–34; Carol Clover, *Men, Women and Chain Saws: Gender in the Modern Horror Film* (London: BFI, 1992); and Barbara Creed, *The Monstrous-Feminine: Film, Feminism, Psychoanalysis* (London: Routledge, 1993).

10 For my earlier postfeminist approach to women see Rikke Schubart, *Super Bitches and Action Babes: The Female Hero in Popular Cinema, 1970–2006* (Jefferson: McFarland, 2007); and Rikke Schubart, "Woman With Dragons: Daenerys, Pride, and Postfeminist Possibilities" in *Women of Ice and Fire: Gender, Game of Thrones, and Multiple Media Engagements*, edited by Rikke Schubart and Anne Gjelsvik (NY: Bloomsbury, 2016), Chapter 5, 105–130.

11 Melissa Hines, *Brain Gender* (New York: Oxford University Press, 2004), 4.

12 Cordelia Fine, *The Delusions of Gender: How Our Minds, Society, and Neurosexism Create Difference* (New York: W. W. Norton & Company, 2010), Kindle edition, 238.

13 Deborah Cameron, "Evolution, Language and the Battle of the Sexes: A Feminist Linguist Encounters Evolutionary Psychology," *Australian Feminist Studies* 30, no. 86 (2015): 351–358. The theme of this issue is feminist encounters with evolutionary psychology.

14 Jane M. Ussher, *Managing the Monstrous Feminine: Regulating the Reproductive Body* (London: Routledge, 2006), 116.

15 Claude M. Steele, *Whistling Vivaldi and Other Clues to How Stereotypes Affect Us* (New York: W.W. Norton & Company, 2010), Kindle edition.

16 There is an excellent discussion of postfeminism in Sarah Projansky, *Watching Rape: Film and Television in Postfeminist Culture* (New York: New York University Press, 2001); I discuss feminism and postfeminism in Schubart and Gjelsvik, *Women of Ice and Fire*, "Introduction," 5–41; a classical use of ecofeminism is Donna Haraway, *Simians, Cyborgs, and Women: The Reinvention of Nature* (London: Free Association Books, 1991); for neofeminism see Hilary Radner, *Neo-Feminist Cinema: Girly Films, Chick Flicks and Consumer Culture* (New York: Routledge, 2011); for a discussion of first, second, and third wave feminism and postfeminism see Stéphanie Genz, "Third Way/ve: The Politics of Postfeminism" in *Feminist Theory* 7, no. 3 (2006): 333–353; for postfeminism see also Benjamin A. Brabon and Stéphanie Genz, eds., *Postfeminist Gothic: Critical Interventions in Contemporary Culture*

(Basingstoke: Palgrave Macmillan, 2007); for fourth wave feminism see Julia Schuster, "Invisible Feminists? Social Media and Young Women's Political Participation," *Political Science* 65, no. 1 (2013): 8–24, and Ealasaid Munro, "Feminism: A Fourth Wave?" Political Studies Association (no date or year), available online: https://www.psa.ac.uk/insight-plus/feminism-fourth-wave (accessed September 8, 2016).

17 Ecosophy was coined by Norwegian philosopher Arne Næss, see Næss, "The Shallow and the Deep, Long-Range Ecology Movement. A Summary," *Inquiry: An Interdisciplinary Journal of Philosophy* 16 (1973): 95–100. For a defense of the Norwegian wolves' rights to live in Norway, see Næss, "Philosophy of Wolf Policies I: General Principles and Preliminary Exploration of Selected Norms," *Conservation Biology* 1, no. 1, May (1987): 22–34.

18 Haraway, *Simians, Cyborgs, and Women*, 198.

19 James B. Twitchell, *Dreadful Pleasures: An Anatomy of Modern Horror* (New York: Oxford University Press, 1985), 7.

20 Clover, *Men, Women and Chain Saws*, 53.

21 Isabel Cristina Pinedo, *Recreational Terror: Women and the Pleasures of Horror Film Viewing* (New York: State University of New York Press, 1997).

22 Erin Harrington, *Women, Monstrosity and Horror Film: Gynaehorror* (Abingdon: Routledge, 2017), Kindle edition.

23 Noël Carroll, *The Philosophy of Horror, or Paradoxes of the Heart* (New York: Routledge, 1990), 193, 194.

24 Murray Smith, "Gangsters, Cannibals, Aesthetes, or Apparently Perverse Allegiances" in *Passionate Views*, eds Carl Plantinga and Greg M. Smith (Baltimore: Johns Hopkins University Press, 1999), 217–238. Slumming and moralism is discussed 228–229.

25 Cynthia Freeland, *The Naked and the Undead: Evil and the Appeal of Horror* (Boulder: Westview Press, 2000), 3. Freeland has a wonderful section titled "Methods I Do Not Use" in her introduction (15–21).

26 Grodal, *Embodied Visions*, 88.

27 Julian Hanich, *Cinematic Emotion in Horror Films and Thrillers: The Aesthetic Paradox of Pleasurable Fear* (New York: Routledge, 2010), 19.

28 Tarja Laine, *Feeling Cinema: Emotional Dynamics in Film Studies* (London: Continuum, 2011), 23. See also Tarja Laine, "Cinema as Second Skin: Under the Membrane of Horror Film," *New Review of Film and Television Studies* 4, no. 2 (August 2006): 93–106.

29 Angela Ndalianis, *The Horror Sensorium: Media and the Senses* (Jefferson: McFarland, 2012), 30.

30 Kevin J. Wetmore, *Post-9/11 Horror in American Cinema* (New York: Continuum, 2012), vii.

31 Both quotes are from Christer Bakke Andresen, *Åpen kropp og lukket sinn: Den norske grøsserfilmen fra 2003 til 2015* [Open Body and Closed Mind: The Norwegian Horror Movie from 2003 to 2015] (Trondheim: NTNU, 2016), Ph.D. dissertation, 19.

32 See for instance Carroll 1990; Carroll, "Film, Emotion, and Genre" in *Passionate Views*, Plantinga and Smith, 21–48; Grodal 2009; Laine 2011; and Hanich 2010. Richard S. Lazarus discusses fear as a both negative and positive emotion, and Katerina Bantinaki discusses fear as a positive emotion. As we shall see in Chapter 1, to call emotions positive or negative raises questions. Richard S. Lazarus, *Emotion and Adaptation* (New York: Oxford University Press, 1991), Kindle edition, 234–240. Katerina Bantinaki, "The Paradox of Horror: Fear as Positive Emotion," *The Journal of Aesthetics and Art Criticism* 70, no. 4, Fall (2012): 383–391.

33 Brian Boyd, *On the Origin of Stories: Evolution, Cognition, and Fiction* (Cambridge: Harvard University Press, 2009), Kindle edition, location 4531.

34 Hanich includes thrillers in his analysis of fear in *Cinematic Emotion in Horror Films and Thrillers* (2010). Also, Carroll writes, "we will freely move between what is called horror and what is called science fiction, regarding the boundary between these putative genres as quite fluid," *The Philosophy of Horror*, 14.

35 Helen Gavin and Theresa Porter, *Female Aggression* (Oxford: Wiley Blackwell, 2015), eBook, 28.

36 Hanna Rosin, *The End of Men: And the Rise of Women* (London: Penguin Books, 2013), Kindle Edition, 186.

37 Erik H. Erikson and Joan Erikson, *The Life Circle Completed. Extended Version With New Chapter on the Ninth Stage of Development by Joan M. Erikson* (New York: W.W. Norton & Company, 1998), Kindle edition.

38 Nico H. Frijda, *The Emotions* (Cambridge: Cambridge University Press, 1986); Nico H. Frijda, *The Laws of Emotion* (New Jersey: Lawrence Erlbaum Associates, 2007); Antonio Damasio, *The Feeling of What Happens: Body and Emotion in the Making of Consciousness* (Orlando: Mariner Books, 2000).

39 Michael S. Gazzaniga, *Who's In Charge: Free Will and the Science of the Brain* (New York: HarperCollins, 2011), Kindle edition; Daniel Kahneman, *Thinking, Fast and Slow* (London: Allan Lane, 2011); Thomas Metzinger, *The Ego Tunnel: The Science of the Mind and the Myth of the Self* (New York: Basic Books, 2009).

40 Simon Baron-Cohen, *The Essential Difference: The Truth About the Male and Female Brain* (New York: Basic Books, 2003); Simon Baron-Cohen, *The Science of Evil: On Empathy and the Origins of Cruelty* (New York: Basic Books, 2011).

41 Sergio Pellis and Vivien Pellis, *The Playful Brain: Venturing to the Limits of Neuroscience* (Oxford: Oneworld, 2009), 4.

42 Roger Caillois, *Man, Play and Games* (Chicago: University of Illinois Press, 2001, French original 1958).

43 Jesper Juul, *The Art of Failure: An Essay on the Pain of Playing Video Games* (Cambridge: The MIT Press, 2013), eBook, 13.

44 Gordon M. Burghardt, *The Genesis of Animal Play: Testing the Limits* (Massachusetts: MIT Press, 2005), Kindle edition.

45 Stephen Lyng, "Edgework: A Social Psychological Analysis of Voluntary Risk Taking," *American Journal of Sociology* 95, no. 4 (January 1990): 851–886, 860.
46 Michael J. Apter, *Danger: Our Quest for Excitement* (Oxford: Oneworld Publications, 2007), eBook.
47 Thomas S. Henricks, *Play and the Human Condition* (Urbana: University of Illinois Press, 2015), Kindle edition.
48 Victor Nell, "Cruelty's Rewards: The Gratifications of Perpetrators and Spectators," *Behavioral and Brain Sciences* 29 (2006): 211–257.
49 It could be argued *Insidious 3* (Leigh Whannell, 2015) is an exception. See note 2 in Chapter 10.

1 The Dark Stage

1 Antonio Damasio, *The Feeling of What Happens: Body and Emotion in the Making of Consciousness* (Orlando: Mariner Books, 2000), 315.
2 For a discussion of time travel, lying, and cognitive differences between human and non-human animals, see Thomas Suddendorf, *The Gap: The Science of What Separates Us From Other Animals* (New York: Basic Books, 2013), Kindle edition. See also Marc Bekoff and Jessica Pierce, *Wild Justice: The Moral Lives of Animals* (Chicago: University of Chicago Press, 2009).
3 New Revised Standard Bible (NRS), *The Bible*, Genesis 1:2–3.
4 Daniel Kahneman, *Thinking, Fast and Slow* (London: Allan Lane, 2011), 21.
5 Kahneman, *Thinking, Fast and Slow*, 417.
6 Richard S. Lazarus, *Emotion and Adaptation*, (New York: Oxford University Press, 1991), Kindle edition, 40.
7 Frijda, *The Emotions*, 253.
8 Noël Carroll, "Film, Emotion, and Genre," in *Passionate Views*, eds Carl Plantinga and Greg M. Smith (Baltimore: Johns Hopkins University Press, 1999), 21–48, 23, 24.
9 Carroll, "Film, Emotion, and Genre," 22.
10 Carroll, "Film, Emotion, and Genre," 28.
11 Cass R. Sunstein, *Laws of Fear: Beyond the Precautionary Principle* (New York: Cambridge University Press, 2005), eBook, 3.
12 Sunstein, *Laws of Fear*, 235.
13 Sunstein, *Laws of Fear*, 234.
14 Lazarus, *Emotion and Adaptation*, 235.
15 Hanich's work is seminal: Julian Hanich, *Cinematic Emotion in Horror Films and Thrillers: The Aesthetic Paradox of Pleasurable Fear* (New York: Routledge, 2010).
16 Hanich, *Cinematic Emotion in Horror Films and Thrillers*, 239.

17 Nico H. Frijda, *The Emotions* (Cambridge: Cambridge University Press, 1986), 252.
18 Frijda, *The Emotions*, 252.
19 Carl Plantinga, "Mood and Ethics in Narrative Cinema," Paper presented at symposium on the Moral Psychology of Fiction, Trondheim, September 20–21, 2012, 12. See also Carl Plantinga, "Art Moods and Human Moods in Narrative Cinema" *New Literary History* 43 (2012): 455–475 and Robert Sinnerbrink, "*Stimmung*: Exploring the Aesthetics of Mood," *Screen* 53, no. 2 (Summer, 2012): 148–163.
20 A. D. Craig, "How Do You Feel? Interoception: The Sense of the Physiological Condition of the Body," *Nature Reviews: Neuroscience* 3 (August 2002): 655–666, 655. For a discussion of senses in horror cinema, see Angela Ndalianis, *The Horror Sensorium: Media and the Senses* (Jefferson: McFarland, 2012), 50.
21 I take feeling states and innate drives from Assal Habibi and Antonio Damasio, "Music, Feelings, and the Human Brain," *Psychomusicology: Music, Mind, and Brain* 24, no 1 (2014): 92–102, 99. They call drives "ation programs that are aimed at satisfying basic instinctual physiological needs," 99.
22 For a discussion of affects, see Eric Shouse, "Feeling, Emotion, Affect," *M/C Journal* 8, no. 6 (December, 2005), no page numbers. Website available online: journal.media-culture.org.au/0512/03-shouse.php (accessed February 4, 2012).
23 See Vinciane Despret, *Our Emotional Makeup: Ethnopsychology and Selfhood* (New York: Other Press, 2004) [original in French 1999].
24 Nico H. Frijda, *The Laws of Emotion* (New Jersey: Lawrence Erlbaum Associates, 2007), see for example Chapter 10, "Revenge," 259–283.
25 Bekoff and Pierce, *Wild Justice*.
26 Lazarus, *Emotion and Adaptation*, 240.
27 Lazarus, *Emotion and Adaptation*, 9. The nine laws are: 1) the law of situational meaning; 2) the law of concern; 3) the law of apparent reality; 4) the laws of change, habituation, and comparative feeling; 5) the law of hedonic asymmetry; 6) the law of conservation of emotional momentum; 7) the law of closure; 8) the law of care for consequence; 9) the laws of lightest load and greatest gain. See Frijda, *The Laws of Emotion*, 1–24.
28 Wikipedia, "Mind," https://en.wikipedia.org/wiki/Mind (accessed on November 27, 2017).
29 Craig, "How Do You Feel?" 663.
30 Damasio, *Feeling of What Happens*, 171.
31 Damasio, *Feeling of What Happens*, 229.
32 Damasio, *Feeling of What Happens*, 84–85.
33 Michael S. Gazzaniga, *Who's In Charge: Free Will and the Science of the Brain* (New York: HarperCollins, 2011), Kindle edition, 43.
34 Gazzaniga, *Who's In Charge*, 102.

35 Thomas Metzinger, *The Ego Tunnel: The Science of the Mind and the Myth of the Self* (New York: Basic Books, 2009), 9.
36 Metzinger, *The Ego Tunnel*, 28.
37 Metzinger, *The Ego Tunnel*, 28–29.
38 Torben Grodal, *Embodied Visions: Evolution, Emotion, Culture, and Film* (New York: Oxford University Press, 2009), 88.
39 Kahneman, *Thinking, Fast and Slow*, the cold water experiment is discussed 382–383.
40 Sunstein, *Laws of Fear*, 195.
41 Sunstein, *Laws of Fear*, 154.
42 Sunstein, *Laws of Fear*, 203.
43 Kahneman, *Thinking, Fast and Slow*, 69.
44 Robert Maurer, *Mastering Fear: Harness Emotion to Achieve Excellence in Health, Work, and Relationships* (Wayne N.J.: Career Press, 2016).
45 Robert C. Solomon and Lori D. Stone, "On 'Positive' and 'Negative' Emotions," *Journal for the Theory of Social Behavior* 32, no. 4 (2002): 417–435, 432.
46 Solomon and Stone, "On 'Positive' and 'Negative' Emotions," 432–433.
47 Solomon and Stone, "On 'Positive' and 'Negative' Emotions," 418.
48 The paradox of art involves ideas of positive and negative emotions: If we avoid negative emotions in real life, why do we appreciate them in art? See Jesper Juul, *The Art of Failure: An Essay on the Pain of Playing Video Games* (Cambridge: The MIT Press, 2013), eBook, especially Chapter 2, "The Paradox of Failure and the Paradox of Tragedy," 33–45.
49 Tarja Laine, *Feeling Cinema: Emotional Dynamics in Film Studies* (London: Continuum, 2011), 11.
50 Laine, *Feeling Cinema*, 3.
51 Laine, *Feeling Cinema*, 4.
52 Greg M. Smith, *Film Structure and the Emotion System* (Cambridge: Cambridge University Press, 2007), 12. For a discussion of mood see also Sinnerbrink, "*Stimmung*," see note 26.
53 Margee Kerr, *Scream: Chilling Adventures in the Science of Fear* (New York: Public Affairs, 2015), Kindle edition, 13.
54 Ndalianis, *Horror Sensorium*, 3.
55 Ndalianis, *Horror Sensorium*, 16.
56 Ndalianis, *Horror Sensorium*, 30.
57 Players debrief each other after playing and in interviews they report various thoughts on their experience of the game, which lasts about three hours: "I don't regret doing it but I could have done without it. I have been asked to game master it for friends but I am not sure I want to help them feel so bad for three hours plus the rest of an evening. I think it is a brilliant game," and

another says, "I found myself throughout the last few days continuously going back, and thinking about it [. . .] It's been really good for me to be able to sit down and talk about these things, and also to think about [. . .] why this can be a good experience even if it's not a fun experience" (about the game *The Journey*). Markus Montola, "The Positive Negative Experience in Extreme Role-Playing," *Nordic DiGRA 2010 Proceedings* (Stockholm, 2010), available online: http://www.digra.org/digital-library/publications/the-positive-negative-experience-in-extreme-role-playing/ (accessed October 12, 2016), 7.

58 See Juul, *Art of Failure*, Chapter 2, "The Paradox of Failure and the Paradox of Tragedy," 33–45. See also Jerrold Levinson, "Emotion in Response to Art: A Survey of the Terrain," in *Emotion and the Arts*, eds. Mette Hjort and Sue Laver (New York: Oxford University Press, 1997), 20–34.

59 Grodal, *Embodied Visions*, 101.

60 Margee Kerr, *Scream: Chilling Adventures in the Science of Fear* (New York: Public Affairs, 2015), Kindle edition.

61 Kerr, *Scream*, 213.

62 Kerr, *Scream*, 217.

63 Kerr, *Scream*, 223–224.

64 For an introduction to feminism as a social construction see Christie Launius and Holly Hassel, *Threshold Concepts In Women's and Gender Studies* (New York: Routledge, 2015), Kindle edition.

65 Doreen Kimura, *Sex and Cognition* (Cambridge: MIT Press, 1999). For the evolutionary story of Man the Hunter and Woman the Gatherer see Mary Zeiss Stange, *Woman the Hunter* (Boston: Beacon Press, 1997).

66 Kimura, *Sex and Cognition*, 34.

67 Melissa Hines, *Brain Gender* (New York: Oxford University Press, 2004), 5.

68 Hines, *Brain Gender*, 218–219.

69 Hines, *Brain Gender*, 153–154.

70 Hines, *Brain Gender*, 224–225.

71 Erwin Straus quoted in Iris Marion Young, "Throwing Like a Girl: A Phenomenology of Feminine Body Comportment Motility and Spatiality," *Human Studies* 3 (1980): 137–156, 137.

72 Young, "Throwing Like a Girl," 138.

73 Young, "Throwing Like a Girl," 143.

74 Iris Marion Young, "Lived Body Vs. Gender: Reflections on Social Structure and Subjectivity," *Ratio (new series)* 15, no. 4, December (2002): 410–428. This is Chapter 1 in Iris Marion Young, *On Female Body Experience: "Throwing Lika a Girl" and Other Essays* (New York: Oxford University Press, 2005), Kindle edition. References are to the Kindle edition.

75 John Florio and Ouisie Shapiro, "The Women Succeeding in a Men's Professional Baseball League," *The New Yorker*, August 29, 2016. Available online: http://www.newyorker.com/news/sporting-scene/the-women-succeeding-in-a-mens-professional-baseball-league (accessed October 11, 2016).

76 Jason Laurendeau, "'Gendered Risk Regimes': A Theoretical Consideration of Edgework and Gender," *Sociology of Sport Journal* 25, no. 3, September (2008): 293–309, 304.
77 Young, "Lived Body," location 193, 199.
78 Sandra Lipsitz Bem, "Gender Schema Theory: A Cognitive Account of Sex Typing," *Psychological Review* 88, no. 4 (1981): 354–364, 355.
79 Bem, "Gender Schema," 355.
80 Claude M. Steele, *Whistling Vivaldi and Other Clues to How Stereotypes Affect Us* (New York: W. W. Norton & Company, 2010), Kindle edition, 170.
81 For a discussion of how the mind activates schemas and integrates them into the Active-Self (the on-the-fly self) and into the Chronic-Self (a stable self), see S. Christian Wheeler, Kenneth G. DeMarree, Richard E. Petty, "Understanding the Role of the Self in Prime-to-Behavior Effects: The Active-Self Account," *Personality and Social Psychology Review* 11, no. 3, August (2007): 234–261.
82 Bem, "Gender Schema," 356.
83 For gender as negative stereotype and the math experiment see Margaret Shih, Todd L. Pittinsky and Nalini Ambady, "Stereotype Susceptibility: Identity Salience and Shifts in Quantitative Performance," *Psychological Science* 10, no. 1, January (1999): 80–83. For ethnicity as negative stereotype see S. Christian Wheeler, "Think Unto Others: The Self-Destructive Impact of Negative Racial Stereotypes," *Journal of Experimental Social Psychology* 37 (2001): 173–180. See also Margaret Shih, Jennifer A. Richeson, Nalini Ambady, Kentaro Fujita, "Stereotype Performance Boosts: The Impact of Self-Relevance and the Manner of Stereotype Activation," *Journal of Personality and Social Psychology* 83, no. 3 (2002): 638–647.
84 Steele, *Whistling Vivaldi*, 123. Anxiety is measured as increased heartbeat, quicker pulse, and worse performance. See Steele, *Whistling Vivaldi*, 170–171, and Shih, Pittinsky and Ambady, "Stereotype Susceptibility," 81.
85 Steele, *Whistling Vivaldi*, 169, 173.
86 Stange, *Woman the Hunter*, 29.
87 Deborah Cameron, "Evolution, Language and the Battle of the Sexes: A Feminist Linguist Encounters Evolutionary Psychology," *Australian Feminist Studies* 30, no. 86 (2015): 351–358, 353.
88 Stange, *Woman the Hunter*, Chapter 1 and 2, 12–78. For a refusal that women are less aggressive see Hines, *Brain Gender*, 213–229. For a discussion of how much and how men and women talk see Cameron, "Evolution, Language and the Battle of the Sexes," 356.
89 British linguist Judith Baxter says, "despite the lack of evidence for *biological* sex differences in speech and leadership styles, the view that women leaders are 'transformational' and male leaders are 'transactional' has become mythologised." Judith Baxter, *The Language of Female Leadership* (Basingstoke: Palgrave MacMillan, 2010), eBook, 68.
90 "Just so" stories are evolutionary explanations which cannot be proven. Stange, *Woman the Hunter*, 22.

91 Simone de Beauvoir, *The Second Sex* (London: Vintage Books, 2011, original 1949), Kindle edition, location 671.
92 Stange, *Woman the Hunter*, 43.
93 Baron–Cohen quoted in Fine, *Delusions of Gender: How Our Minds, Society, and Neurosexism Create Difference* (New York: W. W. Norton & Company, 2010), Kindle edition, location 153.
94 Baron–Cohen quoted in Fine, *Delusions of Gender*, location 161.
95 Baron–Cohen quoted in Fine, *Delusions of Gender*, location 234–251.
96 Baron–Cohen quoted in Fine, *Delusions of Gender*, location 2350.
97 For the disappearance of sex difference in math abilities, see Steele, *Whistling Vivaldi*, 178.
98 For women and free climbing see Dianne Chisholm, "Climbing Like a Girl: An Exemplary Adventure in Feminist Phenomenology," *Hypatia* 23, no. 1, January–March (2008): 9–40; for benefits of gender equality in The Olympic Games see Jennifer L Berhahl, Eric Luis Uhlmann, and Feng Bai, "Win-Win: Female *and* Male Athletes From More Gender Equal Nations Perform Better in International Sports Competitions," *Journal of Experimental Social Psychology* 56 (2015): 1–3.
99 Steele, *Whistling Vivaldi*, 166.
100 Steele, *Whistling Vivaldi*, 168.
101 Steele, *Whistling Vivaldi*, 175.
102 Cordelia Fine, *The Delusions of Gender: How Our Minds, Society, and Neurosexism Create Difference* (New York: W. W. Norton & Company, 2010), Kindle edition, 235.
103 For the benefit of failure in learning how to become a better player see Jesper Juul, *The Art of Failure*, 60, and Chapters 3 and 4.
104 Jane Spencer, "Afterword: Feminist Waves," in *Third Wave Feminism: A Critical Exploration*, eds Stacy Gillis, Gillian Howie, Rebecca Munford (Basingstoke: Palgrave Macmillan, 2007), eBook, 298–303, 302.
105 Donna J. Haraway, *Simians, Cyborgs, and Women: The Reinvention of Nature* (London: Free Association Books, 1991), 196.
106 Haraway, *Simians, Cyborgs, and Women*, 192.
107 Brian Boyd, *On the Origin of Stories: Evolution, Cognition, and Fiction* (Cambridge: Harvard University Press, 2009), Kindle edition, location 4531.
108 Karl R. Popper, "Of Clouds and Clocks," Chapter 6 in *Objective Knowledge: An Evolutionary Approach* (Oxford: Oxford University Press, 1973), 206–256, 244.
109 Michael S. Gazzaniga, *Who's In Charge: Free Will and the Science of the Brain* (New York: HarperCollins, 2011), Kindle edition, 216.
110 Popper, "Of Clouds and Clocks," 248–249.
111 Cynthia Freeland, *The Naked and the Undead: Evil and the Appeal of Horror* (Boulder: Westview Press, 2000), 17.

112 Freeland, *The Naked and the Undead*, 15.
113 For third wave, fourth wave, postfeminism, neofeminism, and ecofeminism, see note 16 in the introduction. In addition to the references in note 15, see also Launius and Hassel, *Threshold Concepts*, and *Third Wave Feminism: A Critical Exploration*, eds Stacy Gillis, Gillian Howie, Rebecca Munford (Basingstoke: Palgrave Macmillan, 2007), eBook. For a positive use of postfeminism see Yvonne Tasker and Diane Negra (eds) *Interrogating Postfeminism: Gender and the Politics of Popular Culture* (London: Duke UP, 2007). For a critique of postfeminism see Diane Negra, *What a Girl Wants: Fantasicing the Reclamation of Self in Postfeminism* (London: Routledge, 2009) and Stéphanie Genz, "'I'm not going to fight them, I'm going to fuck them': Sexist Liberalism and Gender (A)politics in *Game of Thrones*," in *Women of Ice and Fire: Gender, Game of Thrones, and Multiple Media Engagements*, Rikke Schubart and Anne Gjelsvik (eds), (NY: Bloomsbury, 2016), 243–266. For a positive use of postfeminism see Rikke Schubart, "Woman With Dragons: Daenerys, Pride, and Postfeminist Possibilities," *Women of Ice and Fire*, Schubart and Gjelsvik (eds), 105–130. On ecofeminism, see for example Karen J. Warren (ed), *Ecofeminist Philosophy: A Western Perspective on What It Is and Why It matters* (Rowman & Littlefield Publishers, 2000) and Mary Phillips and Nick Rumens, *Contemporary Perspectives on Ecofeminism* (London: Routledge, 2015).
114 Spencer, "Afterword: Feminist Waves ," 302.
115 Jane Kalbfleisch quoted in Stéphanie Genz, *Postfemininities in Popular Culture.* (London: Palgrave, 2009), 22.
116 Negra, *What a Girl Wants*, 152, 153.
117 Wheeler, DeMarree, and Petty argue that the Active-Self and the Chronic-Self can use conflicting schemas, because they work in a modular brain that accommodates here-and-now situations which may conflict with one's beliefs. Wheeler, DeMarree, and Petty, "Understanding the Role of the Self in Prime-to-Behavior Effects," 238.
118 Wendy Brown, *Edgework: Critical Essays on Knowledge and Power* (Princeton: Princeton University Press, 2005), 98.
119 Brown, *Edgework*, 111.
120 Brown, *Edgework*, 115.
121 Andrew Tudor, *Theories of Film* (London: Secker & Warburg, 1974), 134.
122 Carroll, "Film, Emotion, and Genre," 38.
123 Katerina Bantinaki, "The Paradox of Horror: Fear as Positive Emotion," *The Journal of Aesthetics and Art Criticism* 70, no. 4, (Fall 2012): 383–391, 383.
124 Jesper Juul, *Half-Real: Video Games Between Real Rules and Fictional Worlds* (Cambridge: MIT Press, 2005), Kindle edition.
125 Gordon M. Burghardt, *The Genesis of Animal Play: Testing the Limits* (Massachusetts: MIT Press, 2005), Kindle edition, location 1822.
126 Roger Caillois, *Man, Play and Games* Chicago: University of Illinois Press, 2001, French original 1958), 9–10.

127 Johan Huizinga, *Homo Ludens: A Study of the Play-Element in Culture* (1944, repr., London: Routledge, 1980), 28, 31.

128 Burghardt, *Genesis of Animal Play*, 97.

129 For horses play fighting see Burghardt, *Genesis of Animal Play*, location 331, and for rats play fighting see Sergio Pellis and Vivien Pellis, *The Playful Brain: Venturing to the Limits of Neuroscience* (Oxford: Oneworld, 2009), Chapter 2, 15–32.

130 Pellis and Pellis, *The Playful Brain*, 136.

131 Pellis and Pellis, *The Playful Brain*, 136.

132 Pellis and Pellis, *The Playful Brain*, 98, 162.

133 Pellis and Pellis, *The Playful Brain*, 81.

134 Pellis and Pellis, *The Playful Brain*, 131.

135 Mihaly Csikszentmihalyi, *Creativity: Flow and the Psychology of Discovery and Invention* (New York: HarperCollins Publishers, 1996), 60.

136 Pellis and Pellis, *The Playful Brain*, 27.

137 Pellis and Pellis, *The Playful Brain*, 154.

138 Brian Sutton-Smith, *The Ambiguity of Play* (Cambridge: Harvard University Press, 2001). Kindle edition, 29.

139 Sutton-Smith, *Ambiguity of Play*, 22.

140 Anthony D. Pellegrini and John Archer, "Sex Differences in Competitive and Aggressive Behavior: A View from Sexual Selection Theory," in *Play and Development: Evolutionary, Sociocultural, and Functional Perspectives (Jean Piaget Symposia Series)*, eds Artin Göncü and Suzanne Gaskins (Oxfordshire: Lawrence Erlbaum Associates, 2007), 231.

141 Percentages of R&T play are from Anthony D. Pellegrini, "The Development and Function of Rough-and-Tumble Play in Childhood and Adolescence: A Sexual Selection Theory Perspective," in *Play and Development*, eds Göncü and Gaskins, 77–98, 89.

142 Anthony D. Pellegrini and John Archer, "Sex Differences in Competitive and Aggressive Behavior, 219–244.

143 The Darwinian sexual selection theory says males compete to spread their genes and males hinder other males in access to females. The explanation is used for many species. Biologist Richard Dawkins reports a study of elephant seals which showed that 4 percent of males account for 88 percent of copulations. "In this case, and in many others, there is a large surplus of bachelor males who probably never get a chance to copulate in their whole lives." Richard Dawkins, *The Selfish Gene* (1976; repr., Oxford University Press, 2006), Kindle edition, location 2893.

144 Pellegrini, "Rough-and-Tumble Play," 91.

145 Frans de Waal, *Good Natured: The Origins of Right and Wrong in Humans and Other Animals* (Cambridge: Harvard University Press, 1996), 124.

146 Vinciane Despret, *Our Emotional Makeup: Ethnopsychology and Selfhood* (New York: Other Press, 2004) [original in French 1999], 164–165.

147 There are several experiments where monkeys are given human toys, and the experiment is to see if female monkeys prefer feminine toys and male monkeys prefer masculine toys. For a 2002 experiment see Gerianne M. Alexander and Melissa Hines, "Sex Differences in Response to Children's Toys in Nonhuman Primates (*Cercopithecus Aethiops Sabaeus*)," *Evolution and Human Behavior* 23 (2002): 467–479; and Chapter 6, "Sex and Play" in Melissa Hines, *Brain Gender* (New York: Oxford University Press, 2004). For a discussion of gender bias and this toy experiment, see Cordelia Fine, *The Delusions of Gender: How Our Minds, Society, and Neurosexism Create Difference* (New York: W. W. Norton & Company, 2010), Kindle edition, 123–126. Another 2008 experiment with monkeys is described in Janice M. Hassett, Erin R. Siebert, and Kim Wallen, "Sex Differences in Rhesus Monkey Toy Preferences Parallel Those of Children," *Hormones and Behavior* 54 (2008): 359–364. For further discussion of monkey versus human play see Christina L. Williams and Kristen E. Pleil, "Toy Story: Why Do Monkey and Human Males Prefer Trucks? Comment on 'Sex Differences in Rhesus Monkey Toy Preferences Parallel Those of Children' by Hassett, Siebert and Wallen," *Hormones and Behavior* 54 (2008): 355–358. For gender bias in science see Letitia Meynell, "Evolutionary Psychology, Ethology, and Essentialism (Because What They Don't Know Can Hurt Us)," *Hypatia* 27, no. 1 (Winter 2012): 3–27; J. Kasi Jackson, "Science Studies Perspectives on Animal Behavior Research: Toward a Deeper Understanding of Gendered Impacts," *Hypatia* 29, no. 4, Fall (2014), 738–754; Carla Fehr, "Feminist Engagement with Evolutionary Psychology," *Hypatia* 27, no. 1, Winter (2012): 50–72.

148 See Hanna Rosin, *The End of Men: And the Rise of Women* (London: Penguin Books), 2013, Kindle Edition, the chapter "A More Perfect Poison: A New Wave of Female Violence" for statistics of the rise of violent crime committed by women, 169–192.

149 Csikszentmihalyi, *Creativity*, 36.

150 Csikszentmihalyi, *Creativity*, 70.

151 Stephen Lyng, "Edgework: A Social Psychological Analysis of Voluntary Risk Taking," *American Journal of Sociology* 95, no. 4 January (1990): 851–886, 855.

152 Lyng, "Edgework," 857.

153 Quoted in Michael J. Apter, *Danger: Our Quest for Excitement* (Oxford: Oneworld Publications, 2007), PDF eBook, 39.

154 Apter, *Danger*, 43.

155 Apter, *Danger*, 73–74.

156 All quotes in this paragraph from Lyng, "Edgework," 860.

157 Mihaly Csikszentmihalyi, *Flow: The Psychology of Happiness* (1990; repr., Ebury Digital, 2013), Kindle edition.

158 Caillois, *Man, Play and Games*, 24.

159 Caillois, *Man, Play and Games*, 138.

160 Margee Kerr, *Scream: Chilling Adventures in the Science of Fear* (New York: Public Affairs, 2015), Kindle edition, 227.

161 Juul, *Half-Real*, 1019–1037. See also Jesper Juul, *The Art of Failure*.

162 Apter, *Danger*, 87–88.
163 Apter, *Danger*, 87–88.
164 See Pellegrini and Archer, "Sex Differences," 234, for covert aggression ("girls are in fact aggressive, but they are more likely to express this by covert means than are boys"). See also Hanna Rosin, *The End of Men: And the Rise of Women* (London: Penguin Books), 2013, Kindle Edition, the chapter "A More Perfect Poison: A New Wave of Female Violence" for statistics of the rise of violent crime committed by women, 169–192.
165 Jennifer Lois, "Peaks and Valleys: The Gendered Emotional Culture of Edgework," *Gender and Society* 15, no. 3 June (2001): 381–406, 387.
166 Lois, "Peaks and Valleys," 389.
167 See Burghardt, *Genesis of Animal Play*, sections 15.3.1 (entitled "Play Can Be Cruel") and 15.3.2 ("Play Can Be Risky and Dangerous"), location 5420–5514.
168 Caillois, *Man, Play and Games*, 24.
169 Victor Nell, "Cruelty's Rewards: The Gratifications of Perpetrators and Spectators," *Behavioral and Brain Sciences* 29 (2006): 211–257, 214.
170 Nell, "Cruelty's Rewards," 215.
171 For a discussion of hunting humans on film see Rikke Schubart, "The Thrill of the Nordic Kill: The Manhunt Movie in the Nordic Thriller" in *Nordic Genre Film: Small Nation Film Cultures in the Global Marketplace*, Tommy Gustafsson and Pietari Kääpä (eds) (Edinburgh: Edinburgh University Press, 2015), 76–90.
172 For a discussion of Nell's argument, see the thirty-two pages of open peer commentary after his article in *Behavioral and Brain Sciences* 29, no. 3 (2006): 224–257.
173 For a discussion of playing with trauma see Toby Smethurst and Stef Craps, "Playing With Trauma: Interreactivity, Empathy, and Complicity in *The Walking Dead* Video Game," *Games and Culture* 10, no. 3 (2015): 269–290.
174 For positive emotions in horror see Rikke Schubart, "Monstrous Appetites and Positive Emotions in *True Blood, The Vampire Diaries* and *The Walking Dead*," *Projections: The Journal for Movies and Mind*, Special Topic: Entertaining Violence, ed. Dirk Eitzen, vol. 7 no. 1 (2013): 43–63.
175 Nell, "Cruelty's Rewards," 213.
176 Thomas S. Henricks, "Play as Self-Realization: Toward a General Theory of Play," *American Journal of Play* 6, no. 2, Winter (2014): 190–213, 198–199.
177 Sutton-Smith, *Ambiguity of Play*, 87.
178 Burghardt, *Genesis of Animal Play*, location 5388.
179 Play researcher Greta Fein says, "I do not think play is about cognition and I don't think playing makes kids especially smarter. It most likely makes them happier," quoted from Sutton-Smith, *Ambiguity of Play*, 32. See also Sutton-Smith, the first two chapters, for a problematization of the functions of play, and for functionality of animal play see location 552–646.
180 Terry Marks-Tarlow, "The Fractal Self at Play," *American Journal of Play*, Summer (2010): 31–62, 35, 42.

2 Mud, Blood, and Magic: Genre and Gender in *Pan's Labyrinth*

1 Gerald Brenan, *The Spanish Labyrinth* (1943; repr., Cambridge: Cambridge University Press, 2014) is the classic historical work about the Spanish Civil War.
2 Reviews by Danish journals *Urban*, *Metroxpress*, and *Jyllandsposten*, quoted on the cover of the Danish rental DVD cover.
3 Kim Newman, "Pan's Labyrinth Review," review in *Empire*, October 27, 2006, available online: http://www.empireonline.com/movies/pan-labyrinth/review/ (accessed November 17, 2016).
4 A. O. Scott, "In Gloom of War, a Child's Paradise," review of *Pan's Labyrinth* in *The New York Times*, December 29, 2006, available online: http://www.nytimes.com/2006/12/29/movies/29laby.html (accessed November 17, 2016).
5 Cass R. Sunstein, *Laws of Fear: Beyond the Precautionary Principle* (New York: Cambridge University Press, 2005), PDF eBook, 187.
6 Daniel Kahneman, *Thinking, Fast and Slow* (London: Allan Lane, 2011), 125–126.
7 Kahneman, *Thinking, Fast and Slow*, 127.
8 Xavier Aldana Reyes, *The Spanish Gothic* (London: Palgrave, 2017), eBook, 216.
9 Reyes, *Spanish Gothic*, 217.
10 Reyes, *Spanish Gothic*, 216.
11 Reyes, *Spanish Gothic*, 220.
12 Max Lüthi, *Once Upon a Time: On the Nature of Fairy Tales* (1962; repr., New York: Frederick Ungar Publishing, 1970), 145.
13 In Charles Perrault's 1697 "Le Petit Chaperon Rouge" Red Riding Hood is eaten by the wolf and in the Brothers Grimm 1812 version of "Rottkäppchen" grandmother and Red Riding Hood are saved by a huntsman. See Marina Warner, Chapter 12, "Granny Bonnets, Wolves' Cover: Seduction III," *From the Beast to the Blonde* (London: Vintage, 1995), 181–201.
14 Donald Haase, "Children, War, and the Imaginative Space of Fairy Tales," *The Lion and the Unicorn* 24, no. 3, September (2000): 360–377, 360.
15 Second World War survivor Ingrid Riedel, quoted in Haase, "Children, War, and the Imaginative Space," 366.
16 J. R. R. Tolkien, "On Fairy-Stories," 1–27, 20, Brainstorm services, available online: http://brainstorm-services.com/wcu-2004/fairystories-tolkien.pdf (accessed December 20, 2015). Tolkien gave "On Fairy-Stories" as a lecture in 1939 and it was published in 1947. For a discussion of Tolkien, Marxist philosopher Ernest Bloch, and the fairy tale as uplifting, see Jack Zipes, Chapter 5, "The Utopian Function of Fairy Tales and Fantasy," *Breaking the Magic Spell: Radical Theories of Folk & Fairy Tales* (Lexington: University Press of Kentucky, 2002), 146–178. "On Fairy-Stories" is reprinted in *The Tolkien Reader* (New York: Ballantine, 1966).

17 For a Marxist view of fairy tales see Zipes, *Breaking the Magic Spell*, 146–178.
18 Maria Tatar, "Test, Tasks, and Trials in the Grimm's Fairy Tales," *Children's Literature* 13 (1985): 31–48, 35.
19 For disobedience see Jennifer Orme, "Narrative Desire and Disobedience in *Pan's Labyrinth*," *Marvels & Tales* 24, no. 2 (2010): 219–234, 220.
20 Tatar, "Test, Tasks, and Trials," 35.
21 Tatar, "Test, Tasks, and Trials," 36–37.
22 Tatar, "Test, Tasks, and Trials," 38.
23 Karen Lury, *The Child in Film: Tears, Fears and Fairy Tales* (New Brunswick: Rutgers University Press, 2010), 6–7, 14.
24 Lury, *The Child in Film*, 111.
25 Lury, *The Child in Film*, 111.
26 Lury, *The Child in Film*, 125.
27 This scene is a visual echo of a scene in *The Spirit of the Beehive* (*El espíritu de laa colmena*, 1973, Victor Erice) where a young girl protagonist adds eyes to a figure. *The Spirit of the Beehive* is set in 1940 after the Civil War, and has a young girl Ana who is obsessed with the *Frankenstein* (1931) film. For a discussion of *Pan's Labyrinth* see Sarah Wright, *The Child in Spanish Cinema* (Manchester: Manchester University Press, 2013), Kindle edition, the section "Prosthetic Memories: *El laberinto del fauno*," location 3096–3161.
28 Emma Wilson, "Children, Emotion and Viewing in Contemporary European Film," *Screen* 46, no. 3, Autumn (2005): 329–340, 332.
29 Wilson, "Children, Emotion and Viewing," 331.
30 Mark Kermode, "Girl Interrupted," interview with Guillermo del Toro, *Sight & Sound* 16, no. 12 (December 2006): 20, available online: http://old.bfi.org.uk/sightandsound/feature/49337 (accessed November 15, 2016).
31 Lury, *The Child in Film*, 133.
32 Almost all films about war and having child protagonists feature boys: *Ivan's Childhood* (*Ivanovo detstvo*, 1962) and *Come and See* (*Idi i smotri*, 1985), war dramas like *Germany Year Zero* (*Germania Anno Zero*, 1948) and *Empire of the Sun* (1987), dramas like *The Ogre* (*Der Unhold*, 1996), *It Happened in Europe* (*Valahol Európában*, 1948), *Diamonds of the Night* (*Démanty noci*, 1962), *Mirror* (*Zerkalo*, 1975), *The Tin Drum* (*Die Blechtrommel*, 1979), and del Toro's ghost story *The Devil's Backbone* (2001). I have only found two films with girl protagonists, *Forbidden Games* (*Jeux interdits*, 1952) and *The Spirit of the Beehive* (*El espíritu de la colmena*, 1973). In these two, the children are not at war locations with soldiers and both girls survive. To my knowledge, Ofelia is the only girl killed in a film about war and with a child protagonist.
33 Tatar, "Test, Tasks, and Trials," 35.
34 Haase, "Children, War, and Imaginative Space," 362.
35 The Black Paintings are from 1819 to 1823, and art historians note that the son's body looks like a woman.

36 Lüthi, *Once Upon a Time*, 86.
37 Haase, "Children, War, and Imaginative Space," 367.
38 Haase, "Children, War, and Imaginative Space," 361.
39 Torben Grodal, *Embodied Visions: Evolution, Emotion, Culture, and Film* (New York: Oxford University Press, 2009), 126.
40 Gary D. Sherman and Jonathan Haidt, "Cuteness and Disgust: The Humanizing and Dehumanizing Effects of Emotion," *Emotion Review* 3, no. 3 (July 2011): 245–251.
41 Sherman and Haidt, "Cuteness and Disgust," 250.
42 Hank Davis and Andrea Javor, "Religion, Death and Horror Movies: Some Striking Evolutionary Parallels," *Evolution and Cognition* 10, no. 1 (2004): 11–18.
43 Kermode, "Girl Interrupted."
44 Tatar, "Test, Tasks, and Trials," 36.
45 Orme, "Narrative Desire and Disobedience," 222.
46 Orme, "Narrative Desire and Disobedience," 223.
47 Orme, "Narrative Desire and Disobedience," 233.
48 Orme, "Narrative Desire and Disobedience," 220.
49 Marcel Mauss, *A General Theory of Magic* (1950; repr., London: Routledge, 1972), 24.
50 Mauss, *A General Theory of Magic*, 9.
51 Bronislaw Malinowski, *Magic, Science and Religion and Other Essays* (New York: Doubleday Anchor Book, 1954), 80.
52 Malinowski, *Magic, Science and Religion*, 84.
53 Malinowski, *Magic, Science and Religion*, 88.
54 Bloch, "The Fairy Tale Moves on its Own in Time" (1930), quoted in Zipes, *Breaking the Magic Spell*, 153.
55 Tolkien, "On Fairy-Stories," 15.
56 Lüthi, *Once Upon a Time*, 77.
57 Kimberley Reynolds, "Fatal Fantasies: The Death of Children in Victorian and Edwardian Fantasy Writing," *Representations of Childhood Death*, eds Gillian Avery and Kimberley Reynolds (New York: Palgrave Macmillan, 1999), 169–188, 177.
58 Scott, "In Gloom of War."
59 Tzvetan Todorov, *The Fantastic: A Structural Approach to a Literary Genre* (Ithaca: Cornell University Press, 1975), 44.
60 Michael Stewart, "Introduction: Film and TV Melodrama: An Overview," in *Melodrama in Contemporary Film and Television*, ed. Michael Stewart (Basingstoke: Palgrave Macmillan, 2014), 1–27, 11.
61 Stewart, *Melodrama*, 12.
62 Grodal, *Embodied Visions*, 142.

63 Grodal, *Embodied Visions*, 118.
64 Grodal, *Embodied Visions*, 140.
65 Orme, "Narrative Desire and Disobedience," 228.
66 See Rikke Schubart, "Utopia and Torture in the Hollywood War Film," *Nordicom Review. Special Issue* Spring (2010): 19–28.
67 Nico H. Frijda, *The Laws of Emotion* (New Jersey: Lawrence Erlbaum Associates, 2007), 5.
68 Robert C. Solomon, "Emotions, Thoughts, and Feelings: Emotions as Engagements with the World," in *Thinking about Feeling: Contemporary Philosophers on Emotions*, ed. Robert C. Solomon (Oxford University Press, 2004), 76–88, 80.
69 Solomon, "Emotions, Thoughts," 81.
70 Solomon, "Emotions, Thoughts," 83.
71 Allison Mackey, "Make It Public! Border Pedagogy and the Transcultural Politics of Hope in Contemporary Cinematic Representations of Children," *College Literature* 37, no. 2 Spring (2010): 171–185, 178.
72 Mackey, "Make It Public!," 179. For another excellent analysis of *Pan's Labyrinth* as linked to the present war on terror rather than to the Spanish Civil War see Anne E. Hardcastle, "Ghosts of the Past and Present: Hauntology and the Spanish Civil War in Guillermo del Toro's *The Devil's Backbone*," *Journal of the Fantastic in the Arts* 15, no. 2 (2005): 120–132.
73 John O. Thompson, "Reflexions on Dead Children in the Cinema and Why there are Not More of Them," *Representations of Childhood Death*, eds Gillian Avery and Kimberley Reynolds (New York: Palgrave Macmillan, 1999), 204–216, 212.
74 Reynolds, "Fatal Fantasies," 170. With the "good death" comes the literary convention of children being taken to a "better place," like the children going to Peter Pan's Neverland, the girl in Hans Christian Andersen's *The Girl With the Matches*, and the boys in Astrid Lindgren's fantasy books *Mio, my Mio* (1954) and *Brothers Lionheart* (1973). Ofelia is also taken to "a better place."
75 Roger Ebert, "Pan's Labyrinth," August 25, 2007, available online: http://www.rogerebert.com/reviews/great-movie-pans-labyrinth–2006 (accessed November 17, 2016).

3 The Bio-Logic of Vengeance in *Let the Right One In*

1 See Chapter 2 for a discussion of moral agent and moral patient. See also Marc Bekoff and Jessica Pierce, *Wild Justice: The Moral Lives of Animals* (Chicago: University of Chicago Press, 2009), 144.
2 For a discussion of coming of age in *Let the Right One In*, see Amanda Howell, "The Mirror and the Window: The Seduction of Innocence and Gothic Coming

of Age in *Låt den Rätte Komma In/Let the Right One In*," *Gothic Studies* 18, no. 1, May (2016): 57–70.

3 Eva Johansson, "*Let the Right One In*: Freezing Horror Story With Vampires in Front" ['Låt den rätte komma in': Isande skräckhistoria med vampyrer i förorten], review in *Svenska Dagbladet*, August 30, 2004, available online: http://www.svd.se/isande-skrackhistoria-med-vampyrer-i-fororten (accessed November 22, 2016). Original text: "'Låt den rätte komma in' omstöper vampyrmyten i gråsjaskig socialrealistisk form, och fyller den med vardagstristess, snabbköp och skolgårdspennalism," translated by the author.

4 Anne Billson defines social realism as "a very broad term for painting (or literature or other art) that comments on contemporary social, political, or economic conditions, usually from a left-wing viewpoint, in a realistic manner." Billson, *Let the Right One In* (Leighton: Auteur, 2011), 18.

5 Mark Kermode, review of *Let the Right One In*, *Sight and Sound*, May 2009, 35, quoted from Billson, *Let the Right One In*, 18.

6 Kim Newman, review of *Let the Right One In*, *Empire*, April 9, 2009, quoted from Billson, *Let the Right One In*, 17.

7 John Ajvide Lindqvist, *Let the Right One In* (London: Quercus, 2009) [original 2004, translation 2007, this version 2009], original title *Lät den rätte komma in*, 11.

8 Lindqvist, *Let the Right One In*, 10.

9 Kurt Gray and Daniel M. Wegner, "Moral Typecasting: Divergent Perceptions of Moral Agents and Moral Patients," *Journal of Personality and Social Psychology* 96, no. 3 (2009): 505–520, 505.

10 Gray and Wegner, "Moral Typecasting," 518.

11 Frans de Waal, *The Age of Empathy: Nature's Lessons for a Kinder Society* (New York: Crown, 2010), 199.

12 Sergio Pellis and Vivien Pellis, *The Playful Brain: Venturing to the Limits of Neuroscience* (Oxford: Oneworld, 2009), 148.

13 Pellis and Pellis, *The Playful Brain*, 144

14 Frans de Waal, *Good Natured: The Origins of Right and Wrong in Humans and Other Animals* (Cambridge: Harvard University Press, 1996).

15 de Waal, *Good Natured*, 145.

16 Gordon M. Burghardt, *The Genesis of Animal Play: Testing the Limits* (Massachusetts: MIT Press, 2005), Kindle edition, 389.

17 Susan Sontag, "Regarding the Torture of Others," *New York Times*, 23 May, 2004. Website available at: http://www.nytimes.com (accessed May 25, 2017). "To 'stack naked men' is like a college fraternity prank, said a caller to Rush Limbaugh and the many millions of Americans who listen to his radio show. Had the caller, one wonders, seen the photographs? No matter. The observation—or is it the fantasy?—was on the mark. What may still be capable of shocking some Americans was Limbaugh's response: 'Exactly!' he exclaimed. 'Exactly my point. This is no different than what happens at the Skull and Bones initiation, and we're going to ruin people's lives over it, and we're going

to hamper our military effort, and then we are going to really hammer them because they had a good time.' 'They' are the American soldiers, the torturers. And Limbaugh went on: 'You know, these people are being fired at every day. I'm talking about people having a good time, these people. You ever heard of emotional release?'"

18 Lindqvist, *Let the Right One In*, 515.
19 Lindqvist, *Let the Right One In*, 116.
20 Lindqvist, *Let the Right One In*, 188.
21 Thank you, Malin! Personal correspondance with film scholar Malin Isaksson, December 2013.
22 Billson, *Let the Right One In*, 65.
23 Billson, *Let the Right One In*, 79.
24 Lindqvist, *Let the Right One In*, 53.
25 Lindqvist, *Let the Right One In*, 339.
26 Lindqvist, *Let the Right One In*, 209. In this conversation with a teacher Oskar is thinking of his father and the father's friend. Oskar does not yet know that Eli is a vampire and a boy.
27 Lindqvist, *Let the Right One In*, 189.
28 Lindqvist, *Let the Right One In*, 339.
29 Bekoff and Pierce, *Wild Justice*, 115, 116.
30 Bekoff and Pierce, *Wild Justice*, 7.
31 Bekoff and Pierce, *Wild Justice*, 8.
32 Bekoff and Pierce, *Wild Justice*, 96.
33 Bekoff and Pierce, *Wild Justice*, ix.
34 de Waal, *Good Natured*, 6–7.
35 Bekoff and Pierce, *Wild Justice*, 115.
36 Robert C. Solomon, *A Passion for Justice: Emotions and the Origin of the Social Contract* (1990; repr., Lanham: Rowman & Littlefield Publishers, 1995), xv.
37 Nico H. Frijda, *The Laws of Emotion* (New Jersey: Lawrence Erlbaum Associates, 2007), Chapter 10, "Revenge" is 259–283, 261.
38 Robert C. Solomon, "Sympathy and Vengeance: The Role of the Emotions in Justice" in *Emotions: Essays on Emotion Theory*, ed. Stephanie H.M. van Goozen et al. (Hillsdale: Lawrence Erlbaum Associates, 1994), 291–311, 296.
39 Susan Jacoby, *Wild Justice* (Harper and Row, 1983), 14.
40 Jacoby, *Wild Justice*, 15.
41 Frijda, *The Laws of Emotion*, 272.
42 Frijda, *The Laws of Emotion*, 267.
43 Frijda, *The Laws of Emotion*, 278.
44 Lindqvist, *Let the Right One In*, 164.
45 King James Version, *The New Testament*, Romans 12:19.

46 Lindqvist, *Let the Right One In*, 390.
47 Jørgen Bruhn, Anne Gjelsvik, Henriette Thune, "Parallel Worlds of Possible Meetings in *Let The Right One In*," *Word & Image* 27, no. 1, March (2011): 2–14, 7.
48 Holger Pötzsch, "Borders, Barriers, and Grievable lives: The Discursive Construction of Self and Other in Audio-Visual Media," *Nordicom Review* 32, no. 2, Autumn (2011): 75–94, 76.
49 Allison Mackey, "Make It Public! Border Pedagogy and the Transcultural Politics of Hope in Contemporary Cinematic Representations of Children," *College Literature* 37, no. 2, Spring (2010): 171–185, 172.
50 Mackey, "Make It Public," 172,
51 Mackey, "Make It Public," 175.
52 Mackey, "Make It Public," 178.
53 Lindqvist, *Let the Right One In*, 391.
54 Lindqvist, *Let the Right One In*, 492.
55 Mackey, "Make It Public," 182.

4 "She Made a Choice": Werewolf Affordances and Female Character Development

1 Heather Schell, "The Big Bad Wolf: Masculinity and Genetics in Popular Culture," *Literature and Medicine* 26, no. 1, Spring (2007): 109–125, 119.
2 For references on female werewolves see Jazmina Cininas, "Beware the Full Moon: Female Werewolves and That Time of the Month," in *Grotesque Femininities: Evil, Women and the Feminine*, ed. Maria Barrett (Oxfordshire: Inter-Disciplinary Press, 2010), 3–27, and Chantal Bourgault du Coudray, *The Curse of the Werewolf: Fantasy, Horror and the Beast Within* (London: I. B. Tauris, 2006).
3 Bourgault du Coudray, *The Curse of the Werewolf*, 12.
4 The 1598 trial of Jacques Roulet is recounted in Sabine Baring-Gould, *The Book of Werewolves* (1865; repr., London: Senate, 1995), 81–84.
5 Baring-Gould, *The Book of Werewolves*, vi.
6 Baring-Gould, *The Book of Werewolves*, 80.
7 Baring-Gould, *The Book of Werewolves*, 81.
8 Bourgault du Coudray, *The Curse of the Werewolf*, 72.
9 James J. Gibson, "The Theory of Affordances," *Perceiving, Acting, and Knowing: Toward an Ecological Psychology* (eds) Robert Shaw and John Bransford (Hillsdale: Lawrence Erlbaum Associates, Publishers, 1977), 67–82, 67.
10 Gibson, "Theory of Affordances," 68, 69.
11 Gibson, "Theory of Affordances," 79.

12 Gibson, "Theory of Affordances," 69.
13 Dennis Danvers, *Wilderness* (New York: Pocket Books, 1992), 305.
14 Bourgault du Coudray, *The Curse of the Werewolf*, 148. Bourgault du Coudray draws from the genre of eco-fiction. For fantastic fiction and ecology see for example Don D. Elgin, *The Comedy of the Fantastic: Ecological Perspectives on the Fantasy Novel* (Praeger, 1985).
15 Mary Zeiss Stange, *Woman the Hunter* (Boston: Beacon Press, 1997), 69. About the Wild Woman, see Clarissa Pinkola Estes, *Women Who Run With the Wolves: Myths and Stories of the Wild Woman Archetype* (New York: Ballantine Books, 1992).
16 Animals can deceive and hide, for instance by camouflage, or by keeping good food to themselves. This may be the biological origin of lying, however, animals are cognitively unable to meta-think and deliberately lie. See Thomas Suddendorf, *The Gap: The Science of What Separates Us From Other Animals* (New York: Basic Books, 2013), Kindle edition.
17 No author, "Playing With Wolves: An Interview With C. J. Rogers," *American Journal of Play*, Summer (2010): 1–30, 10–11.
18 Arne Næss, "The Shallow and the Deep, Long-Range Ecology Movement. A Summary," *Inquiry: An Interdisciplinary Journal of Philosophy* no. 16 (1973): 95–100.
19 For a discussion of the PMS werewolf in *Ginger Snaps*, see April Miller, "The Hair that Wasn't there Before," *Western Folklore* 64, no. 3–4, Summer–Fall (2005): 281–303. For a discussion of the menstrual circle and the female werewolf, see Cininas, "Beware the Full Moon."
20 In the 1980s, several murder trials in the US and UK used a PMS defense to acquit women of murder, arguing they were "a raging animal each month and forced to act out of character." Jane M. Ussher, *Managing the Monstrous Feminine* (London: Routledge, 2006), 26.
21 Barbara Creed, *The Monstrous-Feminine: Film, Feminism, Psychoanalysis* (London: Routledge, 1993), 40, 42.
22 P. Faxneld, "Women Liberated by the Devil in Four Gothic Novels: William Beckford's *Vathek* (1786), Matthew Lewis' *The Monk* (1796), Charlotte Dacre's *Zofloya, or The Moor* (1806) and Charles Maturin's *Melmoth the Wanderer* (1820)," published conference proceedings, *Inter-Disciplinary.Net: Evil, Women and the Feminine* (2009), quoted in Cininas, "Beware the Full Moon," 15.
23 Ussher, *Managing the Monstrous Feminine*, see the chapter "Mad, Bad, Bloody Women: The Shame of Menarche and Pathologising of Premenstrual Change," 18–80, 25.
24 *The Diagnostic and Statistical Manual of Mental Disorders* of the American Psychiatric Association, quoted from Ussher, *Managing the Monstrous Feminine*, 26.
25 Iris Marion Young, Chapter 6 "Menstrual Meditations," *On Female Body Experience: "Throwing Like a Girl" and Other Essays* (New York: Oxford University Press, 2005), Kindle edition, location 1461.

26 Beauvoir quoted in Young, *On Female Body Experience*, location 1366.
27 Cininas, "Beware the Full Moon," 17.
28 Miller quoted in Cininas, "Beware the Full Moon," 16.
29 bell hooks, *Feminism Is for Everybody: Passionate Politics* (New York: Routledge, 2014), Kindle edition, 9.
30 Angela Ndalianis, *The Horror Sensorium: Media and the Senses* (Jefferson: McFarland, 2012), 85.
31 Thomas S. Henricks, "Play as Self-Realization: Toward a General Theory of Play," *American Journal of Play* 6, no. 2, Winter (2014): 190–213, 194.
32 Terry Marks-Tarlow, "The Fractal Self at Play," *American Journal of Play*, Summer (2010): 31–62.
33 Catherine Malabou, *The Ontology of the Accident: An Essay on Destructive Plasticity* (Cambridge: Polity Press, 2012), 5.
34 Malabou, *The Ontology of the Accident*, 1.
35 Malabou, *The Ontology of the Accident*, 6.
36 For a discussion of girls and slut identity, see Jessica Ringrose, "Are You Sexy, Flirty, Or A Slut? Exploring 'Sexualization' and How Teen Girls Perform/Negotiate Digital Sexual Identity on Social Networking Sites" in Rosalind Gill and Christina Scharff (eds), *New Femininities: Postfeminism, Neoliberalism and Subjectivity* (London: Palgrave MacMillan, 2011), eBook, 99–116.
37 Ringrose, "Are You Sexy, Flirty, Or A Slut?", 13.
38 Diane Negra, *What a Girl Wants: Fantasicing the Reclamation of Self in Postfeminism* (London: Routledge, 2009), 9, 153.
39 Shelley Budgeon, "The Contradictions of Successful Femininity: Third-Wave Feminism, Postfeminism and 'New' Femininities," in Rosalind Gill and Christina Scharff (eds), *New Femininities: Postfeminism, Neoliberalism and Subjectivity* (Basingstoke: Palgrave Macmillan, 2011), PDF digital edition, 279–292, 280.
40 Budgeon, "Contradictions," 280.
41 McGreevy, *Hemlock Grove*, 73.
42 Gary Snyder, "The Rediscovery of Turtle Island," essay from 1994, available online: http://dspace.uah.es/dspace/bitstream/handle/10017/4900/therediscoveryofturtleisland.pdf?sequence=1 (accessed January 2, 2017).
43 Snyder, "The Rediscovery of Turtle Island," 10.
44 Næss, "The Shallow and the Deep," 99.
45 Arne Næss, "Philosophy of Wolf Policies I: General Principles and Preliminary Exploration of Selected Norms," *Conservation Biology* 1, no. 1, May (1987): 22–34.
46 Bourgault du Coudray, *The Curse of the Werewolf*, 119, 143.
47 Bourgault du Coudray, *The Curse of the Werewolf*, 147.
48 Kay S. Hymowitz, "The New Girl Order," *City Journal*, Autumn, 2007, available online: http://www.city-journal.org/html/17_4_new_girl_order.html (accessed May 14, 2014).

49 For a discussion of age and the fantasy teen drama see also Rikke Schubart, "'I am Become Death, the Destroyer of Worlds': Managing Massacres and Constructing the Female Teen Leader in *The 100*," in *A Companion to the Action Film*, ed. Jim Kendrick (New Jersey: Wiley Blackwell, forthcoming 2017).

50 For female characters and fantasy television shows see Jes Battis (ed.), *Supernatural Youth: The Rise of the Teen Hero in Literature and Popular Culture* (Plymouth: Lexington Books, 2013).

51 Budgeon, "Contradictions," 281.

52 Martin Fradley, "'Hell Is a Teenage Girl'?: Postfeminism and Contemporary Teen Horror," in *Postfeminism and Contemporary Hollywood Cinema*, eds Joel Gwynne and Nadine Muller (Basingstoke: Palgrave Macmillan, 2013), 204–221, 205, 206.

53 Fradley, "'Hell Is a Teenage Girl,'" 208.

54 For fourth wave feminism, see Pauline Maclaran, "Feminism's Fourth Wave: A Research Agenda for Marketing and Consumer Research," *Journal of Marketing Management* 31, no. 15–16 (2015): 1732–1738; Prudence Chamberlain, "Affective Temporality: Towards a Fourth Wave," *Gender and Education* 28, no. 3 (2016): 458–464; and Elizabeth Evans and Prudence Chamberlain, "Critical Waves: Exploring Feminist Identity, Discourse and Praxis in Western Feminism," *Social Movement Studies* 14, no. 4 (2015): 396–409.

55 Hilary Radner, *Neo-Feminist Cinema: Girly Films, Chick Flicks and Consumer Culture* (New York: Routledge, 2011), 19.

56 Hymowitz, "The New Girl Order."

57 Helen Gurley Brown, *Sex and the Single Girl* (1962; repr., New York: Open Road, 2003), Kindle edition, location 1507.

58 Budgeon, "Contradictions," 284.

59 Radner, *Neo-Feminist Cinema*, 180.

60 Henricks, "Play as Self-Realization," 204.

61 Brown, *Sex and the Single Girl*, location 171.

62 Hymowitz, "New Girl Order."

63 Hymowitz, "New Girl Order," 188.

64 Hymowitz, "New Girl Order," 70.

65 Malabou, *The Ontology of the Accident*, 85.

5 Lust, Trust, and Educational Torture: *The Vampire Diaries*

1 See Joel Stein, "The New Greatest Generation: Why Millennials Will Save Us All," *Time*, May 20 (2013): 28–35. See also English teacher David McCullough Jr.'s address to Wellesley High School's graduation class, a 12-minute talk

titled "You Are Not Special" with 2,7 million hits on YouTube. Available online: https://www.youtube.com/watch?v=_lfxYhtf8o4 (accessed February 22, 2017).

2 For a discussion of the three types of aggression see Chapter 3. For aggression and cruelty see Victor Nell, "Cruelty's Rewards: The Gratifications of Perpetrators and Spectators," *Behavioral and Brain Sciences*, no. 29 (2006): 211–257.

3 Anthony D. Pellegrini, "The Development and Function of Rough-and-Tumble Play in Childhood and Adolescence: A Sexual Selection Theory Perspective," in *Play and Development: Evolutionary, Sociocultural, and Functional Perspectives (Jean Piaget Symposia Series)*, edited by Artin Göncü and Suzanne Gaskins (Psychology Press, 2007), 77–98, 91.

4 Pellegrini, "The Development and Function of Rough-and-Tumble Play," 85.

5 For the extended self, see Thomas S. Henricks, "Play as Self-Realization: Toward a General Theory of Play," *American Journal of Play* 6, no. 2, Winter (2014): 190–213, 198–199.

6 Erik H. Erikson, *Toys and Reason: Stages in the Ritualization of Experience* (New York: W. W. Norton & Company, 1977), Kindle edition, 108.

7 Erikson, *Toys and Reason*, 110.

8 L. J. Smith first *The Vampire Diaries* four-book series is from 1991–1992 and she added a trilogy in 2009–2011. A ghostwriter wrote another trilogy in 2011–2012, and Aubrey Clark wrote three more books in 2013–2014. L. J. Smith had sold the rights to her book series and was fired by the publisher in 2014. Today Smith writes fan fiction to the *Vampire Diaries* set in an alternate world. Her book series *Evensong* is published on Amazon Kindle.

9 Rebecca Williams, "Unlocking *The Vampire Diaries*: Genre, Authorship, and Quality in Teen TV Horror," *Gothic Studies* 15, no. 1 May (2013): 88–99.

10 Williams, "Unlocking *The Vampire Diaries*," 93.

11 See for example *The Essential HBO Reader*, edited by Gary R. Edgerton and Jeffrey P. Jones (Lexington: University Press of Kentucky, 2008).

12 *The Essential HBO Reader*, 89.

13 Online writer David Hinckley quoted in Williams, "Unlocking *The Vampire Diaries*," 90.

14 The most striking example is J. K. Rowling's *Harry Potter* book series, which attracted not only children and adolescents, but adults too. The film adaptations of *Harry Potter*, *Twilight*, and *The Hunger Games* book series likewise attracted a wider audience in terms of age and gender than that mirroring the books' protagonists. This is not new, an earlier teen drama like *Buffy the vampire slayer* (UPN/WB, 1997–2003) also had a wider fan following than teenage girls.

15 Leigh M. McLennon in the chapter "Defining Urban Fantasy and Paranormal Romance: Crossing Boundaries of Genre, Media, Self and Other in New Supernatural Worlds" says a set definition of UF/PR as subgenre is misleading,

because it is a hybrid and shifting genre: "By attempting to categorise and understand UF/PR as a subgenre of horror *or* fantasy *or* mystery *or* romance, and by distinguishing between urban fantasy and paranormal romance as separate subgenres, these definitions obscure the complex generic interplay which actually constitutes UF/PR," 9. Leigh M. McLennon, unpublished PhD. Dissertation, shared with the author during writing. Romance is a genre with primarily female authors, protagonists, and female readers. For statistics on
the gender and age of the romance reader, see the website available online: https://www.rwa.org/p/cm/ld/fid=580 (accessed May 29, 2017).

16 Pamela Regis, *A Natural History of the Romance Novel*, quoted in Maria Lindgren Leavenworth and Malin Isaksson, *Fanged Fan Fiction: Variations on* Twilight, True Blood *and* The Vampire Diaries (Jefferson: McFarland, 2013), 20.

17 Leavenworth and Isaksson, *Fanged Fan Fiction*, 25.

18 For Aristotle's *Poetics* see Wikipedia, available online: https://en.wikipedia.org/wiki/Poetics_(Aristotle) (accessed June 1, 2017).

19 Marlene Zuk, *Sexual Selections: What We Can and Can't Learn About Sex From Animals* (Berkeley: University of California Press, 2002), Kindle edition, 8.

20 Zuk, *Sexual Selections*, 9.

21 Jennifer Lynn Barnes, "Sweet Caroline," in *A Visitor's Guide to Mystic Falls* ed. by Red and Vee (Smart Pop, BenBella Books, 2010), Kindle book, 153.

22 Barnes, "Sweet Caroline," 158.

23 Zoologist Konrad Lorenz in *On Aggression* talks of four big drives: "feeding, reproduction, flight and aggression, which we will here call the 'big drives'." Konrad Lorenz, *On Aggression* (1963; repr., London: Routledge, 2005), PDF eBook, 86.

24 Nico H. Frijda, *The Laws of Emotion* (New Jersey: Lawrence Erlbaum Associates, 2007), Chapter 9, "Sex," 227–258, 228.

25 Frijda, *The Laws of Emotion*, 250.

26 Frijda, *The Laws of Emotion*, 228.

27 Frijda, *The Laws of Emotion*, 228

28 Frijda, *The Laws of Emotion*, 233.

29 Frijda, *The Laws of Emotion*, 234, 235.

30 Frijda, *The Laws of Emotion*, 244.

31 For discussions of trust see Annette Baier, "Trust and Antitrust," *Ethics* 96, no. 2 January (1986): 231–260; Annette Baier "Demoralization, Trust, and the Virtues," in *Setting the Moral Compass: Essays by Women Philosophers*, edited by Cheshire Calhoun (NY: Oxford UP, 2004); Karen Jones, "Trust as an Affective Attitude," *Ethics* 107, no. 1 October (1996): 4–25; Lawrence C. Becker, "Trust as Noncognitive Security About Motives," *Ethics* 107, no. 1, October (1996): 43–61; Lars Hertzberg, "On the Attitude of Trust," *Inquiry: An Interdisciplinary Journal of Philosophy* 31, no. 3 (1988): 307–322; Bernd

Lahno, "On the Emotional Character of Trust," *Ethical Theory and Moral Practice* 4, no. 2, Theme: "Cultivating Emotions," June (2001): 171–189.

32 Baier, "Trust and Antitrust," 242.
33 Becker, "Trust as Noncognitive Security," 43.
34 Baier, "Trust and Antitrust," 258.
35 Becker, "Trust as Noncognitive Security," 50.
36 Lahno, "On the Emotional Character of Trust," 171.
37 Lahno, "On the Emotional Character of Trust," 184.
38 See for example Rikke Schubart, "Utopia and Torture in the Hollywood War Film," *Nordicom Review. NordMedia 2009* June 29 (2009): 19–28.
39 Williams, "Unlocking *The Vampire Diaries*," 89.
40 See *The Vampire Diaries* wiki, available online: http://vampirediaries.wikia.com/wiki/Stefan_Salvatore (accessed October 11, 2015).
41 All actors are older than characters, but male actors are much older than their characters, probably due to the Western convention that the man should be older than the woman in a relationship.
42 The episode "Family Ties" (1.04).
43 Ann Thurber, *Bite Me: Desire and the Female Spectator in* Twilight, The Vampire Diaries, *and* True Blood, unpublished MA dissertation (Faculty of the James T. Laney School of Graduate Studies of Emory University, 2011), 76, available online: https://etd.library.emory.edu/view/record/pid/emory:92d6h (accessed on February 27, 2017).
44 Erikson, *Toys and Reason*, 108.
45 See Wikipedia for numbers of age at marriage, "List of countries by age at first marriage," available online: https://en.wikipedia.org/wiki/List_of_countries_by_age_at_first_marriage#Americas (accessed February 26, 2017).
46 Jeffrey Jensen Arnett, "Emerging Adulthood: A Theory of Development From the Late Teens Through the Twenties," *American Psychologist* 55, no. 5, May (2000): 469–480, 473.
47 Arnett, "Emerging Adulthood," 473.
48 Arnett, "Emerging Adulthood," 477.
49 For the New Girl Order, see Kay S. Hymowitz, "The New Girl Order," *City Journal*, Autumn, 2007, available online: http://www.city-journal.org/html/17_4_new_girl_order.html (accessed May 14, 2014). For a discussion of the psychological girl characteristics and the neofeminist heroine, see also Hilary Radner, *Neo-Feminist Cinema: Girly Films, Chick Flicks and Consumer Culture* (New York: Routledge, 2011).
50 Erik H. Erikson and Joan Erikson, *The Life Circle Completed. Extended Version With New Chapter on the Ninth Stage of Development by Joan M. Erikson* (New York: W. W. Norton & Company, 1998), Kindle edition, 1011–1018.

6 Disgust and Self-Injury: *In My Skin, Martyrs, Black Swan*

1. Erik H. Erikson and Joan Erikson, *The Life Circle Completed. Extended Version With New Chapter on the Ninth Stage of Development by Joan M. Erikson* (New York: W. W. Norton & Company, 1998), Kindle edition, 41.
2. Nikolaj Lübecker, "Lars von Trier's *Dogville*: A Feel-Bad Film," in *The New Extremism in Cinema*, edited by Tanya Horeck and Tina Rendall, 157–168 (Edinburgh: Edinburgh University Press, 2013); and Markus Montola, "The Positive Negative Experience in Extreme Role-Playing," *Nordic DiGRA 2010 Proceedings* (Stockholm, 2010), available online: http://www.digra.org/digital-library/publications/the-positive-negative-experience-in-extreme-role-playing/ (accessed October 12, 2016).
3. Daniel Kelly, *Yuck! The Nature and Moral Significance of Disgust* (Cambridge: MIT Press, 2011), Kindle edition, 17. For disgust, see also Chuck Kleinhans, "Cross-Cultural Disgust: Some Problems in the Analysis of Contemporary Horror Cinema," *Jump Cut*, no. 51, Spring (2009). Available online: https://www.ejumpcut.org/archive/jc51.2009/crosscultHorror/index.html (accessed July 2, 2009).
4. Rachel Herz, *That's Disgusting: Unraveling the Mysteries of Repulsion* (New York: W. W. Norton & Company, 2012), Kindle edition, 49.
5. Jonathan Haidt, Clark McCauley, and Paul Rozin, "Individual Differences in Sensitivity to Disgust: A Scale Sampling Seven Domains of Disgust Elicitors," *Personality and Individual Differences* 16, no. 5, May (1994): 701–713, 712. See also Chapter 2, "Poisons and Parasites: The Entanglement Thesis and the Evolution of Disgust" in Kelly, *Yuck!*, location 875–1214 for a discussion of the biological underpinnings of core disgust.
6. Haidt, McCauley, and Rozin, "Individual Differences," 712.
7. Haidt, McCauley, and Rozin, "Individual Differences," 712.
8. Haidt, McCauley, and Rozin, "Individual Differences," 712.
9. Valerie Curtis and Adam Biran, "Dirt, Disgust, and Disease: Is Hygiene in Our Genes?" *Perspectives in Biology and Medicine* 44, no. 1, Winter (2001): 17–31, 29.
10. Curtis and Biran, "Dirt, Disgust, and Disease," 21.
11. Aurel Kolnai quoted in Angela Ndalianis, "Corpse Contagion and the Aesthetics of Disgust," keynote presentation at the "B for BAD cinema. Aesthetics, politics and cultural value" Conference, April 16–18, 2009, Melbourne, Australia.
12. Herz, *That's Disgusting*, 47.
13. For a discussion of the aesthetics of French Extremity, see Tim Palmer "Style and Sensation in the Contemporary French Cinema of the Body," *Journal of Film and Video* 58, no. 3, Fall (2006): 22–32.
14. James Quandt, "Flesh & Blood: Sex and Violence in Recent French Cinema,"

ArtForum, February 2004, available online: https://www.artforum.com/inprint/issue=200402&id=6199 (accessed June 2, 2017).

15 Tanya Horeck and Tina Kendell, eds., *The New Extremism in Cinema: From France to Europe* (Edinburgh: Edinburgh University Press, 2011), 7.
16 Quandt, "Flesh & Blood."
17 The words come from respectively directors Bruno Dumont and (Austrian) Michael Haneke, quoted in Horeck and Kendell, *The New Extremism*, 6.
18 David Edelstein, "Now Playing at Your Local Multiplex: Torture Porn," *New York Magazine*, January 28, 2006, available online: http://nymag.com/movies/features/15622/ (accessed June 1, 2017).
19 Edelstein, "Now Playing at Your Local Multiplex: Torture Porn."
20 Hans T. Sternudd, "The Discourse of Cutting: A Study of Visual Representations of Self-Injury on the Internet," in *Making Sense of Pain: Critical and Interdisciplinary Perspectives*, edited by Jane Fernandez, 237–248 (Freeland: Inter-Disciplinary Press, 2010), PDF eBook, 237.
21 Sarah Naomi Shaw, "Shifting Conversations on Girls' and Women's Self-Injury: An Analysis of the Clinical Literature in Historical Context," *Feminism and Psychology* 12, no. 2 (2002): 191–219, 198, 201, 195.
22 Shaw, "Shifting Conversations," 204–205.
23 Sternudd, "The Discourse of Cutting," 241.
24 Sternudd, "The Discourse of Cutting," 241
25 The quote is from Sternudd, "The Discourse of Cutting," 238, and is his phrasing, a conclusion drawn from his research in self-injurers communication on blogs. About pride and shame: "I think the thing about being proud about one's scar and at the same time ashamed is weird. I want big scars because it feels wonderful to cut but also for people to see. At the same time I feel ashamed and don't want anyone to know and wear long-sleeved shirts. I don't get it." Anonymous self-injurer quoted in Anna Johansson, "Rakbladsflikkor: Om Kvinnlig Självskada som Identitet och Symbolspråk" [Razorblade Girls: About Female Self-Injury as Identity and Symbolic Language], *Nåtverket* 14 (2004): 100–114, 106, 111. Translation from Swedish by author.
26 Tim Palmer, "Under Your Skin: Marina de Van and the Contemporary French Cinema du Corps," *Studies in French Cinema* 6 no. 3, Fall (2006): 171–181, 176.
27 Palmer, "Under Your Skin," 175.
28 Palmer, "Under Your Skin," 175.
29 Palmer, "Under Your Skin," 176.
30 Inga Bryden, "Cut'n'Slash: Remodelling the 'Freakish' Female Form," in *Controversies in Body Theology*, edited by Marcella Althaus-Reid Maria and Lisa Isherwood, 29–48 (London: SCM Press).
31 Bryden, "Cut'n'Slash."
32 Geoffrey Macnab, "Sadean Woman," *Sight & Sound*, December (2004): 20–22, 22.

33 Asbjørn Grønstad, "Abject Desire: *Anatomie de l'enfer* and the Unwatchable," *Studies in French Cinema* 6, no. 3 (2006): 161–169, 162, 164.

34 Marina de Van quoted in Palmer, "Under Your Skin," 179.

35 Murray Smith, "Gangsters, Cannibals, Aesthetes, or Apparently Perverse Allegiances," in *Passionate Views*, edited by Carl Plantinga and Greg M. Smith (Baltimore: Johns Hopkins University Press, 1999), 217–238, 229.

36 Smith, "Gangsters, Cannibals, Aesthetes," 230.

37 A. R. Favazza and K. Conterio, "Female Habitual Self-Mutilators," *Acta Psychiatr Scand* 79, no. 3 (1989): 283–289, 286

38 Favazza and Conterio, "Female Habitual Self-Mutilators," 286.

39 Thomas Elsaesser and Malte Hagener, *Film Theory: An Introduction through the Senses* (New York: Routledge, 2010), 154.

40 See Darren Jorgensen, "The Impossible Thought of *Lingchi* in Georges Bataille's *The Tears of Eros*," *Kritikos* 5, March–April (2008), available online: http://intertheory.org/jorgensen.htm (accessed June 2, 2017.

41 These quotes are from Lisa Coulthard's discussion of Austrian director Michael Haneke in Horeck and Kendell, *The New Extremism*, 183.

42 James Quandt, "More Moralism from that 'Wordy Fuck'," in Horeck and Kendell, *The New Extremism*, 209–213, 211. This is a comment to his 2004 article and the responses it generated.

43 Lübecker, "Lars von Trier's *Dogville*," 165.

44 Lübecker, "Lars von Trier's *Dogville*," 168.

45 William Brown, "Violence in Extreme Cinema and the Ethics of Spectatorship." *Projections: The Journal for Movies and Mind* 7, no. 1 (2013): 25–42. Special Topic: Entertaining Violence, edited by Dirk Eitzen, 31, 36. From "What I want to emphasize . . ." is on page 36.

46 Barbara Jane Brickman, "'Delicate' Cutters: Gendered Self-Mutilation and Attractive Flesh in Medical Discourse," *Body and Society* 10, no. 4 (2004): 87–111, 92.

47 Brickman, "'Delicate' Cutters," 92.

48 Brickman, "'Delicate' Cutters," quoting a study from 1961, 91.

49 Brickman, "'Delicate' Cutters," quoting a study from 1969, 91–92.

50 Brickman, "'Delicate' Cutters," 97.

51 Elaine Showalter, *Sexual Anarchy* (1990), 134, quoted in Bryden, "Cut'n'Slash."

52 Shaw, "Shifting Conversations," 206.

53 Margee Kerr, *Scream: Chilling Adventures in the Science of Fear* (New York: Public Affairs, 2015), Kindle edition, 227

54 Herz, *That's Disgusting*, 42.

55 Haidt, McCauley, and Rozin, "Individual Differences," 709, 711, 711.

56 Haidt, McCauley, and Rozin, "Individual Differences," 709, 711, 711.

57 Klastrup quoted in Cindy Poromba, "Critical Potential on the Brink of the

Magic Circle," *Situated Play*, Proceedings of DiGRA 2007 Conference, 772–778, available online: http://www.digra.org/digital-library/publications/critical-potential-on-the-brink-of-the-magic-circle/ (accessed June 2, 2017), 775.

58 Poromba, "Critical Potential," 772.
59 Markus Montola, "The Positive Negative Experience in Extreme Role-Playing," paper presented at Nordic DiGRA 2010, available online: http://www.digra.org/wp-content/uploads/digital-library/10343.56524.pdf (accessed June 2, 2017), 8-page PDF download, 8.
60 Montola, "The Positive Negative Experience," 5.
61 Player quoted in Montola, "The Positive Negative Experience," 6.
62 Gary D. Sherman and Jonathan Haidt, "Cuteness and Disgust: The Humanizing and Dehumanizing Effects of Emotion," *Emotion Review* 3, no. 3 (July 2011): 245–251, 247.

7 The Maternal Myth: Birth, Breatfeeding, Mothering

1 Marlene Zuk, *Sexual Selections: What We Can and Can't Learn About Sex From Animals* (Berkeley: University of California Press, 2002), Kindle edition, 50.
2 Review of *The Babadook* in *Film Experience*, February 26, 2014, available online: http://if.com.au/2014/02/26/article/Aussie-Thriller-THE-BABADOOK-Set-For-An-Australian-Release/IBTVLYLLYL.html (accessed March 18, 2017).
3 Susan Douglas and Meredith Michaels, *The Mommy Myth: The Idealization of Motherhood and How It Has Undermined Women* (New York: Free Press, 2004).
4 Sarah Arnold, *Maternal Horror Film: Melodrama and Motherhood* (Basingstoke: Palgrave Macmillan, 2013), 51, 67.
5 Arnold, *Maternal Horror Film*, 23.
6 Jane M. Ussher, *Managing the Monstrous Feminine* (London: Routledge, 2006), 94.
7 Ussher, *Managing the Monstrous Feminine*, 94.
8 Arnold, *Maternal Horror Film*, 39.
9 Heather Addison, Mary Kate Goodwin-Kelly, and Elaine Roth, eds., *Motherhood Misconceived: Representing the Maternal in U.S. Films* (New York: New York State University Press, 2009), 7.
10 Ussher, *Managing the Monstrous Feminine*, 87.
11 Ussher, *Managing the Monstrous Feminine*, 81.
12 Ussher, *Managing the Monstrous Feminine*, 163.
13 Theresa Porter, "Woman as Molester: Implications for Society," in *Grotesque Femininities: Evil, Women and the Feminine*, ed. Maria Barrett (Oxford: Inter-Disciplinary Press, 2010), 84.
14 E. Weldon quoted in Porter, "Woman as Molester," 85.

15 "Parental Descent: Jennifer Kent's *The Babadook* is a Spooky Tale of a Mother in Crisis," no author, *Film Journal International*, November 14, 2014, available online: http://www.filmjournal.com/content/parental-descent-jennifer-kent's-'-babadook'-spooky-tale-mother-crisis (accessed March 19, 2017).

16 For an analysis of the maternal body and *Inside*, see also Erin Harrington, *Women, Monstrosity and Horror Film: Gynaehorror* (Abingdon: Routledge, 2017, Kindle edition), 1–2, 116–120.

17 tonymurphylee, "One of the most shocking and effective horror films I have ever seen," IMDB viewer comment to *Inside*, available on: http://www.imdb.com/title/tt0856288/ (accessed December 10, 2015).

18 tonymurphylee, "One of the most shocking."

19 callanvass, "One of the Rare Horror Movies That Nearly Rendered Me Speechless," IMDB viewer comment to *Inside*, available online: http://www.imdb.com/title/tt0856288/reviews?filter=prolific;filter=prolific;start=10 (accessed December 14, 2015).

20 Julian Hanich, *Cinematic Emotion in Horror Films and Thrillers: The Aesthetic Paradox of Pleasurable Fear* (New York: Routledge, 2010), 203–204.

21 Hanich, *Cinematic Emotion*, 156.

22 Hanich, *Cinematic Emotion*, 208.

23 Richard S. Lazarus, *Emotion and Adaptation* (New York: Oxford University Press, 1991), Kindle edition, 237.

24 Barbara Creed, *The Monstrous-Feminine: Film, Feminism, Psychoanalysis*. (London: Routledge, 1993), 51.

25 The list is on the website Screenrant, available online: http://screenrant.com/10-worst-movie-pregnancies/ (accessed December 11, 2015).

26 Asbjørn Grønstad, "Abject Desire: *Anatomie de l'enfer* and the Unwatchable," *Studies in French Cinema* 6, no. 3 (2006): 161–169, 163–164.

27 Ussher, *Managing the Monstrous Feminine*, xiii.

28 Vernon J. Geberth, "Homicides Involving the Theft of a Fetus From a Pregnant Victim," *Law and Order* 54, no. 3 March (2006), no page numbers, available online: http://www.practicalhomicide.com/Research/LOmar2006.htm (accessed December 14, 2015).

29 This was the case of Dynal Lane who was arrested in 2015 and charged with attempted murder and kidnapping. This type of crime is referred to as fetal abduction, cesarean kidnapping, and wombraiding. Abby Ohlheiser and Elahe Izadi, "Pregnant Colorado Woman Stabbed, Her Baby 'Removed,' After Answering Craigslist Ad," *The Washington Post*, March 19, 2015, available online: https://www.washingtonpost.com/news/morning-mix/wp/2015/03/19/a-pregnant-colorado-woman-was-stabbed-her-baby-removed-when-she-answered-a-craigslist-ad-for-baby-clothes/ (accessed December 14, 2015). For wombraider cases see Wikipedia, "Fetal Abduction," available online: https://en.wikipedia.org/wiki/Fetal_abduction (accessed December 14, 2015).

30 Geberth, "Homicides Involving the Theft."

31 For a discussion of disgust, see Jonathan Haidt, Clark McCauley, and Paul

Rozin. "Individual Differences in Sensitivity to Disgust: A Scale Sampling Seven Domains of Disgust Elicitors." *Personality and Individual Differences* 16, no. 5, May (1994): 701–713; for moral disgust, see Rachel Herz, *That's Disgusting: Unraveling the Mysteries of Repulsion* (New York: W. W. Norton & Company, 2012), Kindle edition.

32 Michael Ordona, "'Grace' Skillfully Preys on Motherhood Pangs," *Los Angeles Times*, August 14, 2009, available online: http://articles.latimes.com/2009/aug/14/entertainment/et-capsules14 (accessed December 16, 2015).

33 Ussher, *Managing the Monstrous Feminine*, 89.

34 Ussher, *Managing the Monstrous Feminine*, 107.

35 E. Ann Kaplan, *Motherhood and Representation: The Mother in Popular Culture and Melodrama* (London: Routledge, 1992), 14.

36 Patricia's character calls for a deeper reading than I offer here. She is a complex character: a trained doctor and a midwife, a feminist, a homosexual, a vegan, an economically independent woman who sells her clinic and buys a mobile home, and changes her hair from dark and long to dyed blond and short. Her change in lifestyle and clothes can be read as disguise, as what psychoanalysis calls masquerade, or as a postfeminist choice between performances of femininity.

37 No author, "Parental Descent."

38 For a discussion of Henricks and play as self-realization, see Chapter 1, the section "Play." See also Thomas S. Henricks, *Play and the Human Condition* (Urbana: University of Illinois Press, 2015), Kindle edition, and Thomas S. Henricks, "Play as Self-Realization: Toward a General Theory of Play," *American Journal of Play* 6, no. 2 Winter (2014): 190–213.

39 Carole Hooven, John Mordechai Gottman, Lynn Fainsilber Katz, "Parental Meta-Emotion Structure Predicts Family and Child Outcomes," *Cognition and Emotion* 9, no. 2–3 (1995): 229–264, 229.

40 Hooven et. al., "Parental Meta-Emotion Structure," 231.

41 Lazarus, *Emotion and Adaptation*, 239–240. For a discussion of facing anxiety with mindfulness instead of denial see Horst Mitmansgruber, Thomas N. Beck, Stefan Höfer, and Gerhard Schüßler, "When You Don't Like What You Feel: Experiential Avoidance, Mindfulness and Meta-Emotion in Emotion Regulation," *Personality and Individual Differences* 46 (2009): 448–453.

42 Douglas and Michaels, *The Mommy Myth*, 23, 28.

43 Brian Sutton-Smith, *The Ambiguity of Play* (Cambridge: Harvard University Press, 2001), Kindle edition, 151.

44 Greta quoted in Henricks, *Play and the Human Condition*, location 2068.

45 Sutton-Smith, *Ambiguity of Play*, 172.

46 Sutton-Smith, *Ambiguity of Play*, 166.

47 Amanda Howell. "Haunting the Art House: *The Babadook* and International Art Cinema Horror." Later published as Amanda Howell, "Haunted Art House: *The Babadook* and International Art Cinema Horror," in *Australian Cinema in the 2000s*, edited by Mark Ryan and Brian Goldsmith (Palgrave-MacMillan 2017), 119–139.

48 Howell, "Haunted Art House."
49 Henricks, *Play and the Human Condition*, location 2066. For play as play therapy and as self-healing see Dorothy G. Singer and Jerome L. Singer, *The House of Make Believe: Children's Play and the Developing Imagination* (Cambridge: Harvard University Press, 1990), Chapter 9, "Play as Healing," 199–229.
50 Jason Laurendeau, "'Gendered Risk Regimes': A Theoretical Consideration of Edgework and Gender," *Sociology of Sport Journal* 25, no. 3 September (2008): 293–309, 306.
51 No author, "Parental Descent."
52 Helen Gavin and Theresa Porter, *Female Aggression* (Oxford: Wiley Blackwell, 2015), Kindle edition, 50.
53 Justyna Hanna Budzik, "Early Film Tricks in the Digital Era: The Power of *Fantasy* in Jennifer Kent's *The Babadook*," paper presented at the conference "The Fantastic in a Transmedia Era: New Theories, Texts, Contexts," University of Southern Denmark, November 24–25, 2015.
54 Ussher, *Managing the Monstrous Feminine*, 170.

8 Home and Road: Carol's Change in *The Walking Dead*

1 Anthony Giddens, *Modernity and Self-Identity* (Redwood City: Stanford University Press, 1991), 75.
2 Definition of middle age is from *The Diagnostic and Statistical Manual of Mental Disorders*, American Psychiatric Association, which in Edition IV (1994) defines it as 45–65. Psychologist Erik Erikson defines middle adulthood as 40–65. "Middle Age," Wikipedia, available online: http://en.wikipedia.org/wiki/Middle_age (accessed March 25, 2015).
3 Erik H. Erikson and Joan Erikson, *The Life Circle Completed. Extended Version With New Chapter on the Ninth Stage of Development by Joan M. Erikson* (New York: W.W. Norton & Company, 1998), Kindle edition, location 987.
4 Sylvia Henneberg, "Moms do Badly, But Grandmas do Worse: The Nexus of Sexism and Ageism in Children's Classics," *Journal of Aging Studies* 24 (2010): 125–134.
5 Jason Mittell, *Complex TV: The Poetics of Contemporary Television Storytelling* (New York: NYU Press, 2015).
6 The first episode in season five, "No Sanctuary," was seen by 17.3 million viewers, of which 8.7 million were in the adult 18–49 age demographic. Walkingdead.wiki.com, available online: http://walkingdead.wikia.com/wiki/Season_5 (accessed May 7, 2015).
7 Erikson, *Life Circle*, location 1005.
8 From issue 7 the monthly comic was drawn by artist Charlie Adlard. At time of

writing (March 2017) it is at issue 165, a fourteen-year-long uninterrupted epic which has expanded transmedially into AMC's horror television series *The Walking Dead* (2010–), the live aftershow *Talking Dead* (2011–), the spin-off prequel horror series *Fear the Walking Dead* (AMC, 2015–), and independent storylines in digital games for multiple platforms and in novels.

9   Kirkman quoted from the Walking Dead Wiki website, available online: http://walkingdead.wikia.com/wiki/Carol_(Comic_Series) (accessed May 1, 2015).

10 Claude M. Steele, *Whistling Vivaldi and Other Clues to How Stereotypes Affect Us*, (New York: W.W. Norton & Company, 2010), Kindle edition, 169.

11 Thomas S. Henricks, *Play and the Human Condition* (Urbana: University of Illinois Press, 2015), Kindle edition, location 1661.

12 Henricks, *Play and the Human Condition*, location 1678.

13 Iris Marion Young, *On Female Body Experience: "Throwing Like a Girl" and Other Essays* (New York: Oxford University Press, 2005), Kindle edition, location 1829.

14 Young, *On Female Body Experience*, location 1696.

15 M. Jeanne Peterson, "No Angels in the House: The Victorian Myth and the Paget Woman," *American Historical Review* 89, no. 3 (1984): 677–708, 677.

16 Young, *On Female Body Experience*, location 2065.

17 Mikhail Bakhtin discusses the chronotope in the essay "Forms of Time and of the Chronotope in the Novel" (1937–1938), published in 1975 in English as part of *The Dialogic Imagination* (Austin: University of Texas Press: 1982). The quote is from Wikipedia, available online: http://en.wikipedia.org/wiki/Chronotope (accessed May 9, 2015).

18 For a discussion of the road movie as genre see Alexandra Ganser, Julia Pühringer, and Markus Rheindorf, "Bakhtin's Chronotope on the Road: Space, Time, and Place in Road Movies Since the 1970s," *Linguistics and Literature* 4, no. 1 (2006): 1–17.

19 Ganser, Pühringer and Rheindorf, "Bakhtin's Chronotope," 5.

20 Ganser, Pühringer and Rheindorf, "Bakhtin's Chronotope," 11.

21 Giddens, *Modernity and Self-Identity*, 70.

22 Giddens, *Modernity and Self-Identity*, 73.

23 Giddens, *Modernity and Self-Identity*, 75.

24 Giddens, *Modernity and Self-Identity*, 79.

25 Giddens, *Modernity and Self-Identity*, 81.

26 For a discussion of battle mind see Merete Wedell-Wedellsborg, *Battle Mind: At præstere under pres* [Battle mind: To perform under pressure] (Copenhagen: Akademisk forlag, 2015). In English see A. C. Castro et al., *Battlemind Training: Transitioning Home from Combat* (Walter Reed Army Institute of Research, 2006).

27 For a discussion of the character Carol see *The Walking Dead* wiki page, http://walkingdead.wikia.com/wiki/Carol_Peletier_(TV_Series) (accessed March 18, 2015).

28 For a discussion of crystallized and fluid knowledge, see Chapter 9, "Creative aging," Mihaly Csikszentmihalyi, *Creativity: Flow and the Psychology of Discovery and Invention*, (New York, HarperCollins Publishers, 1996), 211–234, Kindle edition, 213.
29 Henricks, *Play and the Human Condition*, location 1674.
30 George Mandler, "Emotions and the Psychology of Freedom," in *Emotions: Essays on Emotion Theory*, eds. Stephanie H. M. von Goozen, Nanne E. Van de Poll, Joseph A. Sergeant (New Jersey: Lawrence Erlbaumm Ass. Publishers, 1994), 241–262, 246.
31 Mandler, "Psychology of Freedom," 248.
32 Mandler, "Psychology of Freedom," 252.
33 Marc Bekoff and Jessica Pierce, *Wild Justice: The Moral Lives of Animals* (Chicago: University of Chicago Press, 2009), 148.
34 The Golden Rule dates back to written sources about 2000 BC. "The Golden Rule," Wikipedia, available online: https://en.wikipedia.org/wiki/Golden_Rule (accessed March 22, 2017).
35 I understand the difference between morals and ethics as the first being morally good behavior and the latter being what *a specific society decides* to be morally good. Thus, morals are natural and ethics culturally constructed.
36 Marlene Zuk, *Sexual Selections: What We Can and Can't Learn About Sex From Animals* (Berkeley: University of California Press, 2002), Kindle edition, location 1051.
37 Zuk, *Sexual Selections*, location 1059.
38 Jonathon D. Brown and Margaret A. Marshall, "Self-Esteem and Emotion: Some Thoughts About Feelings," *Personality and Social Psychology Bulletin* 27, no. 5, May (2001): 575–584, 582.
39 Kirkman quoted on the Internet page "Quotes On Caryl" dedicated to the Carol-Daryl relationship, available online: http://daryl-x-carol.deviantart.com/journal/Quotes-On-Caryl-345028343 (accessed May 29, 2015).
40 Fan comment, "Quotes On Caryl."
41 Greg Nicotero, director of nineteen episodes of *The Walking Dead*, one the central episode "No Sanctuary" (5.01), "Quotes On Caryl."
42 Melissa McBride, "Quotes On Caryl."

9 Age Anxiety and Chills: Jessica Lange and *American Horror Story*

1 Mihaly Csikszentmihalyi, *Creativity: Flow and the Psychology of Discovery and Invention* (New York, HarperCollins Publishers, 1996), Kindle edition, 346.
2 For a nuanced discussion of the ageing woman, the horror subgenre of "hagsploitation," and menopause in horror, see Erin Harrington, *Women,*

Monstrosity and Horror Film: Gynaehorror (Abingdon: Routledge, 2017, Kindle edition), 234–258.

3 Mary McNamara, "Review: 'American Horror Story: Coven' Casts a Wicked Spell," *Los Angeles Times*, October 9, 2013, available online: http://www.latimes.com/entertainment/tv/showtracker/la-et-st-american-horror-story-coven-20131009-story.html (accessed March 23, 2017). For a recent analysis of Lange in *AHS*, see Harrington, *Women, Monstrosity and Horror Film*, 258–265.

4 Luke Holland, television review, "American Horror Story: Freak Show is the strongest season of the show so far," December 2, 2014, *The Guardian*, available online: http://www.theguardian.com/tv-and-radio/2014/dec/02/american-horror-story-season-four-freak-show-review (accessed July 18, 2015).

5 Interest is the same as curiosity. Noël Carroll in *The Philosophy of Horror, or Paradoxes of the Heart* (New York: Routledge, 1990) sees the viewer's cognitive curiosity about what violates our cognitive schemas explains our fascination with horror. See Chapter 1 and later in this chapter for Carrol and curiosity.

6 "Life on Mars" is from the 1971 Bowie album *Hunky Dory* and was released as single in 1973 and as music video in 1973.

7 Paul J. Silvia, "What is Interesting? Exploring the Appraisal Structure of Interest," *Emotion* 5, no. 1 (2005): 89–102, 89.

8 Habibi and Damasio define drives as "action programs that are aimed at satisfying basic instinctual physiological needs. Examples include hunger, thirst, libido, exploration and play, care of progeny, and attachment to mates." Assal Habibi and Antonio Damasio, "Music, Feelings, and the Human Brain," *Psychomusicology: Music, Mind, and Brain* 24, no. 1 (2014): 92–102, 99.

9 The description of the phases of interest are from the website metainterest, available online: https://sites.google.com/site/metainterest/tenet_1 (accessed July 13, 2015).

10 Emily Nussbaum, review of Season One: Murder House, "Shock Value," October 30, 2011, *New York Magazine TV Review*, available online: http://nymag.com/arts/tv/reviews/american-horror-story-nussbaum-2011-11/#print (accessed July 16, 2015).

11 Nussbaum, "Shock Value."

12 Silvia, "What is Interesting?" 90.

13 Paul J. Silvia, *Exploring the Psychology of Interest* (New York: Oxford University Press, 2006), Kindle edition, location 491.

14 For a discussion of the neurochemical elements of wanting and liking in interest see Jordan Litman, "Curiosity and the Pleasures of Learning: Wanting and Liking New Information," *Cognition and Emotion* 19, no. 6 (2005): 793–814.

15 Anne Jerslev, "The Elderly Female Face in Beauty and Fashion Ads: Joan Didion for Céline," *European Journal of Cultural Studies*, accepted and forthcoming in 2017, PDF 1–17, 2.

16 Sylvia Henneberg, "Moms do Badly, But Grandmas do Worse: The Nexus of Sexism and Ageism in Children's Classics," *Journal of Aging Studies* 24 (2010): 125–134.
17 Henneberg, "Moms do Badly," 130.
18 Susan Pickard, "Biology as Destiny? Rethinking Embodiment in 'deep' Old Age," *Ageing and Society* 34 (2014): 1279–1291, 1280.
19 Henneberg, "Moms do Badly," 129.
20 "Old Age," Wikipedia, available online: http://en.wikipedia.org/wiki/Old_age#Official_definitions (accessed March 25, 2015).
21 For a feminist discussion of age ideology and deep old age see Pickard, "Biology as Destiny."
22 Jerslev, "The Elderly Female Face," 4.
23 Jerslev, "The Elderly Female Face," 7.
24 Susan M. Behuniak, "The Living Dead? The Construction of People With Alzheimer's Disease as Zombies," Old Age," *Ageing and Society* 31 (2011): 70–92, 73.
25 Pickard, "Biology as Destiny," 1280.
26 These praxises were observed around patients suffering from Alzheimer's disease. Behuniak, "The Living Dead," 74.
27 For the me-me-me generation see Chapter 7, note 1.
28 Brian Tallericao, "TV Review: 'American Horror Story: Coven' Casts a Spell," October 9, 2013, available online: http://www.hollywoodchicago.com/news/22642/tv-review-american-horror-story-coven-casts-a-spell#ixzz3fqVYEksJ (accessed July 14, 2015).
29 Eva Krainitzki, "Judi Dench's Age-Inappropriateness and the Role of M: Challenging Normative Temporality," *Journal of Aging Studies* 29 (2014): 32–40, 36. Dench first played M in *GoldenEye* (1995). M was modeled on Dame Stella Rimington, the real-life head of the British MI5—Military Intelligence Section 5—between 1992 and 1996. Rimington was 57–61 years old in this period.
30 See Bianca London's article "Meet the New WAGs: No, Not Footballers' Wives . . . the Women Ageing Gracefully," *MailOnline*, December 10, 2012, available online: http://www.dailymail.co.uk/femail/article-2244604/Helen-Mirren-Joanna-Lumley-Meet-new-WAGs--Women-Ageing-Gracefully.html (accessed June 13, 2017).
31 Krainitzki, "Judi Dench," 34.
32 For a discussion of the SYF, see Kay S. Hymowitz, "The New Girl Order," *City Journal*, Autumn 2007, available online: http://www.city-journal.org/html/17_4_new_girl_order.html.2 (accessed March 25, 2015).
33 One of 205 comments to "Meet the New WAGs."
34 Comment to "Meet the New WAGs."
35 LaLaurie is based on the real Delphine LaLaurie who tortured her slaves in New Orleans until 1834, when she fled to France.

36 Theresa Porter, "Woman as Molester: Implications for Society," in *Grotesque Femininities: Evil, Women and the Feminine*, edited by Maria Barrett (Oxford: Inter-Disciplinary Press, 2010), 82.

37 Porter, "Woman as Molester," 84, 85.

38 For mother as evil witch see Maria Barrett, "Karen Matthews the Heartbroken Mother-Come-Cold Hearted Witch: News Discourses of Evil," in *Grotesque Femininities: Evil, Women and the Feminine*, ed. Maria Barrett (Oxford: Inter-Disciplinary Press, 2010), 99–126. For mother as sexual molester see Porter, "Woman as Molester" and Helen Gavin, "Mummy Wouldn't Do That: The Perception and Construction of the Female Child Sex Abuser," *Grotesque Femininities*, 61–78.

39 Wikipedia, see the entry "Freak," available online: Wikipedia (accessed June 13, 2017).

40 Lübecker, Nikolaj. "Lars von Trier's *Dogville*: A Feel-Bad Film." In *The New Extremism in Cinema*, eds Tanya Horeck and Tina Rendall (Edinburgh: Edinburg University Press, 2013), 157–168. See also my discussion of Lübecker and feel-bad emotions in Chapter 6.

41 For chills and music see Habibi and Damasio, "Music, Feelings, and the Human Brain." For being moved and feeling chills in films, see Eugen Wassiliwizky, Valentin Wagner, and Thomas Jacobsen, "Art-Elicited Chills Indicate States of Being Moved," *Psychology of Aesthetics, Creativity, and the Arts* 9, no. 4 (November 2015): 405–416.

42 Lacy Baugher, "American Horror Story: Freak Show' premiere: 5 things you need to know" (a review of season four), *The Baltimore Sun*, October 9, 2014, available online: http://www.baltimoresun.com/entertainment/bthesite/tv-lust/bal-american-horror-story-freak-show-premiere–5-things-you-need-to-know-20141008-story.html#page=1 (accessed July 17, 2015).

43 David Wiegand, "TV Review, 'Freak Show': Fine Acting, Frighteningly Bad Scripts," *SF Gate* website, October 6, 2014, available online: http://www.sfgate.com/entertainment/article/TV-review-Even-great-acting-can-t-keep–5801257.php (accessed July 19, 2015).

44 Katey Rich, "Why *American Horror Story: Freak Show* Includes a David Bowie Song," *Vanity Fair*, October 8, 2014, available online: http://www.vanityfair.com/hollywood/2014/10/american-horror-story-david-bowie (accessed on June 17, 2015).

45 For an analysis of the *Ilsa, She-Wolf of the SS* see Chapter 2, "A Pure Dominatrix: *Ilsa, She-Wolf of the SS*," in Rikke Schubart, *Super Bitches and Action Babes: The Female Hero in Popular Cinema, 1970–2006* (Jefferson: McFarland, 2007), 65–83.

46 Brian Moylan, "American Horror Story: Freak Show Finale Recap: No Freakin' Way," posted January 22, 2015, available online: http://www.vulture.com/2015/01/american-horror-story-recap-season–4-episode–13.html (accessed July 18, 2015).

47 Luke Holland, television review, "American Horror Story."

48 Carroll, *The Philosophy of Horror*, 187.

49 Carroll, *The Philosophy of Horror*, 186.

50 Carroll, *The Philosophy of Horror*, 185.
51 Carole Hooven, John Mordechai Gottman, Lynn Fainsilber Katz, "Parental Meta-Emotion Structure Predicts Family and Child Outcomes," *Cognition and Emotion* 9 (2/3) (1995): 229–264, 231.
52 Thanks to Danish professor Anne Jerslev for reminding me of Joan Riviere. Joan Riviere, "Womanliness as Masquerade," *International Journal of Psychoanalysis* 10 (1929): 303–313, 306.
53 Wassiliwizky et al., "Art-Elicited Chills," 8.
54 Wassiliwizky et al., "Art-Elicited Chills," 2.
55 See also Chapter 6, "Sadness, Melodrama, and Rituals of Loss and Death," in Torben Grodal, *Embodied Visions: Evolution, Emotion, Culture, and Film* (New York: Oxford University Press, 2009), 122–145.
56 Habibi and Damasio, "Music, Feelings, and the Human Brain," 93.
57 Habibi and Damasio, "Music, Feelings, and the Human Brain," 95–96.
58 Habibi and Damasio, "Music, Feelings, and the Human Brain," 94.
59 For music used as therapy see for example the website "The Brain Injury Society," available online: http://www.bisociety.org/music-therapy-helps-heal-brain-injury-victims/ (accessed April 1, 2017).
60 In 2017, FX television series *Feud* premiered, a historical drama based on the shooting of *What Ever Happened to Baby Jane? Feud* stars 68-year-old Jessica Lange and 71-year-old Susan Sarandon as Crawford and Davis, and illustrates how Lange with *AHS* opened a new space in Hollywood for the middle-age female protagonist. Intriguingly, both actresses are old and playing middle-old characters.
61 In November 2009, the same year as her audition, Susan Boyle sang with Elaine Paige in a gala show. Susan Boyle's dream did come true.
62 Elsa's "Let It Go" has more than 500 million views on YouTube and Disney's sing-along version more than a billion.
63 Catherine Malabou, *The Ontology of the Accident: An Essay on Destructive Plasticity* (Cambridge: Polity Press, 2012), 80.

10 Abyss and Peak: The New Old Woman

1 It can be argued that the medium in *Insidious 3* (2015, Leigh Whannell) functions as the protagonist of the film rather than young Stefanie Scott, played by actress Quinn Brenner. Brenner is billed protagonist, however, the medium Elise Rainier (played by then 71-year-old Lin Shaye) is the one who defeats the evil spirit in the spirit world. Thanks to Angela Ndalianis for drawing my attention to this film.
2 Erik H. Erikson and Joan Erikson, *The Life Circle Completed. Extended Version With New Chapter on the Ninth Stage of Development by Joan M. Erikson* (New York: W. W. Norton & Company, 1998), Kindle edition, location 947.

3 Jay Ginn and Sara Arber, "Ageing and Cultural Stereotypes of Older Women," *Ageing and Later Life*, edited by Julia Johnson and Robert Slater (London: Sage, 1993), 60–67.

4 Season one was set in 1891. It looks like season two takes place a year later, however, years are not specified after the start of the show.

5 For an analysis of Vanessa Ives as protagonist, see Rikke Schubart, "The Journey: Vanessa Ives and Edgework as Self-Work," *Refractory: A Journal of Entertainment Media* 29, Special Issue: Penny Dreadful, Summer (2017): no page numbers, 1–16, 8. Available online: http://refractory.unimelb.edu.au/2017/06/14/schubart/ (accessed November 28, 2017).

6 "Proves that you don't need over the top cliff hangers to make good TV," IMDB fan comment to "The Nightcomers" by JonSnowsMother, IMDB, available online: http://www.imdb.com/title/tt3780308/reviews?ref_=tt_ov_rt (accessed May 4, 2017).

7 Maureen Ryan, "'Penny Dreadful' Creator Talks Season 3, Vanessa's Demons and the American West," *Variety*, 4 May 2016, available online: http://variety.com/2016/tv/features/penny-dreadful-john-logan-interview-1201766847/ (accessed May 5, 2017).

8 Michael Logan, "Patti LuPone on *Penny Dreadful*, How She'll End Her Stellar Career and (Yes) Those Damn Cell Phones," *TV-Insider*, April 28, 2016, available online at https://www.tvinsider.com/87551/patti-lupone-on-her-new-penny-dreadful-role-career-cell-phones/ (accessed May 4, 2017).

9 "Viva Patti," fan comment to "The Day Tennyson Died" (3.01) by lor, May 2, 2016, available online at: http://www.imdb.com/title/tt4786300/reviews?ref_=tt_ov_rt (accessed May 4, 2017).

10 Logan quoted in Maureen Ryan, "Creator John Logan and Showtime's David Nevins on the Decision to End 'Penny Dreadful'." *Variety*, 20 June 2016, available online: http://variety.com/2016/tv/news/penny-dreadful-ending-season-3-series-finale-creator-interview-john-logan-david-nevins-1201798946/ (accessed May 5, 2017).

11 Sylvia Henneberg, "Moms do Badly, But Grandmas do Worse: The Nexus of Sexism and Ageism in Children's Classics," *Journal of Aging Studies* 24 (2010): 125–134, 127.

12 Henneberg, "Moms do Badly," 128.

13 Henneberg, "Moms do Badly," 128.

14 Henneberg, "Moms do Badly," 129.

15 See Lizanne Henderson, *Witchcraft and Folk Belief in the Age of Enlightenment Scotland, 1670–1740* (Basingstoke: Palgrave Macmillan, 2016), eBook, 107–109.

16 Dafna Lemish and Varda Muhlbauer, "'Can't Have it All': Representations of Older Women in Popular Culture," *Women & Therapy* 35, 3–4: 165–180, 166.

17 Anne Jerslev, "The Elderly Female Face in Beauty and Fashion Ads: Joan Didion for Céline," *European Journal of Cultural Studies*, forthcoming 2017, no page numbers yet, draft version is 1–17.

18 For a discussion of age appropriate behavior and age anxiety see Chapter 9 and Eva Krainitzki, "Judi Dench's Age-Inappropriateness and the Role of M: Challenging Normative Temporality," *Journal of Aging Studies* 29 (2014): 32–40.
19 Krainitzki, "Judi Dench," 33.
20 Krainitzki, "Judi Dench," 36.
21 Mihaly Csikszentmihalyi, *Creativity: Flow and the Psychology of Discovery and Invention* (New York, HarperCollins Publishers, 1996), Kindle edition, 213.
22 Csikszentmihalyi, *Creativity*, 213.
23 Csikszentmihalyi, *Creativity*, 213.
24 Csikszentmihalyi, *Creativity*, 214.
25 Henderson, *Witchcraft and Folk Belief*, 99.
26 Henderson, *Witchcraft and Folk Belief*, 81.
27 Henderson, *Witchcraft and Folk Belief*, 81.
28 Henderson, *Witchcraft and Folk Belief*, 66.
29 More recent examples of the middle-aged and youth-obsessed witch are *Stardust* (2007, Matthew Vaughn), *Enchanted* (2007, Kevin Lima), and *The Huntsman: Winter's War* (2016, Cedric Nicolas-Troyan).
30 Henderson, *Witchcraft and Folk Belief*, 83.
31 Henderson, *Witchcraft and Folk Belief*, 84.
32 Jerslev, "The Elderly Female Face."
33 Jerslev, "The Elderly Female Face."
34 C. G. Jung, "The Philosophical Tree," in *Alchemical Studies, The Collected Works of C. G. Jung Volume 13*, (Princeton University Press, PDF eBook), 272.
35 Henderson, *Witchcraft and Folk Belief*, 77.
36 Henderson, *Witchcraft and Folk Belief*, 77
37 Ginn and Arber, "Ageing and Cultural Stereotypes," 65.
38 Catherine Malabou, *What Should We Do With Our Brain* (New York: Fordham University Press, 2008), 27.
39 D. J. Conway, *Maiden, Mother, Crone: The Myth and Reality of the Triple Goddess* (St. Paul, MN: Llewellyn Publications, 1994), 77, quoted in Dorothy S. Becvar, "Tracking the Archetype of the Wise Woman/Crone," *ReVision* 28, no. 1 (2005): 20–23, 20.
40 Csikszentmihalyi, *Creativity*, 224–225.
41 Csikszentmihalyi, *Creativity*, 225.
42 Becvar, "Tracking the Archetype," 21.
43 Becvar, "Tracking the Archetype," 21.
44 Becvar, "Tracking the Archetype," 21.
45 F. Needham and T. Outterson, "Report of the Committee appointed to investigate the nature of the phenomena of hypnotism," July 23, 1892. See

"Hypnotherapy," Wikipedia, website available on: https://en.wikipedia.org/wiki/Hypnotherapy#cite_note-Needham–33 (accessed May 28, 2017).

46 Logan, "Patti LuPone on *Penny Dreadful*."
47 Jerslev, "The Elderly Female Face."
48 Jerslev, "The Elderly Female Face."
49 Jerslev, "The Elderly Female Face."
50 Stephanie Green, "Lily Frankenstein: The Gothic New Woman in *Penny Dreadful*," *Refractory: A Journal of Entertainment Media* 29, Special Issue: Penny Dreadful, Summer (2017), section "The Troubling New Woman." Available online: http://refractory.unimelb.edu.au/2017/06/14/green/ (accessed November 28, 2017).
51 Green, "Lily Frankenstein," in the section "The Troubling New Woman."
52 Jerslev, "Elderly Female Face."
53 Becvar, "Tracking the Archetype," 22.
54 Erikson, *Life Circle*, location 1780.
55 Chris Gilleard, Paul Higgs, "The Fourth Age and the Concept of a 'Social Imaginary': A Theoretical Excursus," *Journal of Aging Studies* 27 (2013): 368–376, 368, 375, 374.
56 Ginn and Arber, "Ageing and Cultural Stereotypes," 65.
57 Ginn and Arber, "Ageing and Cultural Stereotypes," 65.
58 Erikson, *Life Circle*, location 1765.
59 Erikson, *Life Circle*, location 1843.
60 Jane M. Ussher, *Managing the Monstrous Feminine* (London: Routledge, 2006), 149.
61 Ussher, *Managing the Monstrous Feminine*, 150.

Exit: Playing the Ball Back to the Universe

1 See the discussion of Csikszentmihalyi and creativity in Chapter 1.
2 John E. Mayfield, *The Engine of Complexity: Evolution as Computation* (Columbia University Press, 2013), Kindle edition, location 4386.
3 Dorothy G. Singer and Jerome L. Singer, *The House of Make-Believe: Children's Play and the Developing Imagination* (Cambridge: Harvard University Press, 1992), 288–289.
4 George Mandler, "Emotions and the Psychology of Freedom," in *Emotions: Essays on Emotion Theory*, edited by Stephanie H. M. von Goozen, Nanne E. Van de Poll, and Joseph A. Sergeant (New Jersey: Lawrence Erlbaumm Ass. Publishers, 1994), 241–62.

Appendix 1

1 Alison Waller, *Constructing Adolescence in Fantastic Realism* (New York: Routledge, 2009), 1–29.
2 Wikipedia, entry "Adolescence," available online: https://en.wikipedia.org/wiki/Adolescence (accessed June 12, 2017).
3 Waller, *Constructing Adolescence*, 6.
4 Waller, *Constructing Adolescence*, 9.
5 For emerging adulthood see Jeffrey Jensen Arnett, "Emerging Adulthood: A Theory of Development From the Late Teens Through the Twenties," *American Psychologist* 55, no. 5, May (2000): 469–480 and Jeffrey Jensen Arnett, *Adolescence and Emerging Adulthood* (London: Pearson, 2012). See also the discussion in Chapter 7 and Chapter 8.
6 See Wikipedia for numbers of age at marriage, "List of countries by age at first marriage," available online: https://en.wikipedia.org/wiki/List_of_countries_by_age_at_first_marriage#Americas (accessed February 26, 2017).
7 "Middle Age," Wikipedia, available online: http://en.wikipedia.org/wiki/Middle_age (accessed June 12, 2015).
8 Chris Gilleard, Paul Higgs, "The Fourth Age and the Concept of a 'Social Imaginary': A Theoretical Excursus," *Journal of Aging Studies* 27 (2013): 368–376. See also Chapter 10 for a discussion of old age.

BIBLIOGRAPHY

Addison, Heather, Mary Kate Goodwin-Kelly, and Elaine Roth, eds. *Motherhood Misconceived: Representing the Maternal in U.S. Films*. New York: New York State University Press, 2009.
Alexander, Gerianne M. and Melissa Hines. "Sex Differences in Response to Children's Toys in Nonhuman Primates (*Cercopithecus Aethiops Sabaeus*)." *Evolution and Human Behavior* 23 (2002): 467–479.
Andresen, Christer Bakke. *Åpen kropp og lukket sinn: Den norske grøsserfilmen fra 2003 til 2015* [Open Body and Closed Mind: The Norwegian Horror Movie from 2003 to 2015]. Trondheim: NTNU, 2016, Ph.D. dissertation.
Apter, Michael J. *Danger: Our Quest for Excitement*. Oxford: Oneworld Publications, 2007. PDF eBook.
Arnett, Jeffrey Jensen. "Emerging Adulthood: A Theory of Development From the Late Teens Through the Twenties." *American Psychologist* 55, no. 5, May (2000): 469–480.
Arnett, Jeffrey Jensen. *Adolescence and Emerging Adulthood*. London: Pearson, 2012.
Arnold, Sarah. *Maternal Horror Film: Melodrama and Motherhood*. Basingstoke: Palgrave Macmillan, 2013.
Avery, Gillian and Kimberley Reynolds, eds. *Representations of Childhood Death*. New York: Palgrave Macmillan, 1999.
Baier, Annette. "Trust and Antitrust." *Ethics* 96, no. 2 January (1986): 231–260.
Baier, Annette. "Demoralization, Trust, and the Virtues." In *Setting the Moral Compass: Essays by Women Philosophers*, edited by Cheshire Calhoun, 176–188. New York: Oxford University Press, 2004.
Bantinaki, Katerina. "The Paradox of Horror: Fear as Positive Emotion." *The Journal of Aesthetics and Art Criticism* 70, no. 4, Fall (2012): 383–391.
Baring-Gould, Sabine. *The Book of Werewolves*. London: Senate, 1995. First published 1865.
Barnes, Jennifer Lynn. "Sweet Caroline." In *A Visitor's Guide to Mystic Falls*, edited by Red and Vee, 143–159. Smart Pop, BenBella Books, 2010. Kindle edition.
Baron-Cohen, Simon. *The Essential Difference: The Truth About the Male and Female Brain*. New York: Basic Books, 2003.
Baron-Cohen, Simon. *The Science of Evil: On Empathy and the Origins of Cruelty*. New York: Basic Books, 2011.
Barrett, Maria. "Karen Matthews the Heartbroken Mother-Come-Cold Hearted Witch: News Discourses of Evil," in *Grotesque Femininities: Evil, Women and the Feminine*, ed. Maria Barrett. Oxford: Inter-Disciplinary Press, 2010), 99–126.

Battis, Jes, ed. *Supernatural Youth: The Rise of the Teen Hero in Literature and Popular Culture*. Plymouth: Lexington Books, 2011.
Baxter, Judith. *The Language of Female Leadership*. Hampshire: Palgrave MacMillan, 2010. PDF eBook.
Beauvoir, Simone de. *The Second Sex*. London: Vintage Books, 2011. First published 1949. Kindle edition.
Becker, Lawrence C. "Trust as Noncognitive Security About Motives." *Ethics* 107, no. 1 October (1996): 43–61.
Becvar, Dorothy S. "Tracking the Archetype of the Wise Woman/Crone." *ReVision* 28, no. 1 (2005): 20–23.
Behuniak, Susan M. "The Living Dead? The Construction of People With Alzheimer's Disease as Zombies," Old Age." *Ageing and Society* 31 (2011): 70–92.
Bekoff, Marc and Jessica Pierce. *Wild Justice: The Moral Lives of Animals*. Chicago: University of Chicago Press, 2009.
Bem, Sandra Lipsitz. "Gender Schema Theory: A Cognitive Account of Sex Typing." *Psychological Review* 88, no. 4 (1981): 354–364.
Berhahl Jennifer L., Eric Luis Uhlmann, and Feng Bai. "Win-Win: Female *and* Male Athletes From More Gender Equal Nations Perform Better in International Sports Competitions." *Journal of Experimental Social Psychology* 56 (2015): 1–3.
Billson, Anne. *Let the Right One In*. Leighton: Auteur, 2011.
Bourgault du Coudray, Chantal. *The Curse of the Werewolf: Fantasy, Horror and the Beast Within*, London: I. B. Tauris, 2006.
Boyd, Brian. *On the Origin of Stories: Evolution, Cognition, and Fiction*. Cambridge: Harvard University Press, 2009. Kindle edition.
Brabon, Benjamin A. and Stéphanie Genz, eds. *Postfeminist Gothic: Critical Interventions in Contemporary Culture*. Basingstoke: Palgrave Macmillan, 2007.
Brickman, Barbara Jane. "'Delicate' Cutters: Gendered Self-Mutilation and Attractive Flesh in Medical Discourse." *Body and Society* 10, no. 4 (2004): 87–111.
Brown, Helen Gurley. *Sex and the Single Girl*. New York: Open Road, 2003. Kindle edition. First published 1962.
Brown, Jonathon D. and Margaret A. Marshall. "Self-Esteem and Emotion: Some Thoughts About Feelings." *Personality and Social Psychology Bulletin* 27, no. 5, May (2001): 575–584.
Brown, Wendy. *Edgework: Critical Essays on Knowledge and Power*. Princeton: Princeton University Press, 2005.
Brown, William. "Violence in Extreme Cinema and the Ethics of Spectatorship." *Projections: The Journal for Movies and Mind* 7, no. 1 (2013): 25–42. Special Topic: Entertaining Violence, edited by Dirk Eitzen.
Bruhn, Jørgen, Anne Gjelsvik, Henriette Thune. "Parallel Worlds of Possible Meetings in *Let the Right One In*." *Word & Image: A Journal of Verbal/visual Enquiry* 27, no. 1 (2011): 2–14.
Bryden, Inga. "Cut'n'Slash: Remodelling the 'Freakish' Female Form." In *Controversies in Body Theology*, edited by Marcella Althaus-Reid Maria and Lisa Isherwood, 29–48. London: SCM Press, 2008.

Budgeon, Shelley. "The Contradictions of Successful Femininity: Third-Wave Feminism, Postfeminism and 'New' Femininities." In *New Femininities: Postfeminism, Neoliberalism and Subjectivity*, edited by Rosalind Gill and Christina Scharff, 279–292. Basingstoke: Palgrave Macmillan, 2011. PDF ebook.

Budzik, Justyna Hanna. "Early Film Tricks in the Digital Era: The Power of *Fantasy* in Jennifer Kent's *The Babadook*." Paper presented at the conference "The Fantastic in a Transmedia Era: New Theories, Texts, Contexts," University of Southern Denmark, November 24–25, 2015.

Burghardt, Gordon M. *The Genesis of Animal Play: Testing the Limits*. Massachusetts: MIT Press, 2005. Kindle edition.

Caillois, Roger. *Man, Play and Games*. Chicago: University of Illinois Press, 2001. First published in French 1958.

Cameron, Deborah. "Evolution, Language and the Battle of the Sexes: A Feminist Linguist Encounters Evolutionary Psychology." *Australian Feminist Studies* 30, no. 86 (2015): 351–358.

Cantor, Joanne and Mary Beth Oliver. "Developmental Differences in Responses to Horror." In *The Horror Film*, edited by Stephen Prince, 224–241. New Brunswick: Rutgers University Press, 2004.

Carroll, Noël. "Film, Emotion, and Genre." In *Passionate Views*, edited by Carl Plantinga and Greg M. Smith, 21–48. Baltimore: Johns Hopkins University Press, 1999.

Carroll, Noël. *The Philosophy of Horror, or Paradoxes of the Heart*. New York: Routledge, 1990.

Chisholm, Dianne. "Climbing Like a Girl: An Exemplary Adventure in Feminist Phenomenology." *Hypatia* 23, no. 1, January–March (2008): 9–40.

Cininas, Jazmina. "Beware of the Full Moon: Female Werewolves and That Time of the Month." In *Grotesque Femininities*, edited by Maria Barrett, 3–27. Oxford: Inter-Disciplinary Press, 2010. Also available online: http://www.inter-disciplinary.net/wp-content/uploads/2009/04/cininas-paper1.pdf (accessed April 24, 2014).

Clover, Carol. *Men, Women and Chain Saws: Gender in the Modern Horror Film*. London: BFI, 1992.

Craig, A. D. "How Do You Feel? Interoception: The Sense of the Physiological Condition of the Body." *Nature Reviews: Neuroscience* 3, August (2002): 655–666.

Creed, Barbara. *The Monstrous-Feminine: Film, Feminism, Psychoanalysis*. London: Routledge, 1993.

Csikszentmihalyi, Mihaly. *Creativity: Flow and the Psychology of Discovery and Invention*, New York: HarperCollins Publishers, 1996. Kindle edition.

Csikszentmihalyi, Mihaly. *Flow: The Psychology of Happiness*. Ebury Digital, 2013. Kindle edition. First published 1990.

Curtis, Valerie and Adam Biran. "Dirt, Disgust, and Disease: Is Hygiene in Our Genes?" *Perspectives in Biology and Medicine* 44, no. 1, Winter (2001): 17–31.

Damasio, Antonio. *The Feeling of What Happens: Body and Emotion in the Making of Consciousness*. Orlando: Mariner Books, 2000.

Danvers, Dennis. *Wilderness*. New York: Pocket Books, 1992.

Davis, Hank and Andrea Javor. "Religion, Death and Horror Movies: Some Striking Evolutionary Parallels." *Evolution and Cognition* 10, no. 1 (2004): 11–18.
Dawkins, Richard. *The Selfish Gene*. Oxford University Press, 2006. First published 1976. Kindle edition.
de Waal, Frans. *The Age of Empathy: Nature's Lessons for a Kinder Society*. New York: Crown, 2010.
de Waal, Frans. *Good Natured: The Origins of Right and Wrong in Humans and Other Animals*. Cambridge: Harvard University Press, 1996.
Despret, Vinciane. *Our Emotional Makeup: Ethnopsychology and Selfhood*. New York: Other Press, 2004. First published in French 1999.
Douglas, Susan J. and Meredith Michaels. *The Mommy Myth: The Idealization of Motherhood and How It Has Undermined Women*. New York: Free Press, 2004.
Ebert, Roger. "Pan's Labyrinth." August 25, 2007. Available online: http://www.rogerebert.com/reviews/great-movie-pans-labyrinth-2006 (accessed November 17, 2016).
Edelstein, David. "Now Playing at Your Local Multiplex: Torture Porn." *New York Magazine*, January 28, 2006. Available online: http://nymag.com/movies/features/15622/ (accessed June 1, 2017).
Elgin, Don D. *The Comedy of the Fantastic: Ecological Perspectives on the Fantasy Novel*. Praeger Publishers, 1985.
Elsaesser, Thomas and Malte Hagener. *Film Theory: An Introduction Through the Senses*. New York: Routledge, 2010.
Erikson, Erik H. *Toys and Reason: Stages in the Ritualization of Experience*. New York: W. W. Norton & Company, 1977. Kindle edition.
Erikson, Erik H. and Joan Erikson. *The Life Circle Completed. Extended Version With New Chapter on the Ninth Stage of Development by Joan M. Erikson*. New York: W. W. Norton & Company, 1998. Kindle edition.
Estes, Clarissa Pinkola. *Women Who Run With the Wolves: Myths and Stories of the Wild Woman Archetype*. New York: Ballantine Books, 1992.
Fagen, Robert. *Animal Play Behavior*. New York: Oxford University Press, 1981.
Fausto-Sterling, Anne. "Beyond Difference: A Biologist's Perspective." *Journal of Social Issues* 53, no. 2 (1997): 233–258.
Fausto-Sterling, Anne. *Sex/Gender: Biology in a Social World*. New York: Routledge, 2012. Kindle edition.
Favazza, A. R. and K. Conterio. "Female Habitual Self-Mutilators." *Acta Psychiatr Scand* 79, no. 3 (1989): 283–289.
Fehr, Carla. "Feminist Engagement with Evolutionary Psychology." *Hypatia* 27, no. 1, Winter (2012): 50–72.
Fine, Cordelia. *The Delusions of Gender: How Our Minds, Society, and Neurosexism Create Difference*. New York: W. W. Norton & Company, 2010. Kindle edition.
Florio, John and Ouisie Shapiro. "The Women Succeeding in a Men's Professional Baseball League," *The New Yorker*, August 29, 2016. Available online: http://www.newyorker.com/news/sporting-scene/the-women-succeeding-in-a-mens-professional-baseball-league (accessed October 11, 2016).

Fradley, Martin. "'Hell Is a Teenage Girl'?: Postfeminism and Contemporary Teen Horror." In *Postfeminism and Contemporary Hollywood Cinema*, edited by Joel Gwynne and Nadine Muller, 204–221. Basingstoke: Palgrave Macmillan, 2013.
Freeland, Cynthia. *The Naked and the Undead: Evil and the Appeal of Horror*. Boulder: Westview Press, 2000.
Frijda, Nico H. *The Emotions*. Cambridge: Cambridge University Press, 1986.
Frijda, Nico H. *The Laws of Emotion*. New Jersey: Lawrence Erlbaum Associates, 2007.
Ganser, Alexandra, Julia Pühringer, and Markus Rheindorf. "Bakhtin's Chronotope on the Road: Space, Time, and Place in Road Movies Since the 1970s." *Linguistics and Literature* 4, no. 1 (2006): 1–17.
Gavin, Helen and Theresa Porter. *Female Aggression*. Oxford: Wiley Blackwell, 2015. Kindle edition.
Gazzaniga, Michael S. *Who's In Charge: Free Will and the Science of the Brain*. New York: HarperCollins, 2011. Kindle edition.
Geberth, Vernon J. "Homicides Involving the Theft of a Fetus From a Pregnant Victim." *Law and Order* 54, no. 3 March (2006), no page numbers, available online: http://www.practicalhomicide.com/Research/LOmar2006.htm (accessed December 14, 2015).
Genz, Stéphanie, "'I'm not going to fight them, I'm going to fuck them': Sexist Liberalism and Gender (A)politics in *Game of Thrones*." In *Women of Ice and Fire: Gender, Game of Thrones, and Multiple Media Engagements*, Rikke Schubart and Anne Gjelsvik, eds. NY: Bloomsbury, 2016, 243–266
Genz, Stéphanie. *Postfemininities in Popular Culture*. London: Palgrave, 2009.
Genz, Stéphanie. "Singled Out: Postfeminism's 'New Woman' and the Dilemma of Having It All." *The Journal of Popular Culture* 43, no. 1 (2010): 97–119.
Genz, Stéphanie. "Third Way/ve: The Politics of Postfeminism." *Feminist Theory* 7, no. 3 (2006): 333–353.
Gibson, James J. "The Theory of Affordances." *Perceiving, Acting, and Knowing: Toward an Ecological Psychology*, edited by Robert Shaw and John Bransford, 67–82. Hillsdale: Lawrence Erlbaum Associates, Publishers, 1977.
Giddens, Anthony. *Modernity and Self-Identity*. Redwood City: Stanford University Press, 1991.
Gill, Rosalind and Christina Scharff, eds. *New Femininities: Postfeminism, Neoliberalism and Subjectivity*. London: Palgrave MacMillan, 2011. PDF eBook.
Gilleard, Chris and Paul Higgs. "The Fourth Age and the Concept of a 'Social Imaginary': A Theoretical Excursus." *Journal of Aging Studies* 27 (2013): 368–376.
Gillis, Stacy, Gillian Howie, and Rebecca Munford, eds. *Third Wave Feminism: A Critical Exploration. Expanded Second Edition*. New York: Palgrave MacMillan, 2007. PDF eBook.
Ginn, Jay and Sara Arber. "Ageing and Cultural Stereotypes of Older Women." In *Ageing and Later Life*, edited by Julia Johnson and Robert Slater, 60–67. London: Sage, 1993.
Gordon, Joan and Veronica Hollinger, eds. *Blood Read: The Vampire as Metaphor in Contemporary Culture*. Philadelphia: University of Pennsylvania Press, 1997.

Grant, Barry Keith, ed. *The Dread of Difference: Gender and the Horror Film.* Austin: University of Texas Press, 1996.

Gray, Kurt and Daniel M. Wegner. "Moral Typecasting: Divergent Perceptions of Moral Agents and Moral Patients." *Journal of Personality and Social Psychology* 96, no. 3 (2009): 505–520.

Green, Stephanie. "Lily Frankenstein: The Gothic New Woman in *Penny Dreadful.*" *Refractory: A Journal of Entertainment Media* 29, Special Issue: Penny Dreadful, Summer (2017): section "The Troubling New Woman." Available online: http://refractory.unimelb.edu.au/2017/06/14/green/ (accessed May 28, 2017).

Grodal, Torben. *Embodied Visions: Evolution, Emotion, Culture, and Film.* New York: Oxford University Press, 2009.

Grønstad, Asbjørn. "Abject Desire: *Anatomie de l'enfer* and the Unwatchable." *Studies in French Cinema* 6, no 3 (2006): 161–169.

Göncü, Artin and Suzanne Gaskins, eds. *Play and Development: Evolutionary, Sociocultural, and Functional Perspectives (Jean Piaget Symposia Series).* Oxfordshire: Lawrence Erlbaum Associates, 2007.

Haase, Donald. "Children, War, and the Imaginative Space of Fairy Tales." *The Lion and the Unicorn* 24, no. 3, September (2000): 360–377.

Habibi, Assal and Antonio Damasio. "Music, Feelings, and the Human Brain." *Psychomusicology: Music, Mind, and Brain* 24, no. 1 (2014): 92–102.

Haidt, Jonathan, Clark McCauley, and Paul Rozin. "Individual Differences in Sensitivity to Disgust: A Scale Sampling Seven Domains of Disgust Elicitors." *Personality and Individual Differences* 16, no. 5, May (1994): 701–713.

Hanich, Julian. *Cinematic Emotion in Horror Films and Thrillers: The Aesthetic Paradox of Pleasurable Fear.* New York: Routledge, 2010.

Haraway, Donna J. *Simians, Cyborgs, and Women: The Reinvention of Nature.* London: Free Association Books, 1991.

Hardcastle, Anne E. "Ghosts of the Past and Present: Hauntology and the Spanish Civil War in Guillermo del Toro's *The Devil's Backbone.*" *Journal of the Fantastic in the Arts* 15, no. 2 (2005): 120–132.

Harrington, Erin. *Women, Monstrosity and Horror Film: Gynaehorror.* Abingdon: Routledge, 2017. Kindle edition.

Hassett, Janice M., Erin R. Siebert, and Kim Wallen. "Sex Differences in Rhesus Monkey Toy Preferences Parallel Those of Children." *Hormones and Behavior* 54 (2008): 359–364.

Henderson, Lizanne. *Witchcraft and Folk Belief in the Age of Enlightenment Scotland, 1670–1740.* Basingstoke: Palgrave Macmillan, 2016. eBook, 107–109.

Henneberg, Sylvia. "Moms do Badly, But Grandmas do Worse: The Nexus of Sexism and Ageism in Children's Classics." *Journal of Aging Studies* 24 (2010): 125–134.

Henricks, Thomas S. *Play and the Human Condition.* Urbana: University of Illinois Press, 2015. Kindle edition.

Henricks, Thomas S. "Play as Self-Realization: Toward a General Theory of Play." *American Journal of Play* 6, no. 2, Winter (2014): 190–213.

Hertzberg, Lars. "On the Attitude of Trust." *Inquiry: An Interdisciplinary Journal of Philosophy* 31, no. 3 (1988): 307–322.

Herz, Rachel. *That's Disgusting: Unraveling the Mysteries of Repulsion.* New York: W. W. Norton & Company, 2012. Kindle edition.

Hines, Melissa. *Brain Gender*. New York: Oxford University Press, 2004.
Holland, Luke. Television review, "American Horror Story: Freak Show is the strongest season of the show so far," December 2, 2014, *The Guardian*, available online: http://www.theguardian.com/tv-and-radio/2014/dec/02/american-horror-story-season-four-freak-show-review (accessed July 18, 2015).
hooks, bell. *Feminism Is For Everybody: Passionate Politics*. New York: Routledge, 2014. Kindle edition.
Hooven, Carole, John Mordechai Gottman, and Lynn Fainsilber Katz. "Parental Meta-Emotion Structure Predicts Family and Child Outcomes." *Cognition and Emotion* 9, no. 2–3 (1995): 229–264.
Horeck, Tanya and Tina Kendell, eds. *The New Extremism in Cinema: From France to Europe*. Edinburgh: Edinburgh University Press, 2011.
Howell, Amanda. "Haunted Art House: *The Babadook* and International Art Cinema Horror." In *Australian Screen in the 2000s*, edited by Mark Ryan and Ben Goldsmith. Palgrave-Macmillan, 2017.
Howell, Amanda. "The Mirror and the Window: The Seduction of Innocence and Gothic Coming of Age in *Låt den Rätte Komma In/Let the Right One In*." *Gothic Studies* 18, no. 1, May (2016): 57–70.
Huizinga, Johan. *Homo Ludens: A Study of the Play-Element in Culture*. London: Routledge, 1980. First published 1944.
Hymowitz, Kay S. "The New Girl Order." *City Journal*, Autumn, 2007. Available online: http://www.city-journal.org/html/17_4_new_girl_order.html (accessed May 14, 2014).
Jackson, J. Kasi. "Science Studies Perspectives on Animal Behavior Research: Toward a Deeper Understanding of Gendered Impacts." *Hypatia* 29, no. 4, Fall (2014): 738–754.
Jacoby, Susan. *Wild Justice: The Evolution of Revenge*. New York: Harper and Row, 1983.
Jerslev, Anne. "The Elderly Female Face in Beauty and Fashion Ads: Joan Didion for Céline." *European Journal of Cultural Studies*, June 15, 2017, no. 00(0), pdf-download, 1–14.
Johansson, Anna. "Rakbladsflikkor: Om Kvinnlig Självskada som Identitet och Symbolspråk" [Razorblade Girls: About Female Self-Injury as Identity and Symbolic Language]. *Nätverket* 14 (2004): 100–114.
Johansson, Eva. "*Let the Right One In*: Freezing Horror Story With Vampires in Front" ['Låt den rätte komma in': Isande skräckhistoria med vampyrer i förorten]. Review in *Svenska Dagbladet*, August 30, 2004. Available online: http://www.svd.se/isande-skrackhistoria-med-vampyrer-i-fororten (accessed November 22, 2016).
Jones, Karen. "Trust as an Affective Attitude." *Ethics* 107, no. 1 October (1996): 4–25.
Jorgensen, Darren. "The Impossible Thought of *Lingchi* in Georges Bataille's *The Tears of Eros*." *Kritikos* 5, March–April (2008). Available online: http://intertheory.org/jorgensen.htm (accessed June 2, 2017).
Jung, C. G. "The Philosophical Tree." In *Alchemical Studies, The Collected Works of C. G. Jung, Volume 13*. Princeton University Press, PDF eBook.
Juul, Jesper. *The Art of Failure: An Essay on the Pain of Playing Video Games*. Cambridge: The MIT Press, 2013. PDF eBook.

Juul, Jesper. *Half-Real: Video Games Between Real Rules and Fictional Worlds.* Cambridge: The MIT Press, 2005. Kindle edition.

Kahneman, Daniel. *Thinking, Fast and Slow.* London: Allan Lane, 2011.

Kaplan, E. Ann. *Motherhood and Representation: The Mother in Popular Culture and Melodrama.* London: Routledge, 1992.

Kelly, Daniel. *Yuck! The Nature and Moral Significance of Disgust.* Cambridge: MIT Press, 2011. Kindle edition.

Kermode, Mark. "Girl Interrupted," interview with Guillermo del Toro, *Sight & Sound* 16, no. 12 (December 2006): 20, available online: http://old.bfi.org.uk/sightandsound/feature/49337 (accessed November 15, 2016).

Kerr, Margee. *Scream: Chilling Adventures in the Science of Fear.* New York: Public Affairs, 2015. Kindle edition.

Kimura, Doreen. *Sex and Cognition.* Cambridge: MIT Press, 1999.

Kleinhans, Chuck. "Cross-Cultural Disgust: Some Problems in the Analysis of Contemporary Horror Cinema." *Jump Cut*, no. 51, Spring (2009). Available online: https://www.ejumpcut.org/archive/jc51.2009/crosscultHorror/index.html (accessed July 2, 2009).

Kolnau, Aurel, Barry Smith and Carolyn Korsmeyer. *On Disgust.* Open Court, 2003.

Krainitzki, Eva. "Judi Dench's Age-Inappropriateness and the Role of M: Challenging Normative Temporality," *Journal of Aging Studies* 29 (2014): 32–40.

Laine, Tarja. "Cinema as Second Skin: Under the Membrane of Horror Film." *New Review of Film and Television Studies* 4, no. 2, August (2006): 93–106.

Laine, Tarja. *Feeling Cinema: Emotional Dynamics in Film Studies.* London: Continuum, 2011.

Lahno, Bernd. "On the Emotional Character of Trust." *Ethical Theory and Moral Practice* 4, no. 2, Theme: "Cultivating Emotions," June (2001): 171–189.

Launius, Christie and Holly Hassel. *Threshold Concepts In Women's and Gender Studies.* New York: Routledge, 2015. Kindle edition.

Laurendeau, Jason. "'Gendered Risk Regimes': A Theoretical Consideration of Edgework and Gender." *Sociology of Sport Journal* 25, no. 3, September (2008): 293–309.

Lazarus, Richard S. *Emotion and Adaptation.* New York: Oxford University Press, 1991. Kindle edition.

Leavenworth, Maria Lindgren and Malin Isaksson. *Fanged Fan Fiction: Variations on* Twilight, True Blood *and* The Vampire Diaries. Jefferson: McFarland, 2013.

Levinson, Jerrold. "Emotion in Response to Art: A Survey of the Terrain." In *Emotion and the Arts*, edited by Mette Hjort and Sue Laver, 20–34. New York: Oxford University Press, 1997.

Lindqvist, John Ajvide. *Let the Right One In.* Original title *Låt den rätte komma*. First printed 2004, translated 2007, this version 2009. London: Quercus, 2009.

Litman, Jordan. "Curiosity and the Pleasures of Learning: Wanting and Liking New Information." *Cognition and Emotion* 19, no. 6 (2005): 793–814.

Logan, Michael. "Patti LuPone on *Penny Dreadful*, How She'll End Her Stellar Career and (Yes) Those Damn Cell Phones." *TV–Insider*, April 28, 2016. Available online: https://www.tvinsider.com/87551/patti-lupone-on-her-new-penny-dreadful-role-career-cell-phones/ (accessed May 4, 2017).

Lois, Jennifer. "Peaks and Valleys: The Gendered Emotional Culture of Edgework." *Gender and Society* 15, no. 3 June (2001): 381–406.
London, Bianca. "Meet the New WAGs: No, Not Footballers' Wives. . . the Women Ageing Gracefully." *MailOnline*, December 10, 2012. Available online: http://www.dailymail.co.uk/femail/article-2244604/Helen-Mirren-Joanna-Lumley-Meet-new-WAGs--Women-Ageing-Gracefully.html (accessed June 13, 2017).
Lorenz, Konrad. *On Aggression*. London: Routledge, 2005. PDF eBook. First published 1963.
Lübecker, Nikolaj. "Lars von Trier's *Dogville*: A Feel-Bad Film." In *The New Extremism in Cinema*, edited by Tanya Horeck and Tina Rendall, 157–168. Edinburgh: Edinburgh University Press, 2013.
Lury, Karen. *The Child in Film: Tears, Fears and Fairy Tales*. New Brunswick: Rutgers University Press, 2010.
Lüthi, Max. *Once Upon a Time: On the Nature of Fairy Tales*. New York: Frederick Ungar Publishing, 1970. First published 1962.
Lyng, Stephen. "Edgework: A Social Psychological Analysis of Voluntary Risk Taking." *American Journal of Sociology* 95, no. 4, January (1990): 851–886.
Macnab, Geoffrey. "Sadean Woman." *Sight & Sound*, December (2004): 20–22.
Mack-Canty, Colleen. "Third-Wave Feminism and the Need to Reweave the Nature/Culture Duality." *NWSA Journal* 16, no. 3, Fall [2004]: 154–179.
Mackey, Allison. "Make It Public! Border Pedagogy and the Transcultural Politics of Hope in Contemporary Cinematic Representations of Children." *College Literature* 37, no. 2, Spring (2010): 171–185.
Malabou, Catherine. *What Should We Do With Our Brain*. New York: Fordham University Press, 2008.
Malabou, Catherine. *The Ontology of the Accident: An Essay on Destructive Plasticity*. Cambridge: Polity, 2012.
Malinowski, Bronislaw. *Magic, Science and Religion and Other Essays*. New York: Doubleday Anchor Book, 1954.
Mandler, George. "Emotions and the Psychology of Freedom." In *Emotions: Essays on Emotion Theory*, edited by Stephanie H.M. von Goozen, Nanne E. Van de Poll, and Joseph A. Sergeant, 241–262. New Jersey: Lawrence Erlbaumm Ass. Publishers, 1994.
Marks-Tarlow, Terry. "The Fractal Self at Play." *American Journal of Play*, Summer (2010): 31–62.
Maurer, Robert. *Mastering Fear: Harness Emotion to Achieve Excellence in Health, Work, and Relationships*. Wayne N.J.: Career Press, 2016.
Mauss, Marcel. *A General Theory of Magic*. London: Routledge, 1972. First published 1950.
Mayfield, John E. *The Engine of Complexity: Evolution as Computation*. Columbia University Press, 2013. Kindle edition.
McGreevy, Brian. *Hemlock Grove, or, The Wise Wolf*. New York: Farrar, Straus and Giroux, 2013.
McLennon, Leigh M. "Defining Urban Fantasy and Paranormal Romance: Crossing Boundaries of Genre, Media, Self and Other in New Supernatural Worlds." *Refractory: A Journal of Entertainment Media* 23, June (2014). Available online: http://refractory.unimelb.edu.au/2014/06/26/uf-mclennon/ (accessed June 3, 2017).

Metzinger, Thomas. *The Ego Tunnel: The Science of the Mind and the Myth of the Self*. New York: Basic Books, 2009.
Meynell, Letitia. "Evolutionary Psychology, Ethology, and Essentialism (Because What They Don't Know Can Hurt Us)." *Hypatia* 27, no. 1, Winter (2012): 3–27.
Miller, April. "The Hair that Wasn't there Before." *Western Folklore* 64, no. 3–4, Summer–Fall (2005): 281–303.
Mitmansgruber, Horst, Thomas N. Beck, Stefan Höfer, and Gerhard Schüßler. "When You Don't Like What You Feel: Experiential Avoidance, Mindfulness and Meta-Emotion in Emotion Regulation." *Personality and Individual Differences* 46 (2009): 448–453.
Mittell, Jason. *Complex TV: The Poetics of Contemporary Television Storytelling*. New York: NYU Press, 2015.
Montola, Markus. "The Positive Negative Experience in Extreme Role-Playing." In *Nordic DiGRA 2010 Proceedings*. Stockholm, 2010. Available online: http://www.digra.org/digital-library/publications/the-positive-negative-experience-in-extreme-role-playing/ (accessed June 2, 2017).
Munro, Ealasaid. "Feminism: A Fourth Wave?" Political Studies Association (no date or year). Available online: https://www.psa.ac.uk/insight-plus/feminism-fourth-wave (accessed September 8, 2016).
Murray, Gabrielle. "*Hostel II*: Representations of the Body in Pain and the Cinema Experience in Torture-Porn." *Jump Cut: A Review of Contemporary Media* no. 50, Spring (2008). Available online: http://www.ejumpcut.org/currentissue/TortureHostel2/text.html (accessed May 19, 2008).
Næss, Arne. "Philosophy of Wolf Policies I: General Principles and Preliminary Exploration of Selected Norms." *Conservation Biology* 1, no. 1, May (1987): 22–34.
Næss, Arne. "The Shallow and the Deep, Long-Range Ecology Movement. A Summary." *Inquiry: An Interdisciplinary Journal of Philosophy* no. 16 (1973): 95–100.
Ndalianis, Angela. "Corpse Contagion and the Aesthetics of Disgust." Keynote presentation at "B for BAD cinema. Aesthetics, politics and cultural value" Conference. 16–18 April, 2009, Melbourne, Australia.
Ndalianis, Angela. *The Horror Sensorium: Media and the Senses*. Jefferson: McFarland, 2012.
Negra, Diane. *What a Girl Wants: Fantasicing the Reclamation of Self in Postfeminism*. London: Routledge, 2009.
Nell, Victor. "Cruelty's Rewards: The Gratifications of Perpetrators and Spectators." *Behavioral and Brain Sciences* no. 29 (2006): 211–257.
Newman, Kim. "Pan's Labyrinth Review." Review in *Empire*, October 27, 2006. Available online: http://www.empireonline.com/movies/pan-labyrinth/review/ (accessed November 17, 2016).
No author. "Parental Descent: Jennifer Kent's *The Babadook* is a Spooky Tale of a Mother in Crisis,", *Film Journal International,* November 14, 2014. Available online: http://www.filmjournal.com/content/parental-descent-jennifer-kent's-'-babadook'-spooky-tale-mother-crisis (accessed March 19, 2017).
No author. "Playing With Wolves: An Interview With C. J. Rogers." *American Journal of Play*, Summer (2010): 1–30.

Nussbaum, Emily. Review of Season One: Murder House, "Shock Value," October 30, 2011, *New York Magazine TV Review*, available online: http://nymag.com/arts/tv/reviews/american-horror-story-nussbaum-2011-11/#print (accessed July 16, 2015).

Oliver, Mary Beth and Meghan Sanders. "The Appeal of Horror and Suspense." In *The Horror Film*, edited by Stephen Prince. New Brunswick: Rutgers University Press, 2004, 242–259.

Orme, Jennifer. "Narrative Desire and Disobedience in *Pan's Labyrinth*." *Marvels & Tales* 24, no. 2 (2010): 219–234.

Palmer, Tim. *Brutal Intimacy: Analyzing Contemporary French Cinema*. Middletown: Wesleyan University Press, 2011.

Palmer, Tim. "Style and Sensation in the Contemporary French Cinema of the Body." *Journal of Film and Video* 58, no. 3, Fall (2006): 22–32.

Palmer, Tim. "Under Your Skin: Marina de Van and the Contemporary French Cinema du Corps." *Studies in French Cinema* 6, no. 3, Fall (2006): 171–181.

Pellegrini, Anthony D. "The Development and Function of Rough-and-Tumble Play in Childhood and Adolescence: A Sexual Selection Theory Perspective." In *Play and Development: Evolutionary, Sociocultural, and Functional Perspectives (Jean Piaget Symposia Series)*, edited by Göncü and Gaskins. Oxfordshire: Lawrence Erlbaum Associates, 2007, 77–98.

Pellegrini, Anthony D. and John Archer. "Sex Differences in Competitive and Aggressive Behavior: A View from Sexual Selection Theory." In *Play and Development: Evolutionary, Sociocultural, and Functional Perspectives (Jean Piaget Symposia Series)*, edited by Göncü and Gaskins. Oxfordshire: Lawrence Erlbaum Associates, 2007, 219–244.

Pellis, Sergio and Vivien Pellis. *The Playful Brain: Venturing to the Limits of Neuroscience*. Oxford: Oneworld, 2009.

Peterson, M. Jeanne. "No Angels in the House: The Victorian Myth and the Paget Woman." *American Historical Review* 89, no. 3 (1984): 677–708.

Phillips, Mary and Nick Rumens. *Contemporary Perspectives on Ecofeminism*. London: Routledge, 2015.

Pickard, Susan. "Biology as Destiny? Rethinking Embodiment in 'deep' Old Age." *Ageing and Society* 34 (2014): 1279–1291.

Pinedo, Isabel Cristina. *Recreational Terror: Women and the Pleasures of Horror Film Viewing*. New York: State University of New York Press, 1997.

Plantinga, Carl. "Mood and Ethics in Narrative Cinema." Paper presented at symposium on the Moral Psychology of Fiction, Trondheim, September 20–21, 2012.

Plantinga, Carl. "Art Moods and Human Moods in Narrative Cinema." *New Literary History* 43, (2012): 455–475.

Plantinga, Carl and Greg M. Smith, eds. *Passionate Views*. Baltimore: Johns Hopkins University Press, 1999.

Popper, Karl R. *Objective Knowledge: An Evolutionary Approach*. Oxford: Oxford University Press, 1973.

Poromba, Cindy. "Critical Potential on the Brink of the Magic Circle." *Situated Play*, Proceedings of DiGRA 2007 Conference, 772–778. Available online: http://www.digra.org/digital-library/publications/critical-potential-on-the-brink-of-the-magic-circle/ (accessed June 2, 2017).

Porter, Theresa. "Woman as Molester: Implications for Society." In *Grotesque Femininities: Evil, Women and the Feminine*, edited by Maria Barrett. Oxford: Inter-Disciplinary Press, 2010.

Pötzsch, Holger. "Borders, Barriers, and Grievable lives: The Discursive Construction of Self and Other in Audio-Visual Media," *Nordicom Review* 32, no. 2, Autumn (2011): 75–94.

Prince, Stephen, ed. *The Horror Film*. New Brunswick: Rutgers University Press, 2004.

Projansky, Sarah. *Watching Rape: Film and Television in Postfeminist Culture*. New York: New York University Press, 2001.

Quandt, James. "Flesh & Blood: Sex and Violence in Recent French Cinema." *ArtForum*. February, 2004. Available online: https://www.artforum.com/inprint/issue=200402&id=6199 (accessed June 2).

Quandt, James. "More Moralism from that 'Wordy Fuck'." In *The New Extremism in Cinema*, edited by Tanya Horeck and Tina Rendall, 209–213. Edinburgh: Edinburgh University Press, 2013.

Radner, Hilary. *Neo-Feminist Cinema: Girly Films, Chick Flicks and Consumer Culture*. New York: Routledge, 2011.

Reyes, Xavier Aldana. *The Spanish Gothic*. London: Palgrave, 2017. eBook.

Reynolds, Kimberley. "Fatal Fantasies: The Death of Children in Victorian and Edwardian Fantasy Writing." In *Representations of Childhood Death*, edited by Gillian Avery and Kimberley Reynolds, 169–188. New York: Palgrave Macmillan, 1999.

Ringrose, Jessica. "Are You Sexy, Flirty, Or A Slut? Exploring 'Sexualization' and How Teen Girls Perform/Negotiate Digital Sexual Identity on Social Networking Sites." In *New Femininities: Postfeminism, Neoliberalism and Subjectivity*, edited by Rosalind Gill and Christina Scharff, 99–116. London: Palgrave MacMillan, 2011. PDF eBook.

Riviere, Joan. "Womanliness as Masquerade." *International Journal of Psychoanalysis* 10 (1929): 303–313.

Rosin, Hanna. *The End of Men: And the Rise of Women*. London: Penguin Books, 2013. Kindle Edition.

Ryan, Maureen. "Creator John Logan and Showtime's David Nevins on the Decision to End 'Penny Dreadful'." *Variety*, 20 June 2016. Available online: http://variety.com/2016/tv/news/penny-dreadful-ending-season–3-series-finale-creator-interview-john-logan-david-nevins–1201798946/ (accessed May 5, 2017).

Ryan, Maureen. "'Penny Dreadful' Creator Talks Season 3, Vanessa's Demons and the American West." *Variety*, 4 May, 2016. Available online: http://variety.com/2016/tv/features/penny-dreadful-john-logan-interview–1201766847/ (accessed May 5, 2017).

Schell, Heather. "The Big Bad Wolf: Masculinity and Genetics in Popular Culture." *Literature and Medicine* 26, no. 1, Spring (2007): 109–125.

Schubart, Rikke. "*Hostel II*, Torture-Porn, and the New Horror Heroine," paper presented at the *Bad Cinema Conference*, Melbourne, 2008. Available online: https://www.academia.edu/10937740/Hostel_II_Torture_Porn_and_the_New_Horror_Heroine (accessed June 3, 2017).

Schubart, Rikke. "'I am Become Death, the Destroyer of Worlds': Managing Massacres and Constructing the Female Teen Leader in *The 100*." In

A Companion to the Action Film, edited by Jim Kendrick. New Jersey: Wiley Blackwell, forthcoming 2018.

Schubart, Rikke. "The Journey: Vanessa Ives and Edgework as Self-Work." *Refractory: A Journal of Entertainment Media* 29, Special Issue: Penny Dreadful (2017): no page numbers. Available online: http://refractory.unimelb.edu.au/2017/06/14/schubart/ (accessed November 30, 2017).

Schubart, Rikke. "Monstrous Appetites and Positive Emotions in *True Blood*, *The Vampire Diaries* and *The Walking Dead*." *Projections: The Journal for Movies and Mind* 7, no. 1 (2013): 43–63. Special Topic: Entertaining Violence, ed. Dirk Eitzen.

Schubart, Rikke. *Super Bitches and Action Babes: The Female Hero in Popular Cinema, 1970–2006*. Jefferson: McFarland, 2007.

Schubart, Rikke. "The Thrill of the Nordic Kill: The Manhunt Movie in the Nordic Thriller." In *Nordic Genre Film: Small Nation Film Cultures in the Global Marketplace*, edited by Tommy Gustafsson and Pietari Kääpä, 76–90. Edinburgh: Edinburgh University Press, 2015.

Schubart, Rikke. "Utopia and Torture in the Hollywood War Film." *Nordicom Review. NordMedia 2009*, June 29 (2009): 19–28.

Schubart, Rikke. "Woman With Dragons: Daenerys, Pride, and Postfeminist Possibilities." In *Women of Ice and Fire: Gender, Game of Thrones, and Multiple Media Engagements*, edited by Rikke Schubart and Anne Gjelsvik, 105–130. New York: Bloomsbury, 2016.

Schubart, Rikke and Anne Gjelsvik, eds. *Women of Ice and Fire: Gender, Game of Thrones, and Multiple Media Engagements*. New York: Bloomsbury, 2016.

Schuster, Julia. "Invisible Feminists? Social Media and Young Women's Political Participation." *Political Science* 65, no. 1 (2013): 8–24.

Scott, A. O. "In Gloom of War, a Child's Paradise." Review of *Pan's Labyrinth* in *The New York Times*, December 29, 2006. Available online: http://www.nytimes.com/2006/12/29/movies/29laby.html (accessed November 17, 2016).

Shaw, Sarah Naomi. "Shifting Conversations on Girls' and Women's Self-Injury: An Analysis of the Clinical Literature in Historical Context." *Feminism and Psychology* 12, no. 2 (2002): 191–219.

Sherman, Gary D. and Jonathan Haidt. "Cuteness and Disgust: The Humanizing and Dehumanizing Effects of Emotion." *Emotion Review* 3, no. 3, July (2011): 245–251.

Shih, Margaret, Todd L. Pittinsky and Nalini Ambady. "Stereotype Susceptibility: Identity Salience and Shifts in Quantitative Performance." *Psychological Science* 10, no. 1, January (1999): 80–83.

Shih, Margaret and Jennifer A. Richeson, Nalini Ambady, Kentaro Fujita. "Stereotype Performance Boosts: The Impact of Self-Relevance and the Manner of Stereotype Activation." *Journal of Personality and Social Psychology* 83, no. 3 (2002): 638–647.

Shouse, Eric. "Feeling, Emotion, Affect." *M/C Journal* 8, no. 6 (2005). Available online: journal.media-culture.org.au/0512/03-shouse.php (accessed on February 4, 2012).

Silvia, Paul J. *Exploring the Psychology of Interest*. New York: Oxford University Press, 2006. Kindle edition.

Silvia, Paul J. "What is Interesting? Exploring the Appraisal Structure of Interest." *Emotion 5*, no. 1 (2005): 89–102.

Singer, Dorothy G. and Jerome L. Singer. *The House of Make-Believe: Children's Play and the Developing Imagination*. Cambridge: Harvard University Press, 1992.

Sinnerbrink, Robert. "*Stimmung*: Exploring the Aesthetics of Mood." *Screen 53*, no. 2, Summer (2012): 148–163.

Smethurst, Toby and Stef Craps. "Playing With Trauma: Interreactivity, Empathy, and Complicity in *The Walking Dead* Video Game." *Games and Culture* 10, no. 3 (2015): 269–290.

Smith, Greg M. *Film Structure and the Emotion System*. Cambridge: Cambridge University Press, 2007.

Smith, Murray. "Gangsters, Cannibals, Aesthetes, or Apparently Perverse Allegiances." In *Passionate Views*, edited by Carl Plantinga and Greg M. Smith, 217–238. Baltimore: Johns Hopkins University Press, 1999.

Snyder, Gary. "The Rediscovery of Turtle Island." Essay from 1994. PDF available online: http://dspace.uah.es/dspace/bitstream/handle/10017/4900/therediscoveryofturtleisland.pdf?sequence=1 (accessed on January 2, 2017).

Solomon, Robert C. "Emotions, Thoughts, and Feelings: Emotions as Engagements with the World." In *Thinking about Feeling: Contemporary Philosophers on Emotions*, edited by Robert C. Solomon, 76–88. Oxford University Press, 2004.

Solomon, Robert C. *A Passion for Justice: Emotions and the Origin of the Social Contract*. Lanham: Rowman & Littlefield Publishers, 1995. First published 1990.

Solomon, Robert C. "Sympathy and Vengeance: The Role of the Emotions in Justice." In *Emotions: Essays on Emotion Theory*, edited by Stephanie H.M. van Goozen et al., 291–311. Hillsdale: Lawrence Erlbaum Associates, 1994.

Solomon, Robert C. and Lori D. Stone. "On 'Positive' and 'Negative' Emotions." *Journal for the Theory of Social Behavior* 32, no. 4 (2002): 417–435.

Spencer, Jane. "Afterword: Feminist Waves." In *Third Wave Feminism: A Critical Exploration*, edited by Stacy Gillis, Gillian Howie, and Rebecca Munford, 298–303. Basingstoke: Palgrave Macmillan, 2007. PDF eBook.

Staiger, Janet. *Perverse Spectators: The Practices of Film Reception*. New York: New York University Press, 2000.

Staiger, Janet. *Media Reception Studies*. New York: New York University Press, 2005.

Stange, Mary Zeiss. *Woman the Hunter*. Boston: Beacon Press, 1997.

Steele, Claude M. *Whistling Vivaldi and Other Clues to How Stereotypes Affect Us*. New York: W. W. Norton & Company, 2010. Kindle edition.

Stein, Joel. "The New Greatest Generation: Why Millennials Will Save Us All." *Time*, May 20 (2013): 28–35.

Sternudd, Hans T. "The Discourse of Cutting: A Study of Visual Representations of Self-Injury on the Internet." In *Making Sense of Pain: Critical and Interdisciplinary Perspectives*, edited by Jane Fernandez, 237–248. Freeland: Inter-Disciplinary Press, 2010. PDF eBook.

Stewart, Michael, ed. *Melodrama in Contemporary Film and Television*. Basingstoke: Palgrave Macmillan, 2014.

Suddendorf, Thomas. *The Gap: The Science of What Separates Us From Other Animals*. New York: Basic Books, 2013. Kindle edition
Sunstein, Cass R. *Laws of Fear: Beyond the Precautionary Principle*. New York: Cambridge University Press, 2005. PDF eBook
Sutton-Smith, Brian. *The Ambiguity of Play*. Cambridge: Harvard University Press, 2001. Kindle edition.
Tasker, Yvonne and Diane Negra, eds. *Interrogating Postfeminism: Gender and the Politics of Popular Culture*. London: Duke UP, 2007.
Tatar, Maria. "Test, Tasks, and Trials in the Grimm's Fairy Tales." *Children's Literature* 13 (1985): 31–48.
Thompson, John O. "Reflexions on Dead Children in the Cinema and Why there are Not More of Them." In *Representations of Childhood Death*, edited by Gillian Avery and Kimberley Reynolds, 204–216. New York: Palgrave Macmillan, 1999.
Thurber, Ann. *Bite Me: Desire and the Female Spectator in* Twilight, The Vampire Diaries, *and* True Blood. MA dissertation. Faculty of the James T. Laney School of Graduate Studies of Emory University, 2011. Available online: https://etd.library.emory.edu/view/record/pid/emory:92d6h (accessed February 27, 2017).
Todorov, Tzvetan. *The Fantastic: A Structural Approach to a Literary Genre*. Ithaca: Cornell University Press, 1975.
Tolkien, J. R. R. "On Fairy-Stories." PDF 1–27. Brainstorm services, available online: http://brainstorm-services.com/wcu-2004/fairystories-tolkien.pdf (accessed December 20, 2015).
Tudor, Andrew. *Theories of Film*. London: Secker & Warburg, 1974.
Twitchell, James B. *Dreadful Pleasures: An Anatomy of Modern Horror*. New York: Oxford University Press, 1985.
Ussher, Jane M. *Managing the Monstrous Feminine: Regulating the Reproductive Body*. London: Routledge, 2006.
Waller, Alison. *Constructing Adolescence in Fantastic Realism*. New York: Routledge, 2009.
Warner, Marina. *From the Beast to the Blonde*. London: Vintage, 1995.
Warren, Karen J., ed. *Ecofeminist Philosophy: A Western Perspective on What It Is and Why It matters*. Rowman & Littlefield Publishers, 2000.
Wassiliwizky Eugen, Valentin Wagner, and Thomas Jacobsen. "Art-Elicited Chills Indicate States of Being Moved." *Psychology of Aesthetics, Creativity, and the Arts* 9, no. 4 (November 2015): 405–416.
Wedell-Wedellsborg, Merete. *Battle Mind: How to Navigate in Chaos and Perform Under Pressure*. Copenhagen: Akademisk forlag, 2015.
Wetmore, Kevin J. *Post–9/11 Horror in American Cinema*. New York: Continuum, 2012.
Wheeler, S. Christian. "Think Unto Others: The Self-Destructive Impact of Negative Racial Stereotypes." *Journal of Experimental Social Psychology* 37 (2001): 173–180.
Wheeler, S. Christian, Kenneth G. DeMarree, Richard E. Petty. "Understanding the Role of the Self in Prime-to-Behavior Effects: The Active-Self Account." *Personality and Social Psychology Review* 11, no. 3, August (2007): 234–261.
Williams, Christina L. and Kristen E. Pleil. "Toy Story: Why Do Monkey and Human Males Prefer Trucks? Comment on 'Sex Differences in Rhesus Monkey

Toy Preferences Parallel Those of Children' by Hassett, Siebert and Wallen." *Hormones and Behavior* 54 (2008): 355–358.

Williams, Linda. "Film Bodies: Gender, Genre, and Excess" In *Film Theory and Criticism: Introductory Readings*, edited by Leo Braudy and Marshall Cohen, 701–715. New York: Oxford University Press, 1999. Essay first published 1991.

Williams, Linda. "When the Woman Looks." In *The Dread of Difference: Gender and the Horror Film*, edited by Barry Keith Grant, 15–34. Austin: University of Texas Press, 1996. Essay first published 1983.

Williams, Rebecca. "Unlocking *The Vampire Diaries*: Genre, Authorship, and Quality in Teen TV Horror." *Gothic Studies* 15, no. 1 May (2013): 88–99.

Wilson, Emma. "Children, Emotion and Viewing in Contemporary European Film." *Screen* 46, no. 3, Autumn (2005): 329–340.

Wright, Sarah. *The Child in Spanish Cinema*. Manchester: Manchester University Press, 2013. Kindle edition.

Young, Iris Marion. "Lived Body Vs. Gender: Reflections on Social Structure and Subjectivity." *Ratio (new series)* 15, no. 4, December (2002): 410–428.

Young, Iris Marion. *On Female Body Experience: "Throwing Lika a Girl" and Other Essays*. New York: Oxford University Press, 2005. Kindle edition.

Young, Iris Marion. "Throwing Like a Girl: A Phenomenology of Feminine Body Comportment Motility and Spatiality." *Human Studies* 3 (1980): 137–156.

Zipes, Jack. *Breaking the Magic Spell: Radical Theories of Folk & Fairy Tales*. Lexington: University Press of Kentucky, 2002.

Zuk, Marlene. *Sexual Selections: What We Can and Can't Learn About Sex From Animals*. Berkeley: University of California Press, 2002. Kindle edition.

FILMOGRAPHY

Listed by English title first, original title in parenthesis, year, director, and nationality if other than US.

Horror Heroine Films

Alien 1979 Ridley Scott, UK/US
Aliens 1986 James Cameron
Babadook, The 2014 Jennifer Kent, Australia
Black Swan 2010 Darren Aronofsky
Brood, The 1979 David Cronenberg, Canada
Curse, The 1999 Jacqueline Garry
Dark Touch 2013 Marina de Van, France/Ireland/Sweden
Descent, The 2005 Neil Marshall, UK
Don't Knock Twice 2016 Caradog W. James, UK
Don't Look Back (Ne te retourne pas) 2009 Marina de Van, France
Frontier (Frontière(s)) 2007 Xavier Gens, France/Switzerland
Ginger Snaps 2000 John Fawcett, Canada/US
Grace 2009 Paul Solet
Hostel: Part II 2007 Eli Roth
House of Voices (Saint Ange) 2004 Pascal Laugier, France
In My Skin (Dans ma peau) 2002 Marina de Van, France
Inside (À L'intérieur) 2007 Alexandre Bustillo and Julien Maury, France
Insidious 3 2015 Leigh Whannell
Let Me In 2010 Matt Reeves
Let the Right One In (Låt den rätte komma in) 2008 Tomas Alfredson, Sweden
Mama 2013 Andrés Muschietti, Canada/Spain
Martyrs 2008 Pascal Laugier, France
Twilight Saga: New Moon, The 2009 Chris Weitz
Orphanage, The (El orfanato) 2007 Juan Antonio Bayona, Spain
Others, The 2001 Alejandro Amenábar, Spain/US
Pan's Labyrinth (El laberinto del fauno) 2006 Guillermo del Toro, Spain/Mexico/US
She-Wolf of London 1946 Jean Yarbrough
Tall Man, The 2012 Pascal Laugier
Twilight 2008 Catherine Hardwicke
Twilight Saga: Breaking Dawn – Part 1, The 2011 Bill Condon
Twilight Saga: Breaking Dawn – Part 2, The 2012 Bill Condon

Twilight Saga: Eclipse, The 2010 David Slade
Vvitch: A New-England Folktale, The 2015 Robert Eggers
Visit, The 2015 M. Night Shyamalan
What Ever Happened to Baby Jane 1962 Robert Aldrich
Wolf Girl 2001 Thom Fitzgerald

Horror Heroine Television Series

American Horror Story 2011– FX
Bitten 2014–2016 Space
Exorcist, The 2016– Fox
Feud 2017– FX
Hemlock Grove 2013–2015 Netflix
Once Upon a Time 2011– ABC
Penny Dreadful 2014–2016 Showtime/Sky
True Blood 2008–2014 HBO
Vampire Diaries, The 2009–2017 CW
Walking Dead, The 2010– AMC
Wilderness 1996, three-part mini-series, UK

Other Films

Anatomy of Hell (*Anatomie de l'enfer*) 2004 Catherine Breillat, France/Portugal
Blade II 2002 Guillermo del Toro
Book of Eli, The 2010 Albert Hughes and Allen Hughes
Cabin in the Woods, The 2012 Drew Goddard
Cabinet of Dr. Caligari, The (*Das Cabinet des Dr. Caligari*) 1920 Fritz Lang, Germany
Carne 1991 Gaspar Noé, France
Carriers 2009 David Pastor and Àlex Pastor
Come and See (*Idi i smotri*) 1985 Elem Klimov, Soviet Union
Cronos 1993 Guillermo del Toro, Mexico
Demon Seed 1977 Donald Cammell
Devil's Backbone, The (*El espinazo del diablo*) 2001 Guillermo del Toro, Spain/Mexico/France/Argentina
Diamonds of the Night (*Démanty noci*) 1962 Jan Nemec, Czechoslovakia
Dogville 2003 Lars von Trier, Denmark
Easy Rider 1969 Dennis Hopper
Edward Scissorhands 1990 Tim Burton
Empire of the Sun 1987 Steven Spielberg
Enchanted 2007 Kevin Lima
Forbidden Games (*Jeux interdits*) 1952 René Clément, France
Freaks 1932 Tod Browning
Frozen 2013 Chris Buck and Jennifer Lee
Germany Year Zero (*Germania Anno Zero*) 1948 Roberto Rossellini, Italy

Gladiator 2000 Ridley Scott
Goodnight Mommy (Ich seh, ich seh) 2014 Severin Fiala, Veronika Franz, Austria
Great Ecstasy of Robert Carmichael, The 2005 Thomas Clay
Hero (Ying xiong) 2002 Zhang Yimou, China
Hostel 2005 Eli Roth
Human Centipede, The 2009 Tom Six
Huntsman: Winter's War, The 2016 Cedric Nicolas-Troyan
Ilsa, She-Wolf of the SS 1975 Don Edmonds
Incident in a Ghost Land 2018 Pascal Laugier, France/Canada
Irreversible (Irréversible) 2002 Gaspar Noé, France
It Happened in Europe (Valahol Európában) 1948 Géza von Radványi, Hungary
Ivan's Childhood (Ivanovo detstvo) 1962 Andrei Tarkovsky, Soviet Union
King Kong 1976 John Guillermin
Lara Croft: Tomb Raider 2001 Simon West
Maid in Manhattan 2002 Wayne Wang
Mean Girls 2004 Mark Waters
Mimic 1997 Guillermo del Toro
Mirror (Zerkalo) 1975 Andrei Tarkovsky, Soviet Union
Nanny, The 1965 Seth Holt
Ogre, The (Der Unhold) 1996 Volker Schlöndorff, Germany/France/UK
Passion of Joan of Arc, The (La Passion de Jeanne d'Arc) 1928 Carl Theodor Dreyer, France
Postman Always Rings Twice, The 1981 Bob Rafelson
Predator 1987 John McTiernan
Pretty Woman 1990 Garry Marshall
Psycho 1960 Alfred Hitchcock
Pulp Fiction 1994 Quentin Tarantino
Road, The 2009 John Hillcoat
Romance 1999 Catherine Breillat, France
Rosemary's Baby 1968 Roman Polanski
Saving Private Ryan 1998 Steven Spielberg
Saw 2004 James Wan
See the Sea (Regarde la mer) 1997 François Ozon
Sex and the City 2008 Michael Patrick King
Shining, The 1980 Stanley Kubrick
Silence of the Lambs, The 1991 Jonathan Demme
Sitcom 1998 François Ozon
Skyfall 2012 Sam Mendes
Spirit of the Beehive, The (El espíritu de la colmena) 1973 Victor Erice, Spain
Stake Land 2010 Jim Mickle
Stardust 2007 Matthew Vaughn
Teen Wolf 1985 Rod Daniel
Thelma & Louise 1991 Ridley Scott
Them (Ils) 2006 David Moreau, Xavier Palud, France/Romania
Tin Drum, The (Die Blechtrommel) 1979 Volker Schlöndorff, West Germany/France/Poland/Yugoslavia
Tootsie 1982 Sydney Pollack
Trouble Every Day 2003 Claire Denis, France

Twentynine Palms 2003 Bruno Dumont, France
Village of the Damned 1960 Wolf Rilla
Werewolf of London 1935 Stuart Walker
When Harry Met Sally... 1989 Rob Reiner
Wizard of Oz, The 1939 Victor Fleming
World War Z 2013 Marc Forster
Wolf 1994 Mike Nichols
Wolf Creek 2005 Greg McLean, Australia
Wolf Man, The 1941 George Waggner
Wolfman, The 2010 Joe Johnston

Other Television Series

Gossip Girl 2007–2012 CW
Pretty Little Liars 2010–2017 ABC
Teen Wolf 2011 MTV

Documentaries

Into the Mind 2013 Eric Crosland, Dave Mossop

Musicals

Evita 1980
Gypsy 2008
Misérables, Les 1985

Computer Games

Resident Evil 1996 Capcom

INDEX

Note: Page numbers followed by n indicate numbered endnotes. Italics refer to most important entries where several pages are indexed.

101 Dalmatians 234

À *L'intérieur* see *Inside*
abyss *see* old
accidentialize (Malabou) 154, 273
adolescence *130–2*, *149–50*, 218, 267, 275, 276–7; adolescence (definition) 276
adolescent (noun) 10, 12, 131–2, 149, 154, 164, 205, 275, 277, 305 n.14; adolescent (adj) 41, 60, 71, 120, 131, 177, 277
adult *see* age
Aeschylus 93
Aestheticism (movement) 163
affects, the (emotion) 8, 12, 18, *20–1*, 22, 32, 65, 248, 286 n.22
affordances 12, 52, 99, 100, *101–3*, 107, 121, 123, 125–6, 153, 274, 301 n.9
age-anxious 10, 13, 229, 241, 262
age: adult (definition) 276; child (definition) 275; middle age (definition) 277; teenager (definition) 276; young adult (definition) 276; young adult (commercial definition) 276–7 (*see also* life stage; old)
ageism 13, 227, 230, *234–5*, 243, 257, 267
aggression (Nell) *11–12*, *50–2*, 55, 129, 280, 305 n.2: angry 12, *51–2*, 90, 101, 104, 123, 125, 129, 159, 187; drive 20, 306 n.23; intermale *51–2*; predatory *51–2*, 101, 123,

129; sex-related *51–2*; territorial *51–2*, 125, 129–30
Aldrich, Robert 249
Alexander, Gerianne M. 293 n.147
Alfredson, Tomas 12, *79–80*, 86, 94, 96
Alice's Adventures in Wonderland 67, 68
Alien (film) 177; series 187
Alien, the (monster) 184, 187
alienist 10, 13, *253–6*, *262–4*, 266–7, 269, 271
Aliens 186
American Horror Story (and *AHS*) 13, 227, 229–31, 235, 237–8, 240–1, 243–4, 246, 248–9, 320 n.60; "Murder House" (season one) 230, 234; "Asylum" (season two) 230, 234, 243; "Coven" (season three) 229–30, 233–4, 238, 241; "Bitchcraft" (3.01) 233, 236–7; "The Replacements" (3.03) 236; "Burn, Witch, Burn" (3.05) 239; "The Dead" (3.07) 235, 240; "Go to Hell" (3.12) 234; "The Seven Wonders" (3.13) 238; "Freak Show" (season four) 229, 231, 242–3, 245; "Monsters Among Us" (4.01) 241; "Edward Mordrake Part 2" (4.04) 244–5; "Show Stoppers" (4.12) 244
amygdala 27, 156
Anatomy of Hell (*Anatomie de l'enfer*) 163
anchor points 25, *59–61*, 63, 66, 74

anecdotes (narrative ecology) 3, 32, 281 n.4
angel in the house 211–12
anger (emotion) 9, 18, 20, 53, 144, 156, 159, 194
angst 183
animal play 11, 16, *41–50*, 55
anthropocentric world view 102, 116; non-anthropocentric world view 102, 116
anxiety *19*, 21, 34, 109, 167, 183, 223; age 229–30, 233–4; denial and repression 183, 195–6; disorders 266; and excitement 47–50, 56, 109, 113; to master 199–200; performance 170, 260; self-injury 167; separation 71; social expectations 162; status 117 (*see also* age–anxious; fear)
apocalypse 52, 207–8, 210–11, 213, 217, 221, 255–6; post-apocalypse 217; post-apocalyptic 52, 206, 212, 216–18, 224
Apple, Fiona 244; "Criminal" (song) 244
Apter, Michael J. 11, 47–50, 193
Arber, Sara 263, 270
Archer, John 44, 55
Arendt, Hannah 213
Arnett, Jeffrey Jensen 130, 132, 149, 277
Arnold, Sarah 178–9
Aronofsky, Darren 12, 153, 155, 171
Artaud, Antonin 169
Auschwitz-Birkenau 69, 217; Birkenau concentration camp 70
awe (emotion) 19, 112 (*see also* fear)

Babadook (monster) 12, 177, 193, 196–202
Babadook, The (film) 12, 19, 177–8, 180, 192–3, 195–6, 198–201, 231
Babel 76, 96
Baier, Annette 141–4
Bakhtin, Mikhal 215, 315 n.17, 315 n.18
Baring-Gould, Sabine 100
Baron-Cohen, Simon 11, 35, 163

BASE jumping 11, 32, 46, *55*
basic horror narrative *see* horror
Bataille, Georges 168
battle mind 221, 315 n.26
beauty and the beast 70–1
beauty myth, the 171, 173, 175, 261
Beauvoir, Simone de 30, 35, 39, 168
Becker, Lawrence C. 142
Becvar, Dorothy S. 266, 270
Behuniak, Susan M. 235
being attracted (as emotion) 135
being charmed (as emotion) 135
being in love (as emotion) 135
being moved (emotional state) 246–8, 319 n.41 (*see also* chills)
Bekoff, Marc and Jessica Pierce 20, 90–1, 224–5
Bem, Sandra Lipsitz 33
Bible, the 17, 218, 260
bioculturalism 4–6, 38, 40, 177
Biran, Adam 156
Bitten 12, 30, 99–100, 119–21, 123–5, 149: "Summons" (1.01) 120, 123; "Bitten" (1.05) 119, 123; "Prisoner" (1.08) 125; "Vengeance" (1.09) 122; "Settling" (1.11) 125; "Caged" (1.12) 30; "Ready" (1.13) 125; "Rule of Anger" (3.06) 126
Black Swan 12, 53, 153–5, 170, 173, 187; and disgust 153–5, 171–2
Blade II 62
Blockhead Hans 65
Book of Eli, The 217–18
border pedagogy 76, 95–6
Bourgault du Coudray, Chantal 101, 105, 116, 118–19
Bowie, David 229–31, 241–8, 317 n.6; "Heroes" (song) 245; "Life on Mars" (song) 230, 244
Boyd, Brian 38
brain; circuits (Nell) 51–2; cognitive abilities 6, 38, 43–4, 46, 48, 92, 224; female brain, the 35; hormones in the, 43; male brain, the 35, 163; modular 39, 291 n.117; structure 23, 31
Brechtian 169
Breillat, Catherine 163, 184

Brickman, Barbara Jane 170–1
Brood, The 177
Brown, Helen Gurley 122, 125–6, 139
Brown, Jonathan D. 227
Brown, Wendy 40
Brown, William 169
Bruhn, Jørgen 94
Bryden, Inga 162, 171
Buck, Chris 238
Budgeon, Shelley 117
Budzik, Justyna Hanna 200
Burghardt, Gordon M. 11, *41*–2, 50, 55–6, 84, 292 n.129
Bustillo, Alexandre 2, 178

Cabin in the Woods, The 15
Cabinet of Dr. Caligari, The (Das Cabinet des Dr. Caligari) 201
Caillois, Roger 11, 41, 49–50, 55
Cameron, Deborah 6, 11, *34*, 289 n.88
Carriers 217
Carroll, Noël 4, 7, 9, 18–19, 40, 54, 92, 243, 246–7, 284 n.34, 317 n.5
catharsis 169
chiaroscuro 160–1
child *see* age
child's perspective, a 65–6, 79–81
Children of Men 76, 96
chills 229–30, 241–2, 246–9
Chronos (Greek god of eternal time) 70
chronos (Greek time) 215
chronotope 215, 315 n.17, 315 n.18
Cinderella 65, 238
cinema brut 157
cinema du corps 157
cinema of sensation 157
Clover, Carol 7, 26, 54 (*see also* final girl)
Clytemnestra 93
cognitive: dissonance 53, 77–8; philosopher 4, 10, 18, 23; philosophy 10; psychologist 6, 30–1, 33, 35, 71, 163, 223; psychology 5–6, 10, 33, 247; software 11, 36–7, 256, 267, 274
Come and See (Idi i smotri) 237 n.32
coming-of-age 80, 114–15, 119
comparative biology 281 n.4

competition: aggression 11, 52; agon 41; character Caroline 134, 136; character Nina 172; male sexual competition 44–5, 130–1, 135; social horror 53, 231
complex television 206
consciousness 5, 10–11, *16–17, 21*–2, 41, 47, 118 (*see also* mind)
consequentialism 225
Conterio, K. 167
Craig, A. D. 20–1
creative horror *see* horror
creative play *see* play
creativity: 179; and play 3, 9, 11, 43, 55–6; System 1 25; fourth narrative 60; and interest 231; Csikszentmihalyi 46, 229, 260, 265
Creed, Barbara: 7, 26, 54; abject 140; maternal body 184; menstrual blood 109, mother 179, 177
crone 206, 227, 234, *264*–6
Cronos (film) 62–3, 66
Cronus (Greek Titan) 70
Cruella De Vil 234
cruelty: boy's play *83*–4; lycanthrope 100; Nell *50–1*; Theatre of Cruelty 169
crystallized: abilities 259–60, 265; intelligence 259; knowledge 222, 315 n.28; mental abilities 265 (*see also* fluid)
Csikszentmihalyi, Mihaly 43, 46, 49, 126, 222, 229, 246, 259–60, 265, 273
curiosity (emotion) 27, 230–2, 243, 264; Csikszentmihalyi 229; Carroll 7, 54, 246–7; magic 74; *Inside* 60, 162–3 (*see also* interest)
Curse, The 99
Curtis, Valerie 156
cut n slash 161–2
cute 71; cuteness 71; cuteness factor 71

Damasio, Antonio 10, *16–17, 21*–2, *24*–5, 28, 33, 36, 232; "Music, Feelings, and the Human Brain" 247–8, 286 n.21
Dans ma peau see In My Skin

Danvers, Dennis 104
dark eroticism 114, 168
dark stage 3–4, 9–10, 15, 17, 21, 24–5, 28–9, 41, 54–6, 132, 140–1, 153, 175, 202, 208, 246, 269–71, 273
Dark Touch 170
Darwin, Charles 191; Darwinian machine 9, 38; Darwinian theory 38; Darwinian sexual selection theory 292 n.143
de Van, Marina 2, 12, 153, 159–64, 170–1, 175
de Waal, Frans 45, 83
Decadence (movement) 163, 268
default; rules 25, 60–1, 63–4, 66, 70, 74, 78; values 59, 75, 77
Del Rey, Lana 244; "Gods and Monsters" (song) 244
del Toro, Guillermo 2, 12, 59, 62–3, 66, 68, 70, 73–4, 77, 79; *The Devil's Backbone* 298 n.72
Deleuze, Gilles 7
delicate cutter 158, *170–1*
Demon Seed 187
Denis, Claire 157
deontology 225; deontologism 225
Descent, The 15, 22, 28
desire (as sexual emotion) 104, 113–14, 122, 125, *135–7*, 139
desire (psychology): Callois 49; curiosity 232; female 113; for freedom 223; for information 232; for something 7, 54, 187, 190, 210, 238, 240, 259, 269, 276; magic 74; male 101; narrative 73; repressed 199; revenge and justice 90–3; Tolkien 74; 210, 223;
despair (emotion) 9, 52–3, 86, 253, 266
Despret, Vinciane 20, 45
Devil, the 100, 187, 255, 259, 261–3, 269
Devil's Backbone, The (*El espinazo del diablo*) 62–3, 66
Diamonds of the Night (*Démanty noci*) 296 n.32
Dietrich, Marlene 244
Dike (Greek goddess) 93
disbelief *see* suspension of disbelief
discontent of civilization 8

disgust (emotion): disgust 2–3, 7, 9, 18, 20, 25, 41, 52–4, 141, *153–7*, 174, 176, 206, 245; animal-reminder, 156; anticipation 172; and body breaches 184; core 153, *156–7*, 167, 189; and cuteness 71; emotional 156; exposure therapy 154, *173–4*; extreme 173–4; face 155; and gender 174; Kolnai 157; and maternal body 179; moral 153, *156–7*, 167, 173, 175, 185, 189; self-disgust, to 174; and self-injury 153, 171–3; sensitive 154, *173–4*, 176 (*see also* terror management theory; *Black Swan*; *Grace*; *Inside*; *Martyrs*)
Disney 70, 242, 247, 261, 320 n.62
Dogville 169
Don't Knock Twice 253
Don't Look Back (*Ne te retourne pas*) 170
Douglas, Susan J. 196
Dr. Jekyll 101; *Penny Dreadful* 254
Dracula 101; *Penny Dreadful* 254–6, 263–4, 266, 269–70; Bram Stoker *Dracula* 262
drama (genre) 81, 119, 122, 133, 153, 157; historical 320 n.60; psychological 9, 12, 153, 170, 172; realist 119; revenge 91; social realist 80; teen 132–3, 304 n.49, 305 n.14; television series 206, 255; torture 153; war 296 n.32
dread (emotion) 8–9, 19, 88, *183* (*see also* fear)

Easy Rider 215
ecofeminism *see* feminism
ecological theory 100, 265 (*see also* psychology; philosophy)
ecology 105; deep 117, 283 n.17
ecosophy 6–7, 118, 283 n.17
Edelstein, David 158, 166 (*see also* torture porn)
edgework 11, *47–50*, 54–6, 78, 141, 175, 194, 199, 201, 231, 268–9, 273–4; mental edgework 48–9, 55–6, 199; gender 50
ego tunnel, the 23, 32, 56

El laberinto del fauno see *Pan's Labyrinth*
Elsaesser, Thomas 168
emerging adult 10, 130, 132, *149*, 219, 269, 275, 277
emotional: dialogue 8, 26, 28–9, 48, 54, 60, 65, 78, 157, 163–4, 210; engagement 9, 23, 27, 48, 55, 71, 140, 149, 153–4, 163, 184; ninja 26, 28–9; robustness 9, 11, 43, 55–6, 174
emotions: basic 18, 20–1, 155–6; challenging 1, 4, 9, 15, *17*, 25, 28, 38, 41, *49*, 55, 141, 153, 227; epistemological 230, 242; meta- 20, 53, 84, 194, 198, 246, 273, 313 n.41; mixed 3; multiple 9, 27; negative 1–4, 7, *9*, 25–6, 247, 284 n.32; positive 1, 3, 9, 242, 281 n.3, 284 n.32, 294 n.174
Empire of the Sun 67–8
Enchanted 322, n.29
Epictetus 223
Erikson, Erik H.: adolescence *132*, *149*–50, 277; adulthood 154, 205–6, 276; life stages *10*, 13, 60, 275; middle adulthood 230, 205–6, 132; old age 253, 265, 269; play 114
Erikson, Joan: 10; ninth stage 10, 13, 253, 271; old age 235
essentialism 11, 32
ethics 4–5; Aristotle 26, 223, 225; Erikson 205; freedom 205, 208, *224*; global 75; *Inside* 184; and morals 8, 26, 91, 224; Nietzsche 40; play 273; society 7, 54; vengeance 91; viewing violence 158, 163, 169; virtue ethics *223*–5, 227; werewolf 102; Wilde 164
ethology 91; narrative 281 n.4
Eudaimonia 224–5
Euripides 93
Evita 255
evofeminism *see* feminism
evolutionary: explanations 35; perspective 26, 185, 208; story 34; theory 38, 44, 156
excitement-seeking instinct 11, 49

existential explosive plasticity 100, *115*–17, 119, 126, 140, 249
Exorcist, The (television series) 227, 230
extreme play *see* play

face: disgust 155; gape 155–6, 172; play 41
fairy tale (genre) 12, 59–60, *63*–6, 69–75, 77–8, 179, 256–7, 260; Bloch 64, 74; Perrault 100; princess 195; Tolkien 64, 70, *73*–4; and women 205, 234 (*see also* Lüthi)
fairy-tale (adj): book 64; end 76, 256; expectations 64; fantasy 60; female characters 234, 256; frog 115; hero 65; heroine 65–6, 70–1, 73, 256; and Nazism 70; rules 60, 63–4, 70, 74; stories 72; time 69; villains 234; violence 70
fairy-tale tests (the three tests): *64*; task 64–5, *69*–70, 72; test 62, *64*, 66, *69*; trial 64, 72, 75
fascism 63, 73, 78
Fausto-Sterling, Anne 39
Favazza, A. R. 167
Fawcett, John 12, 100, 107–8
fear (emotion): 2–3, 7, 9, *25*–7, 155; basic emotion 18–19; Carroll 9, 246; children and war 64; chills 242; curiosity 243; edgework 47, 49; experimental studies 247; feel 22; Hanich 8, (definition) *19*, 183; innate 71; Kerr 28; Lazarus (definition) *19*; Nell *51*–2; physical sensations of 54; Sunstein (definition) *19*, 24–5; wolves and werewolves 123 (*see also* anxiety; awe; dread; fright; panic; play with fear; fear of)
FEAR circuit, the (Nell) 51–2
Fear Factory 174
fear of: age 233 (*see also* age-anxious); children 95; failure 49, 55; women 262
fear: choice based on 227; master 10, 56, 199, 271, 274; overcome 173; play with 15–16, 21, *40*–1, 153, 200, 273

feel-bad experience (Lübecker) 154, 169
feeling-of-a-feeling (Damasio) 16, 22
feelings (type of emotion) 18, 20–2, 25, 32, 247–8, 274, 286 n.21
Fein, Greta 197, 294 n.179
female aggression 180
female sex offender 180 (*see also* molester)
feminism: ecofeminism 6, 39–40, 106, 121, 282–3 n.16, 291 n.113; evofeminism 4–7, 37–40, 107, 206, 282 n.6; first wave 282–3 n.16; fourth wave 6, 39–40, 121, 282–3 n.16; neofeminism 6, 39–40, *121–2*, 126, 282–3 n.16; postfeminism 5–6, *39–40*, 117, 121–2, 282 n.6, 282–3 n.16; second wave 6, 110, 116–17, 121, 127, 191, 282–3 n.16; third wave 6, 117, 121, 127, 282–3 n.16
feminist: biology 11, 317 n.21 (*see also* Zuk, Fausto-Sterling); psychology 11 (*see also* Fine, Ussher); phenomenology 5, 11, 290, n.98 (*see also* Young, Beauvoir, Haraway)
Feud 320 n.60
fight-or-flight 27, 51, 156, 183
final girl 7, 26, 205
Fine, Cordelia 6, 35–6, 39, 274, 293 n.147
first wave feminism *see* feminism
Flaubert, Gustave 256
fluid: abilities 259–60; knowledge 222, 315 n.28 (*see also* crystallized knowledge)
Forbidden Games (Jeux interdits) 296 n.32
fourth age *see* age
fourth wave feminism *see* feminism
Fradley, Martin 121
frame (Apter): confidence 47; detachment 47–8, 194; protective 47, 194; safety-zone 47–8
Frankenstein (*Penny Dreadful*) 254, 264, 266, 269
Frankenstein's monster (*Penny Dreadful*) 101, 256

freak 143; Bryden 162, 309 n.30; "Freak Show" 240–8, *242*; freak circus 13, 229–30, 242; *Grace* 189
Freaks 243
free will 5, 10, 17, 77; Gazzaniga 38; Carol 222, 224; animals 256; *Penny Dreadful* 263
freedom (emotion) 13, 222–4, 227, 248, 274
Freeland, Cynthia 7, 9, *38–9*, 54
Freud, Sigmund 8, 23, 163, 191
fright *19*, 183 (*see also* fear)
Frijda, Nico H. 10, 18, *20–1*, 36, 76, 91–2, 35–7
Frontier (Frontière(s)) 157
Frozen 238, 242–4, 247–8

games: brink 174; forbidden 174; rough 175
Gang Rape (game) 175
Gavin, Helen 179–80, 200
Gazzaniga, Michael S. 10, 22–4, 36, 38–9, 222
gender difference 11, 29, *31–3*, 36, 46, 56, 131
gender script: 6, 32; Carol 206; children and 44; Elsa 243; Fiona 235; *Ginger Snaps* 107, 109, 117; *In My Skin* 175; *Penny Dreadful* 254; mother and 178; negative 4; society's 32, 154; Ussher 271; *Vampire Diaries* 129; *Wilderness* 105
gender stereotype, the 10–13, *33–4*, 36–7, 40, 44–5; *Let the Right One In* (movie) 86; middle age 205, 230; negotiate 274
Genz, Stéphanie 39, 282–3 n.16
Germany Year Zero (Germania Anno Zero) 296 b.32
gerotranscendence 271
ghost 12, 19, 177–8, 192, 194, 240, 245, 253
Gibson, James J. *100–2*, 274
Giddens, Anthony 205, 218, 220
Ginger Snaps 12, 100, *107–9*, 112–13, 116, 121, 139, 302 n.19
Ginn, Jay 263, 270

INDEX

girl: New Girl Order, the 120, 122, 125, 133, 237; Modern Girl 122; New Girl 120; single 125–6, 139; *see also* Brown, Helen Gurley
Giroux, Henry 96
Gjelsvik, Anne 94
Gladiator 75–6
Golden Rule, the 224–5, 316 n.34
Goodnight Mommy (*Ich seh, ich seh*) 198
Gothic literature 254
Gothic New Woman 268
Gottman, John Mordechai 194
Goya, Francisco 70
Grace 12, 178, *187–92*, 198
Grande, Sarah 268
Great Ecstasy of Robert Carmichael, The 169
Grey, Dorian 254, 269
Grodal, Torben 4, 8, 24, 28–9, 54, 75
Grønstad, Asbjørn 163, 184
Guattari, Félix 7
gustatory cortex 155
Gypsy 255

Haase, Donald 64
Habibi, Assal 232, 247–8
habitat (biology) 102–4, 110, 210
Hagener, Malte 168
Haidt, Jonathan 71, 156, 174–5, 184
Hanich, Julian 8–9, 19, 54, 172, *183*
Haraway, Donna 7, 38
hard-wired 11, 17, 35, 224
hardware 11, 36 (*see also* cognitive software)
Harrington, Erin 7, 54
Heidegger, Martin 211
Hellboy 62
Hemlock Grove (television show) 12, 99–100, *110–19*, 124, 227, 230; "The Angel" (1.02) 111–12; "Hello, Handsome" (1.05) 112; "What Peter Can Live Without" (1.09) 116; "Children of the Night" (1.12) 112
Hemlock Grove, or, The Wise Wolf (novel) 118
Henderson, Lizanne 260, 262

Henneberg, Sylvia 205, 234, 238, 256, 264
Henricks, Thomas S. 11, 53, 114, 125–6, 187, 208, 222, 248
Hero (*Ying xiong*) 75
Herz, Rachel 156
hesitation (emotion) 75–6
heuristics 10, 21, 24, 60, 71
Hines, Melissa 6, 31
Hitchcock, Alfred 166, 177
home (trope) 13, 205–6, *210–18*, 220, 227
home-invasion 53, 187
hooks, bell 110
Hooven, Carole 194
hope (emotion) 3, 49, 52–3, 74, 95
Horeck, Tanya 157
horror (as emotion): suggested 8, 19, 183; direct 8, 19, 183
horror (as narrative): basic 11, 52–3, 55, 60, 231; creative 15, 53–5, 164, 193, 231; identity 11–12, 15, 52–5, 60, 90, 100–1, 103, 112, 159, 164, 178, 187, 193, 220, 231; social horror 11, 15, 52–4, 60, 100, 103, 112, 129, 135, 141, 187, 231; survival 11, 15, 52–4, 60, 101, 206, 220–2, 224
horror genre 7–10, 40–1, 62, 132
horror heroine, the: *American Horror Story* 229–30, 242, 249; child 12; middle-age 13; *Pan's Labyrinth* 60; *Penny Dreadful* 253; *Walking Dead, The* 205–6, 218; werewolf 101–2, 121
Hostel 2 see *Hostel: Part II*
Hostel 53, 60, 112, 174
Hostel: Part II 1, 3, 53, 112, 147, 166, 281 n.1
House of Voices (*Saint Ange*) 164, 194, 198
Howell, Amanda 198, 298 n.2
Huizinga, Johan 41, 55–6
Human Centipede, The 174
humanism 4, 6, 118; post-human 118; 282 n.6
Huntsman: Winter's War, The 322 n.29
Hymowitz, Kay S. 120, 122, 126, 133, 307 n.49

identity horror *see* horror
Ilsa, She-Wolf of the SS 244, 319 n.45
In My Skin (*Dans ma peau*) 2, 12, 153–4, *157–64*, 166, 170–1, 174–5
Incident in a Ghost Land 170
incremental story 30, *36–7*, 56; narrative 206, 208, 274
information gaps 232, 246
Inside (À L'intérieur) 160–1, 163, 167
interest (emotion) 3, 8, 13, *229–33*, 242, 245–6
interface 8, 27, *29*, 54
Into the Mind (documentary) 47
invitation (Greg M. Smith) *26–7*, 29, 48
Irreversible (*Irréversible*) 157–8
It Happened in Europe (*Valahol Európában*) 296 n.32
Ivan's Childhood (*Ivanovo detstvo*) 67

Jacobsen, Thomas 247
Jerslev, Anne 233, 235, 254, 257, 261, 267–8, 270
Jones, Karen 306 n.31
Journey, The (LARP game) 175, 287 n.57
Jung, C. G. 261–2
just so story *see* story
justice (emotion) 20, *89–93*
Justitia (Roman goddess) 93
Juul, Jesper 41, 49

Kahneman, Daniel 10, 17, 22, *24–5*, 59, 61, 66, 78, 125, 265
Kaplan, E. Ann 178, 191
Katz, Lynn Fainsilber 194
Kendell, Tina 157
Kent, Jennifer 12, 19, 177, 180, 192–3, 196, 199, 201
Kerr, Margee *28–9*, 49, 173, 281 n.5
Kierkegaard, Søren 183
Kimura, Doreen 30, 32
King Kong 274
King, Martin Luther 223
Kirkman, Robert 206–7, 227
Kolnai, Aurel 157

Lahno, Bernd 145–6
Laine, Tarja 8, 26

Lara Croft: Tomb Raider 185
Laugier, Pascal 12, 153, 164–5, 170–1, 194
Laurendeau, Jason 32
Lee, Jennifer 238
Let Me In 12, 79–80, 85–8, 96
Let the Right One In (*Låt den rätte komma in*) (book) 80–1, 299 n.3
Let the Right One In (*Låt den rätte komma in*) (movie) 12, 79–81, 83, *85–91*, *93–6*, 110, 194, 298 n.2
life stage 10, 13, *55*, 60, 114–15, 131, 149, 230, 253, 265–6, 269, 275–6: eight 10; ninth 10, 253 (*see also* age; Erikson, Erik; Erikson, Joan)
Lily Frankenstein (*Penny Dreadful*) 268, 322 n.50
Lindqvist, John Ajvide 12, 80
Little Red Riding Hood 100
Live Action Role Play (LARP) 46
lived body, the 30, *32*
Lori D. Stone 26
love (emotion) 9, 20, 53, 80–1, 130, *135–7*, *139–41*, 240
Lübecker, Nikolaj 169, 242
Lucifer (*Penny Dreadful*) 264
Luhrmann, Baz 244
LuPone, Patti 13, 253–5, 258, 263, 267–8
Lury, Karen 65–7, 72, 76
lust (emotion) 2, 8–9, 12, 53, 125, 129, 135–7, 139, 141
Lüthi, Max 64, 70, 74
lycanthropy *100–1*, 103–5, 109, 117, 126–7
Lycaon (Greek king) 100
Lyng, Stephen 11, 47, 49, 55

Mackey, Allison 76, *95–6*
Madame Bovary (novel) 256
magic 59–60, 63, 70, 72–4, 77–8, 174, 192–3, 260; magic circle, the 11, 28, 37, 41, 173–4, 193, 199–200, 273
Maid in Manhattan 122
maiden 265
Malabou, Catherine 100, *115–16*, 126, 140, 154, 249, 273
Maleficent 234

Mama 62, 194
Man the Hunter 29, 34, 38, 51, 106, 265, 288 n.65 (*see also* Woman the Gatherer)
Mandler, George 223, 248, 274
Marks-Tarlow, Terry 114–15
Marshall, Margaret A. 227
Marshall, Neil 15
Martyrs 12, 27, 153–4, 157, 164–6, 168–71, 174–5, 245
marvelous, the (genre) 71–2, 75, 77
masquerade 5, 214–15, 248–9, 315 n.36, 321 n.52
maternal: myth 12, 177–8, 180, 201; instinct 177, 180
Maurer, Robert 26
Maury, Julien 2, 178
Mayfield, John E. 273
McCauley, Clark, 156, 174, 184
McGreevy, Brian 111, 118
me-me-me script 129
Medea 93
melodrama (genre) 60, 63, 74–5, 77–8, 178–9
menstruation 107, 109; menses 115; menstruating 109; menarche 107, 109, 275
mentalizing 71
meta-narrative, the 6, 10–11, 30, *34–5*, 38, 40, 43–4, 46, 50, 55, 66, 73, 77–8, 80, 90, 113, 119, 131, 154, 174, 176, 179, 185, 191, 238, 254
meta-thinking 17, 19–20, 51, 55, 60, 125 (*see also* play, emotions)
Metzinger, Thomas 10, 23, 32, 36
Michaels, Meredith 196
Mill, John Stuart 223
Mimic 62
mind 5, 10–11, *16–24*; and stereotype 34–6; and self-injury 167 (*see also* consciousness)
mind-game film 168, 245
Mirror (Zerkalo) 296
Misérables, Les 255
Mittell, Jason 206
molester (sexual): female (*American Horror Story*) 234, 238–9, 318 n.38; male (*Bitten*) 30, 123

momism 196, 211
Montola, Markus 175, 287 n.57
mood *18–21*
Moore, Tony 206
moral agent 80, 82–3, 92, 95, 110, 145, 222, 263, 271 (*see also* moral patient)
moral patient 82–3, 93, 95, 145, 222 (*see also* moral agent)
moral: behavior 90, 175, 224; judgment 26; reasoning 225
morals 26, 224, 316 n.35 (*see also* ethics)
moratorium 132
mother: dead mother plot 238, 256; early modern 191; high-modernist 191; postmodernist 191; self-sacrificing 206, 227, 234 (*see also* maternal myth; stereotype)
motherhood: biological 178; essential 178–80; idealized 179, 191–2, 201; sick 188–9
mountain climbing 11, 47
moved *see* being moved

Næss, Arne 118, 283 n.17
Narnia 73
Ndalianis, Angela 4, 8, 27, 29, 54, 113–14
negative emotions *see* emotions
Negra, Diane 39, 117, 215, 291 n.113
Nell, Victor 11–12, *50–2*, 55, 84, 129, 166
Nemesis (Greek goddess) 93
neofeminism *see* feminism
neoliberal 39, 95, 121, 125, 127, 274
neuro-: neuroeconomist 10, 17; neuropsychologist 6, 11, 22, 31, 35, 42, 50, 84; neurosexism 6, 35; neuroscience 6, 35; neuroscientist 10, 16, 232, 247, 264
New French Extremity 2, 12, 153, *157–8*, 162–4, 168
New Old Woman, the 253–6, 267, 269–71
New Woman, the 254, 268–9, 322 n.50
niche (biology) 52, 102–5, 107, 116, 126

Noé, Gaspar 157, 184
novelty check 232, 242–3, 246, 248
numinous (Erikson): adult 150, 154, 162, 230; role model 164, 205

Ogre, The (*Der Unhold*) 296 n.32
old: abyss (deep old age) 13, 235, 238, 249, 253, 257, 265, 270–1; deep-old 238, 253; fourth age 270, 277, 323 n.55; middle-old 235, 253, 277, 320 n.60; old (definition) 277; old-old 10, 253, 261, 271, 277; third age 270, 277; young-old 271, 253, 262, 270, 277
Once Upon a Time 64
Orme, Jennifer 73, 75–6
Orphanage, The (*El orfanato*) 194, 198
Others, The 62–3
Ovid 100

pain (emotion) 2–3, 8–9, 20–2; identity horror 53; maternal body 190–1; *Martyrs* 165–9; Nell 51; ninja 28; play fighting 42–3, 50, 83–4, 91; self-injury 159–61, 236; *Vampire Diaries* 130, 141–2, 145–8; vengeance 92–3
Pale Man, the 62–3, 69–71, 74
Palmer, Tim 157, 163
Pan's Labyrinth (*El laberinto del fauno*) 2, 12, 59–63, 67–8, 73, 75–9, 95–6
panic 19, 26, 64, 123, 232
paradigm scenario 76–7
paradox of horror, the 169, 284 n.32
parent-child bonding 71
Passion of Joan of Arc, The (*La Passion de Jeanne d'Arc*) 161, 168
passions, the (emotion) 18
Patmore, Coventry 211
pedophilia 80–1, 88–9
Pellegrini, Anthony D. 44, 55, 131
Pellis, Sergio and Vivien Pellis 42–3, 46, 53, 55, 83–4
Penny Dreadful: 13, 253–71; "The Nightcomers" (2.03) 254; "And They Were Enemies" (2.10) 261; "The Day Tennyson Died" (3.01) 262; "Predators Far and Near" (3.02) 267; "Good and Evil Braided Be" (3.03) 268; "A Blade of Grass" (3.04) 269–70; "The Blessed Dark" (3.09) 266
phantasmagoria 197; phantasmagorical 197, 199–200
philosophy: cognitive 10; ecological 7, 119, 282 n.6; existential 39
Pickard, Susan 234
piggy game, the *81–5*, 93, 96
Pinedo, Isabel Cristina 7
Pinkola Este, Clarissa 105
Plantinga, Carl 19
plasticity *see* existential explosive plasticity
play (Callois) agon 41; alea 41; ilinx 41, 49; mimicry 41
play fighting 2–4, 8–9, 11–12, 42–6, 48–50, 55–6, 81, 83–4, 90–1, 130–1, 140–1, 147–8, 166, 169, 193
play: coaching 194–5, 198, 199–201, 231; "complex play" 43; creative 46, 112, 116, 126; cruel 53, 81, 83–4, 91; dark 178, 192, 197–8, 201; deep 197; drive 84; extreme 154; meta-13, 53, 193–5, 198, 200–1, 231, 246; play-with-fiction 193; "play with play" 43–4, *53–5*, 231; play-within-fiction 194, 199; research 11, 46, 49, 197; rough-and-tumble (R&T) 3, 44, 83, 131, 292 n.141; therapy 199; wild 195–7, 274 (*see also* animal play)
playground 1–2, 9, 38, 44, 83, 109, 195
Popper, Karl 1, 5, 38
Poromba, Cindy 174–5
Porter, Theresa 180, 200
positive emotions *see* emotions
post-human 118–19
postfeminism *see* feminism
Postman Always Rings Twice, The 240
Pötzsch, Holger 95
predation 11, 52–3
Predator 52, 221
Pretty Woman 122
Prochaintz, Alain 264
Psycho 166

INDEX

psychological drama *see* drama
psychological thriller *see* thriller
psychology: cognitive 5–6, 10, 33, 247; developmental 5; ecological 5, 12, 101; feminist 11
psychosemiotics 5, 18, 38, 282 n.9
puberty (definition) 275, 276
Pulp Fiction 163

Quandt, James 157–8, 169

R&T *see* play
Radner, Hilary 39, 121–2, 125–6
RAGE circuit (Nell) 51–2
Rembrandt; "Anatomy Lesson, the" (painting) 160
Renfield (*Penny Dreadful*) 262–3, 266
Resident Evil (computer game) 52
Reynolds, Kimberley 74
risk-seeking instinct 11
Riviere, Joan 246–7
road (trope) 13, 205–6, *215–19*, 227
Road, The 52
Romance 163
Romeo and Juliet 87–9, 96
Rosemary's Baby 187
Roth, Eli 1, 112
Rousseau, Jean-Jacques 191, 224
Rozin, Paul 156, 174, 184
Rubens, Peter Paul 70

Saint Ange see *House of Voices*
Saturn (Roman god) 70
Saving Private Ryan 75–6
Saw 166
Schell, Heather 99–100, 126
schema 6, 11, 30, 33, 35, 38, 44, 71, 210–11, 246, 274
Scherer, Klaus 232
science fiction (genre) 9, 76
sciences: social 5; cognitive 5, 21, 25, 264; neuro- 6, 35
Scott, Ridley 75, 177, 191
script: gender 4, 6, 32, 44, 105, 107, 109, 117, 129, 154, 175, 178, 206, 235, 243, 254, 271; mother 12, 177–80, 184–92, 196, 198, 200–2, 238–9; negative 230, 238; positive 13, 247, 254 (*see also* schema; stereotype)
second wave feminism *see* feminism
second-order: map 17, 21–2, 27, 33; account 16
See the Sea (Regarde la mer) 162
SEEKING circuit (Nell) 51–2
self-defense 11–12, 51–5, 90, 104, 110, 123, 129, 131, 159, 187, 196, 207, 222, 231
self-esteem (emotion) 8; *Let the Right One In* 80, 89–90, 92–3, 95–6; *Bitten* 125; *Vampire Diaries* 135, 143, 150; *The Walking Dead* 225, 227
self-injurer 10, 12, *157–9*, 309 n.25; *American Horror Story* 236; *Black Swan* 170–1, 177; *In My Skin* 160; *Martyrs* 165, 167
self-model 23
self: autobiographical 22, 25; body- 21–3; core 22, 25; memorizing 24; mind- 21–2; proto- 22, 25; wide sense of 53, 125–6
sensations 8, *18–21*, 32, 46, 54, 65, 92, 113, 157, 160; "liking" 232; "wanting" 232
sensorium 26, 27–9, 54; horror sensorium 4, 8, 27
separation anxiety 71
Sex and the City (2008 movie) 122
sex difference 11, *29–33*, 36, 43, 45–6, 49, 83, 289 n.89
sexism 6, 13, 35, 257, 267, 293 n.147
sexual enjoyment (as emotion) 135, 137
sexual excitement (as emotion) 135
sexual selection theory 12, 44–5, 51, 130–1, 134–5, 140–1, 292 *n.143*
shame (emotion) 8, 20–1, 84, 92–3, 107, 109–10, 139, 159, 196
Shaw, Sarah Naomi 158, 162, 172
She-Wolf of London 99
Sherman, Gary D. 71, 175
Shining, The 198
Shouse, Eric 286 n.22
Silence of the Lambs, The 163
Silvia, Paul J. 231
Sinnerbrink, Robert 286 n.19, 287 n.52

Sitcom 162
skills: sensorimotor 11, 44, 54, 56; sexual 44; social 9, 11, 42, 44, 53–4, 56, 129
Skyfall 237
Sleeping Beauty 234
Smith, Greg M. 27, 29
Smith, Murray 7, 54–5, 163–4, 168
Snow White (1937 movie) 70, 261
Snow White (character) 71
Snow White (fairy tale) 233, 236, 238
Snyder, Gary 118
social constructivism 32
social horror *see* horror
social realism 80–1, 299 n.4
Solet, Paul 12, 178, 187–8
Solomon, Robert C. 26, 76, 89, 91–2
Spencer, Jane 37
Spielberg, Steven 67–8, 75
Spirit of the Beehive, The (*El espíritu de la colmena*) 296 n.27
stage: *see* life stage; for stage (theatre) *see* dark stage
Stake Land 221
Stange, Mary Zeiss 106
Stardust 322 n.29
Steele, Claude M. 6, *33–4*, 36–7, 206, 208
stereotype: child 66; gender *see* gender stereotype; middle-age 229; mother 12, 201, 239; negative 6, 13, 30, *33–7*, 205–6, 256, 289 n.83; positive 33, 35
Sternudd, Hans T. 158–9, 162
Stewart, Michael 75
story: fixed *36*, 208; incremental 30, 36–7, 56, 206, 208, 274; "just so" 35, 289 n.90
Sunstein, Cass R. 19, *24–5*, 36, 59–61
survival horror *see* horror (as narrative)
suspension of disbelief 28
Sutton-Smith, Brian 43, 192, 197
SYF (single young female) 120, 122, 126, 133, 149, 237
System 1 17, 21–2, 24–5, 27–9, 33, 48, 55, 60, 78, 125, 166, 208, 222, 265, 273
System 2 17, 21–2, 24–5, 27–9, 33, 48, 52, 55, 60, 78, 125, 166–7, 200, 208, 218, 222, 246, 259, 265–6, 273–4

Tall Man, The 170
Tasker, Yvonne 291 n.113
Tatar, Maria 64, 72
Teen Wolf (movie) 110
Teen Wolf (television show) 110
teenager *see* age
terror (emotion) 8, 19, 70, 90–1, 156–7, 174, 178–9, *182–5*, 208
terror management theory, the 156
Theatre of Cruelty 169
Thelma & Louise 191, 216
Them (*Ils*) 53
Themis (Greek Titaness) 93
third age *see* age
third wave feminism *see* feminism
Thompson, John O. 77
thriller (genre) 8–9, 111, 114, 137, 157; psychological thriller 12
Thune, Henriette 94
Thurber, Ann 148
time travel 16
Todorov, Tzvetan 75
Tolkien, J. R. R. fairy stories 64, 74, 295 n.16; fantasy; 70, magic 73; political revolt 77
Tootsie 240
torture porn (genre) 1, 112, 147, *158*, 164, 166
torture: educational 129, 146–7; Lingchi 168, 310 n.40; hundred cuts 168; porn *see* torture porn
transactional 34, 289 n.89
transformational 34, 289 n.89
transnational cinema 59, 62–3, 75
Trouble Every Day 157
True Blood 114, 125, 132–3, 139, 141, 148, 294 n.174
trust (emotion) 3, 8–9, 12, 20, 52–3, 91; *Vampire Diaries* 129–30, *141–50*; wolves 106
Tudor, Andrew 8, 40
Twilight (book series) 120, 132, 148, 305 n.14
Twilight Saga: Breaking Dawn – Part 2, The 117
Twilight: film series 132–3, 139–41, 148; 2008 movie 114, 305 n.14
Twitchell, James B. 7, 54

urban supernatural romance 119
Ussher, Jane M. 6, 109, 178–9, 185, 191, 201, 271
Utopia 40, 298 n.66; utopian 70, 74, 216–18, 295 n.16; *Utopia* (novel) 215, 257

vampire 12, 17, 46, 102; Eli 79–83, 85–90, 92–6; *Hemlock Grove* 111, 113–14, 117; *Vampire Diaries* 125, 129–30, 132–4, 136–48, 150; *Grace* 190; *Penny Dreadful* 254, 269
Vampire Diaries, The 12, 52, 114, 125, 129–30, 132–3, 136, 137–42, 144–5, 148, 305 n.8; "Pilot" (1.01) 134; "The Night of the Comet" (1.02) 136; "Friday Night Bites" (1.03) 135, 137; "Family Ties" (1.04) 137; "You're Undead to Me" (1.05) 144; "Haunted" (1.07) 137; "162 Candles" (1.08) 135; "There Goes the Neighborhood" (1.16) 143; "The Return" (2.01) 139; "Brave New World" (2.02) 138; "Daddy Issues" (2.13) 145; "The Birthday" (3.01) 146; "The Hybrid" (3.02) 146; "The End of the Affair" (3.03) 129, 141–2, 146; "Ghost World" (3.07) 147; "The Ties That Bind" (3.12) 148; "Bringing Out the Dead" (3.13) 148
vargulf 99
vengeance (emotion) 9, 12, 53, 79–82, 89–93, 96
Verfremdung 169
virtue ethics *see* ethics
Visit, The 253, 264
Vvitch: A New-England Folktale, The 253, 261

WAG (women aging gracefully) 235–7
Wagner, Valentin 247
Walking Dead, The (graphic novel) 206–7, 210; issue 2 206; issue 41 207; issue 132 207
Walking Dead, The (television show) 13, 205–6, 209, 211, 213, 215–21, 224, 226–7, 229; "Tell it to the Frogs" (1.03) 207,; "Wildfire" (1.04) 207; "Pretty Much Dead Already" (2.07) 207; "The Killer Within" (3.04) 227; "This Sorrowful Life" (3.15) 207; "Isolation" (4.03) 217; "Indifference" (4.04) 208; "Too Far Gone" (4.08) 217; "After" (4.09) 217; "The Grove" (4.14) 208; "Us" (4.15) 210; "No Sanctuary" (5.01) 217; "Remember" (5.12) 213; "Forget" (5.13) 210; "Spend" (5.14) 214
Waller, Alison 276
Walton, Karen 107
war: Spanish Civil War 59, 63, 70, 295; Second World War 64, 67–8, 295 n.15
Wassiliwizky Eugen 247
Wedell-Wedellsborg, Merete 315 n.26
werewolf 12, 29–31, 35, 99–103; *Bitten* 121, 123, 125–7, 237; *Ginger Snaps* 107–10; *Hemlock Grove* 110–19; *Penny Dreadful* 254, 266; *Vampire Diaries* 140–1, 145–6, 149; *Wilderness* 103–4, 106–7
Werewolf of London 99
Wetmore, Kevin J. 8, 54
What Ever Happened to Baby Jane 248, 320 n.60
When Harry Met Sally… 239
Wilde, Oscar 163, 268
Wilderness (novel) 104
Wilderness (television mini series) 12, 100, 104–7, 113, 266
Williams, Linda 179, 282 n.9
Wilson, Emma 66
Wise Woman, the (archetype) 256
witch 10, 13, 100, 180, 205; *American Horror Story* 229–30, 233–41; *Penny Dreadful* 253–62, 264–5, 271; *Vampire Diaries* 140, 143, 145; *The Walking* Dead 205, 227
witch: trials 260, 262; beliefs 260
Wizard of Oz, The 71
Wolf (1994 movie) 99
wolf 99–100, 102–4, 106–7, 112–13, 117–19, 124–5, 283 n.17, 295 n.13
Wolf Creek 166
Wolf Girl 99

Wolf Man, The (1941 movie) 99
Wolfman, The (2010 movie) 101
Woman the Gatherer 29, 34, 265 (*see also* Man the Hunter)
wombraider 185–7, 312 n.29; wombraiding 12, 185, 312 n.29
World War Z 52

Young, Iris Marion 31–2, 39–40, 67, 109, 118, 211–13

Zeus (Greek god) 100
Zipes, Jack 296 n.17
zombie 10, 17, 42, 52, 157, 183; *American Horror Story* 235, 239; *The Walking Dead* 205–8, 211–13, 118, 221–2, 225
zone (Apter): danger 47, 50, 197; safety 47–8; trauma 47–8, 50, 56, 74, 78, 170, 175, 197
Zuk, Marlene 39, 134–5, 177, 225